NIGHTMARES AND DREAMSCAPES

The long reach of Stephen King's imagination and the no-holds-barred force of his storytelling have never been so richly demonstrated as in this his third collection of short stories. A solitary finger pokes out of a drain. Novelty teeth turn predatory. Flies settle and die on an old pair of sneakers in New York, and the Nevada desert swallows a Cadillac. Meanwhile, the legend of Castle Rock returns . . . and grows on you. There's something here for readers of every stripe and predilection—classic tales of the macabre and the monstrous, cutting-edge explorations of the borderlands between good and evil. In story after story, King takes his readers to places they've never been before.

NIGHTMARES AND DREAMSCAPES

Stephen King

CHIVERS PRESS
BATH

First published in Great Britain 1993
by
Hodder and Stoughton
a division of Hodder and Stoughton Ltd
This Large Print edition published by
Chivers Press
by arrangement with
Hodder and Stoughton Ltd
1994

ISBN 0 7451 7682 8

British Library Cataloguing in Publication Data available

NIGHTMARES
AND
DREAMSCAPES

In memory of
THOMAS WILLIAMS, *1926–1991:*
poet, novelist, and
great American storyteller.

Contents

Introduction

MYTH, BELIEF, FAITH, AND
RIPLEY'S BELIEVE IT OR NOT!

When I was a kid I believed everything I was told, everything I read, and every dispatch sent out by my own overheated imagination. This made for more than a few sleepless nights, but it also filled the world I lived in with colors and textures I would not have traded for a lifetime of restful nights. I knew even then, you see, that there were people in the world — too many of them, actually — whose imaginative senses were either numb or completely deadened, and who lived in a mental state akin to colorblindness. I always felt sorry for them, never dreaming (at least then) that many of these unimaginative types either pitied me or held me in contempt, not just because I suffered from any number of irrational fears but because I was deeply and unreservedly credulous on almost every subject. "There's a boy," some of them must have thought (I know my mother did), "who will buy the Brooklyn Bridge not just once but over and over again, all his life."

There was some truth to that then, I suppose, and if I am to be honest, I suppose there's some truth to it now. My wife still delights in telling people that her husband cast his first Presidential ballot, at the tender age of twenty-one, for Richard Nixon. "Nixon said he had a plan to get us out of Vietnam," she says, usually with a gleeful gleam in her eye, *"and Steve believed him!"*

That's right; Steve believed him. Nor is that all Steve has believed during the often-eccentric course of his forty-five years. I was, for example, the last kid in my neighborhood to decide that all those street-corner Santas meant there was no *real* Santa (I still find no logical merit in the idea; it's like saying that a million disciples prove there is no master). I never questioned my Uncle Oren's assertion that you could tear off a person's shadow with a steel tent-peg (if you struck precisely at high noon, that was) or his wife's claim that every time you shivered, a goose was walking over the place where your grave would someday be. Given the course of *my* life, that must mean I'm slated to end up buried behind Aunt Rhody's barn out in Goose Wallow, Wyoming.

I also believed everything I was told in the schoolyard; little minnows and whale-sized whoppers went down my throat with equal ease. One kid told me with complete certainty that if you put a dime down on a railroad track, the first train to come along would be derailed by it. Another kid told me that a dime left on a railroad track would be perfectly smooshed (that was exactly how he put it — *perfectly smooshed*) by the next train, and what you took off the rail after the train had passed would be a flexible and nearly transparent coin the size of a silver dollar. My own belief was that both things were true: that dimes left on railroad tracks were perfectly smooshed before they derailed the trains which did the smooshing.

Other fascinating schoolyard facts which I absorbed during my years at Center School in Stratford, Connecticut, and Durham Elementary School in Durham, Maine, concerned such diverse subjects as golf-balls (poisonous and corrosive at the center), miscarriages (sometimes born alive, as malformed monsters which had to be killed by health-care individuals ominously referred to as "the special nurses"), black cats (if one crossed your path, you had to fork the sign of the evil eye at it quickly or risk almost certain death before the end of the day), and sidewalk cracks. I probably don't have to explain the potentially dangerous relationship of these latter to the spinal columns of completely innocent mothers.

My primary sources of wonderful and amazing facts in those days were the paperback compilations from *Ripley's Believe It or Not!* which were issued by Pocket Books. It was in *Ripley's* that I discovered you could make a powerful explosive by scraping the celluloid off the backs of playing cards and then tamping the stuff into a length of pipe, that you could drill a hole in your own skull and then plug it with a candle, thereby turning yourself into a kind of human night-light (why anyone would want to do such a thing was a question which never occurred to me until years later), that there were actual giants (one man well over eight feet tall), actual elves (one woman barely eleven inches tall), and actual MONSTERS TOO HORRIBLE TO DESCRIBE . . . except *Ripley's* described them all, in loving detail, and usually with a picture (if I live to be a hundred, I'll never forget

11

the one of the guy with the candle stuck in the center of his shaved skull).

That series of paperbacks was — to me, at least — the world's most wonderful sideshow, one I could carry around in my back pocket and curl up with on rainy weekend afternoons, when there were no baseball games and everyone was tired of Monopoly. Were all of Ripley's fabulous curiosities and human monsters real? In this context that hardly seems relevant. They were real to *me,* and that probably is — during the years from six to eleven, crucial years in which the human imagination is largely formed, they were *very* real to me. I believed them just as I believed you could derail a freight-train with a dime or that the drippy goop in the center of a golf-ball would eat the hand right off your arm if you were careless and got some of it on you. It was in *Ripley's Believe It or Not!* that I first began to see how fine the line between the fabulous and the humdrum could sometimes be, and to understand that the juxtaposition of the two did as much to illuminate the ordinary aspects of life as it did to illuminate its occasional weird outbreaks. Remember it's *belief* we're talking about here, and belief is the cradle of myth. What about reality, you ask? Well, as far as I'm concerned, reality can go take a flying fuck at a rolling doughnut. I've never held much of a brief for reality, at least in my written work. All too often it is to the imagination what ash stakes are to vampires.

I think that myth and imagination are, in fact, nearly interchangeable concepts, and that belief is the wellspring of both. Belief in what? I don't think it matters very much, to tell you the truth. One god or many. Or that a dime can derail a freight-train.

These beliefs of mine had nothing to do with faith; let's be very clear on that subject. I was raised Methodist and hold onto enough of the fundamentalist teachings of my childhood to believe that such a claim would be presumptuous at best and downright blasphemous at worst. I believed all that weird stuff because I was *built* to believe in weird stuff. Other people run races because they were built to run fast, or play basketball because God made them six-foot-ten, or solve long, complicated equations on blackboards because they were built to see the places where the numbers all lock together.

Yet faith comes into it someplace, and I think that place has to do with going back to do the same thing again and again even though you believe in your deepest, truest heart that you will never be able to do it any better than you already have, and that if you press on, there's really no place to go but downhill. You don't have anything to lose when you take your first whack at the *piñata,* but to take a second one (and a third . . . and a fourth . . . and a thirty-fourth) is to risk failure, depression, and, in the case of the short-story writer who works in a pretty well defined genre, self-parody. But we do go on, most of us, and that gets to be hard. I never would have believed that twenty years ago, or even ten, but it does. It gets hard. And I have days when I think this old Wang word-processor stopped running on electricity about five years ago; that from

13

The Dark Half on, it's been running completely on faith. But that's okay; whatever gets the words across the screen, right?

The idea for each of the stories in this book came in a moment of belief and was written in a burst of faith, happiness, and optimism. Those positive feelings have their dark analogues, however, and the fear of failure is a long way from the worst of them. The worst — for me, at least — is the gnawing speculation that I may have already said everything I have to say, and am now only listening to the steady quacking of my own voice because the silence when it stops is just too spooky.

The leap of faith necessary to make the short stories happen has gotten particularly tough in the last few years; these days it seems that everything wants to be a novel, and every novel wants to be approximately four thousand pages long. A fair number of critics have mentioned this, and usually not favorably. In reviews of every long novel I have written, from *The Stand* to *Needful Things,* I have been accused of overwriting. In some cases the criticisms have merit; in others they are just the ill-tempered yappings of men and women who have accepted the literary anorexia of the last thirty years with a puzzling (to me, at least) lack of discussion and dissent. These self-appointed deacons in the Church of Latter-Day American Literature seem to regard generosity with suspicion, texture with dislike, and any broad literary stroke with outright hate. The result is a strange and arid literary climate where a meaningless little fingernail-paring like Nicholson Baker's *Vox* becomes an object of fascinated debate and dissection, and a truly ambitious American novel like Greg Matthews's *Heart of the Country* is all but ignored.

But all that is by the by, not only off the subject but just a tiny bit whimpery, too — after all, was there ever a writer who didn't feel that he or she had been badly treated by the critics? All I started to say before I so rudely interrupted myself was that the act of faith which turns a moment of belief into a real object — i.e., a short story that people will actually want to read — has been a little harder for me to come by in the last few years.

"Well then, don't write them," someone might say (only it's usually a voice I hear inside my own head, like the ones Jessie Burlingame hears in *Gerald's Game*). "After all, you don't need the money they bring in the way you once did."

That's true enough. The days when a check for some four-thousand-word wonder would buy penicillin for one of the kids' ear infections or help meet the rent are long gone. But the logic is more than spurious; it's dangerous. I don't exactly need the money the *novels* bring in, either, you see. If it was just the money, I could hang up my jock and hit the showers . . . or spend the rest of my life on some Caribbean island, catching the rays and seeing how long I could grow my fingernails.

But it *isn't* about the money, no matter what the glossy tabloids may say, and it's not about selling out, as the more arrogant critics really seem to believe. The fundamental things still apply as time goes by, and for me the object hasn't changed — the job is still getting to *you*, Constant Reader, getting you by the short hairs and, hopefully, scaring you so badly you won't be able to go to sleep without leaving the bathroom light on. It's still about first seeing the impossible . . . and then saying it. It's still about making you believe what I believe, at least for a little while.

I don't talk about this much, because it embarrasses me and it sounds pompous, but I still see stories as a great thing, something which not only enhances lives but actually saves them. Nor am I speaking metaphorically. Good writing — good *stories* — are the imagination's firing pin, and the purpose of the imagination, I believe, is to offer us solace and shelter from situations and life-passages which would otherwise prove unendurable. I can only speak from my own experience, of course, but for me, the imagination which so often kept me awake and in terror as a child has seen me through some terrible bouts of stark raving reality as an adult. If the stories which have resulted from that imagination have done the same for some of the people who've read them, then I am perfectly happy and perfectly satisfied — feelings which cannot, so far as I know, be purchased with rich movie deals or multi-million-dollar book contracts.

Still, the short story is a difficult and challenging literary form, and that's why I was so delighted — and so surprised — to find I had enough of them to issue a third collection. It has come at a propitious time, as well, because one of those facts of which I was so sure as a kid (I probably picked it up in *Ripley's Believe It or Not!*, too) was that people completely renew themselves every seven years: every tissue, every organ, every muscle replaced by entirely new cells. I am drawing *Nightmares and Dreamscapes* together in the summer of 1992, seven years after the publication of *Skeleton Crew*, my last collection of short stories, and *Skeleton Crew* was published seven years after *Night Shift*, my first collection. The greatest thing is knowing that, although the leap of faith necessary to translate an idea into reality has become harder (the jumping muscles get a little older every day, you know), it's still perfectly possible. The next greatest thing is knowing that someone still wants to read them — that's you, Constant Reader, should you wonder.

The oldest of these stories (my versions of the killer golf-ball goop and monster miscarriages, if you will) is "It Grows on You," originally published in a University of Maine literary magazine called *Marshroots* . . . although it has been considerably revised for this book, so it could better be what it apparently wanted to be — a final look back at the doomed little town of Castle Rock. The most recent, "The Ten O'Clock People," was written in three fevered days during the summer of 1992.

There are some genuine curiosities here — the first version of my only original teleplay; a Sherlock Holmes story in which Dr. Watson steps forward to solve the case; a Cthulhu Mythos story set in the suburb of London where Peter Straub lived when I first met him; a hardboiled "caper" story of the Richard Bachman stripe; and a slightly different version of a story called "My Pretty Pony," which was originally done as a limited edition from the Whitney Museum, with artwork by Barbara Kruger.

After a great deal of thought, I've also decided to include a lengthy non-fiction piece, "Head Down," which concerns kids and baseball. It was originally published in *The New Yorker*, and I probably worked harder on it than anything else I've written over the last fifteen years. That doesn't make it good, of course, but I know that writing and publishing it gave me enormous satisfaction, and I'm passing it along for that reason. It doesn't really fit in a collection of stories which concern themselves mostly with suspense and the supernatural . . . except somehow it does. The texture is the same. See if you don't think so.

What I've tried hardest to do is to steer clear of the old chestnuts, the trunk stories, and the bottom-of-the-drawer stuff. Since 1980 or so, some critics have been saying I could publish my laundry list and sell a million copies or so, but these are for the most part critics who think that's what I've been doing all along. The people who read my work for pleasure obviously feel differently, and I have made this book with those readers, not the critics, in the forefront of my mind. The result, I think, is an uneven Aladdin's cave of a book, one which completes a trilogy of which *Night Shift* and *Skeleton Crew* are the first two volumes. All the good short stories have now been collected; all the bad ones have been swept as far under the rug as I could get them, and there they will stay. If there is to be another collection, it will consist entirely of stories which have not as yet been written or even considered (stories which have not yet been *believed*, if you will), and I'd

18

guess it will show up in a year which begins with a 2.

Meantime, there are these twenty-odd (and some, I should warn you, are *very* odd). Each contains something I believed for awhile, and I know that some of these things — the finger poking out of the drain, the man-eating toads, the hungry teeth — are a little frightening, but I think we'll be all right if we go together. First, repeat the catechism after me:

I believe a dime can derail a freight-train.

I believe there are alligators in the New York City sewer system, not to mention rats as big as Shetland ponies.

I believe that you can tear off someone's shadow with a steel tent-peg.

I believe that there really *is* a Santa Claus, and that all those red-suited guys you see at Christmas-time really are his helpers.

I believe there is an unseen world all around us.

I believe that tennis balls are full of poison gas, and if you cut one in two and breathe what comes out, it'll kill you.

Most of all, I *do* believe in spooks, I *do* believe in spooks, I *do* believe in spooks.

Okay? Ready? Fine. Here's my hand. We're going now. I know the way. All you have to do is hold on tight . . . and *believe*.

Bangor, Maine
November 6, 1992

Dolan's Cadillac

Revenge is a dish best eaten cold.
— Spanish proverb

I waited and watched for seven years. I saw him come and go — Dolan. I watched him stroll into fancy restaurants dressed in a tuxedo, always with a different woman on his arm, always with his pair of bodyguards bookending him. I watched his hair go from iron-gray to a fashionable silver while my own simply receded until I was bald. I watched him leave Las Vegas on his regular pilgrimages to the West Coast; I watched him return. On two or three occasions I watched from a side road as his Sedan DeVille, the same color as his hair, swept by on Route 71 toward Los Angeles. And on a few occasions I watched him leave his place in the Hollywood Hills in the same gray Cadillac to return to Las Vegas — not often, though. I am a schoolteacher. Schoolteachers and high-priced hoodlums do not have the same freedom of movement; it's just an economic fact of life.

He did not know I was watching him — I never came close enough for him to know that. I was careful.

He killed my wife or had her killed; it comes to the same, either way. Do you want details? You won't get them from me. If you want them, look them up in the back issues of the papers. Her name was Elizabeth. She taught in the same school where I taught and where I teach still. She taught first-graders. They loved her, and I think that some of them may not have forgotten their love still, although they would be teenagers now. *I* loved her and love her still, certainly. She was not beautiful but she was pretty. She was quiet, but she could laugh. I dream of her. Of her hazel eyes. There has never been another woman for me. Nor ever will be.

He slipped — Dolan. That's all you have to know. And Elizabeth was there, at the wrong place and the wrong time, to see the slip. She went to the police, and the police sent her to the FBI, and she was questioned, and she said yes, she would testify. They promised to protect her, but they either slipped or they underestimated Dolan. Maybe it was both. Whatever it was, she got into her car one night and the dynamite wired to the ignition made me a widower. *He* made me a widower — Dolan.

With no witness to testify, he was let free.

He went back to his world, I to mine. The penthouse apartment in Vegas for him, the empty tract home for me. The succession of beautiful women in furs and sequined evening dresses for him, the silence for me. The gray Cadillacs, four of them over the years, for him, and the aging Buick Riviera for me. His hair went silver while mine just went.

But I watched.

I was careful — oh, yes! Very careful. I knew

21

what he was, what he could do. I knew he would step on me like a bug if he saw or sensed what I meant for him. So I was careful.

During my summer vacation three years ago I followed him (at a prudent distance) to Los Angeles, where he went frequently. He stayed in his fine house and threw parties (I watched the comings and goings from a safe shadow at the end of the block, fading back when the police cars made their frequent patrols), and I stayed in a cheap hotel where people played their radios too loud and neon light from the topless bar across the street shone in the window. I fell asleep on those nights and dreamed of Elizabeth's hazel eyes, dreamed that none of it had ever happened, and woke up sometimes with tears drying on my face.

I came close to losing hope.

He was well guarded, you see; so well guarded. He went nowhere without those two heavily armed gorillas with him, and the Cadillac itself was armor plated. The big radial tires it rolled on were of the self-sealing type favored by dictators in small, uneasy countries.

Then, that last time, I saw how it could be done — but I did not see it until after I'd had a very bad scare.

I followed him back to Las Vegas, always keeping at least a mile between us, sometimes two, sometimes three. As we crossed the desert heading east his car was at times no more than a sunflash on the horizon and I thought about Elizabeth, how the sun looked on her hair.

I was far behind on this occasion. It was the middle of the week, and traffic on U.S. 71 was very light. When traffic is light, tailing becomes dangerous — even a grammar-school teacher knows that. I passed an orange sign which read DETOUR 5 MILES and dropped back even farther. Desert detours slow traffic to a crawl, and I didn't want to chance coming up behind the gray Cadillac as the driver babied it over some rutted secondary road.

DETOUR 3 MILES, the next sign read, and below that: BLASTING AREA AHEAD • TURN OFF 2-WAY RADIO.

I began to muse on some movie I had seen years before. In this film a band of armed robbers had tricked an armored car into the desert by putting up false detour signs. Once the driver fell for the trick and turned off onto a deserted dirt road (there are thousands of them in the desert, sheep roads and ranch roads and old government roads that go nowhere), the thieves had removed the signs, assuring isolation, and then had simply laid siege to the armored car until the guards came out.

They killed the guards.

I remembered that.

They killed the guards.

I reached the detour and turned onto it. The road was as bad as I had imagined — packed dirt, two lanes wide, filled with potholes that made my old Buick jounce and groan. The Buick needed new shock absorbers, but shocks are an expense a schoolteacher sometimes has to put off, even when he is a widower with no children and no hobbies except his dream of revenge.

As the Buick bounced and wallowed along, an idea occurred to me. Instead of following Dolan's

Cadillac the next time it left Vegas for L.A. or L.A. for Vegas, I would pass it — get ahead of it. I would create a false detour like the one in the movie, luring it out into the wastes that exist, silent and rimmed by mountains, west of Las Vegas. Then I would remove the signs, as the thieves had done in the movie —

I snapped back to reality suddenly. Dolan's Cadillac was ahead of me, *directly ahead of me,* pulled off to one side of the dusty track. One of the tires, self-sealing or not, was flat. No — not just flat. It was exploded, half off the rim. The culprit had probably been a sharp wedge of rock stuck in the hardpan like a miniature tank-trap. One of the two bodyguards was working a jack under the front end. The second — an ogre with a pig-face streaming sweat under his brush cut — stood protectively beside Dolan himself. Even in the desert, you see, they took no chances.

Dolan stood to one side, slim in an open-throated shirt and dark slacks, his silver hair blowing around his head in the desert breeze. He was smoking a cigarette and watching the men as if he were somewhere else, a restaurant or a ballroom or a drawing room perhaps.

His eyes met mine through the windshield of my car and then slid off with no recognition at all, although he had seen me once, seven years ago (when I had hair!), at a preliminary hearing, sitting beside my wife.

My terror at having caught up with the Cadillac was replaced with an utter fury.

I thought of leaning over and unrolling the passenger window and shrieking: *How dare you forget me? How dare you dismiss me?* Oh, but that would have been the act of a lunatic. It was *good* that he had forgotten me, it was *fine* that he had dismissed me. Better to be a mouse behind the wainscoting, nibbling at the wires. Better to be a spider, high up under the eaves, spinning its web.

The man sweating the jack flagged me, but Dolan wasn't the only one capable of dismissal. I looked indifferently beyond the arm-waver, wishing him a heart attack or a stroke or, best of all, both at the same time. I drove on — but my head pulsed and throbbed, and for a few moments the mountains on the horizon seemed to double and even treble.

If I'd had a gun! I thought. *If only I'd had a gun! I could have ended his rotten, miserable life right then if I'd only had a gun!*

Miles later some sort of reason reasserted itself. If I'd had a gun, the only thing I could have been sure of was getting myself killed. If I'd had a gun I could have pulled over when the man using the bumper-jack beckoned me, and gotten out, and begun spraying bullets wildly around the deserted landscape. I might have wounded someone. Then I would have been killed and buried in a shallow grave, and Dolan would have gone on escorting the beautiful women and making pilgrimages between Las Vegas and Los Angeles in his silver Cadillac while the desert animals unearthed my remains and fought over my bones under the cold moon. For Elizabeth there would have been no revenge — none at all.

The men who travelled with him were trained to kill. I was trained to teach third-graders.

This was not a movie, I reminded myself as I returned to the highway and passed an orange END CONSTRUCTION • THE STATE OF NEVADA THANKS YOU! sign. And if I ever made the mistake of confusing reality with a movie, of thinking that a balding third-grade teacher with myopia could ever be Dirty Harry anywhere outside of his own daydreams, there would never be any revenge, ever.

But *could* there be revenge, ever? *Could* there be?

My idea of creating a fake detour was as romantic and unrealistic as the idea of jumping out of my old Buick and spraying the three of them with bullets — me, who had not fired a gun since the age of sixteen and who had never fired a handgun.

Such a thing would not be possible without a band of conspirators — even the movie I had seen, romantic as it had been, had made that clear. There had been eight or nine of them in two separate groups, staying in touch with each other by walkie-talkie. There had even been a man in a small plane cruising above the highway to make sure the armored car was relatively isolated as it approached the right spot on the highway.

A plot no doubt dreamed up by some overweight screenwriter sitting by his swimming pool with a piña colada by one hand and a fresh supply of Pentel pens and an Edgar Wallace plot-wheel by the other. And even that fellow had needed a small army to fulfill his idea. I was only one man.

It wouldn't work. It was just a momentary false gleam, like the others I'd had over the years — the idea that maybe I could put some sort of poison gas in Dolan's air-conditioning system, or plant a bomb in his Los Angeles house, or perhaps obtain some really deadly weapon — a bazooka, let us say — and turn his damned silver Cadillac into a fireball as it raced east toward Vegas or west toward L.A. along 71.

Best to dismiss it.

But it wouldn't go.

Cut him out, the voice inside that spoke for Elizabeth kept whispering. *Cut him out the way an experienced sheep-dog cuts a ewe out of the flock when his master points. Detour him out into the emptiness and kill him. Kill them all.*

Wouldn't work. If I allowed no other truth, I would at least have to allow that a man who had stayed alive as long as Dolan must have a carefully honed sense of survival — honed to the point of paranoia, perhaps. He and his men would see through the detour trick in a minute.

They turned down this one today, the voice that spoke for Elizabeth responded. *They never even hesitated. They went just like Mary's little lamb.*

But I knew — yes, somehow I did! — that men like Dolan, men who are really more like wolves than men, develop a sort of sixth sense when it comes to danger. I could steal genuine detour signs from some road department shed and set them up in all the right places; I could even add fluorescent orange road cones and a few of those smudge-pots. I could do all that and Dolan would still smell the nervous sweat of my hands on the stage dressing. Right through his bullet-proof windows he would smell it. He would close his eyes and hear Elizabeth's name far back in the snake-pit that passed for his mind.

The voice that spoke for Elizabeth fell silent, and I thought it had finally given up for the day. And then, with Vegas actually in sight — blue and misty and wavering on the far rim of the desert — it spoke up again.

Then don't try to fool him with a fake detour, it whispered. *Fool him with a* real *one*.

I swerved the Buick over to the shoulder and shuddered to a stop with both feet on the brake-pedal. I stared into my own wide, startled eyes in the rear-view mirror.

Inside, the voice that spoke for Elizabeth began to laugh. It was wild, mad laughter, but after a few moments I began to laugh along with it.

The other teachers laughed at me when I joined the Ninth Street Health Club. One of them wanted to know if someone had kicked sand in my face. I laughed along with them. People don't get suspicious of a man like me as long as he keeps laughing along with them. And why shouldn't I laugh? My wife had been dead seven years, hadn't she? Why, she was no more than dust and hair and a few bones in her coffin! So why shouldn't I laugh? It's only when a man like me stops laughing that people wonder if something is wrong.

I laughed along with them even though my muscles ached all that fall and winter. I laughed even though I was constantly hungry — no more second helpings, no more late-night snacks, no more beer, no more before-dinner gin and tonic. But lots of red meat and greens, greens, greens.

I bought myself a Nautilus machine for Christmas.

No — that's not quite right. *Elizabeth* bought me a Nautilus machine for Christmas.

I saw Dolan less frequently; I was too busy working out, losing my pot belly, building up my arms and chest and legs. But there were times when it seemed I could not go on with it, that recapturing anything like real physical fitness was going to be impossible, that I could not live without second helpings and pieces of coffee cake and the occasional dollop of sweet cream in my coffee. When those times came I would park across from one of his favorite restaurants or perhaps go into one of the clubs he favored and wait for him to show up, stepping from the fog-gray Cadillac with an arrogant, icy blonde or a laughing redhead on his arm — or one on each. There he would be, the man who had killed my Elizabeth, there he would be, resplendent in a formal shirt from Bijan's, his gold Rolex winking in the nightclub lights. When I was tired and discouraged I went to Dolan as a man with a raging thirst might seek out an oasis in the desert. I drank his poisoned water and was refreshed.

In February I began to run every day, and then the other teachers laughed at my bald head, which peeled and pinked and then peeled and pinked again, no matter how much sun-block I smeared on it. I laughed right along with them, as if I had not twice nearly fainted and spent long, shuddering minutes with cramps stabbing the muscles of my legs at the end of my runs.

When summer came, I applied for a job with the Nevada Highway Department. The municipal employment office stamped a tentative approval on my form and sent me along to a district foreman named Harvey Blocker. Blocker was a tall man, burned almost black by the Nevada sun. He wore jeans, dusty workboots, and a blue tee-shirt with cut-off sleeves. BAD ATTITUDE, the shirt proclaimed. His muscles were big rolling slabs under his skin. He looked at my application. Then he looked at me and laughed. The application looked very puny rolled up in one of his huge fists.

"You got to be kidding, my friend. I mean, you have *got* to be. We talkin desert sun and desert heat here-none of that yuppie tanning-salon shit. What are you in real life, bubba? An accountant?"

"A teacher," I said. "Third grade."

"Oh, *honey*," he said, and laughed again. "Get out of my face, okay?"

I had a pocket watch — handed down from my great-grandfather, who worked on the last stretch of the great transcontinental railroad. He was there, according to family legend, when they hammered home the golden spike. I took the watch out and dangled it in Blocker's face on its chain.

"See this?" I said. "Worth six, maybe seven hundred dollars."

"This a bribe?" Blocker laughed again. A great old laugher was he. "Man, I've heard of people making deals with the devil, but you're the first one I ever met who wanted to *bribe* himself into hell." Now he looked at me with something like compassion. "You may *think* you understand what you're tryin to get yourself into, but I'm here to tell you you don't have the slightest idea. In July I've seen it go a hundred and seventeen degrees out there west of Indian Springs. It makes strong men cry. And you ain't strong, bubba. I don't have to see you with your shirt off to know you ain't got nothin on your rack but a few yuppie health-club muscles, and they won't cut it out in the Big Empty."

I said, "The day you decide I can't cut it, I'll walk off the job. You keep the watch. No argument."

"You're a fucking liar."

I looked at him. He looked back for some time.

"You're *not* a fucking liar." He said this in tones of amazement.

"No."

"You'd give the watch to Tinker to hold?" He cocked his thumb at a humongous black man in a tie-dyed shirt who was sitting nearby in the cab of a bulldozer, eating a fruit-pie from McDonald's and listening.

"Is he trustworthy?"

"You're damned tooting."

"Then he can hold it until you tell me to take a hike or until I have to go back to school in September."

"And what do I put up?"

I pointed to the employment application in his fist. "Sign that," I said. "That's what you put up."

"You're crazy."

I thought of Dolan and of Elizabeth and said nothing.

"You'd start on shit-work," Blocker warned. "Shovelling hotpatch out of the back of a truck and into potholes. Not because I want your damned watch — although I'll be more than happy

31

to take it — but because that's where everyone starts."

"All right."

"As long as you understand, bubba."

"I do."

"No," Blocker said, "you don't. But you will."

And he was right.

I remember next to nothing about the first couple of weeks — just shovelling hot-top and tamping it down and walking along behind the truck with my head down until the truck stopped at the next pothole. Sometimes we worked on the Strip and I'd hear the sound of jackpot bells ringing in the casinos. Sometimes I think the bells were just ringing in my head. I'd look up and I'd see Harvey Blocker looking at me with that odd look of compassion, his face shimmering in the heat baking off the road. And sometimes I'd look over at Tinker, sitting under the canvas parasol which covered the cab of his 'dozer, and Tinker would hold up my great-granddad's watch and swing it on the chain so it kicked off sunflashes.

The big struggle was not to faint, to hold onto consciousness no matter what. All through June I held on, and the first week of July, and then Blocker sat down next to me one lunch hour while I was eating a sandwich with one shaking hand. I shook sometimes until ten at night. It was the heat. It was either shake or faint, and when I thought of Dolan I somehow managed to keep shaking.

"You still ain't strong, bubba," he said.

"No," I said. "But like the man said, you should

have seen the materials I had to start with."

"I keep expecting to look around and see you passed out in the middle of the roadbed and you keep not doing it. But you gonna."

"No, I'm not."

"Yes, you are. If you stay behind the truck with a shovel, you gonna."

"No."

"Hottest part of the summer still coming on, bubba. Tink calls it cookie-sheet weather."

"I'll be fine."

He pulled something out of his pocket. It was my great-granddad's watch. He tossed it in my lap. "Take this fucking thing," he said, disgusted. "I don't want it."

"You made a deal with me."

"I'm calling it off."

"If you fire me, I'll take you to arbitration," I said. "You signed my form. You —"

"I ain't firing you," he said, and looked away. "I'm going to have Tink teach you how to run a front-end loader."

I looked at him for a long time, not knowing what to say. My third-grade classroom, so cool and pleasant, had never seemed so far away . . . and still I didn't have the slightest idea of how a man like Blocker thought, or what he meant when he said the things he said. I knew that he admired me and held me in contempt at the same time, but I had no idea why he felt either way. *And you don't need to care,* darling, Elizabeth spoke up suddenly inside my mind. *Dolan is your business. Remember Dolan.*

"Why do you want to do that?" I asked at last.

33

He looked back at me then, and I saw he was both furious and amused. But the fury was the emotion on top, I think. "What is it with you, bubba? What do you think I am?"

"I don't —"

"You think I want to kill you for your fucking watch? That what you think?"

"I'm sorry."

"Yeah, you are. Sorriest little motherfucker *I* ever saw."

I put my great-granddad's watch away.

"You ain't *never* gonna be strong, bubba. Some people and plants take hold in the sun. Some wither up and die. You dyin. You know you are, and still you won't move into the shade. Why? Why you pulling this crap on your system?"

"I've got my reasons."

"Yeah, I bet you do. And God help anyone who gets in your way."

He got up and walked off.

Tinker came over, grinning.

"You think you can learn to run a front-end loader?"

"I think so," I said.

"I think so, too," he said. "Ole Blockhead there likes you — he just don't know how to say so."

"I noticed."

Tink laughed. "Tough little motherfucker, ain't you?"

"I hope so," I said.

I spent the rest of the summer driving a front-end loader, and when I went back to school that fall, almost as black as Tink himself, the other teachers stopped laughing at me. Sometimes they looked at me out of the corners of their eyes after I passed, but they had stopped laughing.

I've got my reasons. That's what I told him. And I did. I did not spend that season in hell just on a whim. I had to get in shape, you see. Preparing to dig a grave for a man or a woman may not require such drastic measures, but it was not just a man or woman I had in mind.

It was that damned Cadillac I meant to bury.

By April of the following year I was on the State Highway Commission's mailing list. Every month I received a bulletin called *Nevada Road Signs.* I skimmed most of the material, which concerned itself with pending highway-improvement bills, road equipment that had been bought and sold, State Legislature action on such subjects as sand dune control and new anti-erosion techniques. What I was interested in was always on the last page or two of the bulletin. This section, simply titled The Calendar, listed the dates and sites of roadwork in each coming month. I was especially interested in sites and dates followed by a simple four-letter abbreviation: RPAV. This stood for re-paving, and my experience on Harvey Blocker's crew had showed me that these were the operations which most frequently called for detours. But not *always* — no indeed. Closing a section of road is a step the Highway Commission never takes unless there is no other choice. But sooner or later, I thought, those four letters might spell the end for Dolan. Just four letters, but there were times when I saw them in my dreams: RPAV.

Not that it would be easy, or perhaps even soon

— I knew I might have to wait for years, and that someone else might get Dolan in the meantime. He was an evil man, and evil men live dangerous lives. Four loosely related vectors would have to come together, like a rare conjunction of the planets: travel for Dolan, vacation time for me, a national holiday, and a three-day weekend.

Years, maybe. Or maybe never. But I felt a kind of serenity — a surety that it *would* happen, and that when it did I would be prepared. And eventually it did happen. Not that summer, not that fall, and not the following spring. But in June of last year, I opened *Nevada Road Signs* and saw this in The Calendar:

> JULY 1–JULY 22 (TENT.):
> U.S. 71 MI 440–472 (WESTBND) RPAV

Hands shaking, I paged through my desk calendar to July and saw that July 4th fell on a Monday.

So here were three of the four vectors, for surely there would be a detour somewhere in the middle of such an extensive repaving job.

But Dolan . . . what about Dolan? What about the fourth vector?

Three times before I could remember him going to L.A. during the week of the Fourth of July — a week which is one of the few slow ones in Las Vegas. I could remember three other times when he had gone somewhere else — once to New York, once to Miami, once all the way to London

36

— and a fourth time when he had simply stayed put in Vegas.

If he went . . .

Was there a way I could find out?

I thought on this long and hard, but two visions kept intruding. In the first I saw Dolan's Cadillac speeding west toward L.A. along U.S. 71 at dusk, casting a long shadow behind it. I saw it passing DETOUR AHEAD signs, the last of them warning CB owners to turn off their sets. I saw the Cadillac passing abandoned road equipment — bulldozers, graders, front-end loaders. Abandoned not just because it was after knocking-off time but because it was a weekend, a three-day weekend.

In the second vision everything was the same except the detour signs were gone.

They were gone because I had taken them down.

It was on the last day of school when I suddenly realized how I might be able to find out. I had been nearly drowsing, my mind a million miles away from both school and Dolan, when I suddenly sat bolt-upright, knocking a vase on the side of my desk (it contained some pretty desert flowers my students had brought me as an end-of-school present) to the floor, where it shattered. Several of my students, who had *also* been drowsing, also sat bolt-upright, and perhaps something on my face frightened one of them, because a little boy named Timothy Urich burst into tears and I had to soothe him.

Sheets, I thought, comforting Timmy. *Sheets and pillowcases and bedding and silverware; the rugs; the grounds. Everything has to look just so. He'll want everything just so.*

37

Of course. Having things just so was as much a part of Dolan as his Cadillac.

I began to smile, and Timmy Urich smiled back, but it wasn't Timmy I was smiling at.

I was smiling at Elizabeth.

School finished on June 10th that year. Twelve days later I flew to Los Angeles. I rented a car and checked into the same cheap hotel I had used on other occasions. On each of the next three days I drove into the Hollywood Hills and mounted a watch on Dolan's house. It could not be a *constant* watch; that would have been noticed. The rich hire people to notice interlopers, because all too often they turn out to be dangerous.

Like me.

At first there was nothing. The house was not boarded up, the lawn was not overgrown — heaven forbid! — the water in the pool was doubtless clean and chlorinated. But there was a look of emptiness and disuse all the same — shades pulled against the summer sun, no cars in the central turnaround, no one to use the pool that a young man with a ponytail cleaned every other morning.

I became convinced it was a bust. Yet I stayed, wishing and hoping for the final vector.

On the 29th of June, when I had almost consigned myself to another year of watching and waiting and exercising and driving a front-end loader in the summer for Harvey Blocker (if he would have me again, that was) a blue car marked LOS ANGELES SECURITY SERVICES pulled up at the gate of Dolan's house. A man in a uniform got out and used a key to open the gate. He drove his car in and around the corner. A few moments later he came back on foot, closed the gate, and relocked it.

This was at least a break in the routine. I felt a dim flicker of hope.

I drove off, managed to make myself stay away for nearly two hours, and then drove back, parking at the head of the block instead of the foot this time. Fifteen minutes later a blue van pulled up in front of Dolan's house. Written on the side were the words BIG JOE'S CLEANING SERVICE. My heart leaped up in my chest. I was watching in the rear-view mirror, and I remember how my hands clamped down on the steering wheel of the rental car.

Four women got out of the van, two white, one black, one Chicana. They were dressed in white, like waitresses, but they were not waitresses, of course; they were cleaning women.

The security guard answered when one of them buzzed at the gate, and unlocked it. The five of them talked and laughed together. The security guard attempted to goose one of the women and she slapped his hand aside, still laughing.

One of the women went back to the van and drove it into the turnaround. The others walked up, talking among themselves as the guard closed the gate and locked it again.

Sweat was pouring down my face; it felt like grease. My heart was triphammering.

They were out of my field of vision in the rear-view mirror. I took a chance and looked around.

I saw the back doors of the van swing open.

One of them carried a neat stack of sheets; another had towels; another had a pair of vacuum cleaners.

They trooped up to the door and the guard let them inside.

I drove away, shaking so badly I could hardly steer the car.

They were opening the house. He was coming.

Dolan did not trade in his Cadillac every year, or even every two — the gray Sedan DeVille he was driving as that June neared its end was three years old. I knew its dimensions exactly. I had written the GM company for them, pretending to be a research writer. They had sent me an operator's manual and spec sheet for that year's model. They even returned the stamped, self-addressed envelope I had enclosed. Big companies apparently maintain their courtesy even when they're running in the red.

I had then taken three figures — the Cadillac's width at its widest point, height at its tallest, and length at its longest — to a friend of mine who teaches mathematics at Las Vegas High School. I have told you, I think, that I had prepared for this, and not all my preparation was physical. Most assuredly not.

I presented my problem as a purely hypothetical one. I was trying to write a science fiction story, I said, and I wanted to have my figures exactly right. I even made up a few plausible plot fragments — my own inventiveness rather astonished me.

My friend wanted to know how fast this alien scout vehicle of mine would be going. It was a question I had not expected, and I asked him if it mattered.

"Of course it matters," he said. "It matters a lot. If you want the scout vehicle in your story to fall directly *into* your trap, the trap has to be exactly the right size. Now this figure you've given me is seventeen feet by five feet."

I opened my mouth to say that wasn't exactly right, but he was already holding up his hand.

"Just an approximation," he said. "Makes it easier to figure the arc."

"The what?"

"The arc of descent," he repeated, and I cooled off. That was a phrase with which a man bent on revenge could fall in love. It had a dark, smoothly portentous sound. *The arc of descent.*

I'd taken it for granted that if I dug the grave so that the Cadillac could fit, it *would* fit. It took this friend of mine to make me see that before it could serve its purpose as a grave, it had to work as a trap.

The shape itself was important, he said. The sort of slit-trench I had been envisioning might not work — in fact, the odds of its not working were greater than the odds that it would. "If the vehicle doesn't hit the start of the trench dead-on," he said, "it may not go all the way in at all. It would just slide along on an angle for awhile and when it stopped all the aliens would climb out the passenger door and zap your heroes." The answer, he said, was to widen the entrance end, giving the whole excavation a funnel-shape.

Then there was this problem of speed.

If Dolan's Cadillac was going too fast and the

41

hole was too short, it would fly across, sinking a bit as it went, and either the frame or the tires would strike the lip of the hole on the far side. It would flip over on its roof — but without falling in the hole at all. On the other hand, if the Cadillac was going too slowly and the hole was too long, it might land at the bottom on its nose instead of its wheels, and that would never do. You couldn't bury a Cadillac with the last two feet of its trunk and its rear bumper sticking out of the ground any more than you could bury a man with his legs sticking up.

"So how fast will your scout vehicle be going?"

I calculated quickly. On the open highway, Dolan's driver kept it pegged between sixty and sixty-five. He would probably be driving a little slower than that where I planned to make my try. I could take away the detour signs, but I couldn't hide the road machinery or erase all the signs of construction.

"About twenty rull," I said.

He smiled. "Translation, please?"

"Say fifty earth-miles an hour."

"Ah-hah." He set to work at once with his slip-stick while I sat beside him, bright-eyed and smiling, thinking about that wonderful phrase: *arc of descent.*

He looked up almost at once. "You know," he said, "you might want to think about changing the dimensions of the vehicle, buddy."

"Oh? Why do you say that?"

"Seventeen by five is pretty big for a scout vehicle." He laughed. "That's damn near the size of a Lincoln Mark IV."

I laughed, too. We laughed together.

After I saw the women going into the house with the sheets and towels, I flew back to Las Vegas.

I unlocked my house, went into the living room, and picked up the telephone. My hand trembled a little. For nine years I had waited and watched like a spider in the eaves or a mouse behind a baseboard. I had tried never to give Dolan the slightest clue that Elizabeth's husband was still interested in him — the totally empty look he had given me that day as I passed his disabled Cadillac on the way back to Vegas, furious as it had made me at the time, was my just reward.

But now I would have to take a risk. I would have to take it because I could not be in two places at the same time and it was imperative that I know *if* Dolan was coming, and *when* to make the detour temporarily disappear.

I had figured out a plan coming home on the plane. I thought it would work. I would *make* it work.

I dialed Los Angeles directory assistance and asked for the number of Big Joe's Cleaning Service. I got it and dialed it.

"This is Bill at Rennie's Catering," I said. "We got a party Saturday night at 1121 Aster Drive in Hollywood Hills. I wanted to know if one of your girls would check for Mr. Dolan's big punchbowl in the cabinet over the stove. Could you do that for me?"

I was asked to hold on. I did, somehow, although with the passing of each endless second I became more and more sure that he had smelled a rat and

43

was calling the phone company on one line while I held on the other.

At last — at long, *long* last — he came back on. He sounded upset, but that was all right. That was just how I wanted him to sound.

"*Saturday* night?"

"Yes, that's right. But I don't have a punch-bowl as big as they're going to want unless I call across town, and my impression was that he already has one. I'd just like to be sure."

"Look, mister, my call-sheet says Mr. Dolan ain't expected in until three P.M. *Sunday* afternoon. I'll be glad to have one of my girls check out your punch-bowl, but I want to straighten this other business out first. Mr. Dolan is not a man to fuck around with, if you'll pardon my French —"

"I couldn't agree with you more," I said.

"— and if he's going to show up a day early, I got to send some more girls out there right away."

"Let me double-check," I said. The third-grade reading textbook I use, *Roads to Everywhere,* was on the table beside me. I picked it up and riffled some of the pages close to the phone.

"Oh, boy," I said. "It's my mistake. He's having people in *Sunday* night. I'm really sorry. You going to hit me?"

"Nah. Listen, let me put you on hold again — I'll get one of the girls and have her check on the —"

"No need, if it's *Sunday,*" I said. "My big punch-bowl's coming back from a wedding reception in Glendale Sunday morning."

"Okay. Take it easy." Comfortable. Unsuspicious. The voice of a man who wasn't going to think twice.

I hoped.

I hung up and sat still, working it out in my head as carefully as I could. To get to L.A. by three, he would be leaving Vegas about ten o'clock Sunday morning. And he would arrive in the vicinity of the detour between eleven-fifteen and eleven-thirty, when traffic was apt to be almost non-existent anyway.

I decided it was time to stop dreaming and start acting.

I looked through the want ads, made some telephone calls, and then went out to look at five used vehicles that were within my financial reach. I settled for a battered Ford van that had rolled off the assembly line the same year Elizabeth was killed. I paid cash. I was left with only two hundred and fifty-seven dollars in my savings account, but this did not disturb me in the slightest. On my way home I stopped at a rental place the size of a discount department store and rented a portable air compressor, using my MasterCard as collateral.

Late Friday afternoon I loaded the van: picks, shovels, compressor, a hand-dolly, a toolbox, binoculars, and a borrowed Highway Department jackhammer with an assortment of arrowhead-shaped attachments made for slicing through asphalt. A large square piece of sand-colored canvas, plus a long roll of canvas — this latter had been a special project of mine last summer — and twenty-one thin wooden struts, each five feet long. Last but not least, a big industrial stapler.

On the edge of the desert I stopped at a shopping

center and stole a pair of license plates and put them on my van.

Seventy-six miles west of Vegas, I saw the first orange sign: CONSTRUCTION AHEAD • PASS AT YOUR OWN RISK. Then, a mile or so beyond that, I saw the sign I had been waiting for since . . . well, ever since Elizabeth died, I suppose, although I hadn't always known it.

DETOUR AHEAD 6 MILES

Dusk was deepening toward dark as I arrived and surveyed the situation. It could have been better if I'd planned it, but not much.

The detour was a right turn between two rises. It looked like an old fence-line road which the Highway Department had smoothed and widened to temporarily accommodate the heavier traffic flow. It was marked by a flashing arrow powered by a buzzing battery in a padlocked steel box.

Just beyond the detour, as the highway rose toward the crest of that second rise, the road was blocked off by a double line of road cones. Beyond them (if one was so extraordinarily stupid as to have, first, missed the flashing arrow and, second, run over the road cones without realizing it — I suppose some drivers were) was an orange sign almost as big a billboard, reading ROAD CLOSED • USE DETOUR.

Yet the *reason* for the detour was not visible from here, and that was good. I didn't want Dolan to have the slightest chance of smelling the trap before he fell into it.

Moving quickly — I didn't want to be seen at this — I got out of the van and quickly stacked up some dozen of the road cones, creating a lane wide enough for the van. I dragged the ROAD CLOSED sign to the right, then ran back to the van, got in, and drove through the gap.

Now I could hear an approaching motor.

I grabbed the cones again, replacing them as fast as I could. Two of them spilled out of my hands and rolled down into the gully. I chased after them, panting. I tripped over a rock in the dark, fell sprawling, and got up quickly with dust on my face and blood dripping from one palm. The car was closer now; soon it would appear over the last rise before the detour-junction and in the glow thrown by his high beams the driver would see a man in jeans and a tee-shirt trying to replace road cones while his van stood idling where no vehicle that didn't belong to the Nevada State Highway Department was supposed to be. I got the last cone in place and ran back to the sign. I tugged too hard. It swayed and almost fell over.

As the approaching car's headlights began to brighten on the rise to the east, I suddenly became convinced it was a Nevada State Trooper.

The sign was back where it had been — and if it wasn't, it was close enough. I sprinted for the van, got in, and drove over the next rise. Just as I cleared it, I saw headlights splash over the rise behind me.

Had he seen me in the dark, with my own lights out?

I didn't think so.

I sat back against the seat, eyes closed, waiting for my heart to slow down. At last, as the sound of the car bouncing and bucketing its way down the detour faded out, it did.

I was here — safe behind the detour.

It was time to get to work.

Beyond the rise, the road descended to a long, straight flat. Two-thirds of the way along this straight stretch the road simply ceased to exist — it was replaced by piles of dirt and a long, wide stretch of crushed gravel.

Would they see that and stop? Turn around? Or would they keep on going, confident that there must be an approved way through since they had not seen any detour signs?

Too late to worry about it now.

I picked a spot about twenty yards into the flat, but still a quarter of a mile short of the place where the road dissolved. I pulled over to the side of the road, worked my way into the back of the van, and opened the back doors. I slid out a couple of boards and muscled the equipment. Then I rested and looked up at the cold desert stars.

"Here we go, Elizabeth," I whispered to them.

It seemed I felt a cold hand stroke the back of my neck.

The compressor made a racket and the jack-hammer was even worse, but there was no help for it — the best I could hope for was to be done with the first stage of the work before midnight. If it went on much longer than that I was going to be in trouble anyway, because I had only a limited quantity of gasoline for the compressor.

Never mind. Don't think of who might be listening and wondering what fool would be running a jackhammer in the middle of the night; think about Dolan. Think about the gray Sedan DeVille.

Think about the arc of descent.

I marked off the dimensions of the grave first, using white chalk, the tape measure from my tool-box, and the figures my mathematician friend had worked out. When I was done, a rough rectangle not quite five feet wide by forty-two feet long glimmered in the dark. At the nearer end it flared wide. In the gloom that flare did not look so much like a funnel as it had on the graph paper where my mathematician friend first sketched it. In the gloom it looked like a gaping mouth at the end of a long, straight windpipe. *All the better to eat you with, my dear,* I thought, and smiled in the dark.

I drew twenty more lines across the box, making stripes two feet wide. Last, I drew a single vertical line down the middle, creating a grid of forty-two near-squares, two feet by two and a half. The forty-third segment was the shovel-shaped flare at the end.

Then I rolled up my sleeves, pull-started the compressor, and went back to square one.

The work went faster than I had any right to hope, but not as fast as I had dared to dream — does it ever? It would have been better if I could have used the heavy equipment, but that would come later. The first thing was to carve up the squares of paving. I was not done by midnight and not by three in the morning, when the compressor ran out of gas. I had anticipated this might happen, and was equipped with a siphon for the van's gas tank. I got as far as unscrewing the gas-cap, but when the smell of the gasoline hit me,

49

I simply screwed the cap back on and lay down flat in the back of the van.

No more, not tonight. I couldn't. In spite of the work-gloves I had worn, my hands were covered with big blisters, many of them now weeping. My whole body seemed to vibrate from the steady, punishing beat of the jackhammer, and my arms felt like tuning forks gone mad. My head ached. My *teeth* ached. My back tormented me; my spine felt as if it had been filled with ground glass.

I had cut my way through twenty-eight squares. Twenty-eight.

Fourteen to go.

And that was only the start.

Never, I thought. *It's impossible. Can't be done.*

That cold hand again.

Yes, my darling. Yes.

The ringing in my ears was subsiding a little now; every once in awhile I could hear an approaching engine . . . and then it would subside to a drone on the right as it turned onto the detour and started around the loop the Highway Department had created to bypass the construction.

Tomorrow was Saturday . . . sorry, today. *Today* was Saturday. Dolan was coming on Sunday. No time.

Yes, my darling.

The blast had torn her to pieces.

My darling had been torn to pieces for telling the truth to the police about what she had seen, for refusing to be intimidated, for being brave, and Dolan was still driving around in his Cadillac and drinking twenty-year-old Scotch while his Rolex glimmered on his wrist.

I'll try, I thought, and then I fell into a dreamless sleep that was like death.

I woke up with the sun, already hot at eight o'clock, shining in my face. I sat up and screamed, my throbbing hands flying to the small of my back. Work? Cut up another fourteen chunks of asphalt? I couldn't even *walk*.

But I could walk, and I did.

Moving like a very old man on his way to a shuffleboard game, I worked my way to the glove compartment and opened it. I had put a bottle of Empirin there in case of such a morning after.

Had I thought I was in shape? Had I *really?*

Well! That was quite funny, wasn't it?

I took four of the Empirin with water, waited fifteen minutes for them to dissolve in my stomach, and then wolfed a breakfast of dried fruit and cold Pop-Tarts.

I looked over to where the compressor and the jackhammer waited. The yellow skin of the compressor already seemed to sizzle in the morning sunshine. Leading up to it on either side of my incision were the neatly cut squares of asphalt.

I didn't want to go over there and pick up that jackhammer. I thought of Harvey Blocker saying, *You ain't* never *gonna be strong, bubba. Some people and plants take hold in the sun. Some wither up and die . . . Why you pulling this crap on your system?*

"She was in pieces," I croaked. "I loved her and she was in pieces."

As a cheer it was never going to replace "Go, Bears!" or "Hook em, horns!" but it got me moving. I siphoned gas from the van's tank, gagging

at the taste and the stink, holding onto my breakfast only by a grim act of will. I wondered briefly
what I was going to do if the road-crew had drained
the diesel from their machines before going home
for the long weekend, and quickly shoved the
thought out of my mind. It made no sense to worry
over things I couldn't control. More and more I
felt like a man who has jumped out of the bay
of a B-52 with a parasol in his hand instead of
a parachute on his back.

I carried the gasoline can over to the compressor
and poured it into the tank. I had to use my left
hand to curl the fingers of my right around the
handle of the compressor's starter-cord. When I
pulled, more blisters broke, and as the compressor
started up, I saw thick pus dripping out of my
fist.

Never make it.

Please, darling.

I walked over to the jackhammer and started
in again.

The first hour was the worst, and then the steady
pounding of the jackhammer combined with the
Empirin seemed to numb everything — my back,
my hands, my head. I finished cutting out the last
block of asphalt by eleven. It was time to see how
much I remembered of what Tinker had told me
about jump-starting road equipment.

I went staggering and flapping back to my van
and drove a mile and a half down the road to where
the road construction was going on. I saw my machine almost at once: a big Case-Jordan bucket-
loader with a grapple-and-pincers attachment on
the back. $135,000 worth of rolling stock. I had

driven a Caterpillar for Blocker, but this one would be pretty much the same.

I hoped.

I climbed up into the cab and looked at the diagram printed on the head of the stick-shift. It looked just the same as the one on my Cat. I ran the pattern once or twice. There was some resistance at first because some grit had found its way into the gearbox — the guy who drove this baby hadn't put down his sand-flaps and his foreman hadn't checked him. Blocker would have checked. And docked the driver five bucks, long weekend or not.

His eyes. His half-admiring, half-contemptuous eyes. What would he think of an errand like this?

Never mind. This was no time to be thinking of Harvey Blocker; this was a time to be thinking of Elizabeth. And Dolan.

There was a piece of burlap on the steel floor of the cab. I lifted it, looking for the key. There was no key there, of course.

Tink's voice in my mind: *Shit, a kid could jump-start one of these babies, whitebread. Ain't nothin to it. At least a car's got a ignition lock on it — new ones do, anyway. Look here. No, not where the key goes, you ain't got no key, why you want to look where the key goes? Look under here. See these wires hangin down?*

I looked now and saw the wires hanging down, looking just as they had when Tinker pointed them out to me: red, blue, yellow, and green. I pared the insulation from an inch of each and then took a twist of copper wire from my back pocket.

Okay, whitebread, lissen up 'cause we maybe goan

53

give Q and A later, you dig me? You gonna wire the red and the green. You won't forget that, 'cause it's like Christmas. That takes care of your ignition.

I used my wire to hold the bare places on the red and green wires of the Case-Jordan's ignition together. The desert wind hooted, thin, like the sound of someone blowing over the top of a soda bottle. Sweat ran down my neck and into my shirt, where it caught and tickled.

Now you just got the blue and the yellow. You ain't gonna wire em; you just gonna touch em together and you gonna make sho you ain't touchin no bare wire wither own self when you do it neither, 'less you wanna make some hot electrified water in your Jockeys, m'man. The blue and the yellow the ones turn the starter. Off you go. When you feel like you had enough of a joyride, you just pull the red and green wires apart. Like turnin off the key you don't have.

I touched the blue and yellow wires together. A big yellow spark jumped up and I recoiled, striking the back of my head on one of the metal posts at the rear of the cab. Then I leaned forward and touched them together again. The motor turned over, coughed, and the bucket-loader took a sudden spasmodic lurch forward. I was thrown into the rudimentary dashboard, the left side of my face striking the steering bar. I had forgotten to put the damned transmission in neutral and had almost lost an eye as a result. I could almost hear Tink laughing.

I fixed that and then tried the wires again. The motor turned over and turned over. It coughed once, puffing a dirty brown smoke signal into the air to be torn away by the ceaseless wind, and then the motor just went on cranking. I kept trying to tell myself the machine was just in rough shape — a man who'd go off without putting the sand-flaps down, after all, was apt to forget anything — but I became more and more sure that they had drained the diesel, just as I had feared.

And then, just as I was about to give up and look for something I could use to dipstick the loader's fuel tank (*all the better to read the bad news with, my dear*), the motor bellowed into life.

I let the wires go — the bare patch on the blue one was smoking — and goosed the throttle. When it was running smoothly, I geared it into first, swung it around, and started back toward the long brown rectangle cut neatly into the westbound lane of the highway.

The rest of the day was a long bright hell of roaring engine and blazing sun. The driver of the Case-Jordan had forgotten to mount his sand-flaps, but he had remembered to take his sun umbrella. Well, the old gods laugh sometimes, I guess. No reason why. They just do. And I guess the old gods have a twisted sense of humor.

It was almost two o'clock before I got all of the asphalt chunks down into the ditch, because I had never achieved any real degree of delicacy with the pincers. And with the spade-shaped piece at the end, I had to cut it in two and then drag each of the chunks down into the ditch by hand. I was afraid that if I used the pincers I would break them.

When all the asphalt pieces were down in the ditch, I drove the bucket-loader back down to the road equipment. I was getting low on fuel; it was time to siphon. I stopped at the van, got the hose . . . and found myself staring, hypnotized, at the big jerrican of water. I tossed the siphon away for the time being and crawled into the back of the van. I poured water over my face and neck and chest and screamed with pleasure. I knew that if I drank I would vomit, but I had to drink. So I did and I vomited, not getting up to do it but only turning my head to one side and then crab-crawling as far away from the mess as I could.

Then I slept again and when I woke up it was nearly dusk and somewhere a wolf was howling at a new moon rising in the purple sky.

In the dying light the cut I had made really did look like a grave — the grave of some mythical ogre. Goliath, maybe.

Never, I told the long hole in the asphalt.

Please, Elizabeth whispered back. *Please . . . for me.*

I got four more Empirin out of the glove compartment and swallowed them down.

"For you," I said.

I parked the Case-Jordan with its fuel tank close to the tank of a bulldozer, and used a crowbar to pry off the caps on both. A 'dozer-jockey on a state crew might get away with forgetting to drop the sand-flaps on his vehicle, but with forgetting to lock the fuel-cap, in these days of $1.05 diesel? Never.

I got the fuel running from the 'dozer into my loader and waited, trying not to think, watching the moon rise higher and higher in the sky. After awhile I drove back to the cut in the asphalt and started to dig.

Running a bucket-loader by moonlight was a lot easier than running a jackhammer under the broiling desert sun, but it was still slow work because I was determined that the floor of my excavation should have exactly the right slant. As a consequence, I frequently consulted the carpenter's level I'd brought with me. That meant stopping the loader, getting down, measuring, and climbing up into the peak-seat again. No problem ordinarily, but by midnight my body had stiffened up and every movement sent a shriek of pain through my bones and muscles. My back was the worst; I began to fear I had done something fairly unpleasant to it.

But that — like everything else — was something I would have to worry about later.

If a hole five feet deep as well as forty-two feet long and five feet wide had been required, it really *would* have been impossible, of course, bucket-loader or not — I might just as well have planned to send him into outer space, or drop the Taj Mahal on him. The total yield on such dimensions is over a thousand cubic feet of earth.

"You've got to create a funnel shape that will suck your bad aliens in," my mathematician friend had said, "and then you've got to create an inclined plane that pretty much mimes the arc of descent."

He drew one on another sheet of graph paper.

"That means that your intergalactic rebels or whatever they are only need to remove *half* as much earth as the figures initially show. In this case —" He scribbled on a work sheet, and beamed. "Five hundred and twenty-five cubic feet. Chicken-feed. One man could do it."

I had believed so, too, once upon a time, but I had not reckoned on the heat . . . the blisters . . . the exhaustion . . . the steady pain in my back.

Stop for a minute, but not too long. Measure the slant of the trench.

It's not as bad as you thought, is it, darling? At least it's roadbed and not desert hardpan —

I moved more slowly along the length of the grave as the hole got deeper. My hands were bleeding now as I worked the controls. Ram the drop-lever all the way forward until the bucket lay on the ground. Pull back on the drop-lever and shove the one that extended the armature with a high hydraulic whine. Watch as the bright oiled metal slid out of the dirty orange casing, pushing the bucket into the dirt. Every now and then a spark would flash as the bucket slid over a piece of flint. Now raise the bucket . . . swivel it, a dark oblong shape against the stars (and try to ignore the steady throbbing pain in your neck the way you're trying to ignore the even deeper throb of pain in your back) . . . and dump it down in the ditch, covering the chunks of asphalt already there.

Never mind, darling — you can bandage your hands when it's done. When he's *done.*

"She was in pieces," I croaked, and jockeyed the bucket back into place so I could take another two hundred pounds of dirt and gravel out of Dolan's grave.

How the time flies when you are having a good time.

Moments after I had noticed the first faint streaks of light in the east I got down to take another measurement of the floor's incline with the carpenter's level. I was actually getting near the end; I thought I might just make it. I knelt, and as I did I felt something in my back let go. It went with a dull little snap.

I uttered a guttural cry and collapsed on my side on the narrow, slanted floor of the excavation, lips pulled back from my teeth, hands pressing into the small of my back.

Little by little the very worst of the pain passed and I was able to get to my feet.

All right, I thought. *That's it. It's over. It was a good try, but it's over.*

Please, darling, Elizabeth whispered back — impossible as it would have been to believe once upon a time, that whispering voice had begun to take on unpleasant undertones in my mind; there was a sense of monstrous implacability about it. *Please don't give up. Please go on.*

Go on digging? I don't even know if I can walk!

But there's so little left to do! the voice wailed — it was no longer just the voice that *spoke* for Elizabeth, if it had ever been; it *was* Elizabeth. *So little left, darling!*

I looked at my excavation in the growing light and nodded slowly. She was right. The bucket-loader was only five feet from the end; seven at most. But it was the *deepest* five or seven, of course; the five or seven with the most dirt in it.

You can do it, darling — I know you can. Softly cajoling.

But it was not really her voice that persuaded me to go on. What really turned the trick was an image of Dolan lying asleep in his penthouse while I stood here in this hole beside a stinking, rumbling bucket-loader, covered with dirt, my hands in flaps and ruins. Dolan sleeping in silk pajama bottoms with one of his blondes asleep beside him, wearing only the top.

Downstairs, in the glassed-in executive section of the parking garage, the Cadillac, already loaded with luggage, would be gassed and ready to go.

"All right, then," I said. I climbed slowly back into the bucket-loader's seat and revved the engine.

I kept on until nine o'clock and then I quit — there were other things to do, and I was running out of time. My angled hole was forty feet long. It would have to be enough.

I drove the bucket-loader back to its original spot and parked it. I would need it again, and that would mean siphoning more gas, but there was no time for that now. I wanted more Empirin, but there weren't many left in the bottle and I would need them all later today . . . and tomorrow. Oh, yes, tomorrow — Monday, the glorious Fourth.

Instead of Empirin I took a fifteen-minute rest. I could ill-afford the time, but I forced myself to take it just the same. I lay on my back in the van, my muscles jumping and twitching, imagining Dolan.

He would be packing a few last-minute items in a Travel-All now — some papers to look over, a toilet kit, maybe a paperback book or a deck of cards.

Suppose he flies this time? a malicious voice deep inside me whispered, and I couldn't help it — a moan escaped me. He had never flown to L.A. before — always it had been the Cadillac. I had an idea he didn't *like* to fly. Sometimes he did, though — he had flown all the way to London once — and the thought lingered, itching and throbbing like a scaly patch of skin.

It was nine-thirty when I took out the roll of canvas and the big industrial stapler and the wooden struts. The day was overcast and a little cooler — God sometimes grants a favor. Up until then I'd forgotten my bald head in consideration of larger agonies, but now, when I touched it with my fingers, I drew them away with a little hiss of pain. I looked at it in the outside passenger mirror and saw that it was a deep, angry red — almost a plum color.

Back in Vegas Dolan would be making last-minute phone calls. His driver would be bringing the Cadillac around front. There were only about seventy-five miles between me and it, and soon the Cadillac would start to close that distance at sixty miles an hour. I had no time to stand around bemoaning my sunburned pate.

I love your sunburned pate, dear, Elizabeth said beside me.

"Thank you, Beth," I said, and began taking the struts over to the hole.

The work was now light compared to the digging I'd done earlier, and the almost unbearable agony in my back subsided to a steady dull throb.

But what about later? that insinuating voice asked. *What about that, hmmmm?*

Later would have to take care of itself, that was all. It was beginning to look as if the trap was going to be ready, and that was the important thing.

The struts spanned the hole with just enough extra length to allow me to seat them tightly in the sides of the asphalt which formed the top layer of my excavation. This was a job that would have been tougher at night, when the asphalt was hard, but now, at mid-morning, the stuff was sludgy-pliable, and it was like sticking pencils in wads of cooling taffy.

When I had all the struts in, the hole had taken on the look of my original chalk diagram, minus the line down the middle. I positioned the heavy roll of canvas next to the shallow end of the hole and removed the hanks of rope that had tied it shut.

Then I unrolled forty-two feet of Route 71.

Close up, the illusion was not perfect — as stage make-up and set-decoration is never perfect from the first three rows. But from even a few yards away, it was virtually undetectable. It was a dark-gray strip which matched the actual surface of Route 71 exactly. On the far left of the canvas strip (as you faced west) was a broken yellow passing line.

I settled the long strip of canvas over the wooden

understructure, then went slowly along the length of it, stapling the canvas to the struts. My hands didn't want to do the work but I coaxed them.

With the canvas secured, I returned to the van, slid behind the wheel (sitting down caused another brief but agonizing muscle spasm), and drove back to the top of the rise. I sat there for a full minute, looking down at my lumpy, wounded hands as they lay in my lap. Then I got out and looked back down Route 71, almost casually. I didn't want to focus on any one thing, you see; I wanted the whole picture — a gestalt, if you will. I wanted, as much as possible, to see the scene as Dolan and his men were going to see it when they came over the rise. I wanted to get an idea of how right — or how wrong — it was going to feel to them.

What I saw looked better than I could have hoped.

The road machinery at the far end of the straight stretch justified the piles of dirt that had come from my excavation. The asphalt chunks in the ditch were mostly buried. Some still showed — the wind was picking up, and it had blown the dirt around — but that looked like the remnants of an old paving job. The compressor I'd brought in the back of the van looked like Highway Department equipment.

And from here the illusion of the canvas strip was perfect — Route 71 appeared to be utterly untouched down there.

Traffic had been heavy Friday and fairly heavy on Saturday — the drone of motors heading into the detour loop had been almost constant. This morning, however, there was hardly any traffic at all; most people had gotten to wherever they intended to spend the Fourth, or were taking the Interstate forty miles south to get there. That was fine with me.

I parked the van just out of sight over the brow of the rise and lay on my belly until ten-forty-five. Then, after a big milk-truck had gone lumbering slowly up the detour, I backed the van down, opened the rear doors, and threw all the road cones inside.

The flashing arrow was a tougher proposition — at first I couldn't see how I was going to unhook it from the locked battery box without electrocuting myself. Then I saw the plug. It had been mostly hidden by a hard rubber O-ring on the side of the sign-case . . . a little insurance policy against vandals and practical jokers who might find pulling the plug on such a highway sign an amusing prank, I supposed.

I found a hammer and chisel in my toolbox, and four hard blows were sufficient to split the O-ring. I yanked it off with a pair of pliers and pulled the cable free. The arrow stopped flashing and went dark. I pushed the battery box into the ditch and buried it. It was strange to stand there and hear it humming down there in the sand. But it made me think of Dolan, and that made me laugh.

I didn't think Dolan would hum.

He might *scream*, but I didn't think he would *hum*.

Four bolts held the arrow in a low steel cradle. I loosened them as fast as I could, ears cocked for another motor. It was time for one — but not time for Dolan yet, surely.

That got the interior pessimist going again.

What if he flew?

He doesn't like to fly.

What if he's driving but going another way? Going by the Interstate, for instance? Today everyone else is . . .

He always *goes by 71.*

Yes, but what if —

"Shut up," I hissed. "Shut up, damn you, just *shut the fuck up!*"

Easy, darling — easy! Everything will be all right.

I got the arrow into the back of the van. It crashed against the sidewall and some of the bulbs broke. More of them broke when I tossed the cradle in after it.

With that done, I drove back up the rise, pausing at the top to look behind me. I had taken away the arrow and the cones; all that remained now was that big orange warning: ROAD CLOSED • USE DETOUR.

There was a car coming. It occurred to me that if Dolan was early, it had all been for nothing — the goon driving would simply turn down the detour, leaving me to go mad out here in the desert.

It was a Chevrolet.

My heart slowed down and I let out a long, shuddering breath. But there was no more time for nerves.

I drove back to where I had parked to look at my camouflage job and parked there again. I reached under the jumble of stuff in the back of the van and got the jack. Grimly ignoring my screaming back, I jacked up the rear end of the

van, loosened the lug-nuts on the back tire they
would see when

(if)

they came, and tossed it into the back of the
van. More glass broke, and I would just have to
hope there had been no damage done to the tire.
I didn't have a spare.

I went back to the front of the van, got my
old binoculars, and then headed back toward the
detour. I passed it and got to the top of the next
rise as fast as I could — a shambling trot was
really all I could manage by this time.

Once at the top, I trained my binoculars east.

I had a three-mile field of vision, and could see
snatches of the road for two miles east of that.
Six vehicles were currently on the way, strung out
like random beads on a long string. The first was
a foreign car, Datsun or Subaru, I thought, less
than a mile away. Beyond that was a pick-up, and
beyond the pick-up was what looked like a Mustang. The others were just desert-light flashing on
chrome and glass.

When the first car neared — it was a Subaru
— I stood up and stuck my thumb out. I didn't
expect a ride looking the way I did, and I wasn't
disappointed. The expensively coiffed woman behind the wheel took one horrified glance and her
face snapped shut like a fist. Then she was gone,
down the hill and onto the detour.

"Get a bath, buddy!" the driver of the pick-up
yelled at me half a minute later.

The Mustang actually turned out to be an Escort.
It was followed by a Plymouth, the Plymouth by
a Winnebago that sounded as if it were full of

kids having a pillow-fight.

No sign of Dolan.

I looked at my watch. 11:25 A.M. If he was going to show up, it ought to be very soon. This was prime time.

The hands on my watch moved slowly around to 11:40 and there was still no sign of him. Only a late-model Ford and a hearse as black as a raincloud.

He's not coming. He went by the Interstate. Or he flew.

No. He'll come.

He won't, though. You were afraid he'd smell you, and he did. That's why he changed his pattern.

There was another twinkle of light on chrome in the distance. This car was a big one. Big enough to be a Cadillac.

I lay on my belly, elbows propped in the grit of the shoulder, binoculars to my eyes. The car disappeared behind a rise . . . re-emerged . . . slipped around a curve . . . and then came out again.

It was a Cadillac, all right, but it wasn't gray — it was a deep mint green.

What followed was the most agonizing thirty seconds of my life; thirty seconds that seemed to last for thirty years. Part of me decided on the spot, completely and irrevocably, that Dolan had traded in his old Cadillac for a new one. Certainly he had done this before, and although he had never traded for a green one before, there was certainly no law against it.

The other half argued vehemently that Cadillacs were almost a dime a dozen on the highways and byways between Vegas and L.A., and the odds against the green Caddy's being Dolan's Cadillac were a hundred to one.

Sweat ran into my eyes, blurring them, and I put the binoculars down. They weren't going to help me solve this one, anyhow. By the time I was able to see the passengers, it would be too late.

It's almost too late now! Go down there and dump the detour sign! You're going to miss him!

Let me tell you what you're going to catch in your trap if you hide that sign now: two rich old people going to L.A. to see their children and take their grandkids to Disneyland.

Do it! It's him! It's the only chance you're going to have!

That's right. The only chance. So don't blow it by catching the wrong people.

It's Dolan!

It's not!

"Stop it," I moaned, holding my head. "Stop it, stop it."

I could hear the motor now.

Dolan.

The old people.

The lady.

The tiger.

Dolan.

The old —

"Elizabeth, help me!" I groaned.

Darling, that man has never owned a green Cadillac in his life. He never would. Of course *it's not him.*

The pain in my head cleared away. I was able to get to my feet and get my thumb out.

It wasn't the old people, and it wasn't Dolan, either. It was what looked like twelve Vegas chorines crowded in with one old boy who was wearing the biggest cowboy hat and the darkest Foster Grants I'd ever seen. One of the chorines mooned me as the green Cadillac went fishtailing onto the detour.

Slowly, feeling entirely washed out, I raised the binoculars again.

And saw him coming.

There was no mistaking *that* Cadillac as it came around the curve at the far end of my uninterrupted view of the road — it was as gray as the sky overhead, but it stood out with startling clarity against the dull brown rises of land to the east.

It was him — Dolan. My long moments of doubt and indecision seemed both remote and foolish in an instant. It was Dolan, and I didn't have to see that gray Cadillac to know it.

I didn't know if he could smell me, but *I* could smell *him*.

Knowing he was on the way made it easier to pick up my aching legs and run.

I got back to the big DETOUR sign and shoved it facedown into the ditch. I shook a sand-colored piece of canvas over it, then pawed loose sand over its support posts. The overall effect wasn't as good as the fake strip of road, but I thought it would serve.

Now I ran up the second rise to where I had left the van, which was just another part of the picture now — a vehicle temporarily abandoned by the owner, who had gone off somewhere to either get a new tire or have an old one fixed.

I got into the cab and stretched out across the seat, my heart thumping.

Again, time seemed to stretch out. I lay there listening for the engine and the sound didn't come and didn't come and didn't come.

They turned off. He caught wind of you at the last moment anyway . . . or something looked hinky, either to him or to one of his men . . . and they turned off.

I lay on the seat, my back throbbing in long, slow waves, my eyes squinched tightly shut as if that would somehow help me hear better.

Was that an engine?

No — just the wind, now blowing hard enough to drive an occasional sheet of sand against the side of the van.

Not coming. Turned off or turned back.

Just the wind.

Turned off or turned b—

No, it was *not* just the wind. It was a motor, the sound of it was swelling, and a few seconds later a vehicle — one single vehicle — rushed past me.

I sat up and grabbed the wheel — I had to grab *something* — and stared out through the windshield, my eyes bulging, my tongue caught between my teeth.

The gray Cadillac floated down the hill toward the flat stretch, doing fifty or maybe a little more. The brake lights never went on. Not even at the end. They never saw it; never had so much as the slightest idea.

What happened was this: all at once the Cadillac

seemed to be driving *through* the road instead of *on* it. This illusion was so persuasive that I felt a moment of confused vertigo even though I had created the illusion myself. Dolan's Cadillac was hubcap-deep in Route 71, and then it was up to the door-panels. A bizarre thought occurred to me: if the GM company made luxury submarines, this is what they would look like going down.

I could hear thin snapping sounds as the struts supporting the canvas broke under the car. I could hear the sound of canvas rippling and ripping.

All of it happened in only three seconds, but they are three seconds I will remember my whole life.

I had an impression of the Cadillac now running with only its roof and the top two or three inches of the polarized windows visible, and then there was a big toneless thud and the sound of breaking glass and crimping metal. A large puff of dust rose in the air and the wind pulled it apart.

I wanted to go down there — wanted to go down right away — but first I had to put the detour to rights. I didn't want us to be interrupted.

I got out of the van, went around to the back, and pulled the tire back out. I put it on the wheel and tightened the six lug-nuts as fast as I could, using only my fingers. I could do a more thorough job later; in the meantime I only needed to back the van down to the place where the detour diverged from Highway 71.

I jacked the bumper down and hurried back to the cab of the van at a limping run. I paused there for a moment, listening, head cocked.

I could hear the wind.

And from the long, rectangular hole in the road, the sound of someone shouting . . . or maybe screaming.

Grinning, I got back in the van.

I backed rapidly down the road, the van swinging drunkenly back and forth. I got out, opened the back doors, and put out the traffic cones again. I kept my ear cocked for approaching traffic, but the wind had gotten too strong to make that very worthwhile. By the time I heard an approaching vehicle, it would be practically on top of me.

I started down into the ditch, tripped, landed on my prat, and slid to the bottom. I pushed away the sand-colored piece of canvas and dragged the big detour sign up to the top. I set it up again, then went back to the van and slammed the rear doors closed. I had no intention of trying to set the arrow sign up again.

I drove back over the next rise, stopped in my old place just out of sight of the detour, got out, and tightened the lug-nuts on the van's back wheel, using the tire-iron this time. The shouting had stopped, but there was no longer any question about the screaming; it was much louder.

I took my time tightening the nuts. I wasn't worried that they were going to get out and either attack me or run away into the desert, because they couldn't get out. The trap had worked perfectly. The Cadillac was now sitting squarely on its wheels at the far end of the excavation, with less than four inches of clearance on either side. The three men inside couldn't open their doors wide enough to do more than stick out a foot, if that. They couldn't open their windows because they were power-drive and the battery would be so much squashed plastic and metal and acid somewhere in the wreck of the engine.

The driver and the man in the shotgun seat might also be squashed in the wreckage, but this did not concern me; I knew that *someone* was still alive in there, just as I knew that Dolan always rode in back and wore his seatbelt as good citizens are supposed to do.

The lug-nuts tightened to my satisfaction, I drove the van down to the wide, shallow end of the trap and got out.

Most of the struts were completely gone, but I could see the splintered butt ends of a few, still sticking out of the tar. The canvas "road" lay at the bottom of the cut, crumpled and ripped and twisted. It look like a shed snakeskin.

I walked up to the deep end and here was Dolan's Cadillac.

The front end was utterly trashed. The hood had accordioned upward in a jagged fan shape. The engine compartment was a jumble of metal and rubber and hoses, all of it covered with sand and dirt that had avalanched down in the wake of the impact. There was a hissing sound and I could hear fluids running and dripping down there someplace. The chilly alcohol aroma of antifreeze was pungent in the air.

I had been worried about the windshield. There was always a chance that it could have broken inward, allowing Dolan space enough to wriggle up and out. But I hadn't been too worried; I told you that Dolan's cars were built to the sorts of specifications required by tinpot dictators and despotic military leaders. The glass was not supposed to break, and it had not.

The Caddy's rear window was even tougher because its area was smaller. Dolan couldn't break it — not in the time *I* was going to give him, certainly — and he would not dare try to shoot it out. Shooting at bullet-proof glass from close up is another form of Russian Roulette. The slug would leave only a small white fleck on the glass and then ricochet back into the car.

I'm sure he could have found an out, given world enough and time, but I was here now, and I would give him neither.

I kicked a shower of dirt across the Cadillac's roof.

The response was immediate.

"We need some help, please. We're stuck in here."

Dolan's voice. He sounded unhurt and eerily calm. But I sensed the fear underneath, held rigidly in check, and I came as close to feeling sorry for him right then as it was possible for me to come. I could imagine him sitting in the back seat of his telescoped Cadillac, one of his men injured and moaning, probably pinned by the engine block, the other either dead or unconscious.

I imagined it and felt a jittery moment of what I can only term sympathetic claustrophobia. Push the window-buttons — nothing. Try the doors, even though you can see they're going to clunk to a full stop long before you could squeeze through.

Then I stopped trying to imagine, because he

was the one who had bought this, wasn't he? Yes. He had bought his own ticket and paid a full fare.

"Who's there?"

"Me," I said, "but I'm not the help you're looking for, Dolan."

I kicked another fan of grit and pebbles across the gray Cadillac's roof. The screamer started doing his thing again as the second bunch of pebbles rattled across the roof.

"*My legs! Jim, my legs!*"

Dolan's voice was suddenly wary. The man outside, the man on top, knew his name. Which meant this was an extremely dangerous situation.

"*Jimmy, I can see the bones in my legs!*"

"Shut up," Dolan said coldly. It was eerie to hear their voices drifting up like that. I suppose I could have climbed down onto the Cadillac's back deck and looked in the rear window, but I would not have seen much, even with my face pressed right against it. The glass was polarized, as I may already have told you.

I didn't want to see him, anyway. I knew what he looked like. What would I want to see him for? To find out if he was wearing his Rolex and his designer jeans?

"Who are you, buddy?" he asked.

"I'm nobody," I said. "Just a nobody who had a good reason to put you where you are right now."

And with an eerie, frightening suddenness, Dolan said: "Is your name Robinson?"

I felt as if someone had punched me in the stomach. He had made the connection that fast, winnowing through all the half-remembered names and faces and coming up with exactly the

75

right one. Had I thought him an animal, with the instincts of an animal? I hadn't known the half of it, and it was really just as well I had not, or I never would have had the guts to do what I had done.

I said, "My name doesn't matter. But you know what happens now, don't you?"

The screamer began again — great bubbling, liquid bellows.

"Get me outta here, Jimmy! Get me outta here! For the luvva Jaysus! My legs're broke!"

"Shut up," Dolan said. And then, to me: "I can't hear you, man, the way he's screaming."

I got down on my hands and knees and leaned over. "I said you know what h—"

I suddenly had an image of the wolf dressed up as Gramma telling Red Riding Hood, *All the better to hear you with, my dear . . . come a little closer.* I recoiled, and just in time. The revolver went off four times. The shots were loud where I was; they must have been deafening in the car. Four black eyes opened in the roof of Dolan's Cadillac, and I felt something split the air an inch from my forehead.

"Did I get you, cocksucker?" Dolan asked.

"No," I said.

The screamer had become the weeper. He was in the front seat. I saw his hands, as pale as the hands of a drowned man, slapping weakly at the windshield, and the slumped body next to him. Jimmy had to get him out, he was bleeding, the pain was bad, the pain was *turrible*, the pain was more than he could take, for the luvva Jaysus he was sorry, heartily sorry for his sins,

76

but this was more than —

There was another pair of loud reports. The man in the front seat stopped screaming. The hands dropped away from the windshield.

"There," Dolan said in a voice that was almost reflective. "He ain't hurting anymore and we can hear what we say to each other."

I said nothing. I felt suddenly dazed and unreal. He had killed a man just now. *Killed* him. The feeling that I had underestimated him in spite of all my precautions and was lucky to be alive recurred.

"I want to make you a proposal," Dolan said.

I continued to hold my peace —

"My friend?"

— and to hold it some more.

"Hey! You!" His voice trembled minutely. "If you're still up there, talk to me! What can that hurt?"

"I'm here," I said. "I was just thinking you fired six times. I was thinking you may wish you'd saved one for yourself before long. But maybe there's eight in the clip, or you have reloads."

Now it was his turn to fall silent. Then:

"What are you planning?"

"I think you've already guessed," I said. "I have spent the last thirty-six hours digging the world's longest grave, and now I'm going to bury you in your fucking Cadillac."

The fear in his voice was still reined in. I wanted that rein to snap.

"You want to hear my proposition first?"

"I'll listen. In a few seconds. First I have to get something."

I walked back to the van and got my shovel.

When I got back he was saying "Robinson? Robinson? Robinson?" like a man speaking into a dead phone.

"I'm here," I said. "You talk. I'll listen. And when you're finished I may make a counter-proposal."

When he spoke, he sounded more cheerful. If I was talking counter-proposals, I was talking deal. And if I was talking deal, he was already halfway to being out.

"I'm offering you a million dollars to let me out of here. But, just as important —"

I tossed a shovelful of gritty till down on the rear deck of the Cadillac. Pebbles bounced and rattled off the small rear window. Dirt sifted into the line of the trunk-lid.

"What are you doing?" His voice was sharp with alarm.

"Idle hands do the devil's work," I said. "I thought I'd keep mine busy while I listened."

I dug into the dirt again and threw in another shovelful.

Now Dolan spoke faster, his voice more urgent.

"A million dollars and my personal guarantee that no one will ever touch you . . . not me, not my men, not anyone else's men."

My hands didn't hurt anymore. It was amazing. I shoveled steadily, and in no more than five minutes, the Cadillac's rear deck was drifted deep in dirt. Putting it in, even by hand, was certainly easier than taking it out.

I paused, leaning on the shovel for a moment. "Keep talking."

"Look, this is crazy," he said, and now I could hear bright splinters of panic in his voice. "I mean it's just *crazy.*"

"You got *that* right," I said, and shoveled in more dirt.

He held on longer than I thought any man could, talking, reasoning, cajoling — yet becoming more and more disjointed as the sand and dirt piled up over the rear window, repeating himself, backtracking, beginning to stutter. At one point the passenger door opened as far as it could and banged into the sidewall of the excavation. I saw a hand with black hair on the knuckles and a big ruby ring on the second finger. I sent down a quick four shovelfuls of loose earth into the opening. He screamed curses and yanked the door shut again.

He broke not long after. It was the sound of the dirt coming down that finally got to him, I think. Sure it was. The sound would have been very loud inside the Cadillac. The dirt and stones rattling onto the roof and falling past the window. He must have finally realized he was sitting in an upholstered eight-cylinder fuel-injected coffin.

"Get me out!" he shrieked. *"Please! I can't stand it! Get me out!"*

"You ready for that counter-proposal?" I asked.

"Yes! Yes! Christ! Yes! Yes! Yes!"

"Scream. That's the counter-proposal. That's what I want. Scream for me. If you scream loud enough, I'll let you out."

He screamed piercingly.

79

"That was *good!*" I said, and I meant it. "But it was nowhere near good enough."

I began to dig again, throwing fan after fan of dirt over the roof of the Cadillac. Disintegrating clods ran down the windshield and filled the windshield-wiper slot.

He screamed again, even louder, and I wondered if it was possible for a man to scream loud enough to rupture his own larynx.

"Not bad!" I said, redoubling my efforts. I was smiling in spite of my throbbing back. "You might get there, Dolan — you really might."

"Five million." It was the last coherent thing he said.

"I think not," I replied, leaning on the shovel and wiping sweat off my forehead with the heel of one grimy hand. The dirt covered the roof of the car almost from side to side now. It looked like a starburst . . . or a large brown hand clasping Dolan's Cadillac. "But if you can make a sound come out of your mouth which is as loud, let us say, as eight sticks of dynamite taped to the ignition switch of a 1968 Chevrolet, then I will get you out, and you may count on it."

So he screamed, and I shoveled dirt down on the Cadillac. For some time he did indeed scream very loudly, although I judged he never screamed louder than two sticks of dynamite taped to the ignition switch of a 1968 Chevrolet. Three, at most. And by the time the last of the Cadillac's brightwork was covered and I rested to look down at the dirt-shrouded hump in the hole, he was producing no more than a series of hoarse and broken grunts.

I looked at my watch. It was just past one o'clock. My hands were bleeding again, and the handle of the shovel was slippery. A sheaf of gritty sand flew into my face and I recoiled from it. A high wind in the desert makes a peculiarly unpleasant sound — a long, steady drone that simply goes on and on. It is like the voice of an idiot ghost.

I leaned over the hole. "Dolan?"

No answer.

"Scream, Dolan."

No answer at first — then a series of harsh barks. Satisfactory!

I went back to the van, started it up, and drove the mile and a half back down to the road construction. On the way I tuned to WKXR, Las Vegas, the only station the van's radio would pull in. Barry Manilow told me he wrote the songs that make the whole world sing, a statement I greeted with some skepticism, and then the weather report came on. High winds were forecast; a travellers' advisory had been posted on the main roads between Vegas and the California line. There were apt to be visibility problems because of sheeting sand, the disc jockey said, but the thing to really watch out for was wind-shear. I knew what he was talking about, because I could feel it whipsawing the van.

Here was my Case-Jordan bucket-loader; already I thought of it as mine. I got in, humming the Barry Manilow tune, and touched the blue and yellow wires together again. The loader started up smoothly. This time I'd remembered to take

81

it out of gear. *Not bad, white boy,* I could hear Tink saying in my head. *You learnin.*

Yes I was. Learning all the time.

I sat for a minute, watching membranes of sand skirl across the desert, listening to the bucket-loader's engine rumble and wondering what Dolan was up to. This was, after all, his Big Chance. Try to break the rear window, or crawl over into the front seat and try to break the windshield. I had put a couple of feet of sand and dirt over each, but it was still possible. It depended on how crazy he was by now, and that wasn't a thing I could know, so it really didn't bear thinking about. Other things did.

I geared the bucket-loader and drove back up the highway to the trench. When I got there I trotted anxiously over and looked down, half-expecting to see a man-sized gopher hole at the front or rear of the Cadillac-mound where Dolan had broken some glass and crawled out.

My spadework had not been disturbed.

"Dolan," I said, cheerfully enough, I thought.

There was no answer.

"Dolan!"

No answer.

He's killed himself, I thought, and felt a sick-bitter disappointment. *Killed himself somehow or died of fright.*

"Dolan?"

Laughter drifted up from the mound; bright, irrepressible, totally genuine laughter. I felt my flesh lift itself into large hard lumps. It was the laughter of a man whose mind has broken.

He laughed and he laughed in his hoarse voice.

Then he screamed; then he laughed again. Finally he did both together.

For awhile I laughed with him, or screamed, or whatever, and the wind laughed and screamed at both of us.

Then I went back to the Case-Jordan, lowered the blade, and began to cover him up for real.

In four minutes even the shape of the Cadillac was gone. There was just a hole filled with dirt.

I thought I could hear something, but with the sound of the wind and the steady grumble of the loader's engine, it was hard to tell. I got down on my knees; then I lay down full-length with my head hanging into what remained of the hole.

Far down, underneath all that dirt, Dolan was still laughing. They were sounds like something you might read in a comic book: *Hee-hee-hee, aaah-hah-hah-hah.* There might have been some words, too. It was hard to tell. I smiled and nodded, though.

"Scream," I whispered. "Scream, if you want." But that faint sound of laughter just went on, seeping up from the dirt like a poisonous vapor.

A sudden dark terror seized me — Dolan was behind me! Yes, somehow Dolan had gotten behind me! And before I could turn around he would tumble *me* into the hole and —

I jumped up and whirled around, my mangled hands making rough approximations of fists.

Wind-driven sand smacked me.

There was nothing else.

I wiped my face with my dirty bandanna and

83

got back into the cab of the bucket-loader and went back to work.

The cut was filled in again long before dark. There was even dirt left over, in spite of what the wind had whipped away, because of the area displaced by the Cadillac. It went quickly . . . so quickly.

The tone of my thoughts was weary, confused, and half-delirious as I piloted the loader back down the road, driving it directly over the spot where Dolan was buried.

I parked it in its original place, removed my shirt, and rubbed all of the metal in the cab with it in an effort to remove fingerprints. I don't know exactly why I did that, even to this day, since I must have left them in a hundred other places around the site. Then, in the deep brownish-gray gloom of that stormy dusk, I went back to the van.

I opened one of the rear doors, observed Dolan crouched inside, and staggered back, screaming, one hand thrown up to shield my face. It seemed to me that my heart must explode in my chest.

Nothing — no one — came out of the van. The door swung and banged in the wind like the last shutter on a haunted house. At last I crept back, heart pounding, and peered inside. There was nothing but the jumble of stuff I had left in there — the road-arrow with the broken bulbs, the jack, my toolbox.

"You have got to get hold of yourself," I said softly. "Get hold of yourself."

I waited for Elizabeth to say, *You'll be all right, darling* . . . something like that . . . but there was only the wind.

I got back into the van, started it, and drove halfway back to the excavation. That was as far as I could make myself go. Although I knew it was utterly foolish, I became more and more convinced that Dolan was lurking in the van. My eyes kept going to the rear-view mirror, trying to pick his shadow out of the others.

The wind was stronger than ever, rocking the van on its springs. The dust it pulled up from the desert and drove before it looked like smoke in the headlights.

At last I pulled over to the side of the road, got out, and locked all the doors. I knew I was crazy to even try sleeping outside in this, but I couldn't sleep in there. I just couldn't. So I crawled under the van with my sleeping bag.

I was asleep five seconds after I zipped myself into it.

When I woke up from a nightmare I could not remember — except there had been hands in it, clutching at my throat — I found that *I* had been buried alive. There was sand up my nose, sand in my ears. It was down my throat, choking me.

I screamed and struggled upward, at first convinced that the confining sleeping bag was earth. Then I banged my head on the van's undercarriage and saw flakes of rust silting down.

I rolled out from under into a dawn the color of smutty pewter. My sleeping bag blew away like a tumbleweed the moment my weight was off it. I gave a surprised yell and chased twenty feet after it before realizing it would be the world's worst mistake. Visibility was down to no more than twenty yards, and maybe less. The road was totally gone in places. I looked back at the van and it looked washed-out, barely there, a sepia photograph of a ghost-town relic.

I staggered back to it, found my keys, and got inside. I was still spitting sand and coughing dryly. I got the motor going and drove slowly back the way I had come. There was no need to wait for a weather report; the weather was all the jock could talk about this morning. The worst desert windstorm in Nevada history. All roads closed. Stay home unless you absolutely have to go out, and then stay home anyway.

The glorious Fourth.

Stay in. You're crazy if you go out there. You'll go sandblind.

That I would chance. This was a golden opportunity to cover it up forever — never in my wildest imaginings had I suspected I might get such a chance, but it was here, and I was taking it.

I had brought three or four extra blankets. I tore a long, wide strip from one of them and tied it around my head. Looking like some sort of crazed Bedouin, I stepped out.

I spent all morning carrying chunks of asphalt up from the ditch and placing them back into the trench, trying to be as neat as a mason laying a wall . . . or bricking up a niche. The actual fetching and carrying was not terribly difficult, although I had to unearth most of the asphalt blocks like an archaeologist hunting for artifacts, and every twenty minutes or so I had to repair to the van to get out of the blowing sand and rest my stinging eyes.

I worked slowly west from what had been the shallow end of the excavation, and by quarter past noon — I had started at six — I had reached the final seventeen feet or so. By then the wind had begun to die and I could see occasional ragged patches of blue above me.

I fetched and placed, fetched and placed. Now I was over the spot where I calculated Dolan must be. Was he dead yet? How many cubic feet of air could a Cadillac hold? How soon would that space become unable to support human life, assuming that neither of Dolan's two companions was still breathing?

I knelt by the bare earth. The wind had eroded the impressions of the Case-Jordan's treads but not quite erased them; somewhere beneath those faint indentations was a man wearing a Rolex.

"Dolan," I said chummily, "I've changed my mind and decided to let you out."

Nothing. No sound at all. Dead for sure this time.

I went back and got another square of asphalt. I placed it, and as I started to rise, I heard faint, cackling laughter seeping up through the earth.

I sank back into a crouch with my head forward — if I'd still had hair, it would have been hanging in my face — and remained in that position for some time, listening as he laughed. The sound was faint and without timbre.

When it stopped, I went back and got another asphalt square. There was a piece of the broken yellow line on this one. It looked like a hyphen. I knelt with it.

"For the love of God!" he shrieked. "For the

love of God, Robinson!"

"Yes," I said, smiling. "For the love of God."

I put the chunk of asphalt in neatly next to its neighbor, and although I listened, I heard him no more.

I got back to my place in Vegas that night at eleven o'clock. I slept for sixteen hours, got up, walked toward the kitchen to make coffee, and then collapsed, writhing, on the hall floor as a monstrous back spasm racked me. I scrabbled at the small of my back with one hand while I chewed on the other to stifle the screams.

After awhile I crawled into the bathroom — I tried standing once, but this resulted in another thunderbolt — and used the washstand to pull myself up enough so I could get the second bottle of Empirin in the medicine cabinet.

I chewed three and drew a bath. I lay on the floor while I waited for the tub to fill. When it was, I wriggled out of my pajamas and managed to get into the tub. I lay there for five hours, dozing most of the time. When I got out, I could walk.

A little.

I went to a chiropractor. He told me I had three slipped discs and had suffered a serious lower spinal dislocation. He wanted to know if I had decided to sub for the circus strongman.

I told him I did it digging in my garden.

He told me I was going to Kansas City.

I went.

They operated.

When the anesthesiologist put the rubber cup over my face, I heard Dolan laughing from the

88

hissing blackness inside and knew I was going to die.

The recovery room was a watery tiled green. "Am I alive?" I croaked.

A nurse laughed. "Oh, yes." His hand touched my brow — my brow that went all the way around my head. "What a sunburn you have! My God! Did that hurt, or are you still too doped up?"

"Still too doped up," I said. "Did I talk while I was under?"

"Yes," he said.

I was cold all over. Cold to the bones of me. "What did I say?"

"You said, 'It's dark in here. Let me out!' " And he laughed again.

"Oh," I said.

They never found him — Dolan.

It was the storm. That flukey storm. I'm pretty sure I know what happened, although I think you'll understand when I tell you I never checked too closely.

RPAV — remember that? They were repaving. The storm almost buried the section of 71 which the detour had closed. When they went back to work, they didn't bother to remove the new dunes all at once but only as they went along — why do otherwise? There was no traffic to worry about. So they plowed sand and routed up old paving at the same time. And if the 'dozer operator happened to notice that the sand-crusted asphalt in one section — a section about forty feet long — was breaking in front of his blade in neat, almost geometric pieces, he never said anything. Maybe he was stoned. Or maybe he was just dreaming of stepping out with his baby that evening.

Then came the dumpsters with their fresh loads of gravel, followed by the spreaders and rollers. After them the big tankers would arrive, the ones with the wide sprayer attachments on the backs and their smell of hot tar, so like melting shoe-leather. And when the fresh asphalt had dried, along would come the lining machine, the driver under his big canvas parasol looking back frequently to make sure the broken yellow line was perfectly straight, unaware that he was passing over a fog-gray Cadillac with three people inside, unaware that down in the darkness there was a ruby ring and a gold Rolex that might still be marking off the hours.

One of those heavy vehicles would almost surely have collapsed an ordinary Cadillac; there would have been a lurch, a crunch, and then a bunch of men digging to see what — or who — they had found. But it really *was* more tank than car, and Dolan's very carefulness has so far kept anyone from finding him.

Sooner or later the Cadillac will collapse of course, probably under the weight of a passing semi, and the next vehicle along will see a big broken dent in the westbound lane, and the Highway Department will be notified, and there will be another RPAV. But if there aren't Highway Department workers right there to see what happens, to observe that the heavy weight of a passing truck has caused some hollow object under the road to collapse, I think they will assume the "marsh-hole" (that is what they call them) has been caused by either frost, or a collapsed salt-dome, or possibly a desert temblor. They will repair it and life will go on.

He was reported missing — Dolan.
A few tears were shed.
A columnist in the *Las Vegas Sun* suggested that he might be playing dominos or shooting pool somewhere with Jimmy Hoffa.
Perhaps that is not so far from the truth.

I'm fine.
My back is pretty much okay again. I'm under strict orders not to lift anything which weighs over thirty pounds without help, but I've got a good bunch of third-graders this year, and all the help I could want.
I've driven back and forth over that stretch of road several times in my new Acura automobile. Once I even stopped, got out, and (after checking in both directions to make sure the road was deserted) took a piss on what I was pretty sure was the spot. But I couldn't produce much of a flow, even though my kidneys felt full, and when I drove on I kept checking the rear-view mirror: I had this funny idea, you see, that he was going to rise up from the back seat, his skin charred to a cinnamon color and stretched over his skull like the skin of a mummy, his hair full of sand, his eyes and his Rolex watch glittering.
That was the *last* time I was on 71, actually.

91

Now I take the Interstate when I need to head west.

And Elizabeth? Like Dolan, she has fallen silent. I find that is a relief.

The End of the
Whole Mess

I want to tell you about the end of war, the de-generation of mankind, and the death of the Mes-siah — an epic story, deserving thousands of pages and a whole shelf of volumes, but you (if there are any "you" later on to read this) will have to settle for the freeze-dried version. The direct in-jection works very fast. I figure I've got somewhere between forty-five minutes and two hours, de-pending on my blood-type. I think it's A, which should give me a little more time, but I'll be god-damned if I can remember for sure. If it turns out to be O, you could be in for a lot of blank pages, my hypothetical friend.

In any event, I think maybe I'd better assume the worst and go as fast as I can.

I'm using the electric typewriter — Bobby's word-processor is faster, but the genny's cycle is too irregular to be trusted, even with the line sup-pressor. I've only got one shot at this; I can't risk getting most of the way home and then seeing the whole thing go to data heaven because of an oHm drop, or a surge too great for the suppressor to cope with.

My name is Howard Fornoy. I was a freelance writer. My brother, Robert Fornoy, was the Mes-siah. I killed him by shooting him up with his own discovery four hours ago. *He* called it The Calmative. A Very Serious Mistake might have been a better name, but what's done is done and can't be undone, as the Irish have been saying for centuries . . . which *proves* what assholes they are.

Shit, I can't afford these digressions.

After Bobby died I covered him with a quilt and sat at the cabin's single living-room window for some three hours, looking out at the woods. Used to be you could see the orange glow of the hi-intensity arc-sodiums from North Conway, but no more. Now there's just the White Mountains, looking like dark triangles of crepe paper cut out by a child, and the pointless stars.

I turned on the radio, dialed through four bands, found one crazy guy, and shut it off. I sat there thinking of ways to tell this story. My mind kept sliding away toward all those miles of dark pine-woods, all that nothing. Finally I realized I needed to get myself off the dime and shoot myself up. Shit. I never *could* work without a deadline.

And I've sure-to-God got one now.

Our parents had no reason to expect anything other than what they got: bright children. Dad was a history major who had become a full pro-fessor at Hofstra when he was thirty. Ten years later he was one of six vice-administrators of the National Archives in Washington, D.C., and in line for the top spot. He was a helluva good guy, too — had every record Chuck Berry ever cut and played a pretty mean blues guitar himself. My dad filed by day and rocked by night.

Mom graduated magna cum laude from Drew. Got a Phi Beta Kappa key she sometimes wore on this funky fedora she had. She became a successful CPA in D.C., met my dad, married him, and took in her shingle when she became pregnant with yours truly. I came along in 1980. By '84 she was doing taxes for some of my dad's associates — she called this her "little hobby." By the time Bobby was born in 1987, she was handling taxes, investment portfolios, and estate-planning for a dozen powerful men. I could name them, but who gives a wad? They're either dead or driveling idiots by now.

I think she probably made more out of "her little hobby" each year than my dad made at his job, but that never mattered — they were happy with what they were to themselves and to each other. I saw them squabble lots of times, but I never saw them fight. When I was growing up, the only difference I saw between my mom and my playmates' moms was that their moms used to read or iron or sew or talk on the phone while the soaps played on the tube, and my mom used to run a pocket calculator and write down numbers on big green sheets of paper while the soaps played on the tube.

I was no disappointment to a couple of people with Mensa Gold Cards in their wallets. I maintained A's and B's through my public-school career (the idea that either I or my brother might go to a private school was never even discussed so far as I know). I also wrote well early, with no effort at all. I sold my first magazine piece when I was twenty — it was on how the Continental

Army wintered at Valley Forge. I sold it to an airline magazine for four hundred fifty dollars. My dad, whom I loved deeply, asked me if he could buy that check from me. He gave me his own personal check and had the check from the airline magazine framed and hung it over his desk. A romantic genius, if you will. A romantic *blues-playing* genius, if you will. Take it from me, a kid could do a lot worse. Of course he and my mother both died raving and pissing in their pants late last year, like almost everyone else on this big round world of ours, but I never stopped loving either of them.

I was the sort of child they had every reason to expect — a good boy with a bright mind, a talented boy whose talent grew to early maturity in an atmosphere of love and confidence, a faithful boy who loved and respected his mom and dad.

Bobby was different. *Nobody,* not even Mensa types like our folks, *ever* expects a kid like Bobby. Not *ever.*

I potty-trained two full years earlier than Bob, and that was the only thing in which I ever beat him. But I never felt jealous of him; that would have been like a fairly good American Legion League pitcher feeling jealous of Nolan Ryan or Roger Clemens. After a certain point the comparisons that cause feelings of jealousy simply cease to exist. I've been there, and I can tell you: after a certain point you just stand back and shield your eyes from the flashburns.

Bobby read at two and began writing short essays ("Our Dog," "A Trip to Boston with Mother") at three. His printing was the straggling, struggling galvanic constructions of a six-year-old, and that was startling enough in itself, but there was more: if transcribed so that his still-developing motor control no longer became an evaluative factor, you would have thought you were reading the work of a bright, if extremely naive, fifth-grader. He progressed from simple sentences to compound sentences to complex ones with dizzying rapidity, grasping clauses, sub-clauses, and modifying clauses with an intuitiveness that was eerie. Sometimes his syntax was garbled and his modifiers misplaced, but he had such flaws — which plague most writers all their lives — pretty well under control by the age of five.

He developed headaches. My parents were afraid he had some sort of physical problem — a brain-tumor, perhaps — and took him to a doctor who examined him carefully, listened to him even more carefully, and then told my parents there was nothing wrong with Bobby except stress: he was in a state of extreme frustration because his writing-hand would not work as well as his brain.

"You got a kid trying to pass a mental kidney stone," the doctor said. "I could prescribe something for his headaches, but I think the drug he really needs is a typewriter." So Mom and Dad gave Bobby an IBM. A year later they gave him a Commodore 64 with WordStar for Christmas and Bobby's headaches stopped. Before going on to other matters, I only want to add that he believed for the next three years or so that it was Santa Claus who had left that word-cruncher under our tree. Now that I think of it, that was another place where I beat Bobby: I Santa-trained earlier, too.

There's so much I could tell you about those early days, and I suppose I'll have to tell you a little, but I'll have to go fast and make it brief. The deadline. Ah, the deadline. I once read a very funny piece called "The Essential *Gone with the Wind*" that went something like this:

" '*A war?*' *laughed Scarlett. 'Oh, fiddle-de-dee!*'

"*Boom! Ashley went to war! Atlanta burned! Rhett walked in and then walked out!*

" '*Fiddle-de-dee,*' *said Scarlett through her tears, 'I will think about it tomorrow, for tomorrow is another day.*' "

I laughed heartily over that when I read it; now that I'm faced with doing something similar, it doesn't seem quite so funny. But here goes:

"*A child with an IQ immeasurable by any existing test?*" *smiled India Fornoy to her devoted husband, Richard. "Fiddle-de-dee! We'll provide an atmosphere where his intellect — not to mention that of his not-exactly-stupid older brother — can grow. And we'll raise them as the normal all-American boys they by gosh are!*"

Boom! The Fornoy boys grew up! Howard went to the University of Virginia, graduated cum laude, *and settled down to a freelance writing career! Made a comfortable living! Stepped out with a lot of women and went to bed with quite a few of them! Managed to avoid social diseases both sexual and pharmacological! Bought a Mitsubishi stereo system! Wrote home at least once a week! Published two novels that did pretty well! "Fiddle-de-dee," said Howard, "this is the life for me!*"

And so it was, at least until the day Bobby

showed up unexpectedly (in the best mad-scientist tradition) with his two glass boxes, a bees' nest in one and a wasps' nest in the other, Bobby wearing a Mumford Phys Ed tee-shirt inside-out, on the verge of destroying human intellect and just as happy as a clam at high tide.

Guys like my brother Bobby come along only once every two or three generations, I think — guys like Leonardo da Vinci, Newton, Einstein, maybe Edison. They all seem to have one thing in common: they are like huge compasses which swing aimlessly for a long time, searching for some true north and then homing on it with fearful force. Before that happens such guys are apt to get up to some weird shit, and Bobby was no exception.

When he was eight and I was fifteen, he came to me and said he had invented an airplane. By then I knew Bobby too well to just say "Bullshit" and kick him out of my room. I went out to the garage, where there was this weird plywood contraption sitting on his American Flyer red wagon. It looked a little like a fighter plane, but the wings were raked forward instead of back. He had mounted the saddle from his rocking horse on the middle of it with bolts. There was a lever on the side. There was no motor. He said it was a glider. He wanted me to push him down Carrigan's Hill, which was the steepest grade in D.C.'s Grant Park — there was a cement path down the middle of it for old folks. That, Bobby said, would be his runway.

"Bobby," I said, "you got this puppy's wings on backward."

"No," he said. "This is the way they're supposed to be. I saw something on *Wild Kingdom* about hawks. They dive down on their prey and then reverse their wings coming up. They're double-jointed, see? You get better lift this way."

"Then why isn't the Air Force building them this way?" I asked, blissfully unaware that both the American and the Russian air forces had plans for such forward-wing fighter planes on their drawing boards.

Bobby just shrugged. He didn't know and didn't care.

We went over to Carrigan's Hill and he climbed into the rocking-horse saddle and gripped the lever. "Push me *hard*," he said. His eyes were dancing with that crazed light I knew so well — Christ, his eyes used to light up that way in his cradle sometimes. But I swear to God I never would have pushed him down the cement path as hard as I did if I thought the thing would actually work.

But I *didn't* know, and I gave him one hell of a shove. He went freewheeling down the hill, whooping like a cowboy just off a traildrive and headed into town for a few cold beers. An old lady had to jump out of his way, and he just missed an old geezer leaning over a walker. Halfway down he pulled the handle and I watched, wide-eyed and bullshit with fear and amazement, as his splintery plywood plane separated from the wagon. At first it only hovered inches above it, and for a second it looked like it was going to settle back. Then there was a gust of wind and Bobby's plane took off like someone had it on an invisible cable.

The American Flyer wagon ran off the concrete path and into some bushes. All of a sudden Bobby was ten feet in the air, then twenty, then fifty. He went gliding over Grant Park on a steepening upward plane, whooping cheerily.

I went running after him, screaming for him to come down, visions of his body tumbling off that stupid rocking-horse saddle and impaling itself on a tree, or one of the park's many statues, standing out with hideous clarity in my head. I did not just imagine my brother's funeral; I tell you I *attended* it.

"BOBBY!" I shrieked. "COME DOWN!"

"WHEEEEEEEE!" Bobby screamed back, his voice faint but clearly ecstatic. Startled chess-players, Frisbee-throwers, book-readers, lovers, and joggers stopped whatever they were doing to watch.

"BOBBY THERE'S NO SEATBELT ON THAT FUCKING THING!" I screamed. It was the first time I ever used that particular word, so far as I can remember.

"*Iyyyy'll beeee all riyyyyht . . .*" He was screaming at the top of his lungs, but I was appalled to realize I could barely hear him. I went running down Carrigan's Hill, shrieking all the way. I don't have the slightest memory of just what I was yelling, but the next day I could not speak above a whisper. I *do* remember passing a young fellow in a neat three-piece suit standing by the statue of Eleanor Roosevelt at the foot of the hill. He looked at me and said conversationally, "Tell you what, my friend, I'm having one *hell* of an acid flashback."

I remember that odd misshapen shadow gliding

across the green floor of the park, rising and rippling as it crossed park benches, litter baskets, and the upturned faces of the watching people. I remember chasing it. I remember how my mother's face crumpled and how she started to cry when I told her that Bobby's plane, which had no business flying in the first place, turned upside down in a sudden eddy of wind and Bobby finished his short but brilliant career splattered all over D Street.

The way things turned out, it might have been better for everyone if things had actually turned out that way, but they didn't.

Instead, Bobby banked back toward Carrigan's Hill, holding nonchalantly onto the tail of his own plane to keep from falling off the damned thing, and brought it down toward the little pond at the center of Grant Park. He went air-sliding five feet over it, then four . . . and then he was skiing his sneakers along the surface of the water, sending back twin white wakes, scaring the usually complacent (and overfed) ducks up in honking indignant flurries before him, laughing his cheerful laugh. He came down on the far side, exactly between two park benches that snapped off the wings of his plane. He flew out of the saddle, thumped his head, and started to bawl.

That was life with Bobby.

Not everything was that spectacular — in fact, I don't think *anything* was . . . at least until The Calmative. But I told you the story because I think, this time at least, the extreme case best illustrates the norm: life with Bobby was a constant mind-fuck. By the age of nine he was attending quantum physics and advanced algebra classes at Georgetown University. There was the day he blanked out every radio and TV on our street — and the surrounding four blocks — with his own voice; he had found an old portable TV in the attic and turned it into a wide-band radio broadcasting station. One old black-and-white Zenith, twelve feet of hi-fi flex, a coathanger mounted on the roofpeak of our house, and presto! For about two hours four blocks of Georgetown could receive only WBOB . . . which happened to be my brother, reading some of my short stories, telling moron jokes, and explaining that the high sulfur content in baked beans was the reason our dad farted so much in church every Sunday morning. "But he gets most of em off pretty quiet," Bobby told his listening audience of roughly three thousand, "or sometimes he holds the real bangers until it's time for the hymns."

My dad, who was less than happy about all this, ended up paying a seventy-five-dollar FCC fine and taking it out of Bobby's allowance for the next year.

Life with Bobby, oh yeah . . . and look here, I'm crying. Is it honest sentiment, I wonder, or the onset? The former, I think — Christ knows how much I loved him — but I think I better try to hurry up a little just the same.

Bobby had graduated high school, for all practical purposes, by the age of ten, but he never got a B.A. or B.S., let alone any advanced degree. It was that big powerful compass in his head, swinging around and around, looking for some true north to point at.

He went through a physics period, and a shorter period when he was nutty for chemistry . . . but in the end, Bobby was too impatient with mathematics for either of those fields to hold him. He could do it, but it — and ultimately all so-called hard science — bored him.

By the time he was fifteen, it was archaeology — he combed the White Mountain foothills around our summer place in North Conway, building a history of the Indians who had lived there from arrowheads, flints, even the charcoal patterns of long-dead campfires in the mesolithic caves in the mid-New Hampshire regions.

But that passed, too, and he began to read history and anthropology. When he was sixteen my father and my mother gave their reluctant approval when Bobby requested that he be allowed to accompany a party of New England anthropologists on an expedition to South America.

He came back five months later with the first real tan of his life; he was also an inch taller, fifteen pounds lighter, and much quieter. He was still cheerful enough, or could be, but his little-boy exuberance, sometimes infectious, sometimes wearisome, but always there, was gone. He had grown up. And for the first time I remember him talking about the news . . . how bad it was, I mean. That was 2003, the year a PLO splinter group called the Sons of the Jihad (a name that always sounded to me hideously like a Catholic community service group somewhere in western Pennsylvania) set off a Squirt Bomb in London, polluting sixty per cent of it and making the rest of it extremely unhealthy for people who ever planned to have children (or to live past the age of fifty, for that matter). The year we tried to blockade the Philippines after the Cedeño administration accepted a "small group" of Red Chinese advisors (fifteen thousand or so, according to our spy satellites), and only backed down when it became clear that (a) the Chinese weren't kidding about emptying the holes if we didn't pull back, and (b) the American people weren't all that crazy about committing mass suicide over the Philippine Islands. That was also the year some other group of crazy motherfuckers — Albanians, I think — tried to air-spray the AIDS virus over Berlin.

This sort of stuff depressed everybody, but it depressed the *shit* out of Bobby.

"Why are people so goddam mean?" he asked me one day. We were at the summer place in New Hampshire, it was late August, and most of our stuff was already in boxes and suitcases. The cabin had that sad, deserted look it always got just before we all went our separate ways. For me it meant back to New York, and for Bobby it meant Waco, Texas, of all places . . . he had spent the summer reading sociology and geology texts — how's that for a crazy salad? — and said he wanted to run a couple of experiments down there. He said it in a casual, offhand way, but I had seen my mother looking at him with a peculiar thoughtful scrutiny in the last couple of weeks we were all together. Neither Dad nor I suspected, but I think my mom knew that Bobby's compass needle had finally stopped swinging and had started pointing.

"Why are they so mean?" I asked. "I'm supposed to answer that?"

"*Someone* better," he said. "Pretty soon, too, the way things are going."

"They're going the way they always went," I said, "and I guess they're doing it because people were built to be mean. If you want to lay blame, blame God."

"That's bullshit. I don't believe it. Even that double-X-chromosome stuff turned out to be bullshit in the end. And don't tell me it's just economic pressures, the conflict between the haves and have-nots, because that doesn't explain all of it, either."

"Original sin," I said. "It works for me — it's got a good beat and you can dance to it."

"Well," Bobby said, "maybe it *is* original sin. But what's the instrument, big brother? Have you ever asked yourself that?"

"Instrument? What instrument? I'm not following you."

"I think it's the water," Bobby said moodily.

"Say *what?*"

"The water. Something in the water."

He looked at me.

"Or something that *isn't.*"

The next day Bobby went off to Waco. I didn't see him again until he showed up at my apartment wearing the inside-out Mumford shirt and carrying the two glass boxes. That was three years later.

"Howdy, Howie," he said, stepping in and giving me a nonchalant swat on the back as if it had been only three days.

"Bobby!" I yelled, and threw both arms around him in a bear-hug. Hard angles bit into my chest, and I heard an angry hive-hum.

"I'm glad to see you too," Bobby said, "but you better go easy. You're upsetting the natives."

I stepped back in a hurry. Bobby set down the big paper bag he was carrying and unslung his shoulder-bag. Then he carefully brought the glass boxes out of the bag. There was a beehive in one, a wasps' nest in the other. The bees were already settling down and going back to whatever business bees have, but the wasps were clearly unhappy about the whole thing.

"Okay, Bobby," I said. I looked at him and grinned. I couldn't seem to stop grinning. "What are you up to this time?"

He unzipped the tote-bag and brought out a mayonnaise jar which was half-filled with a clear liquid.

"See this?" he said.

"Yeah. Looks like either water or white lightning."

"It's actually both, if you can believe that. It came from an artesian well in La Plata, a little town forty miles east of Waco, and before I turned it into this concentrated form, there were five gallons of it. I've got a regular little distillery running down there, Howie, but I don't think the government will ever bust me for it." He was grinning, and now the grin broadened. "Water's all it is, but it's still the goddamndist popskull the human race has ever seen."

"I don't have the slightest idea what you're talking about."

"I know you don't. But you will. You know what, Howie?"

"What?"

"If the idiotic human race can manage to hold itself together for another six months, I'm betting it'll hold itself together for all time."

He lifted the mayonnaise jar, and one magnified Bobby-eye stared at me through it with huge solemnity. "This is the big one," he said. "The cure for the worst disease to which *Homo sapiens* falls prey."

"Cancer?"

"Nope," Bobby said. "War. Barroom brawls. Drive-by shootings. The whole mess. Where's your bathroom, Howie? My back teeth are floating."

When he came back he had not only turned the Mumford tee-shirt right-side out, he had combed his hair — nor had his method of doing this changed, I saw. Bobby just held his head under the faucet for awhile then raked everything back with his fingers.

He looked at the two glass boxes and pronounced the bees and wasps back to normal. "Not that a wasps' nest ever approaches anything even closely resembling 'normal,' Howie. Wasps are social insects, like bees and ants, but unlike bees, which are almost always sane, and ants, which have occasional schizoid lapses, wasps are total full-bore lunatics." He smiled. "Just like us good old *Homo saps.*" He took the top off the glass box containing the beehive.

"Tell you what, Bobby," I said. I was smiling, but the smile felt much too wide. "Put the top

108

back on and just *tell* me about it, what do you say? Save the demonstration for later. I mean, my landlord's a real pussycat, but the super's this big bull dyke who smokes Odie Perode cigars and has thirty pounds on me. She —"

"You'll like this," Bobby said, as if I hadn't spoken at all — a habit as familiar to me as his Ten Fingers Method of Hair Grooming. He was never impolite but often totally absorbed. And could I stop him? Aw shit, no. It was too good to have him back. I mean I think I knew even then that something was going to go totally wrong, but when I was with Bobby for more than five minutes, he just hypnotized me. He was Lucy holding the football and promising me this time *for sure,* and I was Charlie Brown, rushing down the field to kick it. "In fact, you've probably seen it done before — they show pictures of it in magazines from time to time, or in TV wildlife documentaries. It's nothing very special, but it *looks* like a big deal because people have got these totally irrational prejudices about bees."

And the weird thing was, he was right — I *had* seen it before.

He stuck his hand into the box between the hive and the glass. In less than fifteen seconds his hand had acquired a living black-and-yellow glove. It brought back an instant of total recall: sitting in front of the TV, wearing footie pajamas and clutching my Paddington Bear, maybe half an hour before bedtime (and surely years before Bobby was born), watching with mingled horror, disgust, and fascination as some beekeeper allowed bees to cover his entire face. They had formed a sort of executioner's hood at first, and then he had brushed them into a grotesque living beard.

Bobby winced suddenly, sharply, then grinned.

"One of em stung me," he said. "They're still a little upset from the trip. I hooked a ride with the local insurance lady from La Plata to Waco — she's got an old Piper Cub — and flew some little commuter airline, Air Asshole, I think it was, up to New Orleans from there. Made about forty connections, but I swear to God it was the cab ride from LaGarbage that got em crazy. Second Avenue's still got more potholes than the Bergenstrasse after the Germans surrendered."

"You know, I think you really ought to get your hand out of there, Bobs," I said. I kept waiting for some of them to fly out — I could imagine chasing them around with a rolled-up magazine for hours, bringing them down one by one, as if they were escapees in some old prison movie. But none of them had escaped . . . at least so far.

"Relax, Howie. You ever see a bee sting a flower? Or even hear of it, for that matter?"

"You don't look like a flower."

He laughed. "Shit, you think *bees* know what a flower looks like? Un-uh! No way, man! They don't know what a flower looks like any more than you or I know what a cloud sounds like. They know I'm sweet because I excrete sucrose dioxin in my sweat . . . along with thirty-seven other dioxins, and those're just the ones we know about."

He paused thoughtfully.

"Although I must confess I *was* careful to, uh, sweeten myself up a little tonight. Ate a box of chocolate-covered cherries on the plane —"

"Oh Bobby, Jesus!"

"— and had a couple of MallowCremes in the taxi coming here."

He reached in with his other hand and carefully began to brush the bees away. I saw him wince once more just before he got the last of them off, and then he eased my mind considerably by replacing the lid on the glass box. I saw a red swelling on each of his hands: one in the cup of the left palm, another high up on the right, near what the palmists call the Bracelets of Fortune. He'd been stung, but I saw well enough what he'd set out to show me: what looked like at least four hundred bees had investigated him. Only two had stung.

He took a pair of tweezers out of his jeans watch-pocket, and went over to my desk. He moved the pile of manuscript beside the Wang Micro I was using in those days and trained my Tensor lamp on the place where the pages had been — fiddling with it until it formed a tiny hard spotlight on the cherrywood.

"Writin anything good, Bow-Wow?" he asked casually, and I felt the hair stiffen on the back of my neck. When was the last time he'd called me Bow-Wow? When he was four? Six? Shit, man, I don't know. He was working carefully on his left hand with the tweezers. I saw him extract a tiny something that looked like a nostril hair and place it in my ashtray.

"Piece on art forgery for *Vanity Fair*," I said. "Bobby, what in hell are you up to this time?"

"You want to pull the other one for me?" he

111

asked, offering me the tweezers, his right hand, and an apologetic smile. "I keep thinking if I'm so goddam smart I ought to be ambidextrous, but my left hand has still got an IQ of about six."

Same old Bobby.

I sat down beside him, took the tweezers, and pulled the bee stinger out of the red swelling near what in his case should have been the Bracelets of Doom, and while I did it he told me about the differences between bees and wasps, the difference between the water in La Plata and the water in New York, and how, goddam! everything was going to be all right with his water and a little help from me.

And oh shit, I ended up running at the football while my laughing, wildly intelligent brother held it, one last time.

"Bees don't sting unless they have to, because it kills them," Bobby said matter-of-factly. "You remember that time in North Conway, when you said we kept killing each other because of original sin?"

"Yes. Hold still."

"Well, if there *is* such a thing, if there's a God who could simultaneously love us enough to serve us His own Son on a cross and send us all on a rocket-sled to hell just because one stupid bitch bit a bad apple, then the curse was just this: He made us like wasps instead of bees. *Shit,* Howie, what are you doing?"

"Hold still," I said, "and I'll get it out. If you want to make a lot of big gestures, I'll wait."

"Okay," he said, and after that he held relatively

still while I extracted the stinger. "Bees are nature's kamikaze pilots, Bow-Wow. Look in that glass box, you'll see the two who stung me lying dead at the bottom. Their stingers are barbed, like fishhooks. They slide in easy. When they pull out, they disembowel themselves."

"Gross," I said, dropping the second stinger in the ashtray. I couldn't see the barbs, but I didn't have a microscope.

"It makes them particular, though," he said.

"I bet."

"Wasps, on the other hand, have smooth stingers. They can shoot you up as many times as they like. They use up the poison by the third or fourth shot, but they can go right on making holes if they like . . . and usually they do. Especially wall-wasps. The kind I've got over there. You gotta sedate em. Stuff called Noxon. It must give em a hell of a hangover, because they wake up madder than ever."

He looked at me somberly, and for the first time I saw the dark brown wheels of weariness under his eyes and realized my kid brother was more tired than I had ever seen him.

"*That's* why people go on fighting, Bow-Wow. On and on and on. We got smooth stingers. Now watch this."

He got up, went over to his tote-bag, rummaged in it, and came up with an eye-dropper. He opened the mayonnaise jar, put the dropper in, and drew up a tiny bubble of his distilled Texas water.

When he took it over to the glass box with the wasps' nest inside, I saw the top on this one was different — there was a tiny plastic slide-piece set into it. I didn't need him to draw me a picture: with the bees, he was perfectly willing to remove the whole top. With the wasps, he was taking no chances.

He squeezed the black bulb. Two drops of water fell onto the nest, making a momentary dark spot that disappeared almost at once. "Give it about three minutes," he said.

"What —"

"No questions," he said. "You'll see. Three minutes."

In that period, he read my piece on art forgery . . . although it was already twenty pages long.

"Okay," he said, putting the pages down. "That's pretty good, man. You ought to read up a little on how Jay Gould furnished the parlor-car of his private train with fake Manets, though — that's a hoot." He was removing the cover of the glass box containing the wasps' nest as he spoke.

"Jesus, Bobby, cut the comedy!" I yelled.

"Same old wimp," Bobby laughed, and pulled the nest, which was dull gray and about the size of a bowling ball, out of the box. He held it in his hands. Wasps flew out and lit on his arms, his cheeks, his forehead. One flew across to me and landed on my forearm. I slapped it and it fell dead to the carpet. I was scared — I mean really scared. My body was wired with adrenaline and I could feel my eyes trying to push their way out of their sockets.

"Don't kill em," Bobby said. "You might as well be killing babies, for all the harm they can do you. That's the whole *point*." He tossed the nest from hand to hand as if it were an overgrown softball. He lobbed it in the air. I watched, horrified, as wasps cruised the living room of my apartment like fighter planes on patrol.

Bobby lowered the nest carefully back into the box and sat down on my couch. He patted the place next to him and I went over, nearly hypnotized. They were everywhere: on the rug, the ceiling, the drapes. Half a dozen of them were crawling across the front of my big-screen TV.

Before I could sit down, he brushed away a couple that were on the sofa cushion where my ass was aimed. They flew away quickly. They were *all* flying easily, crawling easily, moving fast. There was nothing drugged about their behavior. As Bobby talked, they gradually found their way back to their spit-paper home, crawled over it, and eventually disappeared inside again through the hole in the top.

"I wasn't the first one to get interested in Waco," he said. "It just happens to be the biggest town in the funny little non-violent section of what is, per capita, the most violent state in the union. Texans *love* to shoot each other, Howie — I mean, it's like a state hobby. Half the male population goes around armed. Saturday night in the Fort Worth bars is like a shooting gallery where you get to plonk away at drunks instead of clay ducks. There are more NRA card-carriers than there are Methodists. Not that Texas is the only place where people shoot each other, or carve each other up with straight-razors, or stick their kids in the oven if they cry too long, you understand, but they sure do like their firearms."

"Except in Waco," I said.

115

"Oh, they like em there, too," he said. "It's just that they use em on each other a hell of a lot less often."

Jesus. I just looked up at the clock and saw the time. It feels like I've been writing for fifteen minutes or so, but it's actually been over an hour. That happens to me sometimes when I'm running at white-hot speed, but I can't allow myself to be seduced into these specifics. I feel as well as ever — no noticeable drying of the membranes in the throat, no groping for words, and as I glance back over what I've done I see only the normal typos and strike-overs. But I can't kid myself. I've got to hurry up. "Fiddle-de-dee," said Scarlett, and all of that.

The non-violent atmosphere of the Waco area had been noticed and investigated before, mostly by sociologists. Bobby said that when you fed enough statistical data on Waco and similar areas into a computer — population density, mean age, mean economic level, mean educational level, and dozens of other factors — what you got back was a whopper of an anomaly. Scholarly papers are rarely jocular, but even so, several of the better than fifty Bobby had read on the subject suggested ironically that maybe it was "something in the water."

"I decided maybe it was time to take the joke seriously," Bobby said. "After all, there's something in the water of a lot of places that prevents tooth decay. It's called fluoride."

He went to Waco accompanied by a trio of research assistants: two sociology grad-students and a full professor of geology who happened to be on sabbatical and ready for adventure. Within six months, Bobby and the sociology guys had constructed a computer program which illustrated what my brother called the world's only calmquake. He had a slightly rumpled printout in his tote. He gave it to me. I was looking at a series of forty concentric rings. Waco was in the eighth, ninth, and tenth as you moved in toward the center.

"Now look at this," he said, and put a transparent overlay on the printout. More rings; but in each one there was a number. Fortieth ring: 471. Thirty-ninth: 420. Thirty-eighth: 418. And so on. In a couple of places the numbers went up instead of down, but only in a couple (and only by a little).

"What are they?"

"Each number represents the incidence of violent crime in that particular circle," Bobby said. "Murder, rape, assault and battery, even acts of vandalism. The computer assigns a number by a formula that takes population density into account." He tapped the twenty-seventh circle, which held the number 204, with his finger. "There's less than nine hundred people in this whole area, for instance. The number represents three or four cases of spouse abuse, a couple of barroom brawls, an act of animal cruelty — some senile farmer got pissed at a pig and shot a load of rock-salt into it, as I recall — and one involuntary manslaughter."

I saw that the numbers in the central circles dropped off radically: 85, 81, 70, 63, 40, 21, 5.

At the epicenter of Bobby's calmquake was the town of La Plata. To call it a sleepy little town seems more than fair.

The numeric value assigned to La Plata was zero.

"So here it is, Bow-Wow," Bobby said, leaning forward and rubbing his long hands together nervously, "my nominee for the Garden of Eden. Here's a community of fifteen thousand, twenty-four per cent of which are people of mixed blood, commonly called Indios. There's a moccasin factory, a couple of little motor courts, a couple of scrub farms. That's it for work. For play there's four bars, a couple of dance-halls where you can hear any kind of music you want as long as it sounds like George Jones, two drive-ins, and a bowling alley." He paused and added, "There's also a still. I didn't know anybody made whiskey that good outside of Tennessee."

In short (and it is now too late to be anything else), La Plata should have been a fertile breeding-ground for the sort of casual violence you can read about in the Police Blotter section of the local newspaper every day. Should have been but wasn't. There had been only one murder in La Plata during the five years previous to my brother's arrival, two cases of assault, no rapes, no reported incidents of child abuse. There had been four armed robberies, but all four turned out to have been committed by transients . . . as the murder and one of the assaults had been. The local Sheriff was a fat old Republican who did a pretty fair Rodney Dangerfield imitation. He had been known, in fact, to spend whole days in the local coffee shop, tugging the knot in his tie and telling people to take his wife, please. My brother said he thought it was a little more than lame humor; he was pretty sure the poor guy was suffering first-stage Alzheimer's Disease. His only deputy was his nephew. Bobby told me the nephew looked quite a lot like Junior Samples on the old *Hee-Haw* show.

"Put those two guys in a Pennsylvania town similar to La Plata in every way but the geographical," Bobby said, "and they would have been out on their asses fifteen years ago. But in La Plata, they're gonna go on until they die . . . which they'll probably do in their sleep."

"What did you do?" I asked. "How did you proceed?"

"Well, for the first week or so after we got our statistical shit together, we just sort of sat around and stared at each other," Bobby said. "I mean, we were prepared for *something*, but nothing quite like this. Even Waco doesn't prepare you for La Plata." Bobby shifted restlessly and cracked his knuckles.

"Jesus, I hate it when you do that," I said.

He smiled. "Sorry, Bow-Wow. Anyway, we started geological tests, then microscopic analysis of the water. I didn't expect a hell of a lot; everyone in the area has got a well, usually a deep one, and they get their water tested regularly to make sure they're not drinking borax, or something. If there had been something obvious, it would have turned up a long time ago. So we went on to sub-microscopy, and that was when we started to turn up some pretty weird stuff."

"What kind of weird stuff?"

119

"Breaks in chains of atoms, subdynamic electrical fluctuations, and some sort of unidentified protein. Water ain't really H_2O, you know — not when you add in the sulfides, irons, God knows what else happens to be in the aquifer of a given region. And La Plata water — you'd have to give it a string of letters like the ones after a professor emeritus's name." His eyes gleamed. "But the protein was the most interesting thing, Bow-Wow. So far as we know, it's only found in one other place: the human brain."

Uh-oh.

It just arrived, between one swallow and the next: the throat-dryness. Not much as yet, but enough for me to break away and get a glass of ice-water. I've got maybe forty minutes left. And oh Jesus, there's so much I want to tell! About the wasps' nests they found with wasps that wouldn't sting, about the fender-bender Bobby and one of his assistants saw where the two drivers, both male, both drunk, and both about twenty-four (sociological bull moose, in other words), got out, shook hands, and exchanged insurance information amicably before going into the nearest bar for another drink.

Bobby talked for hours — more hours than I have. But the upshot was simple: the stuff in the mayonnaise jar.

"We've got our own still in La Plata now," he said. "This is the stuff we're brewing, Howie; pacifist white lightning. The aquifer under that area of Texas is deep but amazingly large; it's like this incredible Lake Victoria driven into the porous

120

sediment which overlays the Moho. The water is potent, but we've been able to make the stuff I squirted on the wasps even more potent. We've got damn near six thousand gallons now, in these big steel tanks. By the end of the year, we'll have fourteen thousand. By next June we'll have thirty thousand. But it's not enough. We need more, we need it faster . . . and then we need to transport it."

"Transport it where?" I asked him.

"Borneo, to start with."

I thought I'd either lost my mind or misheard him. I really did.

"Look, Bow-Wow . . . sorry. Howie." He was scrumming through his tote-bag again. He brought out a number of aerial photographs and handed them over to me. "You see?" he asked as I looked through them. "You see how fucking perfect it is? It's as if God Himself suddenly busted through our business-as-usual transmissions with something like 'And now we bring you a special bulletin! This is your last chance, assholes! And now we return you to *Days of Our Lives.*' "

"I don't get you," I said. "And I have no idea what I'm looking at." Of course I knew; it was an island — not Borneo itself but an island lying to the west of Borneo identified as Gulandio — with a mountain in the middle and a lot of muddy little villages lying on its lower slopes. It was hard to see the mountain because of the cloud cover. What I meant was that I didn't know what I was looking *for*.

"The mountain has the same name as the island," he said. "Gulandio. In the local patois it

121

means *grace,* or *fate,* or *destiny,* or take your pick. But Duke Rogers says it's really the biggest time-bomb on earth . . . and it's wired to go off by October of next year. Probably earlier."

The crazy thing's this: the story's only crazy if you try to tell it in a speed-rap, which is what I'm trying to do now. Bobby wanted me to help him raise somewhere between six hundred thousand and a million and a half dollars to do the following: first, to synthesize fifty to seventy thousand gallons of what he called "the high-test"; second, to airlift all of this water to Borneo, which had landing facilities (you could land a hang-glider on Gulandio, but that was about all); third, to ship it over to this island named Fate, or Destiny, or Grace; fourth, to truck it up the slope of the volcano, which had been dormant (save for a few puffs in 1938) since 1804, and then to drop it down the muddy tube of the volcano's caldera. Duke Rogers was actually John Paul Rogers, the geology professor. He claimed that Gulandio was going to do more than just erupt; he claimed that it was going to explode, as Krakatoa had done in the nineteenth century, creating a bang that would make the Squirt Bomb that poisoned London look like a kid's firecracker.

The debris from the Krakatoa blow-up, Bobby told me, had literally encircled the globe; the observed results had formed an important part of the Sagan Group's nuclear winter theory. For three months afterward sunsets and sunrises half a world away had been grotesquely colorful as a result of the ash whirling around in both the jet stream and the Van Allen Currents, which lie forty miles below the Van Allen Belt. There had been global changes in climate which lasted five years, and nipa palms, which previously had grown only in eastern Africa and Micronesia, suddenly showed up in both South and North America.

"The North American nipas all died before 1900," Bobby said, "but they're alive and well below the equator. Krakatoa seeded them there, Howie . . . the way I want to seed La Plata water all over the earth. I want people to go out in La Plata water when it rains — and it's going to rain a lot after Gulandio goes bang. I want them to drink the La Plata water that falls in their reservoirs, I want them to wash their hair in it, bathe in it, soak their contact lenses in it. I want whores to *douche* in it."

"Bobby," I said, knowing he was not, "you're crazy."

He gave me a crooked, tired grin. "I ain't crazy," he said. "You want to see crazy? Turn on CNN, Bow . . . Howie. You'll see crazy in living color."

But I didn't need to turn on Cable News (what a friend of mine had taken to calling The Organ-Grinder of Doom) to know what Bobby was talking about. The Indians and the Pakistanis were poised on the brink. The Chinese and the Afghans, ditto. Half of Africa was starving, the other half on fire with AIDS. There had been border skirmishes along the entire Tex-Mex border in the last five years, since Mexico went Communist, and people had started calling the Tijuana crossing point in California Little Berlin because of the wall. The

123

saber-rattling had become a din. On the last day of the old year the Scientists for Nuclear Responsibility had set their black clock to fifteen seconds before midnight.

"Bobby, let's suppose it could be done and everything went according to schedule," I said. "It probably couldn't and wouldn't, but let's suppose. You don't have the slightest idea what the long-term effects might be."

He started to say something and I waved it away.

"Don't even suggest that you do, because you don't! You've had time to find this calmquake of yours and isolate the cause, I'll give you that. But did you ever hear about thalidomide? That nifty little acne-stopper and sleeping pill that caused cancer and heart attacks in thirty-year-olds? Don't you remember the AIDS vaccine in 1997?"

"Howie?"

"*That* one stopped the disease, except it turned the test subjects into incurable epileptics who all died within eighteen months."

"Howie?"

"Then there was —"

"Howie?"

I stopped and looked at him.

"The world," Bobby said, and then stopped. His throat worked. I saw he was struggling with tears. "The world needs heroic measures, man. I don't know about long-term effects, and there's no time to study them, because there's no long-term prospect. Maybe we can cure the whole mess. Or maybe —"

He shrugged, tried to smile, and looked at me

with shining eyes from which two single tears slowly tracked.

"Or maybe we're giving heroin to a patient with terminal cancer. Either way, it'll stop what's happening now. It'll end the world's pain." He spread out his hands, palms up, so I could see the stings on them. "Help me, Bow-Wow. Please help me."

So I helped him.

And we fucked up. In fact I think you could say we fucked up big-time. And do you want the truth? I don't give a shit. We killed all the plants, but at least we saved the greenhouse. Something will grow here again, someday. I hope.

Are you reading this?

My gears are starting to get a little sticky. For the first time in years I'm having to think about what I'm doing. The motor-movements of writing. Should have hurried more at the start.

Never mind. Too late to change things now.

We did it, of course: distilled the water, flew it in, transported it to Gulandio, built a primitive lifting system — half motor-winch and half cog railway — up the side of the volcano, and dropped over twelve thousand five-gallon containers of La Plata water — the brain-buster version — into the murky misty depths of the volcano's caldera. We did all of this in just eight months. It didn't cost six hundred thousand dollars, or a million and a half; it cost over four million, still less than a sixteenth of one per cent of what America spent on defense that year. You want to know how we razed it? I'd tell you if I had more thyme, but my head's falling apart so never mend. I raised

125

most of it myself if it matters to you. Some by hoof and some by croof. Tell you the truth, I din't know I could do it muself until I did. But we did it and somehow the world held together and that volcano — whatever its name wuz, I can't exactly remember now and there izzunt time to go back over the manuscript — it blue just when it was spo

Wait

Okay. A little better. Digitalin. Bobby had it. Heart's beating like crazy but I can think again.

The volcano — Mount Grace, we called it — blue just when Dook Rogers said it would. Everything when skihi and for awhile everyone's attention turned away from whatever and toward the skys. And bimmel-dee-dee, said Strapless!

It happened pretty fast like sex and checks and special effex and everybody got healthy again. I mean
wait

Jesus please let me finish this.

I mean that everybody stood down. Everybody started to get a little purstective on the situation. The wurld started to get like the wasps in Bobbys nest the one he showed me where they didn't stink too much. There was three yerz like an Indian sumer. People getting together like in that old Youngbloods song that went cmon everybody get together rite now, like what all the hippeez wanted, you no, peets and luv and
wt

126

Big blast. Feel like my heart is coming out thru my ears. But if I concentrate every bit of my force, my *concentration* —

It was like an Indian summer, that's what I meant to say, like three years of Indian summer. Bobby went on with his resurch. La Plata. Sociological background etc. You remember the local Sheriff? Fat old Republican with a good Rodney Youngblood imitashun? How Bobby said he had the preliminary simptoms of Rodney's Disease?

concentrate asshole

Wasn't just him; turned out like there was a lot of that going around in that part of Texas. All's Hallows Disease is what I meen. For three yerz me and Bobby were down there. Created a new program. New graff of circkles. I saw what was happen and came back here. Bobby and his to asistants stayed on. One shot hisself Boby said when he showed up here.
Wait one more blas

All right. Last time. Heart beating so fast I can hardly breeve. The new graph, the *last* graph, really only whammed you when it was laid over the calmquake graft. The calmquake graff showed ax of vilence going down as you approached La Plata in the muddle; the Alzheimer's graff showed incidence of premature seenullity going *up* as you approached La Plata. People there were getting very silly very yung.

127

Me and Bobo were careful as we could be for next three years, drink only Parrier Water and wor big long sleekers in the ran. so no war and when everybobby started to get seely we din and I came back here because he my brother I cant remember what his name

Bobby

Bobby when he came here tonight cryeen and I sed Bobby I luv you Bobby sed Ime sorry Bow-wow Ime sorry I made the hole world ful of foals and dumbbels and I sed better fouls and bells than a big black sinder in spaz and he cryed and I cryed Bobby I luv you and he sed will you give me a shot of the spacial wadder and I sed yez and he said wil you ride it down and I sed yez an I think I did but I cant reely remember I see wurds but dont no what they mean

I have a Bobby his nayme is bruther and I theen I an dun riding and I have a bocks to put this into thats Bobby sd full of quiyet air to last a milyun yrz so gudboy gudboy everybrother, Im goin to stob gudboy bobby i love you it wuz not yor falt i love you

    forgivyu
  love yu

               sinned (for the wurld),

               BowWow Forboy

Suffer the Little Children

Miss Sidley was her name, and teaching was her game.

She was a small woman who had to stretch to write on the highest level of the blackboard, which she was doing now. Behind her, none of the children giggled or whispered or munched on secret sweets held in cupped hands. They knew Miss Sidley's deadly instincts too well. Miss Sidley could always tell who was chewing gum at the back of the room, who had a beanshooter in his pocket, who wanted to go to the bathroom to trade baseball cards rather than use the facilities. Like God, she seemed to know everything all at once.

She was graying, and the brace she wore to support her failing back was limned clearly against her print dress. Small, constantly suffering, gimlet-eyed woman. But they feared her. Her tongue was a school-yard legend. The eyes, when focused on a giggler or a whisperer, could turn the stoutest knees to water.

Now, writing the day's list of spelling words on the board, she reflected that the success of her long teaching career could be summed and checked and proven by this one everyday action: she could turn her back on her pupils with confidence. "Vacation," she said, pronouncing the word as she wrote it in her firm, no-nonsense script. "Edward, please use the word *vacation* in a sentence."

"I went on a vacation to New York City," Edward piped. Then, as Miss Sidley had taught, he repeated the word carefully. "Vay-cay-shun."

"Very good, Edward." She began on the next word.

She had her little tricks, of course; success, she firmly believed, depended as much on the little things as on the big ones. She applied the principle constantly in the classroom, and it never failed.

"Jane," she said quietly.

Jane, who had been furtively perusing her Reader, looked up guiltily.

"Close that book right now, please." The book shut; Jane looked with pale, hating eyes at Miss Sidley's back. "And you will remain at your desk for fifteen minutes after the final bell."

Jane's lips trembled. "Yes, Miss Sidley."

One of her little tricks was the careful use of her glasses. The whole class was reflected in their thick lenses and she had always been thinly amused by their guilty, frightened faces when she caught them at their nasty little games. Now she saw a phantomish, distorted Robert in the first row wrinkle his nose. She did not speak. Not yet. Robert would hang himself if given just a little more rope.

"Tomorrow," she pronounced clearly. "Robert, you will please use the word *tomorrow* in a sentence."

Robert frowned over the problem. The classroom was hushed and sleepy in the late-September sun. The electric clock over the door buzzed a rumor of three o'clock dismissal just a half-hour away, and the only thing that kept young heads from drowsing over their spellers was the silent, ominous threat of Miss Sidley's back.

"I am waiting, Robert."

"Tomorrow a bad thing will happen," Robert said. The words were perfectly innocuous, but Miss Sidley, with the seventh sense that all strict disciplinarians have, didn't like them a bit. "Too-mor-row," Robert finished. His hands were folded neatly on the desk, and he wrinkled his nose again. He also smiled a tiny side-of-the-mouth smile. Miss Sidley was suddenly, unaccountably sure Robert knew about her little trick with the glasses.

All right; very well.

She began to write the next word with no word of commendation for Robert, letting her straight body speak its own message. She watched carefully with one eye. Soon Robert would stick out his tongue or make that disgusting finger-gesture they all knew (even the girls seemed to know it these days), just to see if she really knew what he was doing. Then he would be punished.

The reflection was small, ghostly, and distorted. And she had all but the barest corner of her eye on the word she was writing.

Robert changed.

She caught just a flicker of it, just a frightening glimpse of Robert's face changing into something . . . different.

She whirled around, face white, barely noticing the protesting stab of pain in her back.

Robert looked at her blandly, questioningly. His hands were neatly folded. The first signs of an afternoon cowlick showed at the back of his head.

He did not look frightened.

I imagined it, she thought. *I was looking for something, and when there was nothing, my mind just made something up. Very cooperative of it. However —*

"Robert?" She meant to be authoritative; meant for her voice to make the unspoken demand for confession. It did not come out that way.

"Yes, Miss Sidley?" His eyes were a very dark brown, like the mud at the bottom of a slow-running stream.

"Nothing."

She turned back to the board. A little whisper ran through the class.

"*Be quiet!*" she snapped, and turned again to face them. "One more sound and we will all stay after school with Jane!" She addressed the whole class, but looked most directly at Robert. He looked back with childlike innocence: *Who, me? Not* me, *Miss Sidley.*

She turned to the board and began to write, not looking out of the corners of her glasses. The last half-hour dragged, and it seemed that Robert gave her a strange look on the way out. A look that said, *We have a secret, don't we?*

The look wouldn't leave her mind. It was stuck there, like a tiny string of roast beef between two molars — a small thing, actually, but feeling as big as a cinderblock.

She sat down to her solitary dinner at five (poached eggs on toast) still thinking about it. She knew she was getting older and accepted the knowledge calmly. She was not going to be one of those old-maid schoolmarms dragged kicking and screaming from their classes at the age of retire-

132

ment. They reminded her of gamblers unable to leave the tables while they were losing. But *she* was not losing. She had always been a winner.

She looked down at her poached eggs.

Hadn't she?

She thought of the well-scrubbed faces in her third-grade classroom, and found Robert's face most prominent among them.

She got up and switched on another light.

Later, just before she dropped off to sleep, Robert's face floated in front of her, smiling unpleasantly in the darkness behind her lids. The face began to change —

But before she saw exactly what it was changing into, darkness overtook her.

Miss Sidley spent an unrestful night and consequently the next day her temper was short. She waited, almost hoping for a whisperer, a giggler, perhaps a note-passer. But the class was quiet — very quiet. They all stared at her unresponsively, and it seemed that she could feel the weight of their eyes on her like blind, crawling ants.

Stop that! she told herself sternly. *You're acting like a skittish girl just out of teachers college!*

Again the day seemed to drag, and she believed she was more relieved than the children when the last bell rang. The children lined up in orderly rows at the door, boys and girls by height, hands dutifully linked.

"Dismissed," she said, and listened sourly as they shrieked their way down the hall and into the bright sunlight.

What was it I saw when he changed? Something bulbous. Something that shimmered. Something that stared at me, yes, stared and grinned and wasn't a child at all. It was old and it was evil and —

"Miss Sidley?"

Her head jerked up and a little *Oh!* hiccupped involuntarily from her throat.

It was Mr. Hanning. He smiled apologetically. "Didn't mean to disturb you."

"Quite all right," she said, more curtly than she had intended. What had she been thinking? What was wrong with her?

"Would you mind checking the paper towels in the girls' lav?"

"Surely." She got up, placing her hands against the small of her back. Mr. Hanning looked at her sympathetically. *Save it,* she thought. *The old maid is not amused. Or even interested.*

She brushed by Mr. Hanning and started down the hall to the girls' lavatory. A snigger of boys carrying scratched and pitted baseball equipment grew silent at the sight of her and leaked guiltily out the door, where their cries began again.

Miss Sidley frowned after them, reflecting that children had been different in her day. Not more polite — children have never had time for that — and not exactly more respectful of their elders; it was a kind of hypocrisy that had never been there before. A smiling quietness around adults that had never been there before. A kind of quiet contempt that was upsetting and unnerving. As if they were . . .

Hiding behind masks? Is that it?

She pushed the thought away and went into the

134

lavatory. It was a small, L-shaped room. The toilets were ranged along one side of the longer bar, the sinks along both sides of the shorter one.

As she checked the paper-towel containers, she caught a glimpse of her face in one of the mirrors and was startled into looking at it closely. She didn't care for what she saw — not a bit. There was a look that hadn't been there two days before, a frightened, watching look. With sudden shock she realized that the blurred reflection in her glasses of Robert's pale, respectful face had gotten inside her and was festering.

The door opened and she heard two girls come in, giggling secretly about something. She was about to turn the corner and walk out past them when she heard her own name. She turned back to the washbowls and began checking the towel holders again.

"And then he —"

Soft giggles.

"She knows, but —"

More giggles, soft and sticky as melting soap.

"Miss Sidley is —"

Stop it! Stop that noise!

By moving slightly she could see their shadows, made fuzzy and ill-defined by the diffuse light filtering through the frosted windows, holding onto each other with girlish glee.

Another thought crawled up out of her mind.

They knew she was there.

Yes. Yes they did. The little bitches knew.

She would shake them. Shake them until their teeth rattled and their giggles turned to wails, she would thump their heads against the tile walls and she would make them *admit* that they knew.

That was when the shadows changed. They seemed to elongate, to flow like dripping tallow, taking on strange hunched shapes that made Miss Sidley cringe back against the porcelain wash stands, her heart swelling in her chest.

But they went on giggling.

The voices changed, no longer girlish, now sexless and soulless, and quite, quite evil. A slow, turgid sound of mindless humor that flowed around the corner to her like sewage.

She stared at the hunched shadows and suddenly screamed at them. The scream went on and on, swelling in her head until it attained a pitch of lunacy. And then she fainted. The giggling, like the laughter of demons, followed her down into darkness.

She could not, of course, tell them the truth.

Miss Sidley knew this even as she opened her eyes and looked up at the anxious faces of Mr. Hanning and Mrs. Crossen. Mrs. Crossen was holding the bottle of smelling salts from the gymnasium first-aid kit under her nose. Mr. Hanning turned around and told the two little girls who were looking curiously at Miss Sidley to go home now, please.

They both smiled at her — slow, we-have-a-secret smiles — and went out.

Very well, she would keep their secret. For awhile. She would not have people thinking her insane, or that the first feelers of senility had touched her early. She would play their game. Until she could expose their nastiness and rip it out by the roots.

"I'm afraid I slipped," she said calmly, sitting up and ignoring the excruciating pain in her back. "A patch of wetness."

"This is awful," Mr. Hanning said. "Terrible. Are you —"

"Did the fall hurt your back, Emily?" Mrs. Crossen interrupted. Mr. Hanning looked at her gratefully.

Miss Sidley got up, her spine screaming in her body.

"No," she said. "In fact, the fall seems to have worked some minor chiropractic miracle. My back hasn't felt this well in years."

"We can send for a doctor —" Mr. Hanning began.

"Not necessary." Miss Sidley smiled at him coolly.

"I'll call you a taxi from the office."

"You'll do no such thing," Miss Sidley said, walking to the door of the girls' lav and opening it. "I always take the bus."

Mr. Hanning sighed and looked at Mrs. Crossen. Mrs. Crossen rolled her eyes and said nothing.

The next day Miss Sidley kept Robert after school. He did nothing to warrant the punishment, so she simply accused him falsely. She felt no qualms; he was a monster, not a little boy. She must make him admit it.

Her back was in agony. She realized Robert knew; he expected that would help him. But it wouldn't. That was another of her little advantages. Her back had been a constant pain to her for the last twelve years, and there had been many

137

times when it had been this bad — well, *almost* this bad.

She closed the door, shutting the two of them in.

For a moment she stood still, training her gaze on Robert. She waited for him to drop his eyes. He didn't. He looked back at her, and presently a little smile began to play around the corners of his mouth.

"Why are you smiling, Robert?" she asked softly.

"I don't know," Robert said, and went on smiling.

"Tell me, please."

Robert said nothing.

And went on smiling.

The outside sounds of children at play were distant, dreamy. Only the hypnotic buzz of the wall clock was real.

"There's quite a few of us," Robert said suddenly, as if he were commenting on the weather.

It was Miss Sidley's turn to be silent.

"Eleven right here in this school."

Quite evil, she thought, amazed. *Very, incredibly evil.*

"Little boys who tell stories go to hell," she said clearly. "I know many parents no longer make their . . . their *spawn* . . . aware of that fact, but I assure you that it is a *true* fact, Robert. Little boys who tell stories go to hell. Little girls too, for that matter."

Robert's smile grew wider; it became vulpine. "Do you want to see me change, Miss Sidley? Do you want a really good look?"

Miss Sidley felt her back prickle. "Go away," she said curtly. "And bring your mother or your father to school with you tomorrow. We'll get this business straightened out." There. On solid ground again. She waited for his face to crumple, waited for the tears.

Instead, Robert's smile grew wider — wide enough to show his teeth. "It will be just like Show and Tell, won't it, Miss Sidley? Robert — the *other* Robert — he liked Show and Tell. He's still hiding way, way down in my head." The smile curled at the corners of his mouth like charring paper. "Sometimes he runs around . . . it itches. He wants me to let him out."

"Go away," Miss Sidley said numbly. The buzzing of the clock seemed very loud.

Robert changed.

His face suddenly ran together like melting wax, the eyes flattening and spreading like knife-struck egg yolks, nose widening and yawning, mouth disappearing. The head elongated, and the hair was suddenly not hair but straggling, twitching growths.

Robert began to chuckle.

The slow, cavernous sound came from what had been his nose, but the nose was eating into the lower half of his face, nostrils meeting and merging into a central blackness like a huge, shouting mouth.

Robert got up, still chuckling, and behind it all she could see the last shattered remains of the other Robert, the real little boy this alien thing had usurped, howling in maniac terror, screeching to be let out.

She ran.

She fled screaming down the corridor, and the few late-leaving pupils turned to look at her with large and uncomprehending eyes. Mr. Hanning jerked open his door and looked out just as she plunged through the wide glass front doors, a wild, waving scarecrow silhouetted against the bright September sky.

He ran after her, Adam's apple bobbing. "Miss Sidley! *Miss Sidley!*"

Robert came out of the classroom and watched curiously.

Miss Sidley neither heard nor saw. She clattered down the steps and across the sidewalk and into the street with her screams trailing behind her. There was a huge, blatting horn and then the bus was looming over her, the bus driver's face a plaster mask of fear. Air brakes whined and hissed like angry dragons.

Miss Sidley fell, and the huge wheels shuddered to a smoking stop just eight inches from her frail, brace-armored body. She lay shuddering on the pavement, hearing the crowd gather around her.

She turned over and the children were staring down at her. They were ringed in a tight little circle, like mourners around an open grave. And at the head of the grave was Robert, a small sober sexton ready to shovel the first spade of dirt into her face.

From far away, the bus driver's shaken babble: ". . . crazy or somethin . . . my God, another half a foot . . ."

Miss Sidley stared at the children. Their shadows covered her. Their faces were impassive. Some of them were smiling little secret smiles, and Miss

Sidley knew that soon she would begin to scream again.

Then Mr. Hanning broke their tight noose, shooed them away, and Miss Sidley began to sob weakly.

She didn't go back to her third grade for a month. She told Mr. Hanning calmly that she had not been feeling herself, and Mr. Hanning suggested that she see a reputable doctor and discuss the matter with him. Miss Sidley agreed that this was the only sensible and rational course. She also said that if the school board wished for her resignation she would tender it immediately although doing so would hurt her very much. Mr. Hanning, looking uncomfortable, said he doubted if that would be necessary. The upshot was that Miss Sidley came back in late October, once again ready to play the game and now knowing how to play it.

For the first week she let things go on as ever. It seemed the whole class now regarded her with hostile, shielded eyes. Robert smiled distantly at her from his front-row seat, and she did not have the courage to take him to task.

Once, while she was on playground duty, Robert walked over to her, holding a dodgem ball, smiling. "There's so many of us now you wouldn't believe it," he said. "And neither would anyone else." He stunned her by dropping a wink of infinite slyness. "If you, you know, tried to tell em."

A girl on the swings looked across the playground into Miss Sidley's eyes and laughed at her.

Miss Sidley smiled serenely down at Robert.

"Why, Robert, whatever do you mean?"

But Robert only continued smiling as he went back to his game.

Miss Sidley brought the gun to school in her handbag. It had been her brother's. He had taken it from a dead German shortly after the Battle of the Bulge. Jim had been gone ten years now. She hadn't opened the box that held the gun in at least five, but when she did it was still there, gleaming dully. The clips of ammunition were still there, too, and she loaded the gun carefully, just as Jim had shown her.

She smiled pleasantly at her class; at Robert in particular. Robert smiled back and she could see the murky alienness swimming just below his skin, muddy, full of filth.

She had no idea what was now living inside Robert's skin, and she didn't care; she only hoped that the real little boy was entirely gone by now. She did not wish to be a murderess. She decided the real Robert must have died or gone insane, living inside the dirty, crawling thing that had chuckled at her in the classroom and sent her screaming into the street. So even if he was still alive, putting him out of his misery would be a mercy.

"Today we're going to have a Test," Miss Sidley said.

The class did not groan or shift apprehensively; they merely looked at her. She could feel their eyes, like weights. Heavy, smothering.

"It's a very special Test. I will call you down to the mimeograph room one by one and give it to you. Then you may have a candy and go home for the day. Won't that be nice?"

They smiled empty smiles and said nothing.

"Robert, will you come first?"

Robert got up, smiling his little smile. He wrinkled his nose quite openly at her. "Yes, Miss Sidley."

Miss Sidley took her bag and they went down the empty, echoing corridor together, past the sleepy drone of classes reciting behind closed doors. The mimeograph room was at the far end of the hall, past the lavatories. It had been soundproofed two years ago; the big machine was very old and very noisy.

Miss Sidley closed the door behind them and locked it.

"No one can hear you," she said calmly. She took the gun from her bag. "You or this."

Robert smiled innocently. "There are lots of us, though. Lots more than here." He put one small scrubbed hand on the papertray of the mimeograph machine. "Would you like to see me change again?"

Before she could speak, Robert's face began to shimmer into the grotesqueness beneath and Miss Sidley shot him. Once. In the head. He fell back against the paper-lined shelves and slid down to the floor, a little dead boy with a round black hole above his right eye.

He looked very pathetic.

Miss Sidley stood over him, panting. Her cheeks were pale.

The huddled figure didn't move.

It was human.

It was Robert.

No!

It was all in your mind, Emily. All in your mind.
No! No, no, *no!*

She went back up to the room and began to lead them down, one by one. She killed twelve of them and would have killed them all if Mrs. Crossen hadn't come down for a package of composition paper.

Mrs. Crossen's eyes got very big; one hand crept up and clutched her mouth. She began to scream and she was still screaming when Miss Sidley reached her and put a hand on her shoulder. "It had to be done, Margaret," she told the screaming Mrs. Crossen. "It's terrible, but it had to. They are all monsters."

Mrs. Crossen stared at the gaily clothed little bodies scattered around the mimeograph and continued to scream. The little girl whose hand Miss Sidley was holding began to cry steadily and monotonously: *"Waahhh . . . waahhhh . . . waahhhh."*

"Change," Miss Sidley said. "Change for Mrs. Crossen. Show her it had to be done."

The girl continued to weep uncomprehendingly.

"Damn you, *change!*" Miss Sidley screamed. "Dirty bitch, dirty crawling, filthy unnatural *bitch!* Change! God damn you, *change!*" She raised the gun. The little girl cringed, and then Mrs. Crossen was on her like a cat, and Miss Sidley's back gave way.

No trial.

The papers screamed for one, bereaved parents swore hysterical oaths against Miss Sidley, and the city sat back on its haunches in numb shock, but in the end, cooler heads prevailed and there was

144

no trial. The State Legislature called for more stringent teacher exams, Summer Street School closed for a week of mourning, and Miss Sidley went quietly to Juniper Hill in Augusta. She was put in deep analysis, given the most modern drugs, introduced into daily work-therapy sessions. A year later, under strictly controlled conditions, Miss Sidley was put in an experimental encounter-therapy situation.

Buddy Jenkins was his name, psychiatry was his game.

He sat behind a one-way glass with a clipboard, looking into a room which had been outfitted as a nursery. On the far wall, the cow was jumping over the moon and the mouse ran up the clock. Miss Sidley sat in her wheelchair with a story book, surrounded by a group of trusting, drooling, smiling, cataclysmically retarded children. They smiled at her and drooled and touched her with small wet fingers while attendants at the next window watched for the first sign of an aggressive move.

For a time Buddy thought she responded well. She read aloud, stroked a girl's head, consoled a small boy when he fell over a toy block. Then she seemed to see something which disturbed her; a frown creased her brow and she looked away from the children.

"Take me away, please," Miss Sidley said, softly and tonelessly, to no one in particular.

And so they took her away. Buddy Jenkins watched the children watch her go, their eyes wide and empty, but somehow deep. One smiled, and another put his fingers in his mouth slyly. Two little girls clutched each other and giggled.

That night Miss Sidley cut her throat with a bit of broken mirror-glass, and after that Buddy Jenkins began to watch the children more and more. In the end, he was hardly able to take his eyes off them.

The Night Flier

1

In spite of his pilot's license, Dees didn't really get interested until the murders at the airport in Maryland — the third and fourth murders in the series. Then he smelled that special combination of blood and guts which readers of *Inside View* had come to expect. Coupled with a good dimestore mystery like this one, you were looking at the likelihood of an explosive circulation boost, and in the tabloid business, increased circulation was more than the name of the game; it was the Holy Grail.

For Dees, however, there was bad news as well as good. The good news was that he had gotten to the story ahead of the rest of the pack; he was still undefeated, still champeen, still top hog in the sty. The bad news was that the roses really belonged to Morrison . . . so far, at least. Morrison, the freshman editor, had gone on picking away at the damned thing even after Dees, the veteran reporter, had assured him there was nothing there but smoke and echoes. Dees didn't like the idea that Morrison had smelled blood first — hated it, in fact — and this left him with a completely understandable urge to piss the man off. And he knew just how to do it.

"Duffrey, Maryland, huh?"

Morrison nodded.

"Anyone in the straight press pick up on it yet?" Dees asked, and was gratified to see Morrison bristle at once.

"If you mean has anyone suggested there's a serial killer out there, the answer is no," he said stiffly.

But it won't be long, Dees thought.

"But it won't be long," Morrison said. "If there's another one —"

"Gimme the file," Dees said, pointing to the buff-colored folder lying on Morrison's eerily neat desk.

The balding editor put a hand on it instead, and Dees understood two things: Morrison *was* going to give it to him, but not until he had been made to pay a little for his initial unbelief . . . and his lofty I'm-the-veteran-around-here attitude. Well, maybe that was all right. Maybe even the top hog in the sty needed to have his curly little tail twisted every now and then, just to refresh his memory on his place in the scheme of things.

"I thought you were supposed to be over at the Museum of Natural History, talking to the penguin guy," Morrison said. The corners of his mouth curved up in a small but undeniably evil smile. "The one who thinks they're smarter than people *and* dolphins."

Dees pointed to the only other thing on Morrison's desk besides the folder and the pictures of his nerdy-looking wife and three nerdy-looking kids: a large wire basket labelled DAILY BREAD. It currently contained a single thin sheaf of manuscript, six or eight pages held together with one of Dees's distinctive magenta paper-clips, and an envelope marked CONTACT SHEETS DO NOT BEND.

Morrison took his hand off the folder (looking ready to slap it back on if Dees so much as twitched), opened the envelope, and shook out two sheets covered with black-and-white photos not much bigger than postage stamps. Each photo showed long files of penguins staring silently out at the viewer. There was something undeniably creepy about them — to Merton Morrison they looked like George Romero zombies in tuxedos. He nodded and slipped them back into the envelope. Dees disliked all editors on principle, but he had to admit that this one at least gave credit where credit was due. It was a rare attribute, one Dees suspected would cause the man all sorts of medical problems in later life. Or maybe the problems had already started. There he sat, surely not thirty-five yet, with at least seventy per cent of his skull exposed.

"Not bad," Morrison said. "Who took them?"

"*I* did," Dees said. "I *always* take the pix that go with my stories. Don't you ever look at the photo credits?"

"Not usually, no," Morrison said, and glanced at the temp headline Dees had slugged at the top of his penguin story. Libby Grannit in Comp would come up with a punchier, more colorful one, of course — that was, after all, her job — but Dees's instincts were good all the way up to headlines, and he usually found the right street, if not often the actual address and apartment number. ALIEN INTELLIGENCE AT NORTH POLE, this one read.

149

Penguins weren't aliens, of course, and Morrison had an idea that they actually lived at the *South Pole*, but those things hardly mattered. *Inside View* readers were crazy about both Aliens and Intelligence (perhaps because a majority of them felt like the former and sensed in them-selves a deep deficiency of the latter), and *that* was what mattered.

"The headline's a little lacking," Morrison began, "but —"

"— that's what Libby's for," Dees finished for him. "So . . ."

"So?" Morrison asked. His eyes were wide and blue and guileless behind his gold-rimmed glasses. He put his hand back down on top of the folder, smiled at Dees, and waited.

"So what do you want me to say? That I was wrong?"

Morrison's smile widened a millimeter or two. "Just that you *might* have been wrong. That'd do, I guess — you know what a pussycat I am."

"Yeah, tell me about it," Dees said, but he was relieved. He could take a little abasement; it was the actual crawling around on his belly that he didn't like.

Morrison sat looking at him, right hand splayed over the file.

"Okay; I might have been wrong."

"How large-hearted of you to admit it," Morrison said, and handed the file over.

Dees snatched it greedily, took it over to the chair by the window, and opened it. What he read this time — it was no more than a loose assemblage of wire-service stories and clippings from a few

150

small-town weeklies — blew his mind.

I didn't see this before, he thought, and on the heels of that: *Why* didn't I see this before?

He didn't know . . . but he *did* know he might have to re-think that idea of being top hog in the tabloid sty if he missed many more stories like this. He knew something else, as well: if his and Morrison's positions had been reversed (and Dees had turned down the editor's chair at *Inside View* not once but twice over the last seven years), he would have made Morrison crawl on his belly like a reptile before giving him the file.

Fuck that, he told himself. You would have fired his ass right out the door.

The idea that he might be burning out fluttered through his mind. The burnout rate was pretty high in this business, he knew. Apparently you could spend only so many years writing about flying saucers carrying off whole Brazilian villages (usually illustrated by out-of-focus photographs of lightbulbs hanging from strands of thread), dogs that could do calculus, and out-of-work daddies chopping their kids up like kindling wood. Then one day you suddenly snapped. Like Dottie Walsh, who had gone home one night and taken a bath with a dry-cleaning bag wrapped around her head.

Don't be a fool, he told himself, but he was uneasy just the same. The story was sitting there, *right there,* big as life and twice as ugly. How in the hell could he have missed it?

He looked up at Morrison, who was rocked back in his desk chair with his hands laced together over his stomach, watching him. "Well?" Morrison asked.

"Yeah," he said. "This could be big. And that's not all. I think it's the real goods."

"I don't care if it's the real goods or not," Morrison said, "as long as it sells papers. And it's going to sell *lots* of papers, isn't it, Richard?"

"Yes." He got to his feet and tucked the folder under his arm. "I want to run this guy's backtrail, starting with the first one we know about, up in Maine."

"Richard?"

He turned back at the door and saw Morrison was looking at the contact sheets again. He was smiling.

"What do you think if we run the best of these next to a photo of Danny DeVito in that Batman movie?"

"It works for me," Dees said, and went out. Questions and self-doubts were suddenly, blessedly set aside; the old smell of blood was back in his nose, strong and bitterly compelling, and for the time being he only wanted to follow it all the way to the end. The end came a week later, not in Maine, not in Maryland, but much farther south, in North Carolina.

2

It was summertime, which meant the living should have been easy and the cotton high, but nothing was coming easy for Richard Dees as that long day wound its way down toward dark.

The major problem was his inability — at least so far — to get into the small Wilmington airport,

152

which served only one major carrier, a few commuter airlines, and a lot of private planes. There were heavy thunderstorm cells in the area and Dees was circling ninety miles from the airfield, pogoing up and down in the unsteady air and cursing as the last hour of daylight began to slip away. It was 7:45 P.M. by the time he was given landing clearance. That was less than forty minutes before official sundown. He didn't know if the Night Flier stuck to the traditional rules or not, but if he did, it was going to be a close thing.

And the Flier *was* here; of that Dees was sure. He had found the right place, the right Cessna Skymaster. His quarry could have picked Virginia Beach, or Charlotte, or Birmingham, or some point even farther south, but he hadn't. Dees didn't know where he had hidden between leaving Duffrey, Maryland, and arriving here, and didn't care. It was enough to know that his intuition had been correct — his boy had continued to work the windsock circuit. Dees had spent a good part of the last week calling all the airports south of Duffrey that seemed right for the Flier's M.O., making the rounds again and again, using his finger on the Touch-Tone in his Days Inn motel room until it was sore and his contacts on the other end had begun to express their irritation with his persistence. Yet in the end persistence had paid off, as it so often did.

Private planes had landed the night before at all of the most likely airfields, and Cessna Skymaster 337s at all of them. Not surprising, since they were the Toyotas of private aviation. But the Cessna 337 that had landed last night in Wilming-

153

ton was the one he was looking for; no question about it. He was on the guy.

Dead on the guy.

"N471B, vector ILS runway 34," the radio voice drawled laconically into his earphones. "Fly heading 160. Descend and maintain 3,000."

"Heading 160. Leaving 6 for 3,000, roger."

"And be aware we still got some nasty weather down here."

"Roger," Dees said, thinking that ole Farmer John, down there in whatever beer-barrel passed for Air Traffic Control in Wilmington, was sure one hell of a sport to tell him that. He *knew* there was still nasty weather in the area; he could see the thunderheads, some with lightning still going off inside them like giant fireworks, and he had spent the last forty minutes or so circling and feeling more like a man in a blender than one in a twin-engine Beechcraft.

He flicked off the autopilot, which had been taking him around and around the same stupid patch of now-you-see-it, now-you-don't North Carolina farmland for far too long, and grabbed a handful of wheel. No cotton down there, high or otherwise, that he could see. Just a bunch of used-up tobacco patches now overgrown with kudzu. Dees was happy to point his plane's nose toward Wilmington and start down the ramp, monitored by pilot, ATC, and tower, for the ILS approach.

He picked up the microphone, thought about giving ole Farmer John there a yell, asking him if there happened to be anything weird going on downstairs — the dark-and-stormy-night kind of stuff *Inside View* readers loved, perhaps — then racked the mike again. It was still awhile until sunset; he had verified the official Wilmington time on his way down from Washington National. No, he thought, maybe he'd just keep his questions to himself for a little while longer.

Dees believed the Night Flier was a real vampire about as much as he believed it was the Tooth Fairy who had put all those quarters under his pillow when he was a kid, but if the guy *thought* he was a vampire — and this guy, Dees was convinced, really did — that would probably be enough to make him conform to the rules.

Life, after all, imitates art.

Count Dracula with a private pilot's license.

You had to admit, Dees thought, it was a lot better than killer penguins plotting the overthrow of the human race.

The Beech jounced as he passed through a thick membrane of cumulus on his steady downward course. Dees cursed and trimmed the plane, which seemed increasingly unhappy with the weather.

You and me both, babes, Dees thought.

When he came into the clear again, he could see the lights of Wilmington and Wrightsville Beach clearly.

Yes, sir, the fatties who shop at 7-Eleven are gonna love this one, he thought as lightning flashed on the port side. *They're gonna pick up about seventy zillion copies of this baby when they go out for their nightly ration of Twinkies and beer.*

But there was more, and he knew it.

This one could be . . . well . . . just so goddam good.

This one could be *legitimate*.

There was a time when a word like that never would have crossed your mind, ole buddy, he thought. Maybe you *are* burning out.

Still, big stacked headlines danced in his head like sugarplums. INSIDE VIEW REPORTER APPREHENDS CRAZED NIGHT FLIER. EXCLUSIVE STORY ON HOW BLOOD-DRINKING NIGHT FLIER WAS FINALLY CAUGHT. "NEEDED TO HAVE IT," DEADLY DRACULA DECLARES.

It wasn't exactly grand opera — Dees had to admit that — but he thought it sang just the same. He thought it sang like a boid.

He picked up the mike after all and depressed the button. He knew his blood-buddy was still down there, but he also knew he wasn't going to be comfortable until he had made absolutely sure.

"Wilmington, this is N471B. You still got a Skymaster 337 from Maryland down there on the ramp?"

Through static: "Looks like it, old hoss. Can't talk just now. I got air traffic."

"Has it got red piping?" Dees persisted.

For a moment he thought he would get no answer, then: "Red piping, roger. Kick it off, N471B, if you don't want me to see if I can slap an FCC fine on y'all. I got too many fish to fry tonight and not enough skillets."

"Thanks, Wilmington," Dees said in his most courteous voice. He hung up the mike and then gave it the finger, but he was grinning, barely noticing the jolts as he passed through another membrane of cloud. Skymaster, red piping, and he was willing to bet next year's salary that if the doofus in the tower hadn't been so busy, he would have

156

been able to confirm the tail-number as well: N101BL.

One week, by Christ, one little week. That was all it had taken. He had found the Night Flier, it wasn't dark yet, and as impossible as it seemed, there were no police on the scene. If there *had* been cops, and if they had been there concerning the Cessna, Farmer John almost certainly would have said so, sky-jam and bad weather or not. Some things were just too good not to gossip about.

I want your picture, you bastard, Dees thought. Now he could see the approach lights, flashing white in the dusk. I'll get your story in time, but first, the picture. Just one, but I gotta have it.

Yes, because it was the picture that made it real. No fuzzy out-of-focus lightbulbs; no "artist's conception"; a real by-God photo in living black-and-white. He headed down more steeply, ignoring the descent beep. His face was pale and set. His lips were pulled back slightly, revealing small, gleaming white teeth.

In the combined light of dusk and the instrument panel, Richard Dees looked quite a little bit like a vampire himself.

3

There were many things *Inside View* was not — literate, for one, overconcerned with such minor matters as accuracy and ethics, for another — but one thing was undeniable: it was exquisitely attuned to horrors. Merton Morrison was a bit of an asshole (although not as much of one as Dees had thought when he'd first seen the man smoking that dumb fucking pipe of his), but Dees had to give him one thing — he had remembered the things that had made *Inside View* a success in the first place: buckets of blood and guts by the handful.

Oh, there were still pictures of cute babies, plenty of psychic predictions, and Wonder Diets featuring such unlikely ingestibles as beer, chocolate, and potato chips, but Morrison had sensed a sea-change in the temper of the times, and had never once questioned his own judgement about the direction the paper should take. Dees supposed that confidence was the main reason Morrison had lasted as long as he had, in spite of his pipe and his tweed jackets from Asshole Brothers of London. What Morrison knew was that the flower children of the sixties had grown into the cannibals of the nineties. Huggy therapy, political correctness, and "the language of feelings" might be big deals among the intellectual upper class, but the ever-popular common man was still a lot more interested in mass murders, buried scandals in the lives of the stars, and just how Magic Johnson had gotten AIDS.

Dees had no doubt there was still an audience for *All Things Bright and Beautiful*, but the one for *All Shit Grim and Gory* had become a growth stock again as the Woodstock Generation began to discover gray in its hair and lines curving down from the corners of its petulant, self-indulgent mouth. Merton Morrison, whom Dees now recognized as a kind of intuitive genius, had made his own inside view clear in a famous memo issued to all staff and stringers less than a week after he and his pipe had taken up residence in the corner office. By all means, stop and smell the roses on your way to work, this memo suggested, but once you get to there, spread those nostrils — spread them *wide* — and start sniffing for blood and guts.

Dees, who had been *made* for sniffing blood and guts, had been delighted. His nose was the reason he was here, flying into Wilmington. There was a human monster down there, a man who thought he was a vampire. Dees had a name all picked out for him; it burned in his mind as a valuable coin might burn in a man's pocket. Soon he would take the coin out and spend it. When he did, the name would be plastered across the tabloid display racks of every supermarket checkout counter in America, screaming at the patrons in unignorable sixty-point type.

Look out, ladies and sensation seekers, Dees thought. You don't know it, but a very bad man is coming your way. You'll read his real name and forget it, but that's okay. What you'll remember is *my* name for him, the name that's going to put him right up there with Jack the Ripper and the Cleveland Torso Murderer and the Black Dahlia. You'll remember the Night Flier, coming soon to a checkout counter near you. The exclusive story, the exclusive interview . . . but what I want most of all is the exclusive *picture*.

He checked his watch again and allowed himself to relax the tiniest bit (which was all he *could* relax). He still had almost half an hour till dark, and he would be parking next to the white Skymaster with red piping (and N101BL on the tail in a similar red) in less than fifteen minutes.

Was the Flier sleeping in town or in some motel on the way into town? Dees didn't think so. One of the reasons for the Skymaster 337's popularity, besides its relatively low price, was that it was the only plane its size with a belly-hold. It wasn't much bigger than the trunk of an old VW Beetle, true, but it was roomy enough for three big suitcases or five small ones . . . and it could certainly hold a man, provided he wasn't the size of a pro basketball player. The Night Flier could be in the Cessna's belly-hold, provided he was (a) sleeping in the fetal position with his knees drawn up to his chin; or (b) crazy enough to think he was a real vampire; or (c) both of the above.

Dees had his money on (c).

Now, with his altimeter winding down from four to three thousand feet, Dees thought: Nope, no hotel or motel for you, my friend, am I right? When *you* play vampire, you're like Frank Sinatra — you do it your way. Know what I think? I think when the belly-hold of that plane opens, the first thing I'm gonna see is a shower of graveyard earth (even if it isn't, you can bet your upper incisors it will be when the story comes out), and then I'm gonna see first one leg in a pair of tuxedo pants, and then the other, because you are gonna be *dressed,* aren't you? Oh, dear man, I think you are gonna be dressed to the *nines,* dressed to *kill,* and the auto-winder is already on my camera, and when I see that cloak flap in the breeze —

But that was where his thoughts stopped, because that was when the flashing white lights on both runways below him went out.

4

I want to run this guy's backtrail, he had told Merton Morrison, *starting with the first one we know about, up in Maine.*

Less than four hours later he had been at Cumberland County Airport, talking to a mechanic named Ezra Hannon. Mr. Hannon looked as if he had recently crawled out of a gin-bottle, and Dees wouldn't have let him within shouting distance of his own plane, but he gave the fellow his full and courteous attention just the same. Of course he did; Ezra Hannon was the first link in what Dees was beginning to think might prove to be a very important chain.

Cumberland County Airport was a dignified-sounding name for a country landing-field which consisted of two Quonset huts and two crisscrossing runways. One of these runways was actually tarred. Because Dees had never landed on a dirt runway, he requested the tarred one. The bouncing his Beech 55 (for which he was in hock up to his eyebrows and beyond) took when he landed convinced him to try the dirt when he took off again, and when he did he had been delighted to find it as smooth and firm as a coed's breast. The field also had a windsock, of course, and of course it was patched like a pair of old Dad's underdrawers. Places like CCA *always* had a windsock. It was part of their dubious charm, like the

161

old biplane that always seemed to be parked in front of the single hangar.

Cumberland County was the most populous in Maine, but you never would have known it from its cow-patty airport, Dees thought . . . or from Ezra the Amazing Gin-Head Mechanic, for that matter. When he grinned, displaying all six of his remaining teeth, he looked like an extra from the film version of James Dickey's *Deliverance*.

The airport sat on the outskirts of the much plusher town of Falmouth, existing mostly on landing fees paid by rich summer residents. Claire Bowie, the Night Flier's first victim, had been CCA's night traffic controller and owned a quarter interest in the airfield. The other employees had consisted of two mechanics and a second ground controller (the ground controllers also sold chips, cigarettes, and sodas; further, Dees had learned, the murdered man had made a pretty mean cheeseburger).

Mechanics and controllers also served as pump jockeys and custodians. It wasn't unusual for the controller to have to rush back from the bathroom, where he had been swabbing out the john with Janitor-in-a-Drum, to give landing clearance and assign a runway from the challenging maze of two at his disposal. The operation was so high-pressure that during the airport's peak summer season the night controller sometimes got only six hours' worth of good sleep between midnight and 7:00 A.M.

Claire Bowie had been killed almost a month prior to Dees's visit, and the picture the reporter put together was a composite created from the news stories in Morrison's thin file and Ezra the

Amazing Gin-Head Mechanic's much more colorful embellishments. And even when he had made the necessary allowances for his primary source, Dees remained sure that something very strange had happened at this dipshit little airport in early July.

The Cessna 337, tail-number N101BL, had radioed the field for landing clearance shortly before dawn on the morning of July 9th. Claire Bowie, who had been working the night shift at the airfield since 1954, when pilots sometimes had to abort their approaches (a maneuver in those days known simply as "pulling up") because of the cows that sometimes wandered onto what was then the single runway, logged the request at 4:32 A.M. The time of landing he noted as 4:49 A.M.; he recorded the pilot's name as Dwight Renfield, and the point of N101BL's origination as Bangor, Maine. The times were undoubtedly correct. The rest was bullshit (Dees had checked Bangor, and wasn't surprised to find they had never heard of N101BL), but even if Bowie had *known* it was bullshit, it probably wouldn't have made much difference; at CCA, the atmosphere was loose, and a landing fee was a landing fee.

The name the pilot had given was a bizarre joke. Dwight just happened to be the first name of an actor named Dwight Frye, and Dwight Frye had just happened to play, among a plethora of other parts, the role of Renfield, a slavering lunatic whose idol had been the most famous vampire of all time. But radioing UNICOM and asking for landing clearance in the name of Count Dracula might have raised suspicion even in a sleepy little place like this, Dees supposed.

Might have; Dees wasn't really sure. After all, a landing fee was a landing fee, and "Dwight Renfield" had paid his promptly, in cash, as he had also paid to top off his tanks — the money had been in the register the next day, along with a carbon of the receipt Bowie had written out.

Dees knew about the casual, hipshot way private air-traffic had been controlled at the smaller fields in the fifties and sixties, but he was still astonished by the informal treatment the Night Flier's plane had received at CCA. It wasn't the fifties or sixties anymore, after all; this was the era of drug paranoia, and most of the shit to which you were supposed to just say no came into small harbors in small boats, or into small airports in small planes . . . planes like "Dwight Renfield's" Cessna Skymaster. A landing fee was a landing fee, sure, but Dees would have expected Bowie to give Bangor a shout about the missing flight-plan just the same, if only to cover his own ass. But he hadn't. The idea of a bribe had occurred to Dees at this point, but his gin-soaked informant claimed that Claire Bowie was as honest as the day was long, and the two Falmouth cops Dees talked to later on had confirmed Hannon's judgement.

Negligence seemed a likelier answer, but in the end it didn't really matter; *Inside View* readers weren't interested in such esoteric questions as how or why things happened. *Inside View* readers were content to know *what* had happened, and how long it took, and if the person it happened to had had time to scream. And pictures, of course. They wanted pictures. Great big hi-intensity black-and-whites, if possible — the kind that seemed to leap right off the page in a swarm of dots and nail you in the forebrain.

Ezra the Amazing Gin-Head Mechanic had looked surprised and considering when Dees asked where he thought "Renfield" might have gone after landing.

"Dunno," he said. "Motel, I s'pose. Musta tooken a cab."

"You came in at . . . what time did you say? Seven o'clock that morning? July ninth?"

"Uh-huh. Just before Claire left to go home."

"And the Cessna Skymaster was parked and tied down and empty?"

"Yep. Parked right where yours is now." Ezra pointed, and Dees pulled back a little. The mechanic smelled quite a little bit like a very old Roquefort cheese which had been pickled in Gilbey's Gin.

"Did Claire happen to *say* if he called a cab for the pilot? To take him to a motel? Because there don't seem to be any in easy walking distance."

"There ain't," Ezra agreed. "Closest one's the Sea Breeze, and that's two mile away. Maybe more." He scratched his stubbly chin. "But I don't remember Claire saying ary word about callin the fella a cab."

Dees made a mental note to call the cab companies in the area just the same. At that time he was going on what seemed like a reasonable assumption: that the guy he was looking for slept in a bed, like almost everyone else.

"What about a limo?" he asked.

"Nope," Ezra said more positively, "Claire

didn't say nothing about no limbo, and he *woulda* mentioned that."

Dees nodded and decided to call the nearby limo companies, too. He would also question the rest of the staff, but he expected no light to dawn there; this old boozehound was about all there was. He'd had a cup of coffee with Claire before Claire left for the day, and another with him when Claire came back on duty that night, and it looked like that was all she wrote. Except for the Night Flier himself, Ezra seemed to have been the last person to see Claire Bowie alive.

The subject of these ruminations looked slyly off into the distance, scratched the wattles below his chin, then shifted his bloodshot gaze back to Dees. "Claire didn't say nothing about no cab or limbo, but he *did* say something else."

"That so?"

"Yep," Ezra said. He unzipped a pocket of his grease-stained coverall, removed a pack of Chesterfields, lit one up, and coughed a dismal old man's cough. He looked at Dees through the drifting smoke with an expression of half-baked craftiness. "Might not mean nothing, but then again, it might. It sure struck Claire perculyer, though. Must have, because most of the time old Claire wouldn't say shit if he had a mouthful."

"What was it he said?"

"Don't quite remember," Ezra said. "Sometimes, you know, when I forget things, a picture of Alexander Hamilton sorta refreshes my memory."

"How about one of Abe Lincoln?" Dees asked dryly.

After a moment's consideration — a short one — Hannon agreed that sometimes Lincoln also did the trick, and a portrait of this gentleman consequently passed from Dees's wallet to Ezra's slightly palsied hand. Dees thought that a portrait of George Washington *might* have turned the trick, but he wanted to make sure the man was entirely on his side . . . and besides, it all came out of the expense account.

"So give."

"Claire said the guy looked like he must be goin to one hell of a fancy party," Ezra said.

"Oh? Why was that?" Dees was thinking he should have stuck with Washington after all.

"Said the guy looked like he just stepped out of a bandbox. Tuxedo, silk tie, all that stuff." Ezra paused. "Claire said the guy was even wearin a big cloak. Red as a fire engine inside, black as a woodchuck's asshole outside. Said when it spread out behind him, it looked like a goddam bat's wing."

A large word lit in red neon suddenly flashed on in Dees's mind, and the word was BINGO.

You don't know it, my gin-soaked friend, Dees thought, *but you may have just said the words that are going to make you famous.*

"All these questions about Claire," Ezra said, "and you ain't never once ast if *I* saw anything funny."

"Did you?"

"As a matter of fact, I did."

"What was that, my friend?"

Ezra scratched his stubbly chin with long, yellow nails, looked wisely at Dees from the corners of

167

his bloodshot eyes, and then took another puff on his cigarette.

"Here we go again," Dees said, but he produced another picture of Abe Lincoln and was careful to keep his voice and face amiable. His instincts were wide awake now, and they were telling him that Mr. Ginhead wasn't quite squeezed dry. Not yet, anyway.

"That don't seem like enough for all I'm tellin you," Ezra said reproachfully. "Rich city fella like you ought to be able to do better'n ten bucks."

Dees looked at his watch — a heavy Rolex with diamonds gleaming on the face. "Gosh!" he said. "Look how late it's getting! And I haven't even been over to talk with the Falmouth police yet!"

Before he could do more than start to get up, the five had disappeared from between his fingers and had joined its mate in the pocket of Hannon's coverall.

"All right, if you've got something else to tell, tell it," Dees said. The amiability was gone now. "I've got places to go and people to see."

The mechanic thought it over, scratching his wattles and sending out little puffs of ancient, cheesy smell. Then he said, almost reluctantly: "Seen a big pile of dirt under that Skymaster. Right under the luggage bay, it was."

"That so?"

"Ayuh. Kicked it with my boot."

Dees waited. He could do that.

"Nasty stuff. Full of worms."

Dees waited. This was good, useful stuff, but he didn't think the old man was wrung completely dry even yet.

"And maggots," Ezra said. "There was maggots, too. Like where something died."

Dees stayed that night at the Sea Breeze Motel, and was winging his way to the town of Alderton in upstate New York by eight o'clock the next morning.

5

Of all the things Dees didn't understand about his quarry's movements, the thing which puzzled him the most was how *leisurely* the Flier had been. In Maine and in Maryland, he had actually lingered before killing. His only one-night stand had been in Alderton, which he had visited two weeks after doing Claire Bowie.

Lakeview Airport in Alderton was even smaller than CCA — a single unpaved runway and a combined Ops/UNICOM that was no more than a shed with a fresh coat of paint. There was no instrument approach; there was, however, a large satellite dish so none of the flying farmers who used the place would have to miss *Murphy Brown* or *Wheel of Fortune* or anything really important like that.

One thing Dees liked a lot: the unpaved Lakeview runway was just as silky-smooth as the one in Maine had been. I could get used to this, Dees thought as he dropped the Beech neatly onto the surface and began to slow it down. No big thuds over asphalt patches, no potholes that want to ground-loop you after you come in . . . yeah, I could get used to this real easy.

In Alderton, nobody had asked for pictures of

Presidents or friends of Presidents. In Alderton, the whole town — a community of just under a thousand souls — was in shock, not merely the few part-timers who, along with the late Buck Kendall, had run Lakeview Airport almost as a charity (and certainly in the red). There was really no one to talk to, anyway, not even a witness of the Ezra Hannon caliber. Hannon had been bleary, Dees reflected, but at least he had been quotable.

"Must have been a mighty man," one of the part-timers told Dees. "Ole Buck, he dressed out right around two-twenty, and he was easy most of the time, but if you *did* get him riled, he made you sorry. Seen him box down a fella in a carny show that came through P'keepsie two years ago. That kind of fightin ain't legal, accourse, but Buck was short a payment on that little Piper of his, so he boxed that carny fighter down. Collected two hundred dollars and got it to the loan comp'ny about two days before they was gonna send out someone to repo his ride, I guess."

The part-timer shook his head, looking genuinely distressed, and Dees wished he'd thought to uncase his camera. *Inside View* readers would have lapped up that long, lined, mournful face. Dees made a mental note to find out if the late Buck Kendall had had a dog. *Inside View* readers also lapped up pictures of the dead man's dog. You posed it on the porch of the deceased's house and captioned it BUFFY'S LONG WAIT BEGINS, or something similar.

"It's a damn shame," Dees said sympathetically.

The part-timer sighed and nodded. "Guy musta

170

got him from behind. That's the only way I can figger it."

Dees didn't know from which direction Gerard "Buck" Kendall had been gotten, but he knew that this time the victim's throat had not been ripped out. This time there were holes, holes from which "Dwight Renfield" had presumably sucked his victim's blood. Except, according to the coroner's report, the holes were on opposite sides of the neck, one in the jugular vein and the other in the carotid artery. They weren't the discreet little bite marks of the Bela Lugosi era or the slightly gorier ones of the Christopher Lee flicks, either. The coroner's report spoke in centimeters, but Dees could translate well enough, and Morrison had the indefatigable Libby Grannit to explain what the coroner's dry language only partially revealed: the killer either had teeth the size of one of *View*'s beloved Bigfeet, or he had made the holes in Kendall's neck in a much more prosaic fashion with a hammer and a nail.

DEADLY NIGHT FLIER SPIKED VICTIMS, DRANK THEIR BLOOD, both men thought at different places on the same day. *Not bad.*

The Night Flier had requested permission to land at Lakeview Airport shortly after 10:30 P.M. on the night of July 23rd. Kendall had granted permission and had noted a tail-number with which Dees had become very familiar: N101BL. Kendall had noted "name of pilot" as "Dwite Renfield" and the "make and model of aircraft" as "Cessna Skymaster 337." No mention of the red piping, and of course no mention of the sweeping bat-wing cloak that was as red as a fire engine

171

on the inside and as black as a woodchuck's asshole on the outside, but Dees was positive of both, just the same.

The Night Flier had flown into Alderton's Lakeview Airport shortly after ten-thirty, killed that strapping fellow Buck Kendall, drunk his blood, and flown out again in his Cessna sometime before Jenna Kendall came by at five o'clock on the morning of the twenty-fourth to give her husband a fresh-made waffle and discovered his exsanguinated corpse instead.

As Dees stood outside the ramshackle Lakeview hangar/tower mulling these things over, it occurred to him that if you *gave* blood, the most you could expect was a cup of orange juice and a word of thanks. If you *took* it, however — *sucked* it, to be specific — you got headlines. As he turned the rest of a bad cup of coffee out on the ground and headed toward his plane, ready to fly south to Maryland, it occurred to Richard Dees that God's hand might have shaken just a tiny bit when He was finishing off the supposed masterwork of His creative empire.

6

Now, two bad hours after leaving Washington National, things had suddenly gotten a lot worse, and with shocking suddenness. The runway lights had gone out, but Dees now saw that wasn't all that had gone out — half of Wilmington and all of Wrightsville Beach were also dark. ILS was still there, but when Dees snatched the mike and screamed, "What happened? *Talk* to me, Wilmington!" he got nothing back but a screech of static in which a few voices babbled like distant ghosts.

He jammed the mike back, missing the prong. It thudded to the cockpit floor at the end of its curled wire, and Dees forgot it. The grab and the yell had been pure pilot's instinct and no more. He knew what had happened as surely as he knew the sun set in the west . . . which it would do very soon now. A stroke of lightning must have scored a direct hit on a power substation near the airport. The question was whether or not to go in anyway.

"You had clearance," one voice said. Another immediately (and correctly) replied that that was so much bullshit rationalization. You learned what you were supposed to do in a situation like this when you were still the equivalent of a student driver. Logic and the book tell you to head for your alternate and try to contact ATC. Landing under snafu conditions such as these could cost him a violation and a hefty fine.

On the other hand, *not* landing now — *right now* — could lose him the Night Flier. It might also cost a life (or lives), but Dees barely factored this into the equation . . . until an idea went off like a flashbulb in his mind, an inspiration that occurred, as most of his inspirations did, in huge tabloid type:

HEROIC REPORTER SAVES (fill in a number, as large as possible, which was pretty large, given the amazingly generous borders that mark the range of human credulity) FROM CRAZED NIGHT FLIER.

173

Eat *that,* Farmer John, Dees thought, and continued his descent toward Runway 34.

The runway lights down there suddenly flashed on, as if approving his decision, then went out again, leaving blue afterimages on his retinas that turned the sick green of spoiled avocados a moment later. Then the weird static coming from the radio cleared and Farmer John's voice screamed: *"Haul port, N471B: Piedmont, haul starboard: Jesus, oh Jesus, midair, I think we got a midair —"*

Dees's self-preservation instincts were every bit as well honed as those which smelled blood in the bush. He never even saw the Piedmont Airlines 727's strobe lights. He was too busy banking as tightly to port as the Beech could bank — which was as tight as a virgin's cooze, and Dees would be happy to testify to that fact if he got out of this shitstorm alive — as soon as the second word was out of Farmer John's mouth. He had a momentary sight/sense of something huge only inches above him, and then the Beech 55 was taking a beating that made the previous rough air seem like glass. His cigarettes flew out of his breast pocket and streamed everywhere. The half-dark Wilmington skyline tilted crazily. His stomach seemed to be trying to squeeze his heart all the way up his throat and into his mouth. Spit ran up one cheek like a kid whizzing along a greased slide. Maps flew like birds. The air outside now raved with jet thunder as well as the kind nature made. One of the windows in the four-seat passenger compartment imploded, and an asthmatic wind whooped in, skirling everything not tied down back there into a tornado.

"Resume your previous altitude assignment, N471B!" Farmer John was screaming. Dees was aware that he'd just ruined a two-hundred-dollar pair of pants by spraying about a pint of hot piss into them, but he was partially soothed by a strong feeling that old Farmer John had just loaded his Jockey shorts with a truckload or so of fresh Mars Bars. Sounded that way, anyhow.

Dees carried a Swiss Army knife. He took it from his right pants pocket and, holding the wheel with his left hand, cut through his shirt just above the left elbow, bringing blood. Then with no pause, he made another cut, shallow, just below his left eye. He folded the knife shut and stuffed it into the elasticized map pocket in the pilot's door. Gotta clean it later, he thought. And if I forget it, I could be in deep shit. But he knew he wouldn't forget, and considering the things the Night Flier had gotten away with, he thought he'd be okay.

The runway lights came on again, this time for good, he hoped, although their pulsing quality told him they were being powered by a generator. He homed the Beech in again on Runway 34. Blood ran down his left cheek to the corner of his mouth. He sucked some in and then spat a pink mixture of blood and spit onto his IVSI. Never miss a trick; just keep following those instincts and they'd always take you home.

He looked at his watch. Sunset was only fourteen minutes away now. This was cutting it much too close to the bone.

"Pull up, Beech!" Farmer John yelled. *"Are you deaf?"*

Dees groped for the mike's kinked wire without ever taking his eyes from the runway lights. He pulled the wire through his fingers until he got the mike itself. He palmed it and depressed the send button.

"Listen to me, you chicken-fried son of a bitch," he said, and now his lips were pulled all the way back to the gum line. "I missed getting turned into strawberry jam by that 727 because your shit genny didn't kick in when it was supposed to; as a result I had no ATC comm. I don't know how many people on the *airliner* just missed getting turned into strawberry jam, but I bet *you* do, and I know the cockpit crew does. The only reason those guys are still alive is because the captain of that boat was bright enough to allemande right, and I was bright enough to do-si-do, but I have sustained both structural and physical damage. If you don't give me a landing clearance right now, I'm going to land anyway. The only difference is that if I have to land without clearance, I'm going to have you up in front of an FAA hearing. But first I will personally see to it that your head and your asshole change places. Have you got that, *hoss?*"

A long, static-filled silence. Then a very small voice, utterly unlike Farmer John's previous hearty "Hey bo'!" delivery, said, "You're cleared to land Runway 34, N471B."

Dees smiled and homed in on the runway.

He depressed the mike button and said, "I got mean and yelling. I'm sorry. It only happens when I almost die."

No response from the ground.

"Well, fuck you very much," Dees said, and then headed on down, resisting the impulse to take a quick glance at his watch as he did so.

<h1 style="text-align:center">7</h1>

Dees was case-hardened and proud of it, but there was no use kidding himself; what he found in Duffrey gave him the creeps. The Night Flier's Cessna had spent another entire day — July 31st — on the ramp, but that was really only where the creeps began. It was the blood his loyal *Inside View* readers would care about, of course, and that was just as it should be, world without end, amen, amen, but Dees was increasingly aware that blood (or, in the case of good old Ray and Ellen Sarch, the *lack* of blood) was only where this story started. Below the blood were caverns dark and strange.

Dees arrived in Duffrey on August 8th, by then barely a week behind the Night Flier. He wondered again where his batty buddy went between strikes. Disney World? Busch Gardens? Atlanta, maybe, to check out the Braves? Such things were relatively small potatoes right now, with the chase still on, but they would be valuable later on. They would become, in fact, the journalistic equivalent of Hamburger Helper, stretching the leftovers of the Night Flier story through a few more issues, allowing readers to resavor the flavor even after the biggest chunks of raw meat had been digested.

Still, there *were* caverns in this story — dark places into which a man might drop and be lost forever. That sounded both crazy and corny, but

177

by the time Dees began to get a picture of what had gone on in Duffrey, he had actually begun to believe it . . . which meant *that* part of the story would never see print, and not just because it was personal. It violated Dees's single iron-clad rule: Never believe what you publish, and never publish what you believe. It had, over the years, allowed him to keep his sanity while those all about him had been losing theirs.

He had landed at Washington National — a *real* airport for a change — and rented a car to take him the sixty miles to Duffrey, because without Ray Sarch and his wife, Ellen, there *was* no Duffrey Airfield. Aside from Ellen's sister, Raylene, who was a pretty fair Socket Wrench Susie, the two of them had been the whole shebang. There was a single oiled-dirt runway (oiled both to lay the dust and to discourage the growth of weeds) and a control booth not much bigger than a closet attached to the Jet-Aire trailer where the Sarch couple lived. They were both retired, both fliers, both reputedly as tough as nails, and still crazy in love with each other even after almost five decades of marriage.

Further, Dees learned, the Sarches watched the private air-traffic in and out of their field with a close eye; they had a personal stake in the war on drugs. Their only son had died in the Florida Everglades, trying to land in what looked like a clear stretch of water with better than a ton of Acapulco Gold packed into a stolen Beech 18. The water *had* been clear . . . except for a single stump, that was. The Beech 18 hit it, water-looped, and exploded. Doug Sarch had been thrown clear, his body smoking and singed but probably still alive, as little as his grieving parents would want to believe such a thing. He had been eaten by gators, and all that remained of him when the DEA guys finally found him a week later was a dismembered skeleton, a few maggoty scraps of flesh, a charred pair of Calvin Klein jeans, and a sport coat from Paul Stuart in New York. One of the sport-coat pockets had contained better than twenty thousand dollars in cash; another had yielded nearly an ounce of Peruvian flake cocaine.

"It was drugs and the motherfuckers who run em killed my boy," Ray Sarch had said on several occasions, and Ellen Sarch was willing to double and redouble on that one. Her hatred of drugs and drug dealers, Dees was told again and again (he was amused by the nearly unanimous feeling in Duffrey that the murder of the elderly Sarches had been a "gangland hit"), was exceeded only by her grief and bewilderment over the seduction of her son by those very people.

Following the death of their son, the Sarches had kept their eyes peeled for anything or anyone who looked even remotely like a drug transporter. They had brought the Maryland State Police out to the field four times on false alarms, but the State Bears hadn't minded because the Sarches had also blown the whistle on three small transporters and two very big ones. The last had been carrying thirty pounds of pure Bolivian cocaine. That was the kind of bust that made you forget a few false alarms, the sort of bust that made promotions.

So very late in the evening of July 30th comes this Cessna Skymaster with a number and descrip-

179

tion that had gone out to every airfield and airport in America, including the one in Duffrey; a Cessna whose pilot had identified himself as Dwight Renfield, point of origination, Bayshore Airport, Delaware, a field which had never heard of "Renfield" or a Skymaster with tail-number N101BL; the plane of a man who was almost surely a murderer.

"If he'd flown in here, he'd be in the stir now," one of the Bayshore controllers had told Dees over the phone, but Dees wondered. Yes. He wondered very much.

The Night Flier had landed in Duffrey at 11:27 P.M., and "Dwight Renfield" had not only signed the Sarches' logbook but also had accepted Ray Sarch's invitation to come into the trailer, have a beer, and watch a rerun of *Gunsmoke* on TNT. Ellen Sarch had told all of this to the proprietor of the Duffrey Beauty Bar the following day. This woman, Selida McCammon, had identified herself to Dees as one of the late Ellen Sarch's closest friends.

When Dees asked how Ellen had seemed, Selida had paused and then said, "Dreamy, somehow. Like a high-school girl with a crush, almost seventy years old or not. Her color was so high I thought it was make-up, until I started in on her perm. Then I saw that she was just . . . you know . . ." Selida McCammon shrugged. She knew what she meant but not how to say it.

"Het up," Dees suggested, and that made Selida McCammon laugh and clap her hands.

"Het up! That's it! You're a writer, all right!"

"Oh, I write like a boid," Dees said, and offered

180

a smile he hoped looked good-humored and warm. This was an expression he had once practiced almost constantly and continued to practice with fair regularity in the bedroom mirror of the New York apartment he called his home, and in the mirrors of the hotels and motels that were *really* his home. It seemed to work — Selida McCammon answered it readily enough — but the truth was that Dees had never felt good-humored and warm in his life. As a kid he had believed these emotions didn't really exist at all; they were just a masquerade, a social convention. Later on he decided he had been wrong about that; most of what he thought of as "*Reader's Digest* emotions" *were* real, at least for most people. Perhaps even love, the fabled Big Enchilada, was real. That he himself could not feel these emotions was undoubtedly a shame, but hardly the end of the world. There were, after all, people out there with cancer, and AIDS, and the memory-spans of brain-damaged parakeets. When you looked at it that way, you quickly realized that being deprived of a few huggy-kissy emotions was fairly small beans. The important thing was that if you could manage to stretch the muscles of your face in the right directions every now and then, you were fine. It didn't hurt and it was easy; if you could remember to zip up your fly after you took a leak, you could remember to smile and look warm when it was expected of you. And an understanding smile, he had discovered over the years, was the world's best interview tool. Once in awhile a voice inside asked him what his *own* inside view was, but Dees didn't *want* an inside view. He only wanted to write and to take photographs. He was better at the writing, always had been and always would be, and he knew it, but he liked the photographs better just the same. He liked to touch them. To see how they froze people either with their real faces hung out for the whole world to see or with their masks so clearly apparent that they were beyond denial. He liked how, in the best of them, people always looked surprised and horrified. How they looked caught.

If pressed, he would have said the photographs provided all the inside view he needed, and the subject had no relevance here, anyway. What *did* was the Night Flier, his little batty buddy, and how he had waltzed into the lives of Ray and Ellen Sarch a week or so earlier.

The Flier had stepped out of his plane and walked into an office with a red-bordered FAA notice on the wall, a notice which suggested there was a dangerous guy out there driving a Cessna Skymaster 337, tail-number N101BL, who might have murdered two men. This guy, the notice went on, might or might not be calling himself Dwight Renfield. The Skymaster had landed, Dwight Renfield had signed in and had almost surely spent the following day in the belly-hold of his plane. And what about the Sarches, those two sharp-eyed old folks?

The Sarches had said nothing; the Sarches had *done* nothing.

Except that latter wasn't quite right, Dees had discovered. Ray Sarch had certainly done something; he had invited the Night Flier in to watch an old *Gunsmoke* episode and drink a beer with his wife. They had treated him like an old friend.

And then, the next day, Ellen Sarch had made an appointment at the Beauty Bar, which Selida McCammon had found surprising; Ellen's visits were usually as regular as clockwork, and this one was at least two weeks before Selida would next have expected her. Her instructions had been unusually explicit; she had wanted not just the usual cut but a perm . . . and a little color, too.

"She wanted to look younger," Selida McCammon told Dees, and then wiped a tear from one cheek with the side of her hand.

But Ellen Sarch's behavior had been pedestrian compared to that of her husband. He had called the FAA at Washington National and told them to issue a NOTAM, removing Duffrey from the active-airfield grid, at least for the time being. He had, in other words, pulled down the shades and closed up the shop.

On his way home, he'd stopped for gas at the Duffrey Texaco and told Norm Wilson, the proprietor, that he thought he was coming down with the flu. Norm told Dees that he thought Ray was probably right about that — he'd looked pale and wan, suddenly even older than his years.

That night, the two vigilant fire wardens had, in effect, burned to death. Ray Sarch was found in the little control room, his head torn off and cast into the far corner, where it sat on a ragged stump of neck, staring toward the open doorway with wide, glazed eyes, as if there were actually something there to see.

His wife had been found in the bedroom of the Sarch trailer. She was in bed. She was dressed in a peignoir so new it might never have been worn before that night. She was old, a deputy had told Dees (at twenty-five dollars he was a more expensive fuck than Ezra the Amazing Gin-Head Mechanic, but worth it), but you still only had to take one look to know that there was a woman who'd dressed for bed with loving on her mind. Dees had liked the c & w twang so much that he wrote it down in his notebook. Those huge, spike-sized holes were driven into her neck, one in the carotid, the other in the jugular. Her face was composed, her eyes closed, her hands on her bosom.

Although she had lost almost every drop of blood in her body, there were only spots on the pillows beneath her, and a few more spots on the book which lay open on her stomach: *The Vampire Lestat,* by Anne Rice.

And the Night Flier?

Sometime just before midnight on July 31st, or just after it on the morning of August 1st, he had simply flown away. Like a boid.

Or a bat.

8

Dees touched down in Wilmington seven minutes before official sunset. While he was throttling back, still spitting blood out of his mouth from the cut below his eye, he saw lightning strike down with blue-white fire so intense that it nearly blinded him. On the heels of the light came the most deafening thunderclap he had ever heard. His subjective opinion of the sound was confirmed

when another window in the passenger compartment, stellated by the near miss with the Piedmont
727, now coughed inward in a spray of junk-shop
diamonds.

In the brilliant glare he saw a squat, cubelike
building on the port side of Runway 34 impaled
by the bolt. It exploded, shooting fire into the
sky in a column that, although brilliant, did not
even come close to the power of the bolt that had
ignited it.

Like lighting a stick of dynamite with a baby
nuke, Dees thought confusedly, and then: The
genny. That was the genny.

The lights — all of them, the white lights that
marked the edges of the runway and the bright
red bulbs that marked its end — were suddenly
gone, as if they had been no more than candles
puffed out by a strong gust of wind. All at once
Dees was rushing at better than eighty miles an
hour from dark into dark.

The concussive force of the explosion which had
destroyed the airport's main generator struck the
Beech like a fist — did more than strike it, hammered it like a looping haymaker. The Beech, still
hardly knowing it had become a ground-bound
creature again, skittered affrightedly to starboard,
rose, and came down with the right wheel pogoing
up and down over something — *somethings* — that
Dees vaguely realized were landing lights.

Go port! his mind screamed. Go port, you asshole!

He almost did before his colder mind asserted
itself. If he hauled the wheel to port at this speed,
he would ground-loop. Probably wouldn't ex-

185

plode, considering how little fuel was left in the tanks, but it was possible. Or the Beech might simply twist apart, leaving Richard Dees from the gut on down twitching in his seat, while Richard Dees from the gut on up went in a different direction, trailing severed intestines like party-favors and dropping his kidneys on the concrete like a couple of oversized chunks of birdshit.

Ride it out! he screamed at himself. Ride it out, you son of a bitch, ride it out!

Something — the genny's secondary LP tanks, he guessed when he had time for guessing — exploded then, buffeting the Beech even farther to starboard, but that was okay, it got him off the dead landing lights, and all at once he was running with relative smoothness again, port wheel on the edge of Runway 34, starboard wheel on the spooky verge between the lights and the ditch he had observed on the right of the runway. The Beech was still shuddering, but not badly, and he understood that he was running on one flat, the starboard tire shredded by the landing lights it had crushed.

He was slowing down, that was what mattered, the Beech finally beginning to understand that it had become a different thing, a thing that belonged to the land again. Dees was starting to relax when he saw the wide-body Learjet, the one the pilots called Fat Albert, looming ahead of him, parked insanely across the runway where the pilot had stopped on his taxi out to Runway 5.

Dees bore down on it, saw lighted windows, saw faces staring out at him with the gape of idiots in an asylum watching a magic trick, and then, without thinking, he pushed full right rudder, bouncing the Beech off the runway and into the ditch, missing the Lear by approximately an inch and a half. He heard faint screams but was really aware of nothing but the *now* exploding in front of him like a string of firecrackers as the Beech tried to become a thing of the air again, helpless to do so with the flaps down and the engines dropping revs but trying anyway; there was a leap like a convulsion in the dying light of the secondary explosion, and then he was skidding across a taxiway, seeing the General Aviation Terminal for a moment with its corners lit by emergency lights that ran on storage batteries, seeing the parked planes — one of them almost surely the Night Flier's Skymaster — as dark crepe-paper silhouettes against a baleful orange light that was the sunset, now revealed by the parting thunderheads.

I'm going over! he screamed to himself, and the Beech *did* try to roll; the port wing struck a fountain of sparks from the taxiway nearest the terminal and its tip actually broke free, wheeling off into the scrub where friction-heat awoke a dim fire in the wet weeds.

Then the Beech was still, and the only sounds were the snowy roar of static from the radio, the sound of broken bottles fizzing their contents onto the carpet of the passenger compartment, and the frenzied hammering of Dees's own heart. He slammed the pop release on his harness and headed for the pressurized hatch even before he was totally sure he was alive.

What happened later he remembered with eidetic clarity, but from the moment the Beech skidded to a stop on the taxiway, ass-end to the Lear and tilted to one side, to the moment he heard the first screams from the terminal, all he remembered for sure was swinging back to get his camera. He couldn't leave the plane without his camera; the Nikon was the closest thing Dees had to a wife. He'd bought it in a Toledo hockshop when he was seventeen and kept it with him ever since. He had added lenses, but the basic box was about the same now as it had been then; the only modifications had been the occasional scratch or dent that came with the job. The Nikon was in the elasticized pocket behind his seat. He pulled it out, looked at it to make sure it was intact, saw that it was. He slung it around his neck and bent over the hatch.

He threw the lever, jumped out and down, staggered, almost fell, and caught his camera before it could strike the concrete of the taxiway. There was another growl of thunder, but *only* a growl this time, distant and unthreatening. A breeze touched him like the caressing touch of a kind hand on his face . . . but more icily below the belt. Dees grimaced. How he had pissed his pants when his Beech and the Piedmont jet had barely scraped by each other would *also* not be in the story.

Then a thin, drilling shriek came from the General Aviation Terminal — a scream of mingled agony and horror. It was as if someone had slapped Dees across the face. He came back to himself. He centered on his goal again. He looked at his watch. It wasn't working. Either the concussion had broken it or it had stopped. It was one of those amusing antiques you had to wind up, and he couldn't remember when he had last done it.

Was it sunset? It was fucking dark out, yes, but with all the thunderheads massed around the airport, it was hard to tell how much that meant. *Was* it?

Another scream came — no, not a scream, a screech — and the sound of breaking glass.

Dees decided sunset no longer mattered.

He ran, vaguely aware that the genny's auxiliary tanks were still burning and that he could smell gas in the air. He tried to increase his speed but it seemed he was running in cement. The terminal was getting closer, but not very fast. Not fast enough.

"Please, no! Please, no! PLEASE NO! OH PLEASE NO!"

This scream, spiraling up and up, was suddenly cut off by a terrible, inhuman howl. Yet there *was* something human in it, and that was perhaps the most terrible thing of all. In the chancy light of the emergency lamps mounted on the corners of the terminal, Dees saw something dark and flailing shatter more glass in the wall of the terminal that faced the parking area — that wall was almost entirely glass — and come flying out. It landed on the ramp with a soggy thud, rolled, and Dees saw it was a man.

The storm was moving away but lightning still flickered fitfully, and as Dees ran into the parking area, panting now, he finally saw the Night Flier's plane, N101BL painted boldly on the tail. The letters and numbers looked black in this light, but he knew they were red and it didn't matter, anyway. The camera was loaded with fast black-and-white film and armed with a smart flash which would fire only when the light was too low for the film's speed.

The Skymaster's belly-hold hung open like the mouth of a corpse. Below it was a large pile of earth in which things squirmed and moved. Dees saw this, did a double-take, and skidded to a stop. Now his heart was filled not just with fright but with a wild, capering happiness. How good it was thateverything had come together like this!

Yes, he thought, but don't you call it luck — don't you *dare* call it luck. Don't you even call it hunch.

Correct. It wasn't luck that had kept him holed up in that shitty little motel room with the clanky air-conditioner, not hunch — not *precisely* hunch, anyway — that had tied him to the phone hour after hour, calling flyspeck airports and giving the Night Flier's tail-number over and over again. That was pure reporter's instinct, and here was where it all started paying off. Except this was no ordinary payoff; this was the jackpot, El Dorado, that fabled Big Enchilada.

He skidded to a stop in front of the yawning belly-hold and tried to bring the camera up. Almost strangled himself on the strap. Cursed. Unwound the strap. Aimed.

From the terminal came another scream — that of a woman or a child. Dees barely noticed. The thought that there was a slaughter going on in there was followed by the thought that slaughter would only fatten the story, and then both thoughts were gone as he snapped three quick shots of the Cessna, making sure to get the gaping belly-hold and the number on the tail. The auto-winder hummed.

Dees ran on. More glass smashed. There was another thud as another body was ejected onto the cement like a rag doll that had been stuffed full of some thick dark liquid like cough-syrup. Dees looked, saw confused movement, the billowing of something that *might* have been a cape . . . but he was still too far away to tell. He turned. Snapped two more pictures of the plane, these shots dead-on. The gaping belly-hold and the pile of earth would be stark and undeniable in the print.

Then he whirled and ran for the terminal. The fact that he was armed with only an old Nikon never crossed his mind.

He stopped ten yards away. Three bodies out here, two adults, one of each sex, and one that might have been either a small woman or a girl of thirteen or so. It was hard to tell with the head gone.

Dees aimed the camera and fired off six quick shots, the flash flickering its own white lightning, the auto-winder making its contented little whizzing sound.

His mind never lost count. He was loaded with thirty-six shots. He had taken eleven. That left twenty-five. There was more film stuffed into the deep pockets of his slacks, and that was great . . . if he got a chance to reload. You could never count on that, though; with photographs like these, you had to grab while the grabbing was good. It was strictly a fast-food banquet.

Dees reached the terminal and yanked open the door.

9

He thought he had seen everything there was to see, but he had *never* seen anything like this. *Never.*

How many? his mind yammered. How many you got? Six? Eight? Maybe a dozen?

He couldn't tell. The Night Flier had turned the little private terminal into a knacker's shop. Bodies and parts of bodies lay everywhere. Dees saw a foot clad in a black Converse sneaker; shot it. A ragged torso; shot it. Here was a man in a greasy mechanic's coverall who was still alive, and for a weird moment he thought it was Ezra the Amazing Gin-Head Mechanic from Cumberland County Airport, but this guy wasn't just going bald; this guy had entirely made the grade. His face had been chopped wide open from forehead to chin. His nose lay in halves, reminding Dees for some mad reason of a grilled frankfurter, split and ready for the bun.

Dees shot it.

And suddenly, just like that, something inside him rebelled and screamed *No more!* in an imperative voice it was impossible to ignore, let alone deny.

No more, stop, it's over!

He saw an arrow painted on the wall, with the words THIS WAY TO COMFORT STATIONS below it. Dees ran in the direction the arrow pointed, his camera flapping.

The men's room happened to be the first one he came to, but Dees wouldn't have cared if it

192

was the aliens' room. He was weeping in great, harsh, hoarse sobs. He could barely credit the fact that these sounds were coming from him. It had been years since he had wept. He'd been a kid the last time.

He slammed through the door, skidded like a skier almost out of control, and grabbed the edge of the second basin in line.

He leaned over it, and everything came out in a rich and stinking flood, some of it splattering back onto his face, some landing in brownish clots on the mirror. He smelled the take-out chicken Creole he'd eaten hunched over the phone in the motel room — this had been just before he'd hit paydirt and gone racing for his plane — and threw up again, making a huge grating sound like over-stressed machinery about to strip its gears.

Jesus, he thought, dear Jesus, it's not a man, it can't be a man —

That was when he heard the sound.

It was a sound he had heard at least a thousand times before, a sound that was commonplace in any American man's life . . . but now it filled him with a dread and a creeping terror beyond all his experience or belief.

It was the sound of a man voiding into a urinal.

But although he could see all three of the bathroom's urinals in the vomit-splattered mirror, he could see no one at any of them.

Dees thought: Vampires don't cast reflec—

Then he saw reddish liquid striking the porcelain of the center urinal, saw it running down that porcelain, saw it swirling into the geometric arrangement of holes at the bottom.

There was no stream in the air; he saw it only when it struck the dead porcelain.

That was when it became visible.

He was frozen. He stood, hands on the edge of the basin, his mouth and throat and nose and sinuses thick with the taste and smell of chicken Creole, and watched the incredible yet prosaic thing that was happening just behind him.

I am, he thought dimly, watching a vampire take a piss.

It seemed to go on forever — the bloody urine striking the porcelain, becoming visible, and swirling down the drain. Dees stood with his hands planted on the sides of the basin into which he had thrown up, gazing at the reflection in the mirror, feeling like a frozen gear in some vast jammed machine.

I'm almost certainly dead meat, he thought.

In the mirror he saw the chromed handle go down by itself. Water roared.

Dees heard a rustle and flap and knew it was a cape, just as he knew that if he turned around, he could strike the "almost certainly" from his last thought. He stayed where he was, palms biting the edge of the basin.

A low, ageless voice spoke from directly behind him. The owner of the voice was so close Dees could feel its cold breath on his neck.

"You have been following me," the ageless voice said.

Dees moaned.

"Yes," the ageless voice said, as if Dees had disagreed with him. "I know you, you see. I know all about you. Now listen closely, my inquisitive

194

friend, because I say this only once: don't follow me anymore."

Dees moaned again, a doglike sound, and more water ran into his pants.

"Open your camera," the ageless voice said.

My film! part of Dees cried. *My film! All I've got! All I've got! My pictures!*

Another dry, batlike flap of the cape. Although Dees could see nothing, he sensed the Night Flier had moved even closer.

"Now."

His film *wasn't* all he had.

There was his life.

Such as it was.

He saw himself whirling and seeing what the mirror would not, could not, show him; saw himself seeing the Night Flier, his batty buddy, a grotesque thing splattered with blood and bits of flesh and clumps of torn-out hair; saw himself snapping shot after shot while the auto-winder hummed . . . but there would be nothing.

Nothing at all.

Because you couldn't take their pictures, either.

"You're real," he croaked, never moving, his hands seemingly welded to the edge of the basin.

"So are you," the ageless voice rasped, and now Dees could smell ancient crypts and sealed tombs on its breath. "For now, at least. This is your last chance, my inquisitive would-be biographer. Open your camera . . . or I'll do it."

With hands that seemed totally numb, Dees opened his Nikon.

Air hummed past his chilly face; it felt like moving razor blades. For a moment he saw a long

195

white hand, streaked with blood; saw ragged nails silted with filth.

Then his film parted and spooled spinelessly out of his camera.

There was another dry flap. Another stinking breath. For a moment he thought the Night Flier would kill him anyway. Then in the mirror he saw the door of the men's room open by itself.

He doesn't need me, Dees thought. *He must have eaten very well tonight.* He immediately threw up again, this time directly onto the reflection of his own staring face.

The door wheezed shut on its pneumatic elbow.

Dees stayed right where he was for the next three minutes or so; stayed there until the approaching sirens were almost on top of the terminal; stayed there until he heard the cough and roar of an airplane engine.

The engine of a Cessna Skymaster 337, almost undoubtedly.

Then he walked out of the bathroom on legs like stilts, struck the far wall of the corridor outside, rebounded, and walked back into the terminal. He slid in a pool of blood, and almost fell.

"Hold it mister!" a cop screamed behind him. *"Hold it right there! One move and you're dead!"*

Dees didn't even turn around.

"Press, dickface," he said, holding up his camera in one hand and his ID card in the other. He went to one of the shattered windows with exposed film still straggling from his camera like long strips of brown confetti, and stood there watching the Cessna accelerate down Runway 5. For a moment

196

it was a black shape against the billowing fire of the genny and the auxiliary tanks, a shape that looked quite a lot like a bat, and then it was up, it was gone, and the cop was slamming Dees up against the wall hard enough to make his nose bleed and he didn't care, he didn't care about anything, and when the sobs began to tear their way out of his chest again he closed his eyes, and still he saw the Night Flier's bloody urine striking the porcelain, becoming visible, and swirling down the drain.

He thought he would see it forever.

Popsy

Sheridan was cruising slowly down the long blank length of the shopping mall when he saw the little kid push out through the main doors under the lighted sign which read COUSINTOWN. It was a boy-child, perhaps a big three and surely no more than five. On his face was an expression to which Sheridan had become exquisitely attuned. He was trying not to cry but soon would.

Sheridan paused for a moment, feeling the familiar soft wave of self-disgust . . . though every time he took a child, that feeling grew a little less urgent. The first time he hadn't slept for a week. He kept thinking about that big greasy Turk who called himself Mr. Wizard, kept wondering what he did with the children.

"They go on a boat-ride, Mr. Sheridan," the Turk told him, only it came out *Dey goo on a bot-rahd, Messtair Shurdunn.* The Turk smiled. *And if you know what's good for you, you won't ask any more about it,* that smile said, and it said it loud and clear, without an accent.

Sheridan *hadn't* asked any more, but that didn't mean he hadn't kept wondering. Especially afterward. Tossing and turning, wishing he had the whole thing to do over again so he could turn it around, so he could walk away from temptation. The second time had been almost as bad . . . the third time a little less . . . and by the fourth time he had almost stopped wondering about the bot-rahd, and what might be at the end of it for the little kids.

Sheridan pulled his van into one of the handicap parking spaces right in front of the mall. He had one of the special license plates the state gave to crips on the back of his van. That plate was worth its weight in gold, because it kept any mall security cop from getting suspicious, and those spaces were so convenient and almost always empty.

You always pretend you're not going out looking, but you always lift a crip plate a day or two before.

Never mind all that bullshit; he was in a jam and that kid over there could solve some very big problems.

He got out and walked toward the kid, who was looking around with increasing panic. Yes, Sheridan thought, he was five all right, maybe even six — just very frail. In the harsh fluorescent glare thrown through the glass doors the boy looked parchment-white, not just scared but perhaps physically ill. Sheridan reckoned it was just big fear, however. Sheridan usually recognized that look when he saw it, because he'd seen a lot of big fear in his own mirror over the last year and a half or so.

The kid looked up hopefully at the people passing around him, people going into the mall eager to buy, coming out laden with packages, their faces dazed, almost drugged, with something they probably thought was satisfaction.

The kid, dressed in Tuffskin jeans and a Pittsburgh Penguins tee-shirt, looked for help, looked for somebody to look at him and see something was wrong, looked for someone to ask the right question — *You get separated from your dad, son?* would do — looking for a friend.

Here I am, Sheridan thought, approaching. *Here I am, sonny — I'll be your friend.*

He had almost reached the kid when he saw a mall rent-a-cop ambling slowly up the concourse toward the doors. He was reaching in his pocket, probably for a pack of cigarettes. He would come out, see the boy, and there would go Sheridan's sure thing.

Shit, he thought, but at least he wouldn't be seen talking to the kid when the cop came out. That would have been worse.

Sheridan drew back a little and made a business of feeling in his own pockets, as if to make sure he still had his keys. His glance flicked from the boy to the security cop and back to the boy. The boy had started to cry. Not all-out bawling, not yet, but great big tears that looked pinkish in the reflected glow of the red COUSINTOWN sign as they tracked down his smooth cheeks.

The girl in the information booth flagged down the cop and said something to him. She was pretty, dark-haired, about twenty-five; he was sandy-blonde with a moustache. As the cop leaned on his elbows, smiling at her, Sheridan thought they looked like the cigarette ads you saw on the backs of magazines. Salem Spirit. Light My Lucky. He was dying out here and they were in there making chit-chat — whatcha doin after work, ya wanna go and get a drink at that new place, and blah-

blah-blah. Now she was also batting her eyes at him. How cute.

Sheridan abruptly decided to take the chance. The kid's chest was hitching, and as soon as he started to bawl out loud, someone would notice him. Sheridan didn't like moving in with a cop less than sixty feet away, but if he didn't cover his markers at Mr. Reggie's within the next twenty-four hours, he thought a couple of very large men would pay him a visit and perform impromptu surgery on his arms, adding several elbow-bends to each.

He walked up to the kid, a big man dressed in an ordinary Van Heusen shirt and khaki pants, a man with a broad, ordinary face that looked kind at first glance. He bent over the little boy, hands on his legs just above the knees, and the boy turned his pale, scared face up to Sheridan's. His eyes were as green as emeralds, their color accentuated by the light-reflecting tears that washed them.

"You get separated from your dad, son?" Sheridan asked.

"My *Popsy*," the kid said, wiping his eyes. "I . . . I can't find my P-P-Popsy!"

Now the kid *did* begin to sob, and a woman headed in glanced around with some vague concern.

"It's all right," Sheridan said to her, and she went on. Sheridan put a comforting arm around the boy's shoulders and drew him a little to the right . . . in the direction of the van. Then he looked back inside.

The rent-a-cop had his face right down next to the information girl's now. Looked like maybe more than that little girl's Lucky was going to get lit tonight. Sheridan relaxed. At this point there could be a stick-up going on at the bank just up the concourse and the cop wouldn't notice a thing. This was starting to look like a cinch.

"I want my Popsy!" the boy wept.

"Sure you do, of course you do," Sheridan said. "And we're going to find him. Don't you worry."

He drew him a little more to the right.

The boy looked up at him, suddenly hopeful. "Can you? Can you, mister?"

"Sure!" Sheridan said, and grinned heartily. "Finding lost Popsys . . . well, you might say it's kind of a specialty of mine."

"It is?" The kid actually smiled a little, although his eyes were still leaking.

"It sure is," Sheridan said, glancing inside again to make sure the cop, whom he could now barely see (and who would barely be able to see Sheridan and the boy, should he happen to look up), was still enthralled. He was. "What was your Popsy wearing, son?"

"He was wearing his suit," the boy said. "He almost always wears his suit. I only saw him once in jeans." He spoke as if Sheridan should know all these things about his Popsy.

"I bet it was a black suit," Sheridan said.

The boy's eyes lit up. "You *saw* him! Where?"

He started eagerly back toward the doors, tears forgotten, and Sheridan had to restrain himself from grabbing the pale-faced little brat right then and there. That type of thing was no good. Couldn't cause a scene. Couldn't do anything people would remember later. Had to get him in the van. The van had sun-filter glass everywhere except in the windshield; it was almost impossible to see inside unless you had your face smashed right up against it.

Had to get him in the van first.

He touched the boy on the arm. "I didn't see him inside, son. I saw him right over there."

He pointed across the huge parking lot with its endless platoons of cars. There was an access road at the far end of it, and beyond that were the double yellow arches of McDonald's.

"Why would Popsy go over *there?*" the boy asked, as if either Sheridan or Popsy — or maybe both of them — had gone utterly mad.

"I don't know," Sheridan said. His mind was working fast, clicking along like an express train as it always did when it got right down to the point where you had to stop shitting and either do it up right or fuck it up righteously. Popsy. Not Dad or Daddy but Popsy. The kid had corrected him on it. Maybe Popsy meant Granddad, Sheridan decided. "But I'm pretty sure that was him. Older guy in a black suit. White hair . . . green tie . . ."

"Popsy had his blue tie on," the boy said. "He knows I like it the best."

"Yeah, it could have been blue," Sheridan said. "Under these lights, who can tell? Come on, hop in the van, I'll run you over there to him."

"Are you *sure* it was Popsy? Because I don't know why he'd go to a place where they —"

Sheridan shrugged. "Look, kid, if you're sure that wasn't him, maybe you better look for him on your own. You might even find him." And he started brusquely away, heading back toward the van.

The kid wasn't biting. He thought about going back, trying again, but it had already gone on too long — you either kept observable contact to a minimum or you were asking for twenty years in Hammerton Bay. He'd better go on to another mall. Scoterville, maybe. Or —

"Wait, mister!" It was the kid, with panic in his voice. There was the light thud of running sneakers. "Wait up! I told him I was thirsty, he must have thought he had to go way over there to get me a drink. Wait!"

Sheridan turned around, smiling. "I wasn't really going to leave you anyway, son."

He led the boy to the van, which was four years old and painted a nondescript blue. He opened the door and smiled at the kid, who looked up at him doubtfully, his green eyes swimming in that pallid little face, as huge as the eyes of a waif in a velvet painting, the kind they advertised in the cheap weekly tabloids like *The National Enquirer* and *Inside View.*

"Step into my parlor, little buddy," Sheridan said, and produced a grin which looked almost entirely natural. It was really sort of creepy, how good he'd gotten at this.

The kid did, and although he didn't know it, his ass belonged to Briggs Sheridan the minute the passenger door swung shut.

There was only one problem in his life. It wasn't broads, although he liked to hear the swish of a skirt or feel the smooth smoke of silken hose as

204

well as any man, and it wasn't booze, although he had been known to take a drink or three of an evening. Sheridan's problem — his fatal flaw, you might even say — was cards. Any kind of cards, as long as it was the kind of game where wagers were allowed. He had lost jobs, credit cards, the home his mother had left him. He had never, at least so far, been in jail, but the first time he got in trouble with Mr. Reggie, he'd thought jail would be a rest-cure by comparison.

He had gone a little crazy that night. It was better, he had found, when you lost right away. When you lost right away you got discouraged, went home, watched Letterman on the tube, and then went to sleep. When you won a little bit at first, you chased. Sheridan had chased that night and had ended up owing seventeen thousand dollars. He could hardly believe it; he went home dazed, almost elated, by the enormity of it. He kept telling himself in the car on the way home that he owed Mr. Reggie not seven hundred, not seven *thousand,* but *seventeen thousand* iron men. Every time he tried to think about it he giggled and turned up the volume on the radio.

But he wasn't giggling the next night when the two gorillas — the ones who would make sure his arms bent in all sorts of new and interesting ways if he didn't pay up — brought him into Mr. Reggie's office.

"I'll pay," Sheridan began babbling at once. "I'll pay, listen, it's no problem, couple of days, a week at the most, two weeks at the outside —"

"You bore me, Sheridan," Mr. Reggie said.

"I —"

"Shut up. If I give you a week, don't you think I know what you'll do? You'll tap a friend for a couple of hundred if you've got a friend left to tap. If you can't find a friend, you'll hit a liquor store . . . if you've got the guts. I doubt if you do, but anything is possible." Mr. Reggie leaned forward, propped his chin on his hands, and smiled. He smelled of Ted Lapidus cologne. "And if you do come up with two hundred dollars, what will you do with it?"

"Give it to you," Sheridan had babbled. By then he was very close to tears. "I'll give it to you, right away!"

"No you won't," Mr. Reggie said. "You'll take it to the track and try to make it grow. What you'll give me is a bunch of shitty excuses. You're in over your head this time, my friend. Way over your head."

Sheridan could hold back the tears no longer; he began to blubber.

"These guys could put you in the hospital for a long time," Mr. Reggie said reflectively. "You would have a tube in each arm and another one coming out of your nose."

Sheridan began to blubber louder.

"I'll give you this much," Mr. Reggie said, and pushed a folded sheet of paper across his desk to Sheridan. "You might get along with this guy. He calls himself Mr. Wizard, but he's a shitbag just like you. Now get out of here. I'm gonna have you back in here in a week, though, and I'll have your markers on this desk. You either buy them back or I'm going to have my friends tool up on you. And like Booker T. says, once they start,

206

they do it until they're satisfied."

The Turk's real name was written on the folded sheet of paper. Sheridan went to see him, and heard about the kids and the bot-rahds. Mr. Wizard also named a figure which was a fairish bit larger than the markers Mr. Reggie was holding. That was when Sheridan started cruising the malls.

He pulled out of the Cousintown Mall's main parking lot, looked for traffic, then drove across the access road and into the McDonald's in-lane. The kid was sitting all the way forward on the passenger seat, hands on the knees of his Tuffskins, eyes agonizingly alert. Sheridan drove toward the building, swung wide to avoid the drive-thru lane, and kept on going.

"Why are you going around the back?" the kid asked.

"You have to go around to the other doors," Sheridan said. "Keep your shirt on, kid. I think I saw him in there."

"You did? You really did?"

"I'm pretty sure, yeah."

Sublime relief washed over the kid's face, and for a moment Sheridan felt sorry for him — hell, he wasn't a monster or a maniac, for Christ's sake. But his markers had gotten a little deeper each time, and that bastard Mr. Reggie had no compunctions at all about letting him hang himself. It wasn't seventeen thousand this time, or twenty thousand, or even twenty-five thousand. This time it was thirty-five grand, a whole damn marching battalion of iron men, if he didn't want a few new sets of elbows by next Saturday.

He stopped in the back by the trash-compactor. Nobody was parked back here. Good. There was an elasticized pouch on the side of the door for maps and things. Sheridan reached into it with his left hand and brought out a pair of blued-steel Kreig handcuffs. The loop-jaws were open.

"Why are we stopping here, mister?" the kid asked. The fear was back in his voice, but the quality of it had changed; he had suddenly realized that maybe getting separated from good old Popsy in the busy mall wasn't the worst thing that could happen to him, after all.

"We're not, not really," Sheridan said easily. He had learned the second time he'd done this that you didn't want to underestimate even a six-year-old once he had his wind up. The second kid had kicked him in the balls and had damn near gotten away. "I just remembered I forgot to put my glasses on when I started driving. I could lose my license. They're in that glasses-case on the floor there. They slid over to your side. Hand em to me, would you?"

The kid bent over to get the glasses-case, which was empty. Sheridan leaned over and snapped one of the cuffs on the kid's reaching hand as neat as you please. And then the trouble started. Hadn't he just been thinking it was a bad mistake to underestimate even a six-year-old? The brat fought like a timberwolf pup, twisting with a powerful muscularity Sheridan would not have credited had he not been experiencing it. He bucked and fought and lunged for the door, panting and uttering weird birdlike cries. He got the handle. The door swung open, but no domelight came on — Sheridan had broken it after that second outing.

Sheridan got the kid by the round collar of his Penguins tee-shirt and hauled him back in. He tried to clamp the other cuff on the special strut beside the passenger seat and missed. The kid bit his hand twice, bringing blood. God, his teeth were like razors. The pain went deep and sent a steely ache all the way up his arm. He punched the kid in the mouth. The kid fell back into the seat, dazed, Sheridan's blood on his lips and chin and dripping onto the ribbed neck of the tee-shirt. Sheridan locked the other cuff onto the strut and then fell back into his own seat, sucking the back of his right hand.

The pain was really bad. He pulled his hand away from his mouth and looked at it in the weak glow of the dashlights. Two shallow, ragged tears, each maybe two inches long, ran up toward his wrist from just above the knuckles. Blood pulsed in weak little rills. Still, he felt no urge to pop the kid again, and that had nothing to do with damaging the Turk's merchandise, in spite of the almost fussy way the Turk had warned him against that — *demmege the goots end you demmege the velue,* the Turk had said in his greasy accent.

No, he didn't blame the kid for fighting — he would have done the same. He would have to disinfect the wound as soon as he could, though, might even have to have a shot; he had read somewhere that human bites were the worst kind. Still, he couldn't help but admire the kid's guts.

He dropped the transmission into drive and pulled around the hamburger stand, past the drivethru window, and back onto the access road. He

209

turned left. The Turk had a big ranch-style house in Taluda Heights, on the edge of the city. Sheridan would go there by secondary roads, just to be safe. Thirty miles. Maybe forty-five minutes, maybe an hour.

He passed a sign which read THANK YOU FOR SHOPPING THE BEAUTIFUL COUSINTOWN MALL, turned left, and let the van creep up to a perfectly legal forty miles an hour. He fished a handkerchief out of his back pocket, folded it over the back of his right hand, and concentrated on following his headlights to the forty grand the Turk had promised for a boy-child.

"You'll be sorry," the kid said.

Sheridan looked impatiently around at him, pulled from a dream in which he had just won twenty straight hands and had Mr. Reggie grovelling at *his* feet for a change, sweating bullets and begging him to stop, what did he want to do, break him?

The kid was crying again, and his tears still had that odd pinkish cast, even though they were now well away from the bright lights of the mall. Sheridan wondered for the first time if the kid might have some sort of communicable disease. He supposed it was a little late to start worrying about such things, so he put it out of his mind.

"When my *Popsy* finds you you'll be sorry," the kid elaborated.

"Yeah," Sheridan said, and lit a cigarette. He turned off State Road 28 and onto an unmarked stretch of two-lane blacktop. There was a long marshy area on the left, unbroken woods on the right.

The kid pulled at the handcuffs and made a sobbing noise.

"Quit it. Won't do you any good."

Nevertheless, the kid pulled again. And this time
there was a groaning, protesting sound Sheridan
didn't like at *all*. He looked around and was
amazed to see that the metal strut on the side of
the seat — a strut he had welded in place himself
— was twisted out of shape. *Shit!* he thought.
*He's got teeth like razors and now I find out he's
also strong as a fucking ox. If this is what he's like
when he's sick, God forbid I should have grabbed him
on a day when he was feeling well.*

He pulled over onto the soft shoulder and said,
"Stop it!"

"I *won't!*"

The kid yanked at the handcuff again and Sheridan saw the metal strut bend a little more. Christ,
how could *any* kid do that?

It's panic, he answered himself. *That's how he
can do it.*

But none of the others had been able to do it,
and many of them had been a lot more terrified
than this kid by this stage of the game.

He opened the glove compartment in the center
of the dash. He brought out a hypodermic needle.
The Turk had given it to him, and cautioned him
not to use it unless he absolutely had to. Drugs,
the Turk said (pronouncing it *drocks*) could
demmege the merchandise.

"See this?"

The kid gave the hypo a glimmering sideways
glance and nodded.

"You want me to use it?"

211

The kid shook his head at once. Strong or not, he had any kid's instant terror of the needle, Sheridan was happy to see.

"That's very smart. It would put out your lights." He paused. He didn't want to say it — hell, he was a nice guy, really, when he didn't have his ass in a sling — but he had to. "Might even kill you."

The kid stared at him, lips trembling, cheeks papery with fear.

"You stop yanking the cuff, I put away the needle. Deal?"

"Deal," the kid whispered.

"You promise?"

"Yes." The kid lifted his lip, showing white teeth. One of them was spotted with Sheridan's blood.

"You promise on your mother's name?"

"I never had a mother."

"Shit," Sheridan said, disgusted, and got the van rolling again. He moved a little faster now, and not only because he was finally off the main road. The kid was a spook. Sheridan wanted to turn him over to the Turk, get his money, and split.

"My Popsy's really strong, mister."

"Yeah?" Sheridan asked, and thought: *I bet he is, kid. Only guy in the old folks' home who can bench-press his own truss, right?*

"He'll find me."

"Uh-huh."

"He can smell me."

Sheridan believed it. *He* could smell the kid. That fear had an odor was something he had learned on his previous expeditions, but this was

212

unreal — the kid smelled like a mixture of sweat, mud, and slowly cooking battery acid. Sheridan was becoming more and more sure that something was seriously wrong with the kid . . . but soon that would be Mr. Wizard's problem, not his, and *caveat emptor,* as those old fellows in the togas used to say; *caveat* fucking *emptor.*

Sheridan cracked his window. On the left, the marsh went on and on. Broken slivers of moonlight glimmered in the stagnant water.

"Popsy can fly."

"Yeah," Sheridan said, "after a couple of bottles of Night Train, I bet he flies like a sonofabitchin eagle."

"Popsy —"

"Enough of the Popsy shit, kid — okay?"

The kid shut up.

Four miles farther on, the marsh on the left broadened into a wide empty pond. Sheridan made a turn onto a stretch of hardpan dirt that skirted the pond's north side. Five miles west of here he would turn right onto Highway 41, and from there it would be a straight shot into Taluda Heights.

He glanced toward the pond, a flat silver sheet in the moonlight . . . and then the moonlight was gone. Blotted out.

Overhead there was a flapping sound like big sheets on a clothesline.

"Popsy!" the kid cried.

"Shut up. It was only a bird."

But suddenly he was spooked, very spooked. He looked at the kid. The kid's lip was drawn back from his teeth again. His teeth were very white, very big.

No . . . not big. Big wasn't the right word. *Long* was the right word. Especially the two at the top at each side. The . . . what did you call them? The canines.

His mind suddenly started to fly again, clicking along as if he were on speed.

I told him I was thirsty.

Why would Popsy go to a place where they —

(*?eat was he going to say eat?*)

He'll find me.

He can smell me.

Popsy can fly.

Something landed on the roof of the van with a heavy clumsy thump.

"Popsy!" the kid screamed again, almost delirious with delight, and suddenly Sheridan could not see the road anymore — a huge membranous wing, pulsing with veins, covered the windshield from side to side.

Popsy can fly.

Sheridan screamed and jumped on the brake, hoping to tumble the thing on the roof off the front. There was that groaning, protesting sound of metal under stress from his right again, this time followed by a short bitter snap. A moment later the kid's fingers were clawing into his face, pulling open his cheek.

"*He stole me, Popsy!*" the kid was screeching at the roof of the van in that birdlike voice. "*He stole me, he stole me, the bad man stole me!*"

You don't understand, kid, Sheridan thought. He groped for the hypo and found it. *I'm not a bad guy, I just got in a jam.*

Then a hand, more like a talon than a real hand, smashed through the side window and ripped the hypo from Sheridan's grasp — along with two of his fingers. A moment later Popsy peeled the entire driver's-side door out of its frame, the hinges now bright twists of meaningless metal. Sheridan saw a billowing cape, black on the outside, lined with red silk on the inside, and the creature's tie . . . and although it was actually a cravat, it was blue all right — just as the boy had said.

Popsy yanked Sheridan out of the car, talons sinking through his jacket and shirt and deep into the meat of his shoulders; Popsy's green eyes suddenly turned as red as blood-roses.

"We came to the mall because my grandson wanted some Ninja Turtle figures," Popsy whispered, and his breath was like flyblown meat. "The ones they show on TV. All the children want them. You should have left him alone. You should have left *us* alone."

Sheridan was shaken like a rag doll. He shrieked and was shaken again. He heard Popsy asking solicitously if the kid was still thirsty; heard the kid saying yes, very, the bad man had scared him and his throat was *so* dry. He saw Popsy's thumbnail for just a second before it disappeared under the shelf of his chin, the nail ragged and thick. His throat was cut with that nail before he realized what was happening, and the last things he saw before his sight dimmed to black were the kid, cupping his hands to catch the flow the way Sheridan himself had cupped his hands under the back-

215

yard faucet for a drink on a hot summer day when he was a kid, and Popsy, stroking the boy's hair gently, with grandfatherly love.

It Grows on You

New England autumn and the thin soil now shows in patches through the ragweed and goldenrod, waiting for snow still four weeks distant. The culverts are clogged with leaves, the sky has gone a perpetual gray, and cornstalks stand in leaning rows like soldiers who have found some fantastic way to die on their feet. Pumpkins, sagging inward now with softrot, are piled against crepuscular sheds, smelling like the breath of old women. There is no heat and no cold at this time of year, only pallid air which is never still, beating through the bare fields under white skies where birds fly south in chevron shapes. That wind blows dust up from the soft shoulders of back roads in dancing dervishes, parts the played-out fields as a comb parts hair, and sniffs its way into junked cars up on blocks in back yards.

The Newall house out on Town Road #3 overlooks that part of Castle Rock known as the Bend. It is somehow impossible to sense anything good about this house. It has a deathly look which can be only partially explained by its lack of paint. The front lawn is a mass of dried hummocks which the frost will soon heave into even more grotesque postures. Thin smoke rises from Brownie's Store at the foot of the hill. Once the Bend was a fairly important part of Castle Rock, but that time passed around the time Korea got over. On the old band-stand across the road from Brownie's two small children roll a red firetruck between them. Their faces are tired and washed out, the faces of old men, almost. Their hands actually seem to cut the air as they roll the truck between them, pausing only to swipe at their endlessly running noses every now and again.

In the store Harley McKissick is presiding, corpulent and redfaced, while old John Clutterbuck and Lenny Partridge sit by the stove with their feet up. Paul Corliss is leaning against the counter. The store has a smell that is ancient — a smell of salami and flypaper and coffee and tobacco; of sweat and dark brown Coca-Cola; of pepper and cloves and O'Dell Hair Tonic, which looks like semen and turns hair into sculpture. A fly-specked poster advertising a beanhole bean supper held in 1986 still leans in the window next to one advertising an appearance of "Country" Ken Corriveau at the 1984 Castle County Fair. The light and heat of almost ten summers has fallen on this latter poster, and now Ken Corriveau (who has been out of the country-music business for at least half of those ten years and now sells Fords over in Chamberlain) looks simultaneously faded and toasted. At the back of the store is a huge glass freezer that came out of New York in 1933, and everywhere hangs the vague but tremendous smell of coffee-beans.

The old men watch the children and speak in low, desultory tones. John Clutterbuck, whose grandson, Andy, is busy drinking himself to death this fall, has been talking about the town landfill.

218

The landfill stinks like a bugger in the summertime, he says. No one disputes this — it's true — but no one is very interested in the subject, either, because it's *not* summer, it's autumn, and the huge range-oil stove is throwing off a stuporous glow of heat. The Winston thermometer behind the counter says 82. Clutterbuck's forehead has a huge dent above his left eyebrow where he struck his head in a car accident in 1963. Small children sometimes ask to touch it. Old Clut has won a great deal of money from summer people who don't believe the dent in his head will hold the contents of a medium-sized water tumbler.

"Paulson," Harley McKissick says quietly.

An old Chevrolet has pulled in behind Lenny Partridge's oil-burner. On the side is a cardboard sign held with heavy masking tape. GARY PAULSON CHAIR'S CANED ANTIQUE'S BOUGHT & SOLD, the sign reads, with the telephone number to call beneath the words. Gary Paulson gets out of his car slowly, an old man in faded green pants with a huge satchel seat. He drags a knurled cane out after him, holding to the doorframe tightly until he has the cane planted just the way he likes it. The cane has the white plastic handgrip from a child's bike affixed over its dark tip like a condom. It makes small circles in the lifeless dust as Paulson begins his careful trip from his car to the door of Brownie's.

The children on the bandstand look up at him, then follow his glance (fearfully, it seems) to the leaning, crepitating bulk of the Newall house on the ridge above them. Then they go back to their firetruck.

Joe Newall bought in Castle Rock in 1904 and owned in Castle Rock until 1929, but his fortune was made in the nearby mill town of Gates Falls. He was a scrawny man with an angry, hectic face and eyes with yellow corneas. He bought a great parcel of open land out in the Bend — this was when it was quite a thriving village, complete with a profitable little combined wood-milling operation and furniture factory — from The First National Bank of Oxford. The bank got it from Phil Budreau in a foreclosure assisted by County Sheriff Nickerson Campbell. Phil Budreau, well-liked but considered something of a fool by his neighbors, slunk away to Kittery and spent the next twelve years or so tinkering with cars and motorcycles. Then he went off to France to fight the Heinies, fell out of an airplane while on a reconnaissance mission (or so the story has it), and was killed.

The Budreau patch lay silent and fallow for most of those years, while Joe Newall lived in a rented house in Gates Falls and saw to the making of his fortune. He was known more for his employee-severance policies than for the way he'd turned around a mill which had been tottering on the brink of ruination when he'd bought it for a song back in '02. The millworkers called him Firing Joe, because if you missed a single shift you were sent down the road, no excuses accepted or even listened to.

He married Cora Leonard, niece of Carl Stowe, in 1914. The marriage had great merit — in Joe Newall's eyes, certainly — because Cora was Carl's only living relative, and she would no doubt come into a nice little bundle when Carl passed on (as long as Joe remained on good terms with him, that was, and he had no intentions of being on anything less with the old fellow, who had been Damned Shrewd in his day but was considered to have become Rather Soft in his declining years). There were other mills in the area that could be bought for a song and then turned around . . . if, that was, a man had a little capital to use as a lever. Joe soon had his lever; his wife's rich uncle died within a year of the wedding.

So the marriage had merit — oh yes, no doubt about it. Cora herself did not have merit, however. She was a grainbag of a woman, incredibly wide across the hips, incredibly full in the butt, yet almost as flatchested as a boy and possessed of an absurd little pipestem neck upon which her oversized head nodded like a strange pale sunflower. Her cheeks hung like dough, her lips like strips of liver; her face was as silent as a full moon on a winter night. She sweated huge dark patches around the armholes of her dresses even in February, and she carried a dank smell of perspiration with her always.

Joe began a house for his wife on the Budreau patch in 1915, and a year later it seemed finished. It was painted white and enclosed twelve rooms that sprouted from many strange angles. Joe Newall was not popular in Castle Rock, partly because he made his money out of town, partly because Budreau, his predecessor, had been such an all-around nice fellow (though a fool, they always reminded each other, as if foolishness and niceness went together and it would be death to forget it), but mostly because his damned house was built with out-of-town labor. Shortly before the gutters and downspouts were hung, an obscene drawing accompanied by a one-syllable Anglo-Saxon word was scrawled on the fanlighted front door in soft yellow chalk.

By 1920 Joe Newall was a rich man. His three Gates Falls mills were going like a house afire, stuffed with the profits of a world war and comfortable with the orders of the newly arisen or (arising) middle class. He began to build a new wing on his house. Most folks in the village pronounced it unnecessary — after all, there were just the two of them up there — and almost all opined it added nothing but ugly to a house most of them already considered ugly beyond almost all measure. This new wing towered one story above the main house and looked blindly down the ridge, which had in those days been covered with straggling pines.

The news that just the two of them were soon to become just the three of them trickled in from Gates Falls, the source most likely being Doris Gingercroft, who was Dr. Robertson's nurse in those days. So the added wing was in the nature of a celebration, it seemed. After six years of wedded bliss and four years of living in the Bend, during which she had been seen only at a distance as she crossed her dooryard, or occasionally picking flowers — crocuses, wild roses, Queen Anne's lace, ladyslipper, paintbrush — in the field beyond the buildings, after all that time, Cora Leonard Newall had Kindled.

She never shopped at Brownie's. Cora did her

222

marketing at the Kitty Korner Store over in Gates Center every Thursday afternoon.

In January of 1921, Cora gave birth to a monster with no arms and, it was said, a tiny clutch of perfect fingers sticking out of one eyesocket. It died less than six hours after mindless contractions had pushed its red and senseless face into the light. Joe Newall added a cupola to the wing seventeen months later, in the late spring of 1922 (in western Maine there is no early spring; only late spring and winter before it). He continued to buy out of town and would have nothing to do with Bill "Brownie" McKissick's store. He also never crossed the threshold of the Bend Methodist Church. The deformed infant which had slid from his wife's womb was buried in the Newall plot in Gates rather than in Homeland. The inscription on the tiny headstone read

SARAH TAMSON TABITHA FRANCINE NEWALL
JANUARY 14, 1921
GOD GRANT SHE LIE STILL.

In the store they talked about Joe Newall and Joe's wife and Joe's house as Brownie's kid Harley, still not old enough to shave (but with his senescence buried inside just the same, hibernating, waiting, perhaps dreaming) but old enough to stack vegetables and haul pecks of potatoes out to the roadside stand whenever called upon to do so, stood by and listened. Mostly it was the house of which they spoke; it was considered to be an affront to the sensibilities and an offense to the eye. "But it grows on you," Clayton Clutterbuck

223

(father of John) sometimes remarked. There was never any answer to this. It was a statement with absolutely no meaning . . . yet at the same time it was a patent fact. If you were standing in the yard at Brownie's, maybe just looking at the berries for the best box when berry-season was on, you sooner or later found your eyes turning up to the house on the ridge the way a weathervane turns to the nor'east before a March blizzard. Sooner or later you had to look, and as time went by, it got to be sooner for most people. Because, as Clayt Clutterbuck said, the Newall place grew on you.

In 1924, Cora fell down the stairs between the cupola and the new wing, breaking her neck and her back. A rumor went through town (it probably originated at a Ladies Aid Bake Sale) that she had been stark naked at the time. She was interred next to her ill-formed, short-lived daughter.

Joe Newall — who, most folks now agreed, undoubtedly contained a touch of the kike — continued to make money hand over fist. He built two sheds and a barn up on the ridge, all of them connected to the main house by way of the new wing. The barn was completed in 1927, and its purpose became clear almost at once — Joe had apparently decided to become a gentleman farmer. He bought sixteen cows from a fellow in Mechanic Falls. He bought a shiny new milking machine from the same fellow. It looked like a metal octopus to those who glanced into the back of the delivery truck and saw it when the driver stopped at Brownie's for a cold bottle of ale before going on up the hill.

With the cows and the milking machine installed, Joe hired a halfwit from Motton to take care of his investment. How this supposedly hardfisted and tough-minded mill-owner could have done such a thing perplexed everyone who turned his mind to the question — that Newall was slipping seemed to be the only answer — but he did, and of course the cows all died.

The county health officer showed up to look at the cows, and Joe showed him a signed statement from a veterinarian (a *Gates Falls* veterinarian, folks said ever after, raising their brows significantly as they said it) certifying that the cows had died of bovine meningitis.

"That means bad luck in English," Joe said.

"Is that supposed to be a joke?"

"Take it the way you want to take it," said Joe. "That's all right."

"Make that idiot shut up, why don't you?" the county health officer said. He was looking down the driveway at the halfwit, who was leaning against the Newall R.F.D. box and howling. Tears ran down his pudgy, dirty cheeks. Every now and then he would draw back and slap himself a good one, like he knew the whole thing was his fault.

"He's all right, too."

"Nothing up here seems all right to me," said the county health man, "least of all sixteen cows layin dead on their backs with their legs stickin up like fence-posts. I can see em from here."

"Good," said Joe Newall, "because it's as close as you'll get."

The county health officer threw the Gates Falls vet's paper down and stamped one of his boots

225

on it. He looked at Joe Newall, his face flushed so bright that the burst squiggles of veins on the sides of his nose stood out purple. "I want to see those cows. Haul one away, if it comes to that."

"No."

"You don't own the world, Newall — I'll get a court order."

"Let's see if you can."

The health officer drove away. Joe watched him. Down at the end of the driveway the halfwit, clad in dung-splattered bib overalls from the Sears and Roebuck mail-order catalogue, went on leaning against the Newall R.F.D. box and howling. He stayed there all that hot August day, howling at the top of his lungs with his flat mongoloid face turned up to the yellow sky. "Bellerin like a calf in the moonlight" was how young Gary Paulson put it.

The county health officer was Clem Upshaw, from Sirois Hill. He might have dropped the matter once his thermostat went down a little, but Brownie McKissick, who had supported him for the office he held (and who let him charge a fair amount of beer), urged him not to. Harley McKissick's dad was not the kind of man who usually resorted to cat's paws — or had to — but he'd wanted to make a point concerning private property with Joe Newall. He wanted Joe to understand that private property is a great thing, yes, an *American* thing, but private property is still stitched to the town, and in Castle Rock people still believed the community came first, even with rich folks that could build a little more house on their house whenever the whim took them. So

226

Clem Upshaw went on down to Lackery, which was the county seat in those days, and got the order.

While he was getting it, a large van drove up past the howling moron and to the barn. When Clem Upshaw returned with his order, only one cow remained, gazing at him with black eyes which had grown dull and distant beneath their covering of hay chaff. Clem determined that this cow at least had died of bovine meningitis, and then he went away. When he was gone, the remover's van returned for the last cow.

In 1928 Joe began another wing. That was when the men who gathered at Brownie's decided the man was crazy. Smart, yes, but crazy. Benny Ellis claimed that Joe had gouged out his daughter's one eye and kept it in a jar of what Benny called "fubbledehyde" on the kitchen table, along with the amputated fingers which had been poking out of the other socket when the baby was born. Benny was a great reader of the horror pulps, magazines that showed naked ladies being carried off by giant ants and similar bad dreams on their covers, and his story about Joe Newall's jar was clearly inspired by his reading matter. As a result, there were soon people all over Castle Rock — not just the Bend — who claimed every word of it was true. Some claimed Joe kept even less mentionable things in the jar.

The second wing was finished in August of 1929 and two nights later a fast-moving jalopy with great sodium circles for eyes screamed juddering into Joe Newall's driveway and the stinking, fly-blown corpse of a large skunk was thrown at the

227

new wing. The animal splattered above one of the windows, throwing a fan of blood across the panes in a pattern almost like a Chinese ideogram.

In September of that year a fire swept the carding room of Newall's flagship mill in Gates Falls, causing fifty thousand dollars' worth of damage. In October the stock market crashed. In November Joe Newall hanged himself from a rafter in one of the unfinished rooms — probably a bedroom, it was meant to be — of the newest wing. The smell of sap in the fresh wood was still strong. He was found by Cleveland Torbutt, the assistant manager of Gates Mills and Joe's partner (or so it was rumored) in a number of Wall Street ventures that were now not worth the puke of a tubercular cocker spaniel. The body was cut down by the county coroner, who happened to be Clem Upshaw's brother Noble.

Joe was buried next to his wife and child on the last day of November. It was a hard, brilliant day and the only person from Castle Rock to attend the service was Alvin Coy, who drove the Hay & Peabody funeral hack. Alvin reported that one of the spectators was a young, shapely woman in a raccoon coat and a black cloche hat. Sitting in Brownie's and eating a pickle straight out of the barrel, Alvin would smile mordantly and tell his cronies that she was a jazz baby if he had ever seen one. She bore not one whit of resemblance to Cora Leonard Newall's side of the family, and she hadn't closed her eyes during the prayer.

Gary Paulson enters the store with exquisite slowness, closing the door carefully behind him.

"Afternoon," Harley McKissick says neutrally.

"Heard you won a turkey down to the Grange last night," says Old Clut as he prepares to light his pipe.

"Yuh," Gary says. He's eighty-four and, like the others, can remember when the Bend was a damned sight livelier than it is now. He lost two sons in two wars — the two before that mess in Viet Nam — and that was a hard thing. His third, a good boy, died in a collision with a pulpwood truck up around Presque Isle — back in 1973, that was. Somehow that one was easier to take, God knows why. Gary sometimes drools from the corners of his lips these days, and makes frequent smacking sounds as he tries to suck the drool back into his mouth before it can get away and start running down his chin. He doesn't know a whole hell of a lot lately, but he knows getting old is a lousy way to spend the last years of your life.

"Coffee?" Harley asks.

"Guess not."

Lenny Partridge, who will probably never recover from the broken ribs he suffered in a strange road-accident two autumns ago, pulls his feet back so the older man can pass by him and lower himself carefully into the chair in the corner (Gary caned the seat of this chair himself, back in '82). Paulson smacks his lips, sucks back spit, and folds his lumpy hands over the head of his cane. He looks tired and haggard.

"It is going to rain a pretty bitch," he says finally. "I'm aching that bad."

"It's a bad fall," Paul Corliss says.

There is silence. The heat from the stove fills

the store that will go out of business when Harley dies or maybe even before he dies if his youngest daughter has her way, it fills the store and coats the bones of the old men, tries to, anyway, and sniffs up against the dirty glass with its ancient posters looking out at the yard where there were gas-pumps until Mobil took them out in 1977. They are old men who have, for the most part, seen their children go away to more profitable places. The store does no business to speak of now, except for a few locals and the occasional through-going summer tourists who think old men like these, old men who sit by the stove in their thermal undershirts even in July, are quaint. Old Clut has always claimed that new people are going to come to this part of the Rock, but the last couple of years things have been worse than ever — it seems the whole goddam town is dying.

"Who is building the new wing on that Christly Newall house?" Gary asks finally.

They look around at him. For a moment the kitchen match Old Clut has just scratched hangs mystically over his pipe, burning down the wood, turning it black. The sulfur node at the end turns gray and curls up. At last, Old Clut dips the match into the bowl and puffs.

"New wing?" Harley asks.

"Yuh."

A blue membrane of smoke from Old Clut's pipe drifts up over the stove and spreads there like a delicate fisherman's net. Lenny Partridge tilts his chin up to stretch the wattles of his neck taut and then runs his hand slowly down his throat, producing a dry rasp.

"No one that *I* know of," Harley says, somehow indicating by his tone of voice that this includes anyone of any consequence, at least in this part of the world.

"They ain't had a buyer on that place since nineteen n eighty-one," Old Clut says. When Old Clut says *they,* he means both Southern Maine Weaving and The Bank of Southern Maine, but he means more: he means The Massachusetts Wops. Southern Maine Weaving came into ownership of Joe's three mills —and Joe's house on the ridge — about a year after Joe took his own life, but as far as the men gathered around the stove in Brownie's are concerned, that name's just a smoke-screen . . . or what they sometimes call The Legal, as in *She swore out a pertection order on him n now he can't even see his own kids because of The Legal.* These men hate The Legal as it impinges upon their lives and the lives of their friends, but it fascinates them endlessly when they consider how some people put it to work in order to further their own nefarious money-making schemes.

Southern Maine Weaving, aka The Bank of Southern Maine, aka The Massachusetts Wops, enjoyed a long and profitable run with the mills Joe Newall saved from extinction, but it's the way they have been unable to get rid of the house that fascinates the old men who spend their days in Brownie's. "It's like a booger you can't flick off the end of your finger," Lenny Partridge said once, and they all nodded. "Not even those spaghetti-suckers from Malden n Revere can get rid of *that* millstone."

Old Clut and his grandson, Andy, are currently

estranged, and it is the ownership of Joe Newall's ugly house which has caused it . . . although there are other, more personal issues swirling around just below the surface, no doubt — there almost always are. The subject came up one night after grandfather and grandson — both widowers now — had enjoyed a pretty decent dinner at Young Clut's house in town.

Young Andy, who had not yet lost his job on the town's police-force, tried (rather self-indulgently) to explain to his grandfather that Southern Maine Weaving had had nothing to do with any of the erstwhile Newall holdings for years, that the actual owner of the house in the Bend was The Bank of Southern Maine, and that the two companies had nothing whatever to do with each other. Old John told Andy he was a fool if he believed that; everyone knew, he said, that both the bank and the textile company were fronts for The Massachusetts Wops, and that the only difference between them was a couple of words. They just hid the more obvious connections with great bunches of paperwork, Old Clut explained — The Legal, in other words.

Young Clut had the bad taste to laugh at that. Old Clut turned red, threw his napkin onto his plate, and got to his feet. *Laugh*, he said. *You just go on. Why not? The only thing a drunk does better'n laugh at what he don't understand is cry over he don't know what.* That made *Andy* mad, and he said something about Melissa being the reason why he drank, and John asked his grandson how long he was going to blame a dead wife for his boozing. Andy turned white when the old man said that, and told him to get out of his house, and John did, and he hasn't been back since. Nor does he want to. Harsh words aside, he can't bear to see Andy going to hell on a handcart like he is.

Speculation or not, this much cannot be denied: the house on the ridge has been empty for eleven years now, no one has ever lived there for long, and The Bank of Southern Maine is usually the organization that ends up trying to sell it through one of the local real estate firms.

"The last people to buy it come from uppa state New York, didn't they?" Paul Corliss asks, and he speaks so rarely they all turn toward him. Even Gary does.

"Yessir," Lenny says. "They was a nice couple. The man was gonna paint the barn red and turn it into some sort of antique store, wasn't he?"

"Ayuh," Old Clut says. "Then their boy got the gun they kep —"

"People are so goddam *careless* —" Harley puts in.

"Did he die?" Lenny asks. "The boy?"

Silence greets the question. It seems no one knows. Then, at last — almost reluctantly — Gary speaks up. "No," he said. "But it blinded him. They moved up to Auburn. Or maybe it was Leeds."

"They was likely people," Lenny said. "I really thought they might make a go of it. But they was set on that house. Believed everybody was pullin their leg about how it was bad luck, on account of they was from Away." He pauses meditatively. "Maybe they think better now . . . wherever they are."

233

There's silence as the old men think of the people from uppa state New York, or maybe of their own failing organs and sensory equipment. In the dimness behind the stove, oil gurgles. Somewhere beyond it, a shutter claps heavily back and forth in the restless autumn air.

"There's a new wing going up on it, all right," Gary says. He speaks quietly but emphatically, as if one of the others has contradicted this statement. "I saw it comin down the River Road. Most of the framing's already done. Damn thing looks like it wants to be a hundred feet long and thirty feet wide. Never noticed it before. Nice maple, looks like. Where does anybody get nice maple like that in this day n age?"

No one answers. No one knows.

At last, very tentatively, Paul Corliss says, "Sure you're not thinking of another house, Gary? Could be you —"

"Could be *shit*," Gary says, just as quietly but even more forcefully. "It's the *Newall* place, a *new wing* on the Newall place, already framed up, and if you still got doubts, just step outside and have a look for yourself."

With that said, there is nothing left to say — they believe him. Neither Paul nor anyone else rushes outside to crane up at the new wing being added to the Newall house, however. They consider it a matter of some importance, and thus nothing to hurry over. More time passes — Harley McKissick has reflected more than once that if time was pulpwood, they'd all be rich. Paul goes to the old water-cooled soft-drink chest and gets an Orange Crush. He gives Harley sixty cents and

Harley rings up the purchase. When he slams the cash-drawer shut again, he realizes the atmosphere in the store has changed somehow. There are other matters to discuss.

Lenny Partridge coughs, winces, presses his hands lightly against his chest where the broken ribs have never really healed, and asks Gary when they are going to have services for Dana Roy.

"Tomorrow," Gary says, "down Gorham. That's where his wife is laid to rest."

Lucy Roy died in 1968; Dana, who was until 1979 an electrician for U.S. Gypsum over in Gates Falls (these men routinely and with no prejudice refer to the company as U.S. Gyp Em), died of intestinal cancer two days before. He lived in Castle Rock all his life, and liked to tell people that he'd only been out of Maine three times in his eighty years, once to visit an aunt in Connecticut, once to see the Boston Red Sox play at Fenway Park ("And they lost, those bums," he always added at this point), and once to attend an electricians' convention in Portsmouth, New Hampshire. "Damn waste of time," he always said of the convention. "Nothin but drinkin and wimmin, and none of the wimmin even worth lookin at, let alone that other thing." He was a crony of these men, and in his passing they feel a queer mixture of sorrow and triumph.

"They took out four feet of his underpinnin," Gary tells the other men. "Didn't do no good. It was all through him."

"*He* knew Joe Newall," Lenny says suddenly. "He was up there with his dad when his dad was puttin in Joe's lectricity — couldn't have been more'n six or eight, I'd judge. I remember he said Joe give him a sucker one time, but he pitched it out'n his daddy's truck on the ride home. Said it tasted sour and funny. Then, later, after they got all the mills runnin again — the late thirties, that would've been — he was in charge of the rewirin. You member that, Harley?"

"Yup."

Now that the subject has come back to Joe Newall by way of Dana Roy, the men sit quietly, conning their brains for anecdotes concerning either man. But when Old Clut finally speaks, he says a startling thing.

"It was Dana Roy's big brother, Will, who throwed that skunk at the side of the house that time. I'm almost sure 'twas."

"Will?" Lenny raises his eyebrows. "Will Roy was too steady to do a thing like that, I would have said."

Gary Paulson says, very quietly: "Ayuh, it *was* Will."

They turn to look at him.

"And 'twas the wife that give Dana a sucker that day he came with his dad," Gary says. "Cora, not Joe. And Dana wa'ant no six or eight; the skunk was throwed around the time of the Crash, and Cora was dead by then. No, Dana maybe remembered some of it, but he couldn't have been no more than two. It was around 1916 that he got that sucker, because it was in '16 that Eddie Roy wired the house. He was never up there again. *Frank* — the middle boy, he's been dead ten or twelve year now — *he* would have been six or eight then, maybe. Frank seen what Cora done

236

to the little one, that much I know, but not when he told Will. It don't matter. Finally Will decided to do somethin about it. By then the woman was dead, so he took it out on the house Joe built for her."

"Never mind that part," Harley says, fascinated. "What'd she do to Dana? That's what *I* want to know."

Gary speaks calmly, almost judiciously. "What Frank told me one night when he'd had a few was that the woman give him the sucker with one hand and reached into his didies with the other. Right in front of the older boy."

"She never!" Old Clut says, shocked in spite of himself.

Gary only looks at him with his yellowed, fading eyes and says nothing.

Silence again, except for the wind and the clapping shutter. The children on the bandstand have taken their firetruck and gone somewhere else with it and still the depthless afternoon continues on and on, the light that of an Andrew Wyeth painting, white and still and full of idiot meaning. The ground has given up its meager yield and waits uselessly for snow.

Gary would like to tell them of the sickroom at Cumberland Memorial Hospital where Dana Roy lay dying with black snot caked around his nostrils and smelling like a fish left out in the sun. He would like to tell them of the cool blue tiles and of nurses with their hair drawn back in nets, young things for the most part with pretty legs and firm young breasts and no idea that 1923 was a real year, as real as the pains which haunt the

237

bones of old men. He feels he would like to ser-monize on the evil of time and perhaps even the evil of certain places, and explain why Castle Rock is now like a dark tooth which is finally ready to fall out. Most of all he would like to inform them that Dana Roy sounded as if someone had stuffed his chest full of hay and he was trying to breathe through it, and that he looked as if he had already started to rot. Yet he can say none of these things because he doesn't know how, and so he only sucks back spit and says nothing.

"No one liked old Joe much," Old Clut says . . . and then his face brightens suddenly. "But by God, he grew on you!"

The others do not reply.

Nineteen days later, a week before the first snow comes to cover the useless earth, Gary Paulson has a surprisingly sexual dream . . . except it is mostly a memory.

On August 14, 1923, while driving by the Newall house in his father's farm truck, thirteen-year-old Gary Martin Paulson happened to observe Cora Leonard Newall turning away from her mailbox at the end of the driveway. She had the newspaper in one hand. She saw Gary and reached down with her free hand to grasp the hem of her housedress. She did not smile. That tremendous moon of a face was pallid and empty as she raised the dress, revealing her sex to him — it was the first time he had ever seen that mystery so avidly discussed by the boys he knew. And, still not smiling but only looking at him gravely, she pistoned her hips at his gaping, amazed face as he passed her by.

And as he passed, his hand dropped into his lap and moments later he ejaculated into his flannel pants.

It was his first orgasm. In the years since, he has made love to a good many women, beginning with Sally Ouelette underneath the Tin Bridge back in '26, and every time he has neared the moment of orgasm — every single one — he has seen Cora Leonard Newall: has seen her standing beside her mailbox under a hot gunmetal sky, has seen her lifting her dress to reveal an almost non-existent thatch of gingery hair beneath the creamy groundswell of her belly, has seen the exclamatory slit with its red lips tinting toward what he knows would be the most deliciously delicate coral

(*Cora*)

pink. Yet it is not the sight of her vulva below that somehow promiscuous swell of gut that has haunted him through all the years, so that every woman became Cora at the moment of release; or it is not *just* that. What always drove him mad with lust when he remembered (and when he made love he was helpless not to) was the way she had pumped her hips at him . . . once, twice, three times. That, and the lack of expression on her face, a neutrality so deep it seemed more like idiocy, as if she were the sum of every very young man's limited sexual understanding and desire — a tight and yearning darkness, no more than that, a limited Eden glowing Cora-pink.

His sex-life has been both delineated and delimited by that experience — a seminal experience if ever there was one — but he has never mentioned it, although he has been tempted more than once when in his cups. He has hoarded it. And it is of this incident that he is dreaming, penis perfectly erect for the first time in almost nine years, when a small blood vessel in his cerebellum ruptures, forming a clot which kills him quietly, considerately sparing him four weeks or four months of paralysis, the flexible tubes in the arms, the catheter, the noiseless nurses with their hair in nets and their fine high breasts. He dies in his sleep, penis wilting, the dream fading like the afterimage of a television picture tube switched off in a dark room. His cronies would be puzzled, however, if any of them were there to hear the last two words he speaks — gasped out but still clear enough:

"*The moon!*"

The day after he is laid to rest in Homeland, a new cupola starts to go up on the new wing on the Newall house.

Chattery Teeth

Looking into the display case was like looking through a dirty pane of glass into the middle third of his boyhood, those years from seven to fourteen when he had been fascinated by stuff like this. Hogan leaned closer, forgetting the rising whine of the wind outside and the gritty *spick-spack* sound of sand hitting the windows. The case was full of fabulous junk, most of it undoubtedly made in Taiwan and Korea, but there was no doubt at all about the pick of the litter. They were the largest Chattery Teeth he'd ever seen. They were also the only ones he'd ever seen with feet — big orange cartoon shoes with white spats. A real scream.

Hogan looked up at the fat woman behind the counter. She was wearing a tee-shirt that said NEVADA IS GOD'S COUNTRY on top (the words swelling and receding across her enormous breasts) and about an acre of jeans on the bottom. She was selling a pack of cigarettes to a pallid young man whose long blonde hair had been tied back in a ponytail with a sneaker shoelace. The young man, who had the face of an intelligent lab-rat, was paying in small change, counting it laboriously out of a grimy hand.

"Pardon me, ma'am?" Hogan asked.

She looked at him briefly, and then the back door banged open. A skinny man wearing a ban-

241

danna over his mouth and nose came in. The wind swirled desert grit around him in a cyclone and rattled the pin-up cutie on the Valvoline calendar thumbtacked to the wall. The newcomer was pulling a handcart. Three wire-mesh cages were stacked on it. There was a tarantula in the one on top. In the cages below it were a pair of rattlesnakes. They were coiling rapidly back and forth and shaking their rattles in agitation.

"Shut the damn door, Scooter, was you born in a barn?" the woman behind the counter bawled.

He glanced at her briefly, eyes red and irritated from the blowing sand. "Gimme a chance, woman! Can't you see I got my hands full here? Ain't you got *eyes*? Christ!" He reached over the dolly and slammed the door. The dancing sand fell dead to the floor and he pulled the dolly toward the storeroom at the back, still muttering.

"That the last of em?" the woman asked.

"All but Wolf." He pronounced it *Woof*. "I'm gonna stick him in the lean-to back of the gas-pumps."

"You ain't not!" the big woman retorted. "Wolf's our star attraction, in case you forgot. You get him in here. Radio says this is gonna get worse before it gets better. A lot worse."

"Just who do you think you're foolin?" The skinny man (her husband, Hogan supposed) stood looking at her with a kind of weary truculence, his hands on his hips. "Damn thing ain't nothin but a Minnesota coydog, as anyone who took more'n half a look could plainly see."

The wind gusted, moaning along the eaves of Scooter's Grocery & Roadside Zoo, throwing sheaves of dry sand against the windows. It *was* getting worse, and Hogan could only hope he would be able to drive out of it. He had promised Lita and Jack he'd be home by seven, eight at the latest, and he was a man who liked to keep his promises.

"Just take care of him," the big woman said, and turned irritably back to the rat-faced boy.

"Ma'am?" Hogan said again.

"Just a minute, hold your water," Mrs. Scooter said. She spoke with the air of one who is all but drowning in impatient customers, although Hogan and the rat-faced boy were in fact the only ones present.

"You're a dime short, Sunny Jim," she told the blonde kid after a quick glance at the coins on the counter-top.

The boy regarded her with wide, innocent eyes. "I don't suppose you'd trust me for it?"

"I doubt if the Pope of Rome smokes Merit 100's, but if he did, I wouldn't trust *him* for it."

The look of wide-eyed innocence disappeared. The rat-faced boy looked at her with an expression of sullen dislike for a moment (this expression looked much more at home on the kid's face, Hogan thought), and then slowly began to investigate his pockets again.

Just forget it and get out of here, Hogan thought. *You'll never make it to L.A. by eight if you don't get moving, windstorm or no windstorm. This is one of those places that have only two speeds — slow and stop. You got your gas and paid for it, so just count yourself ahead of the game and get back on the road before the storm gets any worse.*

243

He almost followed his left brain's good advice
. . . and then he looked at the Chattery Teeth
in the display case again, the Chattery Teeth standing there on those big orange cartoon shoes. And
white spats! They were the real killer. *Jack would
love them,* his right brain told him. *And tell the
truth, Bill, old buddy; if it turns out* Jack *doesn't
want them,* you *do. You may see another set of Jumbo
Chattery Teeth at some point in your life, anything's
possible, but ones that also walk on big orange feet?
Huh-uh. I really doubt it.*

It was the right brain he listened to that time
. . . and everything else followed.

The kid with the ponytail was still going through
his pockets; the sullen expression on his face deep-
ened each time he came up dry. Hogan was no
fan of smoking — his father, a two-pack-a-day
man, had died of lung cancer — but he had visions
of still waiting to be waited on an hour from now.
"Hey! Kid!"

The kid looked around and Hogan flipped him
a quarter.

"Hey! Thanks, m'man!"

"Think nothing of it."

The kid concluded his transaction with the beefy
Mrs. Scooter, put the cigarettes in one pocket, and
dropped the remaining fifteen cents in another.
He made no offer of the change to Hogan, who
hadn't really expected it. Boys and girls like this
were legion these days — they cluttered the highways from coast to coast, blowing along like tum-
bleweeds. Perhaps they had always been there, but
to Hogan the current breed seemed both unpleas-

ant and a little scary, like the rattlers Scooter was now storing in the back room.

The snakes in pissant little roadside menageries like this one couldn't kill you; their venom was milked twice a week and sold to clinics that made drugs with it. You could count on that just as you could count on the winos to show up at the local plasma bank every Tuesday and Thursday. But the snakes could still give you one hell of a painful bite if you got too close and then made them mad. That, Hogan thought, was what the current breed of road-kids had in common with them.

Mrs. Scooter came drifting down the counter, the words on her tee-shirt drifting up and down and side to side as she did. "Whatcha need?" she asked. Her tone was still truculent. The West had a reputation for friendliness, and during the twenty years he had spent selling there Hogan had come to feel the reputation was more often than not deserved, but this woman had all the charm of a Brooklyn shopkeeper who has been stuck up three times in the last two weeks. Hogan supposed that her kind was becoming as much a part of the scene in the New West as the road-kids. Sad but true.

"How much are these?" Hogan asked, pointing through the dirty glass at what the sign identified as JUMBO CHATTERY TEETH — *THEY WALK!* The case was filled with novelty items — Chinese finger-pullers, Pepper Gum, Dr. Wacky's Sneezing Powder, cigarette loads (A Laff Riot! according to the package — Hogan guessed they were more likely a great way to get your teeth knocked out), X-ray glasses, plastic vomit (*So Realistic!*), joy-buzzers.

"I dunno," Mrs. Scooter said. "Where's the box, I wonder?"

The teeth were the only item in the case that wasn't packaged, but they certainly *were* jumbo, Hogan thought — *super*-jumbo, in fact, five times the size of the sets of wind-up teeth which had so amused him as a kid growing up in Maine. Take away the joke feet and they would look like the teeth of some fallen Biblical giant — the cuspids were big white blocks and the canine teeth looked like tentpegs sunk in the improbably red plastic gums. A key jutted from one gum. The teeth were held together in a clench by a thick rubber band.

Mrs. Scooter blew the dust from the Chattery Teeth, then turned them over, looking on the soles of the orange shoes for a price sticker. She didn't find one. "*I* don't know," she said crossly, eyeing Hogan as if he might have taken the sticker off himself. "Only Scooter'd buy a piece of trash like this here. Been around since Noah got off the boat. I'll have to ask him."

Hogan was suddenly tired of the woman and of Scooter's Grocery & Roadside Zoo. They were great Chattery Teeth, and Jack would undoubtedly love them, but he had promised — eight at the latest.

"Never mind," he said. "It was just an —"

"Them teeth was supposed to go for $15.95, if you c'n believe it," Scooter said from behind them. "They ain't just plastic — those're metal teeth painted white. They could give you a helluva bite if they worked . . . but she dropped em on the floor two-three years ago when she was dustin the inside of the case and they're busted."

246

"Oh," Hogan said, disappointed. "That's too bad. I never saw a pair with, you know, feet."

"There are lots of em like that now," Scooter said. "They sell em at the novelty stores in Vegas and Dry Springs. But I never saw a set as big as those. It was funnier'n hell to watch em walk across the floor, snappin like a crocodile. Shame the old lady dropped em."

Scooter glanced at her, but his wife was looking out at the blowing sand. There was an expression on her face which Hogan couldn't quite decipher — was it sadness, or disgust, or both?

Scooter looked back at Hogan. "I could let em go for three-fifty, if you wanted em. We're gettin rid of the novelties, anyway. Gonna put rental videotapes in that counter." He closed the storeroom door. The bandanna was now pulled down, lying on the dusty front of his shirt. His face was haggard and too thin. Hogan saw what might have been the shadow of serious illness lurking just beneath his desert tan.

"You could do no such a thing, Scooter!" the big woman snapped, and turned toward him . . . almost turned *on* him.

"Shutcha head," Scooter replied. "You make my fillins ache."

"I told you to get Wolf —"

"Myra, if you want him back there in the storeroom, go get him yourself." He began to advance on her, and Hogan was surprised — almost wonder-struck, in fact — when she gave ground. "Ain't nothin but a Minnesota coydog anyway. Three dollars even, friend, and those Chattery Teeth are yours. Throw in another buck and you

247

can take Myra's Woof, too. If you got five, I'll deed the whole place to you. Ain't worth a dogfart since the turnpike went through, anyway."

The long-haired kid was standing by the door, tearing the top from the pack of cigarettes Hogan had helped buy and watching this small comic opera with an expression of mean amusement. His small gray-green eyes gleamed, flicking back and forth between Scooter and his wife.

"Hell with you," Myra said gruffly, and Hogan realized she was close to tears. "If you won't get my sweet baby, I will." She stalked past him, almost striking him with one boulder-sized breast. Hogan thought it would have knocked the little man flat if it had connected.

"Look," Hogan said, "I think I'll just shove along."

"Aw, hell," Scooter said. "Don't mind Myra. I got cancer and she's got the change, and it ain't my problem she's havin the most trouble livin with. Take the darn teeth. Bet you got a boy might like em. Besides, it's probably just a cog knocked a little off-track. I bet a man who was handy could get em walkin and chompin again."

He looked around, his expression helpless and musing. Outside, the wind rose to a brief, thin shriek as the kid opened the door and slipped out. He had decided the show was over, apparently. A cloud of fine grit swirled down the middle aisle, between the canned goods and the dog food.

"I was pretty handy myself, at one time," Scooter confided.

Hogan did not reply for a long moment. He could not think of anything — quite literally not one single thing — to say. He looked down at the Jumbo Chattery Teeth standing on the scratched and cloudy display case, nearly desperate to break the silence (now that Scooter was standing right in front of him, he could see that the man's eyes were huge and dark, glittering with pain and some heavy dope . . . Darvon, or perhaps morphine), and he spoke the first words that popped into his head: "Gee, they don't *look* broken."

He picked the teeth up. They were metal, all right — too heavy to be anything else — and when he looked through the slightly parted jaws, he was surprised at the size of the mainspring that ran the thing. He supposed it would take one that size to make the teeth not only chatter but walk, as well. What had Scooter said? *They could give you a helluva bite if they worked.* Hogan gave the thick rubber band an experimental tweak, then stripped it off. He was still looking at the teeth so he wouldn't have to look into Scooter's dark, pain-haunted eyes. He grasped the key and at last he risked a look up. He was relieved to see that now the thin man was smiling a little.

"Do you mind?" Hogan asked.

"Not me, pilgrim — let er rip."

Hogan grinned and turned the key. At first it was all right; there was a series of small, ratcheting clicks, and he could see the mainspring winding up. Then, on the third turn, there was a *spronk!* noise from inside, and the key simply slid bonelessly around in its hole.

"See?"

"Yes," Hogan said. He set the teeth down on the counter. They stood there on their unlikely orange feet and did nothing.

Scooter poked the clenched molars on the left-hand side with the tip of one horny finger. The jaws of the teeth opened. One orange foot rose and took a dreamy half-step forward. Then the teeth stopped moving and the whole rig fell sideways. The Chattery Teeth came to rest on the wind-up key, a slanted, disembodied grin out here in the middle of no-man's-land. After a moment or two, the big teeth came together again with a slow click. That was all.

Hogan, who had never had a premonition in his life, was suddenly filled with a clear certainty that was both eerie and sickening. *A year from now, this man will have been eight months in his grave, and if someone exhumed his coffin and pried off the lid, they'd see teeth just like these poking out of his dried-out dead face like an enamel trap.*

He glanced up into Scooter's eyes, glittering like dark gems in tarnished settings, and suddenly it was no longer a question of *wanting* to get out of here; he *had* to get out of here.

"Well," he said (hoping frantically that Scooter would not stick out his hand to be shaken), "gotta go. Best of luck to you, sir."

Scooter *did* put his hand out, but not to be shaken. Instead, he snapped the rubber band back around the Chattery Teeth (Hogan had no idea why, since they didn't work), set them on their funny cartoon feet, and pushed them across the scratched surface of the counter. "Thank you kindly," he said. "And take these teeth. No charge."

"Oh . . . well, thanks, but I couldn't . . ."

"Sure you can," Scooter said. "Take em and give em to your boy. He'll get a kick out of em standin on the shelf in his room even if they don't work. I know a little about boys. Raised up three of em."

"How did you know I had a son?" Hogan asked.

Scooter winked. The gesture was terrifying and pathetic at the same time. "Seen it in your face," he said. "Go on, take em."

The wind gusted again, this time hard enough to make the boards of the building moan. The sand hitting the windows sounded like fine snow. Hogan picked the teeth up by the plastic feet, surprised all over again by how heavy they were.

"Here." Scooter produced a paper bag, almost as wrinkled and crumpled about the edges as his own face, from beneath the counter. "Stick em in here. That's a real nice sportcoat you got there. If you carry them choppers in the pocket, it'll get pulled out of shape."

He put the bag on the counter as if he understood how little Hogan wanted to touch him.

"Thanks," Hogan said. He put the Chattery Teeth in the bag and rolled down the top. "Jack thanks you, too — he's my son."

Scooter smiled, revealing a set of teeth just as false (but nowhere near as large) as the ones in the paper bag. "My pleasure, mister. You drive careful until you get out of the blow. You'll be fine once you get in the foothills."

"I know." Hogan cleared his throat. "Thanks again. I hope you . . . uh . . . recover soon."

"That'd be nice," Scooter said evenly, "but I don't think it's in the cards, do you?"

251

"Uh. Well." Hogan realized with dismay that he didn't have the slightest idea how to conclude this encounter. "Take care of yourself."

Scooter nodded. "You too."

Hogan retreated toward the door, opened it, and had to hold on tight as the wind tried to rip it out of his hand and bang the wall. Fine sand scoured his face and he slitted his eyes against it.

He stepped out, closed the door behind him, and pulled the lapel of his real nice sportcoat over his mouth and nose as he crossed the porch, descended the steps, and headed toward the customized Dodge camper-van parked just beyond the gas-pumps. The wind pulled his hair and the sand stung his cheeks. He was going around to the driver's-side door when someone tugged his arm.

"Mister! Hey, mister!"

He turned. It was the blonde-haired boy with the pale, ratty face. He hunched against the wind and blowing sand, wearing nothing but a tee-shirt and a pair of faded 501 jeans. Behind him, Mrs. Scooter was dragging a mangy beast on a choke-chain toward the back door of the store. Wolf the Minnesota coydog looked like a half-starved German shepherd pup — and the runt of the litter, at that.

"What?" Hogan shouted, knowing very well what.

"Can I have a ride?" the kid shouted back over the wind.

Hogan did not ordinarily pick up hitchhikers — not since one afternoon five years ago. He had stopped for a young girl on the outskirts of Tonopah. Standing by the side of the road, the

252

girl had resembled one of those sad-eyed waifs in the UNICEF posters, a kid who looked like her mother and her last friend had both died in the same housefire about a week ago. Once she was in the car, however, Hogan had seen the bad skin and mad eyes of the long-time junkie. By then it was too late. She'd stuck a pistol in his face and demanded his wallet. The pistol was old and rusty. Its grip was wrapped in tattered electrician's tape. Hogan had doubted that it was loaded, or that it would fire if it was . . . but he had a wife and a kid back in L.A., and even if he had been single, was a hundred and forty bucks worth risking your life over? He hadn't thought so even then, when he had just been getting his feet under him in his new line of work and a hundred and forty bucks had seemed a lot more important than it did these days. He gave the girl his wallet. By then her boyfriend had been parked beside the van (in those days it had been a Ford Econoline, nowhere near as nice as the custom Dodge XRT) in a dirty blue Chevy Nova. Hogan asked the girl if she would leave him his driver's license, and the pictures of Lita and Jack. "Fuck you, sugar," she said, and slapped him across the face, hard, with his own wallet before getting out and running to the blue car.

Hitchhikers were trouble.

But the storm was getting worse, and the kid didn't even have a jacket. What was he supposed to tell him? Fuck you, sugar, crawl under a rock with the rest of the lizards until the wind drops?

"Okay," Hogan said.

"Thanks, man! Thanks a lot!"

The kid ran toward the passenger door, tried it, found it locked, and just stood there, waiting to be let in, hunching his shoulders up around his ears. The wind billowed out the back of his shirt like a sail, revealing glimpses of his thin, pimple-studded back.

Hogan glanced back at Scooter's Grocery & Roadside Zoo as he went around to the driver's door. Scooter was standing at the window, looking out at him. He raised his hand, solemnly, palm out. Hogan raised his own in return, then slipped his key into the lock and turned it. He opened the door, pushed the unlock button next to the power window switch, and motioned for the kid to get in.

He did, then had to use both hands to pull the door shut again. The wind howled around the van, actually making it rock a little from side to side.

"*Wow!*" the kid gasped, and rubbed his fingers briskly through his hair (he'd lost the sneaker lace and the hair now lay on his shoulders in lank clots). "Some storm, huh? Big-time!"

"Yeah," Hogan said. There was a console between the two front seats — the kind of seats the brochures liked to call "captain's chairs" — and Hogan placed the paper bag in one of the cupholders. Then he turned the ignition key. The engine started at once with a good-tempered rumble.

The kid twisted around in his seat and looked appreciatively into the back of the van. There was a bed (now folded back into a couch), a small LP gas stove, several storage compartments where Hogan kept his various sample cases, and a toilet cubicle at the rear.

"Not too tacky, m'man!" the kid said. "All the comforts." He glanced back at Hogan. "Where you headed?"

"Los Angeles."

The kid grinned. "Hey, great! So'm I!" He took out his just-purchased pack of Merits and tapped one loose.

Hogan had put on his headlights and dropped the transmission into drive. Now he shoved the gearshift back into park and turned to the kid. "Let's get a couple of things straight," he said.

The kid gave Hogan his wide-eyed innocent look. "Sure, dude — no prob."

"First, I don't pick up hitchhikers as a rule. I had a bad experience with one a few years back. It vaccinated me, you might say. I'll take you through the Santa Clara foothills, but that's all. There's a truckstop on the other side — Sammy's. It's close to the turnpike. That's where we part company. Okay?"

"Okay. Sure. You bet." Still with the wide-eyed look.

"Second, if you really have to smoke, we part company right now. *That* okay?"

For just a moment Hogan saw the kid's other look (and even on short acquaintance, Hogan was almost willing to bet he only had two): the mean, watchful look. Then he was all wide-eyed innocence again, just a harmless refugee from Wayne's World. He tucked the cigarette behind his ear and showed Hogan his empty hands. As he raised them, Hogan noticed the hand-lettered tattoo on the kid's left bicep: DEF LEPPARD 4-EVER.

"No cigs," the kid said. "I got it."

255

"Fine. Bill Hogan." He held out his hand.

"Bryan Adams," the kid said, and shook Hogan's hand briefly.

Hogan dropped the transmission into drive again and began to roll slowly toward Route 46. As he did, his eyes dropped briefly to a cassette box lying on the dashboard. It was *Reckless,* by Bryan Adams.

Sure, he thought. *You're Bryan Adams and I'm really Don Henley. We just stopped by Scooter's Grocery & Roadside Zoo to get a little material for our next albums, right, dude?*

As he pulled out onto the highway, already straining to see through the blowing dust, he found himself thinking of the girl again, the one outside of Tonopah who had slapped him across the face with his own wallet before fleeing. He was starting to get a very bad feeling about this.

Then a hard gust of wind tried to push him into the eastbound lane, and he concentrated on his driving.

They rode in silence for awhile. When Hogan glanced once to his right he saw the kid was lying back with his eyes closed — maybe asleep, maybe dozing, maybe just pretending because he didn't want to talk. That was okay; Hogan didn't want to talk, either. For one thing, he didn't know what he might have to say to Mr. Bryan Adams from Nowhere, U.S.A. It was a cinch young Mr. Adams wasn't in the market for labels or Universal Product Code readers, which was what Hogan sold. For another, just keeping the van on the road had become something of a challenge.

As Mrs. Scooter had warned, the storm was intensifying. The road was a dim phantom crossed at irregular intervals by tan ribs of sand. These drifts were like speed-bumps, and they forced Hogan to creep along at no more than twenty-five. He could live with that. At some points, however, the sand had spread more evenly across the road's surface, camouflaging it, and then Hogan had to drop down to fifteen miles an hour, navigating by the dim bounceback of his headlights from the reflector-posts which marched along the side of the road.

Every now and then an approaching car or truck would loom out of the blowing sand like a prehistoric phantom with round blazing eyes. One of these, an old Lincoln Mark IV as big as a cabin cruiser, was driving straight down the center of 46. Hogan hit the horn and squeezed right, feeling the suck of the sand against his tires, feeling his lips peel away from his teeth in a helpless snarl. Just as he became sure the oncomer was going to force him into the ditch, the Lincoln swerved back onto its own side just enough for Hogan to make it by. He thought he heard the metallic click of his bumper kissing off the Mark IV's rear bumper, but given the steady shriek of the wind, that was almost certainly his own imagination. He *did* catch just a glimpse of the driver — an old bald-headed man sitting bolt-upright behind the wheel, peering into the blowing sand with a concentrated glare that was almost maniacal. Hogan shook his fist at him, but the old codger did not so much as glance at him. *Probably didn't even realize I was there,* Hogan thought, *let alone how close he came to hitting me.*

For a few seconds he was very close to going off the road anyway. He could feel the sand sucking harder at the rightside wheels, felt the van trying to tip. His instinct was to twist the wheel hard to the left. Instead, he fed the van gas and only urged it in that direction, feeling sweat dampen his last good shirt at the armpits. At last the suck on the tires diminished and he began to feel in control of the van again. Hogan blew his breath out in a long sigh.

"Good piece of driving, man."

His attention had been so focused he had forgotten his passenger, and in his surprise he almost twisted the wheel all the way to the left, which would have put them in trouble again. He looked around and saw the blonde kid watching him. His gray-green eyes were unsettlingly bright; there was no sign of sleepiness in them.

"It was really just luck," Hogan said. "If there was a place to pull over, I would . . . but I know this piece of road. It's Sammy's or bust. Once we're in the foothills, it'll get better."

He did not add that it might take them three hours to cover the seventy miles between here and there.

"You're a salesman, right?"

"As rain."

He wished the kid wouldn't talk. He wanted to concentrate on his driving. Up ahead, fog-lights loomed out of the murk like yellow ghosts. They were followed by an Iroc Z with California plates. The van and the Z crept past each other like old ladies in a nursing-home corridor. In the corner

258

of his eye, Hogan saw the kid take the cigarette from behind his ear and begin to play with it. Bryan Adams indeed. Why had the kid given him a false name? It was like something out of an old Republic movie, the kind of thing you could still see on the late-late show, a black-and-white crime movie where the travelling salesman (probably played by Ray Milland) picks up the tough young con (played by Nick Adams, say) who has just broken out of jail in Gabbs or Deeth or some place like that —

"What do you sell, dude?"

"Labels."

"Labels?"

"That's right. The ones with the Universal Product Code on them. It's a little block with a pre-set number of black bars in it."

The kid surprised Hogan by nodding. "Sure — they whip em over an electric-eye gadget in the supermarket and the price shows up on the cash register like magic, right?"

"Yes. Except it's not magic, and it's not an electric eye. It's a laser reader. I sell those, too. Both the big ones and the portables."

"Far out, dude-mar." The tinge of sarcasm in the kid's voice was faint . . . but it was there.

"Bryan?"

"Yeah?"

"The name's Bill, not m'man, not dude, and most certainly not dude-mar."

He found himself wishing more and more strongly that he could roll back in time to Scooter's, and just say no when the kid asked him for a ride. The Scooters weren't bad sorts; they

259

would have let the kid stay until the storm blew itself out this evening. Maybe Mrs. Scooter would even have given him five bucks to babysit the tarantula, the rattlers, and Woof, the Amazing Minnesota Coydog. Hogan found himself liking those gray-green eyes less and less. He could feel their weight on his face, like small stones.

"Yeah — Bill. Bill the Label Dude."

Bill didn't reply. The kid laced his fingers together and bent his hands backward, cracking the knuckles.

"Well, it's like my old mamma used to say — it may not be much, but it's a living. Right, Label Dude?"

Hogan grunted something noncommittal and concentrated on his driving. The feeling that he had made a mistake had grown to a certainty. When he'd picked up the girl that time, God had let him get away with it. *Please*, he prayed. *One more time, okay, God? Better yet, let me be wrong about this kid — let it just be paranoia brought on by low barometer, high winds, and the coincidence of a name that can't, after all, be that uncommon.*

Here came a huge Mack truck from the other direction, the silver bulldog atop the grille seeming to peer into the flying grit. Hogan squeezed right until he felt the sand piled up along the edge of the road grabbing greedily at his tires again. The long silver box the Mack was pulling blotted out everything on Hogan's left side. It was six inches away — maybe even less — and it seemed to pass forever.

When it was finally gone, the blonde kid asked: "You look like you're doin pretty well, Bill —

rig like this must have set you back at least thirty big ones. So why —"

"It was a lot less than that." Hogan didn't know if "Bryan Adams" could hear the edgy note in his voice, but *he* sure could. "I did a lot of the work myself."

"All the same, you sure ain't staggerin around hungry. So why aren't you up above all this shit, flyin the friendly skies?"

It was a question Hogan sometimes asked himself in the long empty miles between Tempe and Tucson or Las Vegas and Los Angeles, the kind of question you *had* to ask yourself when you couldn't find anything on the radio but crappy synthopop or threadbare oldies and you'd listened to the last cassette of the current best-seller from Recorded Books, when there was nothing to look at but miles of gullywashes and scrubland, all of it owned by Uncle Sam.

He could say that he got a better feel for his customers and their needs by travelling through the country where they lived and sold their goods, and it was true, but it wasn't the reason. He could say that checking his sample cases, which were much too bulky to fit under an airline seat, was a pain in the ass and waiting for them to show up on the conveyor belt at the other end was always an adventure (he'd once had a packing case filled with five thousand soft-drink labels show up in Hilo, Hawaii, instead of Hillside, Arizona). That was *also* true, but it also wasn't the reason.

The reason was that in 1982 he had been on board a Western Pride commuter flight which had crashed in the high country seventeen miles north of Reno. Six of the nineteen passengers on board and both crew-members had been killed. Hogan had suffered a broken back. He had spent four months in bed and another ten in a heavy brace his wife Lita called the Iron Maiden. They (whoever *they* were) said that if you got thrown from a horse, you should get right back on. William I. Hogan said that was bullshit, and with the exception of a white-knuckle, two-Valium flight to attend his father's funeral in New York, he had never been on a plane since.

He came out of these thoughts all at once, realizing two things: he had had the road to himself since the passage of the Mack, and the kid was still looking at him with those unsettling eyes, waiting for him to answer the question.

"I had a bad experience on a commuter flight once," he said. "Since then, I've pretty much stuck to transport where you can coast into the breakdown lane if your engine quits."

"You sure have had a lot of bad experiences, Bill-dude," the kid said. A tone of bogus regret crept into his voice. "And now, so sorry, you're about to have another one." There was a sharp metallic click. Hogan looked over and was not very surprised to see the kid was holding a switchknife with a glittering eight-inch blade.

Oh shit, Hogan thought. Now that it was here, now that it was right in front of him, he didn't feel very scared. Only tired. *Oh shit, and only four hundred miles from home. Goddam.*

"Pull over, Bill-dude. Nice and slow."

"What do you want?"

"If you really don't know the answer to that

262

one, you're even dumber than you look." A little smile played around the corners of the kid's mouth. The homemade tattoo on the kid's arm rippled as the muscle beneath it twitched. "I want your dough, and I guess I want your rolling whore-house too, at least for awhile. But don't worry — there's this little truckstop not too far from here. Sammy's. Close to the turnpike. Someone'll give you a ride. The people who don't stop will look at you like you're dogshit they found on their shoes, of course, and you might have to beg a little, but I'm sure you'll get a ride in the end. Now *pull over.*"

Hogan was a little surprised to find that he felt angry as well as tired. Had he been angry that other time, when the road-girl had stolen his wallet? He couldn't honestly remember.

"Don't pull that shit on me," he said, turning to the kid. "I gave you a ride when you needed one, and I didn't make you beg for it. If it wasn't for me, you'd still be eating sand with your thumb out. So why don't you just put that thing away. We'll —"

The kid suddenly lashed forward with the knife, and Hogan felt a thread of burning pain across his right hand. The van swerved, then shuddered as it passed over another of those sandy speed-bumps.

"Pull *over*, I said. You're either walking, Label Dude, or you're lying in the nearest gully with your throat cut and one of your own price-reading gadgets jammed up your ass. And you wanna know something? I'm gonna chain-smoke all the way to Los Angeles, and every time I finish a cigarette

I'm gonna butt it out on your fuckin dashboard."

Hogan glanced down at his hand and saw a diagonal line of blood which stretched from the last knuckle of his pinky to the base of his thumb. And here was the anger again . . . only now it was really rage, and if the tiredness was still there, it was buried somewhere in the middle of that irrational red eye. He tried to summon a mental picture of Lita and Jack to damp that feeling down before it got the better of him and made him do something crazy, but the images were fuzzy and out of focus. There *was* a clear image in his mind, but it was the wrong one — it was the face of the girl outside of Tonopah, the girl with the snarling mouth below the sad poster-child eyes, the girl who had said *Fuck you, sugar* before slapping him across the face with his own wallet.

He stepped down on the gas-pedal and the van began to move faster. The red needle moved past thirty.

The kid looked surprised, then puzzled, then angry. "What are you doing? I told you to pull over! Do you want your guts in your lap, or what?"

"I don't know," Hogan said. He kept his foot on the gas. Now the needle was trembling just above forty. The van ran across a series of dunelets and shivered like a dog with a fever. "What do *you* want, kid? How about a broken neck? All it takes is one twist of the wheel. I fastened *my* seatbelt. I notice you forgot yours."

The kid's gray-green eyes were huge now, glittering with a mixture of fear and fury. You're supposed to pull over, those eyes said. That's the way it's supposed to work when I'm holding a knife on you — don't you *know* that?

"You won't wreck us," the kid said, but Hogan thought he was trying to convince himself.

"Why not?" Hogan turned toward the kid again. "After all, I'm pretty sure I'll walk away, and the van's insured. You call the play, asshole. What about that?"

"You —" the kid began, and then his eyes widened and he lost all interest in Hogan. *"Look out!"* he screamed.

Hogan snapped his eyes forward and saw four huge white headlamps bearing down on him through the flying wrack outside. It was a tanker truck, probably carrying gasoline or propane. An air-horn beat the air like the cry of a gigantic, enraged goose: *WHONK! WHONK! WHONNNK!*

The van had drifted while Hogan was trying to deal with the kid; now *he* was the one halfway across the road. He yanked the wheel hard to the right, knowing it would do no good, knowing it was already too late. But the approaching truck was also moving, squeezing over just as Hogan had tried to squeeze over in order to accommodate the Mark IV. The two vehicles danced past each other though the blowing sand with less than a gasp between them. Hogan felt his rightside wheels bite into the sand again and knew that this time he didn't have a chance in hell of holding the van on the road — not at forty-plus miles an hour. As the dim shape of the big steel tank (CARTER'S FARM SUPPLIES & ORGANIC FERTILIZER was painted along the side) slid from view, he felt the steering wheel go mushy in his hands, dragging farther to the right. And from the corner of his eye, he saw the kid leaning forward with his knife.

What's the matter with you, are you crazy? he wanted to scream at the kid, but it would have been a stupid question even if he'd had time enough to articulate it. Sure the kid was crazy — you only had to take a good look into those gray-green eyes to see it. Hogan must have been crazy himself to give the kid a ride in the first place, but none of that mattered now; he had a situation to cope with here, and if he allowed himself the luxury of believing this couldn't be happening to him — if he allowed himself to think that for even a single second — he would probably be found tomorrow or the next day with his throat cut and his eyes nibbled out of their sockets by the buzzards. This was really happening; it was a true thing.

The kid tried his level best to plant the blade in Hogan's neck, but the van had begun to tilt by then, running deeper and deeper into the sand-choked gully. Hogan recoiled back from the blade, letting go of the wheel entirely, and thought he had gotten clear until he felt the wet warmth of blood drench the side of his neck. The knife had unzipped his right cheek from jaw to temple. He flailed with his right hand, trying to get the kid's wrist, and then the van's left front wheel struck a rock the size of a pay telephone and the van flipped high and hard, like a stunt vehicle in one of those movies this rootless kid undoubtedly loved. It rolled in midair, all four wheels turning, still doing thirty miles an hour according to the speedometer, and Hogan felt his seatbelt lock painfully across his chest and belly. It was like reliving the plane-crash — now, as then, he could not get it through his head that this was really happening.

The kid was thrown upward and forward, still holding onto the knife. His head bounced off the roof as the van's top and bottom swapped places. Hogan saw his left hand waving wildly, and realized with amazement that the kid was *still* trying to stab him. He was a rattler, all right, Hogan had been right about that, but no one had milked his poison sacs.

Then the van struck the desert hardpan, peeling off the luggage racks, and the kid's head connected with the roof again, much harder this time. The knife was jolted from his hand. The cabinets at the rear of the van sprang open, spraying sample-books and laser label-readers everywhere. Hogan was dimly aware of an inhuman screaming sound — the long, drawn-out squall of the XRT's roof sliding across the gravelly desert surface on the far side of the gully — and thought: *So this is what it would be like to be inside a tin can when someone was using the opener.*

The windshield shattered, blowing inward in a sagging shield clouded by a million zig-zagging cracks. Hogan shut his eyes and threw his hands up to shield his face as the van continued to roll, thumping down on Hogan's side long enough to shatter the driver's-side window and admit a rattle of rocks and dusty earth before staggering upright again. It rocked as if meaning to go over on the kid's side . . . and then came to rest.

Hogan sat where he was without moving for perhaps five seconds, eyes wide, hands gripping the armrests of his chair, feeling a little like Captain

Kirk in the aftermath of a Klingon attack. He was aware there was a lot of dirt and crumbled glass in his lap, and something else as well, but not what the something else was. He was also aware of the wind, blowing more dirt through the van's broken windows.

Then his vision was temporarily blocked by a swiftly moving object. The object was a mottle of white skin, brown dirt, raw knuckles, and red blood. It was a fist, and it struck Hogan squarely in the nose. The agony was immediate and intense, as if someone had fired a flare-gun directly into his brain. For a moment his vision was gone, swallowed in a vast white flash. It had just begun to come back when the kid's hands suddenly clamped around his neck and he could no longer breathe.

The kid, Mr. Bryan Adams from Nowhere, U.S.A., was leaning over the console between the front seats. Blood from perhaps half a dozen different scalp-wounds had flowed over his cheeks and forehead and nose like warpaint. His gray-green eyes stared at Hogan with fixed, lunatic fury.

"Look what you did, you fuck!" the kid shouted. *"Look what you did to me!"*

Hogan tried to pull back, and got half a breath when the kid's hold slipped momentarily, but with his seatbelt still buckled — and still locked down as well, from the feel — there was really nowhere he could go. The kid's hands were back almost at once, and this time his thumbs were pressing into his windpipe, pinching it shut.

Hogan tried to bring his own hands up, but the kid's arms, as rigid as prison bars, blocked him. He tried to knock the kid's arms away, but they

268

wouldn't budge. Now he could hear another wind — a high, roaring wind inside his own head.

"Look what you did, you stupid shit! I'm bleedin!"

The kid's voice, but farther away than it had been.

He's killing me, Hogan thought, and a voice replied: *Right — fuck you, sugar.*

That brought the anger back. He groped in his lap for whatever was there besides dirt and glass. It was a paper bag with some bulky object — Hogan couldn't remember exactly what — inside it. Hogan closed his hand around it and pistoned his fist upward toward the shelf of the kid's jaw. It connected with a heavy thud. The kid screamed in surprised pain, and his grip on Hogan's throat was suddenly gone as he fell over backward.

Hogan pulled in a deep, convulsive breath and heard a sound like a teakettle howling to be taken off the burner. *Is that me, making that sound? My God, is that me?*

He dragged in another breath. It was full of flying dust, it hurt his throat and made him cough, but it was heaven all the same. He looked down at his fist and saw the shape of the Chattery Teeth clearly outlined against the brown bag.

And suddenly felt them *move.*

There was something so shockingly human in this movement that Hogan shrieked and dropped the bag at once; it was as if he had picked up a human jawbone which had tried to speak to his hand.

The bag hit the kid's back and then tumbled to the van's carpeted floor as "Bryan Adams" pushed himself groggily to his knees. Hogan heard

269

the rubber band snap . . . and then the unmistakable click-and-chutter of the teeth themselves, opening and closing.

It's probably just a cog knocked a little off-track, Scooter had said. *I bet a man who was handy could get em walkin and chompin again.*

Or maybe just a good knock would do it, Hogan thought. *If I live through this and ever get back that way, I'll have to tell Scooter that all you have to do to fix a pair of malfunctioning Chattery Teeth is roll your van over and then use them to hit a psychotic hitchhiker who's trying to strangle you: so simple even a child could do it.*

The teeth clattered and smacked inside the torn brown bag; the sides fluttered, making it look like an amputated lung which refused to die. The kid crawled away from the bag without even looking at it — crawled toward the back of the van, shaking his head from side to side, trying to clear it. Blood flew from the clots of his hair in a fine spray.

Hogan found the clasp of his seatbelt and pushed the pop-release. Nothing happened. The square in the center of the buckle did not give even a little and the belt itself was still locked as tight as a cramp, cutting into the middle-aged roll of fat above the waistband of his trousers and pushing a hard diagonal across his chest. He tried rocking back and forth in the seat, hoping that would unlock the belt. The flow of blood from his face increased, and he could feel his cheek flapping back and forth like a strip of dried wallpaper, but that was all. He felt panic struggling to break through amazed shock, and twisted his head over his right shoulder to see what the kid was up to.

It turned out to be no good. He had spotted his knife at the far end of the van, lying atop a litter of instructional manuals and brochures. He grabbed it, flicked his hair away from his face, and peered back over his own shoulder at Hogan. He was grinning, and there was something in that grin that made Hogan's balls simultaneously tighten and shrivel until it felt as if someone had tucked a couple of peach-pits into his Jockey shorts.

Ah, here it is! the kid's grin said. *For a minute or two there I was worried — quite seriously worried — but everything is going to come out all right after all. Things got a little improvisational there for awhile, but now we're back to the script.*

"You stuck, Label Dude?" the kid asked over the steady shriek of the wind. "You are, ain't you? Good thing you buckled your belt, right? Good thing for me."

The kid tried to get up, almost made it, and then his knees gave way. An expression of surprise so magnified it would have been comic under other circumstances crossed his face. Then he flicked his blood-greasy hair out of his face again and began to crawl toward Hogan, his left hand wrapped around the imitation-bone handle of the knife. The Def Leppard tattoo ebbed and flowed with each flex of his impoverished bicep, making Hogan think of the way the words on Myra's tee-shirt — NEVADA IS GOD'S COUNTRY — had rippled when she moved.

Hogan grasped the seatbelt buckle with both hands and drove his thumbs against the pop-release as enthusiastically as the kid had driven his

271

into Hogan's windpipe. There was absolutely no response. The belt was frozen. He craned his neck to look at the kid again.

The kid had made it as far as the fold-up bed and then stopped. That expression of large, comic surprise had resurfaced on his face. He was staring straight ahead, which meant he was looking at something on the floor, and Hogan suddenly remembered the teeth. They were still chattering away.

He looked down in time to see the Jumbo Chattery Teeth march from the open end of the torn paper bag on their funny orange shoes. The molars and the canines and the incisors chopped rapidly up and down, producing a sound like ice in a cocktail-shaker. The shoes, dressed up in their tony white spats, almost seemed to *bounce* along the gray carpet. Hogan found himself thinking of Fred Astaire tap-dancing his way across a stage and back again, Fred Astaire with a cane tucked under his arm and a straw boater tipped saucily forward over one eye.

"Oh shit!" the kid said, half-laughing. "Is *that* what you were dickerin for back there? Oh, man! I kill *you*, Label Dude, I'm gonna be doin the world a favor."

The key, Hogan thought. *The key on the side of the teeth, the one you use to wind them up . . . it isn't turning.*

And he suddenly had another of those precognitive flashes; he understood exactly what was going to happen. The kid was going to reach for them.

The teeth abruptly stopped walking and chattering. They simply stood there on the slightly tilted floor of the van, jaws slightly agape. Eyeless, they still seemed to peer quizzically up at the kid.

"Chattery Teeth," Mr. Bryan Adams, from Nowhere, U.S.A., marvelled. He reached out and curled his right hand around them, just as Hogan had known he would.

"Bite him!" Hogan shrieked. "Bite his fucking fingers *right off!*"

The kid's head snapped up, the gray-green eyes wide with startlement. He gaped at Hogan for a moment — that big expression of totally dumb surprise — and then he began to laugh. His laughter was high and shrieky, a perfect complement to the wind howling through the van and billowing the curtains like long ghost-hands.

"Bite me! *Bite* me! *Biiiite me!*" the kid chanted, as if it were the punchline to the funniest joke he'd ever heard. "Hey, Label Dude! I thought *I* was the one who bumped my head!"

The kid clamped the handle of the switchblade in his own teeth and stuck the forefinger of his left hand between the Jumbo Chattery Teeth. *"Ite ee!"* he said around the knife. He giggled and wiggled his finger between the oversized jaws. *"Ite ee! Oh on, ite ee!"*

The teeth didn't move. Neither did the orange feet. Hogan's premonition collapsed around him the way dreams do upon waking. The kid wiggled his finger between the Chattery Teeth one more time, began to pull it out . . . then began screaming at the top of his lungs. *"Oh shit! SHIT! MotherFUCKER!"*

For a moment Hogan's heart leaped in his chest,

and then he realized that, although the kid was still screaming, what he was really doing was *laughing*. Laughing at him. The teeth had remained perfectly still the whole time.

The kid lifted the teeth up for a closer look as he grasped his knife again. He shook the long blade at the Chattery Teeth like a teacher shaking his pointer at a naughty student. "You shouldn't bite," he said. "That's very bad behav—"

One of the orange feet took a sudden step forward on the grimy palm of the kid's hand. The jaws opened at the same time, and before Hogan was fully aware of what was happening, the Chattery Teeth had closed on the kid's nose.

This time Bryan Adams's scream was real — a thing of agony and ultimate surprise. He flailed at the teeth with his right hand, trying to bat them away, but they were locked on his nose as tightly as Hogan's seatbelt was locked around his middle. Blood and filaments of torn gristle burst out between the canines in red strings. The kid jack-knifed backward and for a moment Hogan could see only his flailing body, lashing elbows, and kicking feet. Then he saw the glitter of the knife.

The kid screamed again and bolted into a sitting position. His long hair had fallen over his face in a curtain; the clamped teeth stuck out like the rudder of some strange boat. The kid had somehow managed to insert the blade of his knife between the teeth and what remained of his nose.

"Kill him!" Hogan shouted hoarsely. He had lost his mind; on some level he understood that he *must* have lost his mind, but for the time being, that didn't matter. "*Go on, kill him!*"

The kid shrieked — a long, piercing firewhistle sound — and twisted the knife. The blade snapped, but not before it had managed to pry the disembodied jaws at least partway open. The teeth fell off his face and into his lap. Most of the kid's nose fell off with them.

The kid shook his hair back. His gray-green eyes were crossed, trying to look down at the mangled stump in the middle of his face. His mouth was drawn down in a rictus of pain; the tendons in his neck stood out like pulley-wires.

The kid reached for the teeth. The teeth stepped nimbly backward on their orange cartoon feet. They were nodding up and down, marching in place, grinning at the kid, who was now sitting with his ass on his calves. Blood drenched the front of his tee-shirt.

The kid said something then that confirmed Hogan's belief that he, Hogan, had lost his mind; only in a fantasy born of delirium would such words be spoken.

"Give bme bag by *dose,* you sud-of-a-bidtch!"

The kid reached for the teeth again and this time they ran *forward,* under his snatching hand, between his spread legs, and there was a meaty *chump!* sound as they closed on the bulge of faded blue denim just below the place where the zipper of the kid's jeans ended.

Bryan Adams's eyes flew wide open. So did his mouth. His hands rose to the level of his shoulders, springing wide open, and for a moment he looked like some strange Al Jolson imitator preparing to sing "Mammy." The switchknife flew over his shoulder to the back of the van.

"*Jesus! Jesus! Jeeeeeee—*"

The orange feet were pumping rapidly, as if doing a Highland Fling. The pink jaws of the Jumbo Chattery Teeth nodded rapidly up and down, as if saying *yes! yes! yes!* and then shook back and forth, just as rapidly, as if saying *no! no! no!*

"*— eeeeeeEEEEEEEE —*"

As the cloth of the kid's jeans began to rip — and that was not all that was ripping, by the sound — Bill Hogan passed out.

He came to twice. The first time must have been only a short while later, because the storm was still howling through and around the van, and the light was about the same. He started to turn around, but a monstrous bolt of pain shot up his neck. Whiplash, of course, and probably not as bad as it could have been . . . or would be tomorrow, for that matter.

Always supposing he lived until tomorrow.

The kid. I have to look and make sure he's dead.

No, you don't. Of course he's dead. If he wasn't, you would be.

Now he began to hear a new sound from behind him — the steady chutter-click-chutter of the teeth.

They're coming for me. They've finished with the kid, but they're still hungry, so they're coming for me.

He placed his hands on the seatbelt buckle again, but the pop-release was still hopelessly jammed, and his hands seemed to have no strength, anyway.

The teeth grew steadily closer — they were right

276

in back of his seat, now, from the sound — and Hogan's confused mind read a rhyme into their ceaseless chomping: *Clickety-clickety-clickety-clack! We are the teeth, and we're coming back! Watch us walk, watch us chew, we ate him, now we'll eat you!*

Hogan closed his eyes.

The clittering sound stopped.

Now there was only the ceaseless whine of the wind and the *spick-spack* of sand striking the dented side of the XRT van.

Hogan waited. After a long, long time, he heard a single click, followed by the minute sound of tearing fibers. There was a pause, then the click and the tearing sound was repeated.

What's it doing?

The third time the click and the small tearing sound came, he felt the back of his seat moving a little and understood. The teeth were pulling themselves up to where he was. Somehow they were pulling themselves up to him.

Hogan thought of the teeth closing on the bulge below the zipper of the kid's jeans and willed himself to pass out again. Sand flew in through the broken windshield, tickled his cheeks and forehead.

Click . . . rip. Click . . . rip. Click . . . rip.

The last one was very close. Hogan didn't want to look down, but he was unable to help himself. And beyond his right hip, where the seat-cushion met the seat's back, he saw a wide white grin. It moved upward with agonizing slowness, pushing with the as-yet-unseen orange feet as it nipped a small fold of gray seat-cover between its incisors

. . . then the jaws let go and it lurched convulsively upward.

This time what the teeth fastened on was the pocket of Hogan's slacks, and he passed out again.

When he came to the second time, the wind had dropped and it was almost dark; the air had taken on a queer purple shade Hogan could not remember ever having seen in the desert before. The skirls of sand running across the desert floor beyond the sagging ruin of the windshield looked like fleeing ghost-children.

For a moment he could remember nothing at all of what had happened to land him here; the last clear memory he could touch was of looking at his gas-gauge, seeing it was down to an eighth, then looking up and seeing a sign at the side of the road which said SCOOTER'S GROCERY & ROADSIDE · ZOO · GAS · SNAX · COLD BEER · *SEE LIVE RATLLESNAKE'S!*

He understood that he could hold onto this amnesia for awhile, if he wanted to; given a little time, his subconscious might even be able to wall off certain dangerous memories permanently. But it could also be dangerous *not* to remember. *Very dangerous.* Because —

The wind gusted. Sand rattled against the badly dented driver's side of the van. It sounded almost like

(*teeth! teeth! teeth!*)

The fragile surface of his amnesia shattered, letting everything pour through, and all the heat fell from the surface of Hogan's skin. He uttered a rusty squawk as he remembered the sound

(*chump!*)

the Chattery Teeth had made as they closed on the kid's balls, and he closed his hands over his own crotch, eyes rolling fearfully in their sockets as he looked for the runaway teeth.

He didn't see them, but the ease with which his shoulders followed the movement of his hands was new. He looked down at his lap and slowly removed his hands from his crotch. His seatbelt was no longer holding him prisoner. It lay on the gray carpet in two pieces. The metal tongue of the pull-up section was still buried inside the buckle, but beyond it there was only ragged red fabric. The belt had not been cut; it had been gnawed through.

He looked up into the rear-view mirror and saw something else: the back doors of the van were standing open, and there was only a vague, man-shaped red outline on the gray carpet where the kid had been. Mr. Bryan Adams, from Nowhere, U.S.A., was gone.

So were the Chattery Teeth.

Hogan got out of the van slowly, like an old man afflicted with a terrible case of arthritis. He found that if he held his head perfectly level, it wasn't too bad . . . but if he forgot and moved it in any direction, a series of exploding bolts went off in his neck, shoulders, and upper back. Even the thought of allowing his head to roll backward was unbearable.

He walked slowly to the rear of the van, running his hand lightly over the dented, paint-peeled surface, hearing and feeling the glass as it crunched under his feet. He stood at the far end of the driver's side for a long time. He was afraid to turn the corner. He was afraid that, when he did, he would see the kid squatting on his hunkers, holding the knife in his left hand and grinning that empty grin. But he couldn't just stand here, holding his head on top of his strained neck like a big bottle of nitroglycerine, while it got dark around him, so at last Hogan went around.

Nobody. The kid was really gone. Or so it seemed at first.

The wind gusted, blowing Hogan's hair around his bruised face, then dropped away completely. When it did, he heard a harsh scraping noise coming from about twenty yards beyond the van. He looked in that direction and saw the soles of the kid's sneakers just disappearing over the top of a dry-wash. The sneakers were spread in a limp V. They stopped moving for a moment, as if whatever was hauling the kid's body needed a few moments' rest to recoup its strength, and then they began to move again in little jerks.

A picture of terrible, unendurable clarity suddenly rose in Hogan's mind. He saw the Jumbo Chattery Teeth standing on their funny orange feet just over the edge of that wash, standing there in spats so cool they made the coolest of the California Raisins look like hicks from Fargo, North Dakota, standing there in the electric purple light which had overspread these empty lands west of Las Vegas. They were clamped shut on a thick wad of the kid's long blonde hair.

The Chattery Teeth were backing up.

The Chattery Teeth were dragging Mr. Bryan Adams away to Nowhere, U.S.A.

Hogan turned in the other direction and walked slowly toward the road, holding his nitro head straight and steady on top of his neck. It took him five minutes to negotiate the ditch and another fifteen to flag a ride, but he eventually managed both things. And during that time, he never looked back once.

Nine months later, on a clear hot summer day in June, Bill Hogan happened by Scooter's Grocery & Roadside Zoo again . . . except the place had been renamed. MYRA'S PLACE, the sign now said. GAS · COLD BEER · VIDEO'S. Below the words was a picture of a wolf — or maybe just a Woof — snarling at the moon. Wolf himself, the Amazing Minnesota Coydog, was lying in a cage in the shade of the porch overhang. His back legs were sprawled extravagantly, and his muzzle was on his paws. He did not get up when Hogan got out of his car to fill the tank. Of the rattlesnakes and the tarantula there was no sign.

"Hi, Woof," he said as he went up the steps. The cage's inmate rolled over onto his back and allowed his long red tongue to dangle enticingly from the side of his mouth as he stared up at Hogan.

The store looked bigger and cleaner inside. Hogan guessed this was partly because the day outside was not so threatening, but that wasn't all; the windows had been washed, for one thing, and that made a big difference. The board walls had been replaced with pine-panelling that still smelled fresh and sappy. A snackbar with five stools had been added at the back. The novelty case was still there, but the cigarette loads, the joy-buzzers, and Dr. Wacky's Sneezing Powder were gone. The case was filled with videotape boxes. A hand-lettered sign read X-RATED IN BACK ROOM · "B 18 OR B GONE."

The woman at the cash register was standing in profile to Hogan, looking down at a calculator and running numbers on it. For a moment Hogan was sure this was Mr. and Mrs. Scooter's daughter — the female complement to those three boys Scooter had talked about raising. Then she lifted her head and Hogan saw it was Mrs. Scooter herself. It was hard to believe this could be the woman whose mammoth bosom had almost burst the seams of her NEVADA IS GOD'S COUNTRY tee-shirt, but it was. Mrs. Scooter had lost at least fifty pounds and dyed her hair a sleek and shiny walnut-brown. Only the sun-wrinkles around the eyes and mouth were the same.

"Getcha gas?" she asked.

"Yep. Fifteen dollars' worth." He handed her a twenty and she rang it up. "Place looks a lot different from the last time I was in."

"Been a lot of changes since Scooter died, all right," she agreed, and pulled a five out of the register. She started to hand it over, really looked at him for the first time, and hesitated. "Say . . . ain't you the guy who almost got killed the day we had that storm last year?"

He nodded and stuck out his hand. "Bill Hogan."

She didn't hesitate; simply reached over the

counter and gave his hand a single strong pump. The death of her husband seemed to have improved her disposition . . . or maybe it was just that her change of life was finally over.

"I'm sorry about your husband. He seemed like a good sort."

"Scoot? Yeah, he was a fine fella before he took ill," she agreed. "And what about you? You all recovered?"

Hogan nodded. "I wore a neck-brace for about six weeks — not for the first time, either — but I'm okay."

She was looking at the scar which twisted down his right cheek. "He do that? That kid?"

"Yeah."

"Stuck you pretty bad."

"Yeah."

"I heard he got busted up in the crash, then crawled into the desert to die." She was looking at Hogan shrewdly. "That about right?"

Hogan smiled a little. "Near enough, I guess."

"J.T. — he's the State Bear around these parts — said the animals worked him over pretty good. Desert rats are awful impolite that way."

"I don't know anything about that part."

"J.T. said the kid's own mother wouldn't have reckanized him." She put a hand on her reduced bosom and looked at him earnestly. "If I'm lyin, I'm dyin."

Hogan laughed out loud. In the weeks and months since the day of the storm, this was something he found himself doing more often. He had come, it sometimes seemed to him, to a slightly different arrangement with life since that day.

"Lucky he didn't kill you," Mrs. Scooter said. "You had a helluva narrow excape. God musta been with you."

"That's right," Hogan agreed. He looked down at the video case. "I see you took out the novelties."

"Them nasty old things? You bet! That was the first thing I did after —" Her eyes suddenly widened. "Oh, say! Jeepers! I got sumpin belongs to you! If I was to forget, I reckon Scooter'd come back and haunt me!"

Hogan frowned, puzzled, but the woman was already going behind the counter. She stood on tiptoe and brought something down from a high shelf above the rack of cigarettes. It was, Hogan saw with absolutely no surprise at all, the Jumbo Chattery Teeth. The woman set them down beside the cash register.

Hogan stared at that frozen, insouciant grin with a deep sense of *déjà vu*. There they were, the world's biggest set of Chattery Teeth, standing on their funny orange shoes beside the Slim Jim display, cool as a mountain breeze, grinning up at him as if to say, *Hello, there! Did you forget me? I didn't forget YOU, my friend. Not at all.*

"I found em on the porch the next day, after the storm blew itself out," Mrs. Scooter said. She laughed. "Just like old Scoot to give you somethin for free, then stick it in a bag with a hole in the bottom. I was gonna throw em out, but he said he give em to you, and I should stick em on a shelf someplace. He said a travelling man who came in once'd most likely come in again . . . and here you are."

284

"Yes," Hogan agreed. "Here I am."

He picked up the teeth and slipped his finger between the slightly gaping jaws. He ran the pad of the finger along the molars at the back, and in his mind he heard the kid, Mr. Bryan Adams from Nowhere, U.S.A., chanting *Bite me! Bite me! Biiiiite me!*

Were the back teeth still streaked with the dull rust of the boy's blood? Hogan thought he could see *something* way back in there, but perhaps it was only a shadow.

"I saved it because Scooter said you had a boy."

Hogan nodded. "I do." *And,* he thought, *the boy still has a father. I'm holding the reason why. The question is, did they walk all the way back here on their little orange feet because this was home . . . or because they somehow knew what Scooter knew? That sooner or later, a travelling man always comes back to where he's been, the way a murderer is supposed to revisit the scene of his crime?*

"Well, if you still want em, they're still yours," she said. For a moment she looked solemn . . . and then she laughed. "Shit, I probably would have throwed em out anyway, except I forgot about em. Course, they're still broken."

Hogan turned the key jutting out of the gum. It went around twice, making little wind-up clicks, then simply turned uselessly in its socket. Broken. Of course they were. And would be until they decided they didn't *want* to be broken for awhile. And the question wasn't how they had gotten back here, and the question wasn't even *why.*

The question was this: What did they want?

He poked his finger into the white steel grin

285

again and whispered, "Bite me — do you want to?"

The teeth only stood there on their supercool orange feet and grinned.

"They ain't talking, seems like," Mrs. Scooter said.

"No," Hogan said, and suddenly he found himself thinking of the kid. Mr. Bryan Adams, from Nowhere, U.S.A. A lot of kids like him now. A lot of grownups, too, blowing along the highways like tumbleweed, always ready to take your wallet, say *Fuck you, sugar,* and run. You could stop picking up hitchhikers (he had), and you could put a burglar-alarm system in your home (he'd done that, too), but it was still a hard world where planes sometimes fell out of the sky and the crazies were apt to turn up anyplace and there was always room for a little more insurance. He had a wife, after all.

And a son.

It might be nice if Jack had a set of Jumbo Chattery Teeth sitting on his desk. Just in case something happened.

Just in case.

"Thank you for saving them," he said, picking the Chattery Teeth up carefully by the feet. "I think my kid will get a kick out of them even if they are broken."

"Thank Scoot, not me. You want a bag?" She grinned. "I got a plastic one — no holes, guaranteed."

Hogan shook his head and slipped the Chattery Teeth into his sportcoat pocket. "I'll carry them this way," he said, and grinned right back at her.

"Keep them handy."

"Suit yourself." As he started for the door, she called after him: "Stop back again! I make a damn good chicken salad sandwich!"

"I'll bet you do, and I will," Hogan said. He went out, down the steps, and stood for a moment in the hot desert sunshine, smiling. He felt good — he felt good a lot these days. He had come to think that was just the way to be.

To his left, Woof the Amazing Minnesota Coydog got to his feet, poked his snout through the crisscross of wire on the side of his cage, and barked. In Hogan's pocket, the Chattery Teeth clicked together once. The sound was soft, but Hogan heard it . . . and felt them move. He patted his pocket. "Easy, big fella," he said softly.

He walked briskly across the yard, climbed behind the wheel of his new Chevrolet van, and drove away toward Los Angeles. He had promised Lita and Jack he would be home by seven, eight at the latest, and he was a man who liked to keep his promises.

Dedication

Around the corner from the doormen, the limos, the taxis, and the revolving doors at the entrance to Le Palais, one of New York's oldest and grandest hotels, there is another door, this one small, unmarked, and — for the most part — unremarked.

Martha Rosewall approached it one morning at a quarter of seven, her plain blue canvas tote-bag in one hand and a smile on her face. The tote was usual, the smile much more rarely seen. She was not unhappy in her work — being the Chief Housekeeper of floors ten through twelve of Le Palais might not seem an important or rewarding job to some, but to a woman who had worn dresses made out of rice- and flour-sacks as a girl growing up in Babylon, Alabama, it seemed very important indeed, and very rewarding as well. Yet no matter what the job, mechanic or movie-star, on ordinary mornings a person arrives at work with an ordinary expression on his or her face; a look that says *Most of me is still in bed* and not much more. For Martha Rosewall, however, this was no ordinary morning.

Things had begun being not ordinary for her when she arrived home from work the previous afternoon and found the package her son had sent from Ohio. The long-expected and long-awaited had finally come. She had slept only in snatches

last night — she had to keep getting up and checking to make sure the thing he had sent was real,
and that it was still there. Finally she had slept
with it under her pillow, like a bridesmaid with
a piece of wedding cake.

Now she used her key to open the small door
around the corner from the hotel's main entrance
and went down three steps to a long hallway
painted flat green and lined with Dandux laundry
carts. They were piled high with freshly washed
and ironed bed-linen. The hallway was filled with
its clean smell, a smell that Martha always associated, in some vague way, with the smell of freshly
baked bread. The faint sound of Muzak drifted
down from the lobby, but these days Martha heard
it no more than she heard the hum of the service
elevators or the rattle of china in the kitchen.

Halfway down the hall was a door marked
CHIEFS OF HOUSEKEEPING. She went in, hung
up her coat, and passed through the big room
where the Chiefs — there were eleven in all —
took their coffee-breaks, worked out problems of
supply and demand, and tried to keep up with
the endless paperwork. Beyond this room with its
huge desk, wall-length bulletin board, and per-
petually overflowing ashtrays was a dressing room.
Its walls were plain green cinderblock. There were
benches, lockers, and two long steel rods festooned
with the kind of coathangers you can't steal.

At the far end of the dressing room was the
door leading into the shower and bathroom area.
This door now opened and Darcy Sagamore appeared, wrapped in a fluffy Le Palais bathrobe and
a plume of warm steam. She took one look at

Martha's bright face and came to her with her arms out, laughing. "It came, didn't it?" she cried. "You got it! It's written all over your face! Yes sir and yes ma'am!"

Martha didn't know she was going to weep until the tears came. She hugged Darcy and put her face against Darcy's damp black hair.

"That's all right, honey," Darcy said. "You go on and let it all out."

"It's just that I'm so proud of him, Darcy — so damn *proud*."

"Of course you are. That's why you're crying, and that's fine . . . but I want to see it as soon as you stop." She grinned then. "You can hold it, though. If I dripped on *that* baby, I gotta believe you might poke my eye out."

So, with the reverence reserved for an object of great holiness (which, to Martha Rosewall, it was), she removed her son's first novel from the blue canvas tote. She had wrapped it carefully in tissue paper and put it under her brown nylon uniform. She now carefully removed the tissue so that Darcy could view the treasure.

Darcy looked carefully at the cover, which showed three Marines, one with a bandage wrapped around his head, charging up a hill with their guns firing. *Blaze of Glory*, printed in fiery red-orange letters, was the title. And below the picture was this: *A Novel by Peter Rosewall.*

"All right, that's good, *wonderful*, but now show me the other!" Darcy spoke in the tones of a woman who wants to dispense with the merely interesting and go directly to the heart of the matter.

Martha nodded and turned unhesitatingly to the dedication page, where Darcy read: *"This book is dedicated to my mother, MARTHA ROSEWALL. Mom, I couldn't have done it without you."* Below the printed dedication this was added in a thin, sloping, and somehow old-fashioned script: *"And that's no lie. Love you, Mom! Pete."*

"Why, isn't that just the sweetest thing?" Darcy asked, and swiped at her dark eyes with the heel of her hand.

"It's more than sweet," Martha said. She rewrapped the book in the tissue paper. "It's true." She smiled, and in that smile her old friend Darcy Sagamore saw something more than love. She saw triumph.

After punching out at three o'clock, Martha and Darcy frequently stopped in at La Pâtisserie, the hotel's coffee shop. On rare occasions they went into Le Cinq, the little pocket bar just off the lobby, for something a little stronger, and this day was a Le Cinq occasion if there had ever been one. Darcy got her friend comfortably situated in one of the booths, and left her there with a bowl of Goldfish crackers while she spoke briefly to Ray, who was tending bar that afternoon. Martha saw him grin at Darcy, nod, and make a circle with the thumb and forefinger of his right hand. Darcy came back to the booth with a look of satisfaction on her face. Martha regarded her with some suspicion.

"What was *that* about?"

"You'll see."

Five minutes later Ray came over with a silver

ice-bucket on a stand and placed it beside them. In it was a bottle of Perrier-Jouët champagne and two chilled glasses.

"Here, now!" Martha said in a voice that was half-alarmed, half-laughing. She looked at Darcy, startled.

"Hush," Darcy said, and to her credit, Martha did.

Ray uncorked the bottle, placed the cork beside Darcy, and poured a little into her glass. Darcy waved at it and winked at Ray.

"Enjoy, ladies," Ray said, and then blew a little kiss at Martha. "And congratulate your boy for me, sweetie." He walked away before Martha, who was still stunned, could say anything.

Darcy poured both glasses full and raised hers. After a moment Martha did the same. The glasses clinked gently. "Here's to the start of your son's career," Darcy said, and they drank. Darcy tipped the rim of her glass against Martha's a second time. "And to the boy himself," she said. They drank again, and Darcy touched their glasses together yet a third time before Martha could set hers down. "And to a mother's love."

"Amen, honey," Martha said, and although her mouth smiled, her eyes did not. On each of the first two toasts she had taken a discreet sip of champagne. This time she drained the glass.

Darcy had gotten the bottle of champagne so that she and her best friend could celebrate Peter Rosewall's breakthrough in the style it seemed to deserve, but that was not the only reason. She was curious about what Martha had said — *It's more than sweet, it's true.* And she was curious about that expression of triumph.

She waited until Martha had gotten through her third glass of champagne and then she said, "What did you mean about the dedication, Martha?"

"What?"

"You said it wasn't just sweet, it was true."

Martha looked at her so long without speaking that Darcy thought she was not going to answer at all. Then she uttered a laugh so bitter it was shocking — at least to Darcy it was. She'd had no idea that cheerful little Martha Rosewall could be so bitter, in spite of the hard life she had led. But that note of triumph was still there, too, an unsettling counter-point.

"His book is going to be a best-seller and the critics are going to eat it up like ice cream," Martha said. "I believe that, but not because Pete says so . . . although he does, of course. I believe it because that's what happened with *him.*"

"Who?"

"Pete's father," Martha said. She folded her hands on the table and looked at Darcy calmly.

"But —" Darcy began, then stopped. Johnny Rosewall had never written a book in his life, of course. IOUs and the occasional *I fucked yo momma* in spray-paint on brick walls were more Johnny's style. It seemed as if Martha was saying . . .

Never mind the fancy stuff, Darcy thought. *You know perfectly well what she's saying: She might have been married to Johnny when she got pregnant with Pete, but someone a little more intellectual was responsible for the kid.*

Except it didn't fit. Darcy had never met

Johnny, but she had seen half a dozen photos of him in Martha's albums, and she'd gotten to know Pete well — so well, in fact, that during his last two years of high school and first two years of college she'd come to think of him as partly her own. And the physical resemblance between the boy who'd spent so much time in her kitchen and the man in the photo albums . . .

"Well, Johnny was Pete's *biological* father," Martha said, as if reading her mind. "Only have to look at his nose and eyes to see *that*. Just wasn't his *natural* one . . . any more of that bubbly? It goes down so smooth." Now that she was tiddly, the South had begun to resurface in Martha's voice like a child creeping out of its hiding place.

Darcy poured most of the remaining champagne into Martha's glass. Martha held it up by the stem, looking through the liquid, enjoying the way it turned the subdued afternoon light in Le Cinq to gold. Then she drank a little, set the glass down, and laughed that bitter, jagged laugh again.

"You don't have the slightes' idea what I'm talking about, do you?"

"No, honey, I don't."

"Well, I'm going to tell you," Martha said. "After all these years I have to tell someone — now more'n ever, now that he's published his book and broken through after all those years of gettin ready for it to happen. God knows I can't tell *him* — him least of all. But then, lucky sons never know how much their mothers love them, or the sacrifices they make, do they?"

"I guess not," Darcy said. "Martha, hon, maybe you ought to think about if you really want to tell me whatever it is you —"

"No, they don't have a clue," Martha said, and Darcy realized her friend hadn't heard a single word she'd said. Martha Rosewall was off in some world of her own. When her eyes came back to Darcy, a peculiar little smile — one Darcy didn't like much — touched the corners of her mouth. "Not a clue," she repeated. "If you want to know what that word *dedication* really means, I think you have to ask a mother. What do *you* think, Darcy?"

But Darcy could only shake her head, unsure what to say. Martha nodded, however, as if Darcy had agreed completely, and then she began to speak.

There was no need for her to go over the basic facts. The two women had worked together at Le Palais for eleven years and had been close friends for most of that time.

The most basic of those basic facts, Darcy would have said (at least until that day in Le Cinq she would have said it), was that Marty had married a man who wasn't much good, one who was a lot more interested in his booze and his dope — not to mention just about any woman who happened to flip a hip in his direction — than he was in the woman he had married.

Martha had been in New York only a few months when she met him, just a babe in the woods, and she had been two months pregnant when she said *I do*. Pregnant or not, she had told Darcy more than once, she had thought carefully before agreeing to marry Johnny. She was grateful he wanted to stick by her (she was wise enough, even then, to know that many men would have been down the road and gone five minutes after the words "I'm pregnant" were out of the little lady's mouth), but she was not entirely blind to his shortcomings. She had a good idea what her mother and father — especially her father — would make of Johnny Rosewall with his black T-Bird and his tu-tone airtip shoes, bought because Johnny had seen Memphis Slim wearing a pair exactly like them when Slim played the Apollo.

That first child Martha had lost in the third month. After another five months or so, she had decided to chalk the marriage up to profit and loss — mostly loss. There had been too many late nights, too many weak excuses, too many black eyes. Johnny, she said, fell in love with his fists when he was drunk.

"He always looked good," she told Darcy once, "but a good-lookin shitheel is still a shitheel."

Before she could pack her bags, Martha discovered she was pregnant again. Johnny's reaction this time was immediate and hostile: he socked her in the belly with the handle of a broom in an effort to make her miscarry. Two nights later he and a couple of his friends — men who shared Johnny's affection for bright clothes and tu-tone shoes — tried to stick up a liquor store on East 116th Street. The proprietor had a shotgun under the counter. He brought it out. Johnny Rosewall was packing a nickel-plated .32 he'd gotten God knew where. He pointed it at the proprietor, pulled the trigger, and the pistol blew up. One of the fragments of the barrel entered his brain by way of his right eye, killing him instantly.

Martha had worked on at Le Palais until her seventh month (this was long before Darcy Sagamore's time, of course), and then Mrs. Proulx told her to go home before she dropped the kid in the tenth-floor corridor or maybe the laundry elevator. You're a good little worker and you can have your job back later on if you want it, Roberta Proulx told her, but for right now you get yourself gone, girl.

Martha did, and two months later she had borne a seven-pound boy whom she had named Peter, and Peter had, in the fullness of time, written a novel called *Blaze of Glory,* which everyone — including the Book-of-the-Month Club and Universal Pictures — thought destined for fame and fortune.

All this Darcy had heard before. The rest of it — the *unbelievable* rest of it — she heard about that afternoon and evening, beginning in Le Cinq, with champagne glasses before them and the advance copy of Pete's novel in the canvas tote by Martha Rosewall's feet.

"We were living uptown, of course," Martha said, looking down at her champagne glass and twirling it between her fingers. "On Stanton Street, up by Station Park. I've been back since. It's worse than it was — a lot worse — but it was no beauty spot even back then.

"There was a spooky old woman who lived at the Station Park end of Stanton Street back then — folks called her Mama Delorme and lots of them swore she was a *bruja* woman. I didn't believe in anything like that myself, and once I asked Octavia Kinsolving, who lived in the same building as me and Johnny, how people could go on believing such trash in a day when space satellites went whizzing around the earth and there was a cure for just about every disease under the sun. 'Tavia was an educated woman — had been to Juilliard — and was only living on the fatback side of 110th because she had her mother and three younger brothers to support. I thought she would agree with me but she only laughed and shook her head.

" 'Are you telling me you believe in *bruja?*' " I asked her.

" 'No,' she said, 'but I believe in *her*. She is different. Maybe for every thousand — or ten thousand — or million — women who claim to be witchy, there's one who really is. If so, Mama Delorme's the one.'

"I just laughed. People who don't need *bruja* can afford to laugh at it, the same way that people who don't need prayer can afford to laugh at *that*. I'm talkin 'bout when I was first married, you know, and in those days I still thought I could straighten Johnny out. Can you dig it?"

Darcy nodded.

"Then I had the miscarriage. Johnny was the main reason I had it, I guess, although I didn't like to admit that even to myself back then. He was beating on me most the time, and drinking *all* the time. He'd take the money I gave him and then he'd take more out of my purse. When I told him I wanted him to quit hooking from my bag he'd get all woundy-faced and claim he hadn't done any such thing. That was if he was sober.

If he was drunk he'd just laugh.

"I wrote my momma down home — it hurt me to write that letter, and it shamed me, and I cried while I was writing it, but I had to know what she thought. She wrote back and told me to get out of it, to go right away before he put me in the hospital or even worse. My older sister, Cassandra (we always called her Kissy), went that one better. She sent me a Greyhound bus ticket with two words written on the envelope in pink lipstick — GO NOW, it said."

Martha took another small sip of her champagne.

"Well, I didn't. I liked to think I had too much dignity. I suppose it was nothing but stupid pride. Either way, it turned out the same. I stayed. Then, after I lost the baby, I went and got pregnant again — only I didn't know at first. I didn't have any morning sickness, you see . . . but then, I never did with the first one, either."

"You didn't go to this Mama Delorme because you were pregnant?" Darcy asked. Her immediate assumption had been that Martha had thought maybe the witch-woman would give her something that would make her miscarry . . . or that she'd decided on an out-and-out abortion.

"No," Martha said. "I went because 'Tavia said Mama Delorme could tell me for sure what the stuff was I found in Johnny's coat pocket. White powder in a little glass bottle."

"Oh-oh," Darcy said.

Martha smiled without humor. "You want to know how bad things can get?" she asked. "Probably you don't but I'll tell you anyway. Bad is when your man drinks and don't have no steady

299

job. *Really* bad is when he drinks, don't have no job, and beats on you. Even worse is when you reach into his coat pocket, hoping to find a dollar to buy toilet paper with down at the Sunland Market, and find a little glass bottle with a spoon on it instead. And do you know what's worst of all? Looking at that little bottle and just hoping the stuff inside it is cocaine and not horse."

"You took it to Mama Delorme?"

Martha laughed pityingly.

"The whole *bottle?* No *ma'am.* I wasn't getting much fun out of life, but I didn't want to *die.* If he'd come home from wherever he was at and found that two-gram bottle gone, he would have plowed me like a pea-field. What I did was take a little and put it in the cellophane from off a cigarette pack. Then I went to 'Tavia and 'Tavia told me to go to Mama Delorme and I went."

"What was she like?"

Martha shook her head, unable to tell her friend exactly what Mama Delorme had been like, or how strange that half-hour in the woman's third-floor apartment had been, or how she'd nearly run down the crazily leaning stairs to the street, afraid that the woman was following her. The apartment had been dark and smelly, full of the smell of candles and old wallpaper and cinnamon and soured sachet. There had been a picture of Jesus on one wall, Nostradamus on another.

"She was a weird sister if there ever was one," Martha said finally. "I don't have any idea even today how old she was; she might have been seventy, ninety, or a hundred and ten. There was a pink-white scar that went up one side of her nose and her forehead and into her hair. Looked like a burn. It had pulled her right eye down in a kind of droop that looked like a wink. She was sitting in a rocker and she had knitting in her lap. I came in and she said, 'I have three things to tell you, little lady. The first is that you don't believe in me. The second is the bottle you found in your husband's coat is full of White Angel heroin. The third is you're three weeks gone with a boy-child you'll name after his natural father.' "

Martha looked around to make sure no one had taken a seat at one of the nearby tables, satisfied herself that they were still alone, and then leaned toward Darcy, who was looking at her with silent fascination.

"Later, when I could think straight again, I told myself that as far as those first two things went, she hadn't done anything that a good stage magician couldn't do — or one of those mentalist fellows in the white turbans. If 'Tavia Kinsolving had called the old lady to say I was coming, she might have told her *why* I was coming, too. You see how simple it could have been? And to a woman like Mama Delorme, those little touches would be important, because if you want to be *known* as a *bruja* woman, you have to *act* like a *bruja* woman."

"I suppose that's right," Darcy said.

"As for her telling me that I was pregnant, that might have been just a lucky guess. Or . . . well . . . some ladies just *know*."

Darcy nodded. "I had an aunt who was damned good at knowing when a woman had caught pregnant. She'd know sometimes before the woman

301

knew, and sometimes before the woman had any *business* being pregnant, if you see what I mean."

Martha laughed and nodded.

"She said their smell changed," Darcy went on, "and sometimes you could pick up that new smell as soon as a day after the woman in question had caught, if your nose was keen."

"Uh-huh," Martha said. "I've heard the same thing, but in my case none of that applied. She just *knew*, and down deep, underneath the part of me that was trying to make believe it was all just a lot of hokum, I *knew* she knew. To be with her was to believe in *bruja* — her *bruja*, anyway. And it didn't go away, that feeling, the way a dream does when you wake up, or the way your belief in a good faker goes away when you're out of his spell."

"What did you do?"

"Well, there was a chair with a saggy old cane seat near the door and I guess that was lucky for me, because when she said what she did, the world kind of grayed over and my knees came unbolted. I was going to sit down no matter what, but if the chair hadn't been there I would have sat on the floor.

"She just waited for me to get myself back together and went on knitting. It was like she had seen it all a hundred times before. I suppose she had.

"When my heart finally began to slow down I opened my mouth and what came out was 'I'm going to leave my husband.'

" 'No,' she came back right away, 'he gonna leave *you*. You gonna see him out, is all. Stick

302

around, woman. There be a little money. You gonna think he hoit the baby but he dint be doin it.'

" 'How,' I said, but that was all I *could* say, it seemed like, and so I kept saying it over and over. 'How-how-how,' just like John Lee Hooker on some old blues record. Even now, twenty-six years later, I can smell those old burned candles and kerosene from the kitchen and the sour smell of dried wallpaper, like old cheese. I can see her, small and frail in this old blue dress with little polka-dots that used to be white but had gone the yellowy color of old newspapers by the time I met her. She was so *little,* but there was such a feeling of power that came from her, like a bright, bright light —"

Martha got up, went to the bar, spoke with Ray, and came back with a large glass of water. She drained most of it at a draught.

"Better?" Darcy asked.

"A little, yeah." Martha shrugged, then smiled. "It doesn't do to go on about it, I guess. If you'd been there, you'd've felt it. You'd've felt *her.*

" 'How I do anythin or why you married that country piece of shit in the first place ain't neither of them important now,' Mama Delorme said to me. 'What's important now is you got to find the child's natural father.'

"Anyone listening would have thought she was as much as saying I'd been screwing around on my man, but it never even occurred to me to be mad at her; I was too confused to be mad. 'What do you mean?' I asked. '*Johnny's* the child's natural father.'

"She kind of snorted and flapped her hand at me, like she was saying *Pshaw*. 'Ain't nothin natural about *that* man.'

"Then she leaned in closer to me and I started to feel a little scared. There was so much *knowing* in her, and it felt like not very much of it was nice.

" 'Any child a woman get, the man shoot it out'n his pecker, girl,' she said. 'You know that, don't you?'

"I didn't think that was the way they put it in the medical books, but I felt my head going up n down just the same, as if she'd reached across the room with hands I couldn't see and nodded it for me.

" 'That's right,' she said, nodding her ownself. 'That's the way God planned it to be . . . like a seesaw. A man shoots cheerun out'n his pecker, so them cheerun mostly his. But it's a woman who carries em and bears em and has the raisin of em, so them cheerun mostly *hers*. That's the way of the world, but there's a 'ception to every rule, one that *proves* the rule, and this is one of em. The man who put you with child ain't gonna be no natural father to that child — he wouldn't be no natural father to it even if he was gonna be around. He'd hate it, beat it to death before its foist birthday, mos' likely, because he'd know it wasn't his. A man can't always smell that out, or see it, but he will if the child is different enough . . . and this child goan be as different from piss-ignorant Johnny Rosewall as day is from night. So tell me, girl: who *is* the child's natural father?' And she kind of leaned toward me.

304

"All I could do was shake my head and tell her I didn't know what she was talking about. But I think that something in me — something way back in that part of your mind that only gets a real chance to think in your dreams — *did* know. Maybe I'm only making that up because of all I know now, but I don't think so. I think that for just a moment or two *his* name fluttered there in my head.

"I said, 'I don't know what it is you want me to say — I don't know anything about natural fathers or unnatural ones. I don't even know for sure if I'm pregnant, but if I am it *has* to be Johnny's, because he's the only man I've ever slept with!'

"Well, she sat back for a minute, and then she smiled. Her smile was like sunshine, and it eased me a little. 'I didn't mean to scare you, honey,' she said. 'That wasn't none of what I had in my mind at all. It's just that I got the sight, and sometime it's strong. I'll just brew us a cup of tea, and that'll calm you down. You'll like it. It's special to me.'

"I wanted to tell her I didn't want any tea, but it seemed like I couldn't. Seemed like too much of an effort to open my mouth, and all the strength had gone out of my legs.

"She had a greasy little kitchenette that was almost as dark as a cave. I sat in the chair by the door and watched her spoon loose tea into an old chipped china pot and put a kettle on the gas ring. I sat there thinking I didn't want *anything* that was special to her, nor anything that came out of that greasy little kitchenette either. I was thinking I'd take just a little sip to be mannerly and then get my ass out of there as fast as I could and never come back.

"But then she brought over two little china cups just as clean as snow and a tray with sugar and cream and fresh-baked bread-rolls. She poured the tea and it smelled good and hot and strong. It kind of waked me up and before I knew it I'd drunk two cups and eaten one of the bread-rolls, too.

"She drank a cup and ate a roll and we got talking along on more natural subjects — who we knew on the street, whereabouts in Alabama I came from, where I liked to shop, and all that. Then I looked at my watch and seen over an hour and a half had gone by. I started to get up and a dizzy feeling ran through me and I plopped right back in my chair again."

Darcy was looking at her, eyes round.

" 'You doped me,' I said, and I was scared, but the scared part of me was way down inside.

" 'Girl, I want to help you,' she said, 'but you don't want to give up what I need to know and I know damn well you ain't gonna do what you need to do even once you *do* give it up — not without a push. So I fixed her. You gonna take a little nap, is all, but before you do you're gonna tell me the name of your babe's natural father.'

"And, sitting there in that chair with its saggy cane bottom and hearing all of uptown roaring and racketing just outside her living-room window, I saw him as clear as I'm seeing you now, Darcy. His name was Peter Jefferies, and he was just as white as I am black, just as tall as I am

306

short, just as educated as I am ignorant. We were as different as two people could be except for one thing — we both come from Alabama, me from Babylon down in the toolies by the Florida state line, him from Birmingham. He didn't even know I was alive — I was just the nigger woman who cleaned the suite where he always stayed on the eleventh floor of this hotel. And as for me, I only thought of him to stay out of his way because I'd heard him talk and seen him operate and I knew well enough what sort of man he was. It wasn't just that he wouldn't use a glass a black person had used before him without it had been washed; I've seen too much of that in my time to get worked up about it. It was that once you got past a certain point in that man's character, white and black didn't have anything to do with what he was. He belonged to the son-of-a-bitch tribe, and that particular bunch comes in all skin-colors.

"You know what? He was like Johnny in a lot of ways, or the way Johnny would have been if he'd been smart and had an education and if God had thought to give Johnny a great big slug of talent inside of him instead of just a head for dope and a nose for wet pussy.

"I thought nothing of him but to steer clear of him, nothing at all. But when Mama Delorme leaned over me, so close I felt like the smell of cinnamon comin out of her pores was gonna suffocate me, it was his name that came out with never a pause. 'Peter Jefferies,' I said. 'Peter Jefferies, the man who stays in 1163 when he ain't writing his books down there in Alabama. He's the natural father. But he's *white!*'

307

"She leaned closer and said, 'No he ain't, honey. No man's white. Inside where they live, they's all black. You don't believe it, but that's true. It's midnight inside em all, any hour of God's day. But a man can make light out of night, and that's why what comes out of a man to make a baby in a woman is white. Natural got nothing to do with color. Now you close your eyes, honey, because you tired — you *so* tired. Now! Say! Now! Don't you fight! Mama Delorme ain't goan put nothin over on you, child! Just got somethin I goan to put in your hand. Now — no, don't look, just close your hand over it.' I did what she said and felt something square. Felt like glass or plastic.

" 'You gonna remember everythin when it's time for you to remember. For now, just go on to sleep. Shhh . . . go to sleep . . . shhh. . . .'

"And that's just what I did," Martha said. "Next thing I remember, I was running down those stairs like the devil was after me. I didn't remember what I was running *from*, but that didn't make any difference; I ran anyway. I only went back there one more time, and I didn't see her when I did."

Martha paused and they both looked around like women freshly awakened from a shared dream. Le Cinq had begun to fill up — it was almost five o'clock and executives were drifting in for their after-work drinks. Although neither wanted to say so out loud, both suddenly wanted to be somewhere else. They were no longer wearing their uniforms but neither felt she belonged among these men with their briefcases and their talk of stocks, bonds, and debentures.

"I've got a casserole and a six-pack at my place," Martha said, suddenly timid. "I could warm up the one and cool down the other . . . if you want to hear the rest."

"Honey, I think I *got* to hear the rest," Darcy said, and laughed a little nervously.

"And I think I've got to tell it," Martha replied, but she did not laugh. Or even smile.

"Just let me call my husband. Tell him I'll be late."

"You do that," Martha said, and while Darcy used the telephone, Martha checked in her bag one more time just to make sure the precious book was still there.

The casserole — as much of it as the two of them could use, anyway — was eaten, and they had each had a beer. Martha asked Darcy again if she was sure she wanted to hear the rest. Darcy said she did.

"Because some of it ain't very nice. I got to be up front with you about that. Some of it's worse'n the sort of magazines the single men leave behind em when they check out."

Darcy knew the sort of magazines she meant, but could not imagine her trim, clean little friend in connection with any of the things pictured in them. She got them each a fresh beer, and Martha began to speak again.

"I was back home before I woke up all the way, and because I couldn't remember hardly any of what had gone on at Mama Delorme's, I decided the best thing — the safest thing — was to believe it had all been a dream. But the powder I'd taken from Johnny's bottle wasn't a dream; it was still in my dress pocket, wrapped up in the cellophane from the cigarette pack. All I wanted to do right then was get rid of it, and never mind all the *bruja* in the world. Maybe I didn't make a business of going through Johnny's pockets, but he surely made a business of going through mine, 'case I was holding back a dollar or two he might want.

"But that wasn't all I found in my pocket — there was something else, too. I took it out and looked at it and then I knew for sure I'd seen her, although I still couldn't remember much of what had passed between us.

"It was a little square plastic box with a top you could see through and open. There wasn't nothing in it but an old dried-up mushroom — except after hearing what 'Tavia had said about that woman, I thought maybe it might be a toad-stool instead of a mushroom, and probably one that would give you the night-gripes so bad you'd wish it had just killed you outright like some of em do.

"I decided to flush it down the commode along with that powder he'd been sniffing up his nose, but when it came right down to it, I couldn't. Felt like she was right there in the room with me, telling me not to. I was even scairt to look into the livin-room mirror, case I might see her standin behind me.

"In the end, I dumped the little bit of powder I'd taken down the kitchen sink, and I put the little plastic box in the cabinet over the sink. I stood on tiptoe and pushed it in as far as I could

— all the way to the back, I guess. Where I forgot all about it."

She stopped for a moment, drumming her fingers nervously on the table, and then said, "I guess I ought to tell you a little more about Peter Jefferies. *My* Pete's novel is about Viet Nam and what he knew of the Army from his own hitch; Peter Jefferies's books were about what he always called Big Two, when he was drunk and partying with his friends. He wrote the first one while he was still in the service, and it was published in 1946. It was called *Blaze of Heaven*."

Darcy looked at her for a long time without speaking and then said, "Is that so?"

"Yes. Maybe you see where I'm going now. Maybe you get a little more what I mean about natural fathers. *Blaze of Heaven, Blaze of Glory*."

"But if your Pete had read this Mr. Jefferies's book, isn't it possible that —"

"Course it's *possible*," Martha said, making that *pshaw* gesture herself this time, "but that ain't what *happened*. I ain't going to try and convince you of that, though. You'll either be convinced when I get done or you won't. I just wanted to tell you about the man, a little."

"Go to it," Darcy said.

"I saw him pretty often from 1957 when I started working at Le Palais right through until 1968 or so, when he got in trouble with his heart and liver. The way the man drank and carried on, I was only surprised he didn't get in trouble with himself earlier on. He was only in half a dozen times in 1969, and I remember how bad he looked — he was never fat, but he'd lost enough weight by then so he wasn't no more than a stuffed string. Went right on drinking, though, yellow face or not. I'd hear him coughing and puking in the bathroom and sometimes crying with the pain and I'd think, *Well, that's it; that's all; he's got to see what he's doing to himself; he'll quit now.* But he never. In 1970 he was only in twice. He had a man with him that he leaned on and who took care of him. He was still drinking, too, although anybody who took even half a glance at him knew he had no business doing it.

"The last time he came was in February of 1971. It was a different man he had with him, though; I guess the first one must have played out. Jefferies was in a wheelchair by then. When I come in to clean and looked in the bathroom, I seen what was hung up to dry on the shower-curtain rail — continence pants. He'd been a handsome man, but those days were long gone. The last few times I saw him, he just looked *raddled.* Do you know what I'm talking about?"

Darcy nodded. You saw such creatures creeping down the street sometimes, with their brown bags under their arms or tucked into their shabby old coats.

"He always stayed in 1163, one of those corner suites with the view that looks toward the Chrysler Building, and I always used to do for him. After awhile, it got so's he would even call me by name, but it didn't really signify — I wore a name-tag and he could read, that was all. I don't believe he ever once really *saw* me. Until 1960 he always left two dollars on top of the television when he checked out. Then, until '64, it was three. At the very end it was five. Those were very good tips for those days, but he wasn't really tipping me; he was following a custom. Custom's important for people like him. He tipped for the same reason he'd hold the door for a lady; for the same reason he no doubt used to put his milk-teeth under his pillow when he was a little fellow. Only difference was, I was the Cleanin Fairy instead of the Tooth Fairy.

"He'd come in to talk to his publishers or sometimes movie and TV people, and he'd call up his friends — some of them were in publishing, too, others were agents or writers like him — and there'd be a party. Always a party. Most I just knew about by the messes I had to clean up the next day — dozens of empty bottles (mostly Jack Daniel's), millions of cigarette butts, wet towels in the sinks and the tub, leftover room service everywhere. Once I found a whole platter of jumbo shrimp turned into the toilet bowl. There were glass-rings on everything, and people snoring on the sofa and floors, like as not.

"That was mostly, but sometimes there were parties still going on when I started to clean at ten-thirty in the morning. He'd let me in and I'd just kinda clean up around em. There weren't any women at those parties; those ones were strictly stag, and all they ever did was drink and talk about the war. How they got to the war. Who they knew in the war. Where they went in the war. Who got killed in the war. What they saw in the war they could never tell their wives about (although it was all right if a black maid happened to pick

313

up on some of it). Sometimes — not too often — they'd play high-stakes poker as well, but they talked about the war even while they were betting and raising and bluffing and folding. Five or six men, their faces all flushed the way white men's faces get when they start really socking it down, sitting around a glass-topped table with their shirts open and their ties pulled way down, the table heaped with more money than a woman like me will make in a lifetime. And how they did talk about their war! They talked about it the way young women talk about their lovers and their boyfriends."

Darcy said she was surprised the management hadn't kicked Jefferies out, famous writer or not — they were fairly stiff about such goings-on now and had been even worse in years gone by, or so she had heard.

"No, no, no," Martha said, smiling a little. "You got the wrong impression. You're thinking the man and his friends carried on like one of those rock-groups that like to tear up their suites and throw the sofas out the windows. Jefferies wasn't no ordinary grunt, like my Pete; he'd been to West Point, went in a Lieutenant and came out a Major. He was *quality,* from one of those old Southern families who have a big house full of old paintings where everyone's ridin hosses and looking noble. He could tie his tie four different ways and he knew how to bend over a lady's hand when he kissed it. He was *quality,* I tell you."

Martha's smile took on a little twist as she spoke the word; the twist had a look both bitter and derisive.

314

"He and his friends sometimes got a little loud, I guess, but they rarely got rowdy — there's a difference, although it's hard to explain — and they *never* got out of control. If there was a complaint from the neighboring room — because it was a corner suite he stayed in, there was only the one — and someone from the front desk had to call Mr. Jefferies's room and ask him and his guests to tone it down a little, why, they always did. You understand?"

"Yes."

"And that's not all. A quality hotel can work *for* people like Mr. Jefferies. It can protect them. They can go right on partying and having a good time with their booze and their cards or maybe their drugs."

"Did he take drugs?"

"Hell, I don't know. He had plenty of them at the end, God knows, but they were all the kind with prescription labels on them. I'm just saying that quality — it's that white Southern gentleman's idea of quality I'm talking about now, you know — calls to quality. He'd been coming to Le Palais a long time, and you may think it was important to the management that he was a big famous author, but that's only because you haven't been at Le Palais as long as I have. Him being famous *was* important to them, but it was really just the icing on the cake. What was more important was that he'd been coming there a long time, and his father, who was a big landowner down around Porterville, had been a regular guest before him. The people who ran the hotel back then were people who believed in tradition. I know the ones who run it now *say* they believe in it, and maybe they do when it suits them, but in those days they *really* believed in it. When they knew Mr. Jefferies was coming up to New York on the Southern Flyer from Birmingham, you'd see the room right next to that corner suite sort of empty out, unless the hotel was full right up to the scuppers. They never charged him for the empty room next door; they were just trying to spare him the embarrassment of having to tell his cronies to keep it down to a dull roar."

Darcy shook her head slowly. "That's amazing."

"You don't believe it, honey?"

"Oh yes — I believe it, but it's still amazing."

That bitter, derisive smile resurfaced on Martha Rosewall's face. "Ain't nothing too much for *quality* . . . for that Robert E. Lee Stars and Bars *charm* . . . or didn't used to be. Hell, even *I* recognized that he was quality, no sort of a man to go hollering *Yee-haw* out the window or telling Rastus P. Coon jokes to his friends.

"He hated blacks just the same, though, don't be thinking different . . . but remember what I said about him belonging to the son-of-a-bitch tribe? Fact was, when it came to hate, Peter Jefferies was an equal-opportunity employer. When John Kennedy died, Jefferies happened to be in the city and he threw a party. All of his friends were there, and it went on into the next day. I could barely stand to be in there, the things they were saying — about how things would be perfect if only someone would get that brother of his who wouldn't be happy until every decent white kid in the country was fucking while the Beatles played on the stereo and the colored (that's what they called black folks, mostly, 'the colored,' I used to hate that sissy, pantywaist way of saying so much) were running wild through the streets with a TV under each arm.

"It got so bad that I knew I was going to scream at him. I just kept telling myself to be quiet and do my job and get out as fast as I could; I kept telling myself to remember the man was my Pete's natural father if I couldn't remember anything else; I kept telling myself that Pete was only three years old and I needed my job and I would lose it if I couldn't keep my mouth shut.

"Then one of em said, 'And after we get Bobby, let's go get his candy-ass kid brother!' and one of the others said, 'Then we'll get all the male children and *really* have a party!'

" 'That's right!' Mr. Jefferies said. 'And when we've got the last head up on the last castle wall we're going to have a party so big I'm going to hire Madison Square Garden!'

"I had to leave then. I had a headache and belly-cramps from trying so hard to keep my mouth shut. I left the room half-cleaned, which is something I never did before nor have since, but sometimes being black has its advantages; he didn't know I was there, and he sure didn't know when I was gone. Wasn't none of them did."

That bitter derisive smile was on her lips again.

"I don't see how you can call a man like that quality, even as a joke," Darcy said, "or call him the natural father of your unborn child, whatever the circumstances might have been. To me he sounds like a beast."

"No!" Martha said sharply. "He *wasn't* a beast. He was a man. In some ways — in *most* ways — he was a bad man, but a man is what he was. And he *did* have that something you could call 'quality' without a smirk on your face, although it only came out completely in the things he wrote."

"Huh!" Darcy looked disdainfully at Martha from below drawn-together brows. "You read one of his books, did you?"

"Honey, I read them *all*. He'd only written three by the time I went to Mama Delorme's with that white powder in late 1959, but I'd read two of them. In time I got all the way caught up, because he wrote even slower than I read." She grinned. "And that's pretty slow!"

Darcy looked doubtfully toward Martha's bookcase. There were books there by Alice Walker and Rita Mae Brown, *Linden Hills* by Gloria Naylor and *Yellow Back Radio Broke-Down* by Ishmael Reed, but the three shelves were pretty much dominated by paperback romances and Agatha Christie mystery stories.

"Stories about war don't hardly seem like your pick an glory, Martha, if you know what I mean."

"Of course I know," Martha said. She got up and brought them each a fresh beer. "I'll tell you a funny thing, Dee: if he'd been a nice man, I probably never would have read even one of them. And I'll tell you an even funnier one: if he'd been a nice man, I don't think they would have been as good as they were."

318

"What are you talking about, woman?"

"I don't know, exactly. Just listen, all right?"

"All right."

"Well, it didn't take me until the Kennedy as-sassination to figure out what kind of man he was. I knew that by the summer of '58. By then I'd seen what a low opinion he had of the human race in general — not his friends, he would've died for them, but everyone else. Everyone was out looking for a buck to stroke, he used to say — stroking the buck, stroking the buck, everyone was stroking the buck. It seemed like him and his friends thought stroking the buck was a real bad thing, unless they were playing poker and had a whole mess of em spread out on the table. Seemed to me like they stroked them then, all right. Seemed to me like then they stroked them plenty, him included.

"There was a lot of big ugly under his South-ern-gentleman top layer — he thought people who were trying to do good or improve the world were about the funniest things going, he hated the blacks and the Jews, and he thought we ought to H-bomb the Russians out of existence before they could do it to us. Why not? he'd say. They were part of what he called 'the sub-human strain of the race.' To him that seemed to mean Jews, blacks, Italians, Indians, and anyone whose family didn't summer on the Outer Banks.

"I listened to him spout all that ignorance and high-toned filth, and naturally I started to wonder about *why* he was a famous writer . . . how he *could* be a famous writer. I wanted to know what it was the critics saw in him, but I was a lot more interested in what ordinary folks like me saw in him — the people who made his books best-sellers as soon as they came out. Finally I decided to find out for myself. I went down to the Public Library and borrowed his first book, *Blaze of Heaven*.

"I was expecting it'd turn out to be something like in the story of the Emperor's new clothes, but it didn't. The book was about these five men and what happened to them in the war, and what happened to their wives and girlfriends back home at the same time. When I saw on the jacket it was about the war, I kind of rolled my eyes, thinking it would be like all those boring stories they told each other."

"It wasn't?"

"I read the first ten or twenty pages and thought, *This ain't so good. It ain't as bad as I thought it'd be, but nothing's happening.* Then I read another thirty pages and I kind of . . . well, I kind of lost myself. Next time I looked up it was almost midnight and I was two hundred pages into that book. I thought to myself, *You got to go to bed, Martha. You got to go right now, because five-thirty comes early.* But I read another forty pages in spite of how heavy my eyes were getting, and it was quarter to one before I finally got up to brush my teeth."

Martha stopped, looking off toward the darkened window and all the miles of night outside it, her eyes hazed with remembering, her lips pressed together in a light frown. She shook her head a little.

"I didn't know how a man who was so boring when you had to listen to him could write so you didn't never want to close the book, nor ever see it end, either. How a nasty, cold-hearted man like him could still make up characters so real you wanted to cry over em when they died. When Noah got hit and killed by a taxi-cab near the end of *Blaze of Heaven,* just a month after his part of the war was over, I *did* cry. I didn't know how a sour, cynical man like Jefferies could make a body care so much about things that weren't real at all — about things he'd made up out of his own head. And there was something else in that book . . . a kind of sunshine. It was full of pain and bad things, but there was sweetness in it, too . . . and love. . . ."

She startled Darcy by laughing out loud.

"There was a fella worked at the hotel back then named Billy Beck, a nice young man who was majoring in English at Fordham when he wasn't on the door. He and I used to talk sometimes —"

"Was he a brother?"

"God, no!" Martha laughed again. "Wasn't no black doormen at Le Palais until 1965. Black porters and bellboys and car-park valets, but no black doormen. Wasn't considered right. Quality people like Mr. Jefferies wouldn't have liked it.

"Anyway, I asked Billy how the man's books could be so wonderful when he was such a booger in person. Billy asked me if I knew the one about the fat disc jockey with the thin voice, and I said I didn't know what he was talking about. Then he said he didn't know the answer to my question, but he told me something a prof of his had said about Thomas Wolfe. This prof said that some writers — and Wolfe was one of them — were no shakes at all until they sat down to a desk and took up pens in their hands. He said that a pen to fellows like that was like a telephone booth is to Clark Kent. He said that Thomas Wolfe was like a . . ." She hesitated, then smiled. ". . . that he was like a divine wind-chime. He said a wind-chime isn't nothing on its own, but when the wind blows through it, it makes a lovely noise.

"I think Peter Jefferies was like that. He *was* quality, he had been raised quality and he *was,* but the quality in him wasn't nothing he could take credit for. It was like God banked it for him and he just spent it. I'll tell you something you probably won't believe: after I'd read a couple of his books, I started to feel sorry for him."

"Sorry?"

"Yes. Because the books were beautiful and the man who made em was ugly as sin. He really *was* like my Johnny, but in a way Johnny was luckier, because he never dreamed of a better life, and Mr. Jefferies did. His *books* were his dreams, where he let himself believe in the world he laughed at and sneered at when he was awake."

She asked Darcy if she wanted another beer. Darcy said she would pass.

"Well if you change your mind, just holler. And you might change it, because right about here is where the water gets murky."

"One other thing about the man," Martha said. "He wasn't a sexy man. At least not the way you usually think about a man being sexy."

"You mean he was a —"

"No, he wasn't a homosexual, or a gay, or what-

322

ever it is you're supposed to call them these days. He wasn't sexy for men, but he wasn't what you could call sexy for women, either. There were two, maybe three times in all the years I did for him when I seen cigarette butts with lipstick on them in the bedroom ashtrays when I cleaned up, and smelled perfume on the pillows. One of those times I also found an eyeliner pencil in the bathroom — it had rolled under the door and into the corner. I reckon they were call-girls (the pillows never smelled like the kind of perfume decent women wear), but two or three times in all those years isn't much, is it?"

"It sure isn't," Darcy said, thinking of all the panties she had pulled out from under beds, all the condoms she had seen floating in unflushed toilets, all the false eyelashes she had found on and under pillows.

Martha sat without speaking for a few moments, lost in thought, then looked up. "I tell you what!" she said. "That man was sexy for himself! It sounds crazy but it's true. There sure wasn't any shortage of jizz in him — I know that from all the sheets I changed."

Darcy nodded.

"And there'd always be a little jar of cold cream in the bathroom, or sometimes on the table by his bed. I think he used it when he pulled off. To keep from getting chapped skin."

The two women looked at each other and suddenly began giggling hysterically.

"You sure he wasn't the other way, honey?" Darcy asked finally.

"I said *cold* cream, not *Vaseline*," Martha said,

and that did it; for the next five minutes the two women laughed until they cried.

But it wasn't really funny, and Darcy knew it. And when Martha went on, she simply listened, hardly believing what she was hearing.

"It was maybe a week after that time at Mama Delorme's, or maybe it was two," Martha said. "I don't remember. It's been a long time since it all happened. By then I was pretty sure I was pregnant — I wasn't throwing up or nothing, but there's a *feeling* to it. It don't come from places you'd think. It's like your gums and your toenails and the bridge of your nose figure out what's going on before the rest of you. Or you want something like chop suey at three in the afternoon and you say, 'Whoa, now! What's *this?*' But you know what it is. I didn't say a word to Johnny, though — I knew I'd have to, eventually, but I was scared to."

"I don't blame you," Darcy said.

"I was in the bedroom of Jefferies's suite one late morning, and while I did the neatening up I was thinking about Johnny and how I might break the news about the baby to him. Jefferies had gone out someplace — to one of his publishers' meetings, likely as not. The bed was a double, messed up on both sides, but that didn't mean nothing; he was just a restless sleeper. Sometimes when I came in the groundsheet would be pulled right out from underneath the mattress.

"Well, I stripped off the coverlet and the two blankets underneath — he was thin-blooded and always slept under all he could — and then I started to strip the top sheet off backward, and I seen it right away. It was his spend, mostly dried on there.

"I stood there looking at it for . . . oh, I don't know how long. It was like I was hypnotized. I saw him, lying there all by himself after his friends had gone home, lying there smelling nothing but the smoke they'd left behind and his own sweat. I saw him lying there on his back and then starting to make love to Mother Thumb and her four daughters. I saw that as clear as I see you now, Darcy; the only thing I didn't see is what he was thinking about, what sort of pictures he was making in his head . . . and considering the way he talked and how he was when he wasn't writing his books, I'm *glad* I didn't."

Darcy was looking at her, frozen, saying nothing.

"Next thing I knew, this . . . this feeling came over me." She paused, thinking, then shook her head slowly and deliberately. "This *compulsion* came over me. It was like wanting chop suey at three in the afternoon, or ice cream and pickles at two in the morning, or . . . what did *you* want, Darcy?"

"Rind of bacon," Darcy said through lips so numb she could hardly feel them. "My husband went out and couldn't find me any, but he brought back a bag of those pork rinds and I just *gobbled* them."

Martha nodded and began to speak again. Thirty seconds later Darcy bolted for the bathroom, where she struggled briefly with her gorge and then vomited up all the beer she'd drunk.

Look on the bright side, she thought, fumbling weakly for the flush. *No hangover to worry about.* And then, on the heels of that: *How am I going to look her in the eyes? Just how am I supposed to do that?*

It turned out not to be a problem. When she turned around, Martha was standing in the bathroom doorway and looking at her with warm concern.

"You all right?"

"Yes." Darcy tried a smile, and to her immense relief it felt genuine on her lips. "I . . . I just . . ."

"I know," Martha said. "Believe me, I do. Should I finish, or have you heard enough?"

"Finish," Darcy said decisively, and took her friend by the arm. "But in the living room. I don't even want to *look* at the refrigerator, let alone open the door."

"Amen to that."

A minute later they were settled on opposite ends of the shabby but comfortable living-room couch.

"You *sure,* honey?"

Darcy nodded.

"All right." But Martha sat quiet a moment longer, looking down at the slim hands clasped in her lap, conning the past as a submarine commander might con hostile waters through his periscope. At last she raised her head, turned to Darcy, and resumed her story.

"I worked the rest of that day in kind of a daze. It was like I was hypnotized. People talked to me, and I answered them, but I seemed to be hearing them through a glass wall and speaking back to them the same way. *I'm hypnotized, all right,* I remember thinking. *She hypnotized me. That old woman. Gave me one of those post-hypnotic suggestions, like when a stage hypnotist says, 'Someone says the word Chiclets to you, you're gonna get down on all fours and bark like a dog,' and the guy who was hypnotized does it even if no one says Chiclets to him for the next ten years. She put something in that tea and hypnotized me and then told me to do that. That nasty thing.*

"I knew why she would, too — an old woman superstitious enough to believe in stump-water cures, and how you could witch a man into love by putting a little drop of blood from your period onto the heel of his foot while he was sleeping, and cross-tie walkers, and God alone knows what else . . . if a woman like that with a bee in her bonnet about natural fathers could do hypnotism, hypnotizing a woman like me into doing what I did might be just what she would do. Because she would *believe* it. And I had named him to her, hadn't I? Yes indeed.

"It never occurred to me then that I hadn't remembered hardly anything at all about going to Mama Delorme's until after I did what I did in Mr. Jefferies's bedroom. It did that night, though.

"I got through the day all right. I mean, I didn't cry or scream or carry on or anything like that. My sister Kissy acted worse the time she was drawing water from the old well round dusk and a bat flew up from it and got caught in her hair. There was just that feeling that I was behind a wall of

327

glass, and I figured if that was all, I could get along with it.

"Then, when I got home, I all at once got thirsty. I was thirstier than ever in my life — it felt like a sandstorm was going on in my throat. I started to drink water. It seemed like I just couldn't drink enough. And I started to spit. I just spit and spit and spit. Then I started to feel sick to my stomach. I ran down to the bathroom and looked at myself in the mirror and stuck out my tongue to see if I could see anything there, any sign of what I'd done, and of course I couldn't. I thought, *There! Do you feel better now?*

"But I didn't. I felt worse. I knelt down in front of the toilet and I did what you did, Darcy, only I did a lot more of it. I vomited until I thought I was going to pass out. I was crying and begging God to please forgive me, to let me stop puking before I lost the baby, if I really was quick with one. And then I remembered myself standing there in his bedroom with my fingers in my mouth, not even thinking about what I was doing — I tell you I could *see* myself doing it, as if I was looking at myself in a movie. And then I vomited again.

"Mrs. Parker heard me and came to the door and asked if I was all right. That helped me get hold of myself a little, and by the time Johnny came in that night, I was over the worst of it. He was drunk, spoiling for a fight. When I wouldn't give him one he hit me in the eye anyway and walked out. I was almost glad he hit me, because it gave me something else to think about.

"The next day when I went into Mr. Jefferies's suite he was sitting in the parlor, still in his pajamas, scribbling away on one of his yellow legal pads. He always travelled with a bunch of them, held together with a big red rubber band, right up until the end. When he came to Le Palais that last time and I didn't see them, I knew he'd made up his mind to die. I wasn't a bit sorry, neither."

Martha looked toward the living-room window with an expression which held nothing of mercy or forgiveness; it was a cold look, one which reported an utter absence of the heart.

"When I saw he hadn't gone out I was relieved, because it meant I could put off the cleaning. He didn't like the maids around when he was working, you see, and so I figured he might not want house-keeping service until Yvonne came on at three.

"I said, 'I'll come back later, Mr. Jefferies.'

" 'Do it now,' he said. 'Just keep quiet while you do. I've got a bitch of a headache and a hell of an idea. The combination is killing me.'

"Any other time he would have told me to come back, I swear it. It seemed like I could almost hear that old black mama laughing.

"I went into the bathroom and started tidying around, taking out the used towels and putting up fresh ones, replacing the soap with a new bar, putting fresh matches out, and all the time I'm thinking, *You can't hypnotize someone who doesn't want to be hypnotized, old woman. Whatever it was you put in the tea that day, whatever it was you told me to do or how many times you told me to do it, I'm wise to you — wise to you and shut of you.*

"I went into the bedroom and I looked at the bed. I expected it would look to me like a closet does to a kid who's scared of the bogeyman, but I saw it was just a bed. I knew I wasn't going to do anything, and it was a relief. So I stripped it and there was another of those sticky patches, still drying, as if he'd woke up horny an hour or so before and just took care of himself.

"I seen it and waited to see if I was going to feel anything about it. I didn't. It was just the leftovers of a man with a letter and no mailbox to put it in, like you and I have seen a hundred times before. That old woman was no more a *bruja* woman than I was. I might be pregnant or I might not be, but if I was, it was Johnny's child. He was the only man I'd ever lain with, and nothin I found on that white man's sheets — or anywhere else, for that matter — was gonna change that.

"It was a cloudy day, but at the second I thought that, the sun came out like God had put His final amen on the subject. I don't recall ever feeling so relieved. I stood there thanking God everything was all right, and all the time I was sayin that prayer of gratitude I was scoopin that stuff up off the sheet — all of it I could get, anyway — and stickin it in my mouth and swallowin it down.

"It was like I was standing outside myself and watching again. And a part of me was saying, *You're crazy to be doing that, girl, but you're even crazier to be doing it with him right there in the next room; he could get up any second and come in here to use the bathroom and see you. Rugs as thick as they are in this place, you'd never hear him coming. And that would be the end of your job at Le Palais — or any other big hotel in New York, most likely. A girl caught doing a thing like what you're doing would never work in this city again as a chambermaid, at least not in any half-decent hotel.*

"But it didn't make any difference. I went on until I was done — or until some part of me was satisfied — and then I just stood there a minute, looking down at the sheet. I couldn't hear nothing at all from the other room, and it came to me that he was right behind me, standing in the doorway. I knew just what the expression on his face'd be. Used to be a travelling show that came to Babylon every August when I was a girl, and they had a man with it — I *guess* he was a man — that geeked out behind the tent-show. He'd be down a hole and some fella would give a spiel about how he was the missing link and then throw a live chicken down. The geek'd bite the head off it. Once my oldest brother — Bradford, who died in a car accident in Biloxi — said he wanted to go and see the geek. My dad said he was sorry to hear it, but he didn't outright forbid Brad, because Brad was nineteen and almost a man. He went, and me and Kissy meant to ask him what it was like when he came back, but when we saw the expression on his face we never did. That's the expression I thought I'd see on Jefferies's face when I turned around and saw him in the doorway. Do you see what I'm sayin?"

Darcy nodded.

"I *knew* he was there, too — I just knew it. Finally I mustered up enough courage to turn around, thinking I'd beg him not to tell the Chief Housekeeper — beg him on my knees, if I had to — and he wasn't there. It had just been my guilty heart all along. I walked to the door and

331

looked out and seen he was still in the parlor, writing on his yellow pad faster than ever. So I went ahead and changed the bed and freshened the room just like always, but that feeling that I was behind a glass wall was back, stronger than ever.

"I took care of the soiled towels and bed-linen like you're supposed to — out to the hall through the bedroom door. First thing I learned when I came to work at the hotel is you don't *ever* take dirty linen through the sitting room of a suite. Then I came back in to where he was. I meant to tell him I'd do the parlor later, when he wasn't working. But when I saw the way he was acting, I was so surprised that I stopped right there in the doorway, looking at him.

"He was walking around the room so fast that his yellow silk pajamas were whipping around his legs. He had his hands in his hair and he was twirling it every which way. He looked like one of those brainy mathematicians in the old *Saturday Evening Post* cartoons. His eyes were all wild, like he'd had a bad shock. First thing I thought was that he'd seen what I did after all and it had, you know, made him feel so sick it'd driven him half-crazy.

"Turned out it didn't have nothing to do with me at all . . . at least *he* didn't think so. That was the only time he talked to me, other than to ask me if I'd get some more stationery or another pillow or change the setting on the air-conditioner. He talked to me because he *had* to. Something had happened to him — something very big — and he had to talk to somebody or go crazy, I guess.

" 'My head is splitting,' he said.

" 'I'm sorry to hear that, Mr. Jefferies,' I said. 'I can get you some aspirin —'

" 'No,' he said. 'That's not it. It's this idea. It's like I went fishing for trout and hooked a marlin instead. I write books for a living, you see. Fiction.'

" 'Yes, sir, Mr. Jefferies,' I said, 'I have read two of them and thought they were fine.'

" '*Did* you,' he said, looking at me as if maybe I'd gone crazy. 'Well, that's very kind of you to say, anyway. I woke up this morning and I had an idea.'

"*Yes, sir*, I was thinking to myself, *you had an idea, all right, one so hot and so fresh it just kinda spilled out all over the sheet. But it ain't there no more, so you don't have to worry.* And I almost laughed out loud. Only, Darcy, I don't think he would have noticed if I had.

" 'I ordered up some breakfast,' he said, and pointed at the room-service trolley by the door, 'and as I ate it I thought about this little idea. I thought it might make a short story. There's this magazine, you know . . . *The New Yorker* . . . well, never mind.' He wasn't going to explain *The New Yorker* magazine to a pickaninny like me, you know."

Darcy grinned.

" 'But by the time I'd finished breakfast,' he went on, 'it began to seem more like a novelette. And then . . . as I started to rough out some ideas . . .' He gave out this shrill little laugh. 'I don't think I've had an idea this good in ten years. Maybe never. Do you think it would be possible for twin brothers — fraternal, not identical — to end up

333

fighting on opposite sides during World War II?'

" 'Well, maybe not in the *Pacific*,' I said. Another time I don't think I would have had nerve enough to speak to him at all, Darcy — I would have just stood there and gawped. But I still felt like I was under glass, or like I'd had a shot of novocaine at the dentist's and it hadn't quite worn off yet.

"He laughed like it was the funniest thing he'd ever heard and said, 'Ha-ha! No, not *there*, it couldn't happen *there*, but it might be possible in the ETO. And they could come face-to-face during the Battle of the Bulge.'

" 'Well, maybe —' I started, but by then he was walking fast around the parlor again, running his hands through his hair and making it look wilder and wilder.

" 'I know it sounds like Orpheum Circuit melodrama,' he said, 'some silly piece of claptrap like *Under Two Flags* or *Armadale*, but the concept of twins . . . and it could be explained rationally . . . I see just how . . .' He whirled on me. 'Would it have dramatic impact?'

" 'Yes, sir,' I said. '*Everyone* likes stories about brothers that don't know they're brothers.'

" 'Sure they do,' he said. 'And I'll tell you something else —' Then he stopped and I saw the queerest expression come over his face. It was queer, but I could read it letter-perfect. It was like he was waking up to doing something foolish, like a man suddenly realizing he's spread his face with shaving cream and then taken his electric razor to it. He was talking to a nigger hotel maid about what was maybe the best idea he'd ever had

334

— a nigger hotel maid whose idea of a really good story was probably *The Edge of Night*. He'd forgot me saying I'd read two of his books —"

"Or thought it was just flattery to get a bigger tip," Darcy murmured.

"Yeah, that'd fit his concept of human nature like a glove, all right. Anyway, that expression said he'd just realized who he was talking to, that was all.

" 'I think I'm going to extend my stay,' he said. 'Tell them at the desk, would you?' He spun around to start walking again and his leg whanged against the room-service cart. 'And get this fucking thing out of here, all right?'

" 'Would you want me to come back later and —' I started.

" 'Yes, yes, yes,' he says, 'come back later and do whatever you like, but for now just be my good little sweetheart and make everything all gone . . . including yourself.'

"I did just that, and I was never so relieved in my life as when the parlor door shut behind me. I wheeled the room-service trolley over to the side of the corridor. He'd had juice and scrambled eggs and bacon. I started to walk away and then I seen there was a mushroom on his plate, too, pushed aside with the last of the eggs and a little bit of bacon. I looked at it and it was like a light went on in my head. I remembered the mushroom *she'd* given me — old Mama Delorme — in the little plastic box. Remembered it for the first time since that day. I remembered finding it in my dress pocket, and where I'd put it. The one on his plate looked just the same — wrinkled and sort of dried up, like it might be a toadstool instead of a mushroom, and one that would make you powerful sick."

She looked at Darcy steadily.

"He'd eaten part of it, too. More than half, I'd say."

"Mr. Buckley was on the desk that day and I told him Mr. Jefferies was thinking of extending his stay. Mr. Buckley said he didn't think that would present a problem even though Mr. Jefferies had been planning to check out that very afternoon.

"Then I went down to the room-service kitchen and talked with Bedelia Aaronson — you must remember Bedelia — and asked her if she'd seen anyone out of the ordinary around that morning. Bedelia asked who I meant and I said I didn't really know. She said 'Why you asking, Marty?' and I told her I'd rather not say. She said there hadn't been nobody, not even the man from the food service who was always trying to date up the short-order girl.

"I started away and she said, 'Unless you mean the old Negro lady.'

"I turned back and asked what old Negro lady that was.

" 'Well,' Bedelia said, 'I imagine she came in off the street, looking for the john. Happens once or twice a day. Negroes sometimes won't ask the way because they're afraid the hotel people will kick them out even if they're well-dressed . . . which, as I'm sure you know, they often do. Anyway, this poor old soul wandered down here

. . .' She stopped and got a look at me. 'Are you all right, Martha? You look like you're going to faint!'

" 'I'm not going to faint,' I said. 'What was she doing?'

" 'Just wandering around, looking at the breakfast trolleys like she didn't know where she was,' she said. 'Poor old thing! She was eighty if she was a day. Looked like a strong gust of wind would blow her right up into the sky like a kite . . . Martha, you come over here and sit down. You look like the picture of Dorian Gray in that movie.'

" 'What did she look like? Tell me!'

" 'I *did* tell you — an old woman. They all look about the same to me. The only thing different about this one was the scar on her face. It ran all the way up into her hair. It —'

"But I didn't hear any more because that was when I *did* faint.

"They let me go home early and I'd no more than got there than I started feeling like I wanted to spit again, and drink a lot of water, and probably end up in the john like before, sicking my guts out. But for the time being I just sat there by the window, looking out into the street, and gave myself a talking-to.

"What she'd done to me wasn't just hypnosis; by then I knew that. It was more powerful than hypnosis. I still wasn't sure if I believed in any such thing as witchcraft, but she'd done *something* to me, all right, and whatever it was, I was just going to have to ride with it. I couldn't quit my job, not with a husband that wasn't turning out to be worth salt and a baby most likely on the way. I couldn't even request to be switched to a different floor. A year or two before I could have, but I knew there was talk about making me Assistant Chief Housekeeper for Ten to Twelve, and that meant a raise in pay. More'n that, it meant they'd most likely take me back at the same job after I had the baby.

"My mother had a saying: *What can't be cured must be endured.* I thought about going back to see that old black mama and asking her to take it off, but I knew somehow she wouldn't — she'd made up her mind it was best for me, what she was doing, and one thing I've learned as I've made my way through this world, Darcy, is that the only time you can never hope to change someone's mind is when they've got it in their head that they're doing you a help.

"I sat there thinking all that and looking out at the street, all the people coming and going, and I kind of dozed off. Couldn't have been for much more than fifteen minutes, but when I woke up again I knew something else. That old woman wanted me to keep on doing what I'd already done twice, and I couldn't do that if Peter Jefferies went back to Birmingham. So she got into the room-service kitchen and put that mushroom on his tray and he ate part of it and it gave him that idea. Turned out to be a whale of a story, too — *Boys in the Mist,* it was called. It was about just what he told me that day, twin brothers, one of them an American soldier and the other a German one, that meet at the Battle of the Bulge. It turned out to be the biggest seller he ever had."

She paused and added, "I read that in his obituary."

"He stayed another week. Every day when I went in he'd be bent over the desk in the parlor, writing away on one of his yellow pads, still wearing his pajamas. Every day I'd ask him if he wanted me to come back later and he'd tell me to go ahead and make up the bedroom but be quiet about it. Never looking up from his writing while he talked. Every day I went in telling myself that this time I wasn't going to do it, and every day that stuff was there on the sheet, still fresh, and every day every prayer and every promise I'd made myself went flying out the window and I found myself doing it again. It really *wasn't* like fighting a compulsion, where you argue it back and forth and sweat and shiver; it was more like blinking for a minute and finding out it had already happened. Oh, and every day when I came in he'd be holding his head like it was just killing him. What a pair we were! He had my morning-sickness and I had his night-sweats!"

"What do you mean?" Darcy asked.

"It was at night I'd really brood about what I was doing, and spit and drink water and maybe have to throw up a time or two. Mrs. Parker got so concerned that I finally told her I thought I was pregnant but I didn't want my husband to know until I was sure.

"Johnny Rosewall was one self-centered son of a bitch, but I think even he would have known something was wrong with me if he hadn't had fish of his own to fry, the biggest trout in the skillet being the liquor store holdup he and his friends were plannin. Not that I knew about that, of course; I was just glad he was keepin out of my way. It made life at least a little easier.

"Then I let myself into 1163 one morning and Mr. Jefferies was gone. He'd packed his bags and headed back to Alabama to work on his book and think about his war. Oh, Darcy, I can't tell you how happy I was! I felt like Lazarus must have when he found out he was going to have a second go at life. It seemed to me that morning like everything might come right after all, like in a story — I would tell Johnny about the baby and he would straighten up, throw out his dope, and get a regular job. He'd be a proper husband to me and a good father to his son — I was already sure it was going to be a boy.

"I went into the bedroom of Mr. Jefferies's suite and seen the bedclothes messed up like always, the blankets kicked off the end and the sheet all tangled up in a ball. I walked over there feeling like I was in a dream again and pulled the sheet back. I was thinking, *Well, all right, if I have to . . . but it's for the last time.*

"Turned out the last time had already happened. There wasn't a trace of him on that sheet. Whatever spell that old *bruja* woman had put on us, it had run its course. *That's good enough,* I thought. *I'm gonna have the baby, he's gonna have the book, and we're both shut of her magic. I don't care a fig about natural fathers, either, as long as Johnny will be a good dad to the one I've got coming.*"

"I told Johnny that same night," Martha said,

then added dryly: "He didn't cotton onto the idea, as I think you already know."

Darcy nodded.

"Whopped me with the end of that broomstick about five times and then stood over me where I lay crying in the corner and yelled, 'What are you, crazy? We ain't having no *kid!* I think you stone crazy, woman!' Then he turned around and walked out.

"I laid there for awhile, thinking of the first miscarriage and scared to death the pains would start any minute, and I'd be on my way to having another one. I thought of my momma writing that I ought to get away from him before he put me in the hospital, and of Kissy sending me that Greyhound ticket with GO NOW written on the folder. And when I was sure that I wasn't going to miscarry the baby, I got up to pack a bag and get the hell out of there — right away, before he could come back. But I was no more than opening the closet door when I thought of Mama Delorme again. I remembered telling her I was going to leave Johnny, and what she said to me: 'No — he gonna leave *you.* You gonna see him out, is all. Stick around, woman. There be a little money. You gonna think he hoit the baby but he dint be doin it.'

"It was like she was right there, telling me what to look for and what to do. I went into the closet, all right, but it wasn't my own clothes I wanted anymore. I started going through his, and I found a couple of things in that same damned sportcoat where I'd found the bottle of White Angel. That coat was his favorite, and I guess it really said everything anyone needed to know about Johnny Rosewall. It was bright satin . . . cheap-looking. I hated it. Wasn't no bottle of dope I found this time. Was a straight-razor in one pocket and a cheap little pistol in the other. I took the gun out and looked at it, and that same feeling came over me that came over me those times in the bedroom of Mr. Jefferies's suite — like I was doing something just after I woke up from a heavy sleep.

"I walked into the kitchen with the gun in my hand and set it down on the little bit of counter I had beside the stove. Then I opened the overhead cupboard and felt around in back of the spices and the tea. At first I couldn't find what she'd given me and this awful stiflin panic came over me — I was scared the way you get scared in dreams. Then my hand happened on that plastic box and I drew it down.

"I opened it and took out the mushroom. It was a repulsive thing, too heavy for its size, and *warm*. It was like holding a lump of flesh that hasn't quite died. That thing I did in Mr. Jefferies's bedroom? I tell you right now I'd do it two hundred more times before I'd pick up that mushroom again.

"I held it in my right hand and I picked up that cheap little .32 in my left. And then I squeezed my right hand as hard as I could, and I felt the mushroom squelch in my fist, and it sounded . . . well, I know it's almost impossible to believe . . . but it sounded like it screamed. Do you believe that could be?"

Slowly, Darcy shook her head. She did not, in fact, know if she believed it or not, but she was absolutely sure of one thing: she did not *want* to believe it.

"Well, I don't believe it, either. But that's what it sounded like. And one other thing you won't believe, but I do, because I saw it: it bled. That mushroom bled. I saw a little stream of blood come out of my fist and splash onto the gun. But the blood disappeared as soon as it hit the barrel.

"After awhile it stopped. I opened my hand, expecting it would be full of blood, but there was only the mushroom, all wrinkled up, with the shapes of my fingers mashed into it. Wasn't no blood on the mushroom, in my hand, on his gun, nor anywhere. And just as I started to think I'd done nothing but somehow have a dream on my feet, the damned thing twitched in my hand. I looked down at it and for a second or two it didn't look like a mushroom at all — it looked like a little tiny penis that was still alive. I thought of the blood coming out of my fist when I squeezed it and I thought of her saying, 'Any child a woman get, the man shoot it out'n his pecker, girl.' It twitched again — I tell you it *did* — and I screamed and threw it in the trash. Then I heard Johnny coming back up the stairs and I grabbed his gun and ran back into the bedroom with it and put it back into his coat pocket. Then I climbed into bed with all my clothes on, even my shoes, and pulled the blanket up to my chin. He come in and I seen he was bound to make trouble. He had a rug-beater in one hand. I don't know where he got it from, but I knew what he meant to do with it.

" 'Ain't gonna be no baby,' he said. 'You get on over here.'

" 'No,' I told him, 'there ain't going to be a baby. You don't need that thing, either, so put it away. You already took care of the baby, you worthless piece of shit.'

"I knew it was a risk, calling him that, but I thought maybe it would make him believe me, and it did. Instead of beating me up, this big goony stoned grin spread over his face. I tell you, I never hated him so much as I did then.

" 'Gone?' he asked.

" 'Gone,' I said.

" 'Where's the mess?' he asked.

" 'Where do you think?' I said. 'Halfway to the East River by now, most likely.'

"He came over then and tried to kiss me, for Jesus' sake. *Kiss* me! I turned my face away and he went upside my head, but not hard.

" 'You're gonna see I know best,' he says. 'There'll be time enough for kids later on.'

"Then he went out again. Two nights later him and his friends tried to pull that liquor store job and his gun blew up in his face and killed him."

"You think you witched that gun, don't you?" Darcy said.

"No," Martha said calmly. "*She* did . . . by way of me, you could say. She saw I wouldn't help myself, and so she *made* me help myself."

"But you *do* think the gun was witched."

"I don't just *think* so," Martha said calmly.

Darcy went into the kitchen for a glass of water. Her mouth was suddenly very dry.

"That's really the end," Martha said when she came back. "Johnny died and I had Pete. Wasn't until I got too pregnant to work that I found out

344

just how many friends I had. If I'd known sooner, I think I would have left Johnny sooner . . . or maybe not. None of us really knows the way the world works, no matter what we think or say."

"But that's not everything, is it?" Darcy asked.

"Well, there *are* two more things," Martha said. "Little things." But she didn't look as if they were little, Darcy thought.

"I went back to Mama Delorme's about four months after Pete was born. I didn't want to but I did. I had twenty dollars in an envelope. I couldn't afford it but I knew, somehow, that it belonged to her. It was dark. Stairs seemed even narrower than before, and the higher I climbed the more I could smell her and the smells of her place: burned candles and dried wallpaper and the cinnamony smell of her tea.

"That feeling of doing something in a dream — of being behind a glass wall — came over me for the last time. I got up to her door and knocked. There was no answer, so I knocked again. There was still no answer, so I knelt down to slip the envelope under the door. And her voice came from *right on the other side,* as if *she* was knelt down, too. I was never so scared in my life as I was when that papery old voice came drifting out of the crack under that door — it was like hearing a voice coming out of a grave.

" 'He goan be a fine boy,' she said. 'Goan be just like he father. Like he *natural* father.'

" 'I brought you something,' I said. I could barely hear my own voice.

" 'Slip it through, dearie,' she whispered. I slipped the envelope halfway under and she pulled

345

it the rest of the way. I heard her tear it open and I waited. I just waited.

" 'It's enough,' she whispered. 'You get on out of here, dearie, and don't you ever come back to Mama Delorme's again, you hear?'

"I got up and ran out of there just as fast as I could."

Martha went over to the bookcase, and came back a moment or two later with a hardcover. Darcy was immediately struck by the similarity between the artwork on this jacket and that on the jacket of Peter Rosewall's book. This one was *Blaze of Heaven* by Peter Jefferies, and the cover showed a pair of GIs charging an enemy pillbox. One of them had a grenade; the other was firing an M-1.

Martha rummaged in her blue canvas tote-bag, brought out her son's book, removed the tissue paper in which it was wrapped, and laid it tenderly next to the Jefferies book. *Blaze of Heaven; Blaze of Glory.* Side by side, the points of comparison were inescapable.

"*This* was the other thing," Martha said.

"Yes," Darcy said doubtfully. "They *do* look similar. What about the stories? Are they . . . well . . ."

She stopped in some confusion and looked up at Martha from beneath her lashes. She was relieved to see Martha was smiling.

"You askin if my boy copied that nasty honky's book?" Martha asked without the slightest bit of rancor.

"No!" Darcy said, perhaps a little too vehemently.

"Other than that they're both about war, they're nothing alike," Martha said. "They're as different as . . . well, as different as black and white." She paused and then added: "But — there's a feel about them every now and then that's the same . . . somethin you seem to almost catch around corners. It's that sunshine I told you about — that feeling that the world is mostly a lot better than it looks, especially better than it looks to those people who are too smart to be kind."

"Then isn't it possible that your son was *inspired* by Peter Jefferies . . . that he read him in college and . . ."

"Sure," Martha said. "I suppose my Peter did read Jefferies's books — that'd be more likely than not even if it was just a case of like calling to like. But there's something else — something that's a little harder to explain."

She picked up the Jefferies novel, looked at it reflectively for a moment, then looked at Darcy.

"I went and bought this copy about a year after my son was born," she said. "It was still in print, although the bookstore had to special-order it from the publisher. When Mr. Jefferies was in on one of his visits, I got up my courage and asked if he would sign it for me. I thought he might be put out by me asking, but I think he was actually a little flattered. Look here."

She turned to the dedication page of *Blaze of Heaven.*

Darcy read what was printed there and felt an eerie doubling in her mind. *This book is dedicated to my mother,* ALTHEA DIXMONT JEFFERIES, *the finest woman I have ever known.* And below that,

Jefferies had written in black fountain-pen ink that was now fading, "For Martha Rosewall, who cleans up my clutter and never complains." Below this he had signed his name and jotted *August '61*.

The wording of the penned dedication struck her first as contemptuous . . . then as eerie. But before she had a chance to think about it, Martha had opened her son's book, *Blaze of Glory*, to the dedication page and placed it beside the Jefferies book. Once again Darcy read the printed matter: *This book is dedicated to my mother, MARTHA ROSEWALL. Mom, I couldn't have done it without you.* Below that he had written in a pen which looked like a fine-line Flair: *"And that's no lie. Love you, Mom! Pete."*

But she didn't really read this; she only looked at it. Her eyes went back and forth, back and forth, between the dedication page which had been inscribed in August of 1961 and the one which had been inscribed in April of 1985.

"You see?" Martha asked softly.

Darcy nodded. She saw.

The thin, sloping, somehow old-fashioned backhand script was the same in both books . . . and so, given the variations afforded by love and familiarity, were the signatures themselves. Only the tone of the written messages varied, Darcy thought, and there the difference was as clear as the difference between black and white.

The Moving Finger

When the scratching started, Howard Mitla was sitting alone in the Queens apartment where he lived with his wife. Howard was one of New York's lesser-known certified public accountants. Violet Mitla, one of New York's lesser-known dental assistants, had waited until the news was over before going down to the store on the corner to get a pint of ice cream. *Jeopardy* was on after the news, and she didn't care for that show. She said it was because Alex Trebek looked like a crooked evangelist, but Howard knew the truth: *Jeopardy* made her feel dumb.

The scratching sound was coming from the bathroom just off the short squib of hall that led to the bedroom. Howard tightened up as soon as he heard it. It wasn't a junkie or a burglar in there, not with the heavy-gauge mesh he had put over all the windows two years ago at his own expense. It sounded more like a mouse in the basin or the tub. Maybe even a rat.

He waited through the first few questions, hoping the scratching sound would go away on its own, but it didn't. When the commercial came on, he got reluctantly up from his chair and walked to the bathroom door. It was standing ajar, allowing him to hear the scratching sound even better.

Almost certainly a mouse or a rat. Little paws clicking against the porcelain.

"Damn," Howard said, and went into the kitchen.

Standing in the little space between the gas stove and the refrigerator were a few cleaning implements — a mop, a bucket filled with old rags, a broom with a dustpan snugged down over the handle. Howard took the broom in one hand, holding it well down toward the bristles, and the dustpan in the other. Thus armed, he walked reluctantly back through the small living room to the bathroom door. He cocked his head forward. Listened.

Scratch, scratch, scritchy-scratch.

A very small sound. Probably not a rat. Yet that was what his mind insisted on conjuring up. Not just a rat but a *New York* rat, an ugly, bushy thing with tiny black eyes and long whiskers like wire and snaggle teeth protruding from below its V-shaped upper lip. A rat with attitude.

The sound was tiny, almost delicate, but nevertheless —

Behind him, Alex Trebek said, "This Russian madman was shot, stabbed, and strangled . . . all in the same night."

"Who was Lenin?" one of the contestants responded.

"Who was *Rasputin,* peabrain," Howard Mitla murmured. He transferred the dustpan to the hand holding the broom, then snaked his free hand into the bathroom and turned on the light. He stepped in and moved quickly to the tub crammed into the corner below the dirty, mesh-covered window.

He hated rats and mice, hated all little furry things that squeaked and scuttered (and sometimes bit), but he had discovered as a boy growing up in Hell's Kitchen that if you had to dispatch one of them, it was best to do it quickly. It would do him no good to sit in his chair and ignore the sound; Vi had helped herself to a couple of beers during the news, and the bathroom would be her first stop when she returned from the market. If there was a mouse in the tub, she would raise the roof . . . and demand he do his manly duty and dispatch it anyway. Posthaste.

The tub was empty save for the hand-held shower attachment. Its hose lay on the enamel like a dead snake.

The scratching had stopped either when Howard turned on the light or when he entered the room, but now it started again. Behind him. He turned and took three steps toward the bathroom basin, raising the broomhandle as he moved.

The fist wrapped around the handle got to the level of his chin and then froze. He stopped moving. His jaw came unhinged. If he had looked at himself in the toothpaste-spotted mirror over the basin, he would have seen shiny strings of spittle, as gossamer as strands of spiderweb, gleaming between his tongue and the roof of his mouth.

A finger had poked its way out of the drain-hole in the basin.

A human finger.

For a moment it froze, as if aware it had been discovered. Then it began to move again, feeling its wormlike way around the pink porcelain. It reached the white rubber plug, felt its way over it, then descended to the porcelain again. The scratching noise hadn't been made by the tiny claws of a mouse after all. It was the nail on the end of that finger, tapping the porcelain as it circled and circled.

Howard gave voice to a rusty, bewildered scream, dropped the broom, and ran for the bathroom door. He hit the tile wall with his shoulder instead, rebounded, and tried again. This time he got out, swept the door shut behind him, and only stood there with his back pressed against it, breathing hard. His heartbeat was hard, toneless Morse code high up in one side of his throat.

He couldn't have stood there for long — when he regained control of his thoughts, Alex Trebek was still guiding that evening's three contestants through Single Jeopardy — but while he did, he had no sense of time passing, where he was, or even who he was.

What brought him out of it was the electronic whizzing sound that signalled a Daily Double square. "The category is Space and Aviation," Alex was saying. "You currently have seven hundred dollars, Mildred — how much do you wish to wager?" Mildred, who did not have game-show-host projection, muttered something inaudible in response.

Howard moved away from the door and back into the living room on legs which felt like pogo-sticks. He still had the dustpan in one hand. He looked at it for a moment and then let it fall to the carpet. It hit with a dusty little thump.

"I didn't see that," Howard Mitla said in a trembling little voice, and collapsed into his chair.

"All right, Mildred — for five hundred dollars: This Air Force test site was originally known as Miroc Proving Ground."

Howard peered at the TV. Mildred, a mousy little woman with a hearing aid as big as a clock-radio screwed into one ear, was thinking deeply.

"I didn't *see* that," he said with a little more conviction.

"What is . . . Vandenberg Air Base?" Mildred asked.

"What is *Edwards* Air Base, birdbrain," Howard said. And, as Alex Trebek confirmed what Howard Mitla already knew, Howard repeated: "I didn't see that *at all*."

But Violet would be back soon, and he had left the broom in the bathroom.

Alex Trebek told the contestants — and the viewing audience — that it was still anybody's game, and they would be back to play Double Jeopardy, where the scores could *really* change, in two shakes of a lamb's tail. A politician came on and began explaining why he should be re-elected. Howard got reluctantly to his feet. His legs felt a little more like legs and a little less like pogo-sticks with metal fatigue now, but he still didn't want to go back into the bathroom.

Look, he told himself, *this is perfectly simple. Things like this always are. You had a momentary hallucination, the sort of thing that probably happens to people all the time. The only reason you don't hear about them more often is because people don't like to talk about them . . . having hallucinations is embarrassing. Talking about them makes people feel the way you're going to feel if that broom is still on the floor in there when Vi comes back and asks what you were up to.*

"Look," the politician on TV was saying in rich, confidential tones. "When you get right down to cases, it's perfectly simple: do you want an honest, competent man running the Nassau County Bureau of Records, or do you want a man from up-state, a hired gun who's never even —"

"It was air in the pipes, I bet," Howard said, and although the sound which had taken him into the bathroom in the first place had not sounded the slightest bit like air in the pipes, just hearing his own voice — reasonable, under control again — got him moving with a little more authority.

And besides — Vi would be home soon. Any minute, really.

He stood outside the door, listening.

Scratch, scratch, scratch. It sounded like the world's smallest blind man tapping his cane on the porcelain in there, feeling his way around, checking out the old surroundings.

"Air in the pipes!" Howard said in a strong, declamatory voice, and boldly threw the bathroom door open. He bent low, grabbed the broomhandle, and snatched it back out the door. He did not have to take more than two steps into the little room with its faded, lumpy linoleum and its dingy, mesh-crisscrossed view on the airshaft, and he most certainly did not look into the bathroom sink.

He stood outside, listening.

Scratch, scratch. Scritch-scratch.

He returned the broom and dustpan to the little nook in the kitchen between the stove and the

354

refrigerator and then returned to the living room. He stood there for a moment, looking at the bathroom door. It stood ajar, spilling a fan of yellow light into the little squib of hall.

You better go turn off the light. You know how Vi raises the roof about stuff like that. You don't even have to go in. Just reach through the door and flick it off.

But what if something touched his hand while he was reaching for the light switch?

What if another finger touched *his* finger?

How about *that,* fellows and girls?

He could still hear that sound. There was something terribly relentless about it. It was maddening.

Scratch. Scritch. Scratch.

On the TV, Alex Trebek was reading the Double Jeopardy categories. Howard went over and turned up the sound a little. Then he sat down in his chair again and told himself he didn't hear anything from the bathroom, not a single thing.

Except maybe a little air in the pipes.

Vi Mitla was one of those women who move with such dainty precision that they seem almost fragile . . . but Howard had been married to her for twenty-one years, and he knew there was nothing fragile about her at all. She ate, drank, worked, danced, and made love in exactly the same way: *con brio.* She came into the apartment like a pocket hurricane. One large arm curled a brown paper sack against the right side of her bosom. She carried it through into the kitchen without pausing. Howard heard the bag crackle, heard the refrigerator door open and then close again. When she came back, she tossed Howard her coat. "Hang this up for me, will you?" she asked. "I've got to pee. Do I ever! Whew!"

Whew! was one of Vi's favorite exclamations. Her version rhymed with P.U., the child's exclamation for something smelly.

"Sure, Vi," Howard said, and rose slowly to his feet with Vi's dark-blue coat in his arms. His eyes never left her as she went down the hall and through the bathroom door.

"Con Ed loves it when you leave the lights on, Howie," she called back over her shoulder.

"I did it on purpose," he said. "I knew that'd be your first stop."

She laughed. He heard the rustle of her clothes. "You know me too well — people will say we're in love."

You ought to tell her — warn her, Howard thought, and knew he could do nothing of the kind. What was he supposed to say? Watch out, Vi, there's a finger coming out of the basin drain-hole, don't let the guy it belongs to poke you in the eye if you bend over to get a glass of water?

Besides, it had just been a hallucination, one brought on by a little air in the pipes and his fear of rats and mice. Now that some minutes had gone by, this seemed almost plausible to him.

Just the same, he only stood there with Vi's coat in his arms, waiting to see if she would scream. And, after ten or fifteen endless seconds, she did.

"My God, Howard!"

Howard jumped, hugging the coat more tightly to his chest. His heart, which had begun to slow down, began to do its Morse-code number again.

He struggled to speak, but at first his throat was locked shut.

"*What?*" he managed finally. "*What, Vi? What is it?*"

"The towels! Half of em are on the floor! Sheesh! What happened?"

"I don't know," he called back. His heart was thumping harder than ever, and it was impossible to tell if the sickish, pukey feeling deep down in his belly was relief or terror. He supposed he must have knocked the towels off the shelf during his first attempt to exit the bathroom, when he had hit the wall.

"It must be spookies," she said. "Also, I don't mean to nag, but you forgot to put the ring down again."

"Oh — sorry," he said.

"Yeah, that's what you always say," her voice floated back. "Sometimes I think you want me to fall in and drown. I really *do!*" There was a clunk as she put it down herself. Howard waited, heart thumping away, her coat still hugged against his chest.

"He holds the record for the most strikeouts in a single game," Alex Trebek read.

"Who was Tom Seaver?" Mildred snapped right back.

"Roger Clemens, you nitwit," Howard said.

Pwooosh! There went the flush. And the moment he was waiting for (Howard had just realized this consciously) was now at hand. The pause seemed almost endless. Then he heard the squeak of the washer in the bathroom faucet marked H (he kept meaning to replace that washer and kept forget-

357

ting), followed by water flowing into the basin, followed by the sound of Vi briskly washing her hands.

No screams.

Of course not, because there was no *finger*.

"Air in the pipes," Howard said with more assurance, and went to hang up his wife's coat.

She came out, adjusting her skirt. "I got the ice cream," she said, "cherry-vanilla, just like you wanted. But before we try it, why don't you have a beer with me, Howie? It's this new stuff. American Grain, it's called. I never heard of it, but it was on sale so I bought a six-pack. Nothing ventured, nothing grained, am I right?"

"Hardy-har," he said, wrinkling his nose. Vi's penchant for puns had struck him as cute when he first met her, but it had staled somewhat over the years. Still, now that he was over his fright, a beer sounded like just the thing. Then, as Vi went out into the kitchen to get him a glass of her new find, he realized he wasn't over his fright at all. He supposed that having a hallucination was better than seeing a real finger poking out of the drain of the bathroom basin, a finger that was alive and moving around, but it wasn't exactly an evening-maker, either.

Howard sat down in his chair again. As Alex Trebek announced the Final Jeopardy category — it was The Sixties — he found himself thinking of various TV shows he'd seen where it turned out that a character who was having hallucinations either had (a) epilepsy or (b) a brain tumor. He found he could remember a lot of them.

"You know," Vi said, coming back into the room with two glasses of beer, "I don't like the Vietnamese people who run that market. I don't think I'll *ever* like them. I think they're sneaky."

"Have you ever *caught* them doing anything sneaky?" Howard asked. He himself thought the Lahs were exceptional people . . . but tonight he didn't care much one way or the other.

"No," Vi said, "not a thing. And that makes me all the more suspicious. Also, they *smile* all the time. My father used to say, 'Never trust a smiling man.' He also said . . . Howard, are you feeling all right?"

"He said *that?*" Howard asked, making a rather feeble attempt at levity.

"*Très amusant, cheri.* You look as pale as milk. Are you coming down with something?"

No, he thought of saying, *I'm not coming down with something — that's too mild a term for it. I think I might have epilepsy or maybe a brain tumor, Vi — how's that for coming down with something?*

"It's just work, I guess," he said. "I told you about the new tax account. St. Anne's Hospital."

"What about it?"

"It's a rat's nest," he said, and that immediately made him think of the bathroom again — the sink and the drain. "Nuns shouldn't be allowed to do bookkeeping. Someone ought to have put it in the Bible just to make sure."

"You let Mr. Lathrop push you around too much," Vi told him firmly. "It's going to go on and on unless you stand up for yourself. Do you want a heart attack?"

"No." *And I don't want epilepsy or a brain tumor,*

either. Please, God, make it a one-time thing. Okay?
Just some weird mental burp that happens once and
never again. Okay? Please? Pretty please? With some
sugar on it?

"You bet you don't," she said grimly. "Arlene
Katz was saying just the other day that when men
under fifty have heart attacks, they almost never
come out of the hospital again. And you're only
forty-one. You have to stand up for yourself, Howard. Stop being such a pushover."

"I guess so," he said glumly.

Alex Trebek came back on and gave the Final
Jeopardy answer: "This group of hippies crossed
the United States in a bus with writer Ken Kesey."
The Final Jeopardy music began to play. The two
men contestants were writing busily. Mildred, the
woman with the microwave oven in her ear, looked
lost. At last she began to scratch something. She
did it with a marked lack of enthusiasm.

Vi took a deep swallow from her glass. "Hey!"
she said. "Not bad! And only two-sixty-seven a
six-pack!"

Howard drank some himself. It was nothing special, but it was wet, at least, and cool. Soothing.

Neither of the male contestants was even close.
Mildred was also wrong, but she, at least, was in
the ball-park. "Who were the Merry Men?" she
had written.

"Merry *Pranksters,* you dope," Howard said.

Vi looked at him admiringly. "You know all the
answers, Howard, don't you?"

"I only wish I did," Howard said, and sighed.

Howard didn't care much for beer, but that

night he helped himself to three cans of Vi's new find nevertheless. Vi commented on it, said that if she had known he was going to like it that much, she would have stopped by the drugstore and gotten him an IV hookup. Another time-honored Vi-ism. He forced a smile. He was actually hoping the beer would send him off to sleep quickly. He was afraid that, without a little help, he might be awake for quite awhile, thinking about what he had imagined he'd seen in the bathroom sink. But, as Vi had often informed him, beer was full of vitamin P, and around eight-thirty, after she had retired to the bedroom to put on her nightgown, Howard went reluctantly into the bathroom to relieve himself.

First he walked over to the bathroom sink and forced himself to look in.

Nothing.

This was a relief (in the end, a hallucination was still better than an actual finger, he had discovered, despite the possibility of a brain tumor), but he still didn't like looking down the drain. The brass cross-hatch inside that was supposed to catch things like clots of hair or dropped bobby-pins had disappeared years ago, and so there was only a dark hole rimmed by a circle of tarnished steel. It looked like a staring eyesocket.

Howard took the rubber plug and stuck it into the drain.

That was better.

He stepped away from the sink, put up the toilet ring (Vi complained bitterly if he forgot to put it down when he was through, but never seemed to feel any pressing need to put it back up when *she* was), and addressed the john. He was one of those men who only began to urinate immediately when the need was extreme (and who could not urinate at all in crowded public lavatories — the thought of all those men standing in line behind him just shut down his circuits), and he did now what he almost always did in the few seconds between the aiming of the instrument and the commencement of target practice: he recited prime numbers in his mind.

He had reached thirteen and was on the verge of flowing when there was a sudden sharp sound from behind him: *pwuck!* His bladder, recognizing the sound of the rubber plug being forced sharply out of the drain even before his brain did, clamped shut immediately (and rather painfully).

A moment later that sound — the sound of the nail clipping lightly against the porcelain as the questing finger twisted and turned — began again. Howard's skin went cold and seemed to shrink until it was too small to cover the flesh beneath. A single drop of urine spilled from him and plinked in the bowl before his penis actually seemed to shrink in his hand, retreating like a turtle seeking the safety of its shell.

Howard walked slowly and not quite steadily over to the wash-basin. He looked in.

The finger was back. It was a very long finger, but seemed otherwise normal. Howard could see the nail, which was neither bitten nor abnormally long, and the first two knuckles. As he watched, it continued to tap and feel its way around the basin.

Howard bent down and looked under the sink.

The pipe which came out of the floor was no more than three inches in diameter. It was not big enough for an arm. Besides, it made a severe bend at the place where the sink trap was. So just what was that finger attached to? What *could* it be attached to?

Howard straightened up again, and for one alarming moment he felt that his head might simply detach itself from his neck and float away. Small black specks flocked across his field of vision.

I'm going to faint! he thought. He grabbed his right earlobe and yanked it once, hard, the way a frightened passenger who has seen trouble up the line might yank the Emergency Stop cord of a railroad car. The dizziness passed . . . but the finger was still there.

It was *not* a hallucination. How could it be? He could see a tiny bead of water on the nail, and a tiny thread of whiteness beneath it — soap, almost surely soap. Vi had washed her hands after using the john.

It could *be a hallucination, though. It still could be. Just because you see soap and water on it, does that mean you can't be imagining it? And listen, Howard — if you're not imagining it, what's it doing in there? How did it get there in the first place? And how come Vi didn't see it?*

Call her, then — call her in! his mind instructed, and in the next microsecond countermanded its own order. *No! Don't do that! Because if you go on seeing it and she doesn't —*

Howard shut his eyes tight and for a moment lived in a world where there were only red flashes of light and his own crazy heartbeat.

When he opened them again, the finger was still there.

"What are you?" he whispered through tightly stretched lips. "*What* are you, and what are you doing here?"

The finger stopped its blind explorations at once. It swivelled — and then pointed directly at Howard. Howard blundered a step backward, his hands rising to his mouth to stifle a scream. He wanted to tear his eyes away from the wretched, awful thing, wanted to flee the bathroom in a rush (and never mind what Vi might think or say or see) . . . but for the moment he was paralyzed and unable to tear his gaze away from that pink-white digit, which now resembled nothing so much as an organic periscope.

Then it curled at the second knuckle. The end of the finger dipped, touched the porcelain, and resumed its tapping circular explorations once more.

"Howie?" Vi called. "Did you fall in?"

"Be right out!" he called back in an insanely cheery voice.

He flushed away the single drop of pee which had fallen into the toilet, then moved toward the door, giving the sink a wide berth. He *did* catch sight of himself in the bathroom mirror, however; his eyes were huge, his skin wretchedly pale. He gave each of his cheeks a brisk pinch before leaving the bathroom, which had become, in the space of one short hour, the most horrible and inexplicable place he had ever visited in his life.

When Vi came out into the kitchen to see what

was taking him so long, she found Howard looking into the refrigerator.

"What do you want?" she asked.

"A Pepsi. I think I'll go down to Lah's and get one."

"On top of three beers and a bowl of cherry-vanilla ice cream? You'll *bust*, Harold!"

"No, I won't," he said. But if he wasn't able to offload what his kidneys were holding, he might.

"Are you *sure* you feel all right?" Vi was looking at him critically, but her tone was gentler now — tinged with real concern. "Because you look terrible. Really."

"Well," he said reluctantly, "there's been some flu going around the office. I suppose —"

"*I'll* go get you the damned soda, if you really need it," she said.

"No you won't," Howard interposed hastily. "You're in your nightgown. Look — I'll put on my coat."

"When was the last time you had a soup-to-nuts physical, Howard? It's been so long I've forgotten."

"I'll look it up tomorrow," he said vaguely, going into the little foyer where their coats were hung. "It must be in one of the insurance folders."

"Well, you *better!* And if you insist on being crazy and going out, wear my scarf!"

"Okay. Good idea." He pulled on his topcoat and buttoned it facing away from her, so she wouldn't see how his hands were shaking. When he turned around, Vi was just disappearing back into the bathroom. He stood there in fascinated silence for several moments, waiting to hear if she would scream *this* time, and then the water began to run in the basin. This was followed by the sound of Vi brushing her teeth in her usual manner: *con brio.*

He stood there a moment longer, and his mind suddenly offered its verdict in four flat, no-nonsense words: *I'm losing my grip.*

It might be . . . but that didn't change the fact that if he didn't take a whiz very soon, he was going to have an embarrassing accident. That, at least, was a problem he could solve, and Howard took a certain comfort in the fact. He opened the door, began to step out, then paused to pull Vi's scarf off the hook.

When are you going to tell her about this latest fascinating development in the life of Howard Mitla? his mind inquired suddenly.

Howard shut the thought out and concentrated on tucking the ends of the scarf into the lapels of his overcoat.

The Mitla apartment was on the fourth floor of a nine-story building on Hawking Street. To the right and half a block down, on the corner of Hawking and Queens Boulevard, was Lah's Twenty-Four Hour Delicatessen and Convenience Market. Howard turned left and walked to the end of the building. Here was a narrow alleyway which gave on the airshaft at the rear of the building. Trash-bins lined both sides of the alley. Between them were littery spaces where homeless people — some but by no means all of them winos — often made their comfortless newspaper beds. No one seemed to have taken up residence in the

366

alley this evening, for which Howard was profoundly grateful.

He stepped between the first and second bins, unzipped, and urinated copiously. At first the relief was so great that he felt almost blessed in spite of the evening's trials, but as the flow slackened and he began to consider his position again, anxiety started creeping back in.

His position was, in a word, untenable.

Here he was, pissing against the wall of the building in which he had a warm, safe apartment, looking over his shoulder all the while to see if he was being observed. The arrival of a junkie or a mugger while he was in such a defenseless position would be bad, but he wasn't sure that the arrival of someone he knew — the Fensters from 2C, for instance, or the Dattlebaums from 3F — wouldn't be even worse. What could he say? And what might that motormouth Alicia Fenster say to Vi?

He finished, zipped his pants, and walked back to the mouth of the alley. After a prudent look in both directions, he proceeded down to Lah's and bought a can of Pepsi-Cola from the smiling, olive-skinned Mrs. Lah.

"You look pale tonight, Mr. Mit-ra," she said through her constant smile. "Feering all right?"

Oh yes, he thought. *I'm fearing just fine, thank you, Mrs. Lah. Never better on* that *score.*

"I think I might have caught a little bug at the sink," he told her. She began to frown through her smile and he realized what he had said. "At the office, I mean."

"Better bunder up walm," she said. The frown

367

line had smoothed out of her almost ethereal forehead. "Radio say cold weather is coming."

"Thank you," he said, and left. On his way back to the apartment, he opened the Pepsi and poured it out on the sidewalk. Considering the fact that his bathroom had apparently become hostile territory, the last thing he needed tonight was any more to drink.

When he let himself in again, he could hear Vi snoring softly in the bedroom. The three beers had sent her off quickly and efficiently. He put the empty soda can on the counter in the kitchen, then paused outside the bathroom door. After a moment or two, he tilted his head against the wood.

Scratch-scratch. Scritch-scritch-scratch.

"Dirty son of a bitch," he whispered.

He went to bed without brushing his teeth for the first time since his two-week stint at Camp High Pines, when he had been twelve and his mother had forgotten to pack his toothbrush.

And lay in bed beside Vi, wakeful.

He could hear the sound of the finger making its ceaseless exploratory rounds in the bathroom sink, the nail clicking and tap-dancing. He couldn't *really* hear it, not with both doors closed, and he knew this, but he *imagined* he heard it, and that was just as bad.

No, it isn't, he told himself. *At least you* know *you're imagining it. With the finger itself you're not sure.*

This was but little comfort. He still wasn't able to get to sleep, and he was no closer to solving

368

his problem. He *did* know he couldn't spend the rest of his life making excuses to go outside and pee in the alley next to the building. He doubted if he could manage that for even forty-eight hours. And what was going to happen the next time he had to take a dump, friends and neighbors? *There* was a question he'd never seen asked in a round of Final Jeopardy, and he didn't have a clue what the answer might be. Not the alley, though — he was sure of that much, at least.

Maybe, the voice in his head suggested cautiously, *you'll get used to the damned thing.*

No. The idea was insane. He had been married to Vi for twenty-one years, and he still found it impossible to go to the bathroom when she was in there with him. Those circuits just overloaded and shut down. She could sit there cheerily on the john, peeing and talking to him about her day at Dr. Stone's while he shaved, but he could not do the same. He just wasn't built that way.

If that finger doesn't go away on its own, you better be prepared to make some changes in the way you're built, then, the voice told him, *because I think you're going to have to make some modifications in the basic structure.*

He turned his head and glanced at the clock on the bed-table. It was quarter to two in the morning . . . and, he realized dolefully, he had to pee again.

He got up carefully, stole from the bedroom, passed the closed bathroom door with the ceaseless scratching, tapping sounds still coming from behind it, and went into the kitchen. He moved the step-stool in front of the kitchen sink, mounted it, and aimed carefully into the drain, ears cocked all the while for the sound of Vi getting out of bed.

He finally managed . . . but not until he had reached three hundred and forty-seven in his catalogue of prime numbers. It was an all-time record. He replaced the step-stool and shuffled back to bed, thinking: *I can't go on like this. Not for long. I just can't.*

He bared his teeth at the bathroom door as he passed it.

When the alarm went off at six-thirty the next morning, he stumbled out of bed, shuffled down to the bathroom, and went inside.

The drain was empty.

"Thank God," he said in a low, trembling voice. A sublime gust of relief — relief so great it felt like some sort of sacred revelation — blew through him. "Oh, thank G—"

The finger popped up like a Jack popping out of a Jack-in-the-box, as if the sound of his voice had called it. It spun around three times, fast, and then bent as stiffly as an Irish setter on point. And it was pointing straight at him.

Howard retreated, his upper lip rising and falling rapidly in an unconscious snarl.

Now the tip of the finger curled up and down, up and down . . . as if it were waving at him. Good morning, Howard, so nice to be here.

"Fuck you," he muttered. He turned and faced the toilet. He tried resolutely to pass water . . . and nothing. He felt a sudden lurid rush of rage . . . an urge to simply whirl and pounce on the nasty intruder in the sink, to rip it out of its cave, throw it on the floor, and stamp on it in his bare feet.

"Howard?" Vi asked blearily. She knocked on the door. "Almost done?"

"Yes," he said, trying his best to make his voice normal. He flushed the toilet.

It was clear that Vi would not have known or much cared if he sounded normal or not, and she took very little interest in how he looked. She was suffering from an unplanned hangover.

"Not the worst one I ever had, but still pretty bad," she mumbled as she brushed past him, hiked her nightdress, and plopped onto the jakes. She propped her forehead in one hand. "No more of *that* stuff, please and thank you. American Grain, my rosy red ass. Someone should have told those babies you put the fertilizer on the hops *before* you grow em, not after. A headache on three lousy beers! Gosh! Well — you buy cheap, you get cheap. Especially when it's those creepy Lahs doing the selling. Be a dollface and get me some aspirin, will you, Howie?"

"Sure," he said, and approached the sink carefully. The finger was gone again. Vi, it seemed, had once more frightened it off. He got the aspirin out of the medicine cabinet and removed two. When he reached to put the bottle back, he saw the tip of the finger protrude momentarily from the drain. It came out no more than a quarter of an inch. Again it seemed to execute that miniature wave before diving back out of sight.

I'm going to get rid of you, my friend, he thought suddenly. The feeling that accompanied the

371

thought was anger — pure, simple anger — and it delighted him. The emotion cruised into his battered, bewildered mind like one of those huge Soviet ice-breakers that crush and slice their way through masses of pack-ice with almost casual ease. *I am going to get you. I don't know how yet, but I will.*

He handed Vi the aspirin and said, "Just a minute — I'll get you a glass of water."

"Don't bother," Vi said drearily, and crunched both tablets between her teeth. "Works faster this way."

"I'll bet it plays hell on your insides, though," Howard said. He found he didn't mind being in the bathroom very much at all, as long as Vi was in here with him.

"Don't care," she said, more drearily still. She flushed the toilet. "How are you this morning?"

"Not great," he said truthfully.

"You got one, too?"

"A hangover? No. I think it's that flu-bug I told you about. My throat's sore, and I think I'm running a finger."

"What?"

"Fever," he said. "Fever's what I meant to say."

"Well, you better stay home." She went to the sink, selected her toothbrush from the holder, and began to brush vigorously.

"Maybe *you* better, too," he said. He did not want Vi to stay home, however; he wanted her right by Dr. Stone's side while Dr. Stone filled cavities and did root canals, but it would have been unfeeling not to have said *something*.

She glanced up at him in the mirror. Already

372

a little color was returning to her cheeks, a little sparkle to her eye. Vi also recovered *con brio*. "The day I call in sick at work because I've got a hangover will be the day I quit drinking altogether," she said. "Besides, the doc's gonna need me. We're pulling a complete set of uppers. Dirty job, but somebody's gotta do it."

She spat directly into the drain and Howard thought, fascinated: *The next time it pops up, it'll have toothpaste on it. Jesus!*

"You stay home and keep warm and drink plenty of fluids," Vi said. She had adopted her Head Nurse Tone now, the tone which said *If you're not taking all this down, be it on your own head.* "Catch up on your reading. And, by the bye, show that Mr. Hot Shit Lathrop what he's missing when you don't come in. Make him think twice."

"That's not a bad idea at all," Howard said.

She kissed him on the way by and dropped him a wink. "Your Shrinking Violet knows a few of the answers, too," she said. By the time she left to catch her bus half an hour later, she was singing lustily, her hangover forgotten.

The first thing Howard did following Vi's departure was to haul the step-stool over to the kitchen sink and whiz into the drain again. It was easier with Vi out of the house; he had barely reached twenty-three, the ninth prime number, before getting down to business.

With *that* problem squared away — at least for the next few hours — he walked back into the hall and poked his head through the bathroom door. He saw the finger at once, and that was wrong. It was *impossible,* because he was way over here, and the basin should have cut off his view. But it didn't and that meant —

"What are you doing, you bastard?" Howard croaked, and the finger, which had been twisting back and forth as if to test the wind, turned toward him. There was toothpaste on it, just as he had known there would be. It bent in his direction . . . only now it bent in *three places,* and *that* was impossible, too, quite impossible, because when you got to the third knuckle of any given finger, you were up to the back of the hand.

It's getting longer, his mind gibbered. *I don't know how that can happen, but it is — if I can see it over the top of the basin from here, it must be at least three inches long . . . maybe more!*

He closed the bathroom door gently and staggered back into the living room. His legs had once again turned into malfunctioning pogo-sticks. His mental ice-breaker was gone, flattened under a great white weight of panic and bewilderment. No iceberg this; it was a whole glacier.

Howard Mitla sat down in his chair and closed his eyes. He had never felt more alone, more disoriented, or more utterly powerless in his entire life. He sat that way for quite some time, and at last his fingers began to relax on the arms of his chair. He had spent most of the previous night wide awake. Now he simply drifted off to sleep while the lengthening finger in his bathroom drain tapped and circled, circled and tapped.

He dreamed he was a contestant on *Jeopardy* — not the new, big-money version but the original daytime show. Instead of computer screens, a stagehand behind the game-board simply pulled up a card when a contestant called for a particular answer. Alex Trebek had been replaced by Art Fleming with his slicked-back hair and somehow prissy poor-boy-at-the-party smile. The woman in the middle was still Mildred, and she still had a satellite downlink in her ear, but her hair was teased up into a Jacqueline Kennedy bouffant and her wire-rimmed glasses had been replaced by a pair of cat's-eye frames.

And everyone was in black and white, him included.

"Okay, Howard," Art said, and pointed at him. His index finger was a grotesque thing, easily a foot long; it stuck out of his loosely curled fist like a pedagogue's pointer. There was dried toothpaste on the nail. "It's your turn to select."

Howard looked at the board and said, "I'd like Pests and Vipers for one hundred, Art."

The square with $100 on it was removed, revealing an answer which Art now read: "The best way to get rid of those troublesome fingers in your bathroom drain."

"What is . . ." Howard said, and then came up blank. A black-and-white studio audience stared silently at him. A black-and-white camera man dollied in for a close-up of his sweat-streaked black-and-white face. "What is . . . um . . ."

"Hurry up, Howard, you're almost out of time," Art Fleming cajoled, waving his grotesquely elongated finger at Howard, but Howard was a total blank. He was going to miss the question, the hundred bucks would be deducted from his score, he was going to go into the minus column, he was going to be a complete loser, they probably wouldn't even given him the lousy set of encyclopedias . . .

A delivery truck on the street below backfired loudly. Howard sat up with a jerk which almost pitched him out of his chair.

"What is liquid drain-cleaner?" he screamed. *"What is liquid drain-cleaner?"*

It was, of course, the answer. The *correct* answer.

He began to laugh. He was still laughing five minutes later, as he shrugged into his topcoat and stepped out the door.

Howard picked up the plastic bottle the toothpick-chewing clerk in the Queens Boulevard Happy Handyman Hardware Store had just set down on the counter. There was a cartoon woman in an apron on the front. She stood with one hand on her hip while she used the other hand to pour a gush of drain-cleaner into something that was either an industrial sink or Orson Welles's bidet. DRAIN-EZE, the label proclaimed. *TWICE the strength of most leading brands! Opens bathroom sinks, showers, and drains IN MINUTES! Dissolves hair and organic matter!*

"Organic matter," Howard said. "Just what does that mean?"

The clerk, a bald man with a lot of warts on his forehead, shrugged. The toothpick poking out between his lips rolled from one side of his mouth to the other. "Food, I guess. But I wouldn't stand the bottle next to the liquid soap, if you know what I mean."

"Would it eat holes in your *hands?*" Howard asked, hoping he sounded properly horrified.

The clerk shrugged again. "I guess it ain't as powerful as the stuff we used to sell — the stuff with lye in it — but that stuff ain't legal anymore. At least I don't *think* it is. But you see that, don'tcha?" He tapped the skull-and-crossbones POISON logo with one short, stubby finger. Howard got a good look at that finger. He had found himself noticing a lot of fingers on his walk down to the Happy Handyman.

"Yes," Howard said. "I see it."

"Well, they don't put that on just because it looks, you know, sporty. If you got kids, keep it out of their reach. And don't gargle with it." He burst out laughing, the toothpick riding up and down on his lower lip.

"I won't," Howard said. He turned the bottle and read the fine print. *Contains sodium hydroxide and potassium hydroxide. Causes severe burns on contact.* Well, that was pretty good. He didn't know if it was good enough, but there was a way to find out, wasn't there?

The voice in his head spoke up dubiously. *What if you only make it mad, Howard? What then?*

Well . . . so what? It was in the drain, wasn't it?

Yes . . . but it appears to be growing.

Still — what choice did he have? On this subject the little voice was silent.

"I hate to hurry you over such an important purchase," the clerk said, "but I'm by myself

377

this morning and I have some invoices to go over, so —"

"I'll take it," Howard said, reaching for his wallet. As he did so, his eye caught something else — a display below a sign which read FALL CLEARANCE SALE. "What are those?" he asked. "Over there?"

"Those?" the clerk asked. "Electric hedge-clippers. We got two dozen of em last June, but they didn't move worth a damn."

"I'll take a pair," said Howard Mitla. He began to smile, and the clerk later told police he didn't like that smile. Not one little bit.

Howard put his new purchases on the kitchen counter when he got home, pushing the box containing the electric hedge-clippers over to one side, hoping it would not come to *those*. Surely it wouldn't. Then he carefully read the instructions on the bottle of Drain-Eze.

Slowly pour ¼ bottle into drain . . . let stand fifteen minutes. Repeat application if necessary.

But surely it wouldn't come to *that*, either . . . would it?

To make sure it wouldn't, Howard decided he would pour *half* the bottle into the drain. Maybe a little bit more.

He struggled with the safety cap and finally managed to get it off. He then walked through the living room and into the hall with the white plastic bottle held out in front of him and a grim expression — the expression of a soldier who knows he will be ordered over the top of the trench at any moment — on his usually mild face.

Wait a minute! the voice in his head cried out as he reached for the doorknob, and his hand faltered. *This is crazy! You KNOW it's crazy! You don't need drain-cleaner, you need a psychiatrist! You need to lie down on a couch somewhere and tell someone you imagine — that's right, that's the word, IMAGINE — there's a finger stuck in the bathroom sink, a finger that's growing!*

"Oh no," Howard said, shaking his head firmly back and forth. "No way."

He could not — absolutely could not — visualize himself telling this story to a psychiatrist . . . to *anyone*, in fact. Suppose Mr. Lathrop got wind of it? He might, too, through Vi's father. Bill DeHorne had been a CPA in the firm of Dean, Green, and Lathrop for thirty years. He had gotten Howard his initial interview with Mr. Lathrop, had written him a glowing recommendation . . . had, in fact, done everything but give him the job himself. Mr. DeHorne was retired now, but he and John Lathrop still saw a lot of each other. If Vi found out her Howie was going to see a shrink (and how could he keep it from her, a thing like that?), she would tell her mother — Vi told her mother *everything*. Mrs. DeHorne would tell her husband, of course. And Mr. DeHorne —

Howard found himself imagining the two men, his father-in-law and his boss, sitting in leather wingback chairs in some mythic club or other, the kind of wingback chairs that were studded with little gold nailheads. He saw them sipping sherry in this vision; the cut-glass decanter stood on the little table by Mr. Lathrop's right hand. (Howard had never seen either man actually drink sherry, but this morbid fantasy seemed to demand it.) He saw Mr. DeHorne — who was now doddering into his late seventies and had all the discretion of a housefly — lean confidentially forward and say, *You'll never believe what my son-in-law Howard's up to, John. He's going to see a psychiatrist! He thinks there's a finger in his bathroom sink, you see. Do you suppose he might be taking drugs of some sort?*

And maybe Howard didn't really think all that would happen. He thought there was a possibility it might — if not in just that way then in some other — but suppose it didn't? He *still* couldn't see himself going to a psychiatrist. Something in him — a close neighbor of that something that would not allow him to urinate in a public bathroom if there was a line of men behind him, no doubt — simply refused the idea. He would not get on one of those couches and supply the answer — *There's a finger sticking out of the bathroom sink* — so that some goatee-wearing head-shrinker could pelt him with questions. It would be like *Jeopardy* in hell.

He reached for the knob again.

Call a plumber, then! the voice yelled desperately. *At least do that much! You don't have to tell him what you see! Just tell him the pipe's clogged! Or tell him your wife lost her wedding ring down the drain! Tell him ANYTHING!*

But that idea was, in a way, even more useless than the idea of calling a shrink. This was New York, not Des Moines. You could lose the Hope Diamond down your bathroom sink and still wait a week for a plumber to make a housecall. He did not intend to spend the next seven days slink-

380

ing around Queens, looking for gas stations where an attendant would accept five dollars for the privilege of allowing Howard Mitla to move his bowels in a dirty men's room underneath this year's Bardahl calendar.

Then do it fast, the voice said, giving up. *At least do it fast.*

On this Howard's two minds were united. He was, in truth, afraid that if he didn't act fast — and keep on acting — he would not act at all.

And surprise it, if you can. Take off your shoes.

Howard thought this was an extremely useful idea. He acted upon it at once, easing off first one loafer and then the other. He found himself wishing he had thought to put on some rubber gloves in case of backsplatter, and wondered if Vi still kept a pair under the kitchen sink. Never mind, though. He was screwed up to the sticking point. If he paused to go back for the rubber gloves now, he might lose his courage . . . maybe temporarily, maybe for good.

He eased open the bathroom door and slipped inside.

The Mitla bathroom was never what one would call a cheery place, but at this time of day, almost noon, it was at least fairly bright. Visibility wouldn't be a problem . . . and there was no sign of the finger. At least, not yet. Howard tiptoed across the room with the bottle of drain-cleaner clutched tightly in his right hand. He bent over the sink and looked into the round black hole in the center of the faded pink porcelain.

Except it *wasn't* dark. Something was rushing up through that blackness, hurrying up that small-bore, oozy pipe to greet him, to greet its good friend Howard Mitla.

"*Take this!*" Howard screamed, and tilted the bottle of Drain-Eze over the sink. Greenish-blue sludge spilled out and struck the drain just as the finger emerged.

The result was immediate and terrifying. The glop coated the nail and the tip of the finger. It went into a frenzy, whirling like a dervish around and around the limited circumference of the drain, spraying off small blue-green fans of Drain-Eze. Several droplets struck the light-blue cotton shirt Howard was wearing and immediately ate holes in it. These holes fizzed brown lace at the edges, but the shirt was rather too large for him, and none of the stuff got through to his chest or belly. Other drops stippled the skin of his right wrist and palm, but he did not feel these until later. His adrenaline was not just flowing; it was at flood tide.

The finger blurted up from the drain — joint after impossible joint of it. It was now smoking, and it smelled like a rubber boot sizzling on a hot barbecue grill.

"*Take this! Lunch is served, you bastard!*" Howard screamed, continuing to pour as the finger rose to a height of just over a foot, rising out of the drain like a cobra from a snake-charmer's basket. It had almost reached the mouth of the plastic bottle when it wavered, seemed to shudder, and suddenly reversed its field, zipping back down into the drain. Howard leaned farther over the basin to watch it go and saw just a retreating flash of white far down in the dark. Lazy tendrils of smoke drifted up.

He drew a deep breath, and this was a mistake. He inhaled a great double lungful of Drain-Eze fumes. He was suddenly, violently sick. He vomited forcefully into the basin and then staggered away, still gagging and trying to retch.

"I did it!" he shouted deliriously. His head swam with the combined stench of corrosive chemicals and burned flesh. Still, he felt almost exalted. He had met the enemy and the enemy, by God and all the saints, was his. *His!*

"Hidey-ho! Hidey-fucking-ho! I did it! I —"

His gorge rose again. He half-knelt, half-swooned in front of the toilet, the bottle of Drain-Eze still held stiffly out in his right hand, and realized too late that Vi had put both the ring and the lid down this morning when she vacated the throne. He vomited all over the fuzzy pink toilet-seat cover and then fell forward into his own gloop in a dead faint.

He could not have been unconscious for long, because the bathroom enjoyed full daylight for less than half an hour even in the middle of summer — then the other buildings cut off the direct sunlight and plunged the room into gloom again.

Howard raised his head slowly, aware he was coated from hairline to chinline with sticky, foul-smelling stuff. He was even more aware of something else. A clittering sound. It was coming from behind him, and it was getting closer.

He turned his head, which felt like an overfilled sandbag, slowly to his left. His eyes slowly widened. He hitched in breath and tried to scream, but his throat locked.

The finger was coming for him.

It was easily seven feet long now, and getting longer all the time. It curved out of the sink in a stiff arc made by perhaps a dozen knuckles, descended to the floor, then curved again (*Doublejointed!* some distant commentator in his disintegrating mind reported with interest). Now it was tapping and feeling its way across the tile floor toward him. The last nine or ten inches were discolored and smoking. The nail had turned a greenish-black color. Howard thought he could see the whitish shine of bone just below the first of its knuckles. It was quite badly burned, but it was not by any stretch of the imagination dissolved.

"Get away," Howard whispered, and for a moment the entire grotesque, jointed contraption came to a halt. It looked like a lunatic's conception of a New Year's Eve party-favor. Then it slithered straight toward him. The last half a dozen knuckles flexed and the tip of the finger wrapped itself around Howard Mitla's ankle.

"*No!*" he screamed as the smoking Hydroxide Twins — Sodium and Potassium — ate through his nylon sock and sizzled his skin. He gave his foot a tremendous yank. For a moment the finger held — it was very strong — and then he pulled free. He crawled toward the door with a huge clump of vomit-loaded hair hanging in his eyes. As he crawled he tried to look back over his shoulder, but he could see nothing through his coagulated hair. Now his chest had unlocked and he gave voice to a series of barking, frightful screams.

He could not *see* the finger, at least temporarily, but he could *hear* the finger, and now it was coming

384

fast, tictictictictic right behind him. Still trying to look back over his shoulder, he ran into the wall to the left of the bathroom door with his shoulder. The towels fell off the shelf again. He went sprawling and at once the finger was around his *other* ankle, flexing tight with its charred and burning tip.

It began to pull him back toward the sink. It actually began to *pull him back.*

Howard uttered a deep and primitive howl — a sound such as had never before escaped his polite set of CPA vocal cords — and flailed at the edge of the door. He caught it with his right hand and gave a huge, panicky yank. His shirttail pulled free all the way around and the seam under his right arm tore loose with a low purring sound, but he managed to get free, losing only the ragged lower half of one sock.

He stumbled to his feet, turned, and saw the finger feeling its way toward him again. The nail at the end was now deeply split and bleeding.

Need a manicure, bud, Howard thought, and uttered an anguished laugh. Then he ran for the kitchen.

Someone was pounding on the door. Hard.

"Mitla! Hey, Mitla! What's going on in there?"

Feeney, from down the hall. A big loud Irish drunk. Correction: a big loud *nosy* Irish drunk.

"Nothing I can't handle, my bog-trotting friend!" Howard shouted as he went into the kitchen. He laughed again and tossed his hair off his forehead. It went, but fell back in exactly the same jellied clump a second later. "Nothing I can't

385

handle, you better believe that! You can take that right to the bank and put it in your NOW account!"

"*What* did you call me?" Feeney responded. His voice, which had been truculent, now became ominous as well.

"Shut up!" Howard yelled. "I'm busy!"

"I want the yelling to stop or I'm calling the cops!"

"*Fuck off!*" Howard screamed at him. Another first. He tossed his hair off his forehead, and *clump!* Back down it fell.

"I don't have to listen to your shit, you little four-eyes creep!"

Howard raked his hands through his vomit-loaded hair and then flung them out in front of him in a curiously Gallic gesture — *Et voilà!* it seemed to say. Warm juice and shapeless gobbets splattered across Vi's white kitchen cabinets. Howard didn't even notice. The hideous finger had seized each of his ankles once, and they burned as if they were wearing circlets of fire. Howard didn't care about that, either. He seized the box containing the electric hedge-clippers. On the front, a smiling dad with a pipe parked in his gob was trimming the hedge in front of an estate-sized home.

"You having a little drug-party in there?" Feeney inquired from the hall.

"You better get out of here, Feeney, or I'll introduce you to a friend of mine!" Howard yelled back. This struck him as incredibly witty. He threw his head back and yodeled at the kitchen ceiling, his hair standing up in strange jags and quills and glistening with stomach juices. He looked like a man who has embarked upon a violent love-affair with a tube of Brylcreem.

"Okay, that's it," Feeney said. "That's *it*. I'm callin the cops."

Howard barely heard him. Dennis Feeney would have to wait; he had bigger fish to fry. He had ripped the electric hedge-clippers from the box, examined them feverishly, saw the battery compartment, and pried it open.

"C-cells," he muttered, laughing. "Good! That's good! No problem there!"

He yanked open one of the drawers to the left of the sink, pulling with such force that the stop broke off and the drawer flew all the way across the kitchen, striking the stove and landing upside down on the linoleum floor with a bang and a clatter. Amid the general rick-rack — tongs, peelers, graters, paring knives, and garbage-bag ties — was a small treasure-trove of batteries, mostly C-cells and square nine-volts. Still laughing — it seemed he could no longer *stop* laughing — Howard fell on his knees and grubbed through the litter. He succeeded in cutting the pad of his right palm quite badly on the blade of a paring knife before seizing two of the C-cells, but he felt this no more than he felt the burns he had sustained when he had been backsplashed. Now that Feeney had at last shut his braying Irish donkey's mouth, Howard could hear the tapping again. Not coming from the sink now, though — huh-uh, no way. The ragged nail was tapping on the bathroom door . . . or maybe the hall floor. He had neglected to close the door, he now remembered.

"Who gives a fuck?" Howard asked, and then he screamed: *"WHO GIVES A FUCK, I SAID! I'M READY FOR YOU MY FRIEND! I'M COMING TO KICK ASS AND CHEW BUB- BLEGUM AND I'M ALL OUT OF BUBBLE- GUM! YOU'LL WISH YOU'D STAYED DOWN THE DRAIN!"*

He slammed the batteries into the compartment set into the handle of the hedge-clippers and tried the power switch. Nothing.

"Bite my crank!" Howard muttered. He pulled one of the batteries out, reversed it, and put it back in. This time the blades buzzed to life when he pushed the switch, snicking back and forth so rapidly they were only a blur.

He started for the kitchen door, then made him- self switch the gadget off and go back to the counter. He didn't want to waste time putting the battery cover back in place — not when he was primed for battle — but the last bit of sanity still flickering in his mind assured him that he had no choice. If his hand slipped while he was dealing with the thing, the batteries might pop out of the open compartment, and then where would he be? Why, facing the James Gang with an unloaded gun, of course.

So he fiddled the battery cover back on, cursing when it wouldn't fit and turning it in the other direction.

"You wait for me, now!" he called back over his shoulder. "I'm coming! We're not done yet!"

At last the battery cover snapped down. Howard strode briskly back through the living room with the hedge-clippers held at port arms. His hair still stood up in punk-rock quills and spikes. His shirt — now torn out under one arm and burned in several places — flapped against his round, tidy stomach. His bare feet slapped on the linoleum. The tattered remains of his nylon socks swung and dangled about his ankles.

Feeney yelled through the door, "I called them, birdbrain! You got that? I called the cops, and I hope the ones who show up are all bog-trotting Irishmen, just like me!"

"Blow it out your old tan tailpipe," Howard said, but he was really paying no attention to Feeney. Dennis Feeney was in another universe; this was just his quacking, unimportant voice coming in over the sub-etheric.

Howard stood to one side of the bathroom door, looking like a cop in a TV show . . . only someone had handed him the wrong prop and he was packing a hedge-clipper instead of a .38. He pressed his thumb firmly on the power button set high on the handle of the hedge-clippers. He took a deep breath . . . and the voice of sanity, now down to a mere gleam, offered a final thought before packing up for good.

Are you sure you want to trust your life to a pair of electric hedge-clippers you bought on sale?

"I have no choice," Howard muttered, smiling tightly, and lunged inside.

The finger was still there, still arced out of the sink in that stiff curve that reminded Howard of a New Year's Eve party-favor, the kind that makes a farting, honking sound and then unrolls toward the unsuspecting bystander when you blow on it.

It had filched one of Howard's loafers. It was picking the shoe up and slamming it petulantly down on the tiles again and again. From the look of the towels scattered about, Howard guessed the finger had tried to kill several of those before finding the shoe.

A weird joy suddenly suffused Howard — it felt as if the inside of his aching, woozy head had been filled with green light.

"Here I am, you nitwit!" he yelled. *"Come and get me!"*

The finger popped out of the shoe, rose in a monstrous ripple of joints (Howard could actually hear some of its many knuckles cracking), and floated rapidly through the air toward him. Howard turned on the hedge-clippers and they buzzed into hungry life. So far, so good.

The burned, blistered tip of the finger wavered in front of his face, the split nail weaving mystically back and forth. Howard lunged for it. The finger feinted to the left and slipped around his left ear. The pain was amazing. Howard simultaneously felt and heard a grisly ripping sound as the finger tried to tear his ear from the side of his head. He sprang forward, seized the finger in his left fist, and sheared through it. The clippers lugged down as the blades hit the bone, the high buzzing of the motor becoming a rough growl, but it had been built to clip through small, tough branches and there was really no problem. No problem at all. This was Round Two, this was Double Jeopardy, where the scores could *really* change, and Howard Mitla was racking up a bundle. Blood flew in a fine haze and then the stump pulled back. Howard blundered after it, the last ten inches of the finger hanging from his ear like a coathanger for a moment before dropping off.

The finger lunged at him. Howard ducked and it went over his head. It was blind, of course. That was his advantage. Grabbing his ear like that had just been a lucky shot. He lunged with the clippers, a gesture which looked almost like a fencing thrust, and sheared off another two feet of the finger. It thumped to the tiles and lay there, twitching.

Now the rest of it was trying to pull back.

"No you don't," Howard panted. "No you don't, not at *all!*"

He ran for the sink, slipped in a puddle of blood, almost fell, then caught his balance. The finger was blurring back down the drain, knuckle after knuckle, like a freight-train going into a tunnel. Howard seized it, tried to hold it, and couldn't — it went sliding through his hand like a greased and burning length of clothesline. He sliced forward again nevertheless, and managed to cut off the last three feet of the thing just above the point where it was whizzing through his fist.

He leaned over the sink (holding his breath this time) and stared down into the blackness of the drain. Again he caught just a glimpse of retreating white.

"Come on back anytime!" Howard Mitla shouted. *"Come back anytime at all! I'll be right here, waiting for you!"*

He turned around, releasing his breath in a gasp. The room still smelled of drain-cleaner. Couldn't have that, not while there was still work to do. There was a wrapped cake of Dial soap behind the hot-water tap. Howard picked it up and threw it at the bathroom window. It broke the glass and bounced off the crisscross of mesh behind it. He remembered putting that mesh in — remembered how proud of it he had been. He, Howard Mitla, mild-mannered accountant, had been TAKING CARE OF THE OLD HOMESTEAD. Now he knew what TAKING CARE OF THE OLD HOMESTEAD was really all about. Had there been a time when he had been afraid to go into the bathroom because he thought there might be a mouse in the tub, and he would have to beat it to death with a broomhandle? He believed so, but that time — and that version of Howard Mitla — seemed long ago now.

He looked slowly around the bathroom. It was a mess. Pools of blood and two chunks of finger lay on the floor. Another leaned askew in the basin. Fine sprays of blood fanned across the walls and stippled the bathroom mirror. The basin was streaked with it.

"All right," Howard sighed. "Clean-up time, boys and girls." He turned the hedge-clippers on again and began to saw the various lengths of finger he had cut off into pieces small enough to flush down the toilet.

The policeman was young and he *was* Irish — O'Bannion was his name. By the time he finally arrived at the closed door of the Mitla apartment, several tenants were standing behind him in a little knot. With the exception of Dennis Feeney, who wore an expression of high outrage, they all looked worried.

O'Bannion knocked on the door, then rapped, and finally hammered.

"You better break it down," Mrs. Javier said. "I heard him all the way up on the seventh floor."

"The man's insane," Feeney said. "Probably killed his wife."

"No," said Mrs. Dattlebaum. "I saw her leave this morning, just like always."

"Doesn't mean she didn't come back again, does it?" Mr. Feeney asked truculently, and Mrs. Dattlebaum subsided.

"Mr. Mitter?" O'Bannion called.

"It's *Mit*la," Mrs. Dattlebaum said. "With an *l.*"

"Oh, crap," O'Bannion said, and hit the door with his shoulder. It burst open and he went inside, closely followed by Mr. Feeney. "You stay here, sir," O'Bannion instructed.

"The hell I will," Feeney said. He was looking into the kitchen, with its strew of implements on the floor and the splatters of vomit on the kitchen cabinets. His eyes were small and bright and interested. "The guy's my neighbor. And after all, I was the one who made the call."

"I don't care if you made the call on your own private hotline to the Commish," O'Bannion said. "Get the hell out of here or you're going down to the station with this guy Mittle."

"Mit*la,*" Feeney said, and slunk unwillingly toward the door to the hallway, casting glances back at the kitchen as he went.

O'Bannion had sent Feeney back mostly because he didn't want Feeney to see how nervous he was. The mess in the kitchen was one thing. The way the place smelled was another — some sort of chemistry-lab stink on top, some other smell underneath it. He was afraid the underneath smell might be blood.

He glanced behind him to make sure that Feeney had gone back all the way — that he was not lingering in the foyer where the coats were hung — and then he advanced slowly across the living room. When he was beyond the view of the onlookers, he unsnapped the strap across the butt of his pistol and drew it. He went to the kitchen and looked all the way in. Empty. A mess, but empty. And . . . what was that splattered across the cabinets? He wasn't sure, but judging by the smell —

A noise from behind him, a little shuffling sound, broke the thought off and he turned quickly, bringing his gun up.

"Mr. Mitla?"

There was no answer, but the little shuffling sound came again. From down the hall. That meant the bathroom or the bedroom. Officer O'Bannion advanced in that direction, raising his gun and pointing its muzzle at the ceiling. He was now carrying it in much the same way Howard had carried the hedge-clippers.

The bathroom door was ajar. O'Bannion was quite sure this was where the sound had come from, and he knew it was where the worst of the smell was coming from. He crouched, then pushed the door open with the muzzle of his gun.

"Oh my God," he said softly.

The bathroom looked like a slaughterhouse after a busy day. Blood sprayed the walls and ceiling

394

in scarlet bouquets of spatter. There were puddles of blood on the floor, and more blood had run down the inside and outside curves of the bathroom basin in thick trails; that was where the worst of it appeared to be. He could see a broken window, a discarded bottle of what appeared to be drain-cleaner (which would explain the awful smell in here), and a pair of men's loafers lying quite a distance apart from each other. One of them was quite badly scuffed.

And, as the door swung wider, he saw the man.

Howard Mitla had crammed himself as far into the space between the bathtub and the wall as he could get when he had finished his disposal operation. He held the electric hedge-clippers on his lap, but the batteries were flat; bone was a little tougher than branches after all, it seemed. His hair still stood up in its wild spikes. His cheeks and brow were smeared with bright streaks of blood. His eyes were wide but almost totally empty — it was an expression Officer O'Bannion associated with speed-freaks and crackheads.

Holy Jesus, he thought. *The guy was right — he DID kill his wife. He killed somebody, at least. So where's the body?*

He glanced toward the tub but couldn't see in. It was the most likely place, but it also seemed to be the one object in the room which wasn't streaked and splattered with gore.

"Mr. Mitla?" he asked. He wasn't pointing his gun directly at Howard, but the muzzle was most certainly in the neighborhood.

"Yes, that's my name," Howard said in a hollow, courteous voice. "Howard Mitla, CPA, at your ser-

395

vice. Did you come to use the toilet? Go right ahead. There's nothing to disturb you now. I think that problem's been taken care of. At least for the time being."

"Uh, would you mind getting rid of the weapon, sir?"

"Weapon?" Howard looked at him vacantly for a moment, then seemed to understand. "These?" He raised the hedge-clippers, and the muzzle of Officer O'Bannion's gun for the first time came to rest on Howard himself.

"Yes, sir."

"Sure," Howard said. He tossed the clippers indifferently into the bathtub. There was a clatter as the battery-hatch popped out. "Doesn't matter. The batteries are flat, anyway. But . . . what I said about using the toilet? On more mature consideration, I guess I'd advise against it."

"You would?" Now that the man was disarmed, O'Bannion wasn't sure exactly how to proceed. It would have been a lot easier if the victim were on view. He supposed he'd better cuff the guy and then call for backup. All he knew for sure was that he wanted to get out of this smelly, creepy bathroom.

"Yes," Howard said. "After all, consider this, Officer: there are five fingers on a hand . . . just *one* hand, mind you . . . and . . . have you ever thought about how many holes to the underworld there are in an ordinary bathroom? Counting the holes in the faucets, that is? I make it seven." Howard paused and then added, "Seven is a prime — which is to say, a number divisible only by one and itself."

"Would you want to hold out your hands for me, sir?" Officer O'Bannion said, taking his handcuffs from his belt.

"Vi says I know all the answers," Howard said, "but Vi's wrong." He slowly held out his hands.

O'Bannion knelt before him and quickly snapped a cuff on Howard's right wrist. "Who's Vi?"

"My wife," Howard said. His blank, shining eyes looked directly into Officer O'Bannion's. "She's never had any problem going to the bathroom while someone else is in the room, you know. She could probably go while *you* were in the room."

Officer O'Bannion began to have a terrible yet weirdly plausible idea: that this strange little man had killed his wife with a pair of hedge-clippers and then somehow dissolved her body with draincleaner — and all because she wouldn't get the hell out of the bathroom while he was trying to drain the dragon.

He snapped the other cuff on.

"Did you kill your wife, Mr. Mitla?"

For a moment Howard looked almost surprised. Then he lapsed back into that queer, plastic state of apathy again. "No," he said. "Vi's at Dr. Stone's. They're pulling a complete set of uppers. Vi says it's a dirty job, but somebody has to do it. Why would I kill Vi?"

Now that he had the cuffs on the guy, O'Bannion felt a little better, a little more in control of the situation. "Well, it looks like you offed *someone.*"

"It was just a finger," Howard said. He was still holding his hands out in front of him.

397

Light twinkled and ran along the chain between the handcuffs like liquid silver. "But there are more fingers than one on a hand. And what about the hand's *owner?*" Howard's eyes shifted around the bathroom, which had now gone well beyond gloom; it was filling up with shadows again. "I told it to come back anytime," Howard whispered, "but I was hysterical. I have decided I . . . I am not capable. It grew, you see. It grew when it hit the air."

Something suddenly splashed inside the closed toilet. Howard's eyes shifted in that direction. So did Officer O'Bannion's. The splash came again. It sounded as if a trout had jumped in there.

"No, I most definitely *wouldn't* use the toilet," Howard said. "I'd hold it, if I were you, Officer. I'd hold it just as long as I possibly could, and then use the alley beside the building."

O'Bannion shivered.

Get hold of yourself, boyo, he told himself sternly. *You get hold of yourself, or you'll wind up as nutty as this guy.*

He got up to check the toilet.

"Bad idea," Howard said. "A *really* bad idea."

"What exactly happened in here, Mr. Mitla?" O'Bannion asked. "And what have you stored in the toilet?"

"What happened? It was like . . . like . . ." Howard trailed off, and then began to smile. It was a relieved smile . . . but his eyes kept creeping back to the closed lid of the toilet. "It was like *Jeopardy,*" he said. "In fact, it was like *Final* Jeopardy. The category is The Inexplicable. The Final Jeopardy answer is, 'Because they can.' Do you know what the Final Jeopardy *question* is, Officer?"

Fascinated, unable to take his eyes from Howard's, Officer O'Bannion shook his head.

"The Final Jeopardy question," Howard said in a voice that was cracked and roughened from screaming, "is: 'Why do terrible things sometimes happen to the nicest people?' *That's* the Final Jeopardy question. It's all going to take a lot of thought. But I have plenty of time. As long as I stay away from the . . . the holes."

The splash came again. It was heavier this time. The vomitous toilet seat bumped sharply up and down. Officer O'Bannion got up, walked over, and bent down. Howard looked at him with some interest.

"Final Jeopardy, Officer," said Howard Mitla. "How much do you wish to wager?"

O'Bannion thought about it for a moment . . . then grasped the toilet seat and wagered it all.

Sneakers

John Tell had been working at Tabori Studios just
over a month when he first noticed the sneakers.
Tabori was in a building which had once been
called Music City and had been, in the early days
of rock and roll and top-forty rhythm and blues,
a very big deal. Back then you never would have
seen a pair of sneakers (unless they were on the
feet of a delivery boy) above lobby-level. Those
days were gone, though, and so were the big-
money producers with their reet pleats and pointy-
toed snakeskin shoes. Sneakers were now just
another part of the Music City uniform, and when
Tell first glimpsed these, he made no negative as-
sumptions about their owner. Well, maybe one:
the guy really could have used a new pair. These
had been white when they were new, but from
the look of them new had been a long time ago.

That was all he noticed when he first saw the
sneakers in the little room where you so often
ended up judging your neighbor by his footwear
because that was all you ever saw of him. Tell
spied this pair under the door of the first toilet-stall
in the third-floor men's room. He passed them
on his way to the third and last stall. He came
out a few minutes later, washed and dried his
hands, combed his hair, and then went back to
Studio F, where he was helping to mix an album

by a heavy-metal group called The Dead Beats. To say Tell had already forgotten the sneakers would be an overstatement, because they had hardly registered on his mental radar screen to begin with.

Paul Jannings was producing The Dead Beats' sessions. He wasn't famous in the way the old be-bop kings of Music City had been famous — Tell thought rock-and-roll music was no longer strong enough to breed such mythic royalty — but he was fairly well-known, and Tell himself thought he was the best producer of rock-and-roll records currently active in the field; only Jimmy Iovine could come close.

Tell had first seen him at a party following the premiere of a concert film; had, in fact, recognized him from across the room. The hair was graying now, and the sharp features of Jannings's handsome face had become almost gaunt, but there was no mistaking the man who had recorded the legendary Tokyo Sessions with Bob Dylan, Eric Clapton, John Lennon, and Al Kooper some fifteen years earlier. Other than Phil Spector, Jannings was the only record producer Tell could have recognized by sight as well as by the distinctive sound of his recordings — crystal-clear top ends underscored by percussion so heavy it shook your clavicle. It was that Don McLean clarity you heard first on the Tokyo Sessions recordings, but if you wiped the treble, what you heard pulsing along through the underbrush was pure Sandy Nelson.

Tell's natural reticence was overcome by admiration and he had crossed the room to where Jannings was standing, temporarily unengaged. He introduced himself, expecting a quick handshake and a few perfunctory words at most. Instead, the two of them had fallen into a long and interesting conversation. They worked in the same field and knew some of the same people, but even then Tell had known there was more to the magic of that initial meeting than those things; Paul Jannings was just one of those rare men to whom he found he could talk, and for John Tell, talking really was akin to magic.

Toward the end of the conversation, Jannings had asked him if he was looking for work.

"Did you ever know anyone in this business who wasn't?" Tell asked.

Jannings laughed and asked for his phone number. Tell had given it to him, not attaching much importance to the request — it was most likely a gesture of politeness on the other man's part, he'd thought. But Jannings had called him three days later to ask if Tell would like to be part of the three-man team mixing The Dead Beats' first album. "I don't know if it's really possible to make a silk purse out of a sow's ear," Jannings had said, "but since Atlantic Records is footing the bills, why not have a good time trying?" John Tell saw no reason at all why not, and signed on for the cruise immediately.

A week or so after he first saw the sneakers, Tell saw them again. He only registered the fact that it was the same guy because the sneakers were in the same place — under the door of stall number one in the third-floor men's. There was no question that they *were* the same ones; white (once, anyway) high-tops with dirt in the deep creases. He noticed an empty eyelet and thought, *Must not have had your own eyes all the way open when you laced that one up, friend.* Then he went on down to the third stall (which he thought of, in some vague way, as "his"). This time he glanced at the sneakers on his way out, as well, and saw something odd when he did: there was a dead fly on one of them. It lay on the rounded toe of the left sneaker, the one with the empty eyelet, with its little legs sticking up.

When he got back to Studio F, Jannings was sitting at the board with his head clutched in his hands.

"You okay, Paul?"

"No."

"What's wrong?"

"Me. *I* was wrong. I *am* wrong. My career is finished. I'm washed up. Eighty-sixed. Over-done-with-gone."

"What are you talking about?" Tell looked around for Georgie Ronkler and didn't see him anywhere. It didn't surprise him. Jannings had periodic fugues and Georgie always left when he saw one coming on. He claimed his karma didn't allow him to deal with strong emotion. "I cry at supermarket openings," Georgie said.

"You *can't* make a silk purse out of a sow's ear," Jannings said. He pointed with his fist at the glass between the mixing room and the performance studio. He looked like a man giving the old Nazi *Heil Hitler* salute. "At least not out of pigs like those."

"Lighten up," Tell said, although he knew

Jannings was perfectly right. The Dead Beats, composed of four dull bastards and one dull bitch, were personally repulsive and professionally incompetent.

"Lighten *this* up," Jannings said, and flipped him the bird.

"God, I hate temperament," Tell said.

Jannings looked up at him and giggled. A second later they were both laughing. Five minutes after that they were back to work.

The mix — such as it was — ended a week later. Tell asked Jannings for a recommendation and a tape.

"Okay, but you know you're not supposed to play the tape for anyone until the album comes out," Jannings said.

"I know."

"And why you'd ever want to, for *anyone*, is beyond me. These guys make The Butthole Surfers sound like The Beatles."

"Come on, Paul, it wasn't *that* bad. And even if it was, it's over."

He smiled. "Yeah. There's that. And if I ever work in this business again, I'll give you a call."

"That would be great."

They shook hands. Tell left the building which had once been known as Music City, and the thought of the sneakers under the door of stall number one in the third-floor men's john never crossed his mind.

Jannings, who had been in the business twenty-five years, had once told him that when it came to mixing bop (he never called it rock and roll, only bop), you were either shit or Superman. For the two months following the Beats' mixing session, John Tell was shit. He didn't work. He began to get nervous about the rent. Twice he almost called Jannings, but something in him thought that would be a mistake.

Then the music mixer on a film called *Karate Masters of Massacre* died of a massive coronary and Tell got six weeks' work at the Brill Building (which had been known as Tin Pan Alley back in the heyday of Broadway and the Big Band sound), finishing the mix. It was library stuff in the public domain — and a few plinking sitars — for the most part, but it paid the rent. And following his last day on the show, Tell had no more than walked into his apartment before the phone rang. It was Paul Jannings, asking him if he had checked the *Billboard* pop chart lately. Tell said he hadn't.

"It came on at number seventy-nine." Jannings managed to sound simultaneously disgusted, amused, and amazed. "With a *bullet*."

"What did?" But he knew as soon as the question was out of his mouth.

" 'Diving in the Dirt.' "

It was the name of a cut on The Dead Beats' forthcoming *Beat It 'Til It's Dead* album, the only cut which had seemed to Tell and Jannings remotely like single material.

"Shit!"

"Indeed it is, but I have a crazy idea it's gonna go top ten. Have you seen the video?"

"No."

"What a scream. It's mostly Ginger, the chick

405

in the group, playing mudhoney in some generic bayou with a guy who looks like Donald Trump in overalls. It sends what my intellectual friends like to call 'mixed cultural messages.' " And Jannings laughed so hard Tell had to hold the phone away from his ear.

When Jannings had himself under control again, he said, "Anyway, it probably means the album'll go top ten, too. A platinum-plated dog-turd is still a dog-turd, but a platinum reference is platinum all the way through — you understand dis t'ing, Bwana?"

"Indeed I do," Tell said, pulling open his desk drawer to make sure his Dead Beats cassette, unplayed since Jannings had given it to him on the last day of the mix, was still there.

"So what are you doing?" Jannings asked him.

"Looking for a job."

"You want to work with me again? I'm doing Roger Daltrey's new album. Starts in two weeks."

"Christ, yes!"

The money would be good, but it was more than that; following The Dead Beats and six weeks of *Karate Masters of Massacre,* working with the ex-lead singer of The Who would be like coming into a warm place on a cold night. Whatever he might turn out to be like personally, the man could *sing*. And working with Jannings again would be good, too. "Where?"

"Same old stand. Tabori at Music City."

"I'm there."

Roger Daltrey not only could sing, he turned out to be a tolerably nice guy in the bargain. Tell

406

thought the next three or four weeks would be good ones. He had a job, he had a production credit on an album that had popped onto the *Billboard* charts at number forty-one (and the single was up to number seventeen and still climbing), and he felt safe about the rent for the first time since he had come to New York from Pennsylvania four years ago.

It was June, trees were in full leaf, girls were wearing short skirts again, and the world seemed a fine place to be. Tell felt this way on his first day back at work for Paul Jannings until approximately 1:45 P.M. Then he walked into the third-floor bathroom, saw the same once-white sneakers under the door of stall one, and all his good feelings suddenly collapsed.

They are not the same. Can't *be the same.*

They were, though. That single empty eyelet was the clearest point of identification, but everything else about them was also the same. *Exactly* the same, and that included their positions. There was only one real difference that Tell could see: there were more dead flies around them now.

He went slowly into the third stall, "his" stall, lowered his pants, and sat down. He wasn't surprised to find that the urge which had brought him here had entirely departed. He sat still for a little while just the same, however, listening for sounds. The rattle of a newspaper. The clearing of a throat. Hell, even a fart.

No sounds came.

That's because I'm in here alone, Tell thought. *Except, that is, for the dead guy in the first stall.*

The bathroom's outer door banged briskly open.

407

Tell almost screamed. Someone hummed his way over to the urinals, and as water began to splash out there, an explanation occurred to Tell and he relaxed. It was so simple it was absurd . . . and undoubtedly correct. He glanced at his watch and saw it was 1:47.

A regular man is a happy man, his father used to say. Tell's dad had been a taciturn fellow, and that saying (along with *Clean your hands before you clean your plate*) had been one of his few aphorisms. If regularity really *did* mean happiness, then Tell supposed he was a happy man. His need to visit the bathroom came on at about the same time every day, and he supposed the same must be true of his pal Sneakers, who favored Stall #1 just as Tell himself favored Stall #3.

If you needed to pass the stalls to get to the urinals, you would have seen that stall empty lots of times, or with different shoes under it. After all, what are the chances a body could stay undiscovered in a men's-room toilet-stall for . . .

He worked out in his mind the time he'd last been there.

. . . four months, give or take?

No chance at all was the answer to that one. He could believe the janitors weren't too fussy about cleaning the stalls — all those dead flies — but they would have to check on the toilet-paper supply every day or two, right? And even if you left those things out, dead people started to smell after awhile, right? God knew this wasn't the sweetest-smelling place on earth — and following a visit from the fat guy who worked down the hall at Janus Music it was almost uninhabitable

408

— but surely the stink of a dead body would be a lot louder. A lot *gaudier.*

Gaudy? Gaudy? *Jesus, what a word. And how would you know? You never smelled a decomposing body in your life.*

True, but he was pretty sure he'd know what he was smelling if he did. Logic was logic and regularity was regularity and that was the end of it. The guy was probably a pencil-pusher from Janus or a writer for Snappy Kards, on the other side of the floor. For all John Tell knew, the guy was in there composing greeting-card verse right now:

Roses are red and violets are blue,
You thought I was dead but that wasn't true;
I just deliver my mail at the same time as you!

That sucks, Tell thought, and uttered a wild little laugh. The fellow who had banged the door open, almost startling him into a scream, had progressed to the wash-basins. Now the splashing-lathering sound of him washing his hands stopped briefly. Tell could imagine the newcomer listening, wondering who was laughing behind one of the closed stall doors, wondering if it was a joke, a dirty picture, or if the man was just crazy. There were, after all, lots of crazy people in New York. You saw them all the time, talking to themselves and laughing for no appreciable reason . . . the way Tell had just now.

Tell tried to imagine Sneakers also listening and couldn't.

Suddenly he didn't feel like laughing anymore.

Suddenly he just felt like getting out of there.

He didn't want the man at the basin to see him, though. The man would look at him. Just for a moment, but that would be enough to know what he was thinking. People who laughed behind closed toilet-stall doors were not to be trusted.

Click-clack of shoes on the old white hexagonal bathroom tiles, *whooze* of the door being opened, *hisshh* of it settling slowly back into place. You could bang it open but the pneumatic elbow-joint kept it from banging shut. That might upset the third-floor receptionist as he sat smoking Camels and reading the latest issue of *Krrang!*

God, it's so silent *in here! Why doesn't the guy move? At least a little?*

But there was just the silence, thick and smooth and total, the sort of silence the dead would hear in their coffins if they could still hear, and Tell again became convinced that Sneakers was dead, fuck logic, he was dead and *had* been dead for who knew how long, he was sitting in there and if you opened the door you would see some slumped mossy thing with its hands dangling between its thighs, you would see —

For a moment he was on the verge of calling, *Hey Sneaks! You all right?*

But what if Sneakers answered, not in a questioning or irritated voice but in a froggy grinding croak? Wasn't there something about waking the dead? About —

Suddenly Tell was up, up fast, flushing the toilet and buttoning his pants, out of the stall, zipping his fly as he headed for the door, aware that in a few seconds he was going to feel silly but not caring. Yet he could not forbear one glance under the first stall as he passed. Dirty white mislaced sneakers. And dead flies. Quite a few of them.

Weren't any dead flies in my *stall. And just how is it that all this time has gone by and he still hasn't noticed that he missed one of the eyelets? Or does he wear em that way all the time, as some kind of artistic statement?*

Tell hit the door pretty hard coming out. The receptionist just up the hall glanced at him with the cool curiosity he saved for beings merely mortal (as opposed to such deities in human form as Roger Daltrey).

Tell hurried down the hall to Tabori Studios.

"Paul?"

"What?" Jannings answered without looking up from the board. Georgie Ronkler was standing off to one side, watching Jannings closely and nibbling a cuticle — cuticles were all he had left to nibble; his fingernails simply did not exist above the point where they parted company with live flesh and hot nerve-endings. He was close to the door. If Jannings began to rant, Georgie would slip through it.

"I think there might be something wrong in —"

Jannings groaned. "Something *else?*"

"What do you mean?"

"This drum track is what I mean. It's *badly* botched, and I don't know what we can do about it." He flicked a toggle, and drums crashed into the studio. "You hear it?"

"The snare, you mean?"

"Of *course* I mean the snare! It stands out a mile

411

from the rest of the percussion, but it's *married to it!*"

"Yes, but —"

"Yes but Jesus bloody *fuck*. I hate shit like this! Forty tracks I got here, *forty goddam tracks to record a simple bop tune and some IDIOT technician —*"

From the tail of his eye Tell saw Georgie disappear like a cool breeze.

"But look, Paul, if you lower the equalization —"

"The eq's got nothing to do with —"

"Shut up and listen a minute," Tell said soothingly — something he could have said to no one else on the face of the earth — and slid a switch. Jannings stopped ranting and started listening. He asked a question. Tell answered it. Then he asked one Tell *couldn't* answer, but Jannings was able to answer it himself, and all of a sudden they were looking at a whole new spectrum of possibilities for a song called "Answer to You, Answer to Me."

After awhile, sensing that the storm had passed, Georgie Ronkler crept back in.

And Tell forgot all about the sneakers.

They returned to his mind the following evening. He was at home, sitting on the toilet in his own bathroom, reading *Wise Blood* while Vivaldi played mildly from the bedroom speakers (although Tell now mixed rock and roll for a living, he owned only four rock records, two by Bruce Springsteen and two by John Fogerty).

He looked up from his book, somewhat startled. A question of cosmic ludicrousness had suddenly occurred to him: *How long has it been since you took a crap in the evening, John?*

He didn't know, but he thought he might be taking them then quite a bit more frequently in the future. At least one of his habits might change, it seemed.

Sitting in the living room fifteen minutes later, his book forgotten in his lap, something else occurred to him: he hadn't used the third-floor rest room once that day. They had gone across the street for coffee at ten, and he had taken a whiz in the men's room of Donut Buddy while Paul and Georgie sat at the counter, drinking coffee and talking about overdubs. Then, on his lunch hour, he had made a quick pit-stop at the Brew 'n Burger . . . and another on the first floor late that afternoon when he had gone down to drop off a bunch of mail that he could have just as easily stuffed into the mail-slot by the elevators.

Avoiding the third-floor men's? Was that what he'd been doing today without even realizing it? You bet your Reeboks it was. Avoiding it like a scared kid who goes a block out of his way coming home from school so he won't have to go past the local haunted house. Avoiding it like the plague.

"Well, so what?" he said out loud.

He couldn't exactly articulate the so-what, but he knew there was one; there was something just a little too existential, even for New York, about getting spooked out of a public bathroom by a pair of dirty sneakers.

Aloud, very clearly, Tell said: "This has got to stop."

But that was Thursday night and something hap-

413

pened on Friday night that changed everything. That was when the door closed between him and Paul Jannings.

Tell was a shy man and didn't make friends easily. In the rural Pennsylvania town where he had gone to high school, a quirk of fate had put Tell up on stage with a guitar in his hands — the last place he'd ever expected to be. The bassist of a group called The Satin Saturns fell ill with salmonella the day before a well-paying gig. The lead guitarist, who was also in the school band, knew John Tell could play both bass and rhythm. This lead guitarist was big and potentially violent. John Tell was small, humble, and breakable. The guitarist offered him a choice between playing the ill bassist's instrument and having it rammed up his ass to the fifth fret. This choice had gone a long way toward clarifying his feelings about playing in front of a large audience.

But by the end of the third song, he was no longer frightened. By the end of the first set he knew he was home. Years after that first gig, Tell heard a story about Bill Wyman, bassist of The Rolling Stones. According to the story, Wyman actually nodded off during a performance — not in some tiny club, mind you, but in a huge hall — and fell from the stage, breaking his collarbone. Tell supposed lots of people thought the story was apocryphal, but he himself had an idea it was true . . . and he was, after all, in a unique position to understand how something like that could happen. Bassists were the invisible men of the rock world. There were exceptions — Paul McCartney, for one — but they only proved the rule.

Perhaps because of the job's very lack of glamor, there was a chronic shortage of bass players. When The Satin Saturns broke up a month later (the lead guitarist and the drummer got into a fist-fight over a girl), Tell joined a band formed by the Saturns' rhythm man, and his life's course was chosen, as simply and quietly as that.

Tell liked playing in the band. You were up front, looking down on everyone else, not just *at* the party but making the party happen; you were simultaneously almost invisible and absolutely essential. Every now and then you had to sing a little backup, but nobody expected you to make a *speech* or anything.

He had lived that life — part-time student and full-time band gypsy — for ten years. He was good, but not ambitious — there was no fire in his belly. Eventually he drifted into session work in New York, began fooling with the boards, and discovered he liked life even better on the far side of the glass window. During all that time he had made one good friend: Paul Jannings. That had happened fast, and Tell supposed the unique pressures that went with the job had had something to do with it . . . but not everything. Mostly, he suspected, it had been a combination of two factors: his own essential loneliness and Jannings's personality, which was so powerful it was almost overwhelming. And it wasn't so different for Georgie, Tell came to realize following what happened on that Friday night.

He and Paul were having a drink at one of the back tables in McManus's Pub, talking about the mix, the biz, the Mets, whatever, when all of a sudden Jannings's right hand was under the table and gently squeezing Tell's crotch.

Tell moved away so violently that the candle in the center of the table fell over and Jannings's glass of wine spilled. A waiter came over and righted the candle before it could scorch the tablecloth, then left. Tell stared at Jannings, his eyes wide and shocked.

"I'm sorry," Jannings said, and he *did* look sorry . . . but he also looked unperturbed.

"Jesus *Christ,* Paul!" It was all he could think of to say, and it sounded hopelessly inadequate.

"I thought you were ready, that's all," Jannings said. "I suppose I should have been a little more subtle."

"Ready?" Tell repeated. "What do you mean? Ready for *what?*"

"To come out. To give yourself permission to come out."

"I'm not that way," Tell said, but his heart was pounding very hard and fast. Part of it was outrage, part was fear of the implacable certainty he saw in Jannings's eyes, most of it was dismay. What Jannings had done had shut him out.

"Let's let it go, shall we? We'll just order and make up our minds that it never happened." *Until you want it to,* those implacable eyes added.

Oh, it happened, all right, Tell wanted to say, but didn't. The voice of reason and practicality would not allow it . . . would not allow him to risk lighting Paul Jannings's notoriously short fuse. This was, after all, a good job . . . and the job *per se* wasn't all. He could use Roger Daltrey's tape in his portfolio even more than he could use

416

two more weeks' salary. He would do well to be diplomatic and save the outraged-young-man act for another time. Besides, did he really have anything to feel outraged about? It wasn't as if Jannings had raped him, after all.

And that was really just the tip of the iceberg. The rest was this: his mouth closed because that was what his mouth had always done. It did more than close — it snapped shut like a bear-trap, with all his heart below those interlocked teeth and all his head above.

"All right," was all he said, "it never happened."

Tell slept badly that night, and what sleep he did get was haunted by bad dreams: one of Jannings groping him in McManus's was followed by one of the sneakers under the stall door, only in this one Tell opened the door and saw Paul Jannings sitting there. He had died naked, and in a state of sexual excitement that somehow continued even in death, even after all this time. Paul's mouth dropped open with an audible creak. "That's right; I *knew* you were ready," the corpse said on a puff of greenly rotten air, and Tell woke himself up by tumbling onto the floor in a tangle of coverlet. It was four in the morning. The first touches of light were just creeping through the chinks between the buildings outside his window. He dressed and sat smoking one cigarette after another until it was time to go to work.

Around eleven o'clock on that Saturday — they were working six-day weeks to make Daltrey's deadline — Tell went into the third-floor men's room to urinate. He stood just inside the door, rubbing his temples, and then looked around at the stalls.

He couldn't see. The angle was wrong.

Then never mind! Fuck it! Take your piss and get out of here!

He walked slowly over to one of the urinals and unzipped. It took a long time to get going.

On his way out he paused again, head cocked like Nipper the Dog's on the old RCA Victor record labels, and then turned around. He walked slowly back around the corner, stopping as soon as he could see under the door of the first stall. The dirty white sneakers were still there. The building which used to be known as Music City was almost completely empty, Saturday-morning-empty, but the sneakers were still there.

Tell's eyes fixed upon a fly just outside the stall. He watched with an empty sort of avidity as it crawled beneath the stall door and onto the dirty toe of one of the sneakers. There it stopped and simply fell dead. It tumbled into the growing pile of insect corpses around the sneakers. Tell saw with no surprise at all (none he felt, anyway) that among the flies were two small spiders and one large cockroach, lying on its back like an upended turtle.

Tell left the men's room in large painless strides, and his progress back to the studios seemed most peculiar; it was as if, instead of him walking, the building was flowing past him, around him, like river-rapids around a rock.

When I get back I'll tell Paul I don't feel well and take the rest of the day off, he thought, but

418

he wouldn't. Paul had been in an erratic, unpleasant mood all morning, and Tell knew he was part (or maybe all) of the reason why. Might Paul fire him out of spite? A week ago he would have laughed at such an idea. But a week ago he had still believed what he had come to believe in his growing-up: friends were real and ghosts were make-believe. Now he was starting to wonder if maybe he hadn't gotten those two postulates turned around somehow.

"The prodigal returns," Jannings said without looking around as Tell opened the second of the studio's two doors — the one that was called the "dead air" door. "I thought you died in there, Johnny."

"No," Tell said. "Not me."

It *was* a ghost, and Tell found out whose a day before the Daltrey mix — and his association with Paul Jannings — ended, but before that happened a great many other things did. Except they were all the same thing, just little mile-markers, like the ones on the Pennsylvania Turnpike, announcing John Tell's steady progress toward a nervous breakdown. He knew this was happening but could not keep it from happening. It seemed he was not driving this particular road but being chauffeured.

At first his course of action had seemed clear-cut and simple: avoid that particular men's room, and avoid all thoughts and questions about the sneakers. Simply turn that subject off. Make it dark.

Except he couldn't. The image of the sneakers crept up on him at odd moments and pounced like an old grief. He would be sitting home, watching CNN or some stupid chat-show on the tube, and all at once he'd find himself thinking about the flies, or about what the janitor who replaced the toilet paper was obviously not seeing, and then he would look at the clock and see an hour had passed. Sometimes more.

For awhile he was almost convinced it was some sort of malevolent joke. Paul was in on it, of course, and probably the fat guy from Janus Music — Tell had seen them talking together quite frequently, and hadn't they looked at him once and laughed? The receptionist was also a good bet, him with his Camels and his dead, skeptical eyes. Not Georgie, Georgie couldn't have kept the secret even if Paul had hectored him into going along, but anyone else was possible. For a day or two Tell even speculated on the possibility that Roger Daltrey himself might have taken a turn wearing the mislaced white sneakers.

Although he recognized these thoughts as paranoid fantasies, recognition did not lead to dispersion. He would tell them to go away, would insist there was no Jannings-led cabal out to get him, and his mind would say *Yeah, okay, makes sense to me,* and five hours later — or maybe only twenty minutes — he would imagine a bunch of them sitting around Desmond's Steak House two blocks downtown: Paul, the chain-smoking receptionist with the taste for heavy-metal, heavy-leather groups, maybe even the skinny guy from Snappy Kards, all of them eating shrimp cocktails and drinking. And laughing, of course. Laughing at *him,* while the dirty white sneakers they took turns wearing sat under the table in a crumpled brown bag.

Tell could *see* that brown bag. That was how bad it had gotten.

But that short-lived fantasy wasn't the worst. The worst was simply this: the third-floor men's room had acquired a *pull*. It was as if there were a powerful magnet in there and his pockets were full of iron filings. If someone had *told* him something like that he would have laughed (maybe just inside, if the person making the metaphor seemed very much in earnest), but it was really there, a feeling like a swerve every time he passed the men's on his way to the studios or to the elevators. It was a terrible feeling, like being pulled toward an open window in a tall building or watching helplessly, as if from outside yourself, as you raised a pistol to your mouth and sucked the barrel.

He wanted to look again. He realized that one more look was about all it would take to finish him off, but it made no difference. He wanted to look again.

Each time he passed, that mental swerve.

In his dreams he opened that stall door again and again. Just to get a look.

A really *good* look.

And he couldn't seem to tell anyone. He knew it would be better if he did, understood that if he poured it into someone else's ear it would change its shape, perhaps even grow a handle with which he could hold it. Twice he went into bars and managed to strike up conversations with the men next to him. Because bars, he thought, were the places where talk was at its absolute cheapest. Bargain-basement rates.

He had no more than opened his mouth on the

first occasion when the man he had picked began to sermonize on the subject of the Yankees and George Steinbrenner. Steinbrenner had gotten under this man's skin in a big way, and it was impossible to get a word in edgeways with the fellow on any other subject. Tell soon gave up trying.

The second time, he managed to strike up a fairly casual conversation with a man who looked like a construction worker. They talked about the weather, then about baseball (but this man, thankfully, was not nuts on the subject), and progressed to how tough it was to find a good job in New York. Tell was sweating. He felt as if he were doing some heavy piece of manual labor — pushing a wheelbarrow filled with cement up a slight grade, maybe — but he also felt that he wasn't doing too badly.

The guy who looked like a construction worker was drinking Black Russians. Tell stuck to beer. It felt as if he was sweating it out as fast as he put it in, but after he had bought the guy a couple of drinks and the guy had bought Tell a couple of schooners, he nerved himself to begin.

"You want to hear something really strange?" he said.

"You queer?" the guy who looked like a construction worker asked him before Tell could get any further. He turned on his stool and looked at Tell with amiable curiosity. "I mean, it's nothin to me whether y'are or not, but I'm gettin those vibes and I just thought I'd tell you I don't go for that stuff. Have it up front, you know?"

"I'm not queer," Tell said.

"Oh. What's really strange?"

"Huh?"

"You said something was really strange."

"Oh, it really wasn't that strange," Tell said. Then he glanced down at his watch and said it was getting late.

Three days before the end of the Daltrey mix, Tell left Studio F to urinate. He now used the bathroom on the sixth floor for this purpose. He had first used the one on four, then the one on five, but these were stacked directly above the one on three, and he had begun to feel the owner of the sneakers radiating silently up through the floors, seeming to suck at him. The men's room on six was on the opposite side of the building, and that seemed to solve the problem.

He breezed past the reception desk on his way to the elevators, blinked, and suddenly, instead of being in the elevator car, he was in the third-floor bathroom with the door *hisshhing* softly shut behind him. He had never been so afraid. Part of it was the sneakers, but most of it was knowing he had just dropped three to six seconds of consciousness. For the first time in his life his mind had simply shorted out.

He had no idea how long he might have stood there if the door hadn't suddenly opened behind him, cracking him painfully in the back. It was Paul Jannings. "Excuse me, Johnny," he said. "I had no idea you came in here to meditate."

He passed Tell without waiting for a response (he wouldn't have got one in any case, Tell thought later; his tongue had been frozen to the roof of

423

his mouth), and headed for the stalls. Tell was able to walk over to the first urinal and unzip his fly, doing these things only because he thought Paul might enjoy it too much if he turned and scurried out. There had been a time not so long ago when he had considered Paul a friend — maybe his *only* friend, at least in New York. Times had certainly changed.

Tell stood at the urinal for ten seconds or so, then flushed it. He headed for the door, then stopped. He turned around, took two quiet on-tiptoe steps, bent, and looked under the door of the first stall. The sneakers were still there, now surrounded by mounds of dead flies.

So were Paul Jannings's Gucci loafers.

What Tell was seeing looked like a double exposure, or one of the hokey ghost effects from the old *Topper* TV program. First he would be seeing Paul's loafers through the sneakers; then the sneakers would seem to solidify and he would be seeing them through the loafers, as if Paul were the ghost. Except, even when he was seeing through them, Paul's loafers made little shifts and movements, while the sneakers remained as immobile as always.

Tell left. For the first time in two weeks he felt calm.

The next day he did what he probably should have done at once: he took Georgie Ronkler out to lunch and asked him if he had ever heard any strange tales or rumors about the building which used to be called Music City. Why he hadn't thought of doing this earlier was a puzzle to him.

424

He only knew that what had happened yesterday seemed to have cleared his mind somehow, like a brisk slap or a faceful of cold water. Georgie might not know anything, but he might; he had been working with Paul for at least seven years, and a lot of that work had been done at Music City.

"Oh, the ghost, you mean?" Georgie asked, and laughed. They were in Cartin's, a deli-restaurant on Sixth Avenue, and the place was noon-noisy. Georgie bit into his corned-beef sandwich, chewed, swallowed, and sipped some of his cream soda through the two straws poked into the bottle. "Who told you 'bout that, Johnny?"

"Oh, one of the janitors, I guess," Tell said. His voice was perfectly even.

"You sure you didn't see him?" Georgie asked, and winked. This was as close as Paul's long-time assistant could get to teasing.

"Nope." Nor had he, actually. Just the sneakers. And some dead bugs.

"Yeah, well, it's pretty much died down now, but for awhile it was all anybody ever talked about — how the guy was haunting the place. He got it right up there on the third floor, you know. In the john." Georgie raised his hands, trembled them beside his peach-fuzzy cheeks, hummed a few bars of *The Twilight Zone* theme, and tried to look ominous. This was an expression he was incapable of achieving.

"Yes," Tell said. "That's what I heard. But the janitor wouldn't tell me any more, or maybe he didn't know any more. He just laughed and walked away."

"It happened before I started to work with Paul. Paul was the one who told me about it."

"He never saw the ghost himself?" Tell asked, knowing the answer. Yesterday Paul had been *sitting* in it. *Shitting* in it, to be perfectly vulgarly truthful.

"No, he used to laugh about it." Georgie put his sandwich down. "You know how he can be sometimes. Just a little m-mean." If forced to say something even slightly negative about someone, Georgie developed a mild stutter.

"I know. But never mind Paul; who was this ghost? What happened to him?"

"Oh, he was just some dope pusher," Georgie said. "This was back in 1972 or '73, I guess, when Paul was just starting out — he was only an assistant mixer himself, back then. Just before the slump."

Tell nodded. From 1975 until 1980 or so, the rock industry had lain becalmed in the horse latitudes. Kids spent their money on video games instead of records. For perhaps the fiftieth time since 1955, the pundits announced the death of rock and roll. And, as on other occasions, it proved to be a lively corpse. Video games topped out; MTV checked in; a fresh wave of stars arrived from England; Bruce Springsteen released *Born in the U.S.A.;* rap and hip-hop began to turn some numbers as well as heads.

"Before the slump, record-company execs used to deliver coke backstage in their attaché cases before big shows," Georgie said. "I was concert-mixing back then, and I saw it happen. There was one guy — he's been dead since 1978, but you'd know his name if I said it — who used to get a jar of olives from his label before every gig. The jar would come wrapped up in pretty paper with bows and ribbon and everything. Only instead of water, the olives came packed in cocaine. He used to put them in his drinks. Called them b-b-blast-off martinis."

"I bet they were, too," Tell said.

"Well, back then lots of people thought cocaine was almost like a vitamin," Georgie said. "They said it didn't hook you like heroin or f-fuck you over the next day like booze. And this building, man, this building was a regular snowstorm. Pills and pot and hash too, but cocaine was the hot item. And this guy —"

"What was his name?"

Georgie shrugged. "I don't know. Paul never said and I never heard it from anyone in the building — not that I remember, anyway. But he was s-supposed to be like one of the deli delivery boys you see going up and down in the elevators with coffee and doughnuts and b-bagels. Only instead of delivering coffee-and, this guy delivered dope. You'd see him two or three times a week, riding all the way up and then working his way down. He'd have a topcoat slung over his arm and an alligator-skin briefcase in that hand. He kept the overcoat over his arm even when it was hot. That was so people wouldn't see the cuff. But I guess sometimes they did a-a-anyway."

"The *what?*"

"*C-C-Cuff,*" Georgie said, spraying out bits of bread and corned beef and immediately going crimson. "Gee, Johnny, I'm sorry."

427

"No problem. You want another cream soda?"

"Yes, thanks," Georgie said gratefully.

Tell signalled the waitress.

"So he was a delivery boy," he said, mostly to put Georgie at his ease again — Georgie was still patting his lips with his napkin.

"That's right." The fresh cream soda arrived and Georgie drank some. "When he got off the elevator on the eighth floor, the briefcase chained to his wrist would be full of dope. When he got off it on the ground floor again, it would be full of money."

"Best trick since lead into gold," Tell said.

"Yeah, but in the end the magic ran out. One day he only made it down to the third floor. Someone offed him in the men's room."

"Knifed him?"

"What I heard was that someone opened the door of the stall where he was s-sitting and stuck a pencil in his eye."

For just a moment Tell saw it as vividly as he had seen the crumpled bag under the imagined conspirators' restaurant table: a Berol Black Warrior, sharpened to an exquisite point, sliding forward through the air and then shearing into the startled circle of pupil. The pop of the eyeball. He winced.

Georgie nodded. "G-G-Gross, huh? But it's probably not true. I mean, not that part. Probably someone just, you know, stuck him."

"Yes."

"But whoever it was must have had *something* sharp with him, all right," Georgie said.

"He did?"

"Yes. Because the briefcase was gone."

Tell looked at Georgie. He could see this, too. Even before Georgie told him the rest he could see it.

"When the cops came and took the guy off the toilet, they found his left hand in the b-bowl."

"Oh," Tell said.

Georgie looked down at his plate. There was still half a sandwich on it. "I guess maybe I'm f-f-full," he said, and smiled uneasily.

On their way back to the studio, Tell asked, "So the guy's ghost is supposed to haunt . . . what, that bathroom?" And suddenly he laughed, because, gruesome as the story had been, there was something comic in the idea of a ghost haunting a shithouse.

Georgie smiled. "You know people. At first that was what they said. When I started in working with Paul, guys would tell me they'd *seen* him in there. Not *all* of him, just his sneakers under the stall door."

"Just his sneakers, huh? What a hoot."

"Yeah. That's how you'd know they were making it up, or imagining it, because you only heard it from guys who knew him when he was alive. From guys who knew he wore sneakers."

Tell, who had been a know-nothing kid still living in rural Pennsylvania when the murder happened, nodded. They had arrived at Music City. As they walked across the lobby toward the elevators, Georgie said, "But you know how fast the turnover is in this business. Here today and gone tomorrow. I doubt if there's anybody left

429

in the building who was working here then, except maybe for Paul and a few of the j-janitors, and none of *them* would have bought from the guy."

"Guess not."

"No. So you hardly ever hear the story anymore, and no one *s-sees* the guy anymore."

They were at the elevators.

"Georgie, why do you stick with Paul?"

Although Georgie lowered his head and the tips of his ears turned a bright red, he did not sound really surprised at this abrupt shift in direction. "Why not? He takes care of me."

Do you sleep with him, Georgie? The question occurred at once, a natural outgrowth, Tell supposed, of the previous question, but he wouldn't ask. Didn't really *dare* to ask. Because he thought Georgie would give him an honest answer.

Tell, who could barely bring himself to talk to strangers and hardly ever made friends, suddenly hugged Georgie Ronkler. Georgie hugged him back without looking up at him. Then they stepped away from each other, and the elevator came, and the mix continued, and the following evening, at six-fifteen, as Jannings was picking up his papers (and pointedly not looking in Tell's direction), Tell stepped into the third-floor men's room to get a look at the owner of the white sneakers.

Talking with Georgie, he'd had a sudden revelation . . . or perhaps you called something this strong an epiphany. It was this: sometimes you could get rid of the ghosts that were haunting your life if you could only work up enough courage to face them.

There was no lapse in consciousness this time, nor any sensation of fear . . . only that slow steady deep drumming in his chest. All his senses had been heightened. He smelled chlorine, the pink disinfectant cakes in the urinals, old farts. He could see minute cracks in the paint on the wall, and chips on the pipes. He could hear the hollow click of his heels as he walked toward the first stall.

The sneakers were now almost buried in the corpses of dead spiders and flies.

There were only one or two at first. Because there was no need for them to die until the sneakers were there, and they weren't there until I saw them there.

"Why me?" he asked clearly in the stillness.

The sneakers didn't move and no voice answered.

"I didn't *know* you, I never *met* you, I don't take the kind of stuff you sold and never did. So why me?"

One of the sneakers twitched. There was a papery rustle of dead flies. Then the sneaker — it was the mislaced one — settled back.

Tell pushed the stall door open. One hinge shrieked in properly gothic fashion. And there it was. *Mystery guest, sign in, please,* Tell thought.

The mystery guest sat on the john with one hand lying limply on his thigh. He was much as Tell had seen him in his dreams, with this difference: there was only the single hand. The other arm ended in a dusty maroon stump to which several more flies had adhered. It was only now that Tell realized he had never noticed Sneakers's pants (and didn't you always notice the way lowered pants bunched up over the shoes if you happened to

431

glance under a bathroom stall? something help-lessly comic, or just defenseless, or one on account of the other?). He hadn't because they were up, belt buckled, fly zipped. They were bell-bottoms. Tell tried to remember when bells had gone out of fashion and couldn't.

Above the bells Sneakers wore a blue chambray work-shirt with an applique peace symbol on each flap pocket. He had parted his hair on the right. Tell could see dead flies in the part. From the hook on the back of the door hung the topcoat of which Georgie had told him. There were dead flies on its slumped shoulders.

There was a grating sound not entirely unlike the one the hinge had made. It was the tendons in the dead man's neck, Tell realized. Sneakers was raising his head. Now he looked at him, and Tell saw with no sense of surprise whatever that, except for the two inches of pencil protruding from the socket of his right eye, it was the same face that looked out of the shaving mirror at him every day. Sneakers was him and he was Sneakers.

"I *knew* you were ready," he told himself in the hoarse toneless voice of a man who has not used his vocal cords in a long time.

"I'm not," Tell said. "Go away."

"To know the truth of it, I mean," Tell told Tell, and the Tell standing in the stall doorway saw circles of white powder around the nostrils of the Tell sitting on the john. He had been using as well as pushing, it seemed. He had come in here for a short snort; someone had opened the stall door and stuck a pencil in his eye. But who committed murder by pencil? Maybe only someone who committed the crime on . . .

"Oh, call it impulse," Sneakers said in his hoarse and toneless voice. "The world-famous impulse crime."

And Tell — the Tell standing in the stall doorway — understood that was exactly what it had been, no matter what Georgie might think. The killer hadn't looked under the door of the stall and Sneakers had forgotten to flip the little hinged latch. Two converging vectors of coincidence that, under other circumstances, would have called for no more than a mumbled "Excuse me" and a hasty retreat. This time, however, something different had happened. This time it had led to a spur-of-the-moment murder.

"I didn't forget the latch," Sneakers told him in his toneless husk of a voice. "It was broken."

Yes, all right, the latch had been broken. It didn't make any difference. And the pencil? Tell was positive the killer had been holding it in his hand when he pushed open the stall door, but not as a murder weapon. He had been holding it only because sometimes you wanted something to hold — a cigarette, a bunch of keys, a pen or pencil to fiddle with. Tell thought maybe the pencil had been in Sneakers's eye before either of them had any idea that the killer was going to put it there. Then, probably because the killer had also been a customer who knew what was in the briefcase, he had closed the door again, leaving his victim seated on the john, had exited the building, got . . . well, got *something* . . .

"He went to a hardware store five blocks over and bought a hacksaw," Sneakers said in his toneless voice, and Tell suddenly realized it wasn't *his* face anymore; it was the face of a man who looked about thirty, and vaguely Native American. Tell's hair was gingery-blonde, and so had this man's been at first, but now it was a coarse, dull black.

He suddenly realized something else — realized it the way you realize things in dreams: when people see ghosts, they *always* see themselves first. Why? For the same reason deep divers pause on their way to the surface, knowing that if they rise too fast they will get nitrogen bubbles in their blood and suffer, perhaps die, in agony. There were *reality* bends, as well.

"Perception changes once you get past what's natural, doesn't it?" Tell asked hoarsely. "And that's why life has been so weird for me lately. Something inside me's been gearing up to deal with . . . well, to deal with you."

The dead man shrugged. Flies tumbled dryly from his shoulders. "You tell *me*, Cabbage — you got the head on you."

"All right," Tell said. "I *will*. He bought a hacksaw and the clerk put it in a bag for him and he came back. He wasn't a bit worried. After all, if someone had already found you, he'd know; there'd be a big crowd around the door. That's the way he'd figure. Maybe cops already, too. If things looked normal, he'd go on in and get the briefcase."

"He tried the chain first," the harsh voice said. "When that didn't work, he used the saw to cut off my hand."

They looked at each other. Tell suddenly realized he could see the toilet seat and the dirty

434

white tiles of the back wall behind the corpse . . . the corpse that was, finally, becoming a real ghost.

"You know now?" it asked Tell. "Why it was you?"

"Yes. You had to tell someone."

"No — history is shit," the ghost said, and then smiled a smile of such sunken malevolence that Tell was struck by horror. "But *knowing* sometimes does some good . . . if you're still alive, that is." It paused. "You forgot to ask your friend Georgie something important, Tell. Something he might not have been so honest about."

"What?" he asked, but was no longer sure he really wanted to know.

"Who my biggest third-floor customer was in those days. Who was into me for almost eight thousand dollars. Who had been cut off. Who went to a rehab in Rhode Island and got clean two months after I died. Who won't even go near the white powder these days. Georgie wasn't here back then, but I think he knows the answer to all those questions just the same. Because he hears people talk. Have you ever noticed the way people talk around George, as if he isn't there?"

Tell nodded.

"And there's no stutter in his *brain*. I think he knows, all right. He'd never tell, Tell, but I think he knows."

The face began to change again, and now the features swimming out of that primordial fog were saturnine and finely chiseled. Paul Jannings's features.

"No," Tell whispered.

435

"He got better than thirty grand," the dead man with Paul's face said. "It's how he paid for rehab . . . with plenty left over for all the vices he *didn't* give up."

And suddenly the figure on the toilet seat was fading out entirely. A moment later it was gone. Tell looked down at the floor and saw the flies were gone, too.

He no longer needed to go to the bathroom. He went back into the control room, told Paul Jannings he was a worthless bastard, paused just long enough to relish the expression of utter stunned surprise on Paul's face, and then walked out the door. There would be other jobs; he was good enough at what he did to be able to count on that. Knowing it, however, was something of a revelation. Not the day's first, but definitely the day's best.

When he got back to his apartment, he went straight through the living room and to the john. His need to relieve himself had returned — had become rather pressing, in fact — but that was all right; that was just another part of being alive. "A regular man is a happy man," he said to the white tile walls. He turned a little, grabbed the current issue of *Rolling Stone* from where he'd left it on the toilet tank, opened it to the Random Notes column, and began to read.

You Know They Got
a Hell of a Band

When Mary woke up, they were lost. She knew it, and Clark knew it, too, although he didn't want to admit it at first; he was wearing his I'm Pissed So Don't Fuck with Me look, where his mouth kept getting smaller and smaller until you thought it might disappear altogether. And "lost" wasn't how Clark would put it; Clark would say they had "taken a wrong turn somewhere," and it would just about kill him to go even that far.

They'd set off from Portland the day before. Clark worked for a computer company — one of the giants — and it had been his idea that they should see something of the Oregon which lay outside the pleasant but humdrum upper-middle-class suburb of Portland where they lived — an area that was known to its inhabitants as Software City. "They say it's beautiful out there in the boonies," he had told her. "You want to go take a look? I've got a week, and the transfer rumors have already started. If we don't see some of the real Oregon, I think the last sixteen months are going to be nothing but a black hole in my memory."

She had agreed willingly enough (school had let out ten days before and she had no summer classes to teach), enjoying the pleasantly haphazard,

437

catch-as-catch-can feel of the trip, forgetting that spur-of-the-moment vacations often ended up just like this, with the vacationers lost along some back road which blundered its way up the overgrown butt-crack of nowhere. It was an adventure, she supposed — at least you could look at it that way if you wanted — but she had turned thirty-two in January, and she thought thirty-two was maybe just a little too old for adventures. These days her idea of a really nice vacation was a motel with a clean pool, bathrobes on the beds, and a hair-dryer that worked in the bathroom.

Yesterday had been fine, though, the country-side so gorgeous that even Clark had several times been awed to an unaccustomed silence. They had spent the night at a nice country inn just west of Eugene, had made love not once but twice (something she was most definitely *not* too old to enjoy), and this morning had headed south, mean-ing to spend the night in Klamath Falls. They had begun the day on Oregon State Highway 58, and *that* was all right, but then, over lunch in the town of Oakridge, Clark had suggested they get off the main highway, which was pretty well clogged with RVs and logging trucks.

"Well, I don't know . . ." Mary spoke with the dubiousness of a woman who has heard many such proposals from her man, and endured the consequences of a few. "I'd hate to get lost out there, Clark. It looks pretty empty." She had tapped one neatly shaped nail on a spot of green marked Boulder Creek Wilderness Area. "That word is *wilderness,* as in no gas stations, no rest rooms, and no motels."

"Aw, come on," he said, pushing aside the remains of his chicken-fried steak. On the juke, Steve Earle and the Dukes were singing "Six Days on the Road," and outside the dirt-streaked windows, a bunch of bored-looking kids were doing turns and pop-outs on their skateboards. They looked as if they were just marking time out there, waiting to be old enough to blow this town for good, and Mary knew exactly how they felt. "Nothing to it, babe. We take 58 a few more miles east . . . then turn south on State Road 42 . . . see it?"

"Uh huh." She also saw that, while Highway 58 was a fat red line, State Road 42 was only a squiggle of black thread. But she'd been full of meatloaf and mashed potatoes, and hadn't wanted to argue with Clark's pioneering instinct while she felt like a boa constrictor that has just swallowed a goat. What she'd wanted, in fact, was to tilt back the passenger seat of their lovely old Mercedes and take a snooze.

"Then," he pushed on, "there's this road here. It's not numbered, so it's probably only a county road, but it goes right down to Toketee Falls. And from there it's only a hop and a jump over to U.S. 97. So — what do you think?"

"That you'll probably get us lost," she'd said — a wisecrack she rather regretted later. "But I guess we'll be all right as long as you can find a place wide enough to turn the Princess around in."

"Sold American!" he said, beaming, and pulled his chicken-fried steak back in front of him. He began to eat again, congealed gravy and all.

"Uck-a-*doo*," she said, holding one hand up in front of her face and wincing. "How *can* you?"

"It's good," Clark said in tones so muffled only a wife could have understood him. "Besides, when one is travelling, one should eat the native dishes."

"It looks like someone sneezed a mouthful of snuff onto a very old hamburger," she said. "I repeat: uck-a-doo."

They left Oakridge in good spirits, and at first all had gone swimmingly. Trouble hadn't set in until they turned off S.R. 42 and onto the unmarked road, the one Clark had been so sure was going to breeze them right into Toketee Falls. It hadn't seemed like trouble at first; county road or not, the new way had been a lot better than Highway 42, which had been potholed and frost-heaved, even in summer. They had gone along famously, in fact, taking turns plugging tapes into the dashboard player. Clark was into people like Wilson Pickett, Al Green, and Pop Staples. Mary's taste lay in entirely different directions.

"What do you see in all these white boys?" he asked as she plugged in her current favorite — Lou Reed's *New York*.

"Married one, didn't I?" she asked, and that made him laugh.

The first sign of trouble came fifteen minutes later, when they came to a fork in the road. Both forks looked equally promising.

"Holy crap," Clark said, pulling up and popping the glove compartment open so he could get at the map. He looked at it for a long time. "*That* isn't on the map."

"Oh boy, here we go," Mary said. She had been on the edge of a doze when Clark pulled up at the unexpected fork, and she was feeling a little

440

irritated with him. "Want my advice?"

"No," he said, sounding a little irritated himself, "but I suppose I'll get it. And I *hate* it when you roll your eyes at me that way, in case you didn't know."

"What way is that, Clark?"

"Like I was an old dog that just farted under the dinner table. Go on, tell me what you think. Lay it on me. It's your nickel."

"Go back while there's still time. That's my advice."

"Uh-huh. Now if you only had a sign that said REPENT."

"Is that supposed to be funny?"

"I don't know, Mare," he said in a glum tone of voice, and then just sat there, alternating looks through the bug-splattered windshield with a close examination of the map. They had been married for almost fifteen years, and Mary knew him well enough to believe he would almost certainly insist on pushing on . . . not in spite of the unexpected fork in the road, but *because* of it.

When Clark Willingham's balls are on the line, he doesn't back down, she thought, and then put a hand over her mouth to hide the grin that had surfaced there.

She was not quite quick enough. Clark glanced at her, one eyebrow raised, and she had a sudden discomfiting thought: if she could read *him* as easily as a child's storybook after all this time, then maybe he could do the same with her. "Something?" he asked, and his voice was just a little too thin. It was at that moment — even *before* she had fallen asleep, she now realized — that his

441

mouth had started to get smaller. "Want to share, sweetheart?"

She shook her head. "Just clearing my throat."

He nodded, pushed his glasses up on his ever-expanding forehead, and brought the map up until it was almost touching the tip of his nose. "Well," he said, "it's *got* to be the left-hand fork, because that's the one that goes south, toward Toketee Falls. The other one heads east. It's probably a ranch road, or something."

"A ranch road with a yellow line running down the middle of it?"

Clark's mouth grew a little smaller. "You'd be surprised how well-off some of these ranchers are," he said.

She thought of pointing out to him that the days of the scouts and pioneers were long gone, that his testicles were not *actually* on the line, and then decided she wanted a little doze-off in the afternoon sun a lot more than she wanted to squabble with her husband, especially after the lovely double feature last night. And, after all, they were bound to come out *somewhere*, weren't they?

With that comforting thought in her mind and Lou Reed in her ears, singing about the last great American whale, Mary Willingham dozed off. By the time the road Clark had picked began to deteriorate, she was sleeping shallowly and dreaming that they were back in the Oakridge café where they had eaten lunch. She was trying to put a quarter in the jukebox, but the coin-slot was plugged with something that looked like flesh. One of the kids who had been outside in the parking lot walked past her with his skateboard under his arm and his Trailblazers hat turned around on his head.

What's the matter with this thing? Mary asked him.

The kid came over, took a quick look, and shrugged. *Aw, that ain't nothing,* he said. *That's just some guy's body, broken for you and for many. This is no rinky-dink operation we got here; we're talking mass culture, sugar-muffin.*

Then he reached up, gave the tip of her right breast a tweak — not a very friendly one, either — and walked away. When she looked back at the jukebox, she saw it had filled up with blood and shadowy floating things that looked suspiciously like human organs.

Maybe you better give that Lou Reed album a rest, she thought, and within the pool of blood behind the glass, a record floated down onto the turntable — as if at her thought — and Lou began to sing "Busload of Faith."

While Mary was having this steadily more unpleasant dream, the road continued to worsen, the patches spreading until it was really *all* patch. The Lou Reed album — a long one — came to an end, and began to recycle. Clark didn't notice. The pleasant look he had started the day with was entirely gone. His mouth had shrunk to the size of a rosebud. If Mary had been awake, she would have coaxed him into turning around miles back. He knew this, just as he knew how she would look at him if she woke up now and saw this narrow swatch of crumbling hot-top — a road only if one thought in the most charitable of terms — with piney woods pressing in close enough on both sides to keep the patched tar in constant shadow. They had not passed a car headed in the other direction since leaving S.R. 42.

He knew he *should* turn around — Mary *hated* it when he got into shit like this, always forgetting the many times he had found his way unerringly along strange roads to their planned destinations (Clark Willingham was one of those millions of American men who are firmly convinced they have a compass in their heads) — but he continued to push on, at first stubbornly convinced that they *must* come out in Toketee Falls, then just hoping. Besides, there really *was* no place to turn around. If he tried to do it, he would mire the Princess to her hubcaps in one of the marshy ditches which bordered this miserable excuse for a road . . . and God knew how long it would take to get a tow-truck in here, or how far he'd have to walk just to call one.

Then, at last, he *did* come to a place where he could have turned around — another fork in the road — and elected not to do so. The reason was simple: although the right fork was rutted gravel with grass growing up the middle, the leftward-tending branch was once again wide, well-paved, and divided by a bright stroke of yellow. According to the compass in Clark's head, this fork headed due south. He could all but *smell* Toketee Falls. Ten miles, maybe fifteen, twenty at the outside.

He did at least *consider* turning back, however. When he told Mary so later, he saw doubt in her eyes, but it was true. He decided to go on because Mary was beginning to stir, and he was quite sure that the bumpy, potholed stretch of road he'd just

444

driven would wake her up if he turned back . . . and then she would look at him with those wide, beautiful blue eyes of hers. Just look. That would be enough.

Besides, why should he spend an hour and a half going back when Toketee Falls was just a spin and a promise away? *Look at that road,* he thought. *You think a road like that is going to just peter out?*

He put the Princess back in gear, started down the left fork, and sure enough, the road petered out. Over the first hill, the yellow line disappeared again. Over the second, the paving gave out and they were on a rutted dirt track with the dark woods pressing even closer on either side and the sun — Clark was aware of this for the first time — now sliding down the wrong side of the sky.

The pavement ended too suddenly for Clark to brake and baby the Princess onto the new surface, and there was a hard, spring-jarring thud that woke Mary. She sat up with a jerk and looked around with wide eyes. "Where —" she began, and then, to make the afternoon utterly perfect and complete, the smoky voice of Lou Reed sped up until he was gabbling out the lyrics to "Good Evening, Mr. Waldheim" at the speed of Alvin and the Chipmunks.

"Oh!" she said, and punched the eject button. The tape belched out, followed by an ugly brown afterbirth — coils of shiny tape.

The Princess hit a nearly bottomless pothole, lurched hard to the left, and then threw herself up and out like a clipper ship corkscrewing through a stormwave.

"Clark?"

"Don't say anything," he said through clenched teeth. "We're *not* lost. This will turn back to tar in just a minute or two — probably over the next hill. *We are not lost.*"

Still upset by her dream (even though she could not quite remember what it had been), Mary held the ruined tape in her lap, mourning it. She supposed she could buy another one . . . but not out here. She looked at the brooding trees which seemed to belly right up to the road like starving guests at a banquet and guessed it was a long way to the nearest Tower Records.

She looked at Clark, noted his flushed cheeks and nearly nonexistent mouth, and decided it would be politic to keep her own mouth shut, at least for the time being. If she was quiet and non-accusatory, he would be more likely to come to his senses before this miserable excuse for a road petered out in a gravel pit or quicksand bog.

"Besides, I can't very well turn around," he said, as if she had suggested that very thing.

"I can see that," she replied neutrally.

He glanced at her, perhaps wanting to fight, perhaps just feeling embarrassed and hoping to see she wasn't too pissed at him — at least not yet — and then looked back through the windshield. Now there were weeds and grass growing up the center of this road, too, and the way was so narrow that if they *did* happen to meet another car, one of them would have to back up. Nor was that the end of the fun. The ground beyond the wheelruts looked increasingly untrustworthy; the scrubby trees seemed to be jostling each other for position in the wet ground.

446

There were no power-poles on either side of the road. She almost pointed this out to Clark, then decided it might be smarter to hold her tongue about that, too. He drove on in silence until they came around a down-slanting curve. He was hoping against hope that they would see a change for the better on the far side, but the overgrown track only went on as it had before. It was, if anything, a little fainter and a little narrower, and had begun to remind Clark of roads in the fantasy epics he liked to read — stories by people like Terry Brooks, Stephen Donaldson, and, of course, J. R. R. Tolkien, the spiritual father of them all. In these tales, the characters (who usually had hairy feet and pointed ears) took these neglected roads in spite of their own gloomy intuitions, and usually ended up battling trolls or boggarts or mace-wielding skeletons.

"Clark —"

"I know," he said, and hammered the wheel suddenly with his left hand — a short, frustrated stroke that succeeded only in honking the horn. "I *know.*" He stopped the Mercedes, which now straddled the entire road (road? hell, *lane* was now too grand a word for it), slammed the transmission into park, and got out. Mary got out on the other side, more slowly.

The balsam smell of the trees was heavenly, and she thought there was something beautiful about the silence, unbroken as it was by the sound of any motor (even the far-off drone of an airplane) or human voice . . . but there was something spooky about it, as well. Even the sounds she *could* hear — the *tu-whit!* of a bird in the shadowy firs,

447

the sough of the wind, the rough rumble of the Princess's diesel engine — served to emphasize the wall of quiet encircling them.

She looked across the Princess's gray roof at Clark, and it was not reproach or anger in her gaze but appeal: *Get us out of this, all right? Please?*

"Sorry, hon," he said, and the worry she saw in his face did nothing to soothe her. "Really."

She tried to speak, but at first no sound came out of her dry throat. She cleared it and tried again. "What do you think about backing up, Clark?"

He considered it for several moments — the *tu-whit!* bird had time to call again and be answered from somewhere deeper in the forest — before shaking his head. "Only as a last resort. It's at least two miles back to the last fork in the road —"

"You mean there was *another* one?"

He winced a little, dropped his eyes, and nodded. "Backing up . . . well, you see how narrow the road is, and how mucky the ditches are. If we went off . . ." He shook his head and sighed.

"So we go on."

"I think so. If the road goes entirely to hell, of course, I'll *have* to try it."

"But by then we'll be in even deeper, won't we?" So far she was managing, and quite well, she thought, to keep a tone of accusation from creeping into her voice, but it was getting harder and harder to do. She was pissed at him, quite severely pissed, and pissed at herself, as well — for letting him get them into this in the first place, and then for coddling him the way she was now.

"Yes, but I like the odds on finding a wide place

up ahead better than I like the odds on reversing for a couple of miles along this piece of crap. If it turns out we *do* have to back out, I'll take it in stages — back up for five minutes, rest for ten, back up for five more." He smiled lamely. "It'll be an adventure."

"Oh yes, it'll be that, all right," Mary said, thinking again that her definition for this sort of thing was not *adventure* but *pain in the ass.* "Are you sure you aren't pressing on because you believe in your heart that we're going to find Toketee Falls right over the next hill?"

For a moment his mouth seemed to disappear entirely and she braced for an explosion of righteous male wrath. Then his shoulders sagged and he only shook his head. In that moment she saw what he was going to look like thirty years from now, and that frightened her a lot more than getting caught on a back road in the middle of nowhere.

"No," he said. "I guess I've given up on Toketee Falls. One of the great rules of travel in America is that roads without electrical lines running along at least one side of them don't go anywhere."

So he had noticed, too.

"Come on," he said, getting back in. "I'm going to try like hell to get us out of this. And next time I'll listen to you."

Yeah, yeah, Mary thought with a mixture of amusement and tired resentment. *I've heard* that *one before.* But before he could pull the transmission stick on the console down from park to drive, she put her hand over his. "I *know* you will," she said, turning what he'd said into a promise. "Now

449

get us out of this mess."

"Count on it," Clark said.

"And be careful."

"You can count on that, too." He gave her a small smile that made her feel a little better, then engaged the Princess's transmission. The big gray Mercedes, looking very out of place in these deep woods, began to creep down the shadowy track again.

They drove another mile by the odometer and nothing changed but the width of the cart-track they were on: it grew narrower still. Mary thought the scruffy firs now looked not like hungry guests at a banquet but morbidly curious spectators at the site of a nasty accident. If the track got any narrower, they would begin to hear the squall of branches along the sides of the car. The ground *under* the trees, meanwhile, had gone from mucky to swampy; Mary could see patches of standing water, dusty with pollen and fallen pine needles, in some of the dips. Her heart was beating much too fast, and twice she had caught herself gnawing at her nails, a habit she thought she had given up for good the year before she married Clark. She had begun to realize that if they got stuck now, they would almost certainly spend the night camped out in the Princess. And there were animals in these woods — she had heard them crashing around out there. Some of them sounded big enough to be bears. The thought of meeting a bear while they stood looking at their hopelessly mired Mercedes made her swallow something that felt and tasted like a large lintball.

"Clark, I think we'd better give it up and try backing. It's already past three o'clock and —"

"Look," he said, pointing ahead. "Is it a sign?"

She squinted. Ahead, the lane rose toward the crest of a deeply wooded hill. There was a bright blue oblong standing near the top. "Yes," she said. "It's a sign, all right."

"Great! Can you read it?"

"Uh-huh — it says IF YOU CAME THIS FAR, YOU REALLY FUCKED UP."

He shot her a complex look of amusement and irritation. "Very funny, Mare."

"Thank you, Clark. I try."

"We'll go to the top of the hill, read the sign, and see what's over the crest. If we don't see anything hopeful, we'll try backing. Agreed?"

"Agreed."

He patted her leg, then drove cautiously on. The Mercedes was moving so slowly now that they could hear the soft sound of the weeds on the crown of the road whickering against the undercarriage. Mary really could make out the words on the sign now, but at first she rejected them, thinking she had to be mistaken — it was just too crazy. But they drew closer still, and the words didn't change.

"Does it say what I think it does?" Clark asked her.

Mary gave a short, bewildered laugh. "Sure . . . but it must be someone's idea of a joke. Don't you think?"

"I've given up thinking — it keeps getting me into trouble. But I see something that *isn't* a joke. Look, Mary!"

451

Twenty or thirty feet beyond the sign — just before the crest of the hill — the road widened dramatically and was once more both paved and lined. Mary felt worry roll off her heart like a boulder.

Clark was grinning. "Isn't that *beautiful?*"

She nodded happily, grinning herself.

They reached the sign and Clark stopped. They read it again:

Welcome to
Rock and Roll Heaven, Ore.

WE COOK WITH GAS! SO WILL YOU!

Jaycees • Chamber of Commerce • Lions • Elks

"It's *got* to be a joke," she repeated.

"Maybe not."

"A town called Rock and Roll Heaven? Puh-*leeze*, Clark."

"Why not? There's Truth or Consequences, New Mexico, Dry Shark, Nevada, and a town in Pennsylvania called Intercourse. So why not a Rock and Roll Heaven in Oregon?"

She laughed giddily. The sense of relief was really incredible. "You made that up."

"What?"

"Intercourse, Pennsylvania."

"I didn't. Ralph Ginzberg once tried to send a magazine called *Eros* from there. For the postmark. The Feds wouldn't let him. Swear. And who knows? Maybe the town was founded by a bunch of communal back-to-the-land hippies in the sixties. They went establishment — Lions, Elks, Jay-

452

cees — but the original name stayed." He was quite taken with the idea; he found it both funny and oddly sweet. "Besides, I don't think it matters. What matters is we found some honest-to-God pavement again, honey. The stuff you drive on."

She nodded. "So drive on it . . . but be careful."

"You bet." The Princess nosed up onto the pavement, which was not asphalt but a smooth composition surface without a patch or expansion-joint to be seen. "Careful's my middle n—"

Then they reached the crest of the hill and the last word died in his mouth. He stamped on the brake-pedal so hard that their seatbelts locked, then jammed the transmission lever back into park.

"Holy wow!" Clark said.

They sat in the idling Mercedes, open-mouthed, looking down at the town below.

It was a perfect jewel of a town nestled in a small, shallow valley like a dimple. Its resemblance to the paintings of Norman Rockwell and the small-town illustrations of Currier & Ives was, to Mary, at least, inescapable. She tried to tell herself it was just the geography; the way the road wound down into the valley, the way the town was sur-rounded by deep green-black forest — leagues of old, thick firs growing in unbroken profusion be-yond the outlying fields — but it was more than the geography, and she supposed Clark knew it as well as she did. There was something too sweetly balanced about the church steeples, for instance — one on the north end of the town common and the other on the south end. The barn-red building off to the east had to be the schoolhouse, and the big white one off to the west, the one with the bell-tower on top and the satellite dish to one side, had to be the town hall. The homes all looked impossibly neat and cozy, the sorts of domiciles you saw in the house-beautiful ads of pre-World War II magazines like *The Saturday Evening Post* and *American Mercury*.

There should be smoke curling from a chimney or two, Mary thought, and after a little examination, she saw that there was. She suddenly found herself remembering a story from Ray Bradbury's *The Martian Chronicles*. "Mars Is Heaven," it had been called, and in it the Martians had cleverly disguised the slaughterhouse so it had looked like everybody's fondest hometown dream.

"Turn around," she said abruptly. "It's wide enough here, if you're careful."

He turned slowly to look at her, and she didn't care much for the expression on his face. He was eyeing her as if he thought she had gone crazy. "Honey, what are you —"

"I don't like it, that's all." She could feel her face growing warm, but she pushed on in spite of the heat. "It makes me think of a scary story I read when I was a teenager." She paused. "It also makes me think of the candy-house in 'Hansel and Gretel.' "

He went on giving her that patented I Just Don't Believe It stare of his, and she realized he meant to go down there — it was just another part of the same wretched testosterone blast that had gotten them off the main road in the first place. He wanted to *explore*, by Christ. And he wanted a souvenir, of course. A tee-shirt bought in the local

454

drugstore would do, one that said something cute like I'VE BEEN TO ROCK AND ROLL HEAVEN AND YOU KNOW THEY GOT A HELL OF A BAND.

"Honey —" It was the soft, tender voice he used when he intended to jolly her into something or die trying.

"Oh, stop. If you want to do something nice for me, turn us around and drive us back to Highway 58. If you do that, you can have some more sugar tonight. Another double helping, even, if you're up to it."

He fetched a deep sigh, hands on the steering wheel, eyes straight ahead. At last, not looking at her, he said: "Look across the valley, Mary. Do you see the road going up the hill on the far side?"

"Yes, I do."

"Do you see how wide it is? How smooth? How nicely paved?"

"Clark, that is hardly —"

"Look! I believe I even see an honest-to-God *bus* on it." He pointed at a yellow bug trundling along the road toward town, its metal hide glittering hotly in the afternoon sunlight. "That's one more vehicle than we've seen on *this* side of the world."

"I still —"

He grabbed the map which had been lying on the console, and when he turned to her with it, Mary realized with dismay that the jolly, coaxing voice had temporarily concealed the fact that he was seriously pissed at her. "Listen, Mare, and pay attention, because there may be questions later. Maybe I can turn around here and maybe

455

I can't — it's wid*er*, but I'm not as sure as you are that it's wide enough. And the ground *still* looks pretty squelchy to me."

"Clark, please don't yell at me. I'm getting a headache."

He made an effort and moderated his voice. "If we *do* get turned around, it's twelve miles back to Highway 58, over the same shitty road we just travelled —"

"Twelve miles isn't so much." She tried to sound firm, if only to herself, but she could feel herself weakening. She hated herself for it, but that didn't change it. She had a horrid suspicion that this was how men almost *always* got their way: not by being right but by being relentless. They argued like they played football, and if you hung in there, you almost always finished the discussion with cleat-marks all over your psyche.

"No, twelve miles isn't so much," he was saying in his most sweetly reasonable I-am-trying-not-to-strangle-you-Mary voice, "but what about the fifty or so we'll have to tack on going around this patch of woods once we get back on 58?"

"You make it sound as if we had a train to catch, Clark!"

"It just pisses me off, that's all. You take one look down at a nice little town with a cute little name and say it reminds you of *Friday the 13th, Part XX* or some damn thing and you want to go back. And that road over there" — he pointed across the valley — "heads *due south*. It's probably less than half an hour from here to Toketee Falls by that road."

"That's about what you said back in Oakridge

456

— before we started off on the Magical Mystery Tour segment of our trip."

He looked at her a moment longer, his mouth tucked in on itself like a cramp, then grabbed the transmission lever. "Fuck it," he snarled. "We'll go back. But if we meet one car on the way, Mary, just one, we'll end up *backing* into Rock and Roll Heaven. So —"

She put her hand over his before he could disengage the transmission for the second time that day.

"Go on," she said. "You're probably right and I'm probably being silly." *Rolling over like this has got to be bred in the goddam bone,* she thought. *Either that, or I'm just too tired to fight.*

She took her hand away, but he paused a moment longer, looking at her. "Only if you're sure," he said.

And that was really the most ludicrous thing of all, wasn't it? Winning wasn't enough for a man like Clark; the vote also had to be unanimous. She had voiced that unanimity many times when she didn't feel very unanimous in her heart, but she discovered that she just wasn't capable of it this time.

"But I'm *not* sure," she said. "If you'd been *listening* to me instead of just putting up with me, you'd know that. *Probably* you're right and *probably* I'm just being silly — your take on it makes more sense than mine does, I admit that much, at least, and I'm willing to soldier along — but that doesn't change the way I feel. So you'll just have to excuse me if I decline to put on my little cheerleader's skirt and lead the Go

457

Clark Go cheer this time."

"Jesus!" he said. His face was wearing an uncertain expression that made him look uncharacteristically — and somehow hatefully — boyish. "You're in some mood, aren't you, honeybunch?"

"I guess I am," she said, hoping he couldn't see how much that particular term of endearment grated on her. She was thirty-two, after all, and he was almost forty-one. She felt a little too old to be anyone's honeybunch and thought Clark was a little too old to need one.

Then the troubled look on his face cleared and the Clark she liked — the one she really believed she could spend the second half of her life with — was back. "You'd look cute in a cheerleader's skirt, though," he said, and appeared to measure the length of her thigh. "You would."

"You're a fool, Clark," she said, and then found herself smiling at him almost in spite of herself.

"That's correct, ma'am," he said, and put the Princess in gear.

The town had no outskirts, unless the few fields which surrounded it counted. At one moment they were driving down a gloomy, tree-shaded lane; at the next there were broad tan fields on either side of the car; at the next they were passing neat little houses.

The town was quiet but far from deserted. A few cars moved lazily back and forth on the four or five intersecting streets that made up downtown, and a handful of pedestrians strolled the sidewalks. Clark lifted a hand in salute to a bare-chested, potbellied man who was simultaneously watering his lawn and drinking a can of Olympia. The potbellied man, whose dirty hair straggled to his shoulders, watched them go by but did not raise his own hand in return.

Main Street had that same Norman Rockwell ambience, and here it was so strong that it was almost a feeling of *déjà vu*. The walks were shaded by robust, mature oaks, and that was somehow just right. You didn't have to see the town's only watering hole to know that it would be called The Dew Drop Inn and that there would be a lighted clock displaying the Budweiser Clydesdales over the bar. The parking spaces were the slanting type; there was a red-white-and-blue barber pole turning outside The Cutting Edge; a mortar and pestle hung over the door of the local pharmacy, which was called The Tuneful Druggist. The pet shop (with a sign in the window saying WE HAVE SIAMESE IF YOU PLEASE) was called White Rabbit. Everything was so right you could just shit. Most right of all was the town common at the center of town. There was a sign hung on a guy-wire above the bandshell, and Mary could read it easily, although they were a hundred yards away. CONCERT TONIGHT, it said.

She suddenly realized that she *knew* this town — had seen it many times on late-night TV. Never mind Ray Bradbury's hellish vision of Mars or the candy-house in "Hansel and Gretel"; what this place resembled more than either was The Peculiar Little Town people kept stumbling into in various episodes of *The Twilight Zone*.

She leaned toward her husband and said in a low, ominous voice: "We're travelling not through a dimension of sight and sound, Clark, but of *mind*. Look!" She pointed at nothing in particular, but a woman standing outside the town's Western Auto saw the gesture and gave her a narrow, mistrustful glance.

"Look at what?" he asked. He sounded irritated again, and she guessed that this time it was because he knew *exactly* what she was talking about.

"There's a signpost up ahead! We're entering —"

"Oh, cut it out, Mare," he said, and abruptly swung into an empty parking slot halfway down Main Street.

"*Clark!*" she nearly screamed. "What are you *doing?*"

He pointed through the windshield at an establishment with the somehow not-cute name of The Rock-a-Boogie Restaurant.

"I'm thirsty. I'm going in there and getting a great big Pepsi to go. You don't have to come. You can sit right here. Lock all the doors, if you want." So saying, he opened his own door. Before he could swing his legs out, she grabbed his shoulder.

"Clark, please don't."

He looked back at her, and she saw at once that she should have canned the crack about *The Twilight Zone* — not because it was wrong but because it was right. It was that macho thing again. He wasn't stopping because he was thirsty, not really; he was stopping because this freaky little burg had scared him, too. Maybe a little, maybe a lot, she didn't know that, but she *did* know that he had no intention of going on until he had convinced

460

himself he *wasn't* afraid, not one little bit.

"I won't be a minute. Do you want a ginger ale, or something?"

She pushed the button that unlocked her seatbelt. "What I want is not to be left alone."

He gave her an indulgent, I-knew-you'd-come look that made her feel like tearing out a couple of swatches of his hair.

"And what I *also* want is to kick your *ass* for getting us into this situation in the first place," she finished, and was pleased to see the indulgent expression turn to one of wounded surprise. She opened her own door. "Come on. Piddle on the nearest hydrant, Clark, and then we'll get out of here."

"Piddle . . . ? Mary, what in the hell are you *talking* about?"

"*Sodas!*" she nearly screamed, all the while thinking that it was really amazing how fast a good trip with a good man could turn bad. She glanced across the street and saw a couple of long-haired young guys standing there. They were also drinking Olly and checking out the strangers in town. One was wearing a battered top-hat. The plastic daisy stuck in the band nodded back and forth in the breeze. His companion's arms crawled with faded blue tattoos. To Mary they looked like the sort of fellows who dropped out of high school their third time through the tenth grade in order to spend more time meditating on the joys of drive-train linkages and date rape.

Oddly enough, they also looked somehow familiar to her.

They saw her looking. Top-Hat solemnly raised

his hand and twiddled his fingers at her. Mary looked away hurriedly and turned to Clark. "Let's get our cold drinks and get the hell out of here."

"Sure," he said. "And you didn't need to shout at me, Mary. I mean, I was right *beside* you, and —"

"Clark, do you see those two guys across the street?"

"What two guys?"

She looked back in time to see Top-Hat and Tattoos slipping through the barber-shop doorway. Tattoos glanced back over his shoulder, and although Mary wasn't sure, she thought he tipped her a wink.

"They're just going into the barber shop. See them?"

Clark looked, but only saw a closing door with the sun reflecting eye-watering shards of light from the glass. "What about them?"

"They looked familiar to me."

"Yeah?"

"Yeah. But I find it somehow hard to believe that any ofthe people I know moved to Rock and Roll Heaven, Oregon, to take up rewarding, high-paying jobs as street-corner hoodlums."

Clark laughed and took her elbow. "Come on," he said, and led her into The Rock-a-Boogie Restaurant.

The Rock-a-Boogie went a fair distance toward allaying Mary's fears. She had expected a greasy spoon, not much different from the dim (and rather dirty) pit-stop in Oakridge where they'd eaten lunch. They entered a sun-filled, agreeable little diner with a funky fifties feel instead: blue-tiled walls; chrome-chased pie case; tidy yellow-oak floor; wooden paddle fans turning lazily overhead. The face of the wall-clock was circled with thin tubes of red and blue neon. Two waitresses in aqua-colored rayon uniforms that looked to Mary like costumes left over from *American Graffiti* were standing by the stainless-steel pass-through between the restaurant and the kitchen. One was young — no more than twenty and probably not that — and pretty in a washed-out way. The other, a short woman with a lot of frizzy red hair, had a brassy look that struck Mary as both harsh and desperate . . . and there was something else about her, as well: for the second time in as many minutes, Mary had the strong sensation that she *knew* someone in this town.

A bell over the door tinkled as she and Clark entered. The waitresses glanced over. "Hi, there," the younger one said. "Be right with you."

"Naw; might take awhile," the redhead disagreed. "We're awful busy. See?" She swept an arm at the room, deserted as only a small-town restaurant can be as the afternoon balances perfectly between lunch and dinner, and laughed cheerily at her own witticism. Like her voice, the laugh had a husky, splintered quality that Mary associated with Scotch and cigarettes. *But it's a voice I know,* she thought. *I'd swear it is.*

She turned to Clark and saw he was staring at the waitresses, who had resumed their conversation, as if hypnotized. She had to tug his sleeve to get his attention, then tug it again when he headed for the tables grouped on the left side of

463

the room. She wanted them to sit at the counter. She wanted to get their damned sodas in take-out cups and then blow this joint.

"What is it?" she whispered.

"Nothing," he said. "I guess."

"You looked like you swallowed your tongue, or something."

"For a second or two it felt like I had," he said, and before she could ask him to explain, he had diverted to look at the jukebox.

Mary sat down at the counter.

"Be right with you, ma'am," the younger waitress repeated, and then bent closer to hear something else her whiskey-voiced colleague was saying. Looking at her face, Mary guessed the younger woman wasn't really very interested in what the older one had to say.

"Mary, this is a great juke!" Clark said, sounding delighted. "It's all fifties stuff! The Moonglows . . . The Five Satins . . . Shep and the Limelites . . . La Vern Baker! Jeez, La VernBaker singing 'Tweedlee Dee'! I haven't heard that one since I was a kid!"

"Well, save your money. We're just getting take-out drinks, remember?"

"Yeah, yeah."

He gave the Rock-Ola one last look, blew out an irritated breath, and then joined her at the counter. Mary pulled a menu out of the bracket by the salt and pepper shakers, mostly so she wouldn't have to look at the frown-line between his eyes and the way his lower lip stuck out. *Look,* he was saying without saying a word (this, she had discovered, was one of the more questionable long-term effects of being married). *I won our way through the wilderness while you slept, killed the buffalo, fought the Injuns, brought you safe and sound to this nifty little oasis in the wilderness, and what thanks do I get? You won't even let me play "Tweedlee Dee" on the jukebox!*

Never mind, she thought. *We'll be gone soon, so never mind.*

Good advice. She followed it by turning her full attention to the menu. It harmonized with the rayon uniforms, the neon clock, the juke, and the general decor (which, while admirably subdued, could still only be described as Mid-Century Rebop). The hot dog wasn't a hot dog; it was a Hound Dog. The cheeseburger was a Chubby Checker and the double cheeseburger was a Big Bopper. The specialty of the house was a loaded pizza; the menu promised "Everything on It But the (Sam) Cooke!"

"Cute," she said. "Poppa-ooo-mow-mow, and all that."

"What?" Clark asked, and she shook her head.

The young waitress came over, taking her order pad out of her apron pocket. She gave them a smile, but Mary thought it was perfunctory; the woman looked both tired and unwell. There was a coldsore perched above her upper lip, and her slightly bloodshot eyes moved restlessly about the room. They touched on everything, it seemed, but her customers.

"Help you folks?"

Clark moved to take the menu from Mary's hand. She held it away from him and said, "A large Pepsi and a large ginger ale. To go, please."

"Y'all oughtta try the cherry pie!" the redhead called over in her hoarse voice. The younger woman flinched at the sound of it. "Rick just made it! You gonna think you died and went to heaven!" She grinned at them and placed her hands on her hips. "Well, y'all *are* in Heaven, but you know what I mean."

"Thank you," Mary said, "but we're really in a hurry, and —"

"Sure, why not?" Clark said in a musing, distant voice. "Two pieces of cherry pie."

Mary kicked his ankle — *hard* — but Clark didn't seem to notice. He was staring at the redhead again, and now his mouth was hung on a spring. The redhead was clearly aware of his gaze, but she didn't seem to mind. She reached up with one hand and lazily fluffed her improbable hair.

"Two sodas to go, two pieces of pie for here," the young waitress said. She gave them another nervous smile while her restless eyes examined Mary's wedding ring, the sugar shaker, one of the overhead fans. "You want that pie a la mode?" She bent and put two napkins and two forks on the counter.

"Y—" Clark began, and Mary overrode him firmly and quickly. *"No."*

The chrome pie case was behind the far end of the counter. As soon as the waitress walked away in that direction, Mary leaned over and hissed: "Why are you doing this to me, Clark? You *know* I want to get out of here!"

"That waitress. The redhead. Is she —"

"And stop staring at her!" Mary whispered fiercely. "You look like a kid trying to peek up

466

some girl's skirt in study hall!"

He pulled his eyes away . . . but with an effort. "Is she the spit-image of Janis Joplin, or am I crazy?"

Startled, Mary cast another glance at the red-head. She had turned away slightly to speak to the short-order cook through the pass-through, but Mary could still see at least two-thirds of her face, and that was enough. She felt an almost audible click in her head as she superimposed the face of the redhead over the face on record albums she still owned — vinyl albums pressed in a year when nobody owned Sony Walkmen and the concept of the compact disc would have seemed like science fiction, record albums now packed away in cardboard boxes from the neighborhood liquor mart and stowed in some dusty attic alcove; record albums with names like *Big Brother and the Holding Company*, *Cheap Thrills*, and *Pearl*. And the face of Janis Joplin — that sweet, homely face which had grown old and harsh and wounded far too soon. Clark was right; this woman's face was the spitting image of the face on those old albums.

Except it was more than the face, and Mary felt fear swarm into her chest, making her heart feel suddenly light and stuttery and dangerous.

It was the *voice*.

In the ear of her memory she heard Janis's chilling, spiraling howl at the beginning of "Piece of My Heart." She laid that bluesy, boozy shout over the redhead's Scotch-and-Marlboros voice, just as she had laid one face over the other, and knew that if the waitress began to sing that song, her

467

voice would be identical to the voice of the dead girl from Texas.

Because she is the dead girl from Texas. Congratulations, Mary — you had to wait until you were thirty-two, but you've finally made the grade; you've finally seen your first ghost.

She tried to dispute the idea, tried to suggest to herself that a combination of factors, not the least of them being the stress of getting lost, had caused her to make too much of a chance resemblance, but these rational thoughts had no chance against the dead certainty in her guts: she was seeing a ghost.

Life within her body underwent a strange and sudden sea-change. Her heart sped up from a beat to a sprint; it felt like a pumped-up runner bursting out of the blocks in an Olympic heat. Adrenaline dumped, simultaneously tightening her stomach and heating her diaphragm like a swallow of brandy. She could feel sweat in her armpits and moisture at her temples. Most amazing of all was the way color seemed to pour into the world, making everything — the neon around the clock-face, the stainless-steel pass-through to the kitchen, the sprays of revolving color behind the juke's facade — seem simultaneously unreal and *too* real. She could hear the fans paddling the air overhead, a low, rhythmic sound like a hand stroking silk, and smell the aroma of old fried meat rising from the unseen grill in the next room. And at the same time, she suddenly felt herself on the edge of losing her balance on the stool and swooning to the floor in a dead faint.

Get hold of yourself, woman! she told herself fran-

tically. *You're having a panic attack, that's all —
no ghosts, no goblins, no demons, just a good old-
fashioned whole-body panic attack, you've had them
before, at the start of big exams in college, the first
day of teaching at school, and that time before you
had to speak to the P.T.A. You know what it is
and you can deal with it. No one's going to do any
fainting around here, so just get hold of yourself, do
you hear me?*

She crossed her toes inside her low-topped
sneakers and squeezed them as hard as she could,
concentrating on the sensation, using it in an effort
to draw herself back to reality and away from that
too-bright place she knew was the threshold of
a faint.

"Honey?" Clark's voice, from far away. "You
all right?"

"Yes, fine." Her voice was also coming from
far away . . . but she knew it was closer than
it would have been if she'd tried to speak even
fifteen seconds ago. Still pressing her crossed toes
tightly together, she picked up the napkin the waitress had left, wanting to feel its texture — it was
another connection to the world and another way
to break the panicky, irrational (it *was* irrational,
wasn't it? surely it was) feeling which had gripped
her so strongly. She raised it toward her face,
meaning to wipe her brow with it, and saw there
was something written on the underside in ghostly
pencil strokes that had torn the fragile paper into
little puffs. Mary read this message, printed in jagged capital letters:

GET OUT WHILE YOU STILL CAN.

"Mare? What is it?"

469

The waitress with the coldsore and the restless, scared eyes was coming back with their pie. Mary dropped the napkin into her lap. "Nothing," she said calmly. As the waitress set the plates in front of them, Mary forced herself to catch the girl's eyes with her own. "Thank you," she said.

"Don't mention it," the girl mumbled, looking directly at Mary for only a moment before her eyes began to skate aimlessly around the room again.

"Changed your mind about the pie, I see," her husband was saying in his most infuriatingly indulgent Clark Knows Best voice. *Women!* this tone said. *Gosh, aren't they something? Sometimes just leading them to the waterhole isn't enough — you gotta hold their heads down to get em started. All part of the job. It isn't easy being a man, but I do my goldurn best.*

"Well, it looks awfully good," she said, marvelling at the even tone of her voice. She smiled at him brightly, aware that the redhead who looked like Janis Joplin was keeping an eye on them.

"I can't get over how much she looks like —" Clark began, and this time Mary kicked his ankle as hard as she could, no fooling around. He drew in a hurt, hissing breath, eyes popping wide, but before he could say anything, she shoved the napkin with its penciled message into his hand.

He bent his head. Looked at it. And Mary found herself praying — really, really praying — for the first time in perhaps twenty years. *Please, God, make him see it's not a joke. Make him see it's not a joke because that woman doesn't just* look *like Janis Joplin, that woman* is *Janis Joplin, and I've got a*

470

horrible feeling about this town, a really horrible feeling.

He raised his head and her heart sank. There was confusion on his face, and exasperation, but nothing else. He opened his mouth to speak . . . and it went right on opening until it looked as if someone had removed the pins from the place where his jaws connected.

Mary turned in the direction of his gaze. The short-order cook, dressed in immaculate whites and wearing a little paper cap cocked over one eye, had come out of the kitchen and was leaning against the tiled wall with his arms folded across his chest. He was talking to the redhead while the younger waitress stood by, watching them with a combination of terror and weariness.

If she doesn't get out of here soon, it'll just be weariness, Mary thought. *Or maybe apathy.*

The cook was almost impossibly handsome — so handsome that Mary found herself unable to accurately assess his age. Between thirty-five and forty-five, probably, but that was the best she could do. Like the redhead, he looked familiar. He glanced up at them, disclosing a pair of wide-set blue eyes fringed with gorgeous thick lashes, and smiled briefly at them before returning his attention to the redhead. He said something that made her caw raucous laughter.

"My God, that's Rick Nelson," Clark whispered. "It can't be, it's impossible, he died in a plane crash six or seven years ago, but it *is*."

Mary opened her mouth to say he must be mistaken, ready to brand such an idea ludicrous even though she herself now found it impossible to believe that the redheaded waitress was anyone but the years-dead blues shouter Janis Joplin. Before she could say anything, that click — the one which turned vague resemblance into positive identification — came again. Clark had been able to put the name to the face first because Clark was nine years older, Clark had been listening to the radio and watching *American Bandstand* back when Rick Nelson had been Ricky Nelson and songs like "Be-Bop Baby" and "Lonesome Town" were happening hits, not just dusty artifacts restricted to the golden oldie stations which catered to the now-graying baby boomers. Clark saw it first, but now that he had pointed it out to her, she could not unsee it.

What had the redheaded waitress said? *Y'all oughtta try the cherry pie! Rick just made it!*

There, not twenty feet away, the fatal plane crash victim was telling a joke — probably a dirty one, from the looks on their faces — to the fatal drug o.d.

The redhead threw back her head and bellowed her rusty laugh at the ceiling again. The cook smiled, the dimples at the corners of his full lips deepening prettily. And the younger waitress, the one with the coldsore and the haunted eyes, glanced over at Clark and Mary, as if to ask *Are you watching this? Are you seeing this?*

Clark was still staring at the cook and the waitress with that alarming expression of dazed knowledge, his face so long and drawn that it looked like something glimpsed in a funhouse mirror.

They'll see that, if they haven't already, Mary thought, *and we'll lose any chance we still have of getting out of this nightmare. I think you better take charge of this situation, kiddo, and quick. The question is, what are you going to do?*

She reached for his hand, meaning to grab it and squeeze it, then decided that wouldn't do enough to alter his slack-jawed expression. She reached further and squeezed his balls instead . . . as hard as she dared. Clark jerked as if someone had zapped him with a laser and swung toward her so fast he almost fell off his stool.

"I left my wallet in the car," she said. Her voice sounded brittle and too loud in her own ears. "Would you get it for me, Clark?"

She looked at him, lips smiling, eyes locked on his with complete concentration. She had read, probably in some shit-intensive woman's magazine while waiting to get her hair done, that when you lived with the same man for ten or twenty years, you forged a low-grade telepathic link with your partner. This link, the article went on to suggest, came in mighty handy when your hubby was bringing the boss home to dinner without phoning ahead or when you wanted him to bring a bottle of Amaretto from the liquor store and a carton of whipping cream from the supermarket. Now she tried — tried with all her might — to send a far more important message.

Go, Clark. Please go. I'll give you ten seconds, then come on the run. And if you're not in the driver's seat with the key in the ignition, I have a feeling we could be seriously fucked here.

And at the same time, a deeper Mary was saying timidly: *This is all a dream, isn't it? I mean . . . it is, isn't it?*

Clark was looking at her carefully, his eyes watering from the tweak she had given him . . . but at least he wasn't complaining about it. His eyes shifted to the redhead and the short-order cook for a moment, saw they were still deep in their own conversation (now *she* appeared to be the one who was telling a joke), and then shifted back to her.

"It might have slid under the seat," she said in her too-loud, too-brittle voice before he could reply. "It's the red one."

After another moment of silence — one that seemed to last forever — Clark nodded slightly. "Okay," he said, and she could have blessed him for his nicely normal tone, "but no fair stealing my pie while I'm gone."

"Just get back before I finish mine and you'll be okay," she said, and tucked a forkful of cherry pie into her mouth. It had absolutely no taste at all to her, but she smiled. God, yes. Smiled like the Miss New York Apple Queen she had once been.

Clark started to get off his stool, and then, from somewhere outside, came a series of amplified guitar chops — not chords but only open strums. Clark jerked, and Mary shot out one hand to clutch his arm. Her heart, which had been slowing down, broke into that nasty, scary sprint again.

The redhead and the cook — even the younger waitress, who, thankfully, didn't look like anyone famous — glanced casually toward the plate-glass windows of the Rock-a-Boogie.

"Don't let it get you, hon," the redhead said. "They're just startin to tune up for the concert tonight."

"That's right," the short-order cook said. He regarded Mary with his drop-dead blue eyes. "We have a concert here in town most every night."

Yes, Mary thought. *Of course. Of course you do.*

A voice both toneless and godlike rolled across from the town common, a voice almost loud enough to rattle the windows. Mary, who had been to her share of rock shows, was able to place it in a clear context at once — it called up images of bored, long-haired roadies strolling around the stage before the lights went down, picking their way with easy grace between the forests of amps and mikes, kneeling every now and then to patch two power-cords together.

"Test!" this voice cried. *"Test-one, test-one, test-one!"*

Another guitar chop, still not a chord but close this time. Then a drum-run. Then a fast trumpet riff lifted from the chorus of "Instant Karma," accompanied by a light rumble of bongos. CONCERT TONIGHT, the Norman Rockwell sign over the Norman Rockwell town common had said, and Mary, who had grown up in Elmira, New York, had been to quite a few free concerts-on-the-green as a child. Those really *had* been Norman Rockwell concerts, with the band (made up of guys wearing their Volunteer Fire Department kit in lieu of the band uniforms they couldn't afford) tootling their way through slightly off-key Sousa marches and the local Barber Shop Quartet (Plus Two) harmonizing on things like "Shenandoah" and "I've Got a Gal from Kalamazoo."

She had an idea that the concerts in Rock and Roll Heaven might be quite different from those childhood musicales where she and her friends had run around waving sparklers as twilight drew on for night.

She had an idea that *these* concerts-on-the-green might be closer to Goya than to Rockwell.

"I'll go get your wallet," he said. "Enjoy your pie."

"Thank you, Clark." She put another tasteless forkful of pie in her mouth and watched him head for the door. He walked in an exaggerated slow-motion saunter that struck her feverish eye as absurd and somehow horrid: *I don't have the slightest idea that I'm sharing this room with a couple of famous corpses,* Clark's ambling, sauntering stride was saying. *What, me worry?*

Hurry up! she wanted to scream. *Forget about the gunslinger strut and move your ass!*

The bell jingled and the door opened as Clark reached for the knob, and two more dead Texans came in. The one wearing the dark glasses was Roy Orbison. The one wearing the hornrims was Buddy Holly.

All my exes come from Texas, Mary thought wildly, and waited for them to lay their hands on her husband and drag him away.

" 'Scuse me, sir," the man in the dark glasses said politely, and instead of grabbing Clark, he stepped aside for him. Clark nodded without speaking — Mary was suddenly quite sure he *couldn't* speak — and stepped out into the sunshine.

Leaving her alone in here with the dead. And that thought seemed to lead naturally to another one, even more horrible: Clark was going to drive off without her. She was suddenly sure of it. Not because he wanted to, and certainly not because he was a coward — this situation went beyond questions of courage and cowardice, and she supposed that the only reason they both weren't gibbering and drooling on the floor was because it had developed so *fast* — but because he just wouldn't be able to *do* anything else. The reptile that lived on the floor of his brain, the one in charge of self-preservation, would simply slither out of its hole in the mud and take charge of things.

You've got to get out of here, Mary, the voice in her mind — the one that belonged to her own reptile — said, and the tone of that voice frightened her. It was more reasonable than it had any right to be, given the situation, and she had an idea that sweet reason might give way to shrieks of madness at any moment.

Mary took one foot off the rail under the counter and put it on the floor, trying to ready herself mentally for flight as she did so, but before she could gather herself, a narrow hand fell on her shoulder and she looked up into the smiling, knowing face of Buddy Holly.

He had died in 1959, a piece of trivia she remembered from that movie where he had been played by Gary Busey. 1959 was over thirty years gone, but Buddy Holly was still a gawky twenty-three-year-old who looked seventeen, his eyes swimming behind his glasses and his adam's apple bobbing up and down like a monkey on a stick. He was wearing an ugly plaid jacket and a string tie. The tie's clasp was a large chrome steer-head. The face and the taste of a country bumpkin, you would have said, but there was something in the set of the mouth that was too wise, somehow, too *dark,* and for a moment the hand gripped her shoulder so tightly she could feel the tough pads of callus on the ends of the fingers — guitar calluses.

"Hey there, sweet thang," he said, and she could smell clove gum on his breath. There was a silvery crack, hair-thin, zig-zagging across the left lens of his glasses. "Ain't seen *you* roun' these parts before."

Incredibly, she was lifting another forkful of pie toward her mouth, her hand not hesitating even when a clot of cherry filling plopped back onto her plate. More incredibly, she was slipping the fork through a small, polite smile.

"No," she said. She was somehow positive that she couldn't let this man see she had recognized him; if he did, any small chance she and Clark might still have would evaporate. "My husband and I are just . . . you know, passing through."

And was Clark passing through even now, desperately keeping to the posted speed limit while the sweat trickled down his face and his eyes rolled back and forth from the mirror to the windshield and back to the mirror again? Was he?

The man in the plaid sportcoat grinned, revealing teeth that were too big and much too sharp. "Yep, I know how that is, all right — y'all seen hoot, n now you're on your way to holler. That about the size of it?"

"I thought *this* was hoot," Mary said primly, and that made the newcomers first look at each other, eyebrows raised, and then shout with laughter. The young waitress looked from one to the other with her frightened, bloodshot eyes.

"That ain't half-bad," Buddy Holly said. "You and y'man ought to think about hangin on a little while, though. Stay for the concert tonight, at least. We put on one heckuva show, if I do say so myself." Mary suddenly realized that the eye behind the cracked lens had filled up with blood. As Holly's grin widened, pushing the corners of his eyes into a squint, a single scarlet drop spilled over his lower lid and tracked down his cheek like a tear. "Isn't that right, Roy?"

"Yes, ma'am, it is," the man in the shades said. "You have to see it to believe it."

"I'm sure that's true," Mary said faintly. Yes, Clark was gone. She was sure of it now. The Testosterone Kid had run like a rabbit, and she supposed that soon enough the frightened young girl with the coldsore would lead her into the back room, where her own rayon uniform and order pad would be waiting.

"It's somethin to write home about," Holly told her proudly. "I mean to *say*." The drop of blood fell from his face and pinked onto the seat of the stool Clark had so recently vacated. "Stick around. You'll be glad y'did." He looked to his friend for support.

The man in the dark glasses had joined the cook and the waitresses; he dropped his hand onto the hip of the redhead, who put her own hand over it and smiled up at him. Mary saw that the nails on the woman's short, stubby fingers had been gnawed to the quick. A Maltese cross hung in the open V of Roy Orbison's shirt. He nodded and flashed a smile of his own. "Love to have you, ma'am, and not just for the night, either — draw up and set a spell, we used to say down home."

"I'll ask my husband," she heard herself saying, and completed the thought in her mind: *If I ever see him again, that is.*

"You do that, sugarpie!" Holly told her. "You just do that very thing!" Then, incredibly, he was giving her shoulder one final squeeze and walking away, leaving her a clear path to the door. Even more incredibly, she could see the Mercedes's distinctive grille and peace-sign hood ornament still outside.

Buddy joined his friend Roy, winked at him (producing another bloody tear), then reached behind Janis and goosed her. She screamed indignantly, and as she did, a flood of maggots flew from her mouth. Most struck the floor between her feet, but some clung to her lower lip, squirming obscenely.

The young waitress turned away with a sad, sick grimace, raising one blocking hand to her face. And for Mary Willingham, who suddenly understood they had very likely been playing with her all along, running ceased to be something she had planned and became an instinctive reaction. She was up and off the stool like a shot and sprinting for the door.

"Hey!" the redhead screamed. "Hey, you didn't pay for the pie! Or the sodas, either! This ain't no Dine and Dash, you crotch! Rick! Buddy! Get her!"

Mary grabbed for the doorknob and felt it slip through her fingers. Behind her, she heard the

480

thump of approaching feet. She grabbed the knob again, succeeded in turning it this time, and yanked the door open so hard she tore off the overhead bell. A narrow hand with hard calluses on the tips of the fingers grabbed her just above the elbow. This time the fingers were not just squeezing but pinching; she felt a nerve suddenly go critical, first sending a thin wire of pain from her elbow all the way up to the left side of her jaw and then numbing her arm.

She swung her right fist back like a short-handled croquet mallet, connecting with what felt like the thin shield of pelvic bone above a man's groin. There was a pained snort — they could feel pain, apparently, dead or not — and the hand holding her arm loosened. Mary tore free and bolted through the doorway, her hair standing out around her head in a bushy corona of fright.

Her frantic eyes locked on the Mercedes, still parked on the street. She blessed Clark for staying. And he had caught *all* of her brainwave, it seemed; he was sitting behind the wheel instead of grovelling under the passenger seat for her wallet, and he keyed the Princess's engine the moment she came flying out of the Rock-a-Boogie.

The man in the flower-decorated top-hat and his tattooed companion were standing outside the barber shop again, watching expressionlessly as Mary yanked open the passenger door. She thought she now recognized Top-Hat — she had three Lynyrd Skynyrd albums, and she was pretty sure he was Ronnie Van Zant. No sooner had she realized that than she knew who his illustrated companion was: Duane Allman, killed when his motorcycle skidded beneath a tractor-trailer rig twenty years ago. He took something from the pocket of his denim jacket and bit into it. Mary saw with no surprise at all that it was a peach.

Rick Nelson burst out of the Rock-a-Boogie. Buddy Holly was right behind him, the entire left side of his face now drenched in blood.

"Get in!" Clark screamed at her. *"Get in the fucking car, Mary!"*

She threw herself into the passenger bucket head-first and he was backing out before she could even make a try at slamming the door. The Princess's rear tires howled and sent up clouds of blue smoke. Mary was thrown forward with neck-snapping force when Clark stamped the brake, and her head connected with the padded dashboard. She groped behind her for the open door as Clark cursed and yanked the transmission down into drive.

Rick Nelson threw himself onto the Princess's gray hood. His eyes blazed. His lips were parted over impossibly white teeth in a hideous grin. His cook's hat had fallen off, and his dark-brown hair hung around his temples in oily snags and corkscrews.

"You're coming to the show!" he yelled.

"Fuck you!" Clark yelled back. He found drive and floored the accelerator. The Princess's normally sedate diesel engine gave a low scream and shot forward. The apparition continued to cling to the hood, snarling and grinning in at them.

"Buckle your seatbelt!" Clark bellowed at Mary as she sat up.

She snatched the buckle and jammed it home,

watching with horrified fascination as the thing on the hood reached forward with its left hand and grabbed the windshield wiper in front of her. It began to haul itself forward. The wiper snapped off. The thing on the hood glanced at it, tossed it overboard, and reached for the wiper on Clark's side.

Before he could get it, Clark tramped on the brake again — this time with both feet. Mary's seatbelt locked, biting painfully into the underside of her left breast. For a moment there was a terrible feeling of *pressure* inside her, as if her guts were being shoved up into the funnel of her throat by a ruthless hand. The thing on the hood was thrown clear of the car and landed in the street. Mary heard a brittle crunching sound, and blood splattered the pavement in a starburst pattern around its head.

She glanced back and saw the others running toward the car. Janis was leading them, her face twisted into a haglike grimace of hate and excitement.

In front of them, the short-order cook sat up with the boneless ease of a puppet. The big grin was still on his face.

"Clark, they're coming!" Mary screamed.

He glanced briefly into the rear-view, then floored the accelerator again. The Princess leaped ahead. Mary had time to see the man sitting in the street raise one arm to shield his face, and wished that was all she'd had time to see, but there was something else, as well, something worse: beneath the shadow of his raised arm, she saw he was still grinning.

Then two tons of German engineering hit him and bore him under. There were crackling sounds that reminded her of a couple of kids rolling in a pile of autumn leaves. She clapped her hands over her ears — too late, too late — and screamed.

"Don't bother," Clark said. He was looking grimly into the rear-view mirror. "We couldn't have hurt him too badly — he's getting up again."

"What?"

"Except for the tire-track across his shirt, he's —" He broke off abruptly, looking at her. "Who hit you, Mary?"

"What?"

"Your mouth is bleeding. Who hit you?"

She put a finger to the corner of her mouth, looked at the red smear on it, then tasted it. "Not blood — pie," she said, and uttered a desperate, cracked laugh. "Get us out of here, Clark, please get us out."

"You bet," he said, and turned his attention back to Main Street, which was wide and — for the time being, at least — empty. Mary noticed that, guitars and amps on the town common or not, there were no power-lines on Main Street, either. She had no idea where Rock and Roll Heaven was getting its power (well . . . maybe *some* idea), but it certainly wasn't from Central Oregon Power and Light.

The Princess was gaining speed as all diesels seem to — not fast, but with a kind of relentless strength — and chumming a dark brown cloud of exhaust behind her. Mary caught a blurred glimpse of a department store, a bookstore, and a maternity shop called Rock and Roll Lullabye.

She saw a young man with shoulder-length brown curls standing outside The Rock Em & Sock Em Billiards Emporium, his arms folded across his chest and one snakeskin boot propped against the whitewashed brick. His face was handsome in a heavy, pouting way, and Mary recognized him at once.

So did Clark. "That was the Lizard King himself," he said in a dry, emotionless voice.

"I know. I saw."

Yes — she saw, but the images were like dry paper bursting into flame under a relentless, focused light which seemed to fill her mind; it was as if the intensity of her horror had turned her into a human magnifying glass, and she understood that if they got out of here, no memories of this Peculiar Little Town would remain; the memories would be just ashes blowing in the wind. That was the way these things worked, of course. A person could not retain such hellish images, such hellish *experiences*, and remain rational, so the mind turned into a blast-furnace, crisping each one as soon as it was created.

That must be why most people can still afford the luxury of disbelieving in ghosts and haunted houses, she thought. *Because when the mind is turned toward the terrifying and the irrational, like someone who is turned and made to look upon the face of Medusa, it forgets. It has to forget. And God! Except for getting out of this hell, forgetting is the only thing in the world I want.*

She saw a little cluster of people standing on the tarmac of a Cities Service station at an intersection near the far end of town. They wore frightened, ordinary faces above faded ordinary clothes. A man in an oil-stained mechanic's coverall. A woman in a nurse's uniform — white once, maybe, now a dingy gray. An older couple, she in orthopedic shoes and he with a hearing aid in one ear, clinging to each other like children who fear they are lost in the deep dark woods. Mary understood without needing to be told that these people, along with the younger waitress, were the *real* residents of Rock and Roll Heaven, Oregon. They had been caught the way a pitcher-plant catches bugs.

"*Please* get us out of here, Clark," she said. "*Please.*" Something tried to come up her throat and she clapped her hands over her mouth, sure she was going to upchuck. Instead of vomiting, she uttered a loud belch that burned her throat like fire and tasted of the pie she had eaten in the Rock-a-Boogie.

"We'll be okay. Take it easy, Mary."

The road — she could no longer think of it as Main Street now that she could see the end of town just ahead — ran past the Rock and Roll Heaven Municipal Fire Department on the left and the school on the right (even in her heightened state of terror, there seemed something existential about a citadel of learning called the Rock and Roll Grammar School). Three children stood in the playground adjacent to the school, watching with apathetic eyes as the Princess tore past. Up ahead, the road curved around an outcrop with a guitar-shaped sign planted on it: YOU ARE NOW LEAVING ROCK AND ROLL HEAVEN • GOODNIGHT SWEETHEART GOODNIGHT.

Clark swung the Princess into the curve without slowing, and on the far side, there was a bus blocking the road.

It was no ordinary yellow schoolbus like the one they had seen in the distance as they entered town; this one raved and rioted with a hundred colors and a thousand psychedelic swoops, an oversized souvenir of the Summer of Love. The windows flocked with butterfly decals and peace signs, and even as Clark screamed and brought his feet down on the brake, she read, with a fatalistic lack of surprise, the words floating up the painted side like overfilled dirigibles: THE MAGIC BUS.

Clark gave it his best, but wasn't quite able to stop. The Princess slid into The Magic Bus at ten or fifteen miles an hour, her wheels locked and her tires smoking fiercely. There was a hollow bang as the Mercedes hit the tie-dyed bus amidships. Mary was thrown forward against her safety harness again. The bus rocked on its springs a little, but that was all.

"Back up and go around!" she screamed at Clark, but she was nearly overwhelmed by a suffocating intuition that it was all over. The Princess's engine sounded choppy, and Mary could see steam escaping from around the front of her crumpled hood; it looked like the breath of a wounded dragon. When Clark dropped the transmission lever down into reverse, the car backfired twice, shuddered like an old wet dog, and stalled.

Behind them, they could hear an approaching siren. She wondered who the town constable would turn out to be. Not John Lennon, whose life's motto had been Question Authority, and not the

Lizard King, who was clearly one of the town's pool-shooting bad boys. Who? And did it really matter? *Maybe,* she thought, *it'll turn out to be Jimi Hendrix.* That sounded crazy, but she knew her rock and roll, probably better than Clark, and she remembered reading somewhere that Hendrix had been a jump-jockey in the 101st Airborne. And didn't they say that ex-service people often made the best law-enforcement officials?

You're going crazy, she told herself, then nodded. Sure she was. In a way it was a relief. "What now?" she asked Clark dully.

He opened his door, having to put his shoulder into it because it had crimped a little in the frame. "We run," he said.

"What's the point?"

"You saw them; do you want to *be* them?"

That rekindled some of her fear. She released the clasp of her seatbelt and opened her own door. Clark came around the Princess and took her hand. As they turned back toward The Magic Bus, his grip tightened painfully as he saw who was stepping off — a tall man in an open-throated white shirt, dark dungarees, and wrap-around sunglasses. His blue-black hair was combed back from his temples in a lush and impeccable duck's ass 'do. There was no mistaking those impossible, almost hallucinatory good looks; not even sunglasses could hide them. The full lips parted in a small, sly smile.

A blue-and-white police cruiser with ROCK AND ROLL HEAVEN P.D. written on the doors came around the curve and screeched to a stop inches from the Princess's back bumper. The man behind the wheel was black, but he wasn't Jimi Hendrix after all. Mary couldn't be sure, but she thought the local law was Otis Redding.

The man in the shades and black jeans was now standing directly in front of them, his thumbs hooked into his belt-loops, his pale hands dangling like dead spiders. "How y'all t'day?" There was no mistaking that slow, slightly sardonic Memphis drawl, either. "Want to welcome you both to town. Hope you can stay with us for awhile. Town ain't much to look at, but we're neighborly, and we take care of our own." He stuck out a hand on which three absurdly large rings glittered. "I'm the mayor round these parts. Name's Elvis Presley."

Dusk, of a summer night.

As they walked onto the town common, Mary was again reminded of the concerts she had attended in Elmira as a child, and she felt a pang of nostalgia and sorrow penetrate the cocoon of shock which her mind and emotions had wrapped around her. So similar . . . but so different, too. There were no children waving sparklers; the only kids present were a dozen or so huddled together as far from the bandshell as they could get, their pale faces strained and watchful. The kids she and Clark had seen in the grammar-school play-yard when they made their abortive run for the hills were among them.

And it was no quaint brass band that was going to play in fifteen minutes or half an hour, either — spread across the bandshell (which looked almost as big as the Hollywood Bowl to Mary's eyes) were the implements and accessories of what had to be the world's biggest — and loudest, judging from the amps — rock-and-roll band, an apocalyptic bebop combination that would, at full throttle, probably be loud enough to shatter window-glass five miles away. She counted a dozen guitars on stands and stopped counting. There were four full drum-sets . . . bongos . . . congas . . . a rhythm section . . . circular stage pop-ups where the backup singers would stand . . . a steel grove of mikes.

The common itself was filled with folding chairs — Mary estimated somewhere between seven hundred and a thousand — but she thought there were no more than fifty spectators actually present, and probably less. She saw the mechanic, now dressed in clean jeans and a Perma-Pressed shirt; the pale, once-pretty woman sitting next to him was probably his wife. The nurse was sitting all by herself in the middle of a long empty row. Her face was turned upward and she was watching the first few glimmering stars come out. Mary looked away from this one; she felt if she looked at that sad, longing face too deeply, her heart would break.

Of the town's more famous residents there was currently no sign. Of course not; their day-jobs were behind them now and they would all be backstage, duding up and checking their cues. Getting ready for tonight's rilly big shew.

Clark paused about a quarter of the way down the grassy central aisle. A puff of evening breeze tousled his hair, and Mary thought it looked as dry as straw. There were lines carved into Clark's forehead and around his mouth that she had never seen before. He looked as if he had lost thirty pounds since lunch in Oakridge. The Testosterone Kid was nowhere in evidence, and Mary had an idea he might be gone for good. She found she didn't care much, one way or the other.

And by the way, sugarpie-honeybunch, how do you think you *look?*

"Where do you want to sit?" Clark asked. His voice was thin and uninterested — the voice of a man who still believes he might be dreaming.

Mary spotted the waitress with the coldsore. She was on the aisle about four rows down, now dressed in a light-gray blouse and cotton skirt. She had thrown a sweater over her shoulders. "There," Mary said, "beside her." Clark led her in that direction without question or objection.

The waitress looked around at Mary and Clark, and Mary saw that her eyes had at least settled down tonight, which was something of a relief. A moment later she realized why: the girl was cataclysmically stoned. Mary looked down, not wanting to meet that dusty stare any longer, and when she did, she saw that the waitress's left hand was wrapped in a bulky white bandage. Mary realized with horror that at least one finger and perhaps two were gone from the girl's hand.

"Hi," the girl said. "I'm Sissy Thomas."

"Hello, Sissy. I'm Mary Willingham. This is my husband, Clark."

"Pleased to meet you," the waitress said.

"Your hand . . ." Mary trailed off, not sure how to go on.

"Frankie did it." Sissy spoke with the deep indifference of one who is riding the pink horse down

491

Dream Street. "Frankie Lymon. Everyone says he was the sweetest guy you'd ever want to meet when he was alive and he only turned mean when he came here. He was one of the first ones . . . the pioneers, I guess you'd say. I don't know about that. If he was sweet before, I mean. I only know he's meaner than cat-dirt now. I don't care. I only wish you'd gotten away, and I'd do it again. Besides, Crystal takes care of me."

Sissy nodded toward the nurse, who had stopped looking at the stars and was now looking at them.

"Crystal takes real good care. She'll fix you up, if you want — you don't need to lose no fingers to want to get stoned in this town."

"My wife and I don't use drugs," Clark said, sounding pompous.

Sissy regarded him without speaking for a few moments. Then she said, "You will."

"When does the show start?" Mary could feel the cocoon of shock starting to dissolve, and she didn't much care for the feeling.

"Soon."

"How long do they go on?"

Sissy didn't answer for nearly a minute, and Mary was getting ready to restate the question, thinking the girl either hadn't heard or hadn't understood, when she said: "A long time. I mean, the show will be over by midnight, they always are, it's a town ordinance, but still . . . they go on a long time. Because time is different here. It might be . . . oh, I dunno . . . I think when the guys really get cooking, they sometimes go on for a year or more."

A cold gray frost began creeping up Mary's arms

and back. She tried to imagine having to sit through a year-long rock show and couldn't do it. *This is a dream and you'll wake up,* she told herself, but that thought, persuasive enough as they stood listening to Elvis Presley in the sunlight by The Magic Bus, was now losing a lot of its force and believability.

"Drivin out this road here wouldn't do you no good nohow," Elvis had told them. "It don't go noplace but Umpqua Swamp. No roads in there, just a lot of polk salad. And quicksand." He had paused then, the lenses of his shades glittering like dark furnaces in the late-afternoon sun. "And other things."

"Bears," the policeman who might be Otis Redding had volunteered from behind them.

"Bears, yep," Elvis agreed, and then his lips had curled up in the too-knowing smile Mary remembered so well from TV and the movies. "And other things."

Mary had begun: "If we stay for the show . . ."

Elvis nodded emphatically. "The show! Oh yeah, you *gotta* stay for the show! We really rock. You just see if we don't."

"Ain't nothin but a stone fact," the policeman had added.

"If we stay for the show . . . can we go when it's over?"

Elvis and the cop had exchanged a glance that had looked serious but felt like a smile. "Well, you know, ma'am," the erstwhile King of Rock and Roll said at last, "we're real far out in the boonies here, and attractin an audience is kinda slow work . . . although once they hear us, *ever-*

493

body stays around for more . . . and we was kinda hopin you'd stick around yourselves for awhile. See a few shows and kind of enjoy our hospitality." He had pushed his sunglasses up on his forehead then, for a moment revealing wrinkled, empty eye-sockets. Then they were Elvis's dark-blue eyes again, regarding them with somber interest.

"I think," he had said, "you might even decide you want to settle down."

There were more stars in the sky now; it was almost full dark. Over the stage, orange spots were coming on, soft as night-blooming flowers, illuminating the mike-stands one by one.

"They gave us jobs," Clark said dully. "*He* gave us jobs. The mayor. The one who looks like Elvis Presley."

"He *is* Elvis," Sissy Thomas said, but Clark just went on staring at the stage. He was not prepared to even *think* this yet, let alone hear it.

"Mary is supposed to go to work in the Be-Bop Beauty Bar tomorrow," he went on. "She has an English degree and a teacher's certificate, but she's supposed to spend the next God-knows-how-long as a shampoo girl. Then he looked at me and he says, 'Whuh bou-*chew*, sir? Whuh-*chore* speciality?' " Clark spoke in a vicious imitation of the mayor's Memphis drawl, and at last a genuine expression began to show in the waitress's stoned eyes. Mary thought it was fear.

"You hadn't ought to make fun," she said. "Makin fun can get you in trouble around here . . . and you don't want to get in trouble." She slowly raised her bandage-wrapped hand. Clark

494

stared at it, wet lips quivering, until she lowered it into her lap again, and when he spoke again, it was in a lower voice.

"I told him I was a computer software expert, and he said there weren't any computers in town . . . although they 'sho would admiah to git a Ticketron outlet or two.' Then the other guy laughed and said there was a stockboy's job open down at the superette, and —"

A bright white spotlight speared the forestage. A short man in a sportcoat so wild it made Buddy Holly's look tame strode into its beam, his hands raised as if to stifle a huge comber of applause.

"Who's that?" Mary asked Sissy.

"Some oldtime disc jockey who used to run a lot of these shows. His name is Alan Tweed or Alan Breed or something like that. We hardly ever see him except here. I think he drinks. He sleeps all day — that I *do* know."

And as soon as the name was out of the girl's mouth, the cocoon which had sheltered Mary disappeared and the last of her disbelief melted away. She and Clark *had* stumbled into Rock and Roll Heaven, but it was actually Rock and Roll Hell. This had not happened because they were evil people; it had not happened because the old gods were punishing them; it had happened because they had gotten lost in the woods, that was all, and getting lost in the woods was a thing that could happen to anybody.

"*Got a great show forya tonight!*" the emcee was shouting enthusiastically into his mike. "*We got the Big Bopper . . . Freddie Mercury, just in from London-Town . . . Jim Croce . . . my main*

495

man Johnny Ace . . ."

Mary leaned toward the girl. "How long have you been here, Sissy?"

"I don't know. It's easy to lose track of time. Six years at least. Or maybe it's eight. Or nine."

"*. . . Keith Moon of The Who . . . Brian Jones of the Stones . . . that cute li'l Florence Ballard of the Supremes . . . Mary Wells . . .*"

Articulating her worst fear, Mary asked: "How old were you when you came?"

"*Cass Elliot . . . Janis Joplin . . .*"

"Twenty-three."

"*King Curtis . . . Johnny Burnette . . .*"

"And how old are you now?"

"*Slim Harpo . . . Bob 'Bear' Hite . . . Stevie Ray Vaughan . . .*"

"Twenty-three," Sissy told her, and on stage Alan Freed went on screaming names at the almost empty town common as the stars came out, first a hundred stars, then a thousand, then too many to count, stars that had come out of the blue and now glittered everywhere in the black; he tolled the names of the drug o.d.'s, the alcohol o.d.'s, the plane crash victims and the shooting victims, the ones who had been found in alleys and the ones who had been found in swimming pools and the ones who had been found in roadside ditches with steering columns poking out of their chests and most of their heads torn off their shoulders; he chanted the names of the young ones and the old ones, but mostly they were the young ones, and as he spoke the names of Ronnie Van Zant and Steve Gaines, she heard the words of one of their songs tolling in her mind, the one that went

Oooh, that smell, can't you smell that smell, and yes, you bet, she certainly *could* smell that smell; even out here, in the clear Oregon air, she could smell it, and when she took Clark's hand it was like taking the hand of a corpse.

"Awwwwwwwlllll RIIIIIYYYYYGHT!" Alan Freed was screaming. Behind him, in the darkness, scores of shadows were trooping onto the stage, lit upon their way by roadies with Penlites. *"Are you ready to PAAAARTY?"*

No answer from the scattered spectators on the common, but Freed was waving his hands and laughing as if some vast audience were going crazy with assent. There was just enough light left in the sky for Mary to see the old man reach up and turn off his hearing aid.

"Are you ready to BOOOOOGIE?"

This time he *was* answered — by a demonic shriek of saxophones from the shadows behind him.

"Then let's go . . . BECAUSE ROCK AND ROLL WILL NEVER DIE!"

As the show-lights came up and the band swung into the first song of that night's long, long concert — "I'll Be Doggone," with Marvin Gaye doing the vocal — Mary thought: *That's what I'm afraid of. That's exactly what I'm afraid of.*

497

Home Delivery

Considering that it was probably the end of the world, Maddie Pace thought she was doing a good job. *Hell* of a good job. She thought, in fact, that she just might be coping with the End of Everything better than anyone else on earth. And she was *positive* she was coping better than any other *pregnant* woman on earth.

Coping.

Maddie Pace, of all people.

Maddie Pace, who sometimes couldn't sleep if, after a visit from Reverend Johnson, she spied a single speck of dust under the dining-room table. Maddie Pace, who, as Maddie Sullivan, used to drive her fiancè, Jack, crazy when she froze over a menu, debating entrées sometimes for as long as half an hour.

"Maddie, why don't you just flip a coin?" he'd asked her once after she had managed to narrow it down to a choice between the braised veal and the lamb chops, and then could get no further. "I've had five bottles of this goddam German beer already, and if you don't make up y'mind pretty damn quick, there's gonna be a drunk lobsterman *under* the table before we ever get any food *on* it!"

So she had smiled nervously, ordered the braised veal, and spent most of the ride home wondering if the chops might not have been tastier, and therefore a better bargain despite their slightly higher price.

She'd had no trouble coping with Jack's proposal of marriage, however; she'd accepted it — and him — quickly, and with tremendous relief. Following the death of her father, Maddie and her mother had lived an aimless, cloudy sort of life on Little Tall Island, off the coast of Maine. "If I wasn't around to tell them women where to squat and lean against the wheel," George Sullivan had been fond of saying while in his cups and among his friends at Fudgy's Tavern or in the back room of Prout's Barber Shop, "I don't know what'n hell they'd do."

When her father died of a massive coronary, Maddie was nineteen and minding the town library weekday evenings at a salary of $41.50 a week. Her mother minded the house — or did, that was, when George reminded her (sometimes with a good hard shot to the ear) that she had a house which needed minding.

When the news of his death came, the two women had looked at each other with silent, panicky dismay, two pairs of eyes asking the same question: *What do we do now?*

Neither of them knew, but they both felt — felt strongly — that he had been right in his assessment of them: they needed him. They were just women, and they needed him to tell them not just what to do, but how to do it, as well. They didn't speak of it because it embarrassed them, but there it was — they hadn't the slightest clue as to what came next, and the idea that they were prisoners of George Sullivan's narrow ideas and expectations did not so much as cross their minds. They were not stupid women, either of them, but they *were* island women.

Money wasn't the problem; George had believed passionately in insurance, and when he dropped down dead during the tiebreaker frame of the League Bowl-Offs at Big Duke's Big Ten in Machias, his wife had come into better than a hundred thousand dollars. And island life was cheap, if you owned your place and kept your garden tended and knew how to put by your own vegetables come fall. The *problem* was having nothing to focus on. The *problem* was how the center seemed to have dropped out of their lives when George went facedown in his Island Amoco bowling shirt just over the foul line of lane nineteen (and goddam if he hadn't picked up the spare his team had needed to win, too). With George gone their lives had become an eerie sort of blur.

It's like being lost in a heavy fog, Maddie thought sometimes. *Only instead of looking for the road, or a house, or the village, or just some landmark like that lightning-struck pine out on the point, I am looking for the wheel. If I can ever find it, maybe I can tell* myself *to squat and lean my shoulder to it.*

At last she found her wheel: it turned out to be Jack Pace. Women marry their fathers and men their mothers, some say, and while such a broad statement can hardly be true all of the time, it was close enough for government work in Maddie's case. Her father had been looked upon by his peers with fear and admiration — "Don't fool with George Sullivan, dear," they'd say. "He'll knock the nose off your face if you so much as look at him wrong."

It was true at home, too. He'd been domineering and sometimes physically abusive, but he'd also known things to want and work for, like the Ford pick-up, the chainsaw, or those two acres that bounded their place to the south. Pop Cook's land. George Sullivan had been known to refer to Pop Cook as one armpit-stinky old bastid, but the old man's aroma didn't change the fact that there was quite a lot of good hardwood left on those two acres. Pop didn't know it because he had gone to living across the reach in 1987, when his arthritis really went to town on him, and George let it be known on Little Tall that what that bastid Pop Cook didn't know wouldn't hurt him none, and furthermore, he would disjoint the man or woman that let light into the darkness of Pop's ignorance. No one did, and eventually the Sullivans got the land, and the hardwood on it. Of course the good wood was all logged off inside of three years, but George said that didn't matter a tinker's damn; land always paid for itself in the end. That was what George said and they believed him, believed *in* him, and they worked, all three of them. He said: You got to put your shoulder to this wheel and *push* the bitch, you got to push ha'ad because she don't move easy. So that was what they did.

In those days Maddie's mother had kept a produce stand on the road from East Head, and there were always plenty of tourists who bought the vegetables she grew (which were the ones George *told* her to grow, of course), and even though they were never exactly what her mother called "the

501

Gotrocks family," they made out. Even in years when lobstering was bad and they had to stretch their finances even further in order to keep paying off what they owed the bank on Pop Cook's two acres, they made out.

Jack Pace was a sweeter-tempered man than George Sullivan had ever thought of being, but his sweet temper only stretched so far, even so. Maddie suspected that he might get around to what was sometimes called home correction — the twisted arm when supper was cold, the occasional slap or downright paddling — in time; when the bloom was off the rose, so as to speak. There was even a part of her that seemed to expect and look forward to that. The women's magazines said marriages where the man ruled the roost were a thing of the past, and that a man who put a hard hand on a woman should be arrested for assault, even if the man in question was the woman in question's lawful wedded husband. Maddie sometimes read articles of this sort down at the beauty shop, but doubted if the women who wrote them had the slightest idea that places like the outer islands even existed. Little Tall *had* produced one writer, as a matter of fact — Selena St. George — but she wrote mostly about politics and hadn't been back to the island, except for a single Thanksgiving dinner, in years.

"I'm not going to be a lobsterman all my life, Maddie," Jack told her the week before they were married, and she believed him. A year before, when he had asked her out for the first time (she'd said yes almost before all the words could get out of his mouth, and she had blushed to the roots

502

of her hair at the sound of her own naked eagerness), he would have said, "I *ain't* going to be a lobsterman all my life." A small change . . . but all the difference in the world. He had been going to night school three evenings a week, taking the old *Island Princess* over and back. He would be dog-tired after a day of pulling pots, but off he'd go just the same, pausing only long enough to shower off the powerful smells of lobster and brine and to gulp two No Dōz with hot coffee. After a while, when she saw he really meant to stick to it, Maddie began putting up hot soup for him to drink on the ferry-ride over. Otherwise he would have had nothing but one of those nasty red hot-dogs they sold in the *Princess*'s snack-bar.

She remembered agonizing over the canned soups in the store — there were so *many!* Would he want tomato? Some people didn't like tomato soup. In fact, some people *hated* tomato soup, even if you made it with milk instead of water. Vegetable soup? Turkey? Cream of chicken? Her helpless eyes roved the shelf display for nearly ten minutes before Charlene Nedeau asked if she could help her with something — only Charlene said it in a sarcastic way, and Maddie guessed she would tell all her friends at high school tomorrow, and they would giggle about it in the girls' room, knowing exactly what was wrong with her — poor mousy little Maddie Sullivan, unable to make up her mind over so simple a thing as a can of *soup*. How she had ever been able to decide to accept Jack Pace's proposal was a wonder and a marvel to all of them . . . but of course they didn't know about the wheel you had to find, and about how, once you found it, you had to have someone to tell you when to stoop and where exactly to push the damned thing.

Maddie had left the store with no soup and a throbbing headache.

When she worked up nerve enough to ask Jack what his favorite soup was, he had said: "Chicken noodle. Kind that comes in the can."

Were there any others he specially liked?

The answer was no, just chicken noodle — the kind that came in the can. That was all the soup Jack Pace needed in his life, and all the answer (on that particular subject, at least) that Maddie needed in hers. Light of step and cheerful of heart, Maddie climbed the warped wooden steps of the store the next day and bought the four cans of chicken noodle soup that were on the shelf. When she asked Bob Nedeau if he had any more, he said he had a whole damn *case* of the stuff out back.

She bought the entire case and left him so flabbergasted that he actually carried the carton out to the truck for her and forgot all about asking why she wanted so *much* — a lapse for which his long-nosed wife and daughter took him sharply to task that evening.

"You just better believe it and never forget," Jack had said that time not long before they tied the knot (she *had* believed it, and had never forgotten). "More than a lobsterman. My dad says I'm full of shit. He says if draggin pots was good enough for his old man, and his old man's old man and all the way back to the friggin Garden of Eden to hear *him* tell it, it ought to be good

504

enough for me. But it ain't — *isn't*, I mean — and I'm going to do better." His eye fell on her, and it was a stern eye, full of resolve, but it was a loving eye, full of hope and confidence, too. "More than a lobsterman is what I mean to be, and more than a lobsterman's wife is what I intend for you to be. You're going to have a house on the mainland."

"Yes, Jack."

"And I'm not going to have any friggin Chevrolet." He drew in a deep breath and took her hands in his. "I'm going to have an *Oldsmobile*."

He looked her dead in the eye, as if daring her to scoff at this wildly upscale ambition. She did no such thing, of course; she said yes, Jack, for the third or fourth time that evening. She had said it to him thousands of times over the year they had spent courting, and she confidently expected to say it a million times before death ended their marriage by taking one of them — or, better, both of them together. *Yes, Jack;* had there ever in the history of the world been two words which made such beautiful music when laid side by side?

"More than a friggin lobsterman, no matter what my old man thinks or how much he laughs." He pronounced this last word in the deeply downeast way: *loffs.* "I'm going to do it, and do you know who's going to help me?"

"Yes," Maddie had responded calmly. "*I* am."

He had laughed and swept her into his arms. "You're damned tooting, my little sweetheart," he'd told her.

And so they were wed, as the fairytales usually put it, and for Maddie those first few months —

505

months when they were greeted almost everywhere with jovial cries of "Here's the newlyweds!"
— *were* a fairytale. She had Jack to lean on, Jack
to help her make decisions, and that was the best
of it. The most difficult household choice thrust
upon her that first year was which curtains would
look best in the living room — there were so *many*
in the catalogue to choose from, and her mother
was certainly no help. Maddie's mother had a hard
time deciding between different brands of toilet
paper.

Otherwise, that year consisted mostly of joy and
security — the joy of loving Jack in their deep
bed while the winter wind scraped over the island
like the blade of a knife across a breadboard, the
security of having Jack to tell her what it was they
wanted, and how they were going to get it. The
loving was good — so good that sometimes when
she thought of him during the days her knees
would feel weak and her stomach fluttery — but
his way of knowing things and her growing trust
in his instincts were even better. So for awhile
it *was* a fairytale, yes.

Then Jack died and things started getting weird.
Not just for Maddie, either.

For everybody.

Just before the world slid into its incomprehen-
sible nightmare, Maddie discovered she was what
her mother had always called "preg," a curt word
that was like the sound you made when you had
to rasp up a throatful of snot (that, at least, was
how it had always sounded to Maddie). By then
she and Jack had moved next to the Pulsifers on

Gennesault Island, which was known simply as Jenny by its residents and those of nearby Little Tall.

She'd had one of her agonizing interior debates when she missed her second period, and after four sleepless nights she made an appointment with Dr. McElwain on the mainland. Looking back, she was glad. If she'd waited to see if she was going to miss a third period, Jack would not have had even one month of joy and she would have missed the concerns and little kindnesses he had showered upon her.

Looking back — now that she was *coping* — her indecision seemed ludicrous, but her deeper heart knew that going to have the test had taken tremendous courage. She had wanted to be more convincingly sick in the mornings so she could be surer; she had longed for nausea to drag her from her dreams. She made the appointment when Jack was out at work, and she went while he was out, but there was no such thing as *sneaking* over to the mainland on the ferry; too many people from both islands saw you. Someone would mention casually to Jack that he or she had seen his wife on the *Princess* t'other day, and then Jack would want to know what it was all about, and if she'd made a mistake, he would look at her like she was a goose.

But it hadn't been a mistake; she was with child (and never mind that word that sounded like someone with a bad cold trying to clear his throat), and Jack Pace had had exactly twenty-seven days to look forward to his first child before a bad swell had caught him and knocked him over the side of *My Lady-Love*, the lobster boat he had inherited

507

from his Uncle Mike. Jack could swim, and he had popped to the surface like a cork, Dave Eamons had told her miserably, but just as he did, another heavy swell came, slewing the boat directly into him, and although Dave would say no more, Maddie had been born and brought up an island girl, and she knew: could, in fact, *hear* the hollow thud as the boat with its treacherous name smashed its way into her husband's head, letting out blood and hair and bone and perhaps the part of his brain that had made him say her name over and over again in the dark of night, when he came into her.

Dressed in a heavy hooded parka and down-filled pants and boots, Jack Pace had sunk like a stone. They had buried an empty casket in the little cemetery at the north end of Jenny Island, and the Reverend Johnson (on Jenny and Little Tall you had your choice when it came to religion: you could be a Methodist, or if that didn't suit you, you could be a lapsed Methodist) had presided over this empty coffin as he had so many others. The service ended, and at the age of twenty-two Maddie had found herself a widow with a bun in the oven and no one to tell her where the wheel was, let alone when to put her shoulder to it or how far to push it.

She thought at first she'd go back to Little Tall, back to her mother, to wait her time, but a year with Jack had given her a little perspective and she knew her mother was as lost — maybe even *more* lost — than she was herself, and that made her wonder if going back would be the right thing to do.

"Maddie," Jack told her again and again (he was dead in the world but not, it seemed, inside her head; inside her head he was as lively as any dead man could possibly get . . . or so she had thought *then*), "the only thing you can ever decide on is not to decide."

Nor was her mother any better. They talked on the phone and Maddie waited and hoped for her mother to just *tell* her to come back home, but Mrs. Sullivan could tell no one over the age of ten anything. "Maybe you ought to come on back over here," she had said once in a tentative way, and Maddie couldn't tell if that meant *please come home* or *please don't take me up on an offer which was really just made for form's sake.* She spent long, sleepless nights trying to decide which it had been and succeeded only in confusing herself more.

Then the weirdness started, and the greatest mercy was that there was only the one small grave-yard on Jenny (and so many of the graves filled with those empty coffins — a thing which had once seemed pitiful to her now seemed another blessing, a grace). There were two on Little Tall, both fairly large, and so it began to seem so much safer to stay on Jenny and wait.

She would wait and see if the world lived or died.

If it lived, she would wait for the baby.

And now she was, after a life of passive obedience and vague resolves that usually passed like dreams an hour or two after she got out of bed, finally *coping*. She knew that part of this was nothing more than the effect of being slammed with one massive shock after another, beginning with the death of her husband and ending with one of the last broadcasts the Pulsifers' high-tech satellite dish had picked up: a horrified young boy who had been pressed into service as a CNN reporter saying that it seemed certain that the President of the United States, the first lady, the Secretary of State, the honorable senior senator from Oregon, and the emir of Kuwait had been eaten alive in the White House East Room by zombies.

"I want to repeat this," the accidental reporter had said, the firespots of his acne standing out on his forehead and chin like stigmata. His mouth and cheeks had begun to twitch; his hands shook spastically. "I want to repeat that a bunch of corpses have just lunched up on the President and his wife and a whole lot of other political hotshots who were at the White House to eat poached salmon and cherries jubilee." Then the kid had begun to laugh maniacally and to scream *Go, Yale! Boola-boola!* at the top of his voice. At last he bolted out of the frame, leaving a CNN news-desk untenanted for the first time in Maddie's memory. She and the Pulsifers sat in dismayed silence as the news-desk disappeared and an ad for Boxcar Willie records — not available in any store, you could get this amazing collection only by dialing the 800 number currently appearing on the bottom of your screen — came on. One of little Cheyne Pulsifer's crayons was on the end table beside the chair Maddie was sitting in, and for some crazy reason she picked it up and wrote the number down on a sheet of scrap paper before Mr. Pulsifer got up and turned off the TV without a single word.

510

Maddie told them good night and thanked them for sharing their TV and their Jiffy Pop.

"Are you sure you're all right, Maddie dear?" Candi Pulsifer asked her for the fifth time that night, and Maddie said she was fine for the fifth time that night, that she was *coping,* and Candi said she *knew* she was, but she was welcome to the upstairs bedroom that used to be Brian's anytime she wanted. Maddie hugged Candi, kissed her cheek, declined with the most graceful thanks she could find, and was at last allowed to escape. She had walked the windy half mile back to her own house and was in her own kitchen before she realized that she still had the scrap of paper on which she had jotted the 800 number. She had dialed it, and there was nothing. No recorded voice telling her all circuits were currently busy or that the number was out of service; no wailing siren sound that indicated a line interruption; no boops or beeps or clicks or clacks. Just smooth silence. That was when Maddie knew for sure that the end had either come or was coming. When you could no longer call the 800 number and order the Boxcar Willie records that were not available in any store, when there were for the first time in her living memory no Operators Standing By, the end of the world was a foregone conclusion.

She felt her rounding stomach as she stood there by the phone on the wall in the kitchen and said it out loud for the first time, unaware that she had spoken: "It will have to be a home delivery. But that's all right, as long as you get ready and stay ready, kiddo. You have to remember that there just isn't any other way. It *has* to be a home delivery."

She waited for fear and none came.

"I can cope with this just fine," she said, and this time she heard herself and was comforted by the sureness of her own words.

A baby.

When the baby came, the end of the world would itself end.

"Eden," she said, and smiled. Her smile was sweet, the smile of a madonna. It didn't matter how many rotting dead people (maybe Boxcar Willie among them, for all she knew) were shambling around the face of the earth.

She would have a baby, she would accomplish her home delivery, and the possibility of Eden would remain.

The first reports came from an Australian hamlet on the edge of the outback, a place with the memorable name of Fiddle Dee. The name of the first American town where the walking dead were reported was perhaps even more memorable: Thumper, Florida. The first story appeared in America's favorite supermarket tabloid, *Inside View*.

DEAD COME TO LIFE IN SMALL FLORIDA TOWN! the headline screamed. The story began with a recap of a film called *Night of the Living Dead*, which Maddie had never seen, and went on to mention another — *Macumba Love* — which she had also never seen. The article was accompanied by three photos. One was a still from *Night of the Living Dead*, showing what appeared to be a

512

bunch of escapees from a loonybin standing outside an isolated farmhouse at night. One was from *Macumba Love,* showing a blonde whose bikini top appeared to be holding breasts the size of prize-winning gourds. The blonde was holding up her hands and screaming in horror at what could have been a black man in a mask. The third purported to be a picture taken in Thumper, Florida. It was a blurred, grainy shot of a person of indeterminate sex standing in front of a video arcade. The article described the figure as being "wrapped in the cerements of the grave," but it could have been someone in a dirty sheet.

No big deal. BIGFOOT RAPES CHOIR BOY last week, dead people coming back to life this week, the dwarf mass murderer next week.

No big deal, at least, until they started to come out in other places, as well. No big deal until the first news film ("You may want to ask your children to leave the room," Tom Brokaw introduced gravely) showed up on network TV, decayed monsters with naked bone showing through their dried skin, traffic accident victims, the morticians' concealing make-up sloughed away so that the ripped faces and bashed-in skulls showed, women with their hair teased into dirt-clogged beehives where worms and beetles still squirmed and crawled, their faces alternately vacuous and informed with a kind of calculating, idiotic intelligence. No big deal until the first horrible stills in an issue of *People* magazine that had been sealed in shrink-wrap and sold with an orange sticker that read NOT FOR SALE TO MINORS!

Then it was a big deal.

513

When you saw a decaying man still dressed in the mud-streaked remnants of the Brooks Brothers suit in which he had been buried tearing at the throat of a screaming woman in a tee-shirt that read PROPERTY OF THE HOUSTON OILERS, you suddenly realized it might be a very big deal indeed.

That was when the accusations and saber rattling had started, and for three weeks the entire world had been diverted from the creatures escaping their graves like grotesque moths escaping diseased cocoons by the spectacle of the two great nuclear powers on what appeared to be an undivertible collision course.

There were no zombies in the United States, Communist Chinese television commentators declared; this was a self-serving lie to camouflage an unforgivable act of chemical warfare against the People's Republic of China, a more horrible (and deliberate) version of what had happened in Bhopal, India. Reprisals would follow if the dead comrades coming out of their graves did not fall down decently dead within ten days. All U.S. diplomatic people were expelled from the mother country and there were several incidents of American tourists being beaten to death.

The President (who would not long after become a Zombie Blue Plate Special himself) responded by becoming a pot (which he had come to resemble, having put on at least fifty pounds since his second-term election) calling a kettle black. The U.S. government, he told the American people, had incontrovertible evidence that the only walking-dead people in China had been set loose deliberately, and while the Head Panda might stand there with his slanty-eyed face hanging out, claiming there were over eight thousand lively corpses striding around in search of the ultimate collectivism, *we* had definite proof that there were less than forty. It was the *Chinese* who had committed an act — a *heinous* act — of chemical warfare, bringing loyal Americans back to life with no urge to consume anything but other loyal Americans, and if these Americans — some of whom had been good Democrats — did not lie down decently dead within the next *five* days, Red China was going to be one large slag pit.

NORAD was at DEFCON-2 when a British astronomer named Humphrey Dagbolt spotted the satellite. Or the spaceship. Or the creature. Or whatever in hell's name it was. Dagbolt was not even a professional astronomer but only an amateur star-gazer from the west of England — no one in particular, you would have said — and yet he almost certainly saved the world from some sort of thermonuclear exchange, if not flat-out atomic war. All in all not a bad week's work for a man with a deviated septum and a bad case of psoriasis.

At first it seemed that the two nose-to-nose political systems did not *want* to believe in what Dagbolt had found, even after the Royal Observatory in London had pronounced his photographs and data authentic. Finally, however, the missile silos closed and telescopes all over the world homed in, almost grudgingly, on Star Wormwood.

The joint American/Chinese space mission to investigate the unwelcome newcomer lifted off from the Lanzhou Heights less than three weeks after the first photographs had appeared in the *Guardian*, and everyone's favorite amateur astronomer was aboard, deviated septum and all. In truth, it would have been hard to have kept Dagbolt off the mission — he had become a world-wide hero, the most renowned Briton since Winston Churchill. When asked by a reporter on the day before lift-off if he was frightened, Dagbolt had brayed his oddly endearing Robert Morley laugh, rubbed the side of his truly enormous nose, and exclaimed, "Petrified, dear boy! Utterly pet-trified!"

As it turned out, he had every reason to be petrified.

They all did.

The final sixty-one seconds of received transmission from the *Xiaoping/Truman* were considered too horrible for release by all three governments involved, and so no formal communiqué was ever issued. It didn't matter, of course; nearly twenty thousand ham operators had been monitoring the craft, and it seemed that at least nineteen thousand of them had been rolling tape when the craft had been — well, was there really any other word for it? — invaded.

Chinese voice: Worms! It appears to be a massive ball of —

American voice: Christ! Look out! It's coming for us!

Dagbolt: Some sort of extrusion is occurring. The portside window is —

Chinese voice: Breach! Breach! To your suits,

516

my friends! (Indecipherable gabble.)

American voice: — and appears to be eating its way in —

Female Chinese voice (Ching-Ling Soong): Oh stop it stop the eyes —

(Sound of an explosion.)

Dagbolt: Explosive decompression has occurred. I see three — er, four — dead, and there are worms . . . everywhere there are worms —

American voice: Faceplate! Faceplate! *Faceplate!* (Screaming.)

Chinese voice: Where is my mamma? Oh dear, where is my mamma?

(Screams. Sounds like a toothless old man sucking up mashed potatoes.)

Dagbolt: The cabin is full of worms — what appear to be worms, at any rate — which is to say that they really *are* worms, one realizes — that have apparently extruded themselves from the main satellite — what we took to be — which is to say one means — the cabin is full of floating body parts. These space-worms apparently excrete some sort of acid —

(Booster rockets fired at this point; duration of the burn is 7.2 seconds. This may have been an attempt to escape or possibly to ram the central object. In either case, the maneuver did not work. It seems likely that the blast-chambers themselves were clogged with worms and Captain Lin Yang — or whichever officer was then in charge — believed an explosion of the fuel tanks themselves to be imminent as a result of the clog. Hence the shutdown.)

American voice: Oh my Christ they're in my

head, *they're eating my fuckin br—*

(Static.)

Dagbolt: I believe that prudence dictates a strategic retreat to the aft storage compartment; the rest of the crew is dead. No question about that. Pity. Brave bunch. Even that fat American who kept rooting around in his nose. But in another sense I don't think —

(Static.)

Dagbolt: — dead after all because Ching-Ling Soong — or rather, Ching-Ling Soong's severed head, one means to say — just floated past me, and her eyes were open and blinking. She appeared to recognize me, and to —

(Static.)

Dagbolt: — keep you —

(Explosion. Static.)

Dagbolt: — around me. I repeat, all around me. Squirming things. They — I say, does anyone know if —

(Dagbolt, screaming and cursing, then just screaming. Sounds of toothless old man again.)

(Transmission ends.)

The *Xiaoping/Truman* exploded three seconds later. The extrusion from the rough ball nicknamed Star Wormwood had been observed from better than three hundred telescopes earthside during the short and rather pitiful conflict. As the final sixty-one seconds of transmission began, the craft began to be obscured by something that certainly *looked* like worms. By the end of the final transmission, the craft itself could not be seen at all — only the squirming mass of things that had attached themselves to it. Moments after the final

518

explosion, a weather satellite snapped a single picture of floating debris, some of which was almost certainly chunks of the worm-things. A severed human leg clad in a Chinese space suit floating among them was a good deal easier to identify.

And in a way, none of it even mattered. The scientists and political leaders of both countries knew exactly where Star Wormwood was located: above the expanding hole in earth's ozone layer. It was sending something down from there, and it was not Flowers by Wire.

Missiles came next. Star Wormwood jigged easily out of their way and then returned to its place over the hole.

On the Pulsifers' satellite-assisted TV, more dead people got up and walked, but now there was a crucial change. In the beginning the zombies had only bitten living people who got too close, but in the weeks before the Pulsifers' high-tech Sony started showing only broad bands of snow, the dead folks started *trying* to get close to the living folks.

They had, it seemed, decided they *liked* what they were biting.

The final effort to destroy the thing was made by the United States. The President approved an attempt to destroy Star Wormwood with a number of orbiting nukes, stalwartly ignoring his previous statements that America had never put atomic SDI weapons in orbit and never would. Everyone else ignored them, as well. Perhaps they were too busy praying for success.

It was a good idea, but not, unfortunately, a workable one. Not a single missile from a single

SDI orbiter fired. This was a total of twenty-four flat-out failures.

So much for modern technology.

And then, after all these shocks on earth and in heaven, there was the business of the one little graveyard right here on Jenny. But even that didn't seem to count much for Maddie because, after all, she had not been there. With the end of civilization now clearly at hand and the island cut off— *thankfully* cut off, in the opinion of the residents — from the rest of the world, old ways had reasserted themselves with unspoken but inarguable force. By then they all knew what was going to happen; it was only a question of when. That, and being ready when it did.

Women were excluded.

It was Bob Daggett, of course, who drew up the watch roster. That was only right, since Bob had been head selectman on Jenny for about a thousand years. The day after the death of the President (the thought of him and the first lady wandering witlessly through the streets of Washington, D.C., gnawing on human arms and legs like people eating chicken legs at a picnic was not mentioned; it was a little much to bear, even if the bastid and his blonde wife *were* Democrats), Bob Daggett called the first men-only Town Meeting on Jenny since sometime before the Civil War. Maddie wasn't there, but she heard. Dave Eamons told her all she needed to know.

"You men all know the situation," Bob said. He looked as yellow as a man with jaundice, and people remembered his daughter, the one still living at home on the island, was only one of four. The other three were other places . . . which was to say, on the mainland.

But hell, if it came down to that, they *all* had folks on the mainland.

"We got one boneyard here on Jenny," Bob continued, "and nothin ain't happened there yet, but that don't mean nothin *will*. Nothin ain't happened yet lots of places . . . but it seems like once it starts, nothin turns to somethin pretty goddam quick."

There was a rumble of assent from the men gathered in the grammar-school gymnasium, which was the only place big enough to hold them. There were about seventy of them in all, ranging in age from Johnny Crane, who had just turned eighteen, to Bob's great-uncle Frank, who was eighty, had a glass eye, and chewed tobacco. There was no spittoon in the gym, of course, so Frank Daggett had brought an empty mayonnaise jar to spit his juice into. He did so now.

"Git down to where the cheese binds, Bobby," he said. "You ain't got no office to run for, and time's a-wastin."

There was another rumble of agreement, and Bob Daggett flushed. Somehow his great-uncle always managed to make him look like an ineffectual fool, and if there was anything in the world he hated worse than looking like an ineffectual fool, it was being called Bobby. He owned property, for Chrissake! And he *supported* the old fart — bought him his goddam chew!

But these were not things he could say; old

Frank's eyes were like pieces of flint.

"Okay," Bob said curtly. "Here it is. We want twelve men to a watch. I'm gonna set a roster in just a couple minutes. Four-hour shifts."

"I can stand watch a helluva lot longer'n four hours!" Matt Arsenault spoke up, and Davey told Maddie that Bob said after the meeting that no welfare-slacker like Matt Arsenault would have had the nerve to speak up like that in a meeting of his betters if that old man hadn't called him Bobby, like he was a kid instead of a man three months shy of his fiftieth birthday, in front of all the island men.

"Maybe you can n maybe you can't," Bob said, "but we got plenty of warm bodies, and nobody's gonna fall asleep on sentry duty."

"I ain't gonna —"

"I didn't say *you,*" Bob said, but the way his eyes rested on Matt Arsenault suggested that he might have *meant* him. "This is no kid's game. Sit down and shut up."

Matt Arsenault opened his mouth to say something more, then looked around at the other men — including old Frank Daggett — and wisely held his peace.

"If you got a rifle, bring it when it's your trick," Bob continued. He felt a little better with Arsenault more or less back in his place. "Unless it's a twenty-two, that is. If you ain't got somethin bigger'n that, come n get one here."

"I didn't know the school kep a supply of em handy," Cal Partridge said, and there was a ripple of laughter.

"It don't now, but it will," Bob said, "because

every man jack of you with more than one rifle bigger than a twenty-two is gonna bring it here." He looked at John Wirley, the school principal. "Okay if we keep em in your office, John?"

Wirley nodded. Beside him, Reverend Johnson was dry-washing his hands in a distraught way.

"Shit on that," Orrin Campbell said. "I got a wife and two kids at home. Am I s'posed to leave em with nothin to defend themselves with if a bunch of cawpses come for an early Thanksgiving dinner while I'm on watch?"

"If we do our job at the boneyard, none will," Bob replied stonily. "Some of you got handguns. We don't want none of those. Figure out which women can shoot and which can't and give em the pistols. We'll put em together in bunches."

"They can play Beano," old Frank cackled, and Bob smiled, too. That was more like it, by the Christ.

"Nights, we're gonna want trucks posted around so we got plenty of light." He looked over at Sonny Dotson, who ran Island Amoco, the only gas station on Jenny. Sonny's main business wasn't gassing cars and trucks — shit, there was no place much on the island to drive, and you could get your go ten cents cheaper on the mainland — but filling up lobster boats and the motorboats he ran out of his jackleg marina in the summer. "You gonna supply the gas, Sonny?"

"Am I gonna get cash slips?"

"You're gonna get your ass saved," Bob said. "When things get back to normal — if they ever do — I guess you'll get what you got coming."

Sonny looked around, saw only hard eyes, and

shrugged. He looked a bit sullen, but in truth he looked more confused than anything, Davey told Maddie the next day.

"Ain't got n'more'n four hunnert gallons of gas," he said. "Mostly diesel."

"There's five generators on the island," Burt Dorfman said (when Burt spoke everyone listened; as the only Jew on the island, he was regarded as a creature both quixotic and fearsome, like an oracle that works about half the time). "They all run on diesel. I can rig lights if I have to."

Low murmurs. If Burt said he could do it, he could. He was a Jewish electrician, and there was a feeling on the outer islands, unarticulated but powerful, that that was the best kind.

"We're gonna light that graveyard up like a friggin stage," Bob said.

Andy Kingsbury stood up. "I heard on the news that sometimes you can shoot one of them things in the head and it'll stay down, and sometimes it won't."

"We've got chainsaws," Bob said stonily, "and what won't stay dead . . . why, we can make sure it won't move too far alive."

And, except for making out the duty roster, that was pretty much that.

Six days and nights passed and the sentries posted around the little graveyard on Jenny were starting to feel a wee bit silly ("I dunno if I'm standin guard or pullin my pud," Orrin Campbell said one afternoon as a dozen men stood around the cemetery gate, playing Liars' Poker) when it happened . . . and when it happened, it happened fast.

Dave told Maddie that he heard a sound like the wind wailing in the chimney on a gusty night, and then the gravestone marking the final resting place of Mr. and Mrs. Fournier's boy Michael, who had died of leukemia at seventeen (bad go, that had been, him being their only child and them being such nice people and all), fell over. A moment later a shredded hand with a moss-caked Yarmouth Academy class ring on one finger rose out of the ground, shoving through the tough grass. The third finger had been torn off in the process.

The ground heaved like (like the belly of a pregnant woman getting ready to drop her load, Dave almost said, and hastily reconsidered) a big wave rolling into a close cove, and then the boy himself sat up, only he wasn't anything you could really recognize, not after almost two years in the ground. There were little splinters of wood sticking out of what was left of his face, Davey said, and pieces of shiny blue cloth in the draggles of his hair. "That was coffin-linin," Davey told her, looking down at his restlessly twining hands. "I know that as well's I know m'own name." He paused, then added: "Thank Christ Mike's dad dint have that trick."

Maddie had nodded.

The men on guard, bullshit-scared as well as revolted, opened fire on the reanimated corpse of the former high-school chess champion and All-Star second baseman, tearing him to shreds. Other shots, fired in wild panic, blew chips off his marble gravestone, and it was just luck that the armed men had been loosely grouped together when the festivities commenced; if they had been divided up into two wings, as Bob Daggett had originally intended, they would very likely have slaughtered each other. As it was, not a single islander was hurt, although Bud Meechum found a rather suspicious-looking hole torn in the sleeve of his shirt the next day.

"Prob'ly wa'ant nothin but a blackberry thorn, just the same," he said. "There's an almighty lot of em out at that end of the island, you know." No one would dispute that, but the black smudges around the hole made his frightened wife think that his shirt had been torn by a thorn with a pretty large caliber.

The Fournier kid fell back, most of him lying still, other parts of him still twitching . . . but by then the whole graveyard seemed to be rippling, as if an earthquake were going on there — but *only* there, noplace else.

Just about an hour before dusk, this had happened.

Burt Dorfman had rigged up a siren to a tractor battery, and Bob Daggett flipped the switch. Within twenty minutes, most of the men in town were at the island cemetery.

Goddam good thing, too, Dave Eamons said, because a few of the deaders almost got away. Old Frank Daggett, still two hours from the heart attack that would carry him off just as the excitement was dying down, organized the new men so they wouldn't shoot each other, either, and for the final ten minutes the Jenny boneyard sounded like Bull Run. By the end of the festivities, the powder smoke was so thick that some men choked on it.

The sour smell of vomit was almost heavier than the smell of gunsmoke . . . it was sharper, too, and lingered longer.

And still some of them wriggled and squirmed like snakes with broken backs — the fresher ones, for the most part.

"Burt," Frank Daggett said. "You got them chainsaws?"

"I got em," Burt said, and then a long, buzzing sound came out of his mouth, a sound like a cicada burrowing its way into tree bark, as he dry-heaved. He could not take his eyes from the squirming corpses, the overturned gravestones, the yawning pits from which the dead had come. "In the truck."

"Gassed up?" Blue veins stood out on Frank's ancient, hairless skull.

"Yeah." Burt's hand was over his mouth. "I'm sorry."

"Work y'fuckin gut all you want," Frank said briskly, "but toddle off n get them saws while you do. And you . . . you . . . you . . . you . . ."

The last "you" was his grandnephew Bob.

"I can't, Uncle Frank," Bob said sickly. He looked around and saw five or six of his friends and neighbors lying crumpled in the tall grass. They had not died; they had swooned. Most of them had seen their own relatives rise out of the ground. Buck Harkness over there lying by an aspen tree had been part of the crossfire that had cut his late wife to ribbons; he had fainted after observing her decayed, worm-riddled brains exploding from the back of her head in a grisly gray splash. "I can't. I c—"

Frank's hand, twisted with arthritis but as hard as stone, cracked across his face.

"You can and you will, chummy," he said.

Bob went with the rest of the men.

Frank Daggett watched them grimly and rubbed his chest, which had begun to send cramped throbs of pain all the way down his left arm to the elbow. He was old but he wasn't stupid, and he had a pretty good idea what those pains were, and what they meant.

"He told me he thought he was gonna have a blow-out, and he tapped his chest when he said it," Dave went on, and placed his hand on the swell of muscle over his own left nipple to demonstrate.

Maddie nodded to show she understood.

"He said, 'If anything happens to me before this mess is cleaned up, Davey, you and Burt and Orrin take over. Bobby's a good boy, but I think he may have lost his guts for at least a little while . . . and you know, sometimes when a man loses his guts, they don't come back.' "

Maddie nodded again, thinking how grateful she was — how very, very grateful — that she was not a man.

"So then we did it," Dave said. "We cleaned up the mess."

Maddie nodded a third time, but this time she must have made some sound, because Dave told her he would stop if she couldn't bear it; he would gladly stop.

"I can bear it," she said quietly. "You might be surprised how much I can bear, Davey." He looked at her quickly, curiously, when she said that, but Maddie had averted her eyes before he could see the secret in them.

Dave didn't know the secret because no one on Jenny knew. That was the way Maddie wanted it, and the way she intended to keep it. There had been a time when she had, perhaps, in the blue darkness of her shock, pretended to be coping. And then something happened that *made* her cope. Four days before the island cemetery vomited up its corpses, Maddie Pace was faced with a simple choice: cope or die.

She had been sitting in the living room, drinking a glass of the blueberry wine she and Jack had put up during August of the previous year — a time that now seemed impossibly distant — and doing something so trite it was laughable. She was Knitting Little Things. Booties, in fact. But what else *was* there to do? It seemed that no one would be going across the reach to the Wee Folks store at the Ellsworth Mall for quite some time.

Something had thumped against the window.

A bat, she thought, looking up. Her needles paused in her hands, though. It seemed that something bigger had moved jerkily out there in the windy dark. The oil lamp was turned up high and kicking too much reflection off the panes for her to be sure. She reached to turn it down and the thump came again. The panes shivered. She heard a little pattering of dried putty falling on the sash. Jack had been planning to reglaze all the windows this fall, she remembered, and then thought, *Maybe that's what he came back for.* That was crazy, he was on the bottom of the ocean, but . . .

She sat with her head cocked to one side, her knitting now motionless in her hands. A little pink bootie. She had already made a blue set. All of a sudden it seemed she could hear so *much*. The wind. The faint thunder of surf on Cricket Ledge. The house making little groaning sounds, like an elderly woman making herself comfortable in bed. The tick of the clock in the hallway.

"Jack?" she asked the silent night that was now no longer silent. "Is it you, dear?" Then the living-room window burst inward and what came through was not really Jack but a skeleton with a few mouldering strings of flesh hanging from it.

His compass was still around his neck. It had grown a beard of moss.

The wind flapped the curtains in a cloud above him as he sprawled, then got up on his hands and knees and looked at her from black sockets in which barnacles had grown.

He made grunting sounds. His fleshless mouth opened and the teeth chomped down. He was hungry . . . but this time chicken noodle soup would not serve. Not even the kind that came in the can.

Gray stuff hung and swung beyond those dark barnacle-encrusted holes, and she realized she was looking at whatever remained of Jack's brain. She sat where she was, frozen, as he got up and came toward her, leaving black kelpy tracks on the carpet, fingers reaching. He stank of salt and fathoms. His hands stretched. His teeth chomped mechanically up and down. Maddie saw he was wearing the remains of the black-and-red-checked shirt she had bought him at L. L. Bean's last Christmas. It had cost the earth, but he had said again and again how warm it was, and look how well it had lasted, how much of it was left even after being under water all this time.

The cold cobwebs of bone which were all that remained of his fingers touched her throat before the baby kicked in her stomach — for the first time — and her shocked horror, which she had believed to be calmness, fled, and she drove one of the knitting needles into the thing's eye.

Making horrid thick choking noises that sounded like the suck of a swill pump, he staggered backward, clawing at the needle, while the half-made pink bootie swung in front of the cavity where his nose had been. She watched as a sea slug squirmed from that nasal cavity and onto the bootie, leaving a trail of slime behind it.

Jack fell over the end table she'd gotten at a yard sale just after they had been married — she hadn't been able to make her mind up about it, had been in agonies about it, until Jack finally said either she was going to buy it for their living room or he was going to give the biddy running the sale twice what she was asking for the goddam thing and then bust it up into firewood with —

— with the —

He struck the floor and there was a brittle, cracking sound as his febrile, fragile form broke in two. The right hand tore the knitting needle, slimed with decaying brain tissue, from his eyesocket and tossed it aside. His top half crawled

531

toward her. His teeth gnashed steadily together.

She thought he was trying to grin, and then the baby kicked again and she remembered how uncharacteristically tired and out of sorts he'd sounded at Mabel Hanratty's yard-sale that day: *Buy it, Maddie, for Chrissake! I'm tired! Want to go home and get m'dinner! If you don't get a move on, I'll give the old bat twice what she wants and bust it up for firewood with my —*

Cold, dank hand clutching her ankle; polluted teeth poised to bite. To kill her and kill the baby. She tore loose, leaving him with only her slipper, which he chewed on and then spat out.

When she came back from the entry, he was crawling mindlessly into the kitchen — at least the top half of him was — with the compass dragging on the tiles. He looked up at the sound of her, and there seemed to be some idiot question in those black eye-sockets before she brought the ax whistling down, cleaving his skull as he had threatened to cleave the end table.

His head fell in two pieces, brains dribbling across the tile like spoiled oatmeal, brains that squirmed with slugs and gelatinous sea worms, brains that smelled like a woodchuck exploded with gassy decay in a high-summer meadow.

Still his hands clashed and clittered on the kitchen tiles, making a sound like beetles.

She chopped . . . chopped . . . chopped.

At last there was no more movement.

A sharp pain rippled across her midsection and for a moment she was gripped by terrible panic: *Is it a miscarriage? Am I going to have a miscarriage?* But the pain left and the baby kicked again, more strongly than before.

She went back into the living room, carrying an ax that now smelled like tripe.

His legs had somehow managed to stand.

"Jack, I loved you so much," she said, "but this isn't you." She brought the ax down in a whistling arc that split him at the pelvis, sliced the carpet, and drove deep into the solid oak floor beneath.

The legs separated, trembled wildly for almost five minutes, and then began to grow quiet. At last even the toes stopped twitching.

She carried him down to the cellar piece by piece, wearing her oven gloves and wrapping each piece with the insulating blankets Jack had kept in the shed and which she had never thrown away — he and the crew threw them over the pots on cold days so the lobsters wouldn't freeze.

Once a severed hand closed upon her wrist. She stood still and waited, her heart drumming heavily in her chest, and at last it loosened again. And that was the end of it. The end of *him*.

There was an unused cistern, polluted, below the house — Jack had been meaning to fill it in. Maddie slid the heavy concrete cover aside so that its shadow lay on the earthen floor like a partial eclipse and then threw the pieces of him down, listening to the splashes. When everything was gone, she worked the heavy cover back into place.

"Rest in peace," she whispered, and an interior voice whispered back that her husband was resting in *pieces,* and then she began to cry, and her cries turned to hysterical shrieks, and she pulled at her hair and tore at her breasts until they were bloody, and she thought, *I am insane, this is what it's like to be insa—*

But before the thought could be completed, she had fallen down in a faint, and the faint became a deep sleep, and the next morning she felt all right.

She would never tell, though.

Never.

"I can bear it," she told Dave Eamons again, thrusting aside the image of the knitting needle with the bootie swinging from the end of it jutting out of the kelp-slimed eyesocket of the thing which had once been her husband, and co-creator of the child in her womb. "Really."

So he told her, perhaps because he had to tell someone or go mad, but he glossed over the worst parts. He told her that they had chainsawed the corpses that absolutely refused to return to the land of the dead, but he did not tell her that some parts had continued to squirm — hands with no arms attached to them clutching mindlessly, feet divorced from their legs digging at the bullet-chewed earth of the graveyard as if trying to run away — and that these parts had been doused with diesel fuel and set afire. Maddie did not have to be told this part. She had seen the pyre from the house.

Later, Gennesault Island's one firetruck had turned its hose on the dying blaze, although there wasn't much chance of the fire spreading, with a brisk easterly blowing the sparks off Jenny's seaward edge. When there was nothing left but a stinking, tallowy lump (and still there were occasional bulges in this mass, like twitches in a tired muscle), Matt Arsenault fired up his old D-9 Caterpillar — above the nicked steel blade and under his faded pillowtick engineer's cap, Matt's face had been as white as cottage cheese — and plowed the whole hellacious mess under.

The moon was coming up when Frank took Bob Daggett, Dave Eamons, and Cal Partridge aside. It was Dave he spoke to.

"I knew it was coming, and here it is," he said.

"What are you talking about, Unc?" Bob asked.

"My heart," Frank said. "Goddam thing has thrown a rod."

"Now, Uncle Frank —"

"Never mind Uncle Frank this n Uncle Frank that," the old man said. "I ain't got time to listen to you play fiddlyfuck on the mouth-organ. Seen half my friends go the same way. It ain't no day at the races, but it could be worse; beats hell out of getting whacked with the cancer-stick.

"But now there's this other sorry business to mind, and all I got to say on that subject is, when I go down I intend to *stay* down. Cal, stick that rifle of yours in my left ear. Dave, when I raise my left arm, you sock yours into my armpit. And Bobby, you put yours right over my heart. I'm gonna say the Lord's Prayer, and when I hit amen, you three fellows are gonna pull your triggers at the same time."

"Uncle Frank — " Bob managed. He was reeling on his heels.

"I told you not to start in on that," Frank said. "And don't you *dare* faint on me, you friggin

535

pantywaist. Now get your country butt over here."

Bob did.

Frank looked around at the three men, their faces as white as Matt Arsenault's had been when he drove the 'dozer over men and women he had known since he was a kid in short pants and Buster Browns.

"Don't you boys frig this up," Frank said. He was speaking to all of them, but his eye might have been particularly trained on his grand-nephew. "If you feel like maybe you're gonna backslide, just remember I'd'a done the same for any of you."

"Quit with the speech," Bob said hoarsely. "I love you, Uncle Frank."

"You ain't the man your father was, Bobby Daggett, but I love you, too," Frank said calmly, and then, with a cry of pain, he threw his left hand up over his head like a guy in New York who has to have a cab in a rip of a hurry, and started in with his last prayer. "Our Father who art in heaven — *Christ,* that hurts! — hallow'd be Thy name — oh, son of a *gun!* — Thy kingdom come, Thy will be done, on earth as it . . . as it . . ."

Frank's upraised left arm was wavering wildly now. Dave Eamons, with his rifle socked into the old geezer's armpit, watched it as carefully as a logger would watch a big tree that looked like it meant to do evil and fall the wrong way. Every man on the island was watching now. Big beads of sweat had formed on the old man's pallid face. His lips had pulled back from the even, yellowy-white of his Roebuckers, and Dave had been able to smell the Polident on his breath.

". . . as it is in heaven!" the old man jerked out. "Lead us not into temptation butdeliverusfromevilohshitonitforeverandeverAMEN!"

All three of them fired, and both Cal Partridge and Bob Daggett fainted, but Frank never did try to get up and walk.

Frank Daggett had meant to *stay* dead, and that was just what he did.

Once Dave started that story he had to go on with it, and so he cursed himself for ever starting. He'd been right the first time; it was no story for a pregnant woman.

But Maddie had kissed him and told him she thought he had done wonderfully, and that Frank Daggett had done wonderfully, too. Dave went out feeling a little dazed, as if he had just been kissed on the cheek by a woman he had never met before.

In a very real sense, that was true.

She watched him go down the path to the dirt track that was one of Jenny's two roads and turn left. He was weaving a little in the moonlight, weaving with tiredness, she thought, but reeling with shock, as well. Her heart went out to him . . . to all of them. She had wanted to tell Dave she loved him and kiss him squarely on the mouth instead of just skimming his cheek with her lips, but he might have taken the wrong meaning from something like that, even though he was boneweary and she was almost five months pregnant.

But she *did* love him, loved *all* of them, because they had gone through hell in order to make this little lick of land forty miles out in the Atlantic safe for her.

And safe for her baby.

"It will be a home delivery," she said softly as Dave went out of sight behind the dark hulk of the Pulsifers' satellite dish. Her eyes rose to the moon. "It will be a home delivery . . . and it will be fine."

Rainy Season

It was half past five in the afternoon by the time John and Elise Graham finally found their way into the little village that lay at the center of Willow, Maine, like a fleck of grit at the center of some dubious pearl. The village was less than five miles from the Hempstead Place, but they took two wrong turns on the way. When they finally arrived on Main Street, both of them were hot and out of sorts. The Ford's air-conditioner had dropped dead on the trip from St. Louis, and it felt about a hundred and ten outside. Of course it wasn't anything at all like that, John Graham thought. As the old-timers said, it wasn't the heat, it was the humidity. He felt that today it would be almost possible to reach out and wring warm dribbles of water from the air itself. The sky overhead was a clear and open blue, but that high humidity made it feel as if it were going to rain any minute. Fuck that — it felt as if it were raining *already*.

"There's the market Milly Cousins told us about," Elise said, and pointed.

John grunted. "Doesn't exactly look like the supermarket of the future."

"No," Elise agreed carefully. They were both being careful. They had been married almost two years and they still loved each other very much, but it had been a long trip across country from St. Louis, especially in a car with a broken radio and air-conditioner. John had every hope they would enjoy the summer here in Willow (they ought to, with the University of Missouri picking up the tab), but he thought it might take as long as a week for them to settle in and settle down. And when the weather turned yellow-dog hot like this, an argument could spin itself out of thin air. Neither of them wanted that kind of start to their summer.

John drove slowly down Main Street toward the Willow General Mercantile and Hardware. There was a rusty sign with a blue eagle on it hanging from one corner of the porch, and he understood this was also the postal substation. The General Mercantile looked sleepy in the afternoon light, with one single car, a beat-to-shit Volvo, parked beside the sign advertising ITALIAN SANDWICHES • PIZZA • GROCS • FISHING LICENCES, but compared with the rest of the town, it seemed to be all but bursting with life. There was a neon beer sign fizzing away in the window, although it would not be dark for almost three hours yet. *Pretty radical,* John thought. *Sure hope the owner cleared that sign with the Board of Selectmen before he put it in.*

"I thought Maine turned into Vacationland in the summer," Elise murmured.

"Judging from what we've seen so far, I think Willow must be a little off the tourist track," he replied.

They got out of the car and mounted the porch steps. An elderly man in a straw hat sat in a rocker with a cane seat, looking at them from shrewd little blue eyes. He was fiddling a home-made cigarette together and dribbling little bits of tobacco on the dog which lay crashed out at his feet. It was a big yellow dog of no particular make or model. Its paws lay directly beneath one of the rocker's curved runners. The old man took no notice of the dog, seemed not even to realize it was there, but the runner stopped a quarter of an inch from the vulnerable paws each time the old man rocked forward. Elise found this unaccountably fascinating.

"Good day to ye, lady n man," the old gentleman said.

"Hello," Elise answered, and offered him a small, tentative smile.

"Hi," John said. "I'm —"

"Mr. Graham," the old man finished placidly. "Mr. and Missus Graham. Ones that took the Hempstead Place for the summer. Heard you was writin some kind of book."

"On the in-migration of the French during the seventeenth century," John agreed. "Word sure gets around, doesn't it?"

"It do travel," the old party agreed. "Small town, don'tcha know." He stuck the cigarette in his mouth, where it promptly fell apart, sprinkling tobacco all over his legs and the dog's limp hide. The dog didn't stir. "Aw, flapdoodle," the old man said, and peeled the uncoiling paper from his lower lip. "Wife doesn't want me to smoke nummore anyway. She says she read it's givin her cancer as well as m'ownself."

"We came into town to get a few supplies," Elise said. "It's a wonderful old house, but the cupboard is bare."

541

"Ayuh," the old man said. "Good to meet you folks. I'm Henry Eden." He hung one bunched hand out in their direction. John shook with him, and Elise followed suit. They both did so with care, and the old man nodded as if to say he appreciated it. "I expected you half an hour ago. Must have taken a wrong turn or two, I guess. Got a lot of roads for such a small town, you know." He laughed. It was a hollow, bronchial sound that turned into a phlegmy smoker's cough. "Got a power of roads in Willow, oh, ayuh!" And laughed some more.

John was frowning a little. "Why would you be expecting us?"

"Lucy Doucette called, said she saw the new folks go by," Eden said. He took out his pouch of Top tobacco, opened it, reached inside, and fished out a packet of rolling papers. "You don't know Lucy, but she says you know her grandniece, Missus."

"This is Milly Cousins's great-aunt we're talking about?" Elise asked.

"Yessum," Eden agreed. He began to sprinkle tobacco. Some of it landed on the cigarette paper, but most went onto the dog below. Just as John Graham was beginning to wonder if maybe the dog was dead, it lifted its tail and farted. So much for *that* idea, he thought. "In Willow, just about everybody's related to everybody else. Lucy lives down at the foot of the hill. I was gonna call you m'self, but since she said you was comin in anyway . . ."

"How did you know we'd be coming *here?*" John asked.

542

Henry Eden shrugged, as if to say *Where else is there to go?*

"Did you want to talk to us?" Elise asked.

"Well, I kinda have to," Eden said. He sealed his cigarette and stuck it in his mouth. John waited to see if it would fall apart, as the other one had. He felt mildly disoriented by all this, as if he had walked unknowingly into some bucolic version of the CIA.

The cigarette somehow held together. There was a charred scrap of sandpaper tacked to one of the arms of the rocker. Eden struck the match on it and applied the flame to his cigarette, half of which incinerated on contact.

"I think you and Missus might want to spend tonight out of town," he finally said.

John blinked at him. "Out of town? Why would we want to do that? We just got here."

"Good idea, though, mister," a voice said from behind Eden.

The Grahams looked around and saw a tall woman with slumped shoulders standing inside the Mercantile's rusty screen door. Her face looked out at them from just above an old tin sign advertising Chesterfield cigarettes — TWENTY-ONE GREAT TOBACCOS MAKE TWENTY WONDERFUL SMOKES. She opened the door and came out on the porch. Her face looked sallow and tired but not stupid. She had a loaf of bread in one hand and a six-pack of Dawson's Ale in the other.

"I'm Laura Stanton," she said. "It's very nice to meet you. We don't like to seem unsociable in Willow, but it's the rainy season here tonight."

John and Elise exchanged bewildered glances.

543

Elise looked at the sky. Except for a few small fair-weather clouds, it was a lucid, unblemished blue.

"I know how it looks," the Stanton woman said, "but that doesn't mean anything, does it, Henry?"

"No'm," Eden said. He took one giant drag on his eroded cigarette and then pitched it over the porch rail.

"You can feel the humidity in the air," the Stanton woman said. "*That's* the key, isn't it, Henry?"

"Well," Eden allowed, "ayuh. But it *is* seven years. To the day."

"The very day," Laura Stanton agreed.

They both looked expectantly at the Grahams.

"Pardon me," Elise said at last. "I don't understand any of this. Is it some sort of local joke?"

This time Henry Eden and Laura Stanton exchanged the glances, then sighed at exactly the same moment, as if on cue.

"I *hate* this," Laura Stanton said, although whether to the old man or to herself John Graham had no idea.

"Got to be done," Eden replied.

She nodded, then sighed. It was the sigh of a woman who has set down a heavy burden and knows she must now pick it up again.

"This doesn't come up very often," she said, "because the rainy season only comes in Willow every seven years —"

"June seventeenth," Eden put in. "Rainy season every seven years on June seventeenth. Never changes, not even in leap-year. It's only one night, but rainy season's what it's always been called.

544

Damned if I know why. Do you know why, Laura?"

"No," she said, "and I wish you'd stop interrupting, Henry. I think you're getting senile."

"Well, pardon me for livin, I just fell off the hearse," the old man said, clearly nettled.

Elise threw John a glance that was a little frightened. *Are these people having us on?* it asked. *Or are they both crazy?*

John didn't know, but he wished heartily that they had gone to Augusta for their supplies; they could have gotten a quick supper at one of the clam-stands along Route 17.

"Now listen," the Stanton woman said kindly. "We reserved a room for you at the Wonderview Motel out on the Woolwich Road, if you want it. The place was full, but the manager's my cousin, and he was able to clear one room out for me. You could come back tomorrow and spend the rest of the summer with us. We'd be glad to have you."

"If this *is* a joke, I'm not getting the point," John said.

"No, it's not a joke," she said. She glanced at Eden, who gave her a brisk little nod, as if to say *Go on, don't quit now.* The woman looked back at John and Elise, appeared to steel herself, and said, "You see, folks, it rains toads here in Willow every seven years. There. Now you know."

"Toads," Elise said in a distant, musing, Tell-me-I'm-dreaming-all-this voice.

"Toads, ayuh!" Henry Eden affirmed cheerfully.

John was looking cautiously around for help, if help should be needed. But Main Street was utterly deserted. Not only that, he saw, but *shuttered*. Not a car moved on the road. Not a single pedestrian was visible on either sidewalk.

We could be in trouble here, he thought. *If these people are as nutty as they sound, we could be in real trouble.* He suddenly found himself thinking of Shirley Jackson's short story "The Lottery" for the first time since he'd read it in junior high school.

"Don't you get the idea that I'm standin here and soundin like a fool 'cause I *want* to," Laura Stanton said. "Fact is, I'm just doin my duty. Henry, too. You see, it doesn't just *sprinkle* toads. It *pours.*"

"Come on," John said to Elise, taking her arm above the elbow. He gave them a smile that felt as genuine as a six-dollar bill. "Nice to meet you folks." He guided Elise down the porch steps, looking back over his shoulder at the old man and the slump-shouldered, pallid woman two or three times as he did. It didn't seem like a good idea to turn his back on them completely.

The woman took a step toward them, and John almost stumbled and fell off the last step.

"It *is* a little hard to believe," she agreed. "You probably think I am just as nutty as a fruitcake."

"Not at all," John said. The large, phony smile on his face now felt as if it were approaching the lobes of his ears. Dear Jesus, why had he ever left St. Louis? He had driven nearly fifteen hundred miles with a busted radio and air-conditioner to meet Farmer Jekyll and Missus Hyde.

"That's all right, though," Laura Stanton said, and the weird serenity in her face and voice made him stop by the ITALIAN SANDWICHES sign, still six feet from the Ford. "Even people who have heard of rains of frogs and toads and birds and such don't have a very clear idea of what happens in Willow every seven years. Take a little advice, though: if you *are* going to stay, you'd be well off to stay in the house. You'll most likely be all right in the house."

"Might want to close y'shutters, though," Eden added. The dog lifted his tail and articulated another long and groaning dog-fart, as if to emphasize the point.

"We'll . . . we'll do that," Elise said faintly, and then John had the Ford's passenger door open and was nearly shovelling her inside.

"You bet," he said through his large frozen grin.

"And come back and see us tomorrow," Eden called as John hurried around the front of the Ford to his side. "You'll feel a mite safer around us tomorrow, I think." He paused, then added: "If you're still around at all, accourse."

John waved, got behind the wheel, and pulled out.

There was silence on the porch for a moment as the old man and the woman with the pale, unhealthy skin watched the Ford head back up Main Street. It left at a considerably higher speed than that at which it had come.

"Well, we done it," the old man said contentedly.

"Yes," she agreed, "and I feel like a horse's ass. I *always* feel like a horse's ass when I see the way they look at us. At me."

547

"Well," he said, "it's only once every seven years. And it has to be done just that way. Because —"

"Because it's part of the ritual," she said glumly.

"Ayuh. It's the ritual."

As if agreeing it was so, the dog flipped up his tail and farted once more.

The woman booted it and then turned to the old man with her hands clamped on her hips. "That is the *stinkiest* mutt in four towns, Henry Eden!"

The dog arose with a grunt and staggered down the porch stairs, pausing only long enough to favor Laura Stanton with a reproachful gaze.

"He can't help it," Eden said.

She sighed, looking up the road after the Ford. "It's too bad," she said. "They seem like such *nice* people."

"Nor can *we* help *that*," Henry Eden said, and began to roll another smoke.

So the Grahams ended up eating dinner at a clam-stand after all. They found one in the neighboring town of Woolwich ("Home of the scenic Wonderview Motel," John pointed out to Elise in a vain effort to raise a smile) and sat at a picnic table under an old, overspreading blue spruce. The clam-stand was in sharp, almost jarring contrast to the buildings on Willow's Main Street. The parking lot was nearly full (most of the cars, like theirs, had out-of-state licence plates), and yelling kids with ice cream on their faces chased after one another while their parents strolled about, slapped blackflies, and waited for their numbers to be announced over the loudspeaker. The stand had a fairly wide menu. In fact, John thought, you could have just about anything you wanted, as long as it wasn't too big to fit in a deep-fat fryer.

"I don't know if I can spend two *days* in that town, let alone two months," Elise said. "The bloom is off the rose for this mother's daughter, Johnny."

"It was a joke, that's all. The kind the natives like to play on the tourists. They just went too far with it. They're probably kicking themselves for that right now."

"They looked serious," she said. "How am I supposed to go back there and face that old man after that?"

"I wouldn't worry about it — judging from his cigarettes, he's reached the stage of life where he's meeting *everyone* for the first time. Even his oldest friends."

Elise tried to control the twitching corners of her mouth, then gave up and burst out laughing. "You're evil!"

"Honest, maybe, but not evil. I won't say he had Alzheimer's, but he *did* look as if he might need a roadmap to find his way to the bathroom."

"Where do you suppose everyone else was? The town looked totally deserted."

"Bean supper at the Grange or a card-party at the Eastern Star, probably," John said, stretching. He peeked into her clam basket. "You didn't eat much, love."

"Love wasn't very hungry."

"I tell you it was just a *joke*," he said, taking her hands. "Lighten up."

"You're really, really sure that's all it was?"

549

"Really-really. I mean, hey — every seven years it rains toads in Willow, Maine? It sounds like an outtake from a Steven Wright monologue."

She smiled wanly. "It doesn't rain," she said, "it pours."

"They subscribe to the old fisherman's credo, I guess — if you're going to tell one, tell a whopper. When I was a kid at sleep-away camp, it used to be snipe hunts. This really isn't much different. And when you stop to think about it, it really isn't that surprising."

"What isn't?"

"That people who make most of their yearly income dealing with summer people should develop a summer-camp mentality."

"That woman didn't *act* like it was a joke. I'll tell you the truth, Johnny — she sort of scared me."

John Graham's normally pleasant face grew stern and hard. The expression did not look at home on his face, but neither did it look faked or insincere.

"I know," he said, picking up their wrappings and napkins and plastic baskets. "And there's going to be an apology made for that. I find foolishness for the sake of foolishness agreeable enough, but when someone scares my wife — hell, they scared *me* a little, too — I draw the line. Ready to go back?"

"Can you find it again?"

He grinned, and immediately looked more like himself. "I left a trail of breadcrumbs."

"How wise you are, my darling," she said, and got up. She was smiling again, and John was glad to see it. She drew a deep breath — it did wonders for the front of the blue chambray work-shirt she was wearing — and let it out. "The humidity seems to have dropped."

"Yeah." John deposited their waste into a trash basket with a left-handed hook shot and then winked at her. "So much for rainy season."

But by the time they turned onto the Hempstead Road, the humidity had returned, and with a vengeance. John felt as if his own tee-shirt had turned into a clammy mass of cob-web clinging to his chest and back. The sky, now turning a delicate shade of evening primrose, was still clear, but he felt that, if he'd had a straw, he could have drunk directly from the air.

There was only one other house on the road, at the foot of the long hill with the Hempstead Place at the top. As they drove past it, John saw the silhouette of a woman standing motionless at one of the windows and looking out at them.

"Well, there's your friend Milly's great-aunt," John said. "She sure was a sport to call the local crazies down at the general store and tell them we were coming. I wonder if they would have dragged out the whoopee cushions and joy-buzzers and chattery teeth if we'd stayed a little longer."

"That dog had his own built-in joy-buzzer."

John laughed and nodded.

Five minutes later they were turning into their own driveway. It was badly overgrown with weeds and dwarf bushes, and John intended to take care of *that* little situation before the summer got much older. The Hempstead Place itself was a rambling country farmhouse, added to by succeeding generations whenever the need — or maybe just the urge — to do some building happened to strike. A barn stood behind it, connected to the house by three rambling, zig-zag sheds. In this flush of early summer, two of the three sheds were almost buried in fragrant drifts of honeysuckle.

It commanded a gorgeous view of the town, especially on a clear night like this one. John wondered briefly just how it could *be* so clear when the humidity was so high. Elise joined him in front of the car and they stood there for a moment, arms around each other's waists, looking at the hills which rolled gently off in the direction of Augusta, losing themselves in the shadows of evening.

"It's beautiful," she murmured.

"And listen," he said.

There was a marshy area of reeds and high grass fifty yards or so behind the barn, and in it a chorus of frogs sang and thumped and snapped the elastics God had for some reason stretched in their throats.

"Well," she said, "the frogs are all present and accounted for, anyway."

"No toads, though." He looked up at the clear sky, in which Venus had now opened her coldly burning eye. "There they are, Elise! Up there! Clouds of toads!"

She giggled.

" 'Tonight in the small town of Willow,' " he intoned, " 'a cold front of toads met a warm front of newts, and the result was —' "

She elbowed him. "*You,*" she said. "Let's go in."

They went in. And did not pass Go. And did not collect two hundred dollars.

They went directly to bed.

Elise was startled out of a satisfying drowse an hour or so later by a thump on the roof. She got up on her elbows. "What was that, Johnny?"

"Huzz," John said, and turned over on his side.

Toads, she thought, and giggled . . . but it was a nervous giggle. She got up and went to the window, and before she looked for anything which might have fallen on the ground, she found herself looking up at the sky.

It was still cloudless, and now shot with a trillion spangled stars. She looked at them, for a moment hypnotized by their simple silent beauty.

Thud.

She jerked back from the window and looked up at the ceiling. Whatever it was, it had hit the roof just overhead.

"John! Johnny! Wake up!"

"Huh? What?" He sat up, his hair all tangled tufts and clock-springs.

"It's started," she said, and giggled shrilly. "The rain of frogs."

"Toads," he corrected. "Ellie, what are you talking ab—"

Thud-thud.

He looked around, then swung his feet out of bed.

"This is ridiculous," he said softly and angrily. "What do you m—"

Thud-CRASH! There was a tinkle of glass downstairs.

553

"Oh, goddam," he said, getting up and yanking on his blue-jeans. "Enough. This is just . . . fucking . . . *enough.*"

Several soft thuds hit the side of the house and the roof. She cringed against him, frightened now. "What do you mean?"

"I mean that crazy woman and probably the old man and some of their friends are out there throwing things at the house," he said, "and I am going to put a stop to it right now. Maybe they've held onto the custom of shivareeing the new folks in this little town, but —"

THUD! SMASH! From the kitchen.

"*God-DAMN!*" John yelled, and ran out into the hall.

"Don't leave me!" Elise cried, and ran after him.

He flicked up the hallway light-switch before plunging downstairs. Soft thumps and thuds struck the house in an increasing rhythm, and Elise had time to think, *How many people from town are out there? How many does it take to do that? And what are they throwing? Rocks wrapped in pillow-cases?*

John reached the foot of the stairs and went into the living room. There was a large window in there which gave on the same view which they had admired earlier. The window was broken. Shards and splinters of glass lay scattered across the rug. He started toward the window, meaning to yell something at them about how he was going to get his shotgun. Then he looked at the broken glass again, remembered that his feet were bare, and stopped. For a moment he didn't know what to do. Then he saw a dark shape lying in the broken glass — the rock one of the imbecilic, interbred

554

bastards had used to break the window, he assumed — and saw red. He might have charged to the window anyway, bare feet or no bare feet, but just then the rock twitched.

That's no rock, he thought. *That's a —*

"John?" Elise asked. The house rang with those soft thuds now. It was as if they were being bombarded with large, rotten-soft hailstones. "John, what is it?"

"A toad," he said stupidly. He was still looking at the twitching shape in the litter of broken glass, and spoke more to himself than to his wife.

He raised his eyes and looked out the window. What he saw out there struck him mute with horror and incredulity. He could no longer see the hills or the horizon — hell, he could barely see the barn, and that was less than forty feet away.

The air was stuffed with falling shapes.

Three more of them came in through the broken window. One landed on the floor, not far from its twitching mate. It came down on a sharp sliver of window-glass and black fluid burst from its body in thick ropes.

Elise screamed.

The other two caught in the curtains, which began to twist and jerk as if in a fitful breeze. One of them managed to disentangle itself. It struck the floor and then hopped toward John.

He groped at the wall with a hand which felt as if it were no part of him at all. His fingers stumbled across the light-switch and flipped it up.

The thing hopping across the glass-littered floor toward him was a toad, but it was also not a toad. Its green-black body was too large, too lumpy.

Its black-and-gold eyes bulged like freakish eggs. And bursting from its mouth, unhinging the jaw, was a bouquet of large, needle-sharp teeth.

It made a thick croaking noise and bounded at John as if on springs. Behind it, more toads were falling in through the window. The ones which struck the floor had either died outright or been crippled, but many others — too many others — used the curtains as a safety-net and tumbled to the floor unharmed.

"Get out of here!" John yelled to his wife, and kicked at the toad which — it was insane, but it was true — was attacking him. It did not flinch back from his foot but sank that mouthful of crooked needles first over and then into his toes. The pain was immediate, fiery, and immense. Without thinking, he made a half-turn and kicked the wall as hard as he could. He felt his toes break, but the toad broke as well, splattering its black blood onto the wainscoting in a half-circle, like a fan. His toes had become a crazy road-sign, pointing in all directions at once.

Elise was standing frozen in the hall doorway. She could now hear window-glass shattering all over the house. She had put on one of John's tee-shirts after they had finished making love, and now she was clutching the neck of it with both hands. The air was full of ugly croaking sounds.

"Get out, Elise!" John screamed. He turned, shaking his bloody foot. The toad which had bitten him was dead, but its huge and improbable teeth were still caught in his flesh like a tangle of fish-hooks. This time he kicked at the air, like a man punting a football, and the toad finally flew free.

The faded living-room carpet was now covered with bloated, hopping bodies. And they were all hopping at *them.*

John ran to the doorway. His foot came down on one of the toads and burst it open. His heel skidded in the cold jelly which popped out of its body and he almost fell. Elise relinquished her death-grip on the neck of her tee-shirt and grabbed him. They stumbled into the hall together and John slammed the door, catching one of the toads in the act of hopping through. The door cut it in half. The top half twitched and juddered on the floor, its toothy, black-lipped mouth opening and closing, its black-and-golden pop-eyes goggling at them.

Elise clapped her hands to the sides of her face and began to wail hysterically. John reached out to her. She shook her head and cringed away from him, her hair falling over her face.

The sound of the toads hitting the roof was bad, but the croakings and chirrupings were worse, because these latter sounds were coming from inside the house . . . and *all over* the house. He thought of the old man sitting on the porch of the General Mercantile in his rocker, calling after them: *Might want to close y'shutters.*

Christ, why didn't I believe him?

And, on the heels of that: *How was I* supposed *to believe him? Nothing in my whole life* prepared *me to believe him!*

And, below the sound of toads thudding onto the ground outside and toads squashing themselves to guts and goo on the roof, he heard a more ominous sound: the chewing, splintering sound of the toads in the living room starting to bite their way through the door. He could actually see it settling more firmly against its hinges as more and more toads crowded their weight against it.

He turned around and saw toads hopping down the main staircase by the dozens.

"Elise!" He grabbed at her. She kept shrieking and pulling away from him. A sleeve of the tee-shirt tore free. He looked at the ragged chunk of cloth in his hand with perfect stupidity for a moment and then let it flutter down to the floor.

"Elise, goddammit!"

She shrieked and drew back again.

Now the first toads had reached the hall floor and were hopping eagerly toward them. There was a brittle tinkle as the fanlight over the door shattered. A toad whizzed through it, struck the carpet, and lay on its back, mottled pink belly exposed, webbed feet twitching in the air.

He grabbed his wife, shook her. *"We have to go down cellar! We'll be safe in the cellar!"*

"*No!*" Elise screamed at him. Her eyes were giant floating zeros, and he understood she was not refusing his idea of retreating to the cellar but refusing *everything*.

There was no time for gentle measures or soothing words. He bunched the front of the shirt she was wearing in his fist and yanked her down the hall like a cop dragging a recalcitrant prisoner to a squad-car. One of the toads which had been in the vanguard of those hurrying down the stairs leaped gigantically and snicked its mouthful of darning-needles shut around a chunk of space occupied by Elise's bare heel a second before.

Halfway down the hall, she got the idea and began to come with him of her own accord. They reached the door. John turned the knob and yanked it, but the door wouldn't move.

"*Goddam!*" he cried, and yanked it again. No good. Nothing.

"*John, hurry!*"

She looked back over her shoulder and saw toads flooding down the hall toward them, taking huge crazy sproings over each other's back, falling on each other, striking the faded rambler-rose wallpaper, landing on their backs and being overrun by their mates. They were all teeth and gold-black eyes and heaving, leathery bodies.

"*JOHN, PLEASE! PL—*"

Then one of them leaped and battened on her left thigh just above the knee. Elise screamed and seized it, her fingers punching through its skin and into its dark liquid workings. She tore it free and for a moment, as she raised her arms, the horrid thing was right in front of her eyes, its teeth gnashing like a piece of some small but homicidal factory machine. She threw it as hard as she could. It cartwheeled in the air and then splattered against the wall just opposite the kitchen door. It did not fall but stuck fast in the glue of its own guts.

"*JOHN! OH JESUS, JOHN!*"

John Graham suddenly realized what he was doing wrong. He reversed the direction of his effort, pushing the door instead of pulling it. It flew open, almost spilling him forward and down the stairs, and he wondered briefly if his mother had had any kids that lived. He flailed at the railing, caught hold of it, and then Elise almost knocked him down again, bolting past him and down the stairs, screaming like a firebell in the night.

Oh she's going to fall, she can't help but fall, she's going to fall and break her neck —

But somehow she did not. She reached the cellar's earth floor and collapsed in a sobbing heap, clutching at her torn thigh.

Toads were leaping and hopping in through the open cellar doorway.

John caught his balance, turned, and slapped the door shut. Several of the toads caught on their side of the door leaped right off the landing, struck the stairs, and fell through the spaces between the risers. Another took an almost vertical leap straight up, and John was suddenly shaken by wild laughter — a sudden bright image of Mr. Toad of Toad Hall on a pogo-stick instead of in a motor-car had come to him. Still laughing, he balled his right hand into a fist and punched the toad dead center in its pulsing, flabby chest at the top of its leap, while it hung in perfect equilibrium between gravity and its own expended energy. It zoomed off into the shadows, and John heard a soft *bonk!* as it struck the furnace.

He scrabbled at the wall in the dark, and his fingers found the raised cylinder which was the old-fashioned toggle light-switch. He flipped it, and that was when Elise began to scream again. A toad had gotten tangled in her hair. It croaked and twisted and turned and bit at her neck, rolling itself into something which resembled a large, misshapen curler.

Elise lurched to her feet and ran in a large circle, miraculously avoiding a tumble over the boxes which had been stacked and stored down here. She struck one of the cellar's support posts, rebounded, then turned and banged the back of her head twice, briskly, against it. There was a thick gushing sound, a squirt of black fluid, and then the toad fell out of her hair, tumbling down the back of her tee-shirt, leaving dribbles of ichor.

She screamed, and the lunacy in that sound chilled John's blood. He half-ran, half-stumbled down the cellar stairs and enfolded her in his arms. She fought him at first and then surrendered. Her screams gradually dissolved into steady weeping.

Then, over the soft thunder of the toads striking the house and the grounds, they heard the croaking of the toads which had fallen down here. She drew away from him, her eyes shifting wildly from side to side in their shiny-white sockets.

"Where are they?" she panted. Her voice was hoarse, almost a bark, from all the screaming she had done. "Where are they, John?"

But they didn't have to look; the toads had already seen *them,* and came hopping eagerly toward them.

The Grahams retreated, and John saw a rusty shovel leaning against the wall. He grabbed it and beat the toads to death with it as they came. Only one got past him. It leaped from the floor to a box and from the box it jumped at Elise, catching the cloth of her shirt in its teeth and dangling there between her breasts, legs kicking.

"Stand still!" John barked at her. He dropped the shovel, took two steps forward, grabbed the toad, and hauled it off her shirt. It took a chunk of cloth with it. The cotton strip hung from one of its fangs as it twisted and pulsed and wriggled in John's hands. Its hide was warty, dry but horridly warm and somehow *busy*. He snapped his hands into fists, popping the toad. Blood and slime squirted out from between his fingers.

Less than a dozen of the little monsters had actually made it through the cellar door, and soon they were all dead. John and Elise clung to each other, listening to the steady rain of toads outside.

John looked over at the low cellar windows. They were packed and dark, and he suddenly saw the house as it must look from the outside, buried in a drift of squirming, lunging, leaping toads.

"We've got to block the windows," he said hoarsely. "Their weight is going to break them, and if that happens, they'll *pour* in."

"With what?" Elise asked in her hoarse bark of a voice. "What can we use?"

He looked around and saw several sheets of plywood, elderly and dark, leaning against one wall. Not much, perhaps, but something.

"That," he said. "Help me to break it up into smaller pieces."

They worked quickly and frantically. There were only four windows in the cellar, and their very narrowness had caused the panes to hold longer than the larger windows upstairs had done. They were just finishing the last when they heard the glass of the first shatter behind the plywood . . . but the plywood held.

They staggered into the middle of the cellar again, John limping on his broken foot.

From the top of the stairway came the sound

of the toads eating their way through the cellar door.

"What do we do if they eat all the way through it?" Elise whispered.

"I don't know," he said . . . and that was when the door of the coal-chute, unused for years but still intact, suddenly swung open under the weight of all the toads which had fallen or hopped into it, and hundreds of them poured out in a high-pressure jet.

This time Elise could not scream. She had damaged her vocal cords too badly for that.

It did not last long for the Grahams in the cellar after the coal-chute door gave way, but until it was over, John Graham screamed quite adequately for both of them.

By midnight, the downpour of toads in Willow had slackened off to a mild, croaking drizzle.

At one-thirty in the morning, the last toad fell out of the dark, starry sky, landed in a pine tree near the lake, hopped to the ground, and disappeared into the night. It was over for another seven years.

Around quarter past five, the first light began to creep into the sky and over the land. Willow was buried beneath a writhing, hopping, complaining carpet of toads. The buildings on Main Street had lost their angles and corners; everything was rounded and hunched and twitching. The sign on the highway which read WELCOME TO WILLOW, MAINE, THE *FRIENDLY* PLACE! looked as if someone had put about thirty shotgun shells through it. The holes, of course, had been made by flying

563

toads. The sign in front of the General Mercantile which advertised ITALIAN SANDWICHES • PIZZA • GROCS • FISHING LICENCES had been knocked over. Toads played leapfrog on and around it. There was a small toad convention going on atop each of the gas-pumps at Donny's Sunoco. Two toads sat upon the slowly swinging iron arm of the weathervane atop the Willow Stove Shop like small misshapen children on a merry-go-round.

At the lake, the few floats which had been put out this early (only the hardiest swimmers dared the waters of Lake Willow before July 4th, however, toads or no toads) were piled high with toads, and the fish were going crazy with so much food almost within reach. Every now and then there was a *plip! plip!* sound as one or two of the toads jostling for place on the floats were knocked off and some hungry trout or salmon's breakfast was served. The roads in and out of town — there were a lot of them for such a small town, as Henry Eden had said — were paved with toads. The power was out for the time being; free-falling toads had broken the power-lines in any number of places. Most of the gardens were ruined, but Willow wasn't much of a farming community, anyway. Several people kept fairly large dairy herds, but they had all been safely tucked away for the night. Dairy farmers in Willow knew all about rainy season and had no wish to lose their milkers to the hordes of leaping, carnivorous toads. What in the hell would you tell the insurance company?

As the light brightened over the Hempstead Place, it revealed drifts of dead toads on the roof, rain-gutters which had been splintered loose by dive-bombing toads, a dooryard that was alive with toads. They hopped in and out of the barn, they stuffed the chimneys, they hopped nonchalantly around the tires of John Graham's Ford and sat in croaking rows on the front seat like a church congregation waiting for the services to start. Heaps of toads, mostly dead, lay in drifts against the building. Some of these drifts were six feet deep.

At 6:05, the sun cleared the horizon, and as its rays struck them, the toads began to melt.

Their skins bleached, turned white, then appeared to become transparent. Soon a vapor which gave off a vaguely swampy smell began to trail up from the bodies and little bubbly rivulets of moisture began to course down them. Their eyes fell in or fell out, depending on their positions when the sun hit them. Their skins popped with an audible sound, and for perhaps ten minutes it sounded as if champagne corks were being drawn all over Willow.

They decomposed rapidly after that, melting into puddles of cloudy white *shmeg* that looked like human semen. This liquid ran down the pitches of the Hempstead Place's roof in little creeks and dripped from the eaves like pus.

The living toads died; the dead ones simply rotted to that white fluid. It bubbled briefly and then sank slowly into the ground. The earth sent up tiny ribands of steam, and for a little while every field in Willow looked like the site of a dying volcano.

By quarter of seven it was over, except for the repairs, and the residents were used to them.

It seemed a small price to pay for another seven years of quiet prosperity in this mostly forgotten Maine backwater.

At five past eight, Laura Stanton's beat-to-shit Volvo turned into the dooryard of the General Mercantile. When Laura got out, she looked paler and sicker than ever. She *was* sick, in fact; she still had the six-pack of Dawson's Ale in one hand, but now all the bottles were empty. She had a vicious hangover.

Henry Eden came out on the porch. His dog walked behind him.

"Get that mutt inside, or I'm gonna turn right around and go home," Laura said from the foot of the stairs.

"He can't help passing gas, Laura."

"That doesn't mean *I* have to be around when he lets rip," Laura said. "I mean it, now, Henry. My head hurts like a bastard, and the last thing I need this morning is listening to that dog play *Hail Columbia* out of its asshole."

"Go inside, Toby," Henry said, holding the door open.

Toby looked up at him with wet eyes, as if to say *Do I have to? Things were just getting interesting out here.*

"Go on, now," Henry said.

Toby walked back inside, and Henry shut the door. Laura waited until she heard the latch snick shut, and then she mounted the steps.

"Your sign fell over," she said, handing him the carton of empties.

"I got eyes, woman," Henry said. He was not

in the best temper this morning, himself. Few people in Willow would be. Sleeping through a rain of toads was a goddam hard piece of work. Thank God it only came once every seven years, or a man would be apt to go shit out of his mind.

"You should have taken it in," she said.

Henry muttered something she didn't quite catch.

"What was that?"

"I said we should have tried harder," Henry said defiantly. "They was a nice young couple. We should have tried harder."

She felt a touch of compassion for the old man in spite of her thudding head, and laid a hand on his arm. "It's the ritual," she said.

"Well, sometimes I just feel like saying frig the ritual!"

"Henry!" She drew her hand back, shocked in spite of herself. But he wasn't getting any younger, she reminded herself. The wheels were getting a little rusty upstairs, no doubt.

"I don't care," he said stubbornly. "They seemed like a real nice young couple. You said so, too, and don't try to say you didn't."

"I *did* think they were nice," she said. "But we can't help that, Henry. Why, you said so yourself just last night."

"I know," he sighed.

"We don't make them stay," she said. "Just the opposite. We warn them out of town. They decide to stay themselves. They *always* decide to stay. They make their own decision. *That*'s part of the ritual, too."

"I know," he repeated. He drew a deep breath

567

and grimaced. "I hate the smell afterward. Whole goddam town smells like clabbered milk."

"It'll be gone by noon. You know that."

"Ayuh. But I just about hope I'm underground when it comes around again, Laura. And if I ain't, I hope somebody else gets the job of meetin whoever comes just before rainy season. I like bein able to pay m'bills when they come due just as well as anybody else, but I tell you, a man gets tired of toads. Even if it is only once every seven years, a man can get damned tired of toads."

"A woman, too," she said softly.

"Well," he said, looking around with a sigh, "I guess we might try puttin some of this damn mess right, don't you?"

"Sure," she said. "And, you know, Henry, we don't make ritual, we only follow it."

"I know, but —"

"And things could change. There's no telling when or why, but they could. This might be the last time we have rainy season. Or next time no one from out of town might come —"

"Don't say that," he said fearfully. "If no one comes, the toads might not go away like they do when the sun hits em."

"There, you see?" she asked. "You have come around to my side of it, after all."

"Well," he said, "it's a long time. Ain't it. Seven years is a long time."

"Yes."

"They *was* a nice young couple, weren't they?"

"Yes," she said again.

"Awful way to go," Henry Eden said with a slight hitch in his voice, and this time she said nothing. After a moment, Henry asked her if she would help him set his sign up again. In spite of her nasty headache, Laura said she would — she didn't like to see Henry so low, especially when he was feeling low over something he could control no more than he could control the tides or the phases of the moon.

By the time they'd finished, he seemed to feel a little better.

"Ayuh," he said. "Seven years is a *hell* of a long time."

It is, she thought, *but it always passes, and rainy season always comes around again, and the outsiders come with it, always two of them, always a man and a woman, and we always tell them exactly what is going to happen, and they don't believe it, and what happens . . . happens.*

"Come on, you old crock," she said, "offer me a cup of coffee before my head splits wide open."

He offered her a cup, and before they had finished, the sounds of hammers and saws had begun in town. Outside the window they could look down Main Street and see people folding back their shutters, talking and laughing.

The air was warm and dry, the sky overhead was a pale and hazy blue, and in Willow, rainy season was over.

My Pretty Pony

The old man sat in the barn doorway in the smell of apples, rocking, wanting not to want to smoke not because of the doctor but because now his heart fluttered all the time. He watched that stupid son of a bitch Osgood do a fast count with his head against the tree and watched him turn and catch Clivey out and laugh, his mouth open wide enough so the old man could observe how his teeth were already rotting in his head and imagine how the kid's breath would smell: like the back part of a wet cellar. Although the whelp couldn't be more than eleven.

The old man watched Osgood laugh his gaspy hee-hawing laugh. The boy laughed so hard he finally had to lean over and put his hands on his knees, so hard the others came out of their hiding places to see what it was, and when they saw, they laughed, too. They all stood around in the morning sun and laughed at his grandson and the old man forgot how much he wanted a smoke. What he wanted now was to see if Clivey would cry. He found he was more curious on this subject than on any other which had engaged his attention over the last several months, including the subject of his own fast-approaching death.

"Caught im out!" the others chanted, laughing. "Caught im, caught im, caught im out!"

Clivey only stood there, stolid as a chunk of rock in a farmer's field, waiting for the razzing to be over so the game could go on with him as It and the embarrassment beginning to be behind him. After a while the game did. Then it was noontime and the other boys went home. The old man watched to see how much lunch Clivey would eat. It turned out to be not much. Clivey just poked at his potatoes, made his corn and his peas change places, and fed little scraps of meat to the dog under the table. The old man watched it all, interested, answering when the others talked to him, but not much listening to their mouths or his own. His mind was on the boy.

When the pie was done he wanted what he couldn't have and so excused himself to take a nap and paused halfway up the stairs because now his heart felt like a fan with a playing card caught in it, and he stood there with his head down, waiting to see if this was the final one (there had been two before), and when it wasn't he went on up and took off all but his underdrawers and lay down on the crisp white coverlet. A rectangular label of sun lay across his scrawny chest; it was cut into three sections by dark strokes of shadow that were the window laths. He put his hands behind his head, drowsing and listening. After awhile he thought he heard the boy crying in his own room down the hall and he thought, *I ought to take care of that.*

He slept an hour, and when he got up the woman was asleep beside him in her slip, and so he took his clothes out into the hallway to dress before going down.

Clivey was outside, sitting on the steps and throwing a stick for the dog, who fetched with more will than the boy tossed. The dog (he had no name, he was just the dog) seemed puzzled.

The old man hailed the boy and told him to take a walk up to the orchard with him and so the boy did.

The old man's name was George Banning. He was the boy's grandfather, and it was from him that Clive Banning learned the importance of having a pretty pony in your life. You had to have one of those even if you were allergic to horses, because without a pretty pony you could have six clocks in every room and so many watches on each wrist you couldn't raise your arms and still you'd never know what time it was.

The instruction (George Banning didn't give advice, only instruction) had taken place on the day Clive got caught out by that idiot Alden Osgood while playing hide and seek. By that time Clive's Grandpa seemed older than God, which probably meant about seventy-two. The Banning homestead was in the town of Troy, New York, which in 1961 was just starting to learn how not to be the country.

The instruction took place in the West Orchard.

His grandfather was standing coatless in a blizzard that was not late snow but early apple blossoms in a high warm wind; Grandpa was wearing his biballs with a collared shirt beneath, a shirt that looked as if it had once been green but was now faded to a no-account olive by dozens or hundreds of washings, and beneath the collared shirt was the round top of a cotton undershirt (the kind with the straps, of course; in those days they made the other kind, but a man like Grandpa would be a strap-undershirt man to the end), and this shirt was clean but the color of old ivory instead of its original white because Gramma's motto, often spoken and stitched into a living-room sampler as well (presumably for those rare times when the woman herself was not there to dispense what wisdom needed dispensing), was this: *Use it, use it, never lose it! Break it in! Wear it out! Keep it safe or do without!* There were apple blossoms caught in Grandpa's long hair, still only half white, and the boy thought the old man was beautiful in the trees.

He had seen Grandpa watching them as they went about their game earlier that day. Watching *him.* Grandpa had been sitting in his rocker at the entrance to the barn. One of the boards squeaked every time Grandpa rocked, and there he sat, a book facedown in his lap, his hands folded atop it, there he sat rocking amid the dim sweet smells of hay and apples and cider. It was this game that caused his Grandpa to offer Clive Banning instruction on the subject of time, and how it was slippery, and how a man had to fight to hold it in his hands almost all the while; the pony was pretty but it had a wicked heart. If you didn't keep a close eye on that pretty pony, it would jump the fence and be out of sight and you'd have to take your rope bridle and go after it, a trip that was apt to tire you all the way to your bones even if it was short.

Grandpa began his instruction by saying that Alden Osgood had cheated. He was supposed to hide his eyes against the dead elm by the chopping block for a full minute, which he would time by counting to sixty. This would give Clivey (so Grandpa had always called him, and he hadn't minded, although he was thinking he would have to fight any boy or man who called him that once he was past the age of twelve) and the others a fair chance to hide. Clivey had still been looking for a place when Alden Osgood got to sixty, turned around, and "caught him out" as he was trying to squirm — as a last resort — behind a pile of apple crates stacked haphazardly beside the press-shed, where the machine that squeezed the blems into cider bulked in the dimness like an engine of torture.

"It wasn't fair," Grandpa said. "You didn't do no bitching about it and that was right, because a natural man *never* does no bitching — they call it bitching because it ain't for men or even boys smart enough to know better and brave enough to do better. Just the same, it wasn't fair. I can say that now because you didn't say it then."

Apple blossoms blowing in the old man's hair. One caught in the dent below his Adam's apple, caught there like a jewel that was pretty simply because some things *were* and couldn't help it, but was *gorgeous* because it lacked duration: in a few seconds it would be brushed impatiently away and left on the ground where it would become perfectly anonymous among its fellows.

He told Grandpa that Alden *had* counted to sixty, just as the rules said he must, not knowing why he wanted to argue the side of the boy who had, after all, shamed him by not even having to find him but had simply "caught him out." Alden — who sometimes slapped like a girl when he was mad — had needed only to turn, see him, then casually put his hand on the dead tree and chant the mystic and unquestioned formula of elimination: "I-see-Clive, my gool-one-two-three!"

Maybe he only argued Alden's case so he and Grandpa wouldn't have to go back yet, so he could watch Grandpa's steel hair blow back in the blizzard of blossoms, so he could admire that transient jewel caught in the hollow at the base of the old man's throat.

"Sure he did," Grandpa said. "Sure he counted to sixty. Now looka this, Clivey! And let it mark your mind!"

There were real pockets in Grandpa's overalls — five of them, counting the kangaroo-like pouch in the bib — but beside the hip pockets there were things that only *looked* like pockets. They were really slits, made so you could reach through to the pants you were wearing underneath (in those days the idea of *not* wearing pants underneath would not have seemed scandalous, only laughable — the behavior of someone who was A Little Soft in the Attic). Grandpa was wearing the inevitable pair of blue-jeans beneath his overalls. "Jew-pants," he called them matter-of-factly, a term that all the farmers Clive knew used. Levi's were either "Jew-pants" or simply "Joozers."

He reached through the righthand slit in his overalls, fumbled at some length in the righthand pocket of the denim trousers beneath, and at last

575

brought out a tarnished silver pocket watch which he put in the boy's unprepared hand. The weight of the watch was so sudden, the ticking beneath its metal skin so lively, that he came within an ace of dropping it.

He looked at Grandpa, his brown eyes wide.

"You ain't gonna drop it," said Grandpa, "and if you did you probably wouldn't stop it — it's been dropped before, even stepped on once in some damned beerjoint in Utica, and it never stopped yet. And if it did stop, it'd be your loss, not mine, because it's yours now."

"What?" He wanted to say he didn't understand but couldn't finish because he thought he did.

"I'm giving it to you," Grandpa said. "Always meant to, but I'll be damned if I'm gonna put it in my will. It'd cost more for the damn law-rights than that thing's worth."

"Grandpa . . . I . . . Jesus!"

Grandpa laughed until he started to cough. He doubled over, coughing and laughing, his face going a plum-purple color. Some of Clive's joy and wonder were lost in concern. He remembered his mother telling him again and again on their way up here that he was not to tire Grandpa out because Grandpa was ill. When Clive had asked him two days before — cautiously — what had made him sick, George Banning had replied with a single mysterious word. It was only on the night after their talk in the orchard, as he was drifting off to sleep with the pocket watch curled warmly in his hand, that Clive realized the word Grandpa had spoken, "ticka," referred not to some dangerous poison-bug but to Grandpa's heart. The doctor had made him stop smoking and said if he tried anything too strenuous, like shovelling snow or trying to hoe the garden, he would end up playing a harp. The boy knew well enough what *that* meant.

"You ain't gonna drop it, and if you did you probably wouldn't stop it," Grandpa had said, but the boy was old enough to know that it *would* stop someday, that people and watches both stopped someday.

He stood, waiting to see if Grandpa was going to stop, but at last his coughing and laughter eased off and he stood up straight again, wiping a runner of snot from his nose with his left hand and then flicking it casually away.

"You're a goddam funny kid, Clivey," he said. "I got sixteen grandchildren, and there's only two of em that I think is gonna amount to duckshit, and you ain't one of em — although you're on the runner-up list — but you're the only one that can make me laugh until my balls ache."

"I didn't mean to make your balls ache," Clive said, and that sent Grandpa off again, although this time he was able to get his laughter under control before the coughing started.

"Loop the chain over your knuckles a time or two, if it'll make you feel easier," Grandpa said. "If you feel easier in your mind, maybe you'll pay attention a little better."

He did as Grandpa suggested and *did* feel better. He looked at the watch in his palm, mesmerized by the lively feel of its mechanism, by the sunstar on its crystal, by the second hand which turned in its own small circle. But it was still Grandpa's watch:

of this he was quite sure. Then, as he had this thought, an apple blossom went skating across the crystal and was gone. This happened in less than a second, but it changed everything. After the blossom, it was true. It was his watch, forever . . . or at least until one of them stopped running and couldn't be fixed and had to be thrown away.

"All right," Grandpa said. "You see the second hand going around all by its ownself?"

"Yes."

"Good. Keep your eye on it. When it gets up to the top, you holler 'Go!' at me. Understand?"

He nodded.

"Okay. When it gets there, you just let her go, Gallagher."

Clive frowned down at the watch with the deep seriousness of a mathematician approaching the conclusion of a crucial equation. He already understood what Grandpa wanted to show him, and he was bright enough to understand that proof was only a formality . . . but one that must be shown just the same. It was a rite, like not being able to leave church until the minister said the benediction, even though all the songs on the board had been sung and the sermon was finally, mercifully, over.

When the second hand stood straight up at twelve on its own separate little dial (*Mine*, he marvelled. *That's* my *second hand on* my *watch*), he hollered *"Go!"* at the top of his lungs, and Grandpa began to count with the greasy speed of an auctioneer selling dubious goods, trying to get rid of them at top prices before his hypnotized audience can wake up and realize it has not just been bilked but outraged.

"One-two-thre', fo'-fi'-six, sev'-ay-nine, ten-'leven," Grandpa chanted, the gnarly blotches on his cheeks and the big purple veins on his nose beginning to stand out again in his excitement. He finished in a triumphant hoarse shout: *"Fiffyn-ine-sixxy!"* As he said this last, the second hand of the pocket watch was just crossing the seventh dark line, marking thirty-five seconds.

"How long?" Grandpa asked, panting and rubbing at his chest with his hand.

Clive told him, looking at Grandpa with undisguised admiration. "That was fast counting, Grandpa!"

Grandpa flapped the hand with which he had been rubbing his chest in a *get out!* gesture, but he smiled. "Didn't count half as fast as that Osgood brat," he said. "I heard that little sucker count twenty-seven, and the next thing I knew he was up somewhere around forty-one." Grandpa fixed him with his eyes, a dark autumnal blue utterly unlike Clive's Mediterranean brown ones. He put one of his gnarled hands on Clive's shoulder. It was knotted with arthritis, but the boy felt the live strength that still slumbered in there like wires in a machine that's turned off. "You remember one thing, Clivey. Time ain't got nothing to do with how fast you can *count.*"

Clive nodded slowly. He didn't understand completely, but he thought he felt the *shadow* of understanding, like the shadow of a cloud passing slowly across a meadow.

Grandpa reached into the pouch pocket in the bib of his overalls and brought out a pack of unfiltered Kools. Apparently Grandpa hadn't stopped smoking after all, dicky heart or not. Still, it seemed to the boy as if maybe Grandpa had cut down drastically, because that pack of Kools looked as if it had done hard travelling; it had escaped the fate of most packs, torn open after breakfast and tossed empty into the gutter at three, a crushed ball. Grandpa rummaged, brought out a cigarette almost as bent as the pack from which it had come. He stuck it in the corner of his mouth, replaced the pack in the bib, and brought out a wooden match which he snapped alight with one practiced flick of his old man's thick yellow thumbnail. Clive watched with the fascination of a child who watches a magician produce a fan of cards from an empty hand. The flick of the thumb was always interesting, but the amazing thing was that *the match did not go out.* In spite of the high wind which steadily combed this hilltop, Grandpa cupped the small flame with an assurance that could afford to be leisurely. He lit his smoke and then was actually *shaking the match,* as if he had negated the wind by simple will. Clive looked closely at the cigarette and saw no black scorch-marks trailing up the white paper from the glowing tip. His eyes had not deceived him, then; Grandpa had taken his light from a straight flame, like a man who takes a light from a candle in a closed room. It was sorcery, pure and simple.

Grandpa removed the cigarette from his mouth and put his thumb and forefinger in, looking for a moment like a man who means to whistle for his dog, or a taxi. Instead he brought them out again wet and pressed them against the match-head. The boy needed no explanation; the only thing Grandpa and his friends out here in the country feared more than sudden freezes was fire. Grandpa dropped the match and ground it under his boot. When he looked up and saw the boy staring at him, he misinterpreted the subject of his fascination.

"I know I ain't supposed to," he said, "and I ain't gonna tell you to lie or even ask you to. If Gramma asks you right out — 'Was that old man smokin up there?' — you go on and tell her I was. I don't need a kid to lie for me." He didn't smile, but his shrewd, side-slanted eyes made Clive feel part of a conspiracy that seemed amiable and sinless. "But then, if Gramma asks *me* right out if you took the Savior's name in vain when I gave you that watch, I'd look her right in the eye and say, 'No'm. He said thanks as pretty as could be and that was *all* he done.' "

Now Clive was the one to burst out laughing, and the old man grinned, revealing his few remaining teeth.

"Course, if she don't ask neither of us nothing, I guess we don't have to *volunteer* nothing . . . do we, Clivey? Does that seem fair?"

"Yes," Clive said. He wasn't a good-looking boy and never became the sort of man women exactly consider handsome, but as he smiled in complete understanding of the old man's rhetorical sleight-of-hand, he *was* beautiful, at least for a moment, and Grandpa ruffled his hair.

"You're a good boy, Clivey."

"Thank you, sir,"

His grandfather stood ruminating, his Kool

burning with unnatural rapidity (the tobacco was dry, and although he puffed seldom, the greedy hilltop wind smoked the cigarette ceaselessly), and Clive thought the old man had said everything he had to say. He was sorry. He loved to hear Grandpa talk. The things Grandpa said continually amazed him because they almost always made sense. His mother, his father, Gramma, Uncle Don — they all said things he was supposed to take to heart, but they *rarely* made sense. Handsome is as handsome does, for instance — what did *that* mean?

He had a sister, Patty, who was six years older. He understood *her* but didn't care because most of what she said out loud was stupid. The rest was communicated in vicious little pinches. The worst of these she called "Peter-Pinches." She told him that, if he ever *told* about the Peter-Pinches, she'd murdalize him. Patty was always talking about people she was going to murdalize; she had a hit-list to rival Murder, Incorporated. It made you want to laugh . . . until you took a good look at her thin, grim face, that was. When you saw what was really there, you lost your desire to laugh. Clive did, anyway. And you had to be careful of her — she *sounded* stupid but was far from it.

"I don't want dates," she had announced at supper one night not long ago — around the time that boys traditionally invited girls to either the Spring Dance at the country club or to the prom at the high school, in fact. "I don't care if I *never* have a date." And she had looked at them with wide-eyed defiance from above her plate of steaming meat and vegetables.

Clive had looked at the still and somehow spooky

face of his sister peering through the steam and remembered something that had happened two months before, when there had still been snow on the ground. He'd come along the upstairs hall-way in his bare feet so she hadn't heard him, and he had looked into the bathroom because the door was open — he hadn't had the slightest idea old Pukey Patty was in there. What he saw had frozen him dead in his tracks. If she had turned her head even a little to the left, she would have seen him.

She didn't, though. She had been too preoccupied with her inspection of herself. She had been standing there as naked as one of the slinky babes in Foxy Brannigan's well-thumbed *Model Delights*, her bath towel lying puddled around her feet. She was no slinky babe, though — Clive knew it, and she knew it too, from the look of her. Tears were rolling down her pimply cheeks. They were big tears and there were a lot of them, but she never made a sound. At last Clive had regained enough of his sense of self-preservation to tiptoe away, and he had never said a word to anyone about the incident, least of all to Patty herself. He didn't know if she would have been mad about her kid brother seeing her bareass, but he had a good idea about how she'd react to the idea that he had seen her bawling (even that weird boohoo-less bawling she'd been doing); for that she would have murdalized him for sure.

"I think boys are dumb and most of them smell like gone-over cottage cheese," she had said on that spring night. She stuck a forkful of roast beef into her mouth. "If a boy ever asked me for a date, I'd laugh."

"You'll change your mind about that, Punkin," Dad said, chewing his roast beef and not looking up from the book beside his plate. Mom had given up trying to get him to stop reading at the table.

"No I *won't*," Patty said, and Clive knew she wouldn't. When Patty said things she most always meant them. That was something Clive understood about her that his parents didn't. He wasn't sure she meant it — you know, *really* — about murdalizing him if he tattled on her about the Peter-Pinches, but he wasn't going to take chances. Even if she didn't actually kill him, she would find some spectacular yet untraceable way to hurt him, that was for sure. Besides, sometimes the Peter-Pinches weren't really pinches at all; they were more like the way Patty sometimes stroked her little half-breed poodle, Brandy, and he knew she was doing it because he was bad, but he had a secret he certainly did not intend to tell her: these other Peter-Pinches, the stroking ones, actually felt sort of good.

When Grandpa opened his mouth, Clive thought he would say *Time to go back t'the house, Clivey,* but instead he told the boy: "I'm going to tell you something, if you want to hear it. Won't take long. You want to hear it, Clivey?"

"Yes, sir!"

"You really do, don't you?" Grandpa said in a bemused voice.

"Yes, sir."

"Sometimes I think I ought to steal you from your folks and keep you around forever. Sometimes I think if I had you on hand most the time,

I'd live forever, goddam bad heart or not."

He removed the Kool from his mouth, dropped it to the ground, and stamped it to death under one workboot, revolving the heel back and forth and then covering the butt with the dirt his heel had loosened just to be sure. When he looked up at Clive again, it was with eyes that gleamed.

"I stopped giving advice a long time ago," he said. "Thirty years or more, I guess. I stopped when I noticed only fools gave it and only fools took it. *Instruction,* now . . . instruction's a different thing. A smart man will give a little from time to time, and a smart man — or boy — will take a little from time to time."

Clive said nothing, only looked at his grandfather with close concentration.

"There are three kinds of time," Grandpa said, "and while all of them are real, only one is *really* real. You want to make sure you know them all and can always tell them apart. Do you understand that?"

"No, sir."

Grandpa nodded. "If you'd said 'Yes, sir,' I would have swatted the seat of your pants and taken you back to the farm."

Clive looked down at the smeared results of Grandpa's cigarette, face hot with blush, proud.

"When a fellow is only a sprat, like you, time is long. Take a for-instance. When May comes, you think school's never gonna let out, that mid-month June will just never come. Ain't that pretty much how it is?"

Clive thought of that last weight of drowsy, chalk-smelling schooldays and nodded.

"And when mid-month June finally *does* come and Teacher gives you your report card and lets you go free, it seems like school's never gonna let back in. Ain't that pretty much right, too?"

Clive thought of that highway of days and nodded so hard his neck actually popped. "Boy, it sure is! I mean, *sir*." Those days. All those days, stretching away across the plains of June and July and over the unimaginable horizon of August. So many days, so many dawns, so many noon lunches of bologna sandwiches with mustard and raw chopped onion and giant glasses of milk while his mom sat silently in the living room with her bottomless glass of wine, watching the soap operas on the TV; so many depthless afternoons when sweat grew in the short hedge of your crewcut and then ran down your cheeks, afternoons when the moment you noticed that your blob of a shadow had grown a boy always came as a surprise, so many endless twilights with the sweat cooling away to nothing but a smell like aftershave on your cheeks and forearms while you played tag or red rover or capture the flag; sounds of bike chains, slots clicking neatly into oiled cogs, smells of honeysuckle and cooling asphalt and green leaves and cut grass, sounds of the slap of baseball cards being laid out on some kid's front walk, solemn and portentous trades which changed the faces of both leagues, councils that went on in the slow shady axial tilt of a July evening until the call of *"Cliiiiive! Supper!"* put an end to that business; and that call was always as expected and yet as shocking as the noon blob that had, by three or so, become a black boy-shape running in the street beside him

— and that boy stapled to his heels had actually become a man by five or so, albeit an extraordinarily skinny one; velvet evenings of television, the occasional rattle of pages as his father read one book after another (he never tired of them; words, words, words, his dad never tired of them, and Clive had meant once to ask him how that could be but lost his nerve), his mother getting up once in a while and going into the kitchen, followed only by his sister's worried, angry eyes and his own simply curious ones; the soft clink as Mom replenished the glass which was never empty after eleven in the morning or so (and their father never looking up from his book, although Clive had an idea he heard it all and knew it all, although Patty had called him a stupid liar and had given him a Peter-Pinch that hurt all day long the one time he had dared to tell her that); the sound of mosquitoes whining against the screens, always so much louder, it seemed, after the sun had gone down; the decree of bedtime, so unfair and unavoidable, all arguments lost before they were begun; his father's brusque kiss, smelling of tobacco, his mother's softer, both sugary and sour with the smell of wine; the sound of his sister telling Mom she ought to go to bed after Dad had gone down to the corner tavern to drink a couple of beers and watch the wrestling matches on the television over the bar; his mom telling Patty to mind her own p's and q's, a conversational pattern that was upsetting in its content but somehow soothing in its predictability; fireflies gleaming in the gloom; a car horn, distant, as he drifted into sleep's long, dark channel; then the next day, which seemed the same but wasn't, not quite. Summer. That was summer. And it did not just seem long; it was long.

Grandpa, watching him closely, seemed to read all this in the boy's brown eyes, to know all the words for all the things the boy never could have found a way to tell, things that could not escape him because his mouth could never articulate the language of his heart. And then Grandpa nodded, as if he wanted to confirm this very idea, and suddenly Clive was terrified that Grandpa would spoil everything by saying something soft and soothing and meaningless. Sure, he would say. I know all about it, Clivey — I was a boy once myself, you know.

But he didn't, and Clive understood he had been stupid to fear the possibility even for a moment. Worse, faithless. Because this was *Grandpa,* and Grandpa *never* talked meaningless shit like other grownups so often did. Instead of speaking softly and soothingly, he spoke with the dry finality of a judge pronouncing a harsh sentence for a capital crime.

"All that changes," he said.

Clive looked up at him, a little apprehensive at the idea but very much liking the wild way the old man's hair blew around his head. He thought Grandpa looked the way the church-preacher would if he really knew the truth about God instead of just guessing. "*Time* does? Are you sure?"

"Yes. When you get to a certain age — right around fourteen, I think, mostly when the two halves of the human race go on and make the mistake of discovering each other — time starts to be *real* time. The *real* real time. It ain't long like it was or short like it gets to be. It does, you know. But for most of your life it's mostly the *real* real time. You know what that is, Clivey?"

"No, sir."

"Then take instruction: *real* real time is your pretty pony. Say it: 'My pretty pony.' "

Feeling dumb, wondering if Grandpa was having him on for some reason ("trying to get your goat," as Uncle Don would have said), Clive said what he wanted him to say. He waited for the old man to laugh, to say, "Boy, I really got your goat that time, Clivey!" But Grandpa only nodded matter-of-factly, in a way that took all the dumb out of it.

"My pretty pony. Those are three words you'll never forget if you're as smart's I think y'might be. My pretty pony. That's the truth of time."

Grandpa took the battered package of cigarettes from his pocket, considered it briefly, then put it back.

"From the time you're fourteen until, oh, I'm gonna say until you're sixty or so, most time is my-pretty-pony time. There's times when it goes back to being long like it was when you were a kid, but those ain't good times anymore. You'd give your soul for some my-pretty-pony time then, let alone short time. If you was to tell Gramma what I'm gonna tell you now, Clivey, she'd call me a blasphemer and wouldn't bring me no hot-water bottle for a week. Maybe two."

Nevertheless, Grandpa's lips twisted into a bitter and unregenerate jag.

"If I was to tell it to that Reverend Chadband

589

the wife sets such a store by, *he'd* trot out the one about how we see through a glass darkly or that old chestnut about how God works in mysterious ways His wonders to perform, but I'll tell you what *I* think, Clivey. I think God must be one mean old son of a bitch to make the only long times a grownup has the times when he is hurt bad, like with crushed ribs or stove-in guts or something like that. A God like that, why, He makes a kid who sticks pins in flies look like that saint who was so good the birds'd come and roost all over him. I think about how long them weeks were after the hay-rick turned turtle on me, and I wonder why God wanted to make living, thinking creatures in the first place. If He needed something to piss on, why couldn't He have just made Him some sumac bushes and left it at that? Or what about poor old Johnny Brinkmayer, who went so slow with the bone cancer last year."

Clive hardly heard that last, although he remembered later, on their ride back to the city, that Johnny Brinkmayer, who had owned what his mother and father called the grocery store and what Grandpa and Gramma still both called "the Mercantile," was the only man Grandpa went to see of an evening . . . and the only man who came to see *Grandpa* of an evening. On the long ride back to town it came to Clive that Johnny Brinkmayer, whom he remembered only vaguely as a man with a very large wart on his forehead and a way of hitching at his crotch as he walked, must have been Grandpa's only real friend. The fact that Gramma tended to turn up her nose when Brinkmayer's name was mentioned — and often complained about the way the man had smelled — only reinforced the idea.

Such reflections could not have come now, anyway, because Clive was waiting breathlessly for God to strike Grandpa dead. Surely He would for such a blasphemy. No one could get away with calling *God the Father Almighty* a mean old son of a bitch, or suggest that the Being who made the universe was no better than a mean third-grader who got his kicks sticking pins into flies.

Clive took a nervous step away from the figure in the bib overalls, who had ceased being his Grandpa and had become instead a lightning rod. Any moment now a bolt would come out of the blue sky, sizzling his Grandpa dead as doggy-doo and turning the apple trees into torches that would signal the old man's damnation to all and sundry. The apple blossoms blowing through the air would be turned into something like the bits of char that went floating up from the incinerator in their backyard when his father burned the week's worth of newspapers on late Sunday afternoons.

Nothing happened.

Clive waited, his dreadful surety eroding, and when a robin twittered cheerily somewhere nearby (as if Grandpa had said nothing more awful than kiss-my-foot), he knew no lightning was going to come. And at the moment of that realization, a small but fundamental change took place in Clive Banning's life. His Grandpa's unpunished blasphemy would not make him a criminal or a bad boy, or even such a small thing as a "problem child" (a phrase that had only recently come into vogue). Yet the true north of belief shifted just a little in Clive's mind, and the way he listened to his Grandpa changed at once. Before, he had *listened* to the old man. Now he *attended* him.

"Times when you're hurt go on forever, seems like," Grandpa was saying. "Believe me, Clivey — a week of being hurt makes the best summer vacation you ever had when you was a kid seem like a weekend. Hell, makes it seem like a Sat'dy mornin! When I think of the seven months Johnny lay there with that . . . that *thing* that was inside him, inside him and eating on his *guts* . . . Jesus, I ain't got no business talkin this way to a kid. Your Gramma's right. I got the sense of a chicken."

Grandpa brooded down at his shoes for a moment. At last he looked up and shook his head, not darkly, but with brisk, almost humorous dismissiveness.

"Ain't a bit of that matters. I said I was gonna give you instruction, and instead I stand here howlin like a woe-dog. You know what a woe-dog is, Clivey?"

The boy shook his head.

"Never mind; that's for another day." Of course there had never been another, because the next time he saw Grandpa, Grandpa was in a box, and Clive supposed that was an important part of the instruction Grandpa had to give that day. The fact that the old man didn't know he was giving it made it no less important. "Old men are like old trains in a switchin yard, Clivey — too many damned tracks. So they loop the damned roundhouse five times before they ever get in."

"That's all right, Grandpa."

"What I mean is that every time I drive for

the point, I go someplace else."

"I know, but those someplace elses are pretty interesting."

Grandpa smiled. "If you're a bullshit artist, Clivey, you are a damned good one."

Clive smiled back, and the darkness of Johnny Brinkmayer's memory seemed to lift from his Grandpa. When he spoke again, his voice was more businesslike.

"Anyway! Never mind that swill. Having long time in pain is just a little extra the Lord throws in. You know how a man will save up Raleigh coupons and trade em in for something like a brass barometer to hang in his den or a new set of steak knives, Clivey?"

Clive nodded.

"Well, that's what pain-time is like . . . only it's more of a *booby* prize than a real one, I guess you'd have to say. Main thing is, when you get old, regular time — my-pretty-pony time — changes to *short* time. It's like when you were a kid, only turned around."

"Backwards."

"Yep."

The idea that time went *fast* when you got old was beyond the ability of the boy's emotions to grasp, but he was bright enough to admit the concept. He knew that if one end of a seesaw went up, the other had to go down. What Grandpa was talking about, he reasoned, must be the same idea: balance and counterbalance. *All right; it's a point of view,* Clive's own father might have said.

Grandpa took the packet of Kools from the kangaroo pouch again, and this time he carefully ex-

593

tracted a cigarette — not just the last one in the packet but the last one the boy would ever see him smoke. The old man crumpled the package and stowed it back in the place from which it had come. He lit this last cigarette as he had the other, with the same effortless ease. He did not ignore the hilltop wind; he seemed somehow to *negate* it.

"When does it happen, Grandpa?"

"I can't exactly tell you that, n it don't happen all at once," Grandpa said, wetting the match as he had its predecessor. "It kinda creeps up, like a cat stalking a squirrel. Finally you notice. And when you *do* notice, it ain't no more fair than the way the Osgood boy counted his numbers was fair."

"Well then, *what* happens? How do you notice?"

Grandpa tapped a roll of ash from his cigarette without taking it from his mouth. He did it with his thumb, knocking on the cigarette the way a man may rap a low knock on a table. The boy never forgot that small sound.

"I think what you notice first must be different for everyone," the old man said, "but for me it started when I was forty-something. I don't remember exactly how old I was, but you want to bet I remember *where* I was . . . in Davis Drug. You know it?"

Clive nodded. His father almost always took him and his sister in there for ice-cream sodas when they were visiting Grandpa and Gramma. His father called them the VanChockstraw Triplets because their orders never varied: their father always had vanilla, Patty chocolate, Clive strawberry. And

594

his father would sit between them and read while they slowly ingested the cold sweet treats. Patty was right when she said you could get away with anything when their father was reading, which was most of the time, but when he put his book away and looked around, you wanted to sit up and put on your prettiest manners, or you were apt to get clouted.

"Well, I was in there," Grandpa resumed, his eyes far off, studying a cloud that looked like a soldier blowing on a bugle moving swiftly across the spring sky, "to get some medicine for your Gramma's arthritis. We'd had rain for a week and it was hurting her like all get-out. And all at once I seen a new store display. Would have been hard to miss. Took up most of one whole aisle, it did. There were masks and cutout decorations of black cats and witches on brooms and things like that, and there were those cardboard punkins they used to sell. They came in a bag with an elastic inside. The idea was, a kid would punch the punkin out of the cardboard and then give his mom an afternoon of peace coloring it in and maybe playing the games on the back. When it was done you hung it on your door for a decoration, or, if the kid's family was too poor to buy him a store mask or too dumb to help him make a costume out of what was around the house, why, you could staple that elastic onto the thing and the kid would wear it. Used to be a lot of kids walking around town with paper bags in their hands and those punkin masks from Davis Drug on their faces come Halloween night, Clivey! And, of course, he had his candy out. Was always that penny-candy counter up there by the soda fountain, you know the one I mean —"

Clive smiled. He knew, all right.

"— but this was different. This was penny candy by the job lot. All that truck like wax bottles and candy corn and root-beer barrels and licorice whips.

"And I thought that old man Davis — there really was a fella named Davis who ran the place back then, it was his father that opened her up right around 1910 — had slipped a cog or two. Holy hell, I'm thinkin to myself, Frank Davis has got his trick-or-treat out before the goddam summer's even over. It crossed my mind to go up to the prescription counter where he was n tell him just that, and then a part of me says, Whoa up a second, George — *you're* the one who's slipped a cog or two. And that wasn't so far wrong, Clivey, because it *wasn't* still summer, and I knew it just as well as I know we're standin here. See, that's what I want you to understand — *that I knew better.*

"Wasn't I already on the lookout for apple pickers from around town, and hadn't I already put in an order for five hundred handbills to get put up over the border in Canada? And didn't I already have my eye on this fella named Tim Warburton who'd come down from Schenectady lookin for work? He had a way about him, looked honest, and I thought he'd make a good foreman during picking time. Hadn't I been meaning to ask him the very next day, and didn't he *know* I was gonna ask because he'd let on he'd be getting his hair cut at such-and-such a place at such-and-such a time? I thought to myself, Suds n body, George, ain't you a little young to be going senile? Yeah, old Frank's got his Halloween candy out a little early, but *summer?* That's gone by, me fine bucko.

"I knew that just fine, but for a second, Clivey — or maybe it was a whole row of seconds — it *seemed* like summer, or like it *had* to be summer, because it was just *being* summer. Get what I mean? It didn't take me long to get September set down straight again in my head, but until I did I felt . . . you know, I felt . . ." He frowned, then reluctantly brought out a word he knew but would not have used in conversation with another farmer, lest he be accused (if only in the other fellow's mind) of being high-flown. "I felt *dismayed.* That's the only goddam way I know how to put it. Dismayed. And that's how it was the first time."

He looked at the boy, who only looked back at him, not even nodding, so deep in concentration was he. Grandpa nodded for both of them and knocked another roll of ash off his cigarette with the side of his thumb. The boy believed Grandpa was so lost in thought that the wind was smoking practically all of this one for him.

"It was like steppin up to the bathroom mirror meanin to do no more'n shave and seein that first gray hair in your head. You get that, Clivey?"

"Yes."

"Okay. And after that first time, it started to happen with *all* the holidays. You'd think they was puttin the stuff out too early, and sometimes you'd even say so to someone, although you always stayed careful to make it sound like you thought the shopkeepers were greedy. That something was wrong with *them*, not *you*. You get *that?*"

"Yes."

"Because," Grandpa said, "a greedy shopkeeper was something a man could understand — and something some men even admired, although I was never one of them. 'So-and-so keeps himself a sharp practice,' they'd say, as if sharp practice, like that butcher fella Radwick that used to always stick his thumb on the scales when he could get away with it, like that was just a honey of a way to be. I never felt that way, but I could understand it. Saying something that made you sound like you had gone over funny in the head, though . . . that was a different kettle of beans. So you'd just say something like 'By God, they'll have the tinsel and the angel's hair out before the hay's in the barn next year,' and whoever you said it to would say that was nothing but the Gospel truth, but it *wasn't* the Gospel truth, and when I hunker right down and study her, Clivey, I know they are putting all those things out pretty near the same time every year.

"Then somethin else happened to me. This might have been five years later, might have been seven. I think I must've been right round fifty, one side or the other. Anyhow, I got called on jury duty. Damn pain in the ass, but I went. The bailiff sweared me up, asked me if I'd do my duty so help me God, and I said I will, just as if I hadn't spent all my life doin my duty about one thing n another so help me God. Then he got out his pen and asked for my address, and I gave it to him neat as you'd like. Then he asked how old I was, and I opened my mouth all primed to say thirty-seven."

598

Grandpa threw back his head and laughed at the cloud that looked like a soldier. That cloud, the bugle part now grown as long as a trombone, had gotten itself halfway from one horizon to the other.

"Why did you want to say that, Grandpa?" Clive thought he had followed everything up to this pretty well, but here was a thicket.

"I wanted to say it because it was the first thing to come into my mind! Hell! Anyhow, I knew it was wrong and so I stopped for a second. I don't think that bailiff or anyone else in the courtroom noticed — seemed like most of em was either asleep or on the doze — and, even if they'd been as wide awake as the fella who just got Widow Brown's broomstick rammed up his buttsky, I don't know as anyone would have made anything of it. Wasn't no more than how, sometimes, a man trying to hit a tricky pitch will kinda take a double pump before he swings. But, shit! Askin a man how damn *old* he is ain't like throwin no spitball. I felt like an ijit. Seemed like for that one second I didn't know *how* old I was if I wasn't thirty-seven. Seemed for a second there like it could have been seven or seventeen or seventy-seven. Then I got it and I said forty-eight or fifty-one or whatever-the-frig. But to lose track of your age, even for a second . . . *shoo!*"

Grandpa dropped his cigarette, brought his heel down upon it, and began the ritual of first murdalizing and then burying it.

"But that's just the *beginning*, Clivey me son," he went on, and, although he spoke only in the Irish vernacular he sometimes affected, the boy thought, I wish I *was* your son. Yours instead of his. "After a bit, it lets go of first, hits second, and before you know it, time has got itself into high gear and you're cruising, the way folks do on the turnpike these days, goin so fast their cars blow the leaves right off'n the trees in the fall."

"What do you mean?"

"Way the seasons change is the worst," the old man said moodily, as if he hadn't heard the boy. "Different seasons stop *bein* different seasons. Seems like Mother has no more'n got the boots n mittens n scarves down from the attic before it's mud season, and you'd think a man'd be *glad* to see mud season gone — shit, *I* always was — but you ain't s'glad t'see it go when it seems like the mud's gone before you done pushed the tractor out of the first jellypot it got stuck in. Then it seems like you no more'n clapped your summer straw on for the first band concert of the year when the poplars start showing their chemises."

Grandpa looked at him then, an eyebrow raised ironically, as if expecting the boy to ask for an explanation, but Clive smiled, delighted by this — he knew what a chemise was, all right, because it was sometimes all that his mother wore until five in the afternoon or so, at least when his father was out on the road, selling appliances and kitchenware and a little insurance when he could. When his father went out on the road his mother got down to the serious drinking, and that was drinking sometimes too serious to allow her to get dressed until the sun was getting ready to go down. Then sometimes she went out, leaving him in Patty's care while she went to visit a sick friend.

Once he said to Patty, "Ma's friends get sick more when Dad's on the road, d'ja notice?" And Patty laughed until tears ran down her face and she said Oh yes, she *had* noticed, she most certainly *had*.

What Grandpa said reminded him of how, once the days finally began to slope down toward school again, the poplars changed somehow. When the wind blew, their undersides turned up exactly the color of his mother's prettiest chemise, a silver color which was as surprisingly sad as it was lovely: a color that signified the end of what you had believed must be forever.

"Then," Grandpa continued, "you start to lose track of things in your own mind. Not too much — it ain't being senile, like old man Hayden down the road, thank God — but it's still a suckardly thing, the way you *lose track*. It ain't like *forgetting* things; that'd be one thing. No, you remember em but you get em in all the wrong places. Like how I was so sure I broke my arm just *after* our boy Billy got killed in that road accident in '58. *That* was a suckardly thing, too. That's one I could task that Reverend Chadband with. Billy, he was followin a gravel truck, doin no more than twenty mile an hour, when a chunk of stone no bigger'n the dial of that pocket watch I gave you fell off the back of the truck, hit the road, bounced up, and smashed the windshield of our Ford. Glass went in Billy's eyes and the doc said he would have been blinded in one of em or maybe even in both if he'd lived, but he didn't live — he went off the road and hit a 'lectric pole. It fell down atop the car and he got fried just the same as any mad dog killer that ever rode Old Sparky at Sing

601

Sing. And him the worst thing he ever did in his life maybe playing sick to keep from hoeing beans when we still kep the garden.

"But I was saying how sure I was I broke my goddam arm *after* — I swore up n down I could remember goin to his funeral with that arm still in the sling! Sarah had to show me the family Bible first and the insurance papers on my arm second before I could believe she had it the right way around; it had been two whole months before, and by the time we buried Billy away, the sling was off. She called me an old fool and I felt like putting one up on the side of her head I was s'mad, but I was mad because I was *embarrassed,* and at least I had the sense to know that n leave her alone. She was only mad because she don't like to think about Bill. He was the apple of her eye, he was."

"Boy!" Clive said.

"It ain't goin *soft;* it's more like when you go down to New York City and there are these fellas on the street corners with nutshells and a beebee under one of em, and they bet you can't tell which nutshell the beebee's under, and you're sure you can, but they shuffle em so goddarn fast they fool you every time. You just lose track. You can't seem to help it."

He sighed, looking around, as if to remember where exactly it was that they were. His face had a momentary look of utter helplessness that disgusted the boy as much as it frightened him. He didn't want to feel that way, but couldn't help it. It was as if Grandpa had pulled open a bandage to show the boy a sore which was a symptom of something awful. Something like leprosy.

"Seems like spring started last week," Grandpa said, "but the blossoms'll be gone tomorrow if the wind keeps up its head, and damn if it don't look like it's gonna. A man can't keep his train of thought when things go as fast as that. A man can't say, Whoa up a minute or two, old hoss, while I get my bearins! There's no one to say it *to*. It's like bein in a cart that's got no driver, if you take my drift. So what do you make of it, Clivey?"

"Well," the boy said, "you're right about one thing, Grandpa — it sounds like an ijit of some kind must've made up the whole thing."

He didn't mean it to be funny, but Grandpa laughed until his face went that alarming shade of purple again, and this time he not only had to lean over and put his hands on the knees of his overalls but then had to sling an arm around the boy's neck to keep from falling down. They both would have gone tumbling if Grandpa's coughing and wheezing hadn't eased just at the moment when the boy felt sure the blood must come bursting out of that face, which was swollen purple with hilarity.

"Ain't you a jeezer!" Grandpa said, pulling back at last. "Ain't you a *one!*"

"Grandpa? Are you all right? Maybe we ought to —"

"Shit, no, I ain't all right. I've had me two heart attacks in the last two years, and if I live another two years no one'll be any more surprised than me. But it ain't no news to the human race, boy. All I ever set out to say was that old or young, fast time or slow time, you can walk a straight

603

line if you remember that pony. Because when you count and say 'my pretty pony' between each number, time can't be nothing but time. You do that, I'm telling you you got the sucker stabled. You can't count *all* the time — that ain't God's plan. I'll go down the primrose lane with that little oily-faced pissant Chadband that far, anyway. But you got to remember that *you* don't own *time;* it's *time* that owns *you.* It goes along outside you at the same speed every second of every day. It don't care a pisshole in the snow for you, but that don't matter if you got a pretty pony. If you got a pretty pony, Clivey, you got the bastard right where its dingle dangles and never mind all the Alden Osgoods in the world."

He bent toward Clive Banning.

"Do you understand that?"

"No, sir."

"I know you don't. Will you remember it?"

"Yes, sir."

Grandpa Banning's eyes studied him so long the boy became uncomfortable and fidgety. At last he nodded. "Yeah, I think you will. Goddam if I don't."

The boy said nothing. In truth, he could think of nothing to say.

"You have taken instruction," Grandpa said.

"I didn't take any instruction if I didn't *understand!*" Clive cried in a frustrated anger so real and so complete it startled him. "I *didn't!*"

"Fuck *understanding,*" the old man said calmly. He slung his arm around the boy's neck again and drew him close — drew him close for the last time before Gramma would find him dead as a stone in bed a month later. She just woke up and there was Grandpa and Grandpa's pony had kicked down Grandpa's fences and gone over all the hills of the world.

Wicked heart, wicked heart. Pretty, but with a wicked heart.

"Understanding and instruction are cousins that don't kiss," Grandpa said that day among the apple trees.

"Then what *is* instruction?"

"Remembrance," the old man said serenely. "Can you remember that pony?"

"Yes, sir."

"What name does it keep?"

The boy paused.

"Time . . . I guess."

"Good. And what color is it?"

The boy thought longer this time. He opened his mind like an iris in the dark. "I don't know," he said at last.

"Me, neither," the old man said, releasing him. "I don't think it has one, and I don't think it matters. What matters is, will you know it?"

"Yes, sir," the boy said at once.

A glittering, feverish eye fastened the boy's mind and heart like a staple.

"*How?*"

"It'll be pretty," Clive Banning said with absolute certainty.

Grandpa smiled. "So!" he said. "Clivey has taken a bit of instruction, and that makes him wiser and me more blessed . . . or the other way around. D'you want a slice of peach pie, boy?"

"Yes, sir!"

605

"Then what are we doin up here? Let's go get her!"

They did.

And Clive Banning never forgot the name, which was time, and the color, which was none, and the look, which was not ugly or beautiful . . . but only pretty. Nor did he ever forget her nature, which was wicked, or what his Grandpa said on the way down, words almost thrown away, lost in the wind: having a pony to ride was better than having no pony at all, no matter how the weather of its heart might lie.

Sorry, Right Number

AUTHOR'S NOTE: Screenplay abbreviations are simple and exist, in this author's opinion, mostly to make those who write screenplays feel like lodge brothers. In any case, you should be aware that CU means *close-up;* ECU means *extreme close-up;* INT. means *interior;* ext. means *exterior;* B.G. means *background;* pov means *point of view.* Probably most of you knew all that stuff to begin with, right?

ACT I

FADE IN ON:

KATIE WEIDERMAN'S MOUTH, ECU

She's speaking into the telephone. Pretty mouth; in a few seconds we'll see that the rest of her is just as pretty.

> KATIE
>
> Bill? Oh, he says he doesn't feel very well, but he's always like that between books . . . can't sleep, thinks every headache is the first symptom of a brain tumor . . . once he gets going on something new, he'll be fine.

SOUND, B.G.: THE TELEVISION.

THE CAMERA DRAWS BACK. KATIE is sitting in the kitchen phone nook, having a good gab with her sister while she idles through some catalogues. We should notice one not-quite-ordinary thing about the phone she's on: it's the sort with two lines. There are LIGHTED BUTTONS to show which ones are engaged. Right now only one — KATIE'S — is. As KATIE CONTINUES HER CONVERSATION, THE CAMERA SWINGS AWAY FROM HER, TRACKS ACROSS THE KITCHEN, and through the arched doorway that leads into the family room.

> KATIE (voice, fading)
> Oh, I saw Janie Charlton today . . . yes! Big as a *house!* . . .

She fades. The TV gets louder. There are three kids: JEFF, eight, CONNIE, ten, and DENNIS, thirteen. *Wheel of Fortune* is on, but they're not watching. Instead they're engaged in that great pastime, Fighting About What Comes On Later.

> JEFF
> Come *onnn!* It was his first *book!*

> CONNIE
> His first *gross* book.

> DENNIS
> We're gonna watch *Cheers* and *Wings,* just like we do every week, Jeff.

608

DENNIS speaks with the utter finality only a big brother can manage. "Wanna talk about it some more and see how much pain I can inflict on your scrawny body, Jeff?" his face says.

> JEFF
> Could we at least tape it?

> CONNIE
> We're taping CNN for Mom. She said she might be on the phone with Aunt Lois for quite awhile.

> JEFF
> How can you tape CNN, for God's sake? It *never stops!*

> DENNIS
> That's what she likes about it.

> CONNIE
> And don't say God's sake, Jeffie — you're not old enough to talk about God except in church.

> JEFF
> Then don't call me Jeffie.

> CONNIE
> Jeffie, Jeffie, Jeffie.

JEFF gets up, walks to the window, and looks out into the dark. He's really upset. DENNIS and CONNIE, in the grand tradition of older brothers and sisters, are delighted to see it.

DENNIS

Poor Jeffie.

CONNIE

I think he's gonna commit suicide.

JEFF (turns to them)

It was his *first* book! Don't you guys even *care?*

CONNIE

Rent it down at the Video Stop tomorrow, if you want to see it so bad.

JEFF

They don't rent R-rated pictures to little kids and you know it!

CONNIE (dreamily)

Shut up, it's Vanna! I *love* Vanna!

JEFF

Dennis —

DENNIS

Go ask Dad to tape it on the VCR in his office and quit being such a totally annoying little booger.

JEFF crosses the room, poking his tongue out at Vanna White as he goes. THE CAMERA FOLLOWS as he goes into the kitchen.

KATIE

. . . so when he asked me if *Polly* had tested strep positive, I had to remind him she's away at prep school . . . and God, Lois, I miss her . . .

JEFF is just passing through, on his way to the stairs.

KATIE
Will you kids *please* be quiet?

JEFF (glum)
They'll be quiet. *Now.*

He goes up the stairs, a little dejected. KATIE looks after him for a moment, loving and worried.

KATIE
They're squabbling again. Polly used to keep them in line, but now that she's away at school . . . I don't know . . . maybe sending her to Bolton wasn't such a hot idea. Sometimes when she calls home she sounds so *unhappy* . . .

INT. BELA LUGOSI AS DRACULA, CU

Drac's standing at the door of his Transylvanian castle. Someone has pasted a comic-balloon coming out of his mouth which reads: "Listen! My children of the night! What music they make!" The poster is on a door but we only see this as JEFF opens it and goes into his father's study.

INT. A PHOTOGRAPH OF KATIE, CU

THE CAMERA HOLDS, THEN PANS SLOWLY

RIGHT. We pass another photo, this one of POLLY, the daughter away at school. She's a lovely girl of sixteen or so. Past POLLY is DENNIS . . . then CONNIE . . . then JEFF.

THE CAMERA CONTINUES TO PAN AND ALSO WIDENS OUT so we can see BILL WEIDERMAN, a man of about forty-four. He looks tired. He's peering into the word-processor on his desk, but his mental crystal ball must be taking the night off, because the screen is blank. On the walls we see framed book-covers. All of them are spooky. One of the titles is *Ghost Kiss.*

JEFF comes up quietly behind his dad. The carpet muffles his feet. BILL sighs and shuts off the word-cruncher. A moment later JEFF claps his hands on his father's shoulders.

JEFF

BOOGA-BOOGA!

BILL

Hi, Jeffie.

He turns in his chair to look at his son, who is disappointed.

JEFF
How come you didn't get scared?

BILL
Scaring is my business. I'm case-hardened. Something wrong?

612

JEFF

Daddy, can I watch the first hour of *Ghost Kiss* and you tape the rest? Dennis and Connie are hogging *everything*.

BILL swivels to look at the book-jacket, bemused.

BILL

You sure you want to watch *that*, champ? It's pretty —

JEFF

Yes!

INT. KATIE, IN THE PHONE NOOK

In this shot, we clearly see the stairs leading to her husband's study behind her.

KATIE

I *really* think Jeff needs the orthodontic work but you know Bill —

The other line rings. The other light stutters.

KATIE

That's just the other line, Bill will —

But now we see BILL and JEFF coming downstairs behind her.

BILL

Honey, where're the blank videotapes? I can't find any in the study and —

KATIE (TO BILL)

Wait!

(TO LOIS)

Gonna put you on hold a sec, Lo.

She does. Now both lines are blinking. She pushes the top one, where the new call has just come in.

KATIE

Hello, Weiderman residence.

SOUND: DESPERATE SOBBING.

SOBBING VOICE (filter)

Take . . . please take . . . t-t-

KATIE

Polly? Is that you? What's wrong?

SOUND: SOBBING. It's awful, heartbreaking.

SOBBING VOICE (filter)

Please — quick —

SOUND: SOBBING . . . Then, CLICK! A broken connection.

KATIE

Polly, calm down! Whatever it is can't be that b—

HUM OF AN OPEN LINE.

JEFF has wandered toward the TV room, hoping

to find a blank tape.

BILL
Who was that?

Without looking at her husband or answering him, KATIE slams the lower button in again.

KATIE
Lois? Listen, I'll call you back. That was Polly, and she sounded very upset. No . . . she hung up. Yes. I will. Thanks.

She hangs up.

BILL (concerned)
It was Polly?

KATIE
Crying her head off. It sounded like she was trying to say "Please take me home" . . . I knew that damn school was bumming her out . . . Why I ever let you talk me into it . . .

She's rummaging frantically on her little phone desk. Catalogues go slithering to the floor around her stool.

KATIE
Connie did you take my address book?

CONNIE (voice)
No, Mom.

BILL pulls a battered book out of his back pocket and pages through it.

                    BILL
I got it. Except —

                    KATIE
I know, damn dorm phone is always busy. Give it to me.

                    BILL
Honey, calm down.

                    KATIE
I'll calm down after I talk to her. She is sixteen, Bill. Sixteen-year-old girls are prone to depressive interludes. Sometimes they even k . . . just give me the damn number!

                    BILL
617-555-8641.

As she punches the numbers, THE CAMERA SLIDES IN TO CU.

                    KATIE
Come on, come on . . . don't be busy . . . just this once . . .

SOUND: CLICKS. A pause. Then . . . the phone starts ringing.

                    KATIE (eyes closed)
Thank You, God.

VOICE (filter)
Hartshorn Hall, this is Frieda. If you want Christine the Sex Queen, she's still in the shower, Arnie.

KATIE
Could you call Polly to the phone? Polly Weiderman? This is Kate Weiderman. Her mother.

VOICE (filter)
Oh, jeez! Sorry. I thought — hang on, please, Mrs. Weiderman.

SOUND: THE PHONE CLUNKS DOWN.

VOICE (filter, and very faint)
Polly? Pol? . . . Phone call! . . . It's your mother!

INT.   A WIDER ANGLE ON THE PHONE NOOK, WITH BILL

BILL
Well?

KATIE
Somebody's getting her. I hope.

JEFF comes back in with a tape.

JEFF
I found one, Dad. Dennis hid em. As usual.

617

BILL

In a minute, Jeff. Go watch the tube.

JEFF

But —

BILL

I won't forget. Now go *on.*

JEFF goes.

KATIE

Come on, come on, come on . . .

BILL

Calm down, Katie.

KATIE (snaps)

If you'd heard her, you wouldn't tell me to calm down! She sounded —

POLLY (filter, cheery voice)

Hi, mom!

KATIE

Pol? Honey? Are you all right?

POLLY (happy, bubbling voice)

Am I *all right?* I aced my bio exam, got a B on my French Conversational Essay, and Ronnie Hansen asked me to the Harvest Ball. I'm so all right that if one more good thing happens to me today, I'll probably blow up like the *Hindenburg.*

KATIE

You didn't just call me up, crying your head off?

We see by KATE's face that she already knows the answer to this question.

POLLY (filter)

Heck no!

KATIE

I'm glad about your test and your date, honey. I guess it was someone else. I'll call you back, okay?

POLLY (filter)

'Kay. Say hi to Dad!

KATIE

I will.

INT. THE PHONE NOOK, WIDER

BILL

She okay?

KATIE

Fine. I could have *sworn* it was Polly, but . . . *she's* walking on air.

BILL

So it was a prank. Or someone who was crying so hard she dialed a wrong number . . . "through a shimmering film of tears," as we veteran hacks like to say.

KATIE

It was not a prank and it was not a wrong number! It was someone in *my family!*

BILL

Honey, you can't know that.

KATIE

No? If Jeffie called up, just crying, would you know it was him?

BILL (struck by this)
Yeah, maybe. I guess I might.

She's not listening. She's punching numbers, fast.

BILL

Who you calling?

She doesn't answer him. SOUND: PHONE RINGS TWICE. Then:

OLDER FEMALE VOICE (filter)
Hello?

KATIE

Mom? Are you . . . (She pauses) Did you call just a few seconds ago?

VOICE (filter)
No, dear . . . why?

620

KATIE

Oh . . . you know these phones. I was talking to Lois and I lost the other call.

VOICE (filter)

Well, it wasn't me. Kate, I saw the *prettiest* dress in La Boutique today, and —

KATIE

We'll talk about it later, Mom, okay?

VOICE (filter)

Kate, are you all right?

KATIE

I have . . . Mom, I think maybe I've got diarrhea. I have to go. 'Bye.

She hangs up. BILL hangs on until she does, then he bursts into wild donkey-brays of LAUGHTER.

BILL

Oh boy . . . diarrhea . . . I gotta remember that the next time my agent calls . . . oh Katie, that was so cool —

KATIE (almost screaming)
This is not funny!

BILL stops laughing.

INT. THE TV ROOM

JEFF and DENNIS have been tussling. They stop.

All three kids look toward the kitchen.

INT. THE PHONE NOOK, WITH BILL AND
KATIE

KATIE

*I tell you it was someone in my family and she
sounded* — oh, you don't understand. I *knew*
that voice.

BILL

But if Polly's okay and your mom's okay . . .

KATIE (positive)

It's Dawn.

BILL

Come on, hon, a minute ago you were sure
it was Polly.

KATIE

It *had* to be Dawn. I was on the phone with
Lois and Mom's okay so Dawn's the only
other one it *could* have been. She's the youngest . . . I could have mistaken her for Polly
. . . and she's out there in that farmhouse
alone with the baby!

BILL (startled)

What do you mean, alone?

KATIE

Jerry's in Burlington! It's Dawn! *Something's
happened to Dawn!*

CONNIE comes into the kitchen, worried.

CONNIE

Mom? Is Aunt Dawn okay?

BILL

So far as we know, she's fine. Take it easy, doll. Bad to buy trouble before you know it's on sale.

KATIE punches numbers and listens. SOUND: The DAH-DAH-DAH of a busy signal. KATIE hangs up. BILL looks a question at her with raised eyebrows.

KATIE

Busy.

BILL

Katie, are you sure —

KATIE

She's the only one left — it had to be her. Bill, I'm scared. Will you drive me out there?

BILL takes the phone from her.

BILL

What's her number?

KATIE

555-6169.

BILL dials. Gets a busy. Hangs up and punches 0.

> OPERATOR (filter)

Operator.

> BILL

I'm trying to reach my sister-in-law, operator. The line is busy. I suspect there may be a problem. Can you break into the call, please?

INT.   THE DOOR TO THE TV ROOM

All three kids are standing there, silent and worried.

INT.   THE PHONE NOOK, WITH BILL AND KATIE

> OPERATOR (filter)

What is your name, sir?

> BILL

William Weiderman. My number is —

> OPERATOR (filter)

Not the William Weiderman that wrote *Spider Doom?!*

> BILL

Yes, that was mine. If —

> OPERATOR (filter)

Oh my God, I just *loved* that book! I love *all* your books! I —

> BILL

I'm delighted you do. But right now my wife

624

is very worried about her sister. If it's possible for you to —

> OPERATOR (filter)
> Yes, I can do that. Please give me your number, Mr. Weiderman, for the records. (SHE GIGGLES.) I *promise* not to give it out.

> BILL
> It's 555-4408.

> OPERATOR (filter)
> And the call number?

> BILL (looks at KATIE)
> Uh . . .

> KATIE
> 555-6169.

> BILL
> 555-6169.

> OPERATOR (filter)
> Just a moment, Mr. Weiderman . . . *Night of the Beast* was also great, by the way. Hold on.

SOUND: TELEPHONIC CLICKS AND CLACKS.

> KATIE
> Is she —

> BILL
> Yes. Just . . .

There's one final CLICK.

>   OPERATOR (filter)
> I'm sorry, Mr. Weiderman, but that line is
> not busy. It's off the hook. I wonder if I
> sent you my copy of *Spider Doom* —

BILL hangs up the phone.

>   KATIE
> Why did you hang up?

>   BILL
> She can't break in. Phone's not busy. It's off
> the hook.

They stare at each other bleakly.

EXT.   A LOW-SLUNG SPORTS CAR PASSES THE
CAMERA NIGHT

INT.   THE CAR, WITH KATIE AND BILL

KATIE's scared. BILL, at the wheel, doesn't look
exactly calm.

>   KATIE
> Hey, Bill — tell me she's all right.

>   BILL
> She's all right.

>   KATIE
> Now tell me what you really think.

BILL

Jeff snuck up behind me tonight and put the old booga-booga on me. He was disappointed as hell when I didn't jump. I told him I was case-hardened. (Pause) I lied.

KATIE

Why did Jerry have to move out there when he's gone half the time? Just her and that little tiny baby? *Why?*

BILL

Shh, Kate. We're almost there.

KATIE

Go faster.

EXT.   THE CAR

He does. That car is smokin.

INT.   THE WEIDERMAN TV ROOM

The tube's still on and the kids are still there, but the horsing around has stopped.

CONNIE

DENNIS, do you think Aunt Dawn's okay?

DENNIS (thinks she's dead, decapitated by a maniac)

Yeah. Sure she is.

INT.   THE PHONE, POV FROM THE TV ROOM

627

Just sitting there on the wall in the phone nook, lights dark, looking like a snake ready to strike.

FADE OUT

ACT II

EXT.   AN ISOLATED FARMHOUSE

A long driveway leads up to it. There's one light on in the living room. Car lights sweep up the driveway. The WEIDERMAN car pulls up close to the garage and stops.

INT.   THE CAR, WITH BILL AND KATIE

KATIE

I'm scared.

BILL bends down, reaches under his seat, and brings out a pistol.

BILL (solemnly)

Booga-booga.

KATIE (total surprise)

How long have you had that?

BILL

Since last year. I didn't want to scare you or the kids. I've got a licence to carry. Come on.

EXT.   BILL AND KATIE

They get out. KATIE stands by the front of the car while BILL goes to the garage and peers in.

> BILL
>
> Her car's here.

THE CAMERA TRACKS WITH THEM to the front door. Now we can hear the TV, PLAYING LOUD. BILL pushes the doorbell. We hear it inside. They wait. KATIE pushes it. Still no answer. She pushes it again and doesn't take her finger off. BILL looks down at:

EXT. THE LOCK, BILL'S POV

Big scratches on it.

EXT. BILL AND KATIE

> BILL (low)
>
> The lock's been tampered with.

KATIE looks, and whimpers. BILL tries the door. It opens. The TV is louder.

> BILL
>
> Stay behind me. Be ready to run if something happens. God, I wish I'd left you home, Kate.

He starts in. KATIE comes after him, terrified, near tears.

INT. DAWN AND JERRY'S LIVING ROOM

From this angle we see only a small section of the room. The TV is much louder. BILL enters the room, gun up. He looks to the right . . . and suddenly all the tension goes out of him. He lowers the gun.

                    KATIE (draws up beside him)
     Bill . . . what . . .

He points.

INT. THE LIVING ROOM, WIDE, BILL AND KATIE'S POV

The place looks like a cyclone hit it . . . but it wasn't robbery and murder that caused this mess; only a healthy eighteen-month-old baby. After a strenuous day of trashing the living room, Baby got tired and Mommy got tired and they fell asleep on the couch together. The baby is in DAWN's lap. There is a pair of Walkman earphones on her head. There are toys — tough plastic Sesame Street and PlaySkool stuff, for the most part — scattered hell to breakfast. The baby has also pulled most of the books out of the bookcase. Had a good munch on one of them, too, by the look. BILL goes over and picks it up. It is *Ghost Kiss*.

                    BILL
     I've had people say they just eat my books up, but this is ridiculous.

He's amused. KATIE isn't. She walks over to her sister, ready to be mad . . . but she sees how really exhausted DAWN looks and softens.

INT.   DAWN AND THE BABY, KATIE'S POV

Fast asleep and breathing easily, like a Raphael painting of Madonna and Child. THE CAMERA PANS DOWN TO: the Walkman. We can hear the faint strains of Huey Lewis and the News. THE CAMERA PANS A BIT FURTHER TO a Princess telephone on the table by the chair. It's off the cradle. Not much; just enough to break the connection and scare people to death.

INT.   KATIE

She sighs, bends down, and replaces the phone. Then she pushes the STOP button on the Walkman.

INT.   DAWN, BILL, AND KATIE

DAWN wakes up when the music stops. Looks at BILL and KATIE, puzzled.

                    DAWN (fuzzed out)
Well . . . hi.

She realizes she's got the Walkman phones on and removes them.

                    BILL
   Hi, Dawn.

                    DAWN (still half asleep)
Shoulda called, guys. Place is a mess.

She smiles. She's radiant when she smiles.

KATIE

We *tried.* The operator told Bill the phone was off the hook. I thought something was wrong. How can you sleep with that music blasting?

DAWN

It's restful.
(Sees the gnawed book BILL's holding)
Oh my God, Bill, I'm sorry! Justin's teething and —

BILL

There are critics who'd say he picked just the right thing to teethe on. I don't want to scare you, beautiful, but somebody's been at your front door lock with a screwdriver or something. Whoever it was forced it.

DAWN

Gosh, no! That was Jerry, last week. I locked us out by mistake and he didn't have his key and the spare wasn't over the door like it's supposed to be. He was mad because he had to take a whiz real bad and so he took the screwdriver to it. It didn't work, either — that's one tough lock. (Pause) By the time I found my key he'd already gone in the bushes.

BILL

If it wasn't forced, how come I could just open the door and walk in?

DAWN (guiltily)
Well . . . sometimes I forget to lock it.

KATIE
You didn't call me tonight, Dawn?

DAWN
Gee, no! I didn't call *anyone!* I was too busy
chasing Justin around! He kept wanting to
eat the fabric softener! Then he got sleepy
and I sat down here and thought I'd listen
to some tunes while I waited for your movie
to come on, Bill, and I fell asleep —

At the mention of the movie BILL starts visibly
and looks at the book. Then he glances at his
watch.

BILL
I promised to tape it for Jeff. Come on, Katie,
we've got time to get back.

KATIE
Just a second.

She picks up the phone and dials.

DAWN
Gee, Bill, do you think Jeffie's old enough
to watch something like that?

BILL
It's network. They take out the blood-
bags.

                    DAWN (confused but amiable)
Oh. That's good.

INT.   KATIE, CU

                    DENNIS (filter)
Hello?

                    KATIE
Just thought you'd like to know your Aunt
Dawn's fine.

                    DENNIS (filter)
Oh! Cool. Thanks, Mom.

INT.   THE PHONE NOOK, WITH DENNIS AND
THE OTHERS

He looks *very* relieved.

                    DENNIS
Aunt Dawn's okay.

INT.   THE CAR, WITH BILL AND KATIE

They drive in silence for awhile.

                    KATIE
You think I'm a hysterical idiot, don't
you?

                    BILL (genuinely surprised)
No! I was scared, too.

                    KATIE
You sure you're not mad?

                    BILL
I'm too relieved. (Laughs) She's sort of a
scatterbrain, old Dawn, but I love her.

        KATIE (leans over and kisses him)
I love *you.* You're a sweet man.

                    BILL
I'm the *boogeyman!*

                    KATIE
I am not fooled, sweetheart.

EXT.   THE CAR

PASSES THE CAMERA AND WE DISSOLVE TO:

INT.   JEFF, IN BED

His room is dark. The covers are pulled up to
his chin.

                    JEFF
You *promise* to tape the rest?

CAMERA WIDENS OUT so we can see BILL, sitting
on the bed.

                    BILL
I promise.

JEFF

I especially liked the part where the dead guy ripped off the punk rocker's head.

BILL

Well . . . they *used* to take out all the blood-bags.

JEFF

What, Dad?

BILL

Nothing. I love you, Jeffie.

JEFF

I love you, too. So does Rambo.

JEFF holds up a stuffed dragon of decidedly un-militant aspect. BILL kisses the dragon, then JEFF.

BILL

'Night.

JEFF

'Night. (As BILL reaches his door) Glad Aunt Dawn was okay.

BILL

Me too.

He goes out.

INT. TV, CU

A guy who looks like he died in a car crash about two weeks prior to filming (and has since been subjected to a lot of hot weather) is staggering out of a crypt. THE CAMERA WIDENS to show BILL, releasing the VCR PAUSE button.

                    KATIE (voice)
Booga-booga.

BILL looks around companionably. THE CAMERA WIDENS OUT MORE to show KATIE, wearing a sexy nightgown.

                    BILL
Same to you. I missed the first forty seconds or so after the break. I had to kiss Rambo.

                    KATIE
You sure you're not mad at me, Bill?

He goes to her and kisses her.

                    BILL
Not even a smidge.

                    KATIE
It's just that I could have sworn it was one of mine. You know what I mean? One of mine?

                    BILL
Yes.

KATIE

I can still hear those sobs. So lost . . . so heartbroken.

BILL

Kate, have you ever thought you recognized someone on the street, and called her, and when she finally turned around it was a total stranger?

KATIE

Yes, once. In Seattle. I was in a mall and I thought I saw my old roommate. I . . . oh. I see what you're saying.

BILL

Sure. There are sound-alikes as well as look-alikes.

KATIE

But . . . *you know your own.* At least I thought so until tonight.

She puts her cheek on his shoulder, looking troubled.

KATIE

I was so *positive* it was Polly . . .

BILL

Because you've been worried about her getting her feet under her at the new school . . . but judging from the stuff she told you tonight, I'd say she's doing just fine in that department. Wouldn't you?

KATIE

Yes . . . I guess I would.

BILL

Let it go, hon.

KATIE (looks at him closely)

I hate to see you looking so tired. Hurry up and have an idea, you.

BILL

Well, I'm trying.

KATIE

You coming to bed?

BILL

Soon as I finish taping this for Jeff.

KATIE (amused)

Bill, that machine was made by Japanese technicians who think of damned near everything. It'll run on its own.

BILL

Yeah, but it's been a long time since I've seen this one, and . . .

KATIE

Okay. Enjoy. I think I'll be awake for a little while. (Pause) I've got a few ideas of my own.

BILL (smiles)

Yeah?

KATIE

Yeah.

She starts out, showing a lot of leg, then turns
in the doorway as something else strikes her.

KATIE

If they show that part where the punk's head
gets —

BILL (guiltily)

I'll edit it.

KATIE

'Night. And thanks again. For everything.

She leaves. BILL sits in his chair.

INT.   TV, CU

A couple is necking in a car. Suddenly the passenger door is ripped open by the dead guy and
we DISSOLVE TO:

INT.   KATIE, IN BED

It's dark. She's asleep. She wakes up . . . sort
of.

KATIE (sleepy)

Hey, big guy —

She feels for him, but his side of the bed is empty,
the coverlet still pulled up. She sits up. Looks at:

INT. A CLOCK ON THE NIGHT-TABLE, KATIE'S POV

It says 2:03 A.M. Then it flashes to 2:04.

INT. KATIE

Fully awake now. And concerned. She gets up, puts on her robe, and leaves the bedroom.

INT. THE TV SCREEN, CU

Snow.

>   KATIE (voice, approaching)
> Bill? Honey? You okay? Bill? Bi—

INT. KATIE, IN BILL'S STUDY

She's frozen, wide-eyed with horror.

INT. BILL, IN HIS CHAIR

He's slumped to one side, eyes closed, hand inside his shirt. DAWN was sleeping. BILL is not.

EXT. A COFFIN, BEING LOWERED INTO A GRAVE

>   MINISTER (voice)
> And so we commit the earthly remains of William Weiderman to the ground, confident of his spirit and soul. "Be ye not cast down, brethren . . ."

EXT.   GRAVESIDE

All the WEIDERMANS are ranged here. KATIE and POLLY wear identical black dresses and veils. CONNIE wears a black skirt and white blouse. DENNIS and JEFF wear black suits. JEFF is crying. He has Rambo the Dragon under his arm for a little extra comfort.

CAMERA MOVES IN ON KATIE. Tears course slowly down her cheeks. She bends and gets a handful of earth. Tosses it into the grave.

> KATIE
> Love you, big guy.

EXT.   JEFF

Weeping.

EXT.   LOOKING DOWN INTO THE GRAVE

Scattered earth on top of the coffin.

DISSOLVE TO:

EXT.   THE GRAVE

A GROUNDSKEEPER pats the last sod into place.

> GROUNDSKEEPER
> My wife says she wishes you'd written a couple more before you had your heart attack, mister. (Pause) I like Westerns, m'self.

THE GROUNDSKEEPER walks away, whistling.

DISSOLVE TO:

EXT. A CHURCH DAY

TITLE CARD: FIVE YEARS LATER

THE WEDDING MARCH is playing. POLLY, older and radiant with joy, emerges into a pelting shower of rice. She's in a wedding gown, her new husband by her side.

Celebrants throwing rice line either side of the path. From behind the bride and groom come others. Among them are KATIE, DENNIS, CONNIE, and JEFF . . . all five years older. With KATIE is another man. This is HANK. In the interim, KATIE has also taken a husband.

POLLY turns and her mother is there.

                    POLLY
  Thank you, Mom.

                  KATIE (crying)
  Oh doll, you're so welcome.

They embrace. After a moment POLLY draws away and looks at HANK. There is a brief moment of tension, and then POLLY embraces HANK, too.

                    POLLY
  Thank you too, Hank. I'm sorry I was such

a creep for so long . . .

> HANK (easily)
> You were never a creep, Pol. A girl only has one father.

> CONNIE
> Throw it! Throw it!

After a moment, POLLY throws her bouquet.

EXT. THE BOUQUET, CU, SLOW MOTION

Turning and turning through the air.

DISSOLVES TO:

INT. THE STUDY, WITH KATIE NIGHT

The word-processor has been replaced by a wide lamp looming over a stack of blueprints. The book jackets have been replaced by photos of buildings. Ones that have first been built in HANK's mind, presumably.

KATIE is looking at the desk, thoughtful and a little sad.

> HANK (voice)
> Coming to bed, Kate?

She turns and THE CAMERA WIDENS OUT to give us HANK. He's wearing a robe over pajamas. She comes to him and gives him a little hug, smiling.

Maybe we notice a few streaks of gray in her hair; her pretty pony has done its fair share of running since BILL died.

                    KATIE
In a little while. A woman doesn't see her first one get married every day, you know.

                    HANK
I know.

THE CAMERA FOLLOWS as they walk from the work area of the study to the more informal area. This is much the same as it was in the old days, with a coffee table, stereo, TV, couch, and BILL's old easy-chair. She looks at this.

                    HANK
You still miss him, don't you?

                    KATIE
Some days more than others. You didn't know, and Polly didn't remember.

                    HANK (gently)
Remember what, doll?

                    KATIE
Polly got married on the five-year anniversary of Bill's death.

                    HANK (hugs her)
Come on to bed, why don't you?

                    KATIE
In a little while.

                    HANK
Okay. Maybe I'll still be awake.

                    KATIE
Got a few ideas, do you?

                    HANK
I might.

                    KATIE
That's nice.

He kisses her, then leaves, closing the door behind him. KATIE sits in BILL's old chair. Close
by, on the coffee table, is a remote control for
the TV and an extension phone. KATIE looks at
the blank TV, and THE CAMERA MOVES IN on
her face. One tear rims one eye, sparkling like
a sapphire.

                    KATIE
I *do* still miss you, big guy. Lots and lots.
Every day. And you know what? It hurts.

The tear falls. She picks up the TV remote and
pushes the ON button.

INT. TV, KATIE'S POV

An ad for Ginsu Knives comes to an end and is
replaced by a STAR LOGO.

ANNOUNCER (voice)
Now back to Channel 63's Thursday night
Star Time Movie . . . *Ghost Kiss.*

The logo DISSOLVES INTO a guy who looks like
he died in a car crash about two weeks ago and
has since been subjected to a lot of hot weather.
He comes staggering out of the same old crypt.

INT. KATIE

Terribly startled — almost horrified. She hits the
OFF button on the remote control. The TV blinks
off.

KATIE's face begins to work. She struggles
against the impending emotional storm, but the
coincidence of the movie is just one thing too
many on what must have already been one of
the most emotionally trying days of her life. The
dam breaks and she begins to sob . . . terrible
heartbroken sobs. She reaches out for the little
table by the chair, meaning to put the remote
control on it, and knocks the phone onto the
floor.

SOUND: The HUM OF AN OPEN LINE.

Her tear-stained face grows suddenly still as she
looks at the telephone. Something begins to fill
it . . . an idea? an intuition? Hard to tell. And
maybe it doesn't matter.

INT. THE TELEPHONE, KATIE'S POV

THE CAMERA MOVES IN TO ECU . . . MOVES IN until the dots in the off-the-hook receiver look like chasms.

SOUND OF OPEN-LINE BUZZ UP TO LOUD.

WE GO INTO THE BLACK . . . and hear

> BILL (voice)
> Who are you calling? Who do you *want* to call? Who *would* you call, if it wasn't too late?

INT. KATIE

There is now a strange hypnotized look on her face. She reaches down, scoops the telephone up, and punches in numbers, seemingly at random.

SOUND: RINGING PHONE.

KATIE continues to look hypnotized. The look holds until the phone is answered . . . *and she hears herself* on the other end of the line.

> KATIE (voice; filter)
> Hello, Weiderman residence.

KATIE — our present-day KATIE with the streaks of gray in her hair — goes on sobbing, yet an expression of desperate hope is trying to be born on her face. On some level she understands that the depth of her grief has allowed a kind of telephonic time-travel. She's trying to talk, to force the words out.

> KATIE (sobbing)
> Take . . . please take . . . t-t-

INT. KATIE, IN THE PHONE NOOK, REPRISE

It's five years ago. BILL is standing beside her, looking concerned. JEFF is wandering off to look for a blank tape in the other room.

> KATIE
> Polly? What's wrong?

INT. KATIE, IN THE STUDY

> KATIE (sobbing)
> *Please — quick —*

SOUND: CLICK OF A BROKEN CONNECTION.

> KATIE (screaming)
> *Take him to the hospital! If you want him to live, take him to the hospital! He's going to have a heart attack! He —*

SOUND: HUM OF AN OPEN LINE.

Slowly, very slowly, KATIE hangs up the telephone. Then, after a moment, she picks it up again. She speaks aloud with no self-consciousness whatever. Probably doesn't even know she's doing it.

> KATIE

I dialed the old number. I dialed —

SLAM CUT TO:

INT.   BILL, IN THE PHONE NOOK WITH KATIE BESIDE HIM

He's just taken the phone from KATIE and is speaking to the operator.

> OPERATOR (filter, GIGGLES)

I *promise* not to give it out.

> BILL

It's 555-

SLAM CUT TO:

INT.   KATIE, IN BILL'S OLD CHAIR, CU

> KATIE (finishes)

-4408.

INT.   THE PHONE, CU

KATIE's trembling finger carefully picks out the number, and we hear the corresponding tones: 555-4408.

INT.   KATIE, IN BILL'S OLD CHAIR, CU

She closes her eyes as the PHONE BEGINS TO RING. Her face is filled with an agonizing mixture of hope and fear. If only she can have one more chance to pass the vital message on, it says . . . just one more chance.

> KATIE (low)
> Please . . . please . . .

> RECORDED VOICE (filter)
> You have reached a non-working number. Please hang up and dial again. If you need assistance —

KATIE hangs up again. Tears stream down her cheeks. THE CAMERA PANS AWAY AND DOWN to the telephone.

INT. THE PHONE NOOK, WITH KATIE AND BILL, REPRISE

> BILL
> So it was a prank. Or someone who was crying so hard she dialed a wrong number . . . "through a shimmering film of tears," as we veteran hacks like to say.

> KATIE
> It was not a prank and it was not a wrong number! It was someone in *my family!*

INT. KATIE (PRESENT DAY) IN BILL'S STUDY

> KATIE
> Yes. Someone in my family. Someone very close. (Pause) *Me.*

She suddenly throws the phone across the room. Then she begins to SOB AGAIN and puts her hands over her face. THE CAMERA HOLDS on her for a moment, then DOLLIES ACROSS TO

INT.   THE PHONE

It lies on the carpet, looking both bland and some-how ominous. CAMERA MOVES IN TO ECU — the holes in the receiver once more look like huge dark chasms. We HOLD, then

FADE TO BLACK.

The Ten O'Clock People

1

Pearson tried to scream but shock robbed his voice and he was able to produce only a low, choked whuffling — the sound of a man moaning in his sleep. He drew in breath to try it again, but before he could get started, a hand seized his left arm just above the elbow in a strong pincers grip and squeezed.

"It'd be a mistake," the voice that went with the hand said. It was pitched only half a step above a whisper, and it spoke directly into Pearson's left ear. "A bad one. Believe me, it would."

Pearson looked around. The thing which had occasioned his desire — no, his *need* — to scream had disappeared inside the bank now, amazingly unchallenged, and Pearson found he *could* look around. He had been grabbed by a good-looking young black man in a cream-colored suit. Pearson didn't know him, but he recognized him; he sight-recognized most of the odd little sub-tribe he'd come to think of as the Ten O'Clock People . . . as, he supposed, they recognized him.

The good-looking young black man was watching him warily.

"Did you see it?" Pearson asked. The words

came out in a high-pitched, nagging whine that was totally unlike his usual confident speaking voice.

The good-looking young black man had let go of Pearson's arm when he became reasonably convinced that Pearson wasn't going to shock the plaza in front of The First Mercantile Bank of Boston with a volley of wild screams; Pearson immediately reached out and gripped the young black man's wrist. It was as if he were not yet capable of living without the comfort of the other man's touch. The good-looking young black man made no effort to pull away, only glanced down at Pearson's hand for a moment before looking back up into Pearson's face.

"I mean, did you *see* it? Horrible! Even if it was make-up . . . or some kind of mask someone put on for a joke . . ."

But it hadn't been make-up and it hadn't been a mask. The thing in the dark-gray Andre Cyr suit and five-hundred-dollar shoes had passed very close to Pearson, almost close enough to touch (*God forbid,* his mind interjected with a helpless cringe of revulsion), and he knew it hadn't been make-up or a mask. Because the flesh on the huge protuberance Pearson supposed was its head had been *in motion,* different parts moving in different directions, like the bands of exotic gases surrounding some planetary giant.

"Friend," the good-looking young black man in the cream-colored suit began, "you need —"

"What was it?" Pearson broke in. "I never saw anything like that in my *life!* It was like something you'd see in a, I don't know, a sideshow . . . or . . . or . . ."

His voice was no longer coming from its usual place inside his head. It seemed to be drifting down from someplace above him, instead — as if he'd fallen into a snare or a crack in the earth and that high-pitched, nagging voice belonged to somebody else, somebody who was speaking down to him.

"Listen, my friend —"

There was something else, too. When Pearson had stepped out through the revolving doors just a few minutes ago with an unlit Marlboro between his fingers, the day had been overcast — threatening rain, in fact. Now everything was not just bright but *overbright*. The red skirt on the pretty blonde standing beside the building fifty feet or so farther down (she was smoking a cigarette and reading a paperback) screamed into the day like a firebell; the yellow of a passing delivery boy's shirt stung like the barb of a wasp. People's faces stood out like the faces in his daughter Jenny's beloved Pop-Up books.

And his lips . . . he couldn't feel his lips. They had gone numb, the way they sometimes did after a big shot of novocaine.

Pearson turned to the good-looking young man in the cream-colored suit and said, "This is ridiculous, but I think I'm going to faint."

"No, you're not," the young man said, and he spoke with such assurance that Pearson believed him, at least temporarily. The hand gripped his arm above the elbow again, but much more gently this time. "Come on over here — you need to sit down."

There were circular marble islands about three feet high scattered around the broad plaza in front of the bank, each containing its own variety of late summer/early fall flowers. There were Ten O'Clock People sitting on the rims of most of these upscale flower tubs, some reading, some chatting, some looking out at the passing rivers of foot-traffic on the sidewalks of Commercial Street, but all of them also doing the thing that made them Ten O'Clock People, the thing Pearson had come downstairs and outside to do himself. The marble island closest to Pearson and his new acquaintance contained asters, their purple miraculously brilliant to Pearson in his heightened state of awareness. Its circular rim was vacant, probably because it was going on for ten past the hour now, and people had begun to drift back inside.

"Sit down," the young black man in the cream-colored suit invited, and although Pearson tried his best, what he ended up doing felt more like falling than sitting. At one moment he was standing beside the reddish-brown marble island, and then somebody pulled the pins in his knees and he landed on his ass. Hard.

"Bend over now," the young man said, sitting down beside him. His face had remained pleasant throughout the entire encounter, but there was nothing pleasant about his eyes; they combed rapidly back and forth across the plaza.

"Why?"

"To get the blood back into your head," the young black man said. "But don't make it *look* like that. Make it look like you're just smelling the flowers."

"Look like to *who?*"

"Just do it, okay?" The smallest tinge of impatience had crept into the young man's voice.

Pearson leaned his head over and took a deep breath. The flowers didn't smell as good as they looked, he discovered — they had a weedy, faintly dog-pissy smell. Still, he thought his head might be clearing just a tiny bit.

"Start saying the states," the black man ordered. He crossed his legs, shook out the fabric of his pants to preserve the crease, and brought a package of Winstons out of an inner pocket. Pearson realized his own cigarette was gone; he must have dropped it in that first shocked moment, when he had seen the monstrous thing in the expensive suit crossing the west side of the plaza.

"The states," he said blankly.

The young black man nodded, produced a lighter that was probably quite a bit less expensive than it looked at first glance, and lit his cigarette. "Start with this one and work your way west," he invited.

"Massachusetts . . . New York, I suppose . . . or Vermont if you start from upstate . . . New Jersey . . ." Now he straightened up a little and began to speak with greater confidence. "Pennsylvania, West Virginia, Ohio, Illinois —"

The black man raised his eyebrows. "West Virginia, huh? You sure?"

Pearson smiled a little. "Pretty sure, yeah. I might have got Ohio and Illinois bass-ackwards, though."

The black man shrugged to show it didn't matter, and smiled. "You don't feel like you're going to faint anymore, though — I can see you don't — and that's the important part. Want a butt?"

657

"Thank you," Pearson said gratefully. He did not just *want* a butt; he felt that he needed one. "I had one, but I lost it. What's your name?"

The black man poked a fresh Winston between Pearson's lips and snapped a light to it. "Dudley Rhinemann. You can call me Duke."

Pearson dragged deeply on the cigarette and looked toward the revolving doors which gave ingress upon all the gloomy depths and cloudy heights of The First Mercantile. "That wasn't just a hallucination, was it?" he asked. "What I saw . . . you saw it, too, right?"

Rhinemann nodded.

"You didn't want him to know I saw him," Pearson said. He spoke slowly, trying to put it together on his own. His voice was back in its usual spot again, and that alone was a big relief.

Rhinemann nodded again.

"But how could I *not* see him? And how could he not know it?"

"Did you see anyone else getting ready to holler themselves into a stroke like you were?" Rhinemann asked. "See anybody else even *looking* the way you were? Me, for instance?"

Pearson shook his head slowly. He now felt more than just frightened; he felt totally lost.

"I got between you and him the best I could, and I don't think he saw you, but for a second or two there it was close. You looked like a man who just saw a mouse crawl out of his meatloaf. You're in Collateral Loans, aren't you?"

"Oh yes — Brandon Pearson. Sorry."

"I'm in Computer Services, myself. And it's okay. Seeing your first batman can do that to you."

Duke Rhinemann stuck out his hand and Pearson shook it, but most of his mind was one turn back. *Seeing your first batman can do that to you,* the young man had said, and once Pearson had jettisoned his initial image of the Caped Crusader swinging his way between the art-deco spires of Gotham City, he discovered that wasn't a bad term at all. He discovered something else, as well, or perhaps rediscovered it: it was good to have a name for something that had frightened you. It didn't make the fright go away, but it went a long way toward rendering the fright manageable.

Now he deliberately replayed what he had seen, thinking *Batman, it was my first batman,* as he did.

He had come out through the revolving doors thinking of only one thing, the same thing he was always thinking about when he came down at ten — how good that first rush of nicotine was going to feel when it hit his brain. It was what made him a part of the tribe; it was his version of phylacteries or tattooed cheeks.

He had first registered the fact that the day had gotten even darker since he'd come in at eight-forty-five, and had thought: *We'll be puffing our cancer-sticks in the pouring rain this afternoon, the whole damned bunch of us.* Not that a little rain would stop them, of course; the Ten O'Clock People were nothing if not persistent.

He remembered sweeping his eyes across the plaza, doing a quick attendance check — so quick it was really almost unconscious. He had seen the girl in the red skirt (and wondered again, as he always did, if anyone who looked that good would

659

be any good in the sack), the young be-bop janitor from the third floor who wore his cap turned around while he was mopping the floors in the john and the snack-bar, the elderly man with the fine white hair and the purple blotches on his cheeks, the young woman with the thick glasses, narrow face, and long straight black hair. He had seen a number of others he vaguely recognized, as well. One of them, of course, had been the good-looking young black man in the cream-colored suit.

If Timmy Flanders had been around, Pearson probably would have joined him, but he wasn't, and so Pearson had moved toward the center of the plaza instead, meaning to sit on one of the marble islands (the very one he was sitting on now, in fact). Once there he would have been in an excellent position to calculate the length and curves of Little Miss Red Skirt's legs — a cheap thrill, granted, but one made do with the materials at hand. He was a well-married man with a wife he loved and a daughter he adored, he'd never come even close to cheating, but as he approached forty, he had discovered certain imperatives surfacing in his blood like sea-monsters. And he didn't know how any man could help staring at a red skirt like that, wondering just a little if the woman was wearing matching underwear beneath.

He had barely gotten moving when the new-comer had turned the corner of the building and begun mounting the plaza steps. Pearson had caught movement in the corner of his eye, and under ordinary circumstances he would have dis-missed it — it was the red skirt he had been concentrating on just then, short, tight, and as bright as the side of a fire engine. But he *had* looked, because, even seen from the corner of his eye and with other things on his mind, he had registered something *wrong* with the face and the head that went with the approaching figure. So he had turned and looked, cancelling sleep for God knew how many nights to come.

The shoes were all right; the dark-gray Andre Cyr suit, looking as solid and as dependable as the door of the bank vault in the basement, was even better; the red tie was predictable but not offensive. All of this was fine, typical top-echelon banker's attire for a Monday morning (and who but a top-echelon banker could come in at ten o'clock in the first place?). It wasn't until you got to the head that you realized that you had either gone crazy or were looking at something for which there was no entry in the *World Book Encyclopedia*.

But why didn't they run? Pearson wondered now, as a raindrop fell on the back of his hand and another fell on the clean white paper of his half-smoked cigarette. *They should have run screaming, the way the people run from the giant bugs in those fifties monster movies.* Then he thought, *But then . . . I didn't run, either.*

True enough, but it wasn't the same. He hadn't run because he'd been frozen in place. He *had* tried to scream, however; it was just that his new friend had stopped him before he could throw his vocal cords back into gear.

Batman. Your first batman.

Above the broad shoulders of this year's most Eminently Acceptable Business Suit and the knot

661

in the red Sulka power-tie had loomed a huge gray-ish-brown head, not round but as misshapen as a baseball that has taken a whole summer's worth of bashing. Black lines — veins, perhaps — pulsed just below the surface of the skull in meaningless roadmap squiggles, and the area that should have been its face but wasn't (not in any human sense, anyway) had been covered with lumps that bulged and quivered like tumors possessed of their own terrible semi-sentient life. Its features were rudi-mentary and pushed to-gether — flat black eyes, perfectly round, that stared avidly from the middle of its face like the eyes of a shark or some bloated insect; malformed ears with no lobes or pinnae. It hadn't had a nose, at least none that Pearson could recognize, although two tusklike protuber-ances had jutted from the spiny tangle of hair that grew just below the eyes. Most of the thing's face had been mouth — a huge black crescent ringed with triangular teeth. To a creature with a mouth like that, Pearson had thought later, bolting one's food would be a sacrament.

His very first thought as he stared at this horrible apparition — an apparition carrying a slim Bally briefcase in one beautifully manicured hand — was *It's the Elephant Man*. But, he now realized, the creature had been nothing at all like the misshapen but essentially human creature in that old movie. Duke Rhinemann was closer to the mark; those black eyes and that drawn-up mouth were features he associated with furry, squeaking things that spent their nights eating flies and their days hang-ing head-down in dark places.

But none of that was what had caused him to

try that first scream; that need had come when the creature in the Andre Cyr suit walked past him, its bright, buglike eyes already fixed on the revolving doors. It was at its closest in that second or two, and it was then that Pearson had seen its tumorous face somehow moving below the mottles of coarse hair which grew from it. He didn't know how such a thing could possibly be, but it *was* — he was watching it happen, observing the man's flesh crawling around the lumpy curves of its skull and rippling along the thick canehead shape of its jaw in alternating bands. Between these he caught glimpses of some gruesome raw pink substance that he didn't even want to think about . . . yet now that he remembered, it seemed that he could not stop thinking about it.

More raindrops splattered on his hands and face. Next to him on the curved lip of marble, Rhinemann took a final drag on his cigarette, pitched it away, and stood up. "Come on," he said. "Starting to rain."

Pearson looked at him with wide eyes, then looked toward the bank. The blonde in the red skirt was just going in, her book now tucked under her arm. She was being closely followed (and closely observed) by the old party with the tycoon's shock of fine white hair.

Pearson flicked his eyes back to Rhinemann and said, "Go in there? Are you serious? That *thing* went in there!"

"I know."

"You want to hear something totally nuts?" Pearson asked, tossing his own cigarette away. He didn't know where he was going now, home, he supposed, but he knew one place he was most assuredly *not* going, and that was back inside The First Mercantile Bank of Boston.

"Sure," Rhinemann agreed. "Why not?"

"That thing looked quite a lot like our revered Chief Executive Officer, Douglas Keefer . . . until you got to the head, that is. Same taste in suits and briefcases."

"What a surprise," Duke Rhinemann said.

Pearson measured him with an uneasy eye. "What do you mean?"

"I think you already know, but you've had a tough morning and so I'll spell it out. That *was* Keefer."

Pearson smiled uncertainly. Rhinemann didn't smile back. He got to his feet, gripped Pearson's arms, and pulled the older man forward until their faces were only inches apart.

"I saved your life just now. Do you believe that, Mr. Pearson?"

Pearson thought about it and discovered that he did. That alien, batlike face with its black eyes and clustered bunches of teeth hung in his mind like a dark flare. "Yes. I guess I do."

"Okay. Then do me the credit of listening carefully as I tell you three things — will you do that?"

"I . . . yes, sure."

"First thing: that *was* Douglas Keefer, CEO of The First Mercantile Bank of Boston, close friend of the Mayor, and, incidentally, honorary chairman of the current Boston Children's Hospital fund-drive. Second thing: there are at least three more bats working in the bank, one of them on your floor. Third thing: you *are* going back in there. If you want to go on living, that is."

Pearson gaped at him, momentarily incapable of reply — if he'd tried, he would have produced only more of those fuzzy whuffling sounds.

Rhinemann took him by the elbow and pulled him toward the revolving doors. "Come on, buddy," he said, and his voice was oddly gentle. "The rain's really starting to come down. If we stay out here much longer we'll attract attention, and people in our position can't afford to do that."

Pearson went along with Rhinemann at first, then thought of the way the black nests of lines on the thing's head had pulsed and squiggled. The image brought him to a cold stop just outside the revolving doors. The smooth surface of the plaza was now wet enough to reveal another Brandon Pearson below him, a shimmery reflection that hung from his own heels like a bat of a different color. "I . . . I don't think I can," he said in a halting, humble voice.

"You can," Rhinemann said. He glanced momentarily down at Pearson's left hand. "Married, I see — with kids?"

"One. A daughter." Pearson was looking into the bank's lobby. The glass panels in the revolving door were polarized, making the big room beyond them look very dark. *Like a cave*, he thought. *A batcave filled with half-blind disease-carriers.*

"You want your wife and kid to read in the paper tomorrow that the cops dragged Da-Da out of Boston Harbor with his throat cut?"

Pearson looked at Rhinemann with wide eyes. Raindrops splattered against his cheeks, his forehead.

"They make it look like junkies did it," Rhinemann said, "and it works. It *always* works. Because they're smart, and because they've got friends in high places. Hell, high places is what they're all about."

"I don't understand you," Pearson said. "I don't understand *any* of this."

"I know you don't," Rhinemann returned. "This is a dangerous time for you, so just do what I tell you. What I'm telling you is to get back to your desk before you're missed, and roll through the rest of the day with a smile on your face. Hold onto that smile, my friend — don't let go of it no matter how greasy it gets." He hesitated, then added: "If you screw up, it's probably gonna get you killed."

The rainwater made bright tracks down the young man's smooth dark face, and Pearson suddenly saw what had been there all along, what he had missed only because of his own shock: this man was terrified, and he had risked a great deal to keep Pearson from stumbling into some awful trap.

"I really can't stay out here any longer," Rhinemann said. "It's dangerous."

"Okay," Pearson said, a little astounded to hear his own voice coming out in normal, even measures. "Then let's go back to work."

Rhinemann looked relieved. "Good man. And whatever you see the rest of the day, *don't show surprise.* You understand?"

"Yes," Pearson said. He didn't understand anything.

"Can you clear your desk early and leave around three?"

Pearson considered it, then nodded. "Yeah. I guess I could do that."

"Good. Meet me around the corner on Milk Street."

"All right."

"You're doin great, man," Rhinemann said. "You're going to be fine. See you at three." He entered the revolving door and gave it a push. Pearson stepped into the segment behind him, feeling as though he had somehow left his mind out there in the plaza . . . all of it, that was, except for the part that already wanted another cigarette.

The day crawled, but everything was all right until he came back from lunch (and two cigarettes) with Tim Flanders. They stepped out of the elevator on the third floor and the first thing Pearson saw was another batman . . . except this one was actually a batwoman wearing black patent-leather heels, black nylon hose, and a formidable silk tweed suit — Samuel Blue was Pearson's guess. The perfect power outfit . . . until you got to the head nodding over it like a mutated sunflower, that was.

"Hullo, gents." A sweet contralto voice spoke from somewhere behind the harelipped hole that was its mouth.

It's Suzanne Holding, Pearson thought. *It can't be, but it is.*

"Hello, Suzy darlin," he heard himself say, and

thought: *If she comes near me . . . tries to touch me . . . I'll scream. I won't be able to help it, no matter what the kid told me.*

"Are you all right, Brand? You look pale."

"A little touch of whatever's going around, I guess," he said, astounded all over again at the natural ease of his voice. "I think I'm getting on top of it, though."

"Good," Suzanne Holding's voice said from behind the bat's face and the strangely motile flesh. "No French kissing until you're all better, though — in fact, don't even breathe on me. I can't afford to be sick with the Japanese coming in on Wednesday."

No problem, sweetheart — no problem, you better believe it.

"I'll try to restrain myself."

"Thanks. Tim, will you come down to my office and look at a couple of spread-sheet summaries?"

Timmy Flanders slipped an arm around the waist of the sexily prim Samuel Blue suit, and before Pearson's wide eyes, he bent and planted a little kiss on the side of the thing's tumor-raddled, hairy face. *That's where Timmy sees her cheek,* Pearson thought, and he felt his sanity suddenly slip like greasy cable wound around the drum of a winch. *Her smooth, perfumed cheek — that's what he's seeing, all right, and what he thinks he's kissing. Oh my God. Oh my God.*

"There!" Timmy exclaimed, and gave the creature a small cavalier's bow. "One kiss and I am your servant, dear lady!"

He tipped Pearson a wink and began walking the monster in the direction of her office. As they

668

passed the drinking fountain, he dropped the arm he had hung about her waist. The short and meaningless little peacock/peahen courting dance — a ritual that had somehow developed over the last ten years or so in business relationships where the boss was female and the aide was male — had now been performed, and they drew away from Pearson as sexual equals, talking nothing but dry numbers.

Marvellous analysis, Brand, Pearson thought distractedly as he turned away from them. *You should have been a sociologist.* And almost had been — it had been his college minor, after all.

As he entered his office he became aware that his whole body was running with a slow slime of sweat. Pearson forgot sociology and began rooting for three o'clock again.

At two-forty-five he steeled himself and poked his head into Suzanne Holding's office. The alien asteroid of her head was tilted toward the blue-gray screen of her computer, but she looked around when he said "Knock-knock," the flesh on her strange face sliding restlessly, her black eyes regarding him with the cold avidity of a shark studying a swimmer's leg.

"I gave Buzz Carstairs the Corporate Fours," Pearson said. "I'm going to take the Individual Form Nines home with me, if that's okay. I've got my backup discs there."

"Is this your coy way of saying you're going AWOL, my dear?" Suzanne asked. The black veins bulged unspeakably on top of her bald skull; the lumps which surrounded her features quivered, and Pearson realized one of them was leaking a thick pinkish substance that looked like blood-stained shaving cream.

He made himself smile. "You caught me."

"Well," Suzanne said, "we'll just have to have the four o'clock orgy without you today, I guess."

"Thanks, Suze." He turned away.

"Brand?"

He turned back, his fear and revulsion threatening to turn into a bright white freeze of panic, suddenly very sure that those avid black eyes had seen through him and that the thing masquerading as Suzanne Holding was going to say, *Let's stop playing games, shall we? Come in and close the door. Let's see if you taste as good as you look.*

Rhinemann would wait awhile, then go on to wherever he was going by himself. *Probably,* Pearson thought, *he'll know what happened. Probably he's seen it before.*

"Yes?" he asked, trying to smile.

She looked at him appraisingly for a long moment without speaking, the grotesque slab of head looming above the sexy lady exec's body, and then she said, "You look a little better this afternoon." The mouth still gaped, the black eyes still stared with all the expression of a Raggedy Ann doll abandoned under a child's bed, but Pearson knew that anyone else would have seen only Suzanne Holding, smiling prettily at one of her junior executives and exhibiting just the right degree of Type A concern. Not exactly Mother Courage, but still caring and interested.

"Good," he said, and decided that was probably too limp. "Great!"

"Now if we could only get you to quit smoking."

"Well, I'm trying," he said, and laughed weakly. The greasy cable around that mental winch slipped again. *Let me go,* he thought. *Let me go, you horrible bitch, let me get out of here before I do something too nutso to be ignored.*

"You'd qualify for an automatic upgrade on your insurance, you know," the monster said. Now the surface of another of those tumors broke open with a rotten little *chup!* sound and more of that pink stuff began to ooze out.

"Yeah, I know," he said. "And I'll give it serious consideration, Suzanne. Really."

"You do that," she said, and swung back toward the glowing computer screen. For a moment he was stunned, unable to grasp his good fortune. The interview was over.

By the time Pearson left the building it was pouring, but the Ten O'Clock People — now they were the Three O'Clock People, of course, but there was no essential difference — were out just the same, huddled together like sheep, doing their thing. Little Miss Red Skirt and the janitor who liked to wear his cap turned around backward were sheltering beneath the same sodden section of the *Boston Globe.* They looked uncomfortable and damp around the edges, but Pearson envied the janitor just the same. Little Miss Red Skirt wore Giorgio; he had smelled it in the elevator on several occasions. And she made little silky rustling noises when she moved, of course.

What the hell are you thinking *about?* he asked himself sternly, and replied in the same mental

671

breath: *Keeping my sanity, thank you very much. Okay by you?*

Duke Rhinemann was standing under the awning of the flower shop just around the corner, his shoulders hunched, a cigarette in the corner of his own mouth. Pearson joined him, glanced at his watch, and decided he could wait a little longer. He poked his head forward a little bit just the same, to catch the tang of Rhinemann's cigarette. He did this without being aware of it.

"My boss is one of them," he told Duke. "Unless, of course, Douglas Keefer is the sort of monster who likes to cross-dress."

Rhinemann grinned ferociously and said nothing.

"You said there were three others. Who are the other two?"

"Donald Fine. You probably don't know him — he's in Securities. And Carl Grosbeck."

"Carl . . . the Chairman of the Board? Jesus!"

"I told you," Rhinemann said. "High places are what these guys're all about — *Hey, taxi!*"

He dashed out from beneath the awning, flagging the maroon-and-white cab he had spotted cruising miraculously empty through the rainy afternoon. It swerved toward them, spraying fans of standing water. Rhinemann dodged agilely, but Pearson's shoes and pantscuffs were soaked. In his current state, it didn't seem terribly important. He opened the door for Rhinemann, who slid in and scooted across the seat. Pearson followed and slammed the door.

"Gallagher's Pub," Rhinemann said. "It's directly across from —"

"I know where Gallagher's is," the driver said, "but we don't go anywhere until you dispose of the cancer-stick, my friend." He tapped the sign clipped to the taximeter. SMOKING IS NOT PERMITTED IN THIS LIVERY, it read.

The two men exchanged a glance. Rhinemann lifted his shoulders in the half-embarrassed, half-surly shrug that has been the principal tribal greeting of the Ten O'Clock People since 1990 or so. Then, without a murmur of protest, he pitched his quarter-smoked Winston out into the driving rain.

Pearson began to tell Rhinemann how shocked he had been when the elevator doors had opened and he'd gotten his first good look at the essential Suzanne Holding, but Rhinemann frowned, gave his head a minute shake, and swivelled his thumb toward their driver. "We'll talk later," he said.

Pearson subsided into silence, contenting himself with watching the rain-streaked highrises of midtown Boston slip by. He found himself almost exquisitely attuned to the little street-life scenes going on outside the taxicab's smeary window. He was especially interested in the little clusters of Ten O'Clock People he observed standing in front of every business building they passed. Where there was shelter, they took it; where there wasn't, they took that, too — simply turned up their collars, hooded their hands protectively over their cigarettes, and smoked anyway. It occurred to Pearson that easily ninety per cent of the posh midtown highrises they were passing were now no-smoking zones, just like the one he and

Rhinemann worked in. It occurred to him further (and this thought came with the force of a revelation) that the Ten O'Clock People were not really a new tribe at all but the raggedy-ass remnants of an old one, renegades running before a new broom that intended to sweep their bad old habit clean out the door of American life. Their unifying characteristic was their unwillingness or inability to quit killing themselves; they were junkies in a steadily shrinking twilight zone of acceptability. An exotic social group, he supposed, but not one that was apt to last very long. He guessed that by the year 2020, 2050 at the latest, the Ten O'Clock People would have gone the way of the dodo.

Oh shit, wait a minute, he thought. *We're just the last of the world's diehard optimists, that's all — most of us don't bother with our seatbelts, either, and we'd love to sit behind home plate at the ballpark if they'd just take down that silly fucking screen.*

"What's so funny, Mr. Pearson?" Rhinemann asked him, and Pearson became aware he was wearing a broad grin.

"Nothing," Pearson said. "Nothing important, at least."

"Okay; just don't freak out on me."

"Would you consider it a freak-out if I asked you to call me Brandon?"

"I guess not," Rhinemann said, and appeared to think it over. "As long as you call me Duke and we don't get down to BeeBee or Buster or anything embarrassing like that."

"I think you're safe on that score. Want to know something?"

"Sure."

"This has been the most amazing day of my life."

Duke Rhinemann nodded without returning Pearson's smile. "And it's not over yet," he said.

2

Pearson thought that Gallagher's had been an inspired choice on Duke's part — a clear Boston anomaly, more Gilley's than Cheers, it was the perfect place for two bank employees to discuss matters which would have left their nearest and dearest with serious questions about their sanity. The longest bar Pearson had ever seen outside of a movie curved around a large square of shiny dance-floor on which three couples were currently dry-humping dreamily as Marty Stuart and Travis Tritt harmonized on "This One's Gonna Hurt You."

In a smaller place the bar proper would have been packed, but the patrons were so well spaced along this amazing length of mahogany-paved racetrack that brass-rail privacy was actually achievable; there was no need for them to search out a booth in the dim nether reaches of the room. Pearson was glad. It would be too easy to imagine one of the batpeople, maybe even a batcouple, sitting (or roosting) in the next booth and listening intently to their conversation.

Isn't that what they call a bunker mentality, old buddy? he thought. *Certainly didn't take you long to get there, did it?*

675

No, he supposed not, but for the time being he didn't care. He was just grateful he would be able to see in all directions while they talked . . . or, he supposed, while Duke talked.

"Bar's okay?" Duke asked, and Pearson nodded.

It looked like one bar, Pearson reflected as he followed Duke beneath the sign which read SMOKING PERMITTED THIS SECTION ONLY, but it was really two . . . the way that, back in the fifties, every lunch-counter below the Mason-Dixon had really been two: one for the white folks and one for the black. And now as then, you could see the difference. A Sony almost the size of a cineplex movie screen overlooked the center of the no-smoking section; in the nicotine ghetto there was only an elderly Zenith bolted to the wall (a sign beside it read: FEEL FREE TO ASK FOR CREDIT, WE WILL FEEL FREE TO TELL YOU TO F!!K OFF). The surface of the bar itself was dirtier down here — Pearson thought at first that this must be just his imagination, but a second glance confirmed the dingy look of the wood and the faint overlapping rings that were the Ghosts of Schooners Past. And, of course, there was the sallow, yellowish odor of tobacco smoke. He swore it came puffing up from the bar-stool when he sat down, like popcorn farts out of an elderly movie-theater seat. The newscaster on their battered, smoke-bleared TV appeared to be dying of zinc poisoning; the same guy playing to the healthy folks farther down the bar looked ready to run the four-forty and then bench-press his weight in blondes.

Welcome to the back of the bus, Pearson thought, looking at his fellow Ten O'Clock People with a

676

species of exasperated amusement. *Oh well, mustn't complain; in another ten years smokers won't even be allowed on board.*

"Cigarette?" Duke asked, perhaps displaying certain rudimentary mind-reading skills.

Pearson glanced at his watch, then accepted the butt, along with another light from Duke's *faux-*classy lighter. He drew deep, relishing the way the smoke slid into his pipes, even relishing the slight swimming in his head. Of *course* the habit was dangerous, potentially lethal; how could anything that got you off like this not be? It was the way of the world, that was all.

"What about you?" he asked as Duke slipped his cigarettes back into his pocket.

"I can wait a little longer," Duke said, smiling. "I got a couple of puffs before we got in the cab. Also, I have to pay off the extra one I had at lunch."

"You ration yourself, huh?"

"Yeah. I usually only allow myself one at lunch, but today I had two. You scared the shit out of me, you know."

"I was pretty scared myself."

The bartender came over, and Pearson found himself fascinated at the way the man avoided the thin ribbon of smoke rising from his cigarette. *I doubt if he even knows he's doing it . . . but if I blew some in his face, I bet he'd come over the top and clean my clock for me.*

"Help you gentlemen?"

Duke ordered Sam Adamses without consulting Pearson. When the bartender left to get them, Duke turned back and said, "Stretch it out. This'd

677

be a bad time to get drunk. Bad time to even get tight."

Pearson nodded and dropped a five-dollar bill on the counter when the bartender came back with the beers. He took a deep swallow, then dragged on his cigarette. There were people who thought a cigarette never tasted better than it did after a meal, but Pearson disagreed; he believed in his heart that it wasn't an apple that had gotten Eve in trouble but a beer and a cigarette.

"So what'd you use?" Duke asked him. "The patch? Hypnosis? Good old American willpower? Looking at you, I'd guess it was the patch."

If it had been Duke's humorous effort at a curve-ball, it didn't work. Pearson had been thinking about smoking a lot this afternoon. "Yeah, the patch," he said. "I wore it for two years, starting just after my daughter was born. I took one look at her through the nursery window and made up my mind to quit the habit. It seemed crazy to go on setting fire to forty or fifty cigarettes a day when I'd just taken on an eighteen-year commitment to a brand-new human being." *With whom I had fallen instantly in love,* he could have added, but he had an idea Duke already knew that.

"Not to mention your life-long commitment to your wife."

"Not to mention my wife," Pearson agreed.

"Plus assorted brothers, sisters-in-law, debt-collectors, rate-payers, and friends of the court."

Pearson burst out laughing and nodded. "Yeah, you got it."

"Not as easy as it sounds, though, huh? When it's four in the morning and you can't sleep, all that nobility erodes fast."

Pearson grimaced. "Or when you have to go upstairs and turn a few cartwheels for Grosbeck and Keefer and Fine and the rest of the boys in the boardroom. The first time I had to do that without grabbing a cigarette before I walked in . . . man, that was tough."

"But you *did* stop completely for at least awhile."

Pearson looked at Duke, only a trifle surprised at this prescience, and nodded. "For about six months. But I never quit in my *mind*, do you know what I mean?"

"Of course I know."

"Finally I started chipping again. That was 1992, right around the time the news stories started coming out about how some people who smoked while they were still wearing the patch had heart attacks. Do you remember those?"

"Uh-huh," Duke said, and tapped his forehead. "I got a complete file of smoking stories up here, my man, alphabetically arranged. Smoking and Alzheimer's, smoking and blood-pressure, smoking and cataracts . . . you know."

"So I had my choice," Pearson said. He was smiling a small, puzzled smile — the smile of a man who knows he has behaved like a horse's ass, is *still* behaving like a horse's ass, but doesn't really know why. "I could quit chipping or quit wearing the patch. So I —"

"*Quit wearing the patch!*" they finished together, and then burst into a gust of laughter that caused a smooth-browed patron in the no-smoking area to glance over at them for a moment, frowning, before returning his attention to the newscast on the tube.

"Life's one fucked-up proposition, isn't it?" Duke asked, still laughing, and started to reach inside his cream-colored jacket. He stopped when he saw Pearson holding out his pack of Marlboros with one cigarette popped up. They exchanged another glance, Duke's surprised and Pearson's knowing, and then burst into another mingled shout of laughter. The smooth-browed guy glanced over again, his frown a little deeper this time. Neither man noticed. Duke took the offered cigarette and lit it. The whole thing took less than ten seconds, but it was long enough for the two men to become friends.

"I smoked like a chimney from the time I was fifteen right up until I got married back in '91," Duke said. "My mother didn't like it, but she appreciated the fact that I wasn't smoking rock or selling it, like half the other kids on my street — I'm talking Roxbury, you know — and so she didn't say too much.

"Wendy and I went to Hawaii for a week on our honeymoon, and the day we got back, she gave me a present." Duke dragged deep and then feathered twin jets of blue-gray smoke from his nose. "She found it in the Sharper Image catalogue, I think, or maybe it was one of the other ones. Had some fancy name, but I don't remember what it was; I just called the goddamned thing Pavlov's Thumbscrews. Still, I loved her like fire — still do, too, you better believe it — so I rared back and gave it my best shot. It wasn't as bad as I

680

thought it would be, either. You know the gadget I'm talking about?"

"You bet," Pearson said. "The beeper. It makes you wait a little longer for each cigarette. Lisabeth — *my* wife — kept pointing them out to me while she was pregnant with Jenny. About as subtle as a wheelbarrow of cement falling off a scaffold, you know."

Duke nodded, smiling, and when the bartender drifted by, he pointed at their glasses and told him to do it again. Then he turned back to Pearson. "Except for using Pavlov's Thumbscrews instead of the patch, the rest of my story's the same as yours. I got all the way to the place where the machine plays a shitty little version of the *Freedom Chorus,* or something, but the habit crept back. It's harder to kill than a snake with two hearts." The bartender brought the fresh beers. Duke paid this time, took a sip of his, and said, "I have to make a telephone call. Take about five minutes."

"Okay," Pearson said. He glanced around, saw the bartender had once more retreated to the relative safety of the no-smoking section (*The unions'll have two bartenders in here by 2005,* he thought, *one for the smokers and one for the non-smokers*), and turned back to Duke again. When he spoke this time, he pitched his voice lower. "I thought we were going to talk about the batmen."

Duke appraised him with his dark-brown eyes for a moment and then said, "We *have* been, my man. We *have* been."

And before Pearson could say anything else, Duke had disappeared into the dim (but almost

681

entirely smokeless) depths of Gallagher's, bound for wherever the pay phones were hidden away.

He was gone closer to ten minutes than to five, and Pearson was wondering if maybe he should go back and check on him when his eye was drawn to the television, where the news anchor was talking about a furor that had been touched off by the Vice President of the United States. The Veep had suggested in a speech to the National Education Association that government-subsidized daycare centers should be re-evaluated and closed wherever possible.

The picture switched to videotape shot earlier that day at some Washington, D.C., convention center, and as the newsclip went from the wide establishing shot and lead-in narration to the close-up of the V.P. at his podium, Pearson gripped the edge of the bar with both hands, squeezing tightly enough to sink his fingers a little way into the padding. One of the things Duke had said that morning on the plaza came back to him: *They've got friends in high places. Hell, high places is what they're all about.*

"We have no grudge against America's working mothers," the misshapen bat-faced monster standing in front of the podium with the blue Vice Presidential seal on it was saying, "and no grudge against the deserving poor. We do feel, however —"

A hand dropped on Pearson's shoulder, and he had to bite his lips together to keep the scream inside them. He looked around and saw Duke. A change had come over the young man — his

682

eyes were sparkling brightly, and there were fine beads of sweat on his brow. Pearson thought he looked as if he'd just won the Publishers Clearing House sweepstakes.

"Don't ever do that again," Pearson said, and Duke froze in the act of climbing back onto his stool. "I think I just ate my heart."

Duke looked surprised, then glanced up at the TV. Understanding dawned on his face. "Oh," he said. "Jesus, I'm sorry, Brandon. Really. I keep forgetting that you came in on this movie in the middle."

"What about the President?" Pearson asked. He strained to keep his voice level and almost made it. "I guess I can live with this asshole, but what about the President? Is he —"

"No," Duke said. He hesitated, then added: "At least, not yet."

Pearson leaned toward him, aware that the strange numbness was stealing back into his lips again. "What do you *mean*, not yet? What's happening, Duke? What are they? Where do they come from? What do they do and what do they want?"

"I'll tell you what I know," Duke said, "but first I want to ask you if you can come to a little meeting with me this evening. Around six? You up for that?"

"Is it about this?"

"Of course it is."

Pearson ruminated. "All right. I'll have to call Lisabeth, though."

Duke looked alarmed. "Don't say anything about —"

683

"Of course not. I'll tell her *La Belle Dame sans Merci* wants to go over her precious spread-sheets again before she shows them to the Japanese. She'll buy that; she knows Holding's all but fudging her frillies about the impending arrival of our friends from the Pacific Rim. Sound okay to you?"

"Yes."

"It sounds okay to me, too, but it feels a little sleazy."

"There's nothing sleazy about wanting to keep as much space as possible between your wife and the bats. I mean, it's not a massage-parlor I want to take you to, bro."

"I suppose not. So talk."

"All right. I guess I better start by telling you about your smoking habits."

The juke, which had been silent for the last few minutes, now began to emit a tired-sounding version of Billy Ray Cyrus's golden clunker, "Achy Breaky Heart." Pearson stared at Duke Rhinemann with confused eyes and opened his mouth to ask what his smoking habits had to do with the price of coffee in San Diego. Only nothing came out. Nothing at all.

"You quit . . . then you started chipping . . . but you were smart enough to know that if you weren't careful, you'd be right back where you started in a month or two," Duke said. "Right?"

"Yes, but I don't see —"

"You will." Duke took his handkerchief out and mopped his brow. Pearson's first impression when the man had come back from using the phone had been that Duke was all but blowing his stack with

684

excitement. He stood by that, but now he realized something else: he was also scared to death. "Just bear with me."

"Okay."

"Anyway, you've worked out an accommodation with your habit. A whatdoyoucallit, *modus vivendi.* You can't bring yourself to quit, but you've discovered that's not the end of the world — it's not like being a coke-addict who can't let go of the rock or a boozehound who can't stop chugging down the Night Train. Smoking's a bastard of a habit, but there really *is* a middle ground between two or three packs a day and total abstinence."

Pearson was looking at him, wide-eyed, and Duke smiled.

"I'm not reading your mind, if that's what you think. I mean, we *know* each other, don't we?"

"I suppose we do," Pearson said thoughtfully. "I just forgot for a minute that we're both Ten O'Clock People."

"We're *what?*"

So Pearson explained a little about the Ten O'Clock People and their tribal gestures (surly glances when confronted by NO SMOKING signs, surly shrugs of acquiescence when asked by some accredited authority to Please Put Your Cigarette Out, Sir), their tribal sacraments (gum, hard candies, toothpicks, and, of course, little Binaca push-button spray cans), and their tribal litanies (*I'm quitting for good next year* being the most common).

Duke listened, fascinated, and when Pearson had finished he said, "Jesus Christ, Brandon! You've found the Lost Tribe of Israel! Crazy fucks all wan-

685

dered off following Joe Camel!"

Pearson burst out laughing, earning another annoyed, puzzled look from the smooth-faced fellow over in NoSmo.

"Anyway, it all fits in," Duke told him. "Let me ask you something — do you smoke around your kid?"

"Christ, no!" Pearson exclaimed.

"Your wife?"

"Nope, not anymore."

"When was the last time you had a butt in a restaurant?"

Pearson considered it and discovered a peculiar thing: he couldn't remember. Nowadays he asked to be seated in the no-smoking section even when he was alone, deferring his cigarette until after he'd finished, paid up, and left. And the days when he had actually smoked between courses were long in the past, of course.

"Ten O'Clock People," Duke said in a marvelling voice. "Man, I love that — I love it that we have a name. And it really *is* like being part of a tribe. It —"

He broke off suddenly, looking out one of the windows. A Boston city cop was walking by, talking to a pretty young woman. She was looking up at him with a sweetly mingled expression of admiration and sex-appeal, totally unaware of the black, appraising eyes and glaring triangular teeth just above her.

"Jesus, would you look at that," Pearson said in a low voice.

"Yeah," Duke said. "It's becoming more common, too. More common every day." He was quiet

686

for a moment, looking into his half-empty beer schooner. Then he seemed to almost physically shake himself out of his revery. "Whatever else we are," he told Pearson, "we're the only people in the whole goddam world who see *them.*"

"What, just *smokers?*" Pearson asked incredulously. Of course he should have seen that Duke was leading him here, but still . . .

"No," Duke said patiently. "*Smokers* don't see them. *Non*-smokers don't see them, either." He measured Pearson with his eyes. "Only people like us see them, Brandon — people who are neither fish nor fowl.

"Only Ten O'Clock People like us."

When they left Gallagher's fifteen minutes later (Pearson had first called his wife, told her his manufactured tale of woe, and promised to be home by ten), the rain had slackened to a fine drizzle and Duke proposed they walk awhile. Not all the way to Cambridge, which was where they would end up, but far enough for Duke to fill in the rest of the background. The streets were nearly deserted, and they could finish their conversation without looking back over their shoulders.

"In a bizarre way, it's sort of like your first orgasm," Duke was saying as they walked through a gauzy groundmist in the direction of the Charles River. "Once that kicks into gear, becomes a part of your life, it's just there for you. Same with this. One day the chemicals in your head balance just right and you *see* one. I've wondered, you know, how many people have just dropped dead of fright at that moment. A lot, I bet."

687

Pearson looked at the bloody smear of a traffic-light reflection on the shiny black pavement of Boylston Street and remembered the shock of his first encounter. "They're so awful. So hideous. The way their flesh seems to move around on their heads . . . there's really no way to say it, is there?"

Duke was nodding. "They're ugly motherfuckers, all right. I was on the Red Line, headed back home to Milton, when I saw my first one. He was standing on the downtown platform at Park Street Station. We went right by him. Good thing for me I was in the train and goin away, because I screamed."

"What happened then?"

Duke's smile had become, at least temporarily, a grimace of embarrassment. "People looked at me, then looked away real quick. You know how it is in the city; there's a nut preachin about how Jesus loves Tupperware on every street corner."

Pearson nodded. He knew how it was in the city, all right. Or thought he had, until today.

"This tall redheaded geek with about a trillion freckles on his face sat down in the seat beside me and grabbed my elbow just about the same way I grabbed yours this morning. His name is Robbie Delray. He's a housepainter. You'll meet him tonight at Kate's."

"What's Kate's?"

"Specialty bookstore in Cambridge. Mysteries. We meet there once or twice a week. It's a good place. Good people, too, mostly. You'll see. Anyway, Robbie grabbed my elbow and said, 'You're not crazy, I saw it too. It's real — it's a batman.' That was all, and he could have been spoutin from the top end of some amphetamine high for all I knew . . . except I *had* seen it, and the relief . . ."

"Yes," Pearson said, thinking back to that morning. They paused at Storrow Drive, waited for a tanker truck to go by, and then hurried across the puddly street. Pearson was momentarily transfixed by a fading spray-painted graffito on the back of a park bench which faced the river. THE ALIENS HAVE LANDED, it said. WE ATE 2 AT LEGAL SEAFOOD.

"Good thing for me you were there this morning," Pearson said. "I was lucky."

Duke nodded. "Yeah, man, you were. When the bats fuck with a dude, they *fuck* with him — the cops usually pick up the pieces in a basket after one of their little parties. You hear that?"

Pearson nodded.

"And nobody knows the victims all had one thing in common — they'd cut down their smoking to between five and ten cigarettes a day. I have an idea that sort of similarity's a little too obscure even for the FBI."

"But why kill us?" Pearson asked. "I mean, some guy goes running around saying his boss is a Martian, they don't send out the National Guard; they put the guy in the boobyhatch!"

"Come on, man, get real," Duke said. "You've *seen* these cuties."

"They . . . like to?"

"Yeah, they like to. But that's getting the cart before the horse. They're like wolves, Brandon, invisible wolves that keep working their way back and forth through a herd of sheep. Now tell me

— what do wolves want with sheep, aside from getting their jollies off every time they kill one?"

"They . . . what are you saying?" Pearson's voice dropped to a whisper. "Are you saying that they *eat* us?"

"They eat some part of us," Duke said. "That's what Robbie Delray believed on the day I met him, and that's what most of us still believe."

"Who's us, Duke?"

"The people I'm taking you to see. We won't all be there, but this time most of us will be. Something's come up. Something big."

"What?"

To that Duke would only shake his head and ask, "You ready for a cab yet? Getting too mildewy?"

Pearson was mildewy, but not ready for a cab. The walk had invigorated him . . . but not just the walk. He didn't think he could tell Duke this — at least not yet — but there was a definite upside to this . . . a *romantic* upside. It was as if he had fallen into some weird but exciting boy's adventure story; he could almost imagine the N. C. Wyeth illustrations. He looked at the nimbuses of white light revolving slowly around the streetlamps which soldiered their way up Storrow Drive and smiled a little. *Something big has come up,* he thought. *Agent X-9 has slipped in with good news from our underground base . . . we've located the batpoison we've been looking for!*

"The excitement wears off, believe me," Duke said dryly.

Pearson turned his head, startled.

"Around the time they fish your second friend

out of Boston Harbor with half his head gone, you realize Tom Swift isn't going to show up and help you whitewash the goddam fence."

"Tom Sawyer," Pearson muttered, and wiped rainwater out of his eyes. He could feel himself flushing.

"They eat something that our brains make, that's what Robbie thinks. Maybe an enzyme, he says, maybe some kind of special electrical wave. He says it might be the same thing that lets us — some of us, anyway — see them, and that to them we're like tomatoes in a farmer's garden, theirs to take whenever they decide we're ripe.

"Me, I was raised Baptist and I'm willing to cut right to the chase — none of that Farmer John crap. I think they're soul-suckers."

"Really? Are you putting me on, or do you really believe that?"

Duke laughed, shrugged, and looked defiant, all at the same time. "Shit, I don't know, man. These things came into my life about the same time I decided heaven was a fairytale and hell was other people. Now I'm all fucked up again. But that doesn't really matter. The important thing, the only thing you have to get straight and keep straight, is that they have *plenty* of reasons to kill us. First because they're afraid of us doing just what we're doing, getting together, organizing, trying to put a hurt on them . . ."

He paused, thought it over, shook his head. Now he looked and sounded like a man holding dialogue with himself, trying yet again to answer some question which has held him sleepless over too many nights.

"Afraid? I don't know if that's exactly true. But they're not taking many chances, about that there's no doubt. And something else there's no doubt about, either — they hate the fact that some of us can see them. They fucking *hate* it. We caught one once and it was like catching a hurricane in a bottle. We —"

"*Caught* one!"

"Yes indeed," Duke said, and offered him a hard, mirthless grin. "We bagged it at a rest area on I-95, up by Newburyport. There were half a dozen of us — my friend Robbie was in charge. We took it to a farmhouse, and when the boatload of dope we'd shot into it wore off — which it did much too fast — we tried to question it, to get better answers to some of the questions you've already asked me. We had it in handcuffs and leg-irons; we had so much nylon rope wrapped around it that it looked like a mummy. You know what I remember best?"

Pearson shook his head. His sense of living between the pages of a boy's adventure story had quite departed.

"How it woke up," Duke said. "There was no in-between. One second it was knocked-out-loaded and the next it was wide-awake, staring at us with those horrible eyes they have. Bat's eyes. They *do* have eyes, you know — people don't always realize that. That stuff about them being blind must have been the work of a good press-agent.

"It wouldn't talk to us. Not a single word. I think it knew it wasn't going to ever leave that barn, but there was no fear in it. Only hate.

Jesus, the hate in its eyes!"

"What happened?"

"It snapped the handcuff-chain like it was tissue-paper. The leg-irons were tougher — and we had it in those special Long John boots you can nail right to the floor — but the nylon boat-rope . . . it started to bite through it where it crossed its shoulders. With those teeth — you've seen them — it was like watching a rat gnaw through twine. We all stood there like bumps on a log. Even Robbie. We couldn't believe what we were seeing . . . or maybe it had us hypnotized. I've wondered about that a lot, you know, if that might not have been possible. Thank God for Lester Olson. We'd used a Ford Econoline van that Robbie and Moira stole, and Lester'd gotten paranoid that it might be visible from the turnpike. He went out to check, and when he came back in and saw that thing almost free except for its feet, he shot it three times in the head. Just pop-pop-pop."

Duke shook his head wonderingly.

"Killed him," Pearson said. "Just pop-pop-pop."

His voice seemed to have risen out of his head again, as it had on the plaza in front of the bank that morning, and a horrid yet persuasive idea suddenly came to him: that there *were* no batpeople. They were a group hallucination, that was all, not much different from the ones peyote users sometimes had during their drug-assisted circle jerks. This one, unique to the Ten O'Clock People, was brought on by just the wrong amount of tobacco. The folks Duke was taking him to meet had killed at least one innocent person while under the influence of this mad idea, and might kill more. Certainly *would* kill more, if given time. And if he didn't get away from this crazed young banker soon, he might end up being a part of it. He had already seen two of the batpeople . . . no, three, counting the cop, and four counting the Vice President. And that just about tore it, the idea that *the Vice President of the United States* —

The look on Duke's face led Pearson to believe that his mind was being read for the third record-breaking time. "You're starting to wonder if maybe we've all gone Looney Tunes, you included," Duke said. "Is that right?"

"Of course it is," Pearson said, a little more sharply than he had intended.

"They disappear," Duke said simply. "I *saw* the one in the barn disappear."

"*What?*"

"Get transparent, turn to smoke, disappear. I know how crazy it sounds, but nothing I could ever say would make you understand how crazy it was to actually *be* there and watch it happen.

"At first you think it's not real even though it's going on right in front of you; you must be dreaming it, or maybe you stepped into a movie somehow, one full of killer special effects like in those old *Star Wars* movies. Then you smell something that's like dust and piss and hot chili-peppers all mixed together. It stings your eyes, makes you want to puke. Lester *did* puke, and Janet sneezed for an hour afterward. She said ordinarily only ragweed or cat-dander does that to her. Anyway, I went up to the chair where he'd been. The ropes were still there, and the handcuffs, and the clothes.

694

The guy's shirt was still buttoned. The guy's tie was still knotted. I reached out and unzipped his pants — careful, like his pecker was gonna fly outta there and rip my nose off — but all I saw was his underwear inside his pants. Ordinary white Jockey shorts. That was all, but that was enough, because *they* were empty, too. Tell you something, my brother — you ain't seen weird until you've seen a guy's clothes all put together in layers like that with no guy left inside em."

"Turn to smoke and disappear," Pearson said. "Jesus Christ."

"Yeah. At the very end, he looked like that." He pointed to one of the streetlights with its bright revolving nimbus of moisture.

"And what happens to . . ." Pearson stopped, unsure for a moment how to express what he wanted to ask. "Are they reported missing? Are they . . ." Then he knew what it was he really wanted to know. "Duke, where's the *real* Douglas Keefer? And the real Suzanne Holding?"

Duke shook his head. "I don't know. Except that, in a way, it's the real Keefer you saw this morning, Brandon, and the real Suzanne Holding, too. We think that maybe the heads we see aren't really there, that our brains are translating what the bats *really* are — their hearts and their souls — into visual images."

"Spiritual telepathy?"

Duke grinned. "You got a way with words, bro — that'll do. You need to talk to Lester. When it comes to the batpeople, he's damn near a poet."

The name rang a clear bell, and after a moment's thought, Pearson thought he knew why.

695

"Is he an older guy with lots of white hair? Looks sort of like an aging tycoon on a soap opera?"

Duke burst out laughing. "Yeah, that's Les."

They walked on in silence for awhile. The river rippled mystically past on their right, and now they could see the lights of Cambridge on the other side. Pearson thought he had never seen Boston looking so beautiful.

"The batpeople come in, maybe no more than a germ you inhale . . ." Pearson began again, feeling his way.

"Yeah, well, some folks go for the germ idea, but I'm not one of em. Because, dig: you never see a batman *janitor* or a batwoman *waitress*. They like *power,* and they're moving into the power neighborhoods. Did you ever hear of a germ that just picked on rich people, Brandon?"

"No."

"Me either."

"These people we're going to meet . . . are they . . ." Pearson was a little amused to find he had to work to bring the next thing out. It wasn't exactly a return to the land of boys' books, but it was close. "Are they resistance fighters?"

Duke considered this, then both nodded and shrugged — a fascinating gesture, as if his body were saying yes and no at the same time. "Not yet," he said, "but maybe, after tonight, we will be."

Before Pearson could ask him what he meant by that, Duke had spotted another cab cruising empty, this one on the far side of Storrow Drive, and had stepped into the gutter to flag it. It made an illegal U-turn and swung over to the curb to pick them up.

In the cab they talked Hub sports — the maddening Red Sox, the depressing Patriots, the sagging Celtics — and left the batpeople alone, but when they got out in front of an isolated frame house on the Cambridge side of the river (KATE'S MYSTERY BOOKSHOP was written on a sign that showed a hissing black cat with an arched back), Pearson took Duke Rhinemann's arm and said, "I have a few more questions."

Duke glanced at his watch. "No time, Brandon — we walked a little too long, I guess."

"Just two, then."

"Jesus, you're like that guy on TV, the one in the old dirty raincoat. I doubt if I can answer them, anyway — I know a hell of a lot less about all this than you seem to think."

"When did it start?"

"See? That's what I mean. I don't know, and the thing we caught sure wasn't going to tell us — that little sweetheart wouldn't even give us its name, rank, and serial number. Robbie Delray, the guy I told you about, says he saw his first one over five years ago, walking a Lhasa Apso on Boston Common. He says there have been more every year since. There still aren't many of them compared to us, but the number has been increasing . . . exponentially? . . . is that the word I want?"

"I hope not," Pearson said. "It's a scary word."

"What's your other question, Brandon? Hurry up."

"What about other cities? Are there more bats? And other people who see them? What do you hear?"

"We don't know. They could be all over the world, but we're pretty sure that America's the only country in the world where more than a handful of people can see them."

"Why?"

"Because this is the only country that's gone bonkers about cigarettes . . . probably because it's the only one where people believe — and down deep they really do — that if they just eat the right foods, take the right combination of vitamins, think enough of the right thoughts, and wipe their asses with the right kind of toilet-paper, they'll live forever and be sexually active the whole time. When it comes to smoking, the battle-lines are drawn, and the result has been this weird hybrid. Us, in other words."

"Ten O'Clock People," Pearson said, smiling.

"Yep — Ten O'Clock People." He looked past Pearson's shoulder. "Moira! Hi!"

Pearson was not exactly surprised to smell Giorgio. He looked around and saw Little Miss Red Skirt.

"Moira Richardson, Brandon Pearson."

"Hello," Pearson said, and took her outstretched hand. "Credit Assistance, isn't it?"

"That's like calling a garbage collector a sanitation technician," she said with a cheerful grin. It was a grin, Pearson thought, that a man could fall in love with, if he wasn't careful. "Credit checks are what I actually do. If you want to buy a new Porsche, I check the records to make sure you're really a Porsche kind of guy . . . in a financial sense, of course."

"Of course," Pearson said, and grinned back at her.

"Cam!" she called. "Come on over here!"

It was the janitor who liked to mop the john with his cap turned around backward. In his streetclothes he seemed to have gained about fifty IQ points and a rather amazing resemblance to Armand Assante. Pearson felt a small pang but no real surprise when he put an arm around Moira Richardson's delectable little waist and a casual kiss on the corner of her delectable little mouth. Then he offered Brandon his hand.

"Cameron Stevens."

"Brandon Pearson."

"I'm glad to see you here," Stevens said. "I thought you were gonna high-side it this morning for sure."

"How many of you were watching me?" Pearson asked. He tried to replay ten o'clock in the plaza and discovered he couldn't — it was lost in a white haze of shock, for the most part.

"Most of us from the bank who see them," Moira said quietly. "But it's okay, Mr. Pearson —"

"Brandon. Please."

She nodded. "We weren't doing anything but rooting for you, Brandon. Come on, Cam."

They hurried up the steps to the porch of the small frame building and slipped inside. Pearson caught just a glimpse of muted light before the door shut. Then he turned back to Duke.

"This is all real, isn't it?" he asked.

Duke looked at him sympathetically. "Unfortunately, yes." He paused, then added, "But there's one good thing about it."

"Oh? What's that?"

Duke's white teeth flashed in the drizzly dark.

"You're about to attend your first smoking-allowed meeting in five years or so," he said. "Come on — let's go in."

3

The foyer and the bookstore beyond it were dark; the light — along with a murmur of voices — was filtering up the steep staircase to their left.

"Well," Duke said, "this is the place. To quote the Dead, what a long strange trip it's been, right?"

"You better believe it," Pearson agreed. "Is Kate a Ten O'Clock Person?"

"The owner? Nope. I only met her twice, but I have an idea she's a total non-smoker. This place was Robbie's idea. As far as Kate knows, we're The Boston Society of Hardboiled Yeggs."

Pearson raised his eyebrows. "Say again?"

"A small group of loyal fans that meets every week or so to discuss the works of Raymond Chandler, Dashiell Hammett, Ross Macdonald, people like that. If you haven't read any of those guys, you probably ought to. It never hurts to be safe. It's not that hard; some of them are actually pretty good."

They descended with Duke in the lead — the staircase was too narrow for them to walk abreast — and passed through an open doorway into a well-lit, low-ceilinged basement room that probably ran the length of the converted frame house above. About thirty folding chairs had been set up, and an easel covered with a blue cloth had been placed before them. Beyond the easel were stacked shipping cartons from various publishers. Pearson was amused to see a framed picture on the lefthand wall, with a sign reading DASHIELL HAMMETT: ALL HAIL OUR FEARLESS LEADER beneath it.

"Duke?" a woman asked from Pearson's left. "Thank God — I thought something had happened to you."

She was someone else Pearson recognized: the serious-looking young woman with the thick glasses and long, straight black hair. Tonight she looked a lot less serious in a pair of tight faded jeans and a Georgetown University tee-shirt beneath which she was clearly braless. And Pearson had an idea that if Duke's wife ever saw the way this young woman was looking at her husband, she would probably drag Duke out of the basement of Kate's by the ear, and never mind all the batpeople in the world.

"I'm fine, darlin," he said. "I was bringing along another convert to the Church of the Fucked-Up Bat, that's all. Janet Brightwood, Brandon Pearson."

Brandon shook her hand, thinking: *You're the one who kept sneezing.*

"It's very nice to meet you, Brandon," she said, and then went back to smiling at Duke, who looked a little embarrassed at the intensity of her gaze. "Want to go for coffee after?" she asked him.

"Well . . . we'll see, darlin. Okay?"

"Okay," she said, and her smile said she'd wait three years to go out for coffee with Duke, if that

701

was the way Duke wanted it.

What am I doing here? Pearson suddenly asked himself. *This is totally insane . . . like an A.A. meeting in a psycho ward.*

The members of the Church of the Fucked-Up Bat were taking ashtrays from a stack on one of the book cartons and lighting up with obvious relish as they took their seats. Pearson estimated that there were going to be few if any folding chairs left over when everyone had gotten settled.

"Got just about everyone," Duke said, leading him to a pair of seats at the end of the back row, far from where Janet Brightwood was presiding over the coffeemaker. Pearson had no idea if this was coincidental or not. "That's good . . . mind the window-pole, Brandon."

The pole, with a hook on the end to open the high cellar windows, was leaning against one whitewashed brick wall. Pearson had inadvertently kicked it as he sat down. Duke grabbed it before it could fall and possibly gash someone, moved it to a marginally safer location, then slipped up the side aisle and snagged an ashtray.

"You *are* a mind-reader," Pearson said gratefully, and lit up. It felt incredibly strange (but rather wonderful) to be doing this as a member of such a large group.

Duke lit his own cigarette, then pointed it at the skinny, freckle-splattered man now standing by the easel. Freckles was deep in conversation with Lester Olson, who had shot the batman, pop-pop-pop, in a Newburyport barn.

"The redhead is Robbie Delray," Duke said, almost reverently. "You'd hardly pick him as The

Savior of His Race if you were casting a miniseries, would you? But he might turn out to be just that."

Delray nodded at Olson, clapped him on the back, and said something that made the white-haired man laugh. Then Olson returned to his seat — front row center — and Delray moved toward the covered easel.

By this time all the seats had been taken, and there were even a few people standing at the back of the room near the coffeemaker. Conversation, animated and jittery, zinged and caromed around Pearson's head like pool-balls after a hard break. A mat of blue-gray cigarette smoke had already gathered just below the ceiling.

Jesus, they're cranked, he thought. *Really cranked. I bet the bomb-shelters in London felt this way back in 1940, during the Blitz.*

He turned to Duke. "Who'd you talk to? Who told you something big was up tonight?"

"Janet," Duke said without looking at him. His expressive brown eyes were fixed on Robbie Delray, who had once saved his sanity on a Red Line train. Pearson thought he saw adoration as well as admiration in Duke's eyes.

"Duke? This is a *really* big meeting, isn't it?"

"For us, yeah. Biggest I've ever seen."

"Does it make you nervous? Having so many of your people in the same place?"

"No," Duke said simply. "Robbie can *smell* bats. He . . . shhhh, here we go."

Robbie Delray, smiling, raised his hands, and the babble quieted almost at once. Pearson saw Duke's look of adoration on many other faces. No-where did he see less than respect.

"Thanks for coming," Delray said quietly. "I think we've finally got what some of us have been waiting four or five years for."

This sparked spontaneous applause. Delray let it go on for a few moments, looking around the room, beaming. Finally he held his hands up for quiet. Pearson discovered a disconcerting thing as the applause (in which he had not participated) tapered off: he didn't like Duke's friend and mentor. He supposed he might be experiencing a touch of jealousy — now that Delray was doing his thing at the front of the room, Duke Rhinemann had clearly forgotten Pearson existed — but he didn't think that was all of it. There was something smug and self-congratulatory in that hands-up, be-quiet gesture; something that expressed a slick politician's almost unconscious contempt for his audience.

Oh, get off it, Pearson told himself. *You can't know* anything *like that.*

True, quite true, and Pearson tried to sweep the intuition out of his mind, to give Delray a chance, if only for Duke's sake.

"Before we begin," Delray went on, "I'd like to introduce you to a brand-new member of the group: Brandon Pearson, from deepest, darkest Medford. Stand up for a second or two, Brandon, and let your new friends see what you look like."

Pearson gave Duke a startled look. Duke grinned, shrugged, then pushed Pearson's shoulder with the heel of his hand. "Go on, they won't bite."

Pearson was not so sure of that. Nevertheless he got up, face hot, all too aware of the people craning around to check him out. He was most particularly aware of the smile on Lester Olson's face — like his hair, it was somehow too dazzling not to be suspect.

His fellow Ten O'Clock People began to applaud again, only this time it was him they were applauding: Brandon Pearson, middle-echelon banker and stubborn smoker. He found himself wondering again if he hadn't somehow found his way into an A.A. meeting that was strictly for (not to mention run by) psychos. When he dropped back into his seat, his cheeks were bright red.

"I could have done without that very well, thanks," he muttered to Duke.

"Relax," Duke said, still grinning. "It's the same for everybody. And you gotta love it, man, don't you? I mean, shit, it's so *nineties*."

"It's nineties, all right, but I don't gotta love it," Pearson said. His heart was pounding too hard and the flush in his cheeks wasn't going away. It felt, in fact, as if it was deepening. *What is this?* he wondered. *A hot-flash? Male menopause? What?*

Robbie Delray bent over, spoke briefly to the bespectacled brunette woman sitting next to Olson, glanced at his watch, then stepped back to the covered easel and faced the group again. His freckled, open face made him look like a Sunday choirboy apt to get up to all sorts of harmless dickens — frogs down the backs of girls' blouses, short-sheeting baby brother's bed, that sort of thing — during the other six days of the week.

"Thanks, folks, and welcome to our place, Brandon," he said.

705

Pearson muttered that he was glad to be here, but it wasn't true — what if his fellow Ten O'Clock People turned out to be a bunch of raving New Age assholes? Suppose he ended up feeling about them as he did about most of the guests he saw on Oprah, or the well-dressed religious nuts who used to pop up on *The P.T.L. Club* at the drop of a hymn? What *then?*

Oh, quit it, he told himself. *You like Duke, don't you?*

Yes, he *did* like Duke, and he thought he was probably going to like Moira Richardson, too . . . once he got past the sexy outer layer and was able to appreciate the person inside, that was. There would undoubtedly be others he'd end up liking as well; he wasn't that hard to please. And he had forgotten, at least temporarily, the underlying reason they were all here in this basement: the batpeople. Given the threat, he could put up with a few nerds and New Agers, couldn't he?

He supposed he could.

Good! Great! Now just sit back, relax, and watch the parade.

He sat back, but found he couldn't relax, at least not completely. Part of it was being the new boy. Part of it was his strong dislike for this sort of forced social interaction — as a rule, he viewed people who used his first name on short notice and without invitation as hijackers of a sort. And part of it . . .

Oh, stop! Don't you get it yet? You have no choice in the matter!

An unpleasant thought, but one it was hard to dispute. He had crossed a line that morning when

706

he had casually turned his head and seen what was *really* living inside Douglas Keefer's clothes these days. He supposed he had known at least that much, but it wasn't until tonight that he had realized how final that line was, how small was the chance of his ever being able to cross back to the other side of it again. To the *safe* side.

No, he couldn't relax. At least not yet.

"Before we get down to business, I want to thank you all for coming on such short notice," Robbie Delray said. "I know it's not always easy to break away without raising eyebrows, and sometimes it's downright dangerous. I don't think it'd be exaggerating to say that we've been through a lot of hell together . . . a lot of high water, too . . ."

A polite, murmured chuckle from the audience. Most of them seemed to be hanging on Delray's every word.

". . . and no one knows any better than I do how difficult it is to be one of the few people who actually know the truth. Since I saw my first bat, five years ago . . ."

Pearson was already fidgeting, experiencing the one sensation he would not have expected tonight: boredom. For the day's strange passage to have ended as it was ending, with a bunch of people sitting in a bookstore basement and listening to a freckled housepainter give what sounded like a bad Rotary Club speech . . .

Yet the others seemed utterly enrapt; Pearson glanced around again to confirm this to himself. Duke's eyes shone with that look of total fascination — a look similar to the look Pearson's child-

707

hood dog, Buddy, had worn when Pearson got its food-dish out of the cupboard under the sink. Cameron Stevens and Moira Richardson sat with their arms around each other and gazed at Robbie Delray with starry absorption. Ditto Janet Brightwood. Ditto the rest of the little group around the Bunn-O-Matic.

Ditto everyone, he thought, *except Brand Pearson. Come on, sweetheart, try to get with the program.*

Except he couldn't, and in a weird way it was almost as if Robbie Delray couldn't, either. Pearson looked back from his scan of the audience just in time to see Delray snatch another quick glance at his watch. It was a gesture Pearson had grown very familiar with since he'd joined the Ten O'Clock People. He guessed that the man was counting down the time to his next cigarette.

As Delray rambled on, some of his other listeners also began to fall out a little — Pearson heard muffled coughs and a few shuffling feet. Delray sailed on regardless, seemingly unaware that, loved resistance leader or no, he was now in danger of overstaying his welcome.

". . . so we've managed the best we can," he was saying, "and we've taken our losses as best we can, too, hiding our tears the way I guess those who fight in the secret wars have always had to, all the time holding onto our belief that a day will come when the secret is out, and we'll —"

— Boink, another quick peek at the old Casio —

"— be able to share our knowledge with all the men and women out there who look but do not see."

Savior of His Race? Pearson thought. *Jesus please help us. This guy sounds more like Jesse Helms during a filibuster.*

He glanced at Duke and was encouraged to see that, while Duke was still listening, he was shifting in his seat and showing signs of coming out of his trance.

Pearson touched his face again and found it was still hot. He lowered the tips of his fingers to his carotid artery and felt his pulse — still racing. It wasn't the embarrassment at having to stand up and be looked over like a Miss America finalist now; the others had forgotten his existence, at least temporarily. No, it was something else. Not a good something else, either.

". . . we've stuck with it and stuck to it, we've done the footwork even when the music wasn't to our taste . . ." Delray was droning.

It's what you felt before, Brand Pearson told himself. *It's the fear that you've stumbled into a group of people sharing the same lethal hallucination.*

"No, it's *not,*" he muttered. Duke turned toward him, eyebrows raised, and Pearson shook his head. Duke turned his attention back to the front of the room.

He was scared, all right, but not of having fallen in with some weird thrill-kill cult. Maybe the people in this room — some of them, at least — *had* killed, maybe that interlude in the Newburyport barn *had* happened, but the energy necessary for such desperate endeavors was not evident here tonight, in this roomful of yuppies being watched over by Dashiell Hammett. All he felt here was sleepy half-headedness, the sort of partial attention that enabled people to get through dull speeches like this without falling asleep or walking out.

"Robbie, get to the point!" some kindred spirit shouted from the back of the room, and there was nervous laughter.

Robbie Delray shot an irritated glance in the direction the voice had come from, then smiled and checked his watch again. "Yeah, okay," he said. "I got rambling, I admit it. Lester, will you help me a sec?"

Lester got up. The two men went behind a stack of book cartons and came back carrying a large leather trunk by the straps. They set it down to the right of the easel.

"Thanks, Les," Robbie said.

Lester nodded and sat back down.

"What's in the case?" Pearson murmured into Duke's ear.

Duke shook his head. He looked puzzled and suddenly a little uncomfortable . . . but maybe not as uncomfortable as Pearson felt.

"Okay, Mac's got a point," Delray said. "I guess I got carried away, but it feels like a historic occasion to me. On with the show."

He paused for effect, then whipped aside the blue cloth on the easel. His audience sat forward on their folding chairs, prepared to be amazed, then sat back with a small collective whoosh of disappointment. It was a black-and-white photograph of what looked to be an abandoned warehouse. It had been enlarged enough so that the eye could easily sort through the litter of papers, condoms, and empty wine-bottles in the loading bays, and read the tangle of spray-painted wit and wisdom on the wall. The biggest of these said RIOT GRRRLS RULE.

A whispered babble of murmurs went through the room.

"Five weeks ago," Delray said impressively, "Lester, Kendra, and I trailed two batmen to this abandoned warehouse in the Clark Bay section of Revere."

The dark-haired woman in the round rimless glasses sitting next to Lester Olson looked around self-importantly . . . and then Pearson was damned if she didn't glance down at *her* watch.

"They were met at this point" — Delray tapped one of the trash-littered loading bays — "by three more batmen and two batwomen. They went inside. Since then, six or seven of us have set up a rotating watch on this place. We have established —"

Pearson glanced around at Duke's hurt, incredulous face. He might as well have had WHY WASN'T I PICKED? tattooed on his forehead.

"— that this is some sort of meeting ground for the bats in the Boston metro area —"

The Boston Bats, Pearson thought, *great name for a baseball team.* And then it came back again, the doubt: *Is this me, sitting here and listening to this craziness? Is it* really?

In the wake of this thought, as if the memory had somehow been triggered by his momentary doubt, he again heard Delray telling the assembled Fearless Bat Hunters that their newest recruit was Brandon Pearson, from deepest, darkest Medford.

He turned back to Duke and spoke quietly into his ear.

711

"When you spoke to Janet on the phone — back in Gallagher's — you told her you were bringing me, right?"

Duke gave him an impatient I'm-trying-to-listen look in which there was still a trace of hurt. "Sure," he said.

"Did you tell her I was from Medford?"

"No," Duke said. "How would I know where you're from? Let me listen, Brand!" And he turned back.

"We have logged over thirty-five vehicles — luxury cars and limos, for the most part — visiting this abandoned warehouse in the middle of nowhere," Delray said. He paused to let this sink in, snatched another quick peek at his watch, and hurried on. "Many of these have visited the site ten or a dozen times. The bats have undoubtedly congratulated themselves on having picked such an out-of-the-way spot for their meeting-hall or social club or whatever it is, but I think they're going to find they've painted themselves into a corner instead. Because . . . pardon me just a sec, guys . . ."

He turned and began a quiet conversation with Lester Olson. The woman named Kendra joined them, her head going back and forth like someone watching a Ping-Pong match. The seated audience watched the whispered conference with expressions of bewilderment and perplexity.

Pearson knew how they felt. *Something big,* Duke had promised, and from the feel of the place when they'd come in, everyone else had been promised the same. "Something big" had turned out to be a single black-and-white photo showing nothing but an abandoned warehouse wallowing in a sea of trash, discarded underwear, and used rubbers. What the fuck is wrong with this picture?

The big deal's got to be in the trunk, Pearson thought. *And by the way, Freckles, how did you know I came from Medford? That's one I'm saving for the Q-and-A after the speech, believe me.*

That feeling — flushed face, pounding heart, above all else the desire for another cigarette — was stronger than ever. Like the anxiety attacks he'd sometimes had back in college. What *was* it? If it wasn't fear, what was it?

Oh, it's fear, all right — it's just not fear of being the only sane man in the snake-pit. You know the bats are real; you're not crazy and neither is Duke and neither is Moira or Cam Stevens or Janet Brightwood. But something is *wrong with this picture just the same . . .* really *wrong. And I think it's* him. *Robbie Delray, housepainter and Savior of His Race. He knew where I was from. Brightwood called him and told him Duke was bringing someone from the First Merc, Brandon Pearson's his name, and Robbie checked on me. Why would he do that? And* how *did he do it?*

In his mind he suddenly heard Duke Rhinemann saying, *They're smart . . . they've got friends in high places. Hell, high places is what they're all about.*

If you had friends in high places, you could check on a fellow in a hurry, couldn't you? Yes. People in high places had access to all the right computer passwords, all the right records, all the numbers that made up all the right vital statistics . . .

Pearson jerked in his seat like a man waking from a terrible dream. He kicked his foot out involuntarily and it struck the base of the window-pole. It started to slide. Meanwhile, the whispering at the front of the room broke up with nods all around.

"Les?" Delray asked. "Would you and Kendra give me another little helping hand?"

Pearson reached to grab the window-pole before it could fall and brain someone — maybe even slice someone's scalp open with the wicked little hook on top. He caught it, started to place it back against the wall, and saw the goblin-face peering in the basement window. The black eyes, like the eyes of a Raggedy Ann doll abandoned under a bed, stared into Pearson's wide blue ones. Strips of flesh rotated like bands of atmosphere around one of the planets astronomers called gas giants. The black snakes of vein under the lumpy, naked skull pulsed. The teeth glimmered in its gaping mouth. "Just help me with the snaps on this darned thing," Delray was saying from the other end of the galaxy. He gave a friendly little chuckle. "They're a little sticky, I guess."

For Brandon Pearson, it was as if time had doubled back on itself to that morning: once again he tried to scream and once again shock robbed his voice and he was able to produce only a low, choked whuffling — the sound of a man moaning in his sleep.

The rambling speech.

The meaningless photograph.

The constant little peeks at the wristwatch.

Does it make you nervous? Having so many of your people in the same place? he had asked, and Duke had replied, smiling: *No. Robbie can smell bats.*

714

This time there was no one to stop him, and this time Pearson's second effort was a total success.

"*IT'S A SET-UP!*" he screamed, leaping to his feet. "*IT'S A SET-UP, WE HAVE TO GET OUT OF HERE!*"

Startled faces craned around to look at him . . . but there were three that didn't have to crane. These belonged to Delray, Olson, and the dark-haired woman named Kendra. They had just solved the latches and opened the trunk. Their faces were full of shock and guilt . . . but no surprise. That particular emotion was absent.

"Siddown, man!" Duke hissed. "Have you gone cra—"

Upstairs, the door crashed open. Bootheels clumped across the floor toward the stairwell.

"What's happening?" Janet Brightwood asked. She spoke directly to Duke. Her eyes were wide and frightened. "What's he *talking* about?"

"*GET OUT!*" Pearson roared. "*GET THE FUCK OUT OF HERE! HE TOLD IT TO YOU BACK-WARD! WE'RE THE ONES IN THE TRAP!*"

The door at the head of the narrow staircase leading to the basement crashed open, and from the shadows up there came the most appalling sounds Pearson had ever heard — it was like listening to a pack of pit-bulls baying over a live baby thrown into their midst.

"*Who's that?*" Janet screamed. "*Who's that up there?*" Yet there was no question on her face; her face knew perfectly well who was up there. *What* was up there.

"*Calm down!*" Robbie Delray shouted to the confused group of people, most of whom were still sitting on their folding chairs. *"They've promised amnesty! Do you hear me? Do you understand what I'm saying? They've given me their solemn —"*

At that moment the cellar window to the left of the one through which Pearson had seen the first batface shattered inward, spraying glass across the stunned men and women in the first row along the wall. An Armani-clad arm snaked through the jagged opening and seized Moira Richardson by the hair. She screamed and beat at the hand holding her . . . which was not really a hand at all, but a bundle of talons tipped with long, chitinous nails.

Without thinking, Pearson seized the window-pole, darted forward, and launched the hook at the pulsing batlike face peering in through the broken window. The hook drove into one of the thing's eyes. A thick, faintly astringent ink pattered down on Pearson's upthrust hands. The bat-man uttered a baying, savage sound — it didn't sound like a scream of pain to Pearson, but he supposed he was allowed to hope — and then it fell backward, pulling the window-pole out of Pearson's hands and into the drizzly night. Before the creature disappeared from view entirely, Pearson saw white mist begin to drift off its tumorous skin, and smelled a whiff of

(*dust urine hot chili-peppers*)

something unpleasant.

Cam Stevens pulled Moira into his arms and looked at Pearson with shocked, disbelieving eyes. All around them were men and women wearing that same blank look, men and women frozen like a herd of deer in the headlights of an oncoming truck.

They don't look much like resistance fighters to me, Pearson thought. *They look like sheep caught in a shearing-pen . . . and the bastard of a judas goat who led them in is standing up there at the front of the room with his co-conspirators.*

The savage baying upstairs was getting closer, but not as fast as Pearson might have expected. Then he remembered how narrow the staircase was — too narrow for two men to walk abreast — and said a little prayer of thanks as he shoved forward. He grabbed Duke by the tie and hauled him to his feet. "Come on," he said. "We're blowing this joint. Is there a back door?"

"I . . . don't know." Duke was rubbing one temple slowly and forcefully, like a man who has a bad headache. "Robbie did this? *Robbie?* Can't be, man . . . can it?" He looked at Pearson with pitiful, stunned intensity.

"I'm afraid so, Duke. Come on."

He got two steps toward the aisle, still holding onto Duke's tie, then stopped. Delray, Olson, and Kendra had been rooting in the trunk, and now they flashed pistol-sized automatic weapons equipped with ridiculous-looking long wire stocks. Pearson had never seen an Uzi outside of the movies and TV, but he supposed that was what these were. Uzis or close relatives, and what the fuck did it matter, anyway? They were *guns.*

"Hold it," Delray said. He appeared to be speaking to Duke and Pearson. He was trying to smile and producing something that looked like the grimace of a death row prisoner who has just been notified it's still on. "Stay right where you are."

Duke kept moving. He was in the aisle now,

and Pearson was right beside him. Others were getting up, following their lead, pressing forward but looking nervously back over their shoulders at the doorway giving on the stairs. Their eyes said they didn't like the guns, but they liked the snarling, baying sounds drifting down from the first floor even less.

"Why, man?" Duke asked, and Pearson saw he was on the verge of tears. He held out his hands, palms up. "Why would you sell us out?"

"Stop, Duke, I'm warning you," Lester Olson said in a Scotch-mellowed voice.

"The rest of you stay back, too!" Kendra snapped. She did not sound mellow at all. Her eyes rolled back and forth in their sockets, trying to cover the whole room at once.

"We never had a chance," Delray told Duke. He sounded as if he were pleading. "They were onto us, they could have taken us *anytime,* but they offered me a deal. Do you understand? I didn't sell out; I *never* sold out. *They* came to *me.*" He spoke vehemently, as if this distinction actually meant something to him, but the shuttling blinks of his eyes signalled a different message. It was as if there were some other Robbie Delray inside, a better Robbie Delray, one who was trying frantically to dissociate himself from this shameful act of betrayal.

"*YOU'RE A FUCKING LIAR!*" Duke Rhinemann shrieked in a voice breaking with hurt betrayal and furious understanding. He leaped at the man who had saved his sanity and perhaps his life on a Red Line train . . . and then everything swooped down at once.

718

Pearson could not have seen it all, yet it seemed that somehow he did. He saw Robbie Delray hesitate, then turn his weapon sideways, as if he intended to club Duke with the barrel instead of shooting him. He saw Lester Olson, who had shot the batman in the Newburyport barn pop-pop-pop before losing his guts and deciding to try and cut a deal, lodge the wire stock of his own gun against the buckle of his belt and pull the trigger. He saw momentary blue licks of fire appear in the ventilation holes in the barrel, and heard a hoarse *hack!hack!hack!hack!* that Pearson supposed was the way automatic weapons sounded in the real world. He heard something invisible slice the air an inch in front of his face; it was like hearing a ghost gasp. And he saw Duke flung backward with blood spraying up from his white shirt and splattering on his cream-colored suit. He saw the man who had been standing directly behind Duke stumble to his knees, hands clapped over his eyes, bright blood oozing out from between the knuckles.

Someone — maybe Janet Brightwood — had shut the door between the staircase and this downstairs room before the meeting started; now it banged open and two batmen wearing the uniforms of the Boston Police squeezed in. Their small, pushed-together faces stared savagely out of their oversized, strangely restless heads.

"Amnesty!" Robbie Delray was screaming. The freckles on his face now stood out like brands; the skin upon which they had been printed was ashy-white. *"Amnesty! I've been promised amnesty*

719

if you'll just stand where you are and put up your hands!"

Several people — those who had been clustered around the coffeemaker, for the most part — *did* raise their hands, although they continued to back away from the uniformed batmen as they did it. One of the bats reached forward with a low grunt, seized a man by the front of his shirt, and yanked him toward it. Almost before Pearson realized it had happened, the thing had torn out the man's eyes. The thing looked at the jellied remains resting on its strange, misshapen palm for a moment, then popped them into its mouth.

As two more bats lunged in through the door, looking around with their blackly gleaming little eyes, the other police-bat drew its service revolver and fired three times, seemingly at random, into the crowd.

"No!" Pearson heard Delray scream. *"No, you promised!"*

Janet Brightwood grabbed the Bunn, lifted it over her head, and threw it at one of the newcomers. It struck with a muted metallic bonging and spewed hot coffee all over the thing. This time there was no mistaking the pain in that shriek. One of the police-bats reached for her. Brightwood ducked, tried to run, was tripped . . . and suddenly she was gone, lost in a stampede toward the front of the room.

Now all the windows were breaking, and somewhere close by Pearson could hear approaching sirens. He saw the bats breaking into two groups and running down the sides of the room, clearly bent on driving the panic-stricken Ten O'Clock

720

People into the storage area behind the easel, which had now been knocked over.

Olson threw down his weapon, grabbed Kendra's hand, and bolted in that direction. A bat-arm snaked down through one of the cellar windows, grabbed a handful of his theatrical white hair, and hauled him upward, choking and gargling. Another hand appeared through the window, and a thumbnail three inches long opened his throat and let out a scarlet flood.

Your days of popping off batmen in barns on the coast are all over, my friend, Pearson thought sickly. He turned toward the front of the room again. Delray stood between the open trunk and the fallen easel, his gun now dangling from one hand, his eyes shocked nearly to vacancy. When Pearson pulled the wire stock from his fingers, the man made no attempt to resist.

"They promised us amnesty," he told Pearson. "They *promised.*"

"Did you really think you could trust things that looked like *that?*" Pearson asked, and then drove the wire stock into the center of Delray's face with all the force he could muster. He heard something break — probably Delray's nose — and the thoughtless barbarian which had awakened within his banker's soul cheered with rude savagery.

He started toward a passage zig-zagging between the stacked cartons — one that had been widened by the people who had already bolted their way through — then paused as gunfire erupted behind the building. Gunfire . . . screams . . . roars of triumph.

Pearson whirled and saw Cam Stevens and Moira

Richardson standing at the head of the aisle between the folding chairs. They wore identical shocked expressions and were holding hands. Pearson had time to think, *That's how Hansel and Gretel must have looked after they finally got out of the candy-house.* Then he bent down, picked up Kendra's and Olson's weapons, and handed one to each.

Two more bats had come in through the rear door. They moved casually, as if all were going according to plan . . . which, Pearson supposed, it was. The action had moved to the rear of the house now — that was where the pen *really* was, not in here, and the bats were doing a lot more than just shearing.

"Come on," he said to Cam and Moira. "Let's get these fucks."

The batmen at the rear of the room were late in realizing that a few of the refugees had decided to turn and fight. One of them spun around, possibly to run, struck a new arrival, and slipped in the spilled coffee. They both went down. Pearson opened fire on the one remaining on its feet. The machine-pistol made its somehow unsatisfying *hack!hack!hack!* sound and the bat was driven backward, its alien face breaking open and letting out a cloud of stinking fog . . . it was as if, Pearson thought, they really *were* just illusions.

Cam and Moira got the idea and opened fire on the remaining bats, catching them in a withering field of fire that knocked them back against the wall and then sent them to the floor, already oozing out of their clothes in an insubstantial mist that to Pearson smelled quite a lot like the asters in the marble flower-islands outside The First Mercantile.

"Come on," Pearson said. "If we go now, we might have a chance."

"But —" Cameron began. He looked around, starting to come out of his daze. That was good; Pearson had an idea they'd all have to be wide-awake if they were going to have a chance of getting out of this.

"Never mind, Cam," Moira said. She had also looked around, and noted the fact that they were the only ones, human or bat, left in here. Everyone else had gone out the back. "Let's just go. I think maybe the door we came in through would be our best bet."

"Yes," Pearson said, "but not for long."

He spared one last look at Duke, who lay on the floor with his face frozen in an expression of pained disbelief. He wished there were time to close Duke's eyes, but there wasn't.

"Let's go," he said, and they went.

By the time they reached the door which gave on the porch — and Cambridge Avenue beyond it — the gunfire coming from the rear of the house had begun to taper off. *How many dead?* Pearson wondered, and the answer which first occurred — *all of them* — was horrible but too plausible to deny. He supposed one or two others might have slipped through, but surely no more. It had been a good trap, set quietly and neatly around them while Robbie Delray ran his gums, stalling for time and checking his watch . . . probably waiting to give some signal which Pearson had pre-empted.

If I'd woken up a little earlier, Duke might still be alive, he thought bitterly. Perhaps true, but if wishes were horses, beggars would ride. This wasn't the time for recriminations.

One police-bat had been left to stand sentry on the porch, but it was turned in the direction of the street, possibly watching for unwanted interference. Pearson leaned through the open door toward it and said, "Hey, you ugly ringmeat ass-hole — got a cigarette?"

The bat turned.

Pearson blew its face off.

4

Shortly after one the next morning, three people — two men and a woman wearing torn nylons and a dirty red skirt — ran beside a freight-train pulling out of the South Station shipping yards. The younger of the two men leaped easily into the square mouth of an empty boxcar, turned, and held out his hands to the woman.

She stumbled and cried out as one of her low heels broke. Pearson put an arm around her waist (he got a heartbreakingly faint whiff of Giorgio below the much fresher smell of her sweat and her fear), ran with her that way, then yelled for her to jump. As she did, he grabbed her hips and boosted her toward Cameron Stevens's reaching hands. She caught them and Pearson gave her a final rough shove to help Stevens haul her aboard.

724

Pearson had fallen behind in his effort to help her, and now he could see the fence which marked the edge of the trainyards not far ahead. The freight was gliding through a hole in the chainlink, but there would be no room for both it and Pearson; if he didn't get aboard, and quickly, he would be left behind in the yard.

Cam glanced around the open boxcar door, saw the approaching fence, and held his hands out again. *"Come on!"* he shouted. *"You can do it!"*

Pearson couldn't have — not back in the old two-pack-a-day life, anyway. Now, however, he was able to find a little extra, both in his legs and in his lungs. He sprinted along the treacherous bed of trash-littered cinders beside the tracks, temporarily outrunning the lumbering train again, holding his hands out and up, stretching his fingers to touch the hands above him as the fence loomed. Now he could see the cruel interlacings of barbed wire weaving in and out of the chainlink diamonds.

The eye of his mind opened wide in that moment and he saw his wife sitting in her chair in the living room, her face puffy with crying and her eyes red. He saw her telling two uniformed policemen that her husband had gone missing. He even saw the stack of Jenny's Pop-Up books on the little table beside her. Was that really going on? Yes; in one form or another, he supposed it was. And Lisabeth, who had never smoked a single cigarette in her whole life, would not be aware of the black eyes and fanged mouths beneath the young faces of the policemen sitting across from her on the couch; she would not see the oozing tumors or the black, pulsing lines which crisscrossed their naked skulls.

Would not know. Would not see.

God bless her blindness, Pearson thought. *Let it last forever.*

He stumbled toward the dark behemoth that was a westbound Conrail freight, toward the orange fluff of sparks which spiraled up from beneath one slowly turning steel wheel.

"*Run!*" Moira shrieked, and leaned out of the boxcar door farther, her hands imploring. "*Please, Brandon — just a little more!*"

"*Hurry up, you gluefoot!*" Cam screamed. "*Watch out for the fucking fence!*"

Can't, Pearson thought. *Can't hurry up, can't watch out for the fence, can't do any more. Just want to lie down. Just want to sleep.*

Then he thought of Duke and managed to put on a little more speed after all. Duke hadn't been old enough to know that sometimes people lose their guts and sell out, that sometimes even the ones you idolize do that, but he had been old enough to grab Brand Pearson's arm and keep him from killing himself with a scream. Duke wouldn't have wanted him to be left behind in this stupid trainyard.

He managed one last sprint toward their outstretched hands, watching the fence now seeming to *leap* toward him out of the corner of his eye, and seized Cam's fingers. He jumped, felt Moira's hand clamp firmly under his armpit, and then he was squirming aboard, pulling his right foot into the boxcar a split second before the fence would have torn it off, loafer and all.

"All aboard for Boy's Adventure," he gasped, "illustrations by N. C. Wyeth!"

"What?" Moira asked. "What did you say?"

He turned over and looked up at them through a matted tangle of hair, resting on his elbows and panting. "Never mind. Who's got a cigarette? I'm *dying* for one."

They gawped at him silently for several seconds, looked at each other, then burst into wild shouts of laughter at exactly the same moment. Pearson guessed that meant they were in love.

As they rolled over and over on the floor of the boxcar, clutching each other and howling, Pearson sat up and slowly began to investigate the inside pockets of his filthy, torn suitcoat.

"Ahhh," he said as his hand entered the second one and felt the familiar shape. He hauled out the battered pack and displayed it. "Here's to victory!"

The boxcar trundled west across Massachusetts with three small red embers glowing in the dark of the open doorway. A week later they were in Omaha, spending the midmorning hours of each day idling along the downtown streets, watching the people who take their coffee-breaks outside even in the pouring rain, looking for Ten O'Clock People, hunting for members of the Lost Tribe, the one that wandered off following Joe Camel.

By November there were twenty of them having meetings in the back room of an abandoned hardware store in La Vista.

They mounted their first raid early the following year, across the river in Council Bluffs, and killed thirty very surprised midwestern bat-bankers and bat-executives. It wasn't much, but Brand Pearson had learned that killing bats had at least one thing in common with cutting down on your cigarette intake: you had to start somewhere.

Crouch End

By the time the woman had finally gone, it was nearly two-thirty in the morning. Outside the Crouch End police station, Tottenham Lane was a small dead river. London was asleep . . . but London never sleeps deeply, and its dreams are uneasy.

PC Vetter closed his notebook, which he'd almost filled as the American woman's strange, frenzied story poured out. He looked at the typewriter and the stack of blank forms on the shelf beside it. "This one'll look odd come morning light," he said.

PC Farnham was drinking a Coke. He didn't speak for a long time. "She was American, wasn't she?" he said finally, as if that might explain most or all of the story she had told.

"It'll go in the back file," Vetter agreed, and looked round for a cigarette. "But I wonder . . ."

Farnham laughed. "You don't mean you believe any part of it? Go on, sir! Pull the other one!"

"Didn't say that, did I? No. But you're new here."

Farnham sat a little straighter. He was twenty-seven, and it was hardly *his* fault that he had been posted here from Muswell Hill to the north, or that Vetter, who was nearly twice his age, had spent his entire uneventful career in the quiet London backwater of Crouch End.

"Perhaps so, sir," he said, "but — with respect, mind — I still think I know a swatch of the old whole cloth when I see one . . . or hear one."

"Give us a fag, mate," Vetter said, looking amused. "There! What a good boy you are." He lit it with a wooden match from a bright red railway box, shook it out, and tossed the match stub into Farnham's ashtray. He peered at the lad through a haze of drifting smoke. His own days of laddie good looks were long gone; Vetter's face was deeply lined and his nose was a map of broken veins. He liked his six of Harp a night, did PC Vetter. "You think Crouch End's a very quiet place, then, do you?"

Farnham shrugged. In truth he thought Crouch End was a big suburban yawn — what his younger brother would have been pleased to call "a fucking Bore-a-Torium."

"Yes," Vetter said, "I see you do. And you're right. Goes to sleep by eleven most nights, it does. But I've seen a lot of strange things in Crouch End. If you're here half as long as I've been, you'll see your share, too. There are more strange things happen right here in this quiet six or eight blocks than anywhere else in London — that's saying a lot, I know, but I believe it. It scares me. So I have my lager, and then I'm not so scared. You look at Sergeant Gordon sometime, Farnham, and ask yourself why his hair is dead white at forty. Or I'd say take a look at Petty, but you can't very well, can you? Petty committed suicide in the summer of 1976. Our hot summer. It was . . . ." Vetter seemed to consider his words. "It was quite bad that summer. Quite bad. There were a lot of us who were afraid they might break through."

"Who might break through what?" Farnham asked. He felt a contemptuous smile turning up the corners of his mouth, knew it was far from politic, but was unable to stop it. In his way, Vetter was raving as badly as the American woman had. He had always been a bit queer. The booze, probably. Then he saw Vetter was smiling right back at him.

"You think I'm a dotty old prat, I suppose," he said.

"Not at all, not at all," Farnham protested, groaning inwardly.

"You're a good boy," Vetter said. "Won't be riding a desk here in the station when you're my age. Not if you stick on the force. Will you stick, d'you think? D'you fancy it?"

"Yes," Farnham said. It was true; he *did* fancy it. He meant to stick even though Sheila wanted him off the police force and somewhere she could count on him. The Ford assembly line, perhaps. The thought of joining the wankers at Ford curdled his stomach.

"I thought so," Vetter said, crushing his smoke. "Gets in your blood, doesn't it? You could go far, too, and it wouldn't be boring old Crouch End you'd finish up in, either. Still, you don't know everything. Crouch End is strange. You ought to have a peek in the back file sometime, Farnham. Oh, a lot of it's the usual . . . girls and boys run away from home to be hippies or punks or whatever it is they call themselves now . . . husbands gone missing (and when you clap an eye to their

731

wives you can most times understand why) . . .
unsolved arsons . . . purse-snatchings . . . all of
that. But in between, there's enough stories to cur-
dle your blood. And some to make you sick to
your stomach."

"True word?"

Vetter nodded. "Some of em very like the one
that poor American girl just told us. She'll not
see her husband again — take my word for it."
He looked at Farnham and shrugged. "Believe me,
believe me not. It's all one, isn't it? The file's there.
We call it the open file because it's more polite
than the back file or the kiss-my-arse file. Study
it up, Farnham. Study it up."

Farnham said nothing, but he actually did intend
to "study it up." The idea that there might be
a whole series of stories such as the one the American woman had told . . . that was disturbing.

"Sometimes," Vetter said, stealing another of
Farnham's Silk Cuts, "I wonder about Dimensions."

"Dimensions?"

"Yes, my good old son — dimensions. Science
fiction writers are always on about Dimensions,
aren't they? Ever read science fiction, Farnham?"

"No," Farnham said. He had decided this was
some sort of elaborate leg-pull.

"What about Lovecraft? Ever read anything by
him?"

"Never heard of him," Farnham said. The last
fiction he'd read for pleasure, in fact, had been
a small Victorian Era pastiche called *Two Gentlemen in Silk Knickers.*

"Well, this fellow Lovecraft was always writing

732

about Dimensions," Vetter said, producing his box of railway matches. "Dimensions close to ours. Full of these immortal monsters that would drive a man mad at one look. Frightful rubbish, of course. Except, whenever one of these people straggles in, I wonder if all of it *was* rubbish. I think to myself then — when it's quiet and late at night, like now — that our whole world, everything we think of as nice and normal and sane, might be like a big leather ball filled with air. Only in some places, the leather's scuffed almost down to nothing. Places where the barriers are thinner. Do you get me?"

"Yes," Farnham said, and thought: *Maybe you ought to give me a kiss, Vetter — I always fancy a kiss when I'm getting my doodle pulled.*

"And then I think, 'Crouch End's one of those thin places.' Silly, but I *do* have those thoughts. Too imaginative, I expect; my mother always said so, anyway."

"Did she indeed?"

"Yes. Do you know what else I think?"

"No, sir — not a clue."

"Highgate's mostly all right, that's what I think — it's just as thick as you'd want between us and the Dimensions in Muswell Hill and Highgate. But now you take Archway and Finsbury Park. *They* border on Crouch End, too. I've got friends in both places, and they know of my interest in certain things that don't seem to be any way rational. Certain crazy stories which have been told, we'll say, by people with nothing to gain by making up crazy stories.

"Did it occur to you to wonder, Farnham, why

the woman would have told us the things she did if they weren't true?"

"Well . . ."

Vetter struck a match and looked at Farnham over it. "Pretty young woman, twenty-six, two kiddies back at her hotel, husband's a young lawyer doing well in Milwaukee or someplace. What's she to gain by coming in and spouting about the sort of things you only used to see in Hammer films?"

"I don't know," Farnham said stiffly. "But there may be an ex—"

"So I say to myself" — Vetter overrode him — "that if there are such things as 'thin spots,' this one would *begin* at Archway and Finsbury Park . . . but the very thinnest part is here at Crouch End. And I say to myself, wouldn't it be a day if the last of the leather between us and what's on the inside that ball just . . . rubbed away? Wouldn't it be a day if even half of what that woman told us was true?"

Farnham was silent. He had decided that PC Vetter probably also believed in palmistry and phrenology and the Rosicrucians.

"Read the back file," Vetter said, getting up. There was a crackling sound as he put his hands in the small of his back and stretched. "I'm going out to get some fresh air."

He strolled out. Farnham looked after him with a mixture of amusement and resentment. Vetter was dotty, all right. He was also a bloody fag-mooch. Fags didn't come cheap in this brave new world of the welfare state. He picked up Vetter's notebook and began leafing through the girl's story again.

And, yes, he would go through the back file. He would do it for laughs.

The girl — or young woman, if you wanted to be politically correct (and all Americans did these days, it seemed) — had burst into the station at quarter past ten the previous evening, her hair in damp strings around her face, her eyes bulging. She was dragging her purse by the strap.

"Lonnie," she said. "Please, you've got to find Lonnie."

"Well, we'll do our best, won't we?" Vetter said. "But you've got to tell us who Lonnie is."

"He's dead," the young woman said. "I know he is." She began to cry. Then she began to laugh — to cackle, really. She dropped her purse in front of her. She was hysterical.

The station was fairly deserted at that hour on a weeknight. Sergeant Raymond was listening to a Pakistani woman tell, with almost unearthly calm, how her purse had been nicked on Hillfield Avenue by a yob with a lot of football tattoos and a great coxcomb of blue hair. Vetter saw Farnham come in from the anteroom, where he had been taking down old posters (HAVE YOU ROOM IN YOUR HEART FOR AN UNWANTED CHILD?) and putting up new ones (SIX RULES FOR SAFE NIGHT-CYCLING).

Vetter waved Farnham forward and Sergeant Raymond, who had looked round at once when he heard the American woman's semi-hysterical voice, back. Raymond, who liked breaking pickpockets' fingers like breadsticks ("Aw, c'mon, mate," he'd say if asked to justify this extra-legal proceeding, "fifty million wogs can't be wrong"), was not the man for a hysterical woman.

"Lonnie!" she shrieked. "Oh, please, they've got Lonnie!"

The Pakistani woman turned toward the young American woman, studied her calmly for a moment, then turned back to Sergeant Raymond and continued to tell him how her purse had been snatched.

"Miss —" PC Farnham began.

"What's going *on* out there?" she whispered. Her breath was coming in quick pants. Farnham noticed there was a slight scratch on her left cheek. She was a pretty little hen with nice bubs — small but pert — and a great cloud of auburn hair. Her clothes were moderately expensive. The heel had come off one of her shoes.

"What's going *on* out there?" she repeated. "Monsters —"

The Pakistani woman looked over again . . . and smiled. Her teeth were rotten. The smile was gone like a conjurer's trick, and she took the Lost and Stolen Property form Raymond was holding out to her.

"Get the lady a cup of coffee and bring it down to Room Three," Vetter said. "Could you do with a cup of coffee, mum?"

"Lonnie," she whispered. "I know he's dead."

"Now, you just come along with old Ted Vetter and we'll sort this out in a jiff," he said, and helped her to her feet. She was still talking in a low moaning voice when he led her away with one arm snugged around her waist. She was rocking unsteadily because of the broken shoe.

Farnham got the coffee and brought it into Room Three, a plain white cubicle furnished with a scarred table, four chairs, and a water cooler in the corner. He put the coffee in front of her.

"Here, mum," he said, "this'll do you good. I've got some sugar if —"

"I can't drink it," she said. "I couldn't —" And then she clutched the porcelain cup, someone's long-forgotten souvenir of Blackpool, in her hands as if for warmth. Her hands were shaking quite badly, and Farnham wanted to tell her to put it down before she slopped the coffee and scalded herself.

"I couldn't," she said again. Then she drank, still holding the cup two-handed, the way a child will hold his cup of broth. And when she looked at them, it was a child's look — simple, exhausted, appealing . . . and at bay, somehow. It was as if whatever had happened had somehow shocked her young; as if some invisible hand had swooped down from the sky and slapped the last twenty years out of her, leaving a child in grownup American clothes in this small white interrogation room in Crouch End.

"Lonnie," she said. "The monsters," she said. "Will you help me? Will you please help me? Maybe he isn't dead. Maybe —

"*I'm an American citizen!*" she cried suddenly, and then, as if she had said something deeply shameful, she began to sob.

Vetter patted her shoulder. "There, mum. I think we can help find your Lonnie. Your husband, is he?"

Still sobbing, she nodded. "Danny and Norma

737

are back at the hotel . . . with the sitter . . . they'll be sleeping . . . expecting him to kiss them when we come in . . ."

"Now if you could just relax and tell us what happened —"

"And *where* it happened," Farnham added. Vetter looked up at him swiftly, frowning.

"But that's just it!" she cried. "I don't *know* where it happened! I'm not even sure *what* happened, except that it was h-huh-*horrible!*"

Vetter had taken out his notebook. "What's your name, mum?"

"Doris Freeman. My husband is Leonard Freeman. We're staying at the Hotel Inter-Continental. We're American citizens." This time the statement of nationality actually seemed to steady her a little. She sipped her coffee and put the mug down. Farnham saw that the palms of her hands were quite red. *You'll feel that later, dearie,* he thought.

Vetter was drudging it all down in his notebook. Now he looked momentarily at PC Farnham, just an unobtrusive flick of the eyes.

"Are you on holiday?" he asked.

"Yes . . . two weeks here and one in Spain. We were supposed to have a week in Barcelona . . . but this isn't helping find Lonnie! Why are you asking me these stupid questions?"

"Just trying to get the background, Mrs. Freeman," Farnham said. Without really thinking about it, both of them had adopted low, soothing voices. "Now you go ahead and tell us what happened. Tell it in your own words."

"Why is it so hard to get a taxi in London?" she asked abruptly.

738

Farnham hardly knew what to say, but Vetter responded as if the question were utterly germane to the discussion.

"Hard to say, mum. Tourists, partly. Why? Did you have trouble getting someone who'd take you out here to Crouch End?"

"Yes," she said. "We left the hotel at three and came down to Hatchard's. Do you know it?"

"Yes, mum," Vetter said. "Lovely big bookshop, isn't it?"

"We had no trouble getting a cab from the Inter-Continental . . . they were lined up outside. But when we came out of Hatchard's, there was nothing. Finally, when one *did* stop, the driver just laughed and shook his head when Lonnie said we wanted to go to Crouch End."

"Aye, they can be right barstards about the suburbs, beggin your pardon, mum," Farnham said.

"He even refused a pound tip," Doris Freeman said, and a very American perplexity had crept into her tone. "We waited for almost half an hour before we got a driver who said he'd take us. It was five-thirty by then, maybe quarter of six. And that was when Lonnie discovered he'd lost the address . . ."

She clutched the mug again.

"Who were you going to see?" Vetter asked.

"A colleague of my husband's. A lawyer named John Squales. My husband hadn't met him, but their two firms were —" She gestured vaguely.

"Affiliated?"

"Yes, I suppose. When Mr. Squales found out we were going to be in London on vacation, he invited us to his home for dinner. Lonnie had always written him at his office, of course, but he had Mr. Squales's home address on a slip of paper. After we got in the cab, he discovered he'd lost it. And all he could remember was that it was in Crouch End."

She looked at them solemnly.

"Crouch End — I think that's an ugly name."

Vetter said, "So what did you do then?"

She began to talk. By the time she'd finished, her first cup of coffee and most of another were gone, and PC Vetter had filled up several pages of his notebook with his blocky, sprawling script.

Lonnie Freeman was a big man, and hunched forward in the roomy back seat of the black cab so he could talk to the driver, he looked to her amazingly as he had when she'd first seen him at a college basketball game in their senior year — sitting on the bench, his knees somewhere up around his ears, his hands on their big wrists dangling between his legs. Only then he had been wearing basketball shorts and a towel slung around his neck, and now he was in a suit and tie. He had never gotten in many games, she remembered fondly, because he just wasn't that good. And he lost addresses.

The cabby listened indulgently to the tale of the lost address. He was an elderly man impeccably turned out in a gray summer-weight suit, the antithesis of the slouching New York cabdriver. Only the checked wool cap on the driver's head clashed, but it was an agreeable clash; it lent him a touch of rakish charm. Outside, the traffic flowed endlessly past on Haymarket; the theater nearby announced that *The Phantom of the Opera* was continuing its apparently endless run.

"Well, I tell you what, guv," the cabby said. "I'll take yer there to Crouch End, and we'll stop at a call box, and you check your governor's address, and off we go, right to the door."

"That's wonderful," Doris said, really meaning it. They had been in London six days now, and she could not recall ever having been in a place where the people were kinder or more civilized.

"Thanks," Lonnie said, and sat back. He put his arm around Doris and smiled. "See? No problem."

"No thanks to you," she mock-growled, and threw a light punch at his midsection.

"Right," the cabby said. "Heigh-ho for Crouch End."

It was late August, and a steady hot wind rattled the trash across the roads and whipped at the jackets and skirts of the men and women going home from work. The sun was settling, but when it shone between the buildings, Doris saw that it was beginning to take on the reddish cast of evening. The cabby hummed. She relaxed with Lonnie's arm around her — she had seen more of him in the last six days than she had all year, it seemed, and she was very pleased to discover that she liked it. She had never been out of America before, either, and she had to keep reminding herself that she was in England, she was going to *Barcelona*, thousands should be so lucky.

Then the sun disappeared behind a wall of buildings, and she lost her sense of direction almost immediately. Cab rides in London did that to you,

741

she had discovered. The city was a great sprawling warren of Roads and Mews and Hills and Closes (even Inns), and she couldn't understand how anyone could get around. When she had mentioned it to Lonnie the day before, he had replied that they got around very carefully . . . hadn't she noticed that all the cabbies kept the *London Streetfinder* tucked cozily away beneath the dash?

This was the longest cab ride they had taken. The fashionable section of town dropped behind them (in spite of that perverse going-around-in-circles feeling). They passed through an area of monolithic housing developments that could have been utterly deserted for all the signs of life they showed (no, she corrected herself to Vetter and Farnham in the small white room; she had seen one small boy sitting on the curb, striking matches), then an area of small, rather tatty-looking shops and fruit stalls, and then — no wonder driving in London was so disorienting to out-of-towners — they seemed to have driven smack into the fashionable section again.

"There was even a McDonald's," she told Vetter and Farnham in a tone of voice usually reserved for references to the Sphinx and the Hanging Gardens.

"*Was* there?" Vetter replied, properly amazed and respectful — she had achieved a kind of total recall, and he wanted nothing to break the mood, at least until she had told them everything she could.

The fashionable section with the McDonald's as its centerpiece dropped away. They came briefly into the clear and now the sun was a solid orange ball sitting above the horizon, washing the streets with a strange light that made all the pedestrians look as if they were about to burst into flame.

"It was then that things began to change," she said. Her voice had dropped a little. Her hands were trembling again.

Vetter leaned forward, intent. "Changed? How? How did things change, Mrs. Freeman?"

They had passed a newsagent's window, she said, and the signboard outside had read SIXTY LOST IN UNDERGROUND HORROR.

"Lonnie, look at that!"

"What?" He craned around, but the newsagent's was already behind them.

"It said, 'Sixty Lost in Underground Horror.' Isn't that what they call the subway? The Underground?"

"Yes — that or the tube. Was it a crash?"

"I don't know." She leaned forward. "Driver, do you know what that was about? Was there a subway crash?"

"A collision, mum? Not that I know of."

"Do you have a radio?"

"Not in the cab, mum."

"Lonnie?"

"Hmmm?"

But she could see that Lonnie had lost interest. He was going through his pockets again (and because he was wearing his three-piece suit, there were a lot of them to go through), having another hunt for the scrap of paper with John Squales's address written on it.

The message chalked on the board played over

and over in her mind, SIXTY KILLED IN TUBE CRASH, it should have read. But . . . SIXTY LOST IN UNDERGROUND HORROR. It made her uneasy. It didn't say "killed," it said "lost," the way news reports in the old days had always referred to sailors who had been drowned at sea.

UNDERGROUND HORROR.

She didn't like it. It made her think of graveyards, sewers, and flabby-pale, noisome things swarming suddenly out of the tubes themselves, wrapping their arms (tentacles, maybe) around the hapless commuters on the platforms, dragging them away to darkness. . . .

They turned right. Standing on the corner beside their parked motorcycles were three boys in leathers. They looked up at the cab and for a moment — the setting sun was almost full in her face from this angle — it seemed that the bikers did not have human heads at all. For that one moment she was nastily sure that the sleek heads of rats sat atop those black leather jackets, rats with black eyes staring at the cab. Then the light shifted just a tiny bit and she saw of course she had been mistaken; there were only three young men smoking cigarettes in front of the British version of the American candy store.

"Here we go," Lonnie said, giving up the search and pointing out the window. They were passing a sign which read "Crouch Hill Road." Elderly brick houses like sleepy dowagers had closed in, seeming to look down at the cab from their blank windows. A few kids passed back and forth, riding bikes or trikes. Two others were trying to ride a skateboard with no notable success. Fathers home from work sat together, smoking and talking and watching the children. It all looked reassuringly normal.

The cab drew up in front of a dismal-looking restaurant with a small spotted sign in the window reading FULLY LICENSED and a much larger one in the center which informed that within one could purchase curries to take away. On the inner ledge there slept a gigantic gray cat. Beside the restaurant was a call box.

"Here you are, guv," the cabdriver said. "You find your friend's address and I'll track him down."

"Fair enough," Lonnie said, and got out.

Doris sat in the cab for a moment and then also emerged, deciding she felt like stretching her legs. The hot wind was still blowing. It whipped her skirt around her knees and then plastered an old ice-cream wrapper to her shin. She removed it with a grimace of disgust. When she looked up, she was staring directly through the plate-glass window at the big gray tom. It stared back at her, one-eyed and inscrutable. Half of its face had been all but clawed away in some long-ago battle. What remained was a twisted pinkish mass of scar tissue, one milky cataract, and a few tufts of fur.

It miaowed at her silently through the glass.

Feeling a surge of disgust, she went to the call box and peered in through one of the dirty panes. Lonnie made a circle at her with his thumb and forefinger and winked. Then he pushed tenpence into the slot and talked with someone. He laughed — soundlessly through the glass. Like the cat. She looked over for it, but now the window was empty. In the dimness beyond she could see chairs up on tables and an old man pushing a broom. When she looked back, she saw that Lonnie was jotting something down. He put his pen away, held the paper in his hand — she could see an address was jotted on it — said one or two other things, then hung up and came out.

He waggled the address at her in triumph. "Okay, that's th—" His eyes went past her shoulder and he frowned. "Where's the stupid *cab* gone?"

She turned around. The taxi had vanished. Where it had stood there was only curbing and a few papers blowing lazily up the gutter. Across the street, two kids were clutching at each other and giggling. Doris noticed that one of them had a deformed hand — it looked more like a claw. She'd thought the National Health was supposed to take care of things like that. The children looked across the street, saw her observing them, and fell into each other's arms, giggling again.

"*I* don't know," Doris said. She felt disoriented and a little stupid. The heat, the constant wind that seemed to blow with no gusts or drops, the almost painted quality of the light . . .

"What time was it then?" Farnham asked suddenly.

"I don't know," Doris Freeman said, startled out of her recital. "Six, I suppose. Maybe twenty past."

"I see, go on," Farnham said, knowing perfectly well that in August sunset would not have begun

— even by the loosest standards — until well past seven.

"Well, what did he *do?*" Lonnie asked, still looking around. It was almost as if he expected his irritation to cause the cab to pop back into view. "Just pick up and leave?"

"Maybe when you put your hand up," Doris said, raising her own hand and making the thumb-and-forefinger circle Lonnie had made in the call box, "maybe when you did that he thought you were waving him on."

"I'd have to wave a long time to send him on with two-fifty on the meter," Lonnie grunted, and walked over to the curb. On the other side of Crouch Hill Road, the two small children were still giggling. "Hey!" Lonnie called. "You kids!"

"You an American, sir?" the boy with the claw-hand called back.

"Yes," Lonnie said, smiling. "Did you see the cab over here? Did you see where it went?"

The two children seemed to consider the question. The boy's companion was a girl of about five with untidy brown braids sticking off in opposite directions. She stepped forward to the opposite curb, formed her hands into a megaphone, and still smiling — she screamed it through her megaphoned hands and her smile — she cried at them: *"Bugger off, Joe!"*

Lonnie's mouth dropped open.

"Sir! Sir! Sir!" the boy screeched, saluting wildly with his deformed hand. Then the two of them took to their heels and fled around the corner and out of sight, leaving only their laughter to echo back.

Lonnie looked at Doris, dumbstruck.

"I guess some of the kids in Crouch End aren't too crazy about Americans," he said lamely.

She looked around nervously. The street now appeared deserted.

He slipped an arm around her. "Well, honey, looks like we hike."

"I'm not sure I want to. Those two kids might've gone to get their big brothers." She laughed to show it was a joke, but there was a shrill quality to the sound. The evening had taken on a surreal quality she didn't much like. She wished they had stayed at the hotel.

"Not much else we can do," he said. "The street's not exactly overflowing with taxis, is it?"

"Lonnie, why would the cabdriver leave us here like that? He seemed so *nice*."

"Don't have the slightest idea. But John gave me good directions. He lives in a street called Brass End, which is a very minor dead-end street, and he said it wasn't in the *Streetfinder*." As he talked he was moving her away from the call box, from the restaurant that sold curries to take away, from the now-empty curb. They were walking up Crouch Hill Road again. "We take a right onto Hillfield Avenue, left halfway down, then our first right . . . or was it left? Anyway, onto Petrie Street. Second left is Brass End."

"And you remember all that?"

"I'm a star witness," he said bravely, and she just had to laugh. Lonnie had a way of making things seem better.

There was a map of the Crouch End area on

the wall of the police station lobby, one considerably more detailed than the one in the *London Streetfinder*. Farnham approached it and studied it with his hands stuffed into his pockets. The station seemed very quiet now. Vetter was still outside — clearing some of the witchmoss from his brains, one hoped — and Raymond had long since finished with the woman who'd had her purse nicked.

Farnham put his finger on the spot where the cabby had most likely let them off (if anything about the woman's story was to be believed, that was). The route to their friend's house looked pretty straightforward. Crouch Hill Road to Hillfield Avenue, then a left onto Vickers Lane followed by a left onto Petrie Street. Brass End, which stuck off from Petrie Street like somebody's afterthought, was no more than six or eight houses long. About a mile, all told. Even Americans should have been able to walk that far without getting lost.

"Raymond!" he called. "You still here?"

Sergeant Raymond came in. He had changed into streets and was putting on a light poplin windcheater. "Only just, my beardless darling."

"Cut it," Farnham said, smiling all the same. Raymond frightened him a little. One look at the spooky sod was enough to tell you he was standing a little too close to the fence that ran between the yard of the good guys and that of the villains. There was a twisted white line of scar running like a fat string from the left corner of his mouth almost all the way to his Adam's apple. He claimed a pickpocket had once nearly cut his throat with a jagged bit of bottle. Claimed that's why he broke their fingers. Farnham thought that was the shit. He thought Raymond broke their fingers because he liked the sound they made, especially when they popped at the knuckles.

"Got a fag?" Raymond asked.

Farnham sighed and gave him one. As he lit it he asked, "Is there a curry shop on Crouch Hill Road?"

"Not to my knowledge, my dearest darling," Raymond said.

"That's what I thought."

"Got a problem, dear?"

"No," Farnham said, a little too sharply, remembering Doris Freeman's clotted hair and staring eyes.

Near the top of Crouch Hill Road, Doris and Lonnie Freeman turned onto Hillfield Avenue, which was lined with imposing and gracious-looking homes — nothing but shells, she thought, probably cut up with surgical precision into apartments and bed-sitters inside.

"So far so good," Lonnie said.

"Yes, it's —" she began, and that was when the low moaning arose.

They both stopped. The moaning was coming almost directly from their right, where a high hedge ran around a small yard. Lonnie started toward the sound, and she grasped his arm. "Lonnie, no!"

"What do you mean, no?" he asked. "Someone's hurt."

She stepped after him nervously. The hedge was

high but thin. He was able to brush it aside and reveal a small square of lawn outlined with flowers. The lawn was very green. In the center of it was a black, smoking patch — or at least that was her first impression. When she peered around Lonnie's shoulder again — his shoulder was too high for her to peer over it — she saw it was a hole, vaguely man-shaped. The tendrils of smoke were emanating from it.

SIXTY LOST IN UNDERGROUND HORROR, she thought abruptly.

The moaning was coming from the hole, and Lonnie began to force himself through the hedge toward it.

"Lonnie," she said, "please, don't."

"Someone's hurt," he repeated, and pushed himself the rest of the way through with a bristly tearing sound. She saw him going toward the hole, and then the hedge snapped back, leaving her nothing but a vague impression of his shape as he moved forward. She tried to push through after him and was scratched by the short, stiff branches of the hedge for her trouble. She was wearing a sleeveless blouse.

"Lonnie!" she called, suddenly very afraid. "Lonnie, come back!"

"Just a minute, hon!"

The house looked at her impassively over the top of the hedge.

The moaning sounds continued, but now they sounded lower — guttural, somehow gleeful. Couldn't Lonnie *hear* that?

"Hey, is somebody down there?" she heard Lonnie ask. "Is there — oh! Hey! *Jesus!*" And suddenly

751

Lonnie screamed. She had never heard him scream before, and her legs seemed to turn to waterbags at the sound. She looked wildly for a break in the hedge, a path, and couldn't see one anywhere. Images swirled before her eyes — the bikers who had looked like rats for a moment, the cat with the pink chewed face, the boy with the claw-hand.

Lonnie! she tried to scream, but no words came out.

Now there were sounds of a struggle. The moaning had stopped. But there were wet, sloshing sounds from the other side of the hedge. Then, suddenly, Lonnie came flying back through the stiff dusty-green bristles as if he had been given a tremendous push. The left arm of his suit-coat was torn, and it was splattered with runnels of black stuff that seemed to be smoking, as the pit in the lawn had been smoking.

"Doris, run!"

"Lonnie, what —"

"Run!" His face pale as cheese.

Doris looked around wildly for a cop. For *any-one*. But Hillfield Avenue might have been a part of some great deserted city for all the life or movement she saw. Then she glanced back at the hedge and saw something else was moving behind there, something that was more than black; it seemed ebony, the antithesis of light.

And it was sloshing.

A moment later, the short, stiff branches of the hedge began to rustle. She stared, hypnotized. She might have stood there forever (so she told Vetter and Farnham) if Lonnie hadn't grabbed her arm roughly and shrieked at her — yes, Lonnie, who never even raised his voice at the kids, had *shrieked* — she might have been standing there yet. Standing there, or . . .

But they ran.

Where? Farnham had asked, but she didn't know. Lonnie was totally undone, in a hysteria of panic and revulsion — that was all she really knew. He clamped his fingers over her wrist like a handcuff and they ran from the house looming over the hedge, and from the smoking hole in the lawn. She knew those things for sure; all the rest was only a chain of vague impressions.

At first it had been hard to run, and then it got easier because they were going downhill. They turned, then turned again. Gray houses with high stoops and drawn green shades seemed to stare at them like blind pensioners. She remembered Lonnie pulling off his jacket, which had been splattered with that black goo, and throwing it away. At last they came to a wider street.

"Stop," she panted. "Stop, I can't keep up!" Her free hand was pressed to her side, where a red-hot spike seemed to have been planted.

And he did stop. They had come out of the residential area and were standing at the corner of Crouch Lane and Norris Road. A sign on the far side of Norris Road proclaimed that they were but one mile from Slaughter Towen.

Town? Vetter suggested.

No, Doris Freeman said. Slaughter *Towen*, with an "e."

Raymond crushed out the cigarette he had cadged from Farnham. "I'm off," he announced, and then looked more closely at Farnham. "My poppet should take better care of himself. He's got big dark circles under his eyes. Any hair on your palms to go with it, my pet?" He laughed uproariously.

"Ever hear of a Crouch Lane?" Farnham asked.

"Crouch Hill Road, you mean."

"No, I mean Crouch Lane."

"Never heard of it."

"What about Norris Road?"

"There's the one cuts off from the high street in Basingstoke —"

"No, here."

"No — *not* here, poppet."

For some reason he couldn't understand — the woman was obviously buzzed — Farnham persisted. "What about Slaughter Towen?"

"Towen, you said? Not Town?"

"Yes, that's right."

"Never heard of it, but if I do, I believe I'll steer clear."

"Why's that?"

"Because in the old Druid lingo, a touen or towen was a place of ritual sacrifice — where they abstracted your liver and lights, in other words." And zipping up his windcheater, Raymond glided out.

Farnham looked after him uneasily. *He made that last up*, he told himself. *What a hard copper like Sid Raymond knows about the Druids you could carve on the head of a pin and still have room for the Lord's Prayer.*

Right. And even if he *had* picked up a piece of information like that, it didn't change the fact that the woman was . . .

"Must be going crazy," Lonnie said, and laughed shakily.

Doris had looked at her watch earlier and saw that somehow it had gotten to be quarter of eight. The light had changed; from a clear orange it had gone to a thick, murky red that glared off the windows of the shops in Norris Road and seemed to face a church steeple across the way in clotted blood. The sun was an oblate sphere on the horizon.

"What happened back there?" Doris asked. "What was it, Lonnie?"

"Lost my jacket, too. Hell of a note."

"You didn't lose it, you took it off. It was covered with —"

"Don't be a fool!" he snapped at her. But his eyes were not snappish; they were soft, shocked, wandering. "I lost it, that's all."

"Lonnie, what happened when you went through the hedge?"

"Nothing. Let's not talk about it. Where are we?"

"Lonnie —"

"I can't remember," he said more softly. "It's all a blank. We were there . . . we heard a sound . . . then I was running. That's all I can remember." And then he added in a frighteningly childish voice: "Why would I throw my jacket away? I liked that one. It matched the pants." He threw back his head, gave voice to a frightening loonlike laugh, and Doris suddenly realized that whatever he had seen beyond the hedge had at least partially

755

unhinged him. She was not sure the same wouldn't have happened to her . . . if she had seen. It didn't matter. They had to get out of here. Get back to the hotel where the kids were.

"Let's get a cab. I want to go home."

"But John —" he began.

"*Never mind John!*" she cried. "It's wrong, everything here is wrong, *and I want to get a cab and go home!*"

"Yes, all right. Okay." Lonnie passed a shaking hand across his forehead. "I'm with you. The only problem is, there aren't any."

There was, in fact, no traffic at all on Norris Road, which was wide and cobbled. Directly down the center of it ran a set of old tram tracks. On the other side, in front of a flower shop, an ancient three-wheeled D-car was parked. Farther down on their own side, a Yamaha motorbike stood aslant on its kickstand. That was all. They could *hear* cars, but the sound was faraway, diffuse.

"Maybe the street's closed for repairs," Lonnie muttered, and then had done a strange thing . . . strange, at least, for him, who was ordinarily so easy and self-assured. He looked back over his shoulder as if afraid they had been followed.

"We'll walk," she said.

"Where?"

"Anywhere. Away from Crouch End. We can get a taxi if we get away from here." She was suddenly positive of that, if of nothing else.

"All right." Now he seemed perfectly willing to entrust the leadership of the whole matter to her.

They began walking along Norris Road toward

the setting sun. The faraway hum of the traffic remained constant, not seeming to diminish, not seeming to grow any, either. It was like the constant push of the wind. The desertion was beginning to nibble at her nerves. She felt they were being watched, tried to dismiss the feeling, and found that she couldn't. The sound of their footfalls

(SIXTY LOST IN UNDERGROUND HORROR)

echoed back to them. The business at the hedge played on her mind more and more, and finally she had to ask again.

"Lonnie, what *was* it?"

He answered simply: "I don't remember. And I don't *want* to."

They passed a market that was closed — a pile of coconuts like shrunken heads seen back-to were piled against the window. They passed a launderette where white machines had been pulled from the washed-out pink plasterboard walls like square teeth from dying gums. They passed a soap-streaked show window with an old SHOP TO LEASE sign in the front. Something moved behind the soap streaks, and Doris saw, peering out at her, the pink and tufted battle-scarred face of a cat. The same gray tom.

She consulted her interior workings and tickings and discovered that she was in a state of slowly building terror. She felt as if her intestines had begun to crawl sluggishly around and around within her belly. Her mouth had a sharp unpleasant taste, almost as if she had dosed with a strong mouthwash. The cobbles of Norris Road bled fresh blood in the sunset.

They were approaching an underpass. And it was dark under there. *I can't,* her mind informed her matter-of-factly. *I can't go under there, anything might be under there, don't ask me because I can't.*

Another part of her mind asked if she could bear for them to retrace their steps, past the empty shop with the travelling cat in it (how had it gotten from the restaurant to here? best not to ask, or even wonder about it too deeply), past the weirdly oral shambles of the launderette, past The Market of the Shrunken Heads. She didn't think she could.

They had drawn closer to the underpass now. A strangely painted six-car train — it was bone-white — lunged over it with startling suddenness, a crazy steel bride rushing to meet her groom. The wheels kicked up bright spinners of sparks. They both leaped back involuntarily, but it was Lonnie who cried out. She looked at him and saw that in the last hour he had turned into someone she had never seen before, had never even suspected. His hair appeared somehow grayer, and while she told herself firmly — as firmly as she could — that it was just a trick of the light, it was the look of his hair that decided her. Lonnie was in no shape to go back. Therefore, the underpass.

"Come on," she said, and took his hand. She took it brusquely so he would not feel her own trembling. "Soonest begun, soonest done." She walked forward and he followed docilely.

They were almost out — it was a very short underpass, she thought with ridiculous relief — when the hand grasped her upper arm.

She didn't scream. Her lungs seemed to have

collapsed like small crumpled paper sacks. Her mind wanted to leave her body behind and just . . . fly. Lonnie's hand parted from her own. He seemed unaware. He walked out on the other side — she saw him for just one moment silhouetted, tall and lanky, against the bloody, furious colors of the sunset, and then he was gone.

The hand grasping her upper arm was hairy, like an ape's hand. It turned her remorselessly toward a heavy slumped shape leaning against the sooty concrete wall. It hung there in the double shadow of two concrete supporting pillars, and the shape was all she could make out . . . the shape, and two luminous green eyes.

"Give us a fag, love," a husky cockney voice said, and she smelled raw meat and deep-fat-fried chips and something sweet and awful, like the residue at the bottom of garbage cans.

Those green eyes were cat's eyes. And suddenly she became horribly sure that if the slumped shape stepped out of the shadows, she would see the milky cataract of eye, the pink ridges of scar tissue, the tufts of gray hair.

She tore free, backed up, and felt something skid through the air near her. A hand? Claws? A spitting, hissing sound —

Another train charged overhead. The roar was huge, brain-rattling. Soot sifted down like black snow. She fled in a blind panic, for the second time that evening not knowing where . . . or for how long.

What brought her back to herself was the realization that Lonnie was gone. She had half collapsed against a dirty brick wall, breathing in great tearing gasps. She was still in Norris Road (at least she believed herself to be, she told the two constables; the wide way was still cobbled, and the tram tracks still ran directly down the center), but the deserted, decaying shops had given way to deserted, decaying warehouses. DAWGLISH & SONS, read the soot-begrimed signboard on one. A second had the name ALHAZRED emblazoned in ancient green across the faded brickwork. Below the name was a series of Arabic pothooks and dashes.

"Lonnie!" she called. There was no echo, no carrying in spite of the silence (no, not complete silence, she told them; there was still the sound of traffic, and it might have been closer, but not much). The word that stood for her husband seemed to drop from her mouth and fall like a stone at her feet. The blood of sunset had been replaced by the cool gray ashes of twilight. For the first time it occurred to her that night might fall upon her here in Crouch End — if she was still indeed *in* Crouch End — and that thought brought fresh terror.

She told Vetter and Farnham that there had been no reflection, no logical train of thought, on her part during the unknown length of time between their arrival at the call box and the final horror. She had simply reacted, like a frightened animal. And now she was alone. She wanted Lonnie, she was aware of that much but little else. Certainly it did not occur to her to wonder why this area, which must surely lie within five miles of Cambridge Circus, should be utterly deserted.

Doris Freeman set off walking, calling for her husband. Her voice did not echo, but her footfalls seemed to. The shadows began to fill Norris Road. Overhead, the sky was now purple. It might have been some distorting effect of the twilight, or her own exhaustion, but the warehouses seemed to lean hungrily over the road. The windows, caked with the dirt of decades — of centuries, perhaps — seemed to be staring at her. And the names on the signboards became progressively stranger, even lunatic, at the very least, unpronounceable. The vowels were in the wrong places, and consonants had been strung together in a way that would make it impossible for any human tongue to get around them. CTHULHU KRYON read one, with more of those Arabic pothooks beneath it. YOGSOGGOTH read another. R'YELEH said yet another. There was one that she remembered particularly: NRTESN NYARLAHOTEP.

"How could you remember such gibberish?" Farnham asked her.

Doris Freeman shook her head, slowly and tiredly. "I don't know. I really don't. It's like a nightmare you want to forget as soon as you wake up, but it won't fade away like most dreams do; it just stays and stays and stays."

Norris Road seemed to stretch on into infinity, cobbled, split by tram tracks. And although she continued to walk — she wouldn't have believed she could run, although later, she said, she did — she no longer called for Lonnie. She was in the grip of a terrible, bone-rattling fear, a fear so great she would not have believed a human being could endure it without going mad or drop-

761

ping dead. It was impossible for her to articulate her fear except in one way, and even this, she said, only began to bridge the gulf which had opened within her mind and heart. She said it was as if she were no longer on earth but on a different planet, a place so alien that the human mind could not even begin to comprehend it. The *angles* seemed different, she said. The *colors* seemed different. The . . . but it was hopeless.

She could only walk under a gnarled-plum sky between the eldritch bulking buildings, and hope that it would end.

As it did.

She became aware of two figures standing on the sidewalk ahead of her — the children she and Lonnie had seen earlier. The boy was using his claw-hand to stroke the little girl's ratty braids.

"It's the American woman," the boy said.

"She's lost," said the girl.

"Lost her husband."

"Lost her way."

"Found the darker way."

"The road that leads into the funnel."

"Lost her hope."

"Found the Whistler from the Stars —"

"— Eater of Dimensions —"

"— the Blind Piper —"

Faster and faster their words came, a breathless litany, a flashing loom. Her head spun with them. The buildings leaned. The stars were out, but they were not *her* stars, the ones she had wished on as a girl or courted under as a young woman, these were crazed stars in lunatic constellations, and her hands went to her ears and her hands did not shut out the sounds and finally she screamed at them:

"Where's my husband? Where's Lonnie? What have you done to him?"

There was silence. And then the girl said: "He's gone beneath."

The boy: "Gone to the Goat with a Thousand Young."

The girl smiled — a malicious smile full of evil innocence. "He couldn't well not go, could he? The mark was on him. You'll go, too."

"Lonnie! *What have you done with —*"

The boy raised his hand and chanted in a high fluting language that she could not understand — but the sound of the words drove Doris Freeman nearly mad with fear.

"The street began to move then," she told Vetter and Farnham. "The cobbles began to undulate like a carpet. They rose and fell, rose and fell. The tram tracks came loose and flew into the air — I remember that, I remember the starlight shining on them — and then the cobbles themselves began to come loose, one by one at first, and then in bunches. They just flew off into the darkness. There was a tearing sound when they came loose. A grinding, tearing sound . . . the way an earthquake must sound. And — something started to *come through —*"

"What?" Vetter asked. He was hunched forward, his eyes boring into her. "What did you see? What was it?"

"Tentacles," she said, slowly and haltingly. "I think it was tentacles. But they were as thick as old banyan trees, as if each of them was made up of a thousand smaller ones . . . and there were

763

pink things like suckers . . . except sometimes they looked like faces . . . one of them looked like Lonnie's face . . . and all of them were in agony. Below them, in the darkness under the street — in the darkness *beneath* — there was something else. Something like *eyes* . . ."

At that point she had broken down, unable to go on for some time, and as it turned out, there was really no more to tell. The next thing she remembered with any clarity was cowering in the doorway of a closed newsagent's shop. She might be there yet, she had told them, except that she had seen cars passing back and forth just up ahead, and the reassuring glow of arc-sodium streetlights. Two people had passed in front of her, and Doris had cringed farther back into the shadows, afraid of the two evil children. But these were not children, she saw; they were a teenage boy and girl walking hand in hand. The boy was saying something about the new Martin Scorsese film.

She'd come out onto the sidewalk warily, ready to dart back into the convenient bolthole of the newsagent's doorway at a moment's notice, but there was no need. Fifty yards up was a moderately busy intersection, with cars and lorries standing at a stop-and-go light. Across the way was a jeweler's shop with a large lighted clock in the show window. A steel accordion grille had been drawn across, but she could still make out the time. It was five minutes of ten.

She had walked up to the intersection then, and despite the streetlights and the comforting rumble of traffic, she had kept shooting terrified glances back over her shoulder. She ached all over. She was limping on one broken heel. She had pulled muscles in her belly and both legs — her right leg was particularly bad, as if she had strained something in it.

At the intersection she saw that somehow she had come around to Hillfield Avenue and Tottenham Road. Under a streetlamp a woman of about sixty with her graying hair escaping from the rag it was done up in was talking to a man of about the same age. They both looked at Doris as if she were some sort of dreadful apparition.

"Police," Doris Freeman croaked. "Where's the police station? I'm an American citizen . . . I've lost my husband . . . I need the police."

"What's happened, then, lovey?" the woman asked, not unkindly. "You look like you've been through the wringer, you do."

"Car accident?" her companion asked.

"No. Not . . . not . . . Please, is there a police station near here?"

"Right up Tottenham Road," the man said. He took a package of Players from his pocket. "Like a cig? You look like you c'd use one."

"Thank you," she said, and took the cigarette although she had quit nearly four years ago. The elderly man had to follow the jittering tip of it with his lighted match to get it going for her.

He glanced at the woman with her hair bound up in the rag. "I'll just take a little stroll up with her, Evvie. Make sure she gets there all right."

"I'll come along as well, then, won't I?" Evvie said, and put an arm around Doris's shoulders. "Now what is it, lovey? Did someone try to mug you?"

"No," Doris said. "It . . . I . . . I . . . the street . . . there was a cat with only one eye . . . the street opened up . . . I *saw* it . . . and they said something about a Blind Piper . . . I've got to find Lonnie!"

She was aware that she was speaking incoherencies, but she seemed helpless to be any clearer. And at any rate, she told Vetter and Farnham, she hadn't been all *that* incoherent, because the man and woman had drawn away from her, as if, when Evvie asked what the matter was, Doris had told her it was bubonic plague.

The man said something then — "Happened again," Doris thought it was.

The woman pointed. "Station's right up there. Globes hanging in front. You'll see it." Moving very quickly, the two of them began to walk away. The woman glanced back over her shoulder once; Doris Freeman saw her wide, gleaming eyes. Doris took two steps after them, for what reason she did not know. "Don't ye come near!" Evvie called shrilly, and forked the sign of the evil eye at her. She simultaneously cringed against the man, who put an arm about her. "Don't you come near, if you've been to Crouch End Towen!"

And with that, the two of them had disappeared into the night.

Now PC Farnham stood leaning in the doorway between the common room and the main filing room — although the back files Vetter had spoken of were certainly not kept here. Farnham had made himself a fresh cup of tea and was smoking the last cigarette in his pack — the woman had also

766

helped herself to several.

She'd gone back to her hotel, in the company of the nurse Vetter had called — the nurse would be staying with her tonight, and would make a judgement in the morning as to whether the woman would need to go in hospital. The children would make that difficult, Farnham supposed, and the woman's being an American almost guaranteed a first-class cock-up. He wondered what she was going to tell the kiddies when they woke up to-morrow, assuming she was capable of telling them anything. Would she gather them round and tell them that the big bad monster of Crouch End Town

(Towen)

had eaten up Daddy like an ogre in a fairy-story?

Farnham grimaced and put down his teacup. It wasn't his problem. For good or for ill, Mrs. Freeman had become sandwiched between the British constabulary and the American Embassy in the great waltz of governments. It was none of his affair; he was only a PC who wanted to forget the whole thing. And he intended to let Vetter write the report. Vetter could afford to put his name to such a bouquet of lunacy; he was an old man, used up. He would still be a PC on the night shift when he got his gold watch, his pension, and his council flat. Farnham, on the other hand, had ambitions of making sergeant soon, and that meant he had to watch every little posey.

And speaking of Vetter, where was he? He'd been taking the night air for quite awhile now.

Farnham crossed the common room and went out. He stood between the two lighted globes and stared across Tottenham Road. Vetter was nowhere in sight. It was past 3:00 A.M., and silence lay thick and even, like a shroud. What was that line from Wordsworth? "All that great heart lying still," or something like.

He went down the steps and stood on the sidewalk, feeling a trickle of unease now. It was silly, of course, and he was angry with himself for allowing the woman's mad story to gain even this much of a foothold in his head. Perhaps he *deserved* to be afraid of a hard copper like Sid Raymond.

Farnham walked slowly up to the corner, thinking he would meet Vetter coming back from his night stroll. But he would go no farther; if the station was left empty even for a few moments, there would be hell to pay if it was discovered. He reached the corner and looked around. It was funny, but all the arc-sodiums seemed to have gone out up here. The entire street looked different without them. Would it have to be reported, he wondered? And where was Vetter?

He would walk just a little farther, he decided, and see what was what. But not far. It simply wouldn't do to leave the station unattended for long.

Just a little way.

Vetter came in less than five minutes after Farnham had left. Farnham had gone in the opposite direction, and if Vetter had come along a minute earlier, he would have seen the young constable standing indecisively at the corner for a moment before turning it and disappearing forever.

"Farnham?"

768

No answer but the buzz of the clock on the wall.

"Farnham?" he called again, and then wiped his mouth with the palm of his hand.

Lonnie Freeman was never found. Eventually his wife (who had begun to gray around the temples) flew back to America with her children. They went on Concorde. A month later she attempted suicide. She spent ninety days in a rest home and came out much improved. Sometimes when she cannot sleep — this occurs most frequently on nights when the sun goes down in a ball of red and orange — she creeps into her closet, knee-walks under the hanging dresses all the way to the back, and there she writes *Beware the Goat with a Thousand Young* over and over with a soft pencil. It seems to ease her somehow to do this.

PC Robert Farnham left a wife and two-year-old twin girls. Sheila Farnham wrote a series of angry letters to her MP, insisting that something was going on, something was being covered up, that her Bob had been enticed into taking some dangerous sort of undercover assignment. He would have done anything to make sergeant, Mrs. Farnham repeatedly told the MP. Eventually that worthy stopped answering her letters, and at about the same time Doris Freeman was coming out of the rest home, her hair almost entirely white now, Mrs. Farnham moved back to Essex, where her parents lived. Eventually she married a man in a safer line of work — Frank Hobbs is a bumper inspector on the Ford assembly line. It had been necessary to get a divorce from her Bob on grounds of desertion, but that was easily managed.

Vetter took early retirement about four months after Doris Freeman had stumbled into the station in Tottenham Lane. He did indeed move into council housing, a two-above-the-shops in Frimley. Six months later he was found dead of a heart attack, a can of Harp Lager in his hand.

And in Crouch End, which is really a quiet suburb of London, strange things still happen from time to time, and people have been known to lose their way. Some of them lose it forever.

The House on Maple Street

Although she was only five, and the youngest of the Bradbury children, Melissa had very sharp eyes and it wasn't really surprising that she was the first to discover something strange had happened to the house on Maple Street while the Bradbury family was summering in England.

She ran and found her older brother, Brian, and told him something was wrong upstairs, on the third floor. She said she would show him, but not until he swore not to tell *anyone* what she had found. Brian swore, knowing it was their step-father Lissa was afraid of; Daddy Lew didn't like it when any of the Bradbury children "got up to foolishness" (that was how he always put it), and he had decided that Melissa was the prime offender in that area. Lissa, who was stupid no more than she was blind, was aware of Lew's prejudices, and had become wary of them. In fact, all of the Brad-bury children had become rather wary of their mother's second husband.

It would probably turn out to be nothing, any-way, but Brian was delighted to be back home and willing enough to humor his baby sister (Brian was two full years her senior), at least for awhile; he followed her down the third-floor hallway with-out so much as a murmur of argument, and he only pulled her braids — he called these braid-pulls "emergency stops" — once.

They had to tiptoe past Lew's study, which was the only finished-off room up here, because Lew was inside, unpacking his notebooks and papers and muttering in an ill-tempered way. Brian's thoughts had actually turned to what might be on TV tonight — he was looking forward to a pig-out on good old American cable after three months of BBC and ITV — when they reached the end of the hall.

What he saw beyond the tip of his little sister's pointing finger drove all thoughts of television from Brian Bradbury's mind.

"Now swear again!" Lissa whispered. "Never tell *anyone*, Daddy Lew or *anyone*, or hope to die!"

"Hope to die," Brian agreed, still staring, and it *was* a half-hour before he told his big sister, Laurie, who was unpacking in her room. Laurie was possessive of her room as only an eleven-year-old girl can be, and she gave Brian the very dickens for coming in without knocking, even though she was completely dressed.

"Sorry," Brian said, "but I gotta show you something. It's *very* weird."

"Where?" She went on putting clothes in her drawers as if she didn't care, as if there was nothing any dopey little seven-year-old could tell her which would be of the *slightest* interest to her, but when it came to eyes, Brian's weren't exactly dull. He could tell when Laurie was interested, and she was interested now.

"Upstairs. Third floor. End of the hall past Daddy Lew's study."

Laurie's nose wrinkled as it always did when

Brian or Lissa called him that. She and Trent remembered their real father, and they didn't like his replacement at all. They made it their business to call him Just Plain Lew. That Lewis Evans clearly did not like this — found it vaguely impertinent, in fact — simply added to Laurie and Trent's unspoken but powerful conviction that it was the right way to address the man their mother (uck!) slept with these days.

"I don't want to go up there," Laurie said. "He's been in a pissy mood ever since we got back. Trent says he'll stay that way until school starts and he can settle back into his rut again."

"His door's shut. We can be quiet. Lissa n me went up and he didn't even know we were there."

"Lissa and *I*."

"Yeah. Us. Anyway, it's safe. The door's shut and he's talking to himself like he does when he's really into something."

"I hate it when he does that," Laurie said darkly. "Our real father never talked to himself, and he didn't use to lock himself in a room by himself, either."

"Well, I don't think he's locked in," Brian said, "but if you're really worried about him coming out, take an empty suitcase. We'll pretend like we're putting it in the closet where we keep them, if he comes out."

"What *is* this amazing thing?" Laurie demanded, putting her fists on her hips.

"I'll show you," Brian said earnestly, "but you have to swear on Mom's name and hope to die if you tell anyone." He paused, thinking, for a moment, and then added: "You specially can't tell

775

Lissa, because I swore to her."

Laurie's ears were finally all the way up. It was probably a big nothing, but she was tired of putting clothes away. It was really amazing how much junk a person could accumulate in just three months. "Okay, I swear."

They took along *two* empty suitcases, one for each of them, but their precautions proved unnecessary; their stepfather never came out of his study. It was probably just as well; he had worked up a grand head of steam, from the sound. The two children could hear him stamping about, muttering, opening drawers, slamming them shut again. A familiar odor seeped out from under the door — to Laurie it smelled like smouldering athletic socks. Lew was smoking his pipe.

She stuck her tongue out, crossed her eyes, and twiddled her fingers in her ears as they tiptoed by.

But a moment later, when she looked at the place Lissa had pointed out to Brian and which Brian now pointed out to her, she forgot Lew just as completely as Brian had forgotten about all the wonderful things he could watch on TV that night.

"What *is* it?" she whispered to Brian. "My gosh, what does it *mean?*"

"I dunno," Brian said, "but just remember, you swore on Mom's name, Laurie."

"Yeah, yeah, but —"

"Say it again!" Brian didn't like the look in her eyes. It was a *telling* look, and he felt she really needed a little reinforcement.

"Yeah, yeah, on Mom's name," she said perfunctorily, "but, Brian, jeezly *crow* —"

"And hope to die, don't forget that part."

"Oh, Brian, you are such a *cheeser!*"

"Never mind, just say you hope to die!"

"Hope to die, hope to die, okay?" Laurie said. "Why do you have to be such a cheeser, Bri?"

"Dunno," he said, smirking in that way she absolutely hated, "just lucky, I guess."

She could have strangled him . . . but a promise *was* a promise, especially one given on the name of your one and only mother, so Laurie held on for over one full hour before getting Trent and showing him. She made him swear, too, and her confidence that Trent would keep *his* promise not to tell was perfectly justified. He was almost fourteen, and as the oldest, he had no one *to* tell . . . except a grownup. Since their mother had taken to her bed with a migraine, that left only Lew, and that was the same as no one at all.

The two oldest Bradbury children hadn't needed to bring up empty suitcases as camouflage this time; their stepfather was downstairs, watching some British fellow lecture on the Normans and Saxons (the Normans and Saxons were Lew's specialty at the college) on the VCR, and enjoying his favorite afternoon snack — a glass of milk and a ketchup sandwich.

Trent stood at the end of the hall, looking at what the other children had looked at before him. He stood there for a long time.

"What *is* it, Trent?" Laurie finally asked. It never crossed her mind that Trent wouldn't know. Trent knew *everything*. So she watched, almost incredulously, as he slowly shook his head.

"I don't know," he said, peering into the crack.

"Some kind of metal, I think. Wish I'd brought a flashlight." He reached into the crack and tapped. Laurie felt a vague sense of disquiet at this, and was relieved when Trent pulled his finger back. "Yeah, it's metal."

"Should it be in there?" Laurie asked. "I mean, *was* it? Before?"

"No," Trent said. "I remember when they re-plastered. That was just after Mom married *him*. There wasn't anything in there then but laths."

"What are they?"

"Narrow boards," he said. "They go between the plaster and the outside wall of the house." Trent reached into the crack in the wall and once again touched the metal which showed dull white in there. The crack was about four inches long and half an inch across at its widest point. "They put in insulation, too," he said, frowning thought-fully and then shoving his hands into the back pockets of his wash-faded jeans. "I remember. Pink, billowy stuff that looked like cotton candy."

"Where is it, then? I don't see any pink stuff."

"Me either," Trent said. "But they *did* put it in. I remember." His eyes traced the four-inch length of the crack. "That metal in the wall is something new. I wonder how much of it there is, and how far it goes. Is it just up here on the third floor, or . . ."

"Or what?" Laurie looked at him with big round eyes. She had begun to be a little frightened.

"Or is it all over the house," Trent finished thoughtfully.

After school the next afternoon, Trent called a

meeting of all four Bradbury children. It got off to a somewhat bumpy start, with Lissa accusing Brian of breaking what she called "your solemn swear" and Brian, who was deeply embarrassed, accusing Laurie of putting their mother's soul in dire jeopardy by telling Trent. Although he wasn't very clear on exactly what a soul was (the Bradburys were Unitarians), he seemed quite sure that Laurie had condemned Mother's to hell.

"Well," Laurie said, "you'll have to take *some* of the blame, Brian. I mean, you were the one who brought Mother into it. You should have had me swear on Lew's name. *He* could go to hell."

Lissa, who was young enough and kind-hearted enough not to wish *anyone* in hell, was so distressed by this line of discourse that she began to cry.

"Hush, all of you," Trent said, and hugged Lissa until she had regained most of her composure. "What's done is done, and I happen to think it all worked out for the best."

"You do?" Brian asked. If Trent said a thing was good, Brian would have died defending it, that went without saying, but Laurie had sworn on Mom's *name*.

"Something this weird needs to be investigated, and if we waste a lot of time arguing over who was right or wrong to break their promise, we'll never get it done."

Trent glanced pointedly up at the clock on the wall of his room, where they had gathered. It was twenty after three. He really didn't have to say any more. Their mother had been up this morning to get Lew his breakfast — two three-minute eggs with whole-wheat toast and marmalade was one of his many daily requirements — but afterward she had gone back to bed, and there she had remained. She suffered from dreadful headaches, migraines that sometimes spent two or even three days snarling and clawing at her defenseless (and often bewildered) brain before decamping for a month or so.

She would not be apt to see them on the third floor and wonder what they were up to, but "Daddy Lew" was a different kettle of fish altogether. With his study just down the hall from the strange crack, they could count on avoiding his notice — and his curiosity — only if they conducted their investigations while he was away, and that was what Trent's pointed glance at the clock had meant.

The family had returned to the States a full ten days before Lew was scheduled to begin teaching classes again, but he could no more stay away from the University once he was back within ten miles of it than a fish could live out of water. He had left shortly after noon, with a briefcase crammed full of papers he had collected at various spots of historical interest in England. He said he was going up to file these papers away. Trent thought that meant he'd cram them into one of his desk drawers, then lock his office and go down to the History Department's Faculty Lounge. There he would drink coffee and gossip with his buddies . . . except, Trent had discovered, when you were a college teacher, people thought you were dumb if you had buddies. You were supposed to say they were your colleagues. So he was away, and that was good, but he might be back at any time between now and five, and that was bad. Still, they had *some* time, and Trent was determined they weren't going to spend it squabbling about who swore what to who.

"Listen to me, you guys," he said, and was gratified to see that they actually *were* listening, their differences and recriminations forgotten in the excitement of an *investigation*. They had also been caught by Trent's inability to explain what Lissa had found. All three of them shared, at least to some extent, Brian's simple faith in Trent — if Trent was puzzled by something, if Trent thought that something was strange and just possibly amazing, they all thought so.

Laurie spoke for all of them when she said: "Just tell us what to do, Trent — we'll do it."

"Okay," Trent said. "We'll need some things." He took a deep breath and began explaining what they were.

Once they were convened around the crack at the end of the third-floor hallway, Trent held Lissa up so she could shine the beam of a small flashlight — it was the one their mother used to inspect their ears, eyes, and noses when they weren't feeling well — into the crack. They could all see the metal; it wasn't shiny enough to throw back a clear reflection of the beam, but it shone silkily just the same. Steel, was Trent's opinion — steel, or some sort of alloy.

"What's an alloy, Trent?" Brian asked.

Trent shook his head. He didn't know exactly. He turned to Laurie and asked her to give him the drill.

Brian and Lissa exchanged an uneasy glance as Laurie passed it over. It had come from the basement workshop, and the basement was the one remaining place in the house which was their real father's. Daddy Lew hadn't been down there a dozen times since he had married Catherine Bradbury. The smaller children knew that as well as Trent and Laurie. They weren't afraid Daddy Lew would notice someone had been using the drill; it was the holes in the wall outside his study they were worried about. Neither one of them said this out loud, but Trent read it on their troubled faces.

"Look," Trent said, holding the drill out so they could get a good look. "This is what they call a needle-point drillbit. See how tiny it is? And since we're only going to drill behind the pictures, I don't think we have to worry."

There were about a dozen framed prints along the third-floor hallway, half of them beyond the study door, on the way to the closet at the end where the suitcases were stored. Most of these were very old (and mostly uninteresting) views of Titusville, where the Bradburys lived.

"He doesn't even look *at* them, let alone *behind* them," Laurie agreed.

Brian touched the tip of the drill with one finger, then nodded. Lissa watched, then copied both the touch and the nod. If Laurie said something was okay, it probably was; if Trent said so, it almost certainly was; if they both said so, there could be no question.

Laurie took down the picture which hung closest to the small crack in the plaster and gave it to Brian. Trent drilled. They stood watching him in a tight little circle of three, like infielders encouraging their pitcher at a particularly tense moment of the game.

The drillbit went easily into the wall, and the hole it made was every bit as tiny as promised. The darker square of wallpaper which had been revealed when Laurie took the print off its hook was also encouraging. It suggested that no one had bothered taking the dark line engraving of the Titusville Public Library off its hook for a very long time.

After a dozen turns of the drill's handle, Trent stopped and reversed, pulling the bit free.

"Why'd you quit?" Brian asked.

"Hit something hard."

"More metal?" Lissa asked.

"I think so. Sure wasn't wood. Let's see." He shone the light in and cocked his head this way and that before shaking it decisively. "My head's too big. Let's boost Lissa."

Laurie and Trent lifted her up and Brian handed her the Pen Lite. Lissa squinted for a time, then said, "Just like in the crack I found."

"Okay," Trent said. "Next picture."

The drill hit metal behind the second, and the third, as well. Behind the fourth — by this time they were quite close to the door of Lew's study — it went all the way in before Trent pulled it out. This time when she was boosted up, Lissa told them she saw "the pink stuff."

"Yeah, the insulation I told you about," Trent said to Laurie. "Let's try the other side of the hall."

They had to drill behind four pictures on the

east side of the corridor before they struck first wood-lath and then insulation behind the plaster . . . and as they were re-hanging the last picture, they heard the out-of-tune snarl of Lew's elderly Porsche turning into the driveway.

Brian, who had been in charge of hanging this picture — he could just reach the hook on tip-toe — dropped it. Laurie reached out and grabbed it by the frame on the way down. A moment later she found herself shaking so badly she had to hand the picture to Trent, or she would have dropped it herself.

"*You* hang it," she said, turning a stricken face to her older brother. "I would have dropped it if I'd been thinking about what I was doing. I really would."

Trent hung the picture, which showed horse-drawn carriages clopping through City Park, and saw it was hanging slightly askew. He reached out to adjust it, then pulled back just before his fingers touched the frame. His sisters and his brother thought he was something like a god; Trent himself was smart enough to know he was only a kid. But even a kid — assuming he was a kid with half a brain — knew that when things like this started to go bad, you ought to leave them alone. If he messed with it anymore, this picture would fall for sure, spraying the floor with broken glass, and somehow Trent knew it.

"Go!" he whispered. "Downstairs! TV room!"

The back door slammed downstairs as Lew came in.

"But it's not *straight!*" Lissa protested. "Trent, it's not —"

"Never *mind!*" Laurie said. "Do what Trent says!"

Trent and Laurie looked at each other, wide-eyed. If Lew went into the kitchen to fix himself a bite to tide himself over until supper, all still might be well. If he didn't, he would meet Lissa and Brian on the stairs. One look at them and he'd know something was going on. The two younger Bradbury children were old enough to close their mouths, but not their faces.

Brian and Lissa went fast.

Trent and Laurie came behind, more slowly, listening. There was a moment of almost unbearable suspense when the only sounds were the little kids' footsteps on the stairs, and then Lew bawled up at them from the kitchen: *"KEEP IT DOWN, CAN'T YOU? YOUR MOTHER'S TAKING A NAP!"*

And if that doesn't wake her up, Laurie thought, *nothing will.*

Late that night, as Trent was drowsing off to sleep, Laurie opened the door of his room, came in, and sat down beside him on the bed.

"You don't like him, but that's not all," she said.

"Who-wha?" Trent asked, peeling a cautious eyelid.

"Lew," she said quietly. "You know who I mean, Trent."

"Yeah," he said, giving up. "And you're right. I don't like him."

"You're scared of him, too, aren't you?"

After a long, long moment, Trent said: "Yeah. A little."

"Just a little?"

"Maybe a little more than a little," Trent said. He winked at her, hoping for a smile, but Laurie only looked at him, and Trent gave up. She wasn't going to be diverted, at least not tonight.

"Why? Do you think he might hurt us?"

Lew shouted at them a lot, but he had never put his hands on them. No, Laurie suddenly remembered, that wasn't quite true. One time when Brian had walked into his study without knocking, Lew had given him a spanking. A hard one. Brian had tried not to cry, but in the end he had. And Mom had cried, too, although she hadn't tried to stop the spanking. But she must have said something to him later on, because Laurie had heard Lew shouting at *her*.

Still, it had been a spanking, not child abuse, and Brian *could* be an insufferable cheese-dog when he put his mind to it.

Had he been putting his mind to it that night? Laurie wondered now. Or had Lew spanked her brother and made him cry over something which had only been an honest little kid's mistake? She didn't know, and had a sudden and unwelcome insight, the sort of thought that made her think Peter Pan had had the right idea about never wanting to grow up: she wasn't sure she *wanted* to know. One thing she did know: who the *real* cheese-dog around here was.

She realized Trent hadn't answered her question, and gave him a poke. "Cat got your tongue?"

"Just thinking," he said. "It's a toughie, you know?"

"Yes," she said soberly. "I know."

This time she let him think.

"Nah," he said at last, and laced his hands together behind his head. "I don't think so, Sprat." She hated to be called that, but tonight she decided to let it go. She couldn't remember Trent ever speaking to her this carefully and seriously. "I don't think he *would* . . . but I think he *could*." He got up on one elbow and looked at her even more seriously. "But I think he's hurting Mom, and I think it gets a little worse for her every day."

"She's sorry, isn't she?" Laurie asked. Suddenly she felt like crying. Why were adults so stupid sometimes about stuff kids could see right away? It made you want to kick them. "She never wanted to go to England in the first place . . . and there's the way he shouts at her sometimes . . ."

"Don't forget the headaches," Trent said flatly. "The ones he says she talks herself into. Yeah, she's sorry, all right."

"Would she ever . . . you know . . ."

"Divorce him?"

"Yes," Laurie said, relieved. She wasn't sure she could have brought the word out herself, and had she realized how much she was her mother's daughter in that regard, she could have answered her own question.

"No," Trent said. "Not Mom."

"Then there's nothing we can do," Laurie sighed.

Trent said in a voice so soft she almost couldn't hear it: "Oh yeah?"

During the next week and a half, they drilled other small holes around the house when there was no one around to see them: holes behind posters in their various rooms, behind the refrigerator in the pantry (Brian was able to squeeze in and just had room to use the drill), in the downstairs closets. Trent even drilled one in a dining-room wall, high up in one corner where the shadows never quite left. He stood on top of the step-ladder while Laurie held it steady.

There was no metal anywhere. Just lath.

The children forgot for a little while.

One day about a month later, after Lew had gone back to teaching full-time, Brian came to Trent and told him there was another crack in the plaster on the third floor, and that he could see more metal behind it. Trent and Lissa came at once. Laurie was still in school, at band practice.

As on the occasion of the first crack, their mother was lying down with a headache. Lew's temper had improved once he was back at school (as Trent and Laurie had been sure it would), but he'd had a crackerjack argument with their mother the night before, about a party he wanted to have for fellow faculty members in the History Department. If there was anything the former Mrs. Bradbury hated and feared, it was playing hostess at faculty parties. Lew had insisted on this one, however, and she had finally given in. Now she was lying in the shadowy bedroom with a damp towel over her eyes and a bottle of Fiorinal on the night-table while Lew was presumably passing around invitations in the Faculty Lounge and clapping his colleagues on the back.

The new crack was on the west side of the hallway, between the study door and the stairwell.

"You sure you saw metal in there?" Trent asked. "We *checked* this side, Bri."

"Look for yourself," Brian said, and Trent did. There was no need of a flashlight; this crack was wider, and there was no question about the metal at the bottom of it.

After a long look, Trent told them he had to go to the hardware store, right away.

"Why?" Lissa asked.

"I want to get some plaster. I don't want him to see that crack." He hesitated, then added: "And I especially don't want him to see the metal inside it."

Lissa frowned at him. "Why not, Trent?"

But Trent didn't exactly know. At least, not yet.

They started drilling again, and this time they found metal behind *all* the walls on the third floor, including Lew's study. Trent snuck in there one afternoon with the drill while Lew was at the college and their mother was out shopping for the upcoming faculty party.

The former Mrs. Bradbury looked very pale and drawn these days — even Lissa had noticed — but when any of the children asked her if she was okay, she always flashed a troubling, overbright smile and told them never better, in the pink, rolling in clover. Laurie, who could be blunt, told her she looked too thin. Oh no, her mother responded, Lew says I was turning into a blob over in England — all those rich teas. She was just trying to get back into fighting trim, that was all.

Laurie knew better, but not even Laurie was blunt enough to call her mother a liar to her face.

If all four of them had come to her at once —
ganged up on her, so to speak — they might have
gotten a different story. But not even Trent
thought of doing that.

One of Lew's advanced degrees was hanging on
the wall over his desk in a frame. While the other
children clustered outside the door, nearly vomiting with terror, Trent removed the framed degree from its hook, laid it on the desk, and drilled
a pinhole in the center of the square where it had
been. Two inches in, the drill hit metal.

Trent carefully rehung the degree — making
very sure *it* wasn't crooked — and came back out.

Lissa burst into tears of relief, and Brian quickly
joined her; he looked disgusted but seemed unable
to help himself. Laurie had to struggle very hard
against her own tears.

They drilled holes at intervals along the stairs
to the second floor and found metal behind these
walls, too. It continued roughly halfway down the
second-floor hallway as it proceeded toward the
front of the house. There was metal behind the walls
of Brian's room, but behind only one wall of
Laurie's.

"It hasn't finished growing in here," Laurie said
darkly.

Trent looked at her, surprised. "Huh?"

Before she could reply, Brian had a brainstorm.

"Try the floor, Trent!" he said. "See if it's there,
too."

Trent thought it over, shrugged, and drilled into
the floor of Laurie's room. The drill went in all
the way with no resistance, but when he peeled
back the rug at the foot of his own bed and tried

there, he soon encountered solid steel . . . or solid whatever-it-was.

Then, at Lissa's insistence, he stood on a stool and drilled up into the ceiling, eyes slitted against the plaster-dust that sifted down into his face.

"Boink," he said after a few moments. "More metal. Let's quit for the day."

Laurie was the only one who saw how deeply troubled Trent looked.

That night after lights-out, it was Trent who came to Laurie's room, and Laurie didn't even pretend to be sleepy. The truth was, neither of them had been sleeping very well for the last couple of weeks.

"What did you mean?" Trent whispered, sitting down beside her.

"About what?" Laurie asked, getting up on one elbow.

"You said it hadn't finished growing in your room. What did you mean?"

"Come on, Trent — you're not dumb."

"No, I'm not," he agreed without conceit. "Maybe I just want to hear you say it, Sprat."

"If you call me that, you never will."

"Okay. Laurie, Laurie, Laurie. You satisfied?"

"Yes. That stuff's growing all over the house." She paused. "No, that's not right. It's growing *under* the house."

"That's not right, either."

Laurie thought about it, then sighed. "Okay," she said. "It's growing *in* the house. It's *stealing* the house. Is that good enough, Mr. Smarty?"

"Stealing the house . . ." Trent sat quietly beside

her on the bed, looking at her poster of Chrissie Hynde and seeming to taste the phrase she had used. At last he nodded and flashed the smile she loved. "Yes — that's good enough."

"Whatever you call it, it acts like it's alive."

Trent nodded. He had already thought of this. He had no idea how metal *could* be alive, but he was damned if he saw any way around her conclusion, at least for the present.

"But that isn't the worst."

"What is?"

"It's *sneaking*." Her eyes, fixed solemnly on his, were big and frightened. "That's the part I really don't like. I don't know what started it or what it means, and I don't really care. But it's *sneaking*."

She ran her fingers into her heavy blonde hair and pushed it back from her temples. It was a fretful, unconscious gesture that reminded Trent achingly of his dad, whose hair had been that exact same shade.

"I feel like something's going to happen, Trent, only I don't know what, and it's like being in a nightmare you can't get all the way out of. Does it feel like that to you sometimes?"

"A little, yeah. But I *know* something's going to happen. I might even know what."

She bolted to a sitting position and grabbed his hands. "You *know?* What? What is it?"

"I can't be sure," Trent said, getting up. "I *think* I know, but I'm not ready to say what I think yet. I have to do some more looking."

"If we drill many more holes, the house is apt to fall down!"

"I didn't say *drilling,* I said *looking.*"

"Looking for *what?*"

"For something that isn't here yet — that hasn't grown yet. But when it does, I don't think it will be able to hide."

"*Tell* me, Trent!"

"Not yet," he said, and planted a small, quick kiss on her cheek. "Besides — curiosity killed the Sprat."

"I *hate* you!" she cried in a low voice, and flopped back down with the sheet over her head. But she felt better for having talked with Trent, and slept better than she had for a week.

Trent found what he was looking for two days before the big party. As the oldest, he perhaps should have noticed that his mother had begun to look alarmingly unhealthy, her skin drawn shiny over her cheekbones, her complexion so pale it had taken on an ugly yellow underlight. He should have noticed how often she was rubbing at her temples, although she denied — almost in a panic — that she had a migraine, or *had* had one for over a week.

He did not notice these things, however. He was too busy looking.

In the four or five days between his after-bedtime talk with Laurie and the day he found what he was looking for, he went through every closet in the big old house at least three times; through the crawlspace above Lew's study five or six times; through the big old cellar half a dozen times.

It was in the cellar that he finally found it.

This was not to say he hadn't found peculiar

things in other places; he most certainly had. There was a knob of stainless steel poking out of the ceiling of a second-floor closet. A curved metal armature of some kind had burst through the side of the luggage-closet on the third floor. It was a dim, polished gray . . . until he touched it. When he did that, it flushed a dusky rose color, and he heard a faint but powerful humming sound deep in the wall. He snatched his hand back as if the armature had been hot (and at first, when it turned a color he associated with the burners on the electric stove, he could have sworn it was). When he did that, the curved metal thing went gray again. The humming stopped at once.

The day before, in the attic, he had observed a cobweb of thin, interlaced cables growing in a low dark corner under the eave. Trent had been crawling around on his hands and knees, not doing anything but getting hot and dirty, when he had suddenly spied this amazing phenomenon. He froze in place, staring through a tangle of hair as the cables spun themselves out of nothing at all (or so it looked, anyway), met, wrapped around each other so tightly they seemed to merge, and then continued spreading until they reached the floor, where they drilled in and anchored themselves in dreamy little puffs of sawdust. They seemed to be creating some sort of limber bracework, and it looked as if it would be *very* strong, able to hold the house together through a lot of buffeting and hard knocks.

What buffeting, though?

What hard knocks?

Again, Trent thought he knew. It was hard to

believe, but he thought he knew.

There was a little closet at the north end of the cellar, far beyond the workshop area and the furnace. Their real father had called this "the wine-cellar," and although he'd put up only about two dozen bottles of plonk (this word had always made their mother giggle), they were all carefully stored in crisscrossing racks he had made himself.

Lew came in here even less frequently than he went into the workshop; he didn't drink wine. And although their mother had often taken a glass or two with their dad, she no longer drank wine either. Trent remembered how sad her face had looked the one time Bri had asked her why she never had a glass of plonk in front of the fire anymore.

"Lew doesn't approve of drinking," she had told Brian. "He says it's a crutch."

There was a padlock on the wine-cellar door, but it was only there to make sure the door didn't swing open and let in the heat from the furnace. The key hung right next to it, but Trent didn't need it. He'd left the padlock undone after his first investigation, and no one had come along to press it shut since then. So far as he knew, no one came to this end of the cellar at all anymore.

He was not much surprised by the sour whiff of spilled wine that greeted him as he approached the door; it was just another proof of what he and Laurie already knew — the changes were winding themselves quietly all through the house. He opened the door, and although what he saw frightened him, it didn't really surprise him.

Metal constructions had burst through two of

the wine-cellar's walls, tearing apart the racks with their diamond-shaped compartments and pushing the bottles of Bollinger and Mondavi and Battiglia onto the floor, where they had broken.

Like the cables in the attic crawlspace, whatever was forming here — growing, to use Laurie's word — hadn't finished yet. It spun itself into being in sheens of light that hurt Trent's eyes and made him feel a little sick to his stomach.

No cables here, however, and no curved struts. What was growing in his real father's forgotten wine-cellar looked like cabinets and consoles and instrument panels. And, as he looked, vague shapes humped themselves up in the metal like the heads of excited snakes, gained focus, became dials and levers and read-outs. There were a few blinking lights. Some of these actually began to blink as he looked at them.

A low sighing sound accompanied this act of creation.

Trent took one cautious step farther into the little room; an especially bright red light, or series of them, had caught his eye. He sneezed as he stepped forward — the machines and consoles pushing across the old concrete had stirred up a great deal of dust.

The lights which had snagged his attention were numbers. They were under a glass strip on a metal construct which was spinning its way out of a console. This new thing looked like some sort of chair, although no one sitting in it would have been very comfortable. At least, no one with a *human* shape, Trent thought with a little shiver.

The glass strip was in one of the arms of this

twisted chair — if it *was* a chair. And the numbers had perhaps caught his eye because they were moving.

72:34:18

became

72:34:17

and then

72:34:16.

Trent looked at his watch, which had a sweep second hand, and used it to confirm what his eyes had already told him. The chair might or might not really be a chair, but the numbers under the glass strip were a digital clock. It was running backward. Counting down, to be perfectly accurate. And what would happen when that read-out finally went from

00:00:01

to

00:00:00

some three days from this very afternoon?

He was pretty sure he knew. Every American boy knows one of two things happen when a backward-running clock finally reads zeros across the board: an explosion or a lift-off.

Trent thought there was too much equipment, too many gadgets, for it to be an explosion.

He thought something had gotten into the house while they were in England. Some sort of spore, perhaps, that had drifted through space for a billion years before being caught in the gravitational pull of the earth, spiraling down through the atmosphere like a bit of milkweed fluff caught in a mild breeze, and finally falling into the chimney of a house in Titusville, Indiana.

Into the *Bradburys'* house in Titusville, Indiana.

It might have been something else entirely, of course, but the spore idea *felt* right to Trent, and although he was the oldest of the Bradbury kids, he was still young enough to sleep well after eating a pepperoni pizza at 9:00 P.M., and to believe completely in his own perceptions and intuitions. And in the end, it didn't really matter, did it? What *mattered* was what had *happened*.

And, of course, what was *going* to happen.

When Trent left the wine-cellar this time, he not only snapped the padlock's arm closed, he took the key as well.

Something terrible happened at Lew's faculty party. It happened at quarter of nine, only forty-five minutes or so after the first guests arrived, and Trent and Laurie later heard Lew shouting at their mother that the only goddam consideration she had shown him was getting up to her foolishness early — if she'd waited until ten o'clock or so, there would have been fifty or more people circulating through the living room, dining room, kitchen, and back parlor.

"What the hell's the matter with you?" Trent and Laurie heard him yelling at her, and when Trent felt Laurie's hand creep into his like a small cold mouse, he held it tightly. "Don't you know what people are going to say about this? Don't you know how people in the department *talk?* I mean, *really*, Catherine — it was like something out of the Three Stooges!"

Their mother's only reply was soft, helpless sobbing, and for just one moment Trent felt a horrible, unwilling burst of hate for her. Why had she married him in the first place? Didn't she deserve this for being such a fool?

Ashamed of himself, he pushed the thought away, made it gone, and turned to Laurie. He was appalled to see tears pouring down her cheeks, and the mute sorrow in her eyes went to his heart like a knife-blade.

"Great party, huh?" she whispered, scrubbing at her cheeks with the heels of her palms.

"Right, Sprat," he said, and hugged her so she could cry against his shoulder without being heard. "It'll make my top-ten list at the end of the year, no sweat."

It seemed that Catherine Evans (who had never wished more bitterly to be Catherine Bradbury again) had been lying to everyone. She had been in the grip of a screaming-blue migraine for not just a day or two days this time but for the last two weeks. During that time she had eaten next to nothing and lost fifteen pounds. She had been serving canapés to Stephen Krutchmer, the head of the History Department, and his wife when the colors went out of everything and the world suddenly swam away from her. She had rolled bonelessly forward, spilling a whole tray of Chinese pork rolls onto the front of Mrs. Krutchmer's expensive Norma Kamali dress, which had been purchased for just this occasion.

Brian and Lissa had heard the commotion and had come creeping down the stairs in their pajamas to see what was going on, although both of them — all four children, for that matter — had been strictly forbidden by Daddy Lew to leave the upper floors of the house once the party began. "University people don't like to see children at faculty parties," Lew had explained brusquely that afternoon. "It sends all sorts of mixed signals."

When they saw their mother on the floor in a circle of kneeling, concerned faculty members (Mrs. Krutchmer was not there; she had run for the kitchen, wanting to get some cold water on the front of her dress before the sauce-stains could set) they had forgotten their stepfather's firm order and had run in, Lissa crying, Brian bellowing in excited dismay. Lissa managed to kick the head of Asian Studies in the left kidney. Brian, who was two years older and thirty pounds heavier, did even better: he knocked the fall semester's guest lecturer, a plump babe in a pink dress and curly-toed evening slippers, smack into the fireplace. She sat there, dazed, in a large puff of gray-black ashes.

"Mom! Mommy!" Brian cried, shaking the former Catherine Bradbury. "*Mommy!* Wake up!"

Mrs. Evans stirred and moaned.

"Get upstairs," Lew said coldly. "Both of you."

When they showed no signs of obeying, Lew put his hand on Lissa's shoulder and tightened it until she squeaked with pain. His eyes blazed at her out of a face which had gone dead pale except for red spots as bright as dimestore rouge in the center of each cheek.

"I'll take care of this," he said through teeth so tightly clamped they refused to entirely unlock even to speak. "You and your brother go upstairs right n—"

"Take your hand off her, you son of a bitch," Trent said clearly.

Lew — and all the party-goers who had arrived early enough to witness this entertaining sideshow — turned toward the archway between the living room and the hallway. Trent and Laurie stood there, side by side. Trent was as pale as his stepfather, but his face was calm and set. There were people at the party — not many but a few — who had known Catherine Evans's first husband, and they agreed later that the resemblance between father and son was extraordinary. That it was, in fact, almost as though Bill Bradbury had come back from the dead to confront his ill-tempered replacement.

"I want you to go upstairs," Lew said. "All four of you. There's nothing here to concern you. Nothing to concern you at all."

Mrs. Krutchmer had come back into the room, the bosom of her Norma Kamali damp but reasonably free of stains.

"Get your hand off Lissa," Trent said.

"And get away from our mother," Laurie said.

Now Mrs. Evans was sitting up, her hands to her head, looking around dazedly. The headache had popped like a balloon, leaving her disoriented and weak but at last out of the agony she had endured for the last fourteen days. She knew she had done something terrible, embarrassed Lew, perhaps even *disgraced* him, but for the moment she was too grateful that the pain had stopped to care. The shame would come later. Now she only wanted to go upstairs — very slowly — and lie down.

"You'll be punished for this," Lew said, looking at his four stepchildren in the nearly perfect shocked silence of the living room. He didn't look at them all at once but one at a time, as if marking the nature and extent of each crime. When his gaze fell on Lissa, she began to cry. "I'm sorry for their misbehavior," he said to the room at large. "My wife is a bit lax with them, I'm afraid. What they need is a good English nanny —"

"Don't be a jackass, Lew," Mrs. Krutchmer said. Her voice was very loud but not very tuneful; she sounded a bit like a jackass in full bray herself. Brian jumped, clutched his sister, and also gave way to tears. "Your wife fainted. They were concerned, that's all."

"Quite right, too," the guest lecturer said, struggling to extract her considerable bulk from the fireplace. Her pink dress was now a splotchy gray and her face was streaked with soot. Only her shoes with their absurd but engaging curly tips seemed to have escaped, but she looked quite unperturbed by the whole thing. "Children *should* care about their mothers. And husbands about their wives."

She looked pointedly at Lew Evans as she said this last, but Lew missed her gaze; he was marking Trent and Laurie's progress as they assisted their mother up the stairs. Lissa and Brian trailed along behind, like an honor guard.

The party went on. The incident was more or less papered over, as unpleasant incidents at faculty parties usually are. Mrs. Evans (who had slept three hours a night at most since her husband had announced his intention of throwing a party) was asleep almost as soon as her head touched the pillow, and the children heard Lew downstairs, booming out *bonhomie* without her. Trent suspected that he was even a little relieved not to have to contend with his scurrying, frightened mouse of a wife anymore.

He never once broke away to come up and check on her.

Not once. Not until the party was over.

After the last guest had been shown out, he walked heavily upstairs and told her to wake up . . . which she did, obedient in this as she had been in everything else since the day when she had made the mistake of telling the minister she did and Lew that she would.

Lew poked his head into Trent's room next and measured the children with his gaze.

"I knew you'd all be in here," he said with a satisfied little nod. "Conspiring. You're going to be punished, you know. Yes indeed. Tomorrow. Tonight I want you to go right to bed and think about it. Now go to your rooms. And no creeping around, either."

Neither Lissa nor Brian did any "creeping around," certainly; they were too exhausted and emotionally wrung out to do anything but go to bed and fall immediately asleep. But Laurie came back down to Trent's room in spite of "Daddy Lew," and the two of them listened in silent dismay as their stepfather upbraided their mother for daring to faint at *his* party . . . and as their mother wept and offered not a word of argument or even demurral.

"Oh, Trent, what are we going to do?" Laurie asked, her voice muffled against his shoulder.

Trent's face was extraordinarily pale and still. "Do?" he said. "Why, we're not going to do anything, Sprat."

"We *have* to! Trent, we *have* to! We have to help her!"

"No, we don't," Trent said. A small and somehow terrible smile played around his lips. "The house is going to do it for us." He looked at his watch and calculated. "At around three-thirty-four tomorrow afternoon, the house is going to do it all."

There were no punishments in the morning; Lew Evans was too preoccupied with his eight o'clock seminar on Consequences of the Norman Conquest. Neither Trent nor Laurie was very surprised at this, but both were extremely grateful. He told them he would see them in his study that night, one by one, and "mete a few fair strokes to each." Once this threat in the form of an obscure quotation had been given, he marched out with his head up and his briefcase clasped firmly in his right hand. Their mother was still asleep when his Porsche snarled its way down the street.

The two younger kids were standing by the kitchen with their arms around each other, looking to Laurie like an illustration from a Grimm's fairytale. Lissa was crying. Brian was keeping a stiff upper lip, at least so far, but he was pale and there were purple pouches under his eyes. "He'll spank us," Brian said to Trent. "And he spanks *hard,* too."

"Nope," Trent said. They looked at him hopefully but dubiously. Lew had, after all, *promised* spankings; even Trent was not to be spared this painful indignity.

"But, Trent —" Lissa began.

"Listen to me," Trent said, pulling a chair out from the table and sitting on it backward in front of the two little ones. "Listen carefully, and don't you miss a single word. It's important, and none of us can screw up."

They stared at him silently with their big green-blue eyes.

"As soon as school is out, I want you two to come right home . . . but only as far as the corner. The corner of Maple and Walnut. Have you got that?"

"Ye-ess," Lissa said hesitantly. "But why, Trent?"

"Never mind," Trent said. His own eyes — also green-blue — were sparkling, but Laurie thought it wasn't a good-humored sparkle; she thought, in fact, that there was something dangerous about it. "Just be there. Stand by the mailbox. You have to be there by three o'clock, three-fifteen at the *latest*. Do you understand?"

"Yes," Brian said, speaking for both of them. "We got it."

"Laurie and I will already be there, or we'll be there right after you get there."

"How are we going to do that, Trent?" Laurie asked. "We don't even get out of school until three o'clock, and I have band practice, and the bus takes —"

"We're not *going* to school today," Trent said.

"No?" Laurie was nonplussed.

Lissa was horrified. "Trent!" she said. "You

can't do that! That's . . . that's . . . *hookey!*"

"And about time, too," Trent said grimly. "Now you two get ready for school. Just remember: the corner of Maple and Walnut at three o'clock, three-fifteen at the absolute latest. And whatever you do, *don't come all the way home.*" He stared at Brian and Lissa so fiercely that they looked back with frightened dismay, drawing together for mutual comfort once again. Even Laurie was frightened. "Wait for us, but don't you *dare* come back into this house," he said. "Not for *anything.*"

When the little kids were gone, Laurie seized his shirt and demanded to know what was going on.

"It has something to do with what's growing in the house, I *know* it does, and if you want me to play hookey and help you, you better tell me what it is, Trent Bradbury!"

"Mellow out, I'll tell you," Trent said. He carefully removed his shirt from Laurie's tight grip. "And quiet down. I don't want you to wake up Mom. She'll make us go to school, and that's no good."

"Well, what *is* it? Tell me!"

"Come on downstairs," Trent said. "I want to show you something."

He led her downstairs to the wine-cellar.

Trent wasn't completely sure Laurie would ride along with what he had in mind — it seemed awfully . . . well, *final* . . . even to him — but she did. If it had just been a matter of enduring a spanking from "Daddy Lew," he didn't think she would have, but Laurie had been as deeply affected by the sight of her mother lying senseless on the living-room floor as Trent had been by his stepfather's unfeeling reaction to it.

"Yeah," Laurie said bleakly. "I think we have to." She was looking at the blinking numbers on the arm of the chair. They now read
07:49:21.

The wine-cellar was no longer a wine-cellar at all. It stank of wine, true enough, and there were the piles of shattered green glass on the floor amid the twisted ruins of their father's wine-racks, but it now looked like a madman's version of the control-bridge on the Starship *Enterprise*. Dials whirled. Digital read-outs flickered, changed, flickered again. Lights blinked and flashed.

"Yeah," Trent said. "I think so, too. That son of a bitch, shouting at her like that!"

"Trent, don't."

"He's a jerk! A bastard! A dickhead!"

But this was just a foul-mouthed version of whistling past the graveyard, and both of them knew it. Looking at the strange agglomeration of instruments and controls made Trent feel almost sick with doubt and unease. He was reminded of a book his dad had read him when he was a child, a Mercer Mayer story where a creature called a Stamp-Eating Trollusk had popped a little girl into an envelope and mailed her To Whom It May Concern. Wasn't that pretty much what he was proposing they do to Lew Evans?

"If we don't do something, he'll kill her," Laurie said in a low voice.

"*Huh?*" Trent whipped his head around so fast

807

it hurt his neck, but Laurie wasn't looking at him. She was looking at the red numbers of the countdown. They reflected backward off the lenses of the spectacles she wore on schooldays. She seemed almost hypnotized, unaware Trent was looking at her, perhaps even unaware that he was there.

"Not on purpose," she said. "He might even be sad. For awhile, anyway. Because I think he *does* love her, sort of, and she loves him. You know — sort of. But he'll make her worse and worse. She'll get sick all the time, and then . . . one day . . ."

She broke off and looked at him, and something in her face scared Trent worse than anything in their strange, changing, *sneaking* house had been able to do.

"Tell me, Trent," she said. Her hand grasped his arm. It was very cold. "Tell me how we're going to do it."

They went up to Lew's study together. Trent was prepared to ransack the place if that was what it took, but they found the key in the top drawer, tucked neatly into an envelope with the word STUDY printed on it in Lew's small, neat, somehow hemorrhoidal printing. Trent pocketed it. They left the house together just as the shower on the second floor went on, meaning their mom was up.

They spent the day in the park. Although neither of them spoke of it, it was the longest day either of them had ever lived through. Twice they saw the beat-cop and hid in the public toilets until he was gone. This was no time to be caught playing truant and bundled off to school.

At two-thirty, Trent gave Laurie a quarter and walked her to the phone booth on the east side of the park.

"Do I have to?" she asked. "I hate to scare her, especially after last night."

"Do you want her in the house when whatever happens, happens?" Trent asked. Laurie dropped the quarter into the telephone with no further protest.

It rang so many times that she became sure their mother had gone out. That might be good, but it might also be bad. It was certainly worrisome. If she was out, it was entirely possible that she might come back before —

"Trent, I don't think she's h—"

"Hello?" Mrs. Evans said in a sleepy voice.

"Oh, hi, Mom," Laurie said. "I didn't think you were there."

"I went back to bed," she said with an embarrassed little laugh. "I can't seem to get enough sleep, all of a sudden. I suppose if I'm asleep I can't think about how horrible I was last night —"

"Oh, Mom, you weren't horrible. When a person faints, it isn't because she *wants* to —"

"Laurie, why are you calling? Is everything okay?"

"Sure, Mom . . . well . . ."

Trent poked her in the ribs. Hard.

Laurie, who had been slumping (growing smaller, it almost seemed), straightened up in a hurry. "I hurt myself in gym. Just . . . you know, a little. It's not bad."

809

"What did you do? Jesus, you're not calling from the hospital, are you?"

"Gosh, no," Laurie said hastily. "It's just a sprained knee. Mrs. Kitt asked if you could come and bring me home early. I don't know if I can walk on it. It really hurts."

"I'll come right away. Try not to move it at all, honey. You could have torn a ligament. Is the nurse there?"

"Not right now. Don't worry, Mom, I'll be careful."

"Will you be in the nurse's office?"

"Yes," Laurie said. Her face was as red as the side of Brian's Radio Flyer wagon.

"I'll be right there."

"Thanks, Mom. Bye."

She hung up and looked at Trent. She drew in a deep breath and then let it out in a long, trembly sigh.

"That was fun," she said in a voice which was close to tears.

He hugged her tight. "You did great," he said. "Lots better than I could have, Spr— Laurie. I'm not sure she would have believed me."

"I wonder if she'll ever believe *me* again?" Laurie asked bitterly.

"She will," Trent said. "Come on."

They went over to the west side of the park, where they could watch Walnut Street. The day had turned cold and dim. Thunderheads were forming overhead, and a chilly wind was blowing. They waited for five endless minutes and then their mother's Subaru passed them, heading rapidly toward Greendowne Middle School, where Trent and Laurie went . . . *where we go when we're not playing hookey, that is,* Laurie thought.

"She's really humming," Trent said. "I hope she doesn't get into an accident, or something."

"Too late to worry about that now. Come on." Laurie had Trent's hand and was pulling him back to the telephone kiosk again. "*You* get to call Lew, you lucky devil."

He put in another quarter and punched the number of the History Department office, referring to a card he had taken from his wallet. He had barely slept a wink the night before, but now that things were set in motion, he found himself cool and calm . . . so cool, in fact, that he was almost refrigerated. He glanced at his watch. Quarter to three. Less than an hour to go. Thunder rumbled faintly in the west.

"History Department," a woman's voice said.

"Hi. This is Trent Bradbury. I need to speak with my stepfather, Lewis Evans, please."

"Professor Evans is in class," the secretary said, "but he'll be out at —"

"I know, he's got Modern British History until three-thirty. But you better get him, just the same. It's an emergency. It concerns his wife." A pointed, calculated pause, and then he added: "My mom."

There was a long pause, and Trent felt a moment of faint alarm. It was as if she were thinking of refusing or dismissing him, emergency or no emergency, and that was most definitely not in the plan.

"He's in Oglethorpe, right next door," she said finally. "I'll get him myself. I'll have him call home as soon as —"

"No, I have to hold on," Trent said.

"But —"

"Please, will you just stop goofing with me and go get him?" he asked, allowing a ragged, harried note into his voice. It wasn't hard.

"All right," the secretary said. It was impossible to tell if she was more disgruntled or worried. "If you could tell me the nature of the —"

"No," Trent said.

There was an offended sniff, and then he was on hold.

"Well?" Laurie asked. She was dancing from foot to foot like someone who needs to go to the bathroom.

"I'm on hold. They're getting him."

"What if he doesn't come?"

Trent shrugged. "Then we're sunk. But he'll come. You wait and see." He wished he could be as confident as he sounded, but he *did* still believe this would work. It *had* to work.

"We left it until awful late."

Trent nodded. They *had* left it until awful late, and Laurie knew why. The study door was solid oak, plenty strong, but neither of them knew anything about the lock. Trent wanted to make sure Lew had only the shortest time possible to test it.

"What if he sees Brian and Lissie on the corner when he comes home?"

"If he gets as hot under the collar as I think he will, he wouldn't notice them if they were on stilts and wearing Day-Glo duncecaps," Trent said.

"Why doesn't he answer the darn *phone?*" Laurie asked, looking at her watch.

"He will," Trent said, and then their stepfather did.

"Hello?"

"It's Trent, Lew. Mom's in your study. Her headache must have come back, because she fainted. I can't wake her up. You better come home right away."

Trent was not surprised at his stepfather's first stated object of concern — it was, in fact, an integral part of his plan — but it still made him so angry his fingers turned white on the telephone.

"My study? My *study?* What the hell was she doing in there?"

In spite of his anger, Trent's voice came out calmly. "Cleaning, I think." And then tossed the ultimate bait to a man who cared a great deal more for work than wife: "There are papers all over the floor."

"I'll be right there," Lew rapped, and then added: "If there are any windows open in there, shut them, for God's sake. There's a storm coming." He hung up without saying goodbye.

"Well?" Laurie asked as Trent hung up.

"He's on his way," Trent said, and laughed grimly. "The son of a bitch was so stirred up he didn't even ask what I was doing home from school. Come on."

They ran back to the intersection of Maple and Walnut. The sky had grown very dark now, and the sound of thunder had become almost constant. As they reached the blue U.S. mailbox on the corner, the streetlights along Maple Street began to come on two by two, marching away from them up the hill.

Lissa and Brian hadn't arrived yet.

"I want to come with you, Trent," Laurie said, but her face proclaimed her a liar. It was very pale, and her eyes were too large, swimming with unshed tears.

"No way," Trent said. "Wait here for Brian and Lissa."

At their names, Laurie turned and looked down Walnut Street. She saw two kids coming, hurrying along with lunchboxes bouncing in their hands. Although they were too far away to make out faces, she was pretty sure it was them, and she told Trent.

"Good. The three of you go behind Mrs. Redland's hedge there and wait for Lew to pass. Then you can come up the street, *but don't go in the house and don't let them, either.* Wait for me outside."

"I'm afraid, Trent." The tears had begun to spill down her cheeks now.

"Me too, Sprat," he said, and kissed her swiftly on the forehead. "But it'll all be over soon."

Before she could say anything else, Trent went running up the street toward the Bradburys' house on Maple Street. He glanced at his watch as he ran. It was twelve past three.

The house had a still, hot air that scared him. It was as if gunpowder had been spilled in every corner, and people he could not see were standing by to light unseen fuses. He imagined the clock in the wine-cellar ticking relentlessly away, now reading

00:19:06.

What if Lew *was* late?

814

No time to worry about that now.

Trent raced up to the third floor through the still, combustible air. He imagined he could feel the house stirring now, coming alive as the count-down neared its conclusion. He tried to tell himself that imagination was *all* it was, but part of him knew better.

He went into Lew's study, opened two or three file-cabinets and desk drawers at random, and threw the papers he found all over the floor. This took only a few moments, but he was just finishing when he heard the Porsche coming up the street. Its engine wasn't snarling today; Lew had wound it up to a scream.

Trent stepped out of the office and into the shad-ows of the third-floor hallway, where they had drilled the first holes what seemed like a century ago. He rammed his hand into his pocket for the key, and his pocket was empty except for an old, crumpled lunch-ticket.

I must have lost it running up the street. It must have bounced right out of my pocket.

He stood there, sweating and frozen, as the Porsche squealed into the driveway. Its engine cut out. The driver's door opened and slammed shut. Lew's footsteps ran for the back door. Thunder crumped like an artillery shell in the sky, a stroke of bright lightning forked through the gloom, and, somewhere deep in the house, a powerful motor turned over, uttered a low, muffled bark, and then began to hum.

Jesus, oh dear Jesus, what do I do? What CAN I do? He's bigger than me! If I try to hit him over the head, he'll —

He had slipped his left hand into his other pocket, and his thoughts broke off as it touched the old-fashioned metal teeth of the key. At some point during the long afternoon in the park, he must have transferred it from one pocket to the other without even being aware of it.

Gasping, heart galloping in his stomach and throat as well as in his chest, Trent faded back down the hall to the luggage-closet, stepped inside, and pulled the accordion-style doors most of the way shut in front of him.

Lew was galumphing up the stairs, bawling his wife's name over and over at the top of his voice. Trent saw him appear, hair standing up in spikes (he must have been running a hand through it as he drove), his tie askew, big drops of sweat standing out on his broad, intelligent forehead, eyes squinted down to furious little slits.

"*Catherine!*" he bawled, and ran down the hall into the office.

Before he could even get all the way in, Trent was out of the luggage-closet and running soundlessly back down the hall. He would have just one chance. If he missed the keyhole . . . if the tumblers failed to turn at the first twist of the key . . .

If either of those things happens, I'll fight with him, he had time to think. *If I can't send him alone, I'll make damn sure to take him with me.*

He grabbed the door and banged it shut so hard that a little film of dust shot out of the cracks between the hinges. He caught one glimpse of Lew's startled face. Then the key was in the lock. He twisted it, and the bolt shot across an instant before Lew struck the door.

"Hey!" Lew shouted. "Hey, you little bastard, what are you doing? Where's Catherine? Let me out of here!"

The knob twisted fruitlessly back and forth. Then it stopped, and Lew rained a fusillade of blows on the door.

"Let me out of here right now Trent Bradbury before you get the worst beating of your goddamned life!"

Trent backed slowly across the hall. When his shoulders struck the far wall, he gasped. The key to the study, which he had removed from the keyhole without even thinking about it, dropped from his fingers and thumped to the faded hall-runner between his feet. Now that it was done, reaction set in. The world began to look wavery, as if he were under water, and he had to fight to keep from fainting himself. Only now, with Lew locked in, his mother sent off on a wild-goose chase, and the other kids safely tucked away behind Mrs. Redland's overgrown yew hedge, did he realize that he had never really expected it would work at all. If "Daddy Lew" was surprised to find himself locked in, Trent Bradbury was absolutely amazed.

The doorknob of the study twisted back and forth in short sharp half-circles.

"LET ME OUT, GODDAMMIT!"

"I'll let you out at quarter of four, Lew," Trent said in an uneven, trembling voice, and then a little giggle escaped him. "If you're still *here* at quarter of four, that is."

Then, from downstairs: "Trent? Trent, are you all right?"

817

Dear God, that was Laurie.

"Are you, Trent?"

And Lissa!

"Hey, *Trent!* Y'okay?"

And Brian.

Trent looked at his watch and was horrified to see it was 3:31 . . . going on 3:32. *And suppose his watch was slow?*

"Get out!" he screamed at them, plunging down the hallway toward the stairs. *"Get out of this house!"*

The third-floor hallway seemed to stretch out before him like taffy; the faster he ran, the farther it seemed to stretch ahead of him. Lew rained blows on the door and curses on the air; thunder boomed; and, from deep within the house came the ever-more-urgent sound of machines waking to life.

He reached the stairwell at last and hurried down, his upper body so far out in front of his legs that he almost fell. Then he was whirling around the newel post and hurtling down the flight of stairs between the second floor and the first, toward where his brother and two sisters waited, looking up at him.

"Out!" he screamed, grabbing them, shoving them toward the open door and the stormy blackness outside. *"Quick!"*

"Trent, what's happening?" Brian asked. "What's happening to the *house?* It's *shaking!*"

It was, too — a deep vibration that rose up through the floor and rattled Trent's eyeballs in their sockets. Plaster-dust began to sift down into his hair.

"No time! Out! Fast! Laurie, help me!"

Trent swept Brian into his arms. Laurie grabbed Lissa under the arms of her dress and stumbled out the door with her.

Thunder bammed. Lightning twisted across the sky. The wind that had been gasping earlier now began to roar like a dragon.

Trent heard an earthquake building under the house. As he ran out through the door with Brian, he saw electric-blue light, so bright it left after-images on his eyes for almost an hour (he reflected later he was lucky not to have been blinded), shoot out through the narrow cellar windows. It cut across the lawn in rays that looked almost solid. He heard the glass break. And, just as he passed through the door, he felt the house *rising* under his feet.

He jumped down the front steps and grabbed Laurie's arm. They stumble-staggered down the walk to the street, which was now as black as night with the coming of the storm.

There they turned back and watched it happen.

The house on Maple Street seemed to gather itself. It no longer looked straight and solid; it seemed to jitter, like a comic-strip picture of a man on a pogo-stick. Huge cracks ran out from it, not only in the cement walk but in the earth surrounding it. The lawn pulled apart in huge pie-shaped turves of grass. Roots strained blackly upward below the green, and the whole front yard seemed to become bubble-shaped, as if it were straining to hold the house before which it had spread so long.

Trent cast his eyes up to the third floor, where

the light in Lew's study still shone. Trent thought the sound of breaking glass had come — was *still* coming — from up there, then dismissed the idea as imagination — how could he hear *anything* in all that racket? It was only a year later that Laurie told him she was quite sure she had heard their stepfather screaming from up there.

The foundation of the house first crumbled, then cracked, then sundered with a croak of exploding mortar. Brilliant cold blue fire lanced out. The children covered their eyes and staggered back. The engines screamed. The earth pulled up and up in a last agonized holding action . . . and then let go. Suddenly the house was a foot above the ground, resting on a pad of bright blue fire.

It was a perfect lift-off.

Atop the center roofpeak, the weathervane spun madly.

The house rose slowly at first, then began to gather speed. It thundered upward on its flaring pad of blue fire, the front door clapping madly back and forth as it went.

"My toys!" Brian bleated, and Trent began to laugh wildly.

The house reached a height of thirty yards, seemed to poise itself for its great leap upward, then *blasted* into the rushing spate of night-black clouds.

It was gone.

Two shingles came floating down like large black leaves.

"Look out, Trent!" Laurie cried out a second or two later, and shoved him hard enough to knock him over. The rubber-backed WELCOME mat thwacked into the street where he had been standing.

Trent looked at Laurie. Laurie looked back.

"That would've smarted like big blue heck if it'd hit you on the head," she told him, "so you just better not call me Sprat anymore, Trent."

He looked at her solemnly for several seconds, then began to giggle. Laurie joined in. So did the little ones. Brian took one of Trent's hands; Lissa took the other. They helped pull him to his feet, and then the four of them stood together, looking at the smoking cellar-hole in the middle of the shattered lawn. People were coming out of their houses now, but the Bradbury children ignored them. Or perhaps it would be truer to say the Bradbury children didn't know they were there at all.

"Wow," Brian said reverently. "Our house took off, Trent."

"Yeah," Trent said.

"Maybe wherever it's going, there'll be people who want to know about the Normans and the Sexies," Lissa said.

Trent and Laurie put their arms around each other and began to shriek with mingled laughter and horror . . . and that was when the rain began to pelt down.

Mr. Slattery from across the street joined them. He didn't have much hair, but what he did have was plastered to his gleaming skull in tight little bunches.

"*What happened?*" he screamed over the thunder, which was almost constant now. "*What happened here?*"

Trent let go of his sister and looked at Mr. Slattery. "True Space Adventures," he said solemnly, and that set them all off again.

Mr. Slattery cast a doubtful, frightened look at the empty cellar-hole, decided discretion was the better part of valor, and retreated to his side of the street. Although it was still pouring buckets, he did not invite the Bradbury children to join him. Nor did they care. They sat down on the curb, Trent and Laurie in the middle, Brian and Lissa on the sides.

Laurie leaned toward Trent and whispered in his ear: "We're free."

"It's better than that," Trent said. "*She* is."

Then he put his arms around all of them — by stretching, he could just manage — and they sat on the curb in the pouring rain and waited for their mother to come home.

The Fifth Quarter

I parked the heap around the corner from Keenan's house, sat in the dark for a moment, then turned off the key and got out. When I slammed the door, I could hear rust flaking off the rocker panels and dropping onto the street. It wasn't going to be like that much longer.

The gun was in a bandolier holster and lay against my ribcage like a fist. It was Barney's .45, and I was glad of that. It lent the whole crazy business a touch of irony. Maybe even a sense of justice.

Keenan's house was an architectural monstrosity spread over a quarter-acre of land, all slanting angles and steep-sloped roofs behind an iron fence. He'd left the gate unlocked, as I'd hoped. Earlier I'd seen him calling someone from the living room, and a hunch too strong to deny told me it had been either Jagger or the Sarge. Probably the Sarge. The waiting was over; this was my night.

I walked to the driveway, staying close to the shrubbery and listening for any strange sound over the cutting whine of the January wind. There wasn't any. It was Friday night, and Keenan's sleep-in maid would be out having a jolly time at somebody's Tupperware party. Nobody home but that bastard Keenan. Waiting for the Sarge. Waiting — although he didn't know it yet — for me.

The carport was open and I slipped inside. The ebony shadow of Keenan's Impala loomed. I tried the back door. The car was also open. Keenan wasn't cut out to be a villain, I reflected; he was much too trusting. I got in the car, sat down, and waited.

Now I could hear the faint sound of jazz on the wind, very quiet, very good. Miles Davis, maybe. Keenan listening to Miles Davis and holding a gin fizz in one manicured hand. Nice for him.

It was a long wait. The hands on my watch crawled from eight-thirty to nine to ten. Time for a lot of thinking. I mostly thought about Barney, and that wasn't strictly a matter of choice. I thought about how he looked in that small boat when I found him, staring up at me and making meaningless cawing noises. He'd been adrift for two days and looked like a boiled lobster. There was black blood encrusted across his midsection where he'd been shot.

He'd steered toward the cottage as best he could, but still it had been mostly luck. Lucky he'd gotten there, lucky he could still talk for a little while. I'd had a fistful of sleeping pills ready if he couldn't talk. I didn't want him to suffer. Not unless there was a reason for it, anyway. As it turned out, there was. He had a story to tell, a real whopper, and he told me almost all of it.

When he was dead, I went back to the boat and got his .45. It was hidden aft in a small compartment, wrapped in a waterproof pouch. Then I towed his boat out into deep water and sank it. If I could have put an epitaph over his head, it would have been the one about how there's a sucker born every minute. Most of them are pretty nice guys, too, I bet — just like Barney. Instead, I started trying to find the men who capped him. It had taken six months to find Keenan and to ascertain that Sarge was, at least, somewhere close by, but I'm a persistent little pup, and here I was.

At ten-twenty, headlights splashed up the curving driveway and I lay on the floor of the Impala. The newcomer drove into the carport, snuggling up close to Keenan's car. It sounded like one of the old Volkswagens. The little engine died and I could hear Sarge grunting softly as he fought his way out of the little car. The porch light went on, and the sound of the door clicking open came to me.

Keenan: "Sarge! You're late! Come on in and have a drink."

Sarge: "Scotch."

I'd unrolled the window before. Now I stuck Barney's .45 through it, holding the stock with both hands. "Stand still," I said.

The Sarge was halfway up the porch steps. Keenan, the perfect host, had come out and was looking down at him, waiting for him to come up so he could after-you him into the house. They were both perfect silhouettes in the light spilling through from inside. I doubted if they could see much of me in the dark, but they could see the gun. It was a big gun.

"Who the hell are you?" Keenan asked.

"Jerry Tarkanian," I said. "Move and I'll put a hole in you big enough to watch television through."

"You sound like a punk," Sarge said. He didn't move, though.

"Just don't move. That's all you've got to worry about." I opened the Impala's back door and got out carefully. The Sarge was staring at me over his shoulder and I could see the glitter of his little eyes. One hand was creeping up the lapel of his 1943-model double-breasted suit.

"Oh, please," I said. "Get your fucking hands up, asshole."

The Sarge put his hands up. Keenan's already were.

"Come down to the foot of the steps. Both of you."

They came down, and out of the direct glare of the light I could see their faces. Keenan looked scared, but the Sarge might have been listening to a lecture on Zen and the art of motorcycle maintenance. He was probably the one who had jobbed Barney.

"Face the wall and lean on it. Both of you."

Keenan: "If you're after money . . ."

I laughed. "Well, I was going to start off by offering you a cut-rate deal on Tupperware, work my way up to the big stuff gradually, but you saw through me. Yeah, I'm after money. Four hundred and eighty thousand dollars, actually. Buried on a little island off Bar Harbor called Carmen's Folly."

Keenan jerked as if he'd been shot, but the Sarge's dipped-in-concrete face never twitched. He turned around and put his hands on the wall, leaning his weight on them. Keenan reluctantly followed suit. I frisked him first and got a stupid little .32 with a three-inch barrel. A gun like that, you could put the muzzle against a guy's head and still miss when you pulled the trigger. I threw it over my shoulder and heard it bounce off one of the cars. Sarge was clean — and it was a relief to step away from him.

"We're going into the house. You first, Keenan, then Sarge, then me. Without incident, okay?"

We all trooped up the steps and into the kitchen. It was one of those germless chrome-and-tile jobs that looks like it was spit whole out of some mass-production womb in the Midwest somewhere, the work of hearty Methodist assholes who all look like Mr. Goodwrench and smell like Cherry Blend tobacco. I doubt if it ever needed anything so vulgar as cleaning; Keenan probably just closed the doors and turned on the hidden sprinklers once a week.

I paraded them through into the living room, another treat for the eyes. It had apparently been done by a pansy decorator who never got over his crush on Ernest Hemingway. There was a flagstone fireplace almost as big as an elevator car, a teak buffet table with a moosehead mounted above it, and a drinks cart stashed below a gunrack loaded with premium artillery. The stereo had turned itself off.

I waved the gun at the couch. "One on each end."

They sat, Keenan on the right, Sarge on the left. The Sarge looked even bigger sitting down. An ugly, dented scar twisted its way through his slightly overgrown crewcut. I put his weight at about two-thirty, and wondered why a man with the size and physical presence of Mike Tyson owned a Volkswagen.

I grabbed an easy chair and dragged it over Keenan's quicksand-colored rug until it was in front and between them. I sat down and let the .45 rest on my thigh. Keenan stared at it like a bird stares at a snake. The Sarge, on the other hand, was staring at me like he was the snake and I was the bird. "Now what?" he asked.

"Let's talk about maps and money," I said.

"I don't know what you're talking about," Sarge said. "All I know is that little boys shouldn't play with guns."

"How's Cappy MacFarland these days?" I asked casually.

It didn't get jack shit from the Sarge, but Keenan popped his cork. "He knows. He knows!" The words shot out of him like bullets.

"Shut up!" the Sarge told him. "Shut up your goddam trap!"

Keenan moaned a little. This was one part of the scenario he had never imagined. I smiled. "He's right, Sarge." I said. "I know. Almost all of it."

"Who are you?"

"No one you know. A friend of Barney's."

"Barney who?" Sarge asked indifferently. "Barney Google, with the goo-goo-googly eyes?"

"He wasn't dead, Sarge. Not quite dead."

Sarge turned a slow and murderous look on Keenan. Keenan shuddered and opened his mouth. "Don't talk," Sarge said to him. "Not one fucking word. I'll snap your neck like a chicken if you do."

Keenan's mouth shut with a snap.

Sarge looked at me again. "What does *almost* all of it mean?"

"Everything but the fine details. I know about the armored car. The island. Cappy MacFarland. How you and Keenan and some bastard named Jagger killed Barney. And the map. I know about that."

"It wasn't the way he told you," Sarge said. "He was going to cross us."

"He couldn't cross the street," I said. "He was just a patsy who could drive."

He shrugged; it was like watching a minor earthquake. "Okay. Be as dumb as you look."

"I knew Barney had something on as early as last March. I just didn't know what. And then one night he had a gun. *This* gun. How did you connect with him, Sarge?"

"A mutual friend — someone who did time with him. We needed a driver who knew eastern Maine and the Bar Harbor area. Keenan and I went to see him and laid it out for him. He liked it."

"I did time with him in the Shank," I said. "I liked him. You couldn't help but like him. He was dumb, but he was a good kid. He needed a keeper more than a partner."

"George and Lennie," Sarge sneered.

"Good to know you spent your own jail time improving what passes for your mind, sweetheart," I said. "We were thinking about a bank in Lewiston. He couldn't wait for me to finish doping it out. So now he's underground."

"Jeepers, this is really sad," Sarge said. "I'm gettin, like, all soft and mushy inside."

I picked up the gun and showed him the muzzle, and for a second or two he was the bird and it was the snake. "One more wisecrack and I'll put a bullet in your belly. Do you believe that?"

His tongue flickered in and out with startling quickness, lapped across his lower lip, and disappeared again. He nodded. Keenan was frozen. He looked like he wanted to retch but didn't quite dare.

"He told me it was big time, a big score," I resumed. "That's all I could get out of him. He took off on April third. Two days later four guys knock over the Portland-Bangor Federated truck just outside of Carmel. All three guards dead. The newspapers said the robbers ran two roadblocks in a souped-up '78 Plymouth. Barney had a '78 up on blocks, thinking about turning it into a stocker. I'm betting Keenan put up the front money for him to turn it into something a little better and a lot faster."

I looked at him. Keenan's face was the color of cheese.

"On May sixth I get a card postmarked Bar Harbor, but that doesn't mean anything — there are dozens of little islands that channel their mail through there. A mailboat does the circuit, picks it up. The card says: 'Mom and family fine, store doing good. See you in July.' It was signed with Barney's middle name. I leased a cottage on the coast, because Barney knew that would be the deal. July comes and goes, no Barney."

"Musta had a terminal hard-on by then, kid, right?" Sarge said. I guess he wanted me to be sure I hadn't buffaloed him.

I looked at him remotely. "He showed up in early August. Courtesy of your buddy Keenan, Sarge. He forgot about the automatic bilge pump in the boat. You thought the chop would sink it quick enough, right, Keenan? But you thought he was dead, too. I had a yellow blanket spread out on Frenchman's Point every day. Visible for miles. Easy to spot. Still, he was lucky."

"*Too* lucky," Sarge almost spat.

"One thing I'm curious about — did he know before the job that the money was new, all the serial numbers recorded? That you couldn't even sell it to a currency-junker in the Bahamas for three or four years?"

"He knew," the Sarge rumbled, and I was surprised to find myself believing him. "And nobody was planning to junk the dough. He knew that, too, kid. I think he was counting on that Lewiston job you mentioned for ready cash, but whatever he was or wasn't counting on, he knew the score and said he could live with it. Christ, why not? Say we had to wait *ten* years to go back for that dough and split it up. What's ten years to a kid like Barney? Shit, he would have been all of thirty-five. I'd be sixty-one."

"What about Cappy MacFarland? Did Barney know about him, too?"

"Yes. Cappy came with the deal. A good man. A pro. He got cancer last year. Inoperable. And he owed me a favor."

"So the four of you went out to Cappy's island," I said. "A little nobody-on-it named Carmen's Folly. Cappy buried the money and made a map."

"That part was Jagger's idea," Sarge said. "We

831

didn't want to split hot money — too tempting. But we didn't want to leave all the swag in one pair of hands, either. Cappy MacFarland was the perfect solution."

"Tell me about the map."

"I thought we'd get to that," Sarge said with a wintry smile.

"Don't tell him!" Keenan cried out hoarsely.

Sarge turned to him and gave him a look that would have melted bar steel. "Shut up. I can't lie and I can't stonewall, thanks to you. You know what I hope, Keenan? I hope you weren't really looking forward to seeing in the new century."

"Your name's in a letter," Keenan said wildly. "If anything happens to me, your name's in a letter!"

"Cappy made a good map," the Sarge said, as if Keenan were not there at all. "He had some draftsman training in Joliet. He cut it into quarters. One for each of us. We were going to have a reunion on July fourth, five years later. Talk it over. Maybe decide to wait another five years, maybe decide to put the pieces together right then. But there was trouble."

"Yes," I said. "I guess that's one way of putting it."

"If it makes you feel any better, it was all Keenan's play. I don't know if Barney knew it or not, but that's how it was. When Jagger and I took off in Cappy's boat, Barney was fine."

"You're a goddam liar!" Keenan squealed.

"Who's got two pieces of the map in his wall safe?" Sarge inquired. "Is it you, dear?"

He looked at me again.

"It was still all right. Half the map still wasn't enough. And am I gonna sit here and say I would have preferred a four-way split to a three-way? I don't think you'd believe it even if it was true. Then, guess what? Keenan calls. Tells me we ought to have a talk. I was expecting it. Looks like you were, too."

I nodded. Keenan had been easier to find than the Sarge — he kept a higher profile. I could have tracked Sarge all the way down eventually, I suppose, but I'd been pretty sure that wouldn't be necessary. Thieves of a feather flock together . . . and the feathers have a tendency to fly, too, when one of the birds is a vulture like Keenan.

"Of course," Sarge went on, "he tells me not to get any lethal ideas. Says he's taken out an insurance policy, my name in an open-in-event-of-my-death letter he'd sent his lawyer. His idea was that the two of us could probably dope out where Cappy'd buried the money if we put three of the four pieces of the map together."

"And split the swag fifty-fifty," I said.

Sarge nodded. Keenan's face was like a moon drifting somewhere in a high stratosphere of terror.

"Where's the safe?" I asked him.

Keenan didn't say anything.

I had done some practicing with the .45. It was a good gun. I liked it. I held it in both hands and shot Keenan in the forearm, just below the elbow. The Sarge didn't even jump. Keenan fell off the couch and curled up in a ball, holding his arm and howling.

"The safe," I said.

Keenan continued to howl.

"I'll shoot you in the knee," I said. "I don't know from personal experience, but I've heard that hurts like a mad bastard."

"The print," he gasped. "The Van Gogh. Don't shoot me anymore, huh?" He looked at me, grinning fearfully.

I motioned to Sarge with the gun. "Stand facing the wall."

The Sarge got up and looked at the wall, arms dangling limply.

"Now you," I said to Keenan. "Go open the safe."

"I'm bleeding to death," Keenan moaned.

I went over and stroked the butt of the .45 up the side of his cheek, laying back skin. "*Now* you're bleeding," I told him. "Go open the safe or you'll bleed more."

Keenan got up, holding his arm and blubbering. He took the print off its hooks with his good hand, revealing an office-gray wall safe. He threw a terrified glance at me and began to twiddle the dial. He made two false starts and had to go back. The third time he got it open. There were some documents and two wads of bills inside. He reached in, fumbled around, and came up with two squares of paper, about three inches on a side.

I swear I didn't mean to kill him. I planned to tie him up and leave him. He was harmless enough; the maid would find him when she got back from her lingerie party or wherever it was she'd gone in her little Dodge Colt, and Keenan wouldn't dare poke his nose out of his house for a week. But it was like Sarge had said. He did have two. And one of them had blood on it.

I shot him again, this time not in the arm. He went down like an empty laundry bag.

Sarge didn't flinch. "I wasn't crapping you. Keenan jobbed your friend. They were both amateurs. Amateurs are stupid."

I didn't answer. I looked down at the squares and shoved them into my pocket. Neither one had an X-marks-the-spot on it.

"What now?" Sarge asked.

"We go to your place."

"What makes you think my piece of the map is there?"

"I don't know. Telepathy, maybe. Besides, if it isn't, we'll go where it is. I'm in no hurry."

"You've got all the answers, huh?"

"Let's go."

We went back out to the carport. I sat in the back of the VW, on the side away from him. His bulk and the size of the car made a surprise play on his part a joke; it would take him five minutes just to get turned around. Two minutes later we were on the road.

It was starting to snow, big, sloppy flakes that clung to the windshield and turned to instant slush when they struck the pavement. It was slippery going, but there wasn't much traffic.

After a half hour on Route 10, he turned off onto a secondary road. Fifteen minutes later we were on a rutted dirt track with snow-freighted pines staring at us on either side. Two miles along we turned into a short, trash-littered driveway.

In the limited sweep of the VW's headlights I could make out a rickety backwoods shack with a patched roof and a twisted TV aerial. There was a snow-covered old Ford in a gully to the left. Out in back was an outhouse and a pile of old tires. Hernando's Hideaway.

"Welcome to Bally's East," Sarge said, and killed the engine.

"If this is a con, I'll kill you."

He seemed to fill three-quarters of the tiny vehicle's front seat. "I know that," he said.

"Get out."

Sarge led the way up to the front door. "Open it," I said. "Then stand still."

He opened the door and stood still. I stood still. We stood still for about three minutes, and nothing happened. The only moving thing was a fat gray squirrel that had ventured into the middle of the yard to curse us in *lingua rodenta*.

"Okay," I said. "Let's go in."

Surprise, it was a dump. The one sixty-watt bulb cast a grungy glow over the whole room, leaving shadows like starved bats in the corners. Newspapers were scattered helter-skelter. Drying clothes were hung on a sagging rope. In one corner there was an ancient Zenith TV. In the opposite corner was a rickety sink and a stark, rust-stained bathtub on claw feet. A hunting rifle stood beside it. The predominant odors were feet, farts, and chili.

"It beats living raw," Sarge said.

I could have argued the point, but didn't. "Where's your piece of the map?"

"In the bedroom."

"Let's go get it."

"Not yet." He turned around slowly, his dipped-in-concrete face hard. "I want your word you ain't going to kill me when you get it."

"How you going to make me keep it?"

"Fuck, I don't know. I guess I'm just gonna hope it was more than the money that got you cranked up. If it was Barney, too — wanting to clean Barney's slate — you did it, it's clean. Keenan capped him and now Keenan's dead. If you want the bundle, too, okay. Maybe three-quarters *will* be enough, and you were right — my piece has got a great big X on it. But you don't get it unless you promise I get something, too: my life."

"How do I know you won't come after me?"

"But I will, sonny," the Sarge said softly.

I laughed. "All right. Throw in Jagger's address and you've got your promise. I'll keep it, too."

The Sarge shook his head slowly. "You don't want to play with Jagger, fella, Jagger will eat you up."

I had dropped the .45 a little. Now I lifted it again.

"All right. He's in Coleman, Massachusetts. A ski lodge. Is that good enough?"

"Yes. Let's get your piece, Sarge."

The Sarge looked me over once more, closely. Then he nodded. We went into the bedroom.

More Colonial charm. The stained mattress on the floor was littered with stroke-books and the walls were papered with photographs of women who appeared to be wearing nothing but a thin coating of Wesson Oil. One look at this place and Dr. Ruth's head would have exploded.

The Sarge didn't hesitate. He picked up the lamp on the night-table and pried the base off it. His quarter of the map was neatly rolled up inside; he held it out wordlessly.

"Throw it," I invited.

The Sarge smiled thinly. "Cautious little pencil-neck, aren't you?"

"I find it pays. Give it up, Sarge."

He tossed it over to me. "Easy come, easy go," he said.

"I'm going to keep my promise," I said. "Consider yourself lucky. Out in the other room."

Cold light flickered in his eyes. "What are you going to do?"

"See that you stay in one place for awhile. Move."

We went out into the main room, a nifty little parade of two. The Sarge stood underneath the naked lightbulb, back to me, his shoulders hunched, anticipating the gunbarrel that was going to groove his head very shortly. I was just lifting the gun to clout him when the light blinked out.

The shack was suddenly pitch black.

I threw myself to the right; Sarge was already gone like a cool breeze. I could hear the thump and tumble of newspapers as he hit the floor in a flat dive. Then silence. Utter and complete.

I waited for my night vision, but when it came it was no help. The place was a mausoleum in which a thousand dim tombstones loomed. And the Sarge knew every one of them.

I knew about Sarge; material on him hadn't been hard to spade up. He'd been a Green Beret in Vietnam, and no one even bothered with his real name anymore; he was just the Sarge, big and murderous and tough.

Somewhere in the dark he was moving in on me. He must have known the place like the back of his hand, because there wasn't a sound, not a squeaking board, not a foot scrape. But I could feel him getting closer and closer, flanking from the left or the right or maybe pulling a tricky one and coming in straight ahead.

The stock of the gun was very sweaty in my hand, and I had to control the urge to fire it wildly, randomly. I was very aware that I had three-quarters of the pie in my pocket. I didn't bother wondering why the lights had gone out. Not until the powerful flashlight stabbed in through the window, sweeping the floor in a wild, random pattern that just happened to catch the Sarge, frozen in a half-crouch seven feet to my left. His eyes glowed greenly in the bright cone of light, like cat's eyes.

He had a glinting razor blade in his right hand, and I suddenly remembered the way his hand had been spidering up his coat lapel in Keenan's carport.

The Sarge said one word into the flash beam. "Jagger?"

I don't know who got him first. A large-caliber pistol fired once behind the flashlight beam, and I pulled the trigger of Barney's .45 twice — pure reflex. The Sarge was thrown back against the wall with force enough to knock him out of one of his boots.

The flashlight snapped off.

I fired one shot at the window, but hit only glass. I lay on my side in the darkness and realized that I hadn't been the only one waiting around for Keenan's greed to resurface. Jagger had been waiting, too. And, although there were twelve rounds of ammunition back in my car, there was only one left in my gun.

You don't want to play with Jagger, fella, the Sarge had said, *Jagger will eat you up.*

I had a pretty good picture of the room in my head now. I got up in a crouch and ran, stepping over Sarge's sprawled legs and into the corner. I got into the bathtub and poked my eyes up over the edge. There was no sound, none at all. The bottom of the tub was gritty with flaked-off bathtub ring. I waited.

About five minutes went by. It seemed like five hours.

Then the light flicked on again, this time in the bedroom window. I ducked my head when it glared through the doorway. It probed briefly and clicked off.

Silence again. A long, loud silence. On the dirty surface of Sarge's porcelain bathtub I saw everything. Keenan, grinning desperately. Barney, with the clotted hole in his gut, due east of his navel. Sarge, standing frozen in the flashlight beam, holding the razor blade professionally between thumb and first finger. Jagger, the dark shadow with no face. And me. The fifth quarter.

Suddenly there was a voice, just outside the door. It was soft and cultured, almost womanish, but not effete. It sounded deadly and competent as hell.

"Hey, beautiful."

I kept quiet. He wasn't getting my number without dialing a little.

When the voice came again, it was by the window. "I'm going to kill you, beautiful. I came to kill them, but you'll do fine."

A pause while he shifted position once more. When the voice came again, it came from the window just over my head — the one above the bathtub. My guts crawled into my throat. If he flashed that light now . . .

"No fifth wheels need apply," Jagger said. "Sorry."

I could barely hear him moving to his next position. It turned out to be back to the doorway. "I've got my quarter with me. You want to come and take it?"

I felt an urge to cough and repressed it.

"Come and get it, beautiful." His voice was mocking. "The whole pie. Come and take it away."

But I didn't have to, and I suppose he knew it. I was holding the chips. I could find the money now. With his single quarter, Jagger had no chance.

This time the silence really spun out. A half-hour, an hour, forever. Eternity squared. My body started to stiffen. Outside, the wind was tuning up, making it impossible to hear anything but rattling snow against the walls. It was very cold. The tips of my fingers were going numb.

Then, around one-thirty, a ghostly stirring sound like crawling rats in the darkness. I stopped breathing. Somehow Jagger had got in. He was right in the middle of the room . . .

Then I got it. *Rigor mortis*, hurried by the cold, was rearranging Sarge for the last time, that was all. I relaxed a little.

That was when the door rammed open and Jagger charged through, ghostly and visible in a mantle of white snow, tall and loose and gangling. I let him have it and the bullet punched a hole through the side of his head. And in the brief gunflash, I saw that what I had holed was a scarecrow with no face, dressed in some farmer's thrown-out pants and shirt. The burlap head fell off the broomstick neck as it hit the floor. Then Jagger was shooting at me.

He was holding a semi-automatic pistol, and the innards of the bathtub were like a great percussive hollow cymbal. Porcelain flew up, bounced off the wall, struck my face. Wood splinters and a single hot spent slug rained down on me.

Then he was charging, never letting up. He was going to shoot me in the tub like a fish in a barrel. I couldn't even put my head up.

It was Sarge who saved me. Jagger stumbled over one big dead foot, staggered, and pumped bullets into the floor instead of over my head. Then I was on my knees. I pretended I was Roger Clemens. I pegged Barney's big .45 at his head.

The gun hit him but didn't stop him. I stumbled over the rim of the tub getting out to tackle him, and Jagger put two groggy shots to my left.

The faint silhouette stepped back, trying to get a bead, one hand holding his ear where the gun had hit him. He shot me through the wrist, and his second shot ripped a groove in my neck. Then, incredibly, he stumbled over Sarge's feet again and fell backward. He brought the gun up again and put one through the roof. It was his last chance. I kicked the gun out of his hand, hearing the wetwood sound of breaking bones. I kicked him in the groin, doubling him up. I kicked him again, this time in the back of the head, and his feet rattled a fast, unconscious tattoo on the floor. He was as good as dead then, but I kicked him again and again, kicked him until there was nothing but pulp and strawberry jam, nothing anyone could ever identify, not by teeth, not by anything. I kicked him until I couldn't swing my leg anymore, and my toes wouldn't move.

I suddenly realized I was screaming and there was no one to hear me but dead men.

I wiped my mouth and knelt over Jagger's body.

He had been lying about his quarter of the map, as it turned out. It didn't surprise me much. No, I take that back. It didn't surprise me at all.

My heap was just where I had left it, around the block from Keenan's house, but now it was just a ghostly hump of snow. I had left Sarge's VW a mile back. I hoped my heater was still working. I was numb all over. I got the door open and winced a little as I sat down inside. The crease in my neck had already clotted over, but my wrist hurt like hell.

The starter cranked for a long time, and the motor finally caught. The heater was working, and the one wiper cleared away most of the snow on the driver's side. Jagger had been lying about his quarter, and it hadn't been in the unobtrusive (and probably stolen) Honda Civic he'd come in. But his address had been in his wallet, and if I actually needed his quarter, I thought there was a pretty good chance I could find it. I didn't think I would; three pieces should be enough, especially since

Sarge's quarter was the one with the X.

I pulled out carefully. I was going to be careful for a long time. The Sarge had been right about one thing: Barney had been a dope. The fact that he'd also been my friend didn't matter anymore. The debt had been paid.

In the meantime, I had a lot to be careful for.

The Doctor's Case

I believe there was only one occasion upon which I actually solved a crime before my slightly fabulous friend, Mr. Sherlock Holmes. I say *believe* because my memory began to grow hazy about the edges as I entered my ninth decade; now, as I approach my centennial, the whole has become downright misty. There *may* have been another occasion, but if so I do not remember it.

I doubt that I shall ever forget this particular case no matter how murky my thoughts and memories may become, and I thought I might as well set it down before God caps my pen forever. It cannot humiliate Holmes now, God knows; he is forty years in his grave. That, I think, is long enough to leave the tale untold. Even Lestrade, who used Holmes upon occasion but never had any great liking for him, never broke his silence in the matter of Lord Hull — he hardly could have done so, considering the circumstances. Even if the circumstances had been different, I somehow doubt he would have. He and Holmes baited each other, and I believe that Holmes may have harbored actual hate in his heart for the policeman (although he never would have admitted to such a low emotion), but Lestrade had a queer respect for my friend.

It was a wet, dreary afternoon and the clock had just rung half past one. Holmes sat by the window, holding his violin but not playing it, looking silently out into the rain. There were times, especially once his cocaine days were behind him, when Holmes would grow moody to the point of surliness when the skies remained stubbornly gray for a week or more, and he had been doubly disappointed on this day, for the glass had been rising since late the night before and he had confidently predicted clearing skies by ten this morning at the latest. Instead, the mist which had been hanging in the air when I arose had thickened into a steady rain, and if there was anything which rendered Holmes moodier than long periods of rain, it was being wrong.

Suddenly he straightened up, tweaking a violin string with a fingernail, and smiled sardonically. "Watson! Here's a sight! The wettest bloodhound you ever saw!"

It was Lestrade, of course, seated in the back of an open wagon with water running into his close-set, fiercely inquisitive eyes. The wagon had no more than stopped before he was out, flinging the driver a coin, and striding toward 221B Baker Street. He moved so quickly that I thought he should run into our door like a battering ram.

I heard Mrs. Hudson remonstrating with him about his decidedly damp condition and the effect it might have on the rugs both downstairs and up, and then Holmes, who could make Lestrade look like a tortoise when the urge struck him, leaped across to the door and called down, "Let him up, Mrs. H. — I'll put a newspaper under his boots if he stays long, but I somehow think, yes, I really do think that . . ."

Then Lestrade was bounding up the stairs, leaving Mrs. Hudson to expostulate below. His color was high, his eyes burned, and his teeth — decidedly yellowed by tobacco — were bared in a wolfish grin.

"Inspector Lestrade!" Holmes cried jovially. "What brings you out on such a —"

No further did he get. Still panting from his climb, Lestrade said, "I've heard gypsies say the devil grants wishes. Now I believe it. Come at once if you'd have a try, Holmes; the corpse is still fresh and the suspects all in a row."

"You frighten me with your ardor, Lestrade!" Holmes cried, but with a sardonic little waggle of his eyebrows.

"Don't play the shrinking violet with me, man — I've come at the run to offer you the very thing for which you in your pride have wished a hundred times or more in my own hearing: the perfect locked-room mystery!"

Holmes had started into the corner, perhaps to get the awful gold-tipped cane which he was for some reason affecting that season. Now he whirled upon our damp visitor, his eyes wide. "Lestrade! Are you serious?"

"Would I have risked wet-lung croup riding here in an open wagon if I were not?" Lestrade countered.

Then, for the only time in my hearing (despite the countless times the phrase has been attributed to him), Holmes turned to me and cried: "Quick, Watson! The game's afoot!"

On our way, Lestrade commented sourly that

Holmes also had the *luck* of the devil; although Lestrade had commanded the wagon-driver to wait, we had no more than emerged from our lodgings when that exquisite rarity clip-clopped down the street: an empty hackney in what had become a driving rain. We climbed in and were off in a trice. As always, Holmes sat on the lefthand side, his eyes darting restlessly about, cataloguing everything, although there was precious little to see on *that* day . . . or so it seemed, at least, to the likes of me. I've no doubt every empty street corner and rain-washed shop window spoke volumes to Holmes.

Lestrade directed the driver to an address in Savile Row, and then asked Holmes if he knew Lord Hull.

"I know *of* him," Holmes said, "but have never had the good fortune of meeting him. Now I suppose I never shall. Shipping, wasn't it?"

"Shipping," Lestrade agreed, "but the good fortune was yours. Lord Hull was, by all accounts (including those of his nearest and — ahem! — dearest), a thoroughly nasty fellow, and as dotty as a puzzle-picture in a child's novelty book. He's finished practicing both nastiness and dottiness for good, however; around eleven o'clock this morning, just" — he pulled out his turnip of a pocket-watch and looked at it — "two hours and forty minutes ago, someone put a knife in his back as he sat in his study with his will on the blotter before him."

"So," Holmes said thoughtfully, lighting his pipe, "you believe the study of this unpleasant Lord Hull is the perfect locked room of my dreams, do you?" His eyes gleamed skeptically through a rising rafter of blue smoke.

"I believe," Lestrade said quietly, "that it is."

"Watson and I have dug such holes before and never struck water," Holmes remarked, and he glanced at me before returning to his ceaseless catalogue of the streets through which we passed. "Do you recall the 'Speckled Band,' Watson?"

I hardly needed to answer him. There had been a locked room in that business, true enough, but there had also been a ventilator, a poisonous snake, and a killer fiendish enough to introduce the latter into the former. It had been the work of a cruelly brilliant mind, but Holmes had seen to the bottom of the matter in almost no time at all.

"What are the facts, Inspector?" Holmes asked.

Lestrade began to lay them before us in the clipped tones of a trained policeman. Lord Albert Hull had been a tyrant in business and a despot at home. His wife had gone in fear of him, and had apparently been justified in doing so. The fact that she had borne him three sons seemed in no way to have moderated his savage approach toward their domestic affairs in general and toward her in particular. Lady Hull had been reluctant to speak of these matters, but her sons had no such reservations; their papa, they said, had missed no opportunity to dig at her, to criticize her, or to jest at her expense . . . all of this when they were in company. When they were alone, he virtually ignored her. Except, Lestrade added, when he felt moved to beat her, which was by no means an uncommon occurrence.

"William, the eldest, told me she always gave

out the same story when she came to the breakfast table with a swollen eye or a mark on her cheek: that she had forgotten to put on her spectacles and had run into a door. 'She ran into doors once and twice a week,' William said. 'I didn't know we had that many doors in the house.' "

"Hmmm," Holmes said. "A cheery fellow! The sons never put a stop to it?"

"She wouldn't allow it," Lestrade said.

"Insanity," I returned. A man who would beat his wife is an abomination; a woman who would allow it an abomination and a perplexity.

"There was a method in her madness, though," Lestrade said. "Method and what you might call 'an informed patience.' She was, after all, twenty years younger than her lord and master. Also, Hull was a heavy drinker and a champion diner. At age seventy, five years ago, he developed gout and angina."

"Wait for the storm to end and then enjoy the sunshine," Holmes remarked.

"Yes," Lestrade said, "but it's an idea which has led many a man and woman through the devil's door, I'll be bound. Hull made sure his family knew both his worth and the provisions of his will. They were little better than slaves."

"With the will as their document of indenture," Holmes murmured.

"Exactly so, old boy. At the time of his death, Hull's worth was three hundred thousand pounds. He never asked them to take his word for this; he had his chief accountant to the house quarterly to detail the balance sheets of Hull Shipping, although he kept the purse-strings firmly in his own hands and tightly closed."

"Devilish!" I exclaimed, thinking of the cruel boys one sometimes sees in Eastcheap or Piccadilly, boys who will hold out a sweet to a starving dog to see it dance . . . and then gobble it themselves while the hungry animal watches. I was shortly to find this comparison even more apt than I would have thought possible.

"On his death, Lady Rebecca was to receive one hundred and fifty thousand pounds. William, the eldest, was to receive fifty thousand; Jory, the middler, forty; and Stephen, the youngest, thirty."

"And the other thirty thousand?" I asked.

"Small bequests, Watson: to a cousin in Wales, an aunt in Brittany (not a cent for Lady Hull's relatives, though), five thousand in assorted bequests to the servants. Oh, and — you'll like this, Holmes — ten thousand pounds to Mrs. Hemphill's Home for Abandoned Pussies."

"You're joking!" I cried, although if Lestrade expected a similar reaction from Holmes, he was disappointed. Holmes merely re-lighted his pipe and nodded as if he had expected this . . . this or something like it. "With babies dying of starvation in the East End and twelve-year-old children working fifty hours a week in the mills, this fellow left ten thousand pounds to a . . . a boarding-hotel for *cats?*"

"Exactly so," Lestrade said pleasantly. "Furthermore, he should have left *twenty-seven times* that amount to Mrs. Hemphill's Abandoned Pussies if not for whatever happened this morning — and whoever did the business."

I could only gape at this, and try to multiply

in my head. While I was coming to the conclusion that Lord Hull had intended to disinherit both wife and children in favor of a rest-home for felines, Holmes was looking sourly at Lestrade and saying something which sounded to me like a total *non sequitur*. "I am going to sneeze, am I not?"

Lestrade smiled. It was a smile of transcendent sweetness. "Yes, my dear Holmes! Often and profoundly, I fear."

Holmes removed his pipe, which he had just gotten drawing to his satisfaction (I could tell by the way he settled back slightly in his seat), looked at it for a moment, and then held it out into the rain. More dumbfounded than ever, I watched him knock out the damp and smouldering tobacco.

"How many?" Holmes asked.

"Ten," Lestrade said with a fiendish grin.

"I suspected it was more than this famous locked room of yours that brought you out in the back of an open wagon on such a wet day," Holmes said sourly.

"Suspect as you like," Lestrade said gaily. "I'm afraid I must go on to the scene of the crime — duty calls, you know — but if you'd like, I could let you and the good doctor out here."

"You are the only man I ever met," Holmes said, "whose wit seems to be sharpened by foul weather. Does that perhaps say something about your character, I wonder? But never mind — that is, perhaps, a subject for another day. Tell me this, Lestrade: when did Lord Hull become sure that he was going to die?"

"*Die?*" I said. "My dear Holmes, whatever gives you the idea that the man believed —"

"It's obvious, Watson," Holmes said. "C.I.B., as I have told you at least a thousand times — character indexes behavior. It amused him to keep them in bondage by means of his will . . ." He looked an aside at Lestrade. "No trust arrangements, I take it? No entailments of any sort?"

Lestrade shook his head. "None whatever."

"Extraordinary!" I said.

"Not at all, Watson; character indexes behavior, remember. He wanted them to soldier along in the belief that all would be theirs when he did them the courtesy of dying, but he never actually intended any such thing. Such behavior would, in fact, have run completely across the grain of his character. D'you agree, Lestrade?"

"As a matter of fact, I do," Lestrade replied.

"Then we are very well to this point, Watson, are we not? All is clear? Lord Hull realizes he is dying. He waits . . . makes absolutely sure that this time it's no mistake, no false alarm . . . and then he calls his beloved family together. When? This morning, Lestrade?"

Lestrade grunted an affirmative.

Holmes steepled his fingers beneath his chin. "He calls them together and tells them he's made a new will, one which disinherits all of them . . . all, that is, save for the servants, his few distant relatives, and, of course, the pussies."

I opened my mouth to speak, only to discover I was too outraged to say anything. The image which kept returning to my mind was that of those cruel boys, making the starving East End curs jump with a bit of pork or a crumb of crust from a meat pie. I must add it never occurred to me to ask whether such a will could be disputed before the bar. Today a man would have a deuce of a time slighting his closest relatives in favor of a cat-hotel, but in 1899, a man's will was a man's will, and unless many examples of insanity — not eccentricity but outright *insanity* — could be proved, a man's will, like God's, was done.

"This new will was properly witnessed?" Holmes asked.

"Indeed it was," Lestrade replied. "Yesterday Lord Hull's solicitor and one of his assistants appeared at the house and were shown into Hull's study. There they remained for about fifteen minutes. Stephen Hull says the solicitor once raised his voice in protest about something — he could not tell what — and was silenced by Hull. Jory, the middle son, was upstairs, painting, and Lady Hull was calling on a friend. But both Stephen and William Hull saw these legal fellows enter, and leave a short time later. William said that they left with their heads down, and although William spoke, asking Mr. Barnes — the solicitor — if he was well, and making some social remark about the persistence of the rain, Barnes did not reply and the assistant seemed actually to cringe. It was as if they were ashamed, William said."

Well, so much for *that* possible loophole, I thought.

"Since we are on the subject, tell me about the boys," Holmes invited.

"As you like. It goes pretty much without saying that their hatred for the pater was exceeded only by the pater's boundless contempt for them . . . although how he could hold Stephen in contempt is . . . well, never mind, I'll keep things in their proper order."

"Yes, please be so kind as to do that," Holmes said dryly.

"William is thirty-six. If his father had given him any sort of allowance, I suppose he would be a bounder. As he had little or none, he has spent his days in various gymnasiums, involved in what I believe is called 'physical culture' — he appears to be an extremely muscular fellow — and his nights in various cheap coffee-houses, for the most part. If he did happen to have a bit of money in his pockets, he was apt to take himself off to a card-parlor, where he would lose it quickly enough. Not a pleasant man, Holmes. A man who has no purpose, no skill, no hobby, and no ambition (save to outlive his father) could hardly be a pleasant man. I had the queerest idea while talking to him that I was interrogating not a man but an empty vase upon which the face of Lord Hull had been lightly stamped."

"A vase waiting to be filled up with pounds sterling," Holmes commented.

"Jory is another matter," Lestrade went on. "Lord Hull saved most of his contempt for him, calling him from his earliest childhood by such endearing pet-names as 'Fish-Face' and 'Keg-Legs' and 'Stoat-Belly.' It's not hard to understand such names, unfortunately; Jory Hull stands no more than five feet tall, if that, is bow-legged, and of a remarkably ugly countenance. He looks a bit like that poet fellow. The pouf."

"Oscar Wilde?" asked I.

Holmes turned a brief, amused glance upon me.

"I think Lestrade means Algernon Swinburne," he said. "Who, I believe, is no more a pouf than you are, Watson."

"Jory Hull was born dead," Lestrade said. "After he remained blue and still for an entire minute, the doctor pronounced him so and put a napkin over his misshapen body. Lady Hull, in her one moment of heroism, sat up, removed the napkin, and dipped the baby's legs into the hot water which had been brought to be used at the birth. The baby began to squirm and squall."

Lestrade grinned and lit a cigarillo with a flourish.

"Hull claimed this immersion had caused the boy's bowed legs, and when he was in his cups, he taxed his wife with it. Told her she should have left well enough alone. Better Jory had been born dead than lived to be what he was, he sometimes said — a scuttling creature with the legs of a crab and the face of a cod."

Holmes's only reaction to this extraordinary (and to my physician's mind rather suspect) story was to comment that Lestrade had gotten a remarkably large body of information in a remarkably short period of time.

"That points up one of the aspects of the case which I thought would appeal to you, my dear Holmes," Lestrade said as we swept into Rotten Row with a splash and a swirl. "They need no coercion to speak; coercion's what it would take to shut em up. They've had to remain silent all too long. And then there's the fact that the new will is gone. Relief loosens tongues beyond measure, I find."

"Gone!" I exclaimed, but Holmes took no notice; his mind still ran upon Jory, the misshapen middle child.

"*Is* he ugly, then?" he asked Lestrade.

"Hardly handsome, but not as bad as some I've seen," Lestrade replied comfortably. "I believe his father continually heaped vituperation on his head because —"

"— because he was the only one who had no need of his father's money to make his way in the world," Holmes finished for him.

Lestrade started. "The devil! How did you know that?"

"Because Lord Hull was reduced to carping at Jory's physical faults. How it must have chafed the old devil to be faced with a potential target so well armored in other respects! Baiting a man for his looks or his posture may be fine for schoolboys or drunken louts, but a villain like Lord Hull had no doubt become used to higher sport. I would venture the opinion that he may have been rather afraid of his bow-legged middle son. What was Jory's key to the cell door?"

"Haven't I told you? He paints," Lestrade said.

"Ah!"

Jory Hull was, as the canvases in the lower halls of Hull House later proved, a very good painter indeed. Not great; I do not mean that at all. But his renderings of his mother and brothers were faithful enough so that, years later, when I saw color photographs for the first time, my mind flashed back to that rainy November afternoon in 1899. And the one of his father perhaps *was* a work of greatness. Certainly it startled (almost intimidated) with the malevolence that seemed to waft out of the canvas like a breath of dank graveyard air. Perhaps it *was* Algernon Swinburne that Jory resembled, but his father's likeness — at least as seen through the middle son's hand and eye — reminded me of an Oscar Wilde character: that nearly immortal *roué*, Dorian Gray.

His canvases were long, slow processes, but he was able to quick-sketch with such nimble rapidity that he might come home from Hyde Park on a Saturday afternoon with as much as twenty pounds in his pockets.

"I'll wager his father enjoyed *that*," Holmes said. He reached automatically for his pipe, then put it back again. "The son of a Peer quick-sketching wealthy American tourists and their sweethearts like a French Bohemian."

Lestrade laughed heartily. "He *raged* over it, as you may imagine. But Jory — good for him! — wouldn't give over his selling stall in Hyde Park . . . not, at least, until his father agreed to an allowance of thirty-five pounds a week. He called it low blackmail."

"My heart bleeds," I said.

"As does mine, Watson," Holmes said. "The third son, Lestrade, quickly — we've almost reached the house, I believe."

As Lestrade had intimated, surely Stephen Hull had the greatest cause to hate his father. As his gout grew worse and his head more muddled, Lord Hull surrendered more and more of the company affairs to Stephen, who was only twenty-eight at the time of his father's death. The responsibilities devolved upon Stephen, and the blame also devolved upon him if his least decision proved amiss. Yet no financial gain accrued to him should he decide well and his father's affairs prosper.

Lord Hull should have looked with favor upon Stephen, as the only one of his children with an interest in and an aptitude for the business he had founded; Stephen was a perfect example of what the Bible calls "the good son." Yet instead of displaying love and gratitude, Lord Hull repaid the young man's largely successful efforts with scorn, suspicion, and jealousy. On many occasions during the last two years of his life, the old man had offered the charming opinion that Stephen "would steal the pennies from a dead man's eyes."

"The b——d!" I cried, unable to contain myself.

"Ignore the new will for a moment," Holmes said, steepling his fingers again, "and return to the old one. Even under the conditions of that marginally more generous document, Stephen Hull would have had cause for resentment. In spite of all his labors, which had not only saved the family fortune but increased it, his reward was still to have been the youngest son's share of the spoils. What, by the way, was to have been the disposition of the shipping company under the provisions of what we might call the Pussy Will?"

I looked carefully at Holmes, but, as always, it was difficult to tell if he had attempted a small *bon mot*. Even after all the years I spent with him and all the adventures we shared, Sherlock Holmes's sense of humor remains a largely undiscovered country, even to me.

"It was to be handed over to the Board of Directors, with no provision for Stephen," Lestrade said, and pitched his cigarillo out the window as the hackney swept up the curving drive of a house which looked extraordinarily ugly to me just then, as it stood amid its brown lawns in the driving rain. "Yet with the father dead and the new will nowhere to be found, Stephen Hull has what the Americans call 'leverage.' The company will have him as managing director. They should have done anyway, but now it will be on Stephen Hull's terms."

"Yes," Holmes said. "Leverage. A good word." He leaned out into the rain. "Stop short, driver!" he cried. "We've not quite done!"

"As you say, guv'nor," the driver returned, "but it's devilish wet out here."

"And you'll go with enough in your pocket to make your innards as wet and devilish as your out'ards," Holmes said. This seemed to satisfy the man, and he stopped thirty yards from the front door of the great house. I listened to the rain tip-tapping on the sides of the coach while Holmes cogitated and then said: "The old will — the one he teased them with — *that* document isn't missing, is it?"

"Absolutely not. It was on his desk, near his body."

"Four excellent suspects! Servants need not apply . . . or so it seems now. Finish quickly, Lestrade — the final circumstances, and the locked room."

Lestrade complied, consulting his notes from time to time. A month previous, Lord Hull had observed a small black spot on his right leg, directly behind the knee. The family doctor was called. His diagnosis was gangrene, an unusual but far from rare result of gout and poor circulation. The doctor told him the leg would have to come off, and well above the site of the infection.

Lord Hull laughed until tears streamed down his cheeks. The doctor, who had expected any reaction but this, was struck speechless. "When they stick me in my coffin, sawbones," Hull said, "it will be with both legs still attached, thank you very much."

The doctor told him that he sympathized with Lord Hull's wish to keep his leg, but that without amputation he would be dead in six months, and he would spend the last two in exquisite pain. Lord Hull asked the doctor what his chances of survival should be if he were to undergo the operation. He was still laughing, Lestrade said, as though it were the best joke he had ever heard. After some hemming and hawing, the doctor said the odds were even.

"Bunk," said I.

"Exactly what Lord Hull said," Lestrade replied, "except he used a term more often used in dosses than in drawing-rooms."

Hull told the doctor that he himself reckoned his chances at no better than one in five. "As to the pain, I don't think it will come to that," he went on, "as long as there's laudanum and a spoon to stir it with in stumping distance."

The next day, Hull finally sprang his nasty surprise — that he was thinking of changing his will. Just how he did not immediately say.

"Oh?" Holmes said, looking at Lestrade from those cool gray eyes that saw so much. "And who, pray, was surprised?"

"None of them, I should think. But you know human nature, Holmes; how people hope against hope."

"And how some plan against disaster," Holmes said dreamily.

This very morning Lord Hull had called his family into the parlor, and when all were settled, he performed an act few testators are granted, one which is usually performed by the wagging tongues of their solicitors after their own have been forever silenced. In short, he read them his new will, leaving the balance of his estate to Mrs. Hemphill's wayward pussies. In the silence which followed he rose, not without difficulty, and favored them all with a death's-head grin. And leaning over his cane, he made the following declaration, which I find as astoundingly vile now as I did when Lestrade recounted it to us in that hackney cab: "So! All is fine, is it not? Yes, very fine! You have served me quite faithfully, woman and boys, for some forty years. Now I intend, with the clearest and most serene conscience imaginable, to cast you hence. But take heart! Things could be worse! If there was time, the pharaohs had their favorite pets — cats, for the most part — killed before they died, so the pets might be there to welcome them into the after-life, to be kicked or petted there, at their masters' whims, forever . . . and forever . . . and forever." Then he laughed at them. He leaned over his cane and laughed from his doughy, dying face, the new will — properly signed and properly witnessed, as all of them had seen — clutched in one claw of a hand.

William rose and said, "Sir, you may be my father and the author of my existence, but you are also the lowest creature to crawl upon the face of the earth since the serpent tempted Eve in the Garden."

"Not at all!" the old monster returned, still laughing. "I know four lower. Now, if you will pardon me, I have some important papers to put away in my safe . . . and some worthless ones to burn in the stove."

"He still had the old will when he confronted them?" Holmes asked. He seemed more interested than startled.

"Yes."

"He could have burned it as soon as the new one was signed and witnessed," Holmes mused. "He had all the previous afternoon and evening to do so. But he didn't, did he? Why not? How say you on that question, Lestrade?"

"He hadn't had enough of teasing them even then, I suppose. He was offering them a chance — a *temptation* — he believed all would refuse."

"Perhaps he believed one of them would not refuse," Holmes said. "Hasn't that idea at least crossed your mind?" He turned his head and searched my face with the momentary beam of his brilliant — and somehow chilling — regard. "*Either* of your minds? Isn't it possible that such a black creature might hold out such a temptation, knowing that if one of his family were to succumb to it and put him out of his misery — Stephen seems most likely from what you say — that one might be caught . . . and swing for the crime of patricide?"

I stared at Holmes in silent horror.

"Never mind," Holmes said. "Go on, Inspector — it's time for the locked room to make its appearance, I believe."

The four of them had sat in paralyzed silence as the old man made his long, slow way up the corridor to his study. There were no sounds but the thud of his cane, the labored rattle of his breathing, the plaintive *miaow* of a cat in the kitchen, and the steady beat of the pendulum in the parlor clock. Then they heard the squeal of hinges as Hull opened his study door and stepped inside.

"Wait!" Holmes said sharply, sitting forward. "No one actually *saw* him go in, did they?"

"I'm afraid that's not so, old chap," Lestrade returned. "Mr. Oliver Stanley, Lord Hull's valet, had heard Lord Hull's progress down the hall. He came from Hull's dressing chamber, went to the gallery railing, and called down to ask if all was well. Hull looked up — Stanley saw him as plainly as I see you right now, old fellow — and said all was absolutely tip-top. Then he rubbed the back of his head, went in, and locked the study door behind him.

"By the time his father had reached the door (the corridor is quite long and it may have taken him as much as two minutes to make his way up it unaided) Stephen had shaken off his stupor and had gone to the parlor door. He saw the exchange between his father and his father's man. Of course Lord Hull was back-to, but Stephen heard his father's voice and described the same characteristic gesture: Hull rubbing the back of his head."

"Could Stephen Hull and this Stanley fellow have spoken before the police arrived?" I asked — shrewdly, I thought.

"Of course they could," Lestrade said wearily. "They probably did. But there was no collusion."

"You feel sure of that?" Holmes asked, but he sounded uninterested.

"Yes. Stephen Hull would lie very well, I think, but Stanley would do it very badly. Accept my professional opinion or not, just as you like, Holmes."

"I accept it."

So Lord Hull passed into his study, the famous locked room, and all heard the click of the lock as he turned the key — the only key there was to that *sanctum sanctorum.* This was followed by a more unusual sound: the bolt being drawn across.

Then, silence.

The four of them — Lady Hull and her sons, so shortly to be blue-blooded paupers — looked at one another in similar silence. The cat miaowed again from the kitchen and Lady Hull said in a distracted voice that if the housekeeper wouldn't give that cat a bowl of milk, she supposed she must. She said the sound of it would drive her mad if she had to listen to it much longer. She left the parlor. Moments later, without a word among them, the three sons also left. William went to his room upstairs, Stephen wandered into the music room, and Jory went to sit upon a bench beneath the stairs where, he had told Lestrade, he had gone since earliest childhood when he was sad or had matters of deep difficulty to think over.

Less than five minutes later a shriek arose from the study. Stephen ran out of the music room, where he had been plinking out isolated notes on the piano. Jory met him at the study door. William was already halfway downstairs and saw them breaking in when Stanley, the valet, came out of Lord Hull's dressing room and went to the gallery railing for the second time. Stanley has testified to seeing Stephen Hull burst into the study; to seeing William reach the foot of the stairs and almost fall on the marble; to seeing Lady Hull come from the dining-room doorway with a pitcher of milk still in one hand. Moments later the rest of the servants had gathered.

"Lord Hull was slumped over his writing-desk with the three brothers standing by. His eyes were open, and the look in them . . . I believe it was surprise. Again, you are free to accept or reject my opinion just as you like, but I tell you it looked very much like surprise to me. Clutched in his hands was his will . . . the old one. Of the new one there was no sign. And there was a dagger in his back."

With this, Lestrade rapped for the driver to go on.

We entered the house between two constables as stone-faced as Buckingham Palace sentinels. Here to begin with was a very long hall, floored in black and white marble tiles like a chessboard. They led to an open door at the end, where two more constables were posted: the entrance to the infamous study. To the left were the stairs, to the right two doors: the parlor and the music room, I guessed.

"The family is gathered in the parlor," Lestrade said.

"Good," Holmes said pleasantly. "But perhaps Watson and I might first have a look at the scene of the crime?"

"Shall I accompany you?"

"Perhaps not," Holmes said. "Has the body been removed?"

"It was still here when I left for your lodgings, but by now it almost certainly will be gone."

"Very good."

Holmes started away. I followed. Lestrade called, "Holmes!"

Holmes turned, eyebrows raised.

"No secret panels, no secret doors. For the third time, take my word or not, as you like."

"I believe I'll wait until . . ." Holmes began and then his breath began to hitch. He scrambled in his pocket, found a napkin probably carried absently away from the eating-house where we had dined the previous evening, and sneezed mightily into it. I looked down and saw a large, scarred tomcat, as out of place here in this grand hall as would have been one of those urchins of whom I had been thinking earlier, twining about Holmes's legs. One of its ears was laid back against its scarred skull. The other was gone, lost in some long-ago alley battle, I supposed.

Holmes sneezed repeatedly and kicked out at the cat. It went with a reproachful backward look rather than with the angry hiss one might have expected from such an old campaigner. Holmes looked at Lestrade over the napkin with reproachful, watery eyes. Lestrade, not in the least put out of countenance, thrust his head forward and grinned like a monkey. "Ten, Holmes," he said. "*Ten.* House is full of felines. Hull loved em." And with that he walked off.

"How long have you suffered this affliction, old fellow?" I asked. I was a bit alarmed.

"Always," he said, and sneezed again. The word *allergy* was hardly known all those years ago, but that, of course, was his problem.

"Do you want to leave?" I asked. I had once seen a case of near asphyxiation as the result of such an aversion, this one to sheep but otherwise similar in all respects.

"He'd like that," Holmes said. I did not need him to tell me whom he meant. Holmes sneezed once more (a large red welt was appearing on his normally pale forehead) and then we passed between the constables at the study door. Holmes closed it behind him.

The room was long and relatively narrow. It was at the end of something like a wing, the main house spreading to either side from an area roughly three-quarters of the way down the hall. There were windows on two sides of the study and it was bright enough in spite of the gray, rainy day. The walls were dotted with colorful shipping charts in handsome teak frames, and among them was mounted an equally handsome set of weather instruments in a brass-bound, glass-fronted case. It contained an anemometer (Hull had the little whirling cups mounted on one of the roofpeaks, I supposed), two thermometers (one registering the outdoor temperature and the other that of the study), and a barometer much like the one which had fooled Holmes into believing the bad weather was about to break. I noticed the glass was still rising, then looked outside. The rain was falling harder than ever, rising glass or no rising glass. We believe we know a great lot, with our instruments and things, but I was old enough then to believe we don't know half as much as we think we do, and old enough now to believe we never will.

Holmes and I both turned to look at the door. The bolt was torn free, but leaning inward, as it should have been. The key was still in the study-side lock, and still turned.

Holmes's eyes, watering as they were, were everywhere at once, noting, cataloguing, storing.

"You are a little better," I said.

"Yes," he said, lowering the napkin and stuffing it indifferently back into his coat pocket. "He may have loved em, but he apparently didn't allow em in here. Not on a regular basis, anyway. What do you make of it, Watson?"

Although my eyes were slower than his, I was also looking around. The double windows were all locked with thumb-turns and small brass side-bolts. None of the panes had been broken. Most of the framed charts and the box of weather instruments were between these windows. The other two walls were filled with books. There was a small coal-stove but no fireplace; the murderer hadn't come down the chimney like Father Christmas, not unless he was narrow enough to fit through a stove-pipe and clad in an asbestos suit, for the stove was still very warm.

The desk stood at one end of this long, narrow,

well-lit room; the opposite end was a pleasantly bookish area, not quite a library, with two high-backed upholstered chairs and a coffee-table between them. On this table was a random stack of volumes. The floor was covered with a Turkish rug. If the murderer had come through a trap-door, I hadn't the slightest idea how he'd gotten back under that rug without disarranging it . . . and it was *not* disarranged, not in the slightest: the shadows of the coffee-table legs lay across it without even a hint of a ripple.

"Did you believe it, Watson?" Holmes asked, snapping me out of what was almost a hypnotic trance. Something . . . something about that coffee-table . . .

"Believe what, Holmes?"

"That all four of them simply walked out of the parlor, in four different directions, four minutes before the murder?"

"I don't know," I said faintly.

"*I* don't believe it; not for a mo—" He broke off. "Watson! Are you all right?"

"No," I said in a voice I could hardly hear myself. I collapsed into one of the library chairs. My heart was beating too fast. I couldn't seem to catch my breath. My head was pounding; my eyes seemed to have suddenly grown too large for their sockets. I could not take them from the shadows of the coffee-table legs upon the rug. "I am most . . . definitely not . . . all right."

At that moment Lestrade appeared in the study doorway. "If you've looked your fill, H—" He broke off. "What the devil's the matter with Watson?"

"I believe," said Holmes in a calm, measured voice, "that Watson has solved the case. Have you, Watson?"

I nodded my head. Not the entire case, perhaps, but most of it. I knew who; I knew how.

"Is it this way with you, Holmes?" I asked. "When you . . . see?"

"Yes," he said, "though I usually manage to keep my feet."

"*Watson's* solved the case?" Lestrade said impatiently. "Bah! Watson's offered a thousand solutions to a hundred cases before this, Holmes, as you very well know, and all of them wrong. It's his *bête noire*. Why, I remember just this last summer —"

"I know more about Watson than you ever shall," Holmes said, "and this time he has hit upon it. I know the look." He began to sneeze again; the cat with the missing ear had wandered into the room through the door which Lestrade had left open. It moved directly toward Holmes with an expression of what seemed to be affection on its ugly face.

"If this is how it is for you," I said, "I'll never envy you again, Holmes. My heart should burst."

"One becomes inured even to insight," Holmes said, with not the slightest trace of conceit in his voice. "Out with it, then . . . or shall we bring in the suspects, as in the last chapter of a detective novel?"

"No!" I cried in horror. I had seen none of them; I had no urge to. "Only I think I must *show* you how it was done. If you and Inspector Lestrade will only step out into the hall for a moment . . ."

The cat reached Holmes and jumped into his lap, purring like the most satisfied creature on earth.

Holmes exploded into a perfect fusillade of sneezes. The red patches on his face, which had begun to fade, burst out afresh. He pushed the cat away and stood up.

"Be quick, Watson, so we can leave this damned place," he said in a muffled voice, and left the room with his shoulders in an uncharacteristic hunch, his head down, and with not a single look back. Believe me when I say that a little of my heart went with him.

Lestrade stood leaning against the door, his wet coat steaming slightly, his lips parted in a detestable grin. "Shall I take Holmes's new admirer, Watson?"

"Leave it," I said, "and close the door when you go out."

"I'd lay a fiver you're wasting our time, old man," Lestrade said, but I saw something different in his eyes: if I'd offered to take him up on the wager, he would have found a way to squirm out of it.

"Close the door," I repeated. "I shan't be long."

He closed the door. I was alone in Hull's study . . . except for the cat, of course, which was now sitting in the middle of the rug, tail curled neatly about its paws, green eyes watching me.

I felt in my pockets and found my own souvenir from last night's dinner — men on their own are rather untidy people, I fear, but there was a reason for the bread other than general slovenliness. I almost always kept a crust in one pocket or the other, for it amused me to feed the pigeons that landed outside the very window where Holmes had been sitting when Lestrade drove up.

"Pussy," said I, and put the bread beneath the coffee-table — the coffee-table to which Lord Hull would have presented his back when he sat down with his two wills, the wretched old one and the even more wretched new one. "Puss-puss-puss."

The cat rose and walked languidly beneath the table to investigate the crust.

I went to the door and opened it. "Holmes! Lestrade! Quickly!"

They came in.

"Step over here," I said, and walked to the coffee-table.

Lestrade looked about and began to frown, seeing nothing; Holmes, of course, began to sneeze again. "Can't we have that wretched thing out of here?" he managed from behind the table-napkin, which was now quite soggy.

"Of course," said I. *But where is the wretched thing, Holmes?"*

A startled expression filled his wet eyes. Lestrade whirled, walked toward Hull's writing-desk, and peered behind it. Holmes knew his reaction should not have been so violent if the cat had been on the far side of the room. He bent and looked beneath the coffee-table, saw nothing but the rug and the bottom row of the two bookcases opposite, and straightened up again. If his eyes had not been spouting like fountains, he should have seen all then; he was, after all, right on top of it. But one must also give credit where credit is due, and the illusion was devilishly good. The empty space beneath his father's coffee-table had been Jory Hull's masterpiece.

"I don't —" Holmes began, and then the cat, who found my friend much more to its liking than any stale crust of bread, strolled out from beneath the table and began once more to twine ecstatically about his ankles. Lestrade had returned, and his eyes grew so wide I thought they might actually fall out. Even having understood the trick, I myself was amazed. The scarred tomcat seemed to be materializing out of thin air; head, body, white-tipped tail last.

It rubbed against Holmes's leg, purring as Holmes sneezed.

"That's enough," I said. "You've done your job and may leave."

I picked it up, took it to the door (getting a good scratch for my pains), and tossed it unceremoniously into the hall. I shut the door behind it.

Holmes was sitting down. "My God," he said in a nasal, clogged voice. Lestrade was incapable of any speech at all. His eyes never left the table and the faded Turkish rug beneath its legs: an empty space that had somehow given birth to a cat.

"I should have seen," Holmes was muttering. "Yes . . . but you . . . how did you understand so *quickly?*" I detected the faintest hurt and pique in that voice, and forgave it at once.

"It was *those,*" I said, and pointed at the rug.

"Of course!" Holmes nearly groaned. He slapped his welted forehead. "Idiot! I'm a perfect *idiot!*"

"Nonsense," I said tartly. "With a houseful of

cats — and one who has apparently picked you out for a special friend — I suspect you were seeing ten of everything."

"What about the rug?" Lestrade asked impatiently. "It's very nice, I'll grant, and probably expensive, but —"

"Not the *rug*," I said. "The *shadows*."

"Show him, Watson," Holmes said wearily, lowering the napkin into his lap.

So I bent and picked one of them off the floor.

Lestrade sat down in the other chair, hard, like a man who has been unexpectedly punched.

"I kept looking at them, you see," I said, speaking in a tone which could not help being apologetic. This seemed all wrong. It was Holmes's job to explain the whos and hows at the end of the investigation. Yet while I saw that he now understood everything, I knew he would refuse to speak in this case. And I suppose a part of me — the part that knew I would probably never have another chance to do something like this — *wanted* to be the one to explain. And the cat was rather a nice touch, I must say. A magician could have done no better with a rabbit and a top-hat.

"I knew something was wrong, but it took a moment for it to sink in. This room is extremely bright, but today it's pouring down rain. Look around and you'll see that not a single object in this room casts a shadow . . . *except for these table-legs*."

Lestrade uttered an oath.

"It's rained for nearly a week," I said, "but both Holmes's barometer and the late Lord Hull's" —

I pointed to it — "said that we could expect sun today. In fact, it seemed a sure thing. So he added the shadows as a final touch."

"Who did?"

"Jory Hull," Holmes said in that same weary tone. "Who else?"

I bent down and reached my hand beneath the right end of the coffee-table. It disappeared into thin air, just as the cat had appeared. Lestrade uttered another startled oath. I tapped the back of the canvas stretched tightly between the forward legs of the coffee-table. The books and the rug bulged and rippled, and the illusion, nearly perfect as it had been, was instantly dispelled.

Jory Hull had painted the nothing under his father's coffee-table, had crouched behind the nothing as his father entered the room, locked the door, and sat at his desk with his two wills, and at last had rushed out from behind the nothing, dagger in hand.

"He was the only one who could execute such an extraordinary piece of realism," I said, this time running my hand down the face of the canvas. We could all hear the low rasping sound it made, like the purr of a very old cat. "The only one who could execute it, and the only one who could hide behind it: Jory Hull, who was no more than five feet tall, bow-legged, slump-shouldered.

"As Holmes said, the surprise of the new will was no surprise. Even if the old man had been secretive about the possibility of cutting the relatives out of the will, which he wasn't, only simpletons could have mistaken the import of the visit from the solicitor and, more important, the assistant. It takes two witnesses to make a will a valid document at Chancery. What Holmes said about some people preparing for disaster was very true. A canvas as perfect as this was not made overnight, or in a month. You may find he had it ready, should it need to be used, for as long as a year —"

"Or five," Holmes interpolated.

"I suppose. At any rate, when Hull announced that he wanted to see his family in the parlor this morning, I imagine Jory knew the time had come. After his father had gone to bed last night, he would have come down here and mounted his canvas. I suppose he may have put down the *faux* shadows at the same time, but if I had been Jory I should have tip-toed in here for another peek at the glass this morning, before the previously announced parlor gathering, just to make sure it was still rising. If the door was locked, I suppose he filched the key from his father's pocket and returned it later."

"Wasn't locked," Lestrade said laconically. "As a rule he kept the door shut to keep the cats out, but rarely locked it."

"As for the shadows, they are just strips of felt, as you now see. His eye was good, they are about where they would have been at eleven this morning . . . if the glass had been right."

"If he expected the sun to be shining, why did he put down shadows at all?" Lestrade grumped. "Sun puts em down as a matter of course, just in case you've never noticed your own, Watson."

Here I was at a loss. I looked at Holmes, who seemed grateful to have *any* part in the answer.

"Don't you see? That is the greatest irony of all! If the sun had shone as the glass suggested it would, the canvas would have *blocked* the shadows. Painted shadow-legs don't cast them, you know. He was caught by shadows on a day when there were none because he was afraid he would be caught by none on a day when his father's barometer said they would almost certainly be everywhere else in the room."

"I still don't understand how Jory got in here without Hull seeing him," Lestrade said.

"That puzzles me as well," Holmes said — dear old Holmes! I doubt that it puzzled him a bit, but that was what he said. "Watson?"

"The parlor where Lord Hull met with his wife and sons has a door which communicates with the music room, does it not?"

"Yes," Lestrade said, "and the music room has a door which communicates with Lady Hull's morning room, which is next in line as one goes toward the back of the house. But from the morning room one can only go back into the hall, Doctor Watson. If there had been *two* doors into Hull's study, I should hardly have come after Holmes on the run as I did."

He said this last in tones of faint self-justification.

"Oh, Jory went back into the hall, all right," I said, "but his father didn't see him."

"Rot!"

"I'll demonstrate," I said, and went to the writing-desk, where the dead man's cane still leaned. I picked it up and turned toward them. "The very instant Lord Hull left the parlor, Jory was up and on the run."

Lestrade shot a startled glance at Holmes; Holmes gave the inspector a cool, ironic look in return. I did not understand those looks then, nor give them much thought at all, if the whole truth be told. I did not fully understand the wider implications of the picture I was drawing for yet awhile. I was too wrapped up in my own re-creation, I suppose.

"He nipped through the first connecting door, ran across the music room, and entered Lady Hull's morning room. He went to the hall door then and peeked out. If Lord Hull's gout had gotten so bad as to have brought on gangrene, he would have progressed no more than a quarter of the way down the hall, and that is optimistic. Now mark me, Inspector Lestrade, and I will show you the price a man pays for a lifetime of rich food and strong drink. If you harbor any doubts when I've done, I shall parade a dozen gout sufferers before you, and each one will show the same ambulatory symptoms I now intend to demonstrate. Please notice above all how fixed my attention is . . . and *where*."

With that I began to stump slowly across the room toward them, both hands clamped tightly on the ball of the cane. I would raise one foot quite high, bring it down, pause, and then draw the other leg along. Never did my eyes look up. Instead, they alternated between the cane and that forward foot.

"Yes," Holmes said quietly. "The good doctor is exactly right, Inspector Lestrade. The gout comes first; then the loss of balance; then (if the sufferer lives long enough), the characteristic stoop brought on by always looking down."

"Jory would have been very aware of how his father fixed his attention when he walked from place to place," I said. "As a result, what happened this morning was diabolically simple. When Jory reached the morning room, he peeped out the door, saw his father studying his feet and the tip of his cane — just as always — and knew he was safe. He stepped out, *right in front of his unseeing father,* and simply nipped into the study. The door, Lestrade informs us, was unlocked, and really, how great would the risk have been? They were in the hall together for no more than three seconds, and probably a little less." I paused. "That hall floor is marble, isn't it? He must have kicked off his shoes."

"He was wearing slippers," Lestrade said in a strangely calm tone of voice, and for the second time, his eyes met Holmes's.

"Ah," I said. "I see. Jory gained the study well ahead of his father and hid behind his cunning stage-flat. Then he withdrew the dagger and waited. His father reached the end of the hall. Jory heard Stanley call down to him, and heard his father call back that he was fine. Then Lord Hull entered his study for the last time . . . closed the door . . . and locked it."

They were both looking at me intently, and I understood some of the godlike power Holmes must have felt at moments like these, telling others what only he could know. And yet, I must repeat that it is a feeling I should not have wanted to have too often. I believe the urge to repeat such a feeling would have corrupted most men — men with less iron in their souls than was possessed by my friend Sherlock Holmes.

"Old Keg-Legs would have made himself as small as possible before the locking-up happened, perhaps knowing (or only suspecting) that his father would have one good look round before turning the key and shooting the bolt. He may have been gouty and going a bit soft about the edges, but that doesn't mean he was going blind."

"Stanley says his eyes were top-hole," Lestrade said. "One of the first things I asked."

"So he looked round," I said, and suddenly I could *see* it, and I suppose this was also the way it was with Holmes; this reconstruction which, while based only upon facts and deduction, seemed to be half a vision. "He saw nothing to alarm him; nothing but the study as it always was, empty save for himself. It is a remarkably open room — I see no closet door, and with the windows on both sides, there are no dark nooks and crannies even on such a day as this.

"Satisfied that he was alone, he closed the door, turned his key, and shot the bolt. Jory would have heard him stump his way across to the desk. He would have heard the heavy thump and wheeze of the chair cushion as his father landed on it — a man in whom gout is well-advanced does not sit so much as position himself over a soft spot and then drop onto it, seat-first — and then Jory would at last have risked a look out."

I glanced at Holmes.

"Go on, old man," he said warmly. "You are doing splendidly. Absolutely first rate." I saw he meant it. Thousands would have called him cold, and they would not have been wrong, precisely, but he also had a large heart. Holmes simply protected it better than most men do.

"Thank you. Jory would have seen his father put his cane aside, and place the papers — the two packets of papers — on the blotter. He did not kill his father immediately, although he could have done; that's what's so gruesomely pathetic about this business, and that's why I wouldn't go into that parlor where they are for a thousand pounds. I wouldn't go in unless you and your men dragged me."

"How do you know he didn't do it immediately?" Lestrade asked.

"The scream came several minutes after the key was turned and the bolt drawn; you said so yourself, and I assume you have enough testimony on that point not to doubt it. Yet it can only be a dozen long paces from door to desk. Even for a gouty man like Lord Hull, it would have taken half a minute, forty seconds at the outside, to cross to the chair and sit down. Add fifteen seconds for him to prop his cane where you found it, and put his wills on the blotter.

"What happened then? What happened during that last minute or two, a short time which must have seemed — to Jory Hull, at least — almost endless? I believe Lord Hull simply sat there, looking from one will to the other. Jory would have been able to tell the difference between the two easily enough; the differing colors of the parchment would have been all the clew he needed.

"He knew his father intended to throw *one* of them into the stove; I believe he waited to see which one it would be. There was, after all, a chance that the old devil was only having a cruel practical joke at his family's expense. Perhaps he would burn the new will, and put the old one back in the safe. Then he could have left the room and told his family the new will was safely put away. Do you know where it is, Lestrade? The safe?"

"Five of the books in that case swing out," Lestrade said briefly, pointing to a shelf in the library area.

"Both family and old man would have been satisfied then; the family would have known their earned inheritances were safe, and the old man would have gone to his grave believing he had perpetrated one of the cruellest practical jokes of all time . . . but he would have gone as God's victim or his own, and not Jory Hull's."

Yet a third time that queer look, half-amused and half-revolted, passed between Holmes and Lestrade.

"Myself, I rather think the old man was only savoring the moment, as a man may savor the prospect of an after-dinner drink in the middle of the afternoon or a sweet after a long period of abstinence. At any rate, the minute passed, and Lord Hull began to rise . . . but with the darker parchment in his hand, and facing the stove rather than the safe. Whatever his hopes may have been, there was no hesitation on Jory's part when the moment came. He burst from hiding, crossed the distance between the coffee-table and the desk in an instant, and plunged the knife into his father's back before he was fully up.

"I suspect the post-mortem will show the thrust clipped through the heart's right ventricle and into the lung — that would explain the quantity of blood expelled onto the desk-top. It also explains why Lord Hull was able to scream before he died, and that's what did for Mr. Jory Hull."

"How so?" Lestrade asked.

"A locked room is a bad business unless you intend to pass murder off as suicide," I said, looking at Holmes. He smiled and nodded at this maxim of his. "The last thing Jory would have wanted was for things to look as they did . . . the locked room, the locked windows, the man with a knife in him where the man himself never could have put it. I think he had never foreseen his father dying with such a squawl. His plan was to stab him, burn the new will, rifle the desk, unlock one of the windows, and escape that way. He would have entered the house by another door, resumed his seat under the stairs, and then, when the body was finally discovered, it would have looked like robbery."

"Not to Hull's solicitor," Lestrade said.

"He might well have kept his silence, however," Holmes mused, and then added brightly, "I'll bet our artistic friend intended to add a few tracks, too. I have found that the better class of murderer almost always likes to throw in a few mysterious tracks leading away from the scene of the crime." He uttered a brief, humorless sound that was more bark than laugh, then looked back from the window nearest the desk to Lestrade and me. "I think we all agree it would have seemed a suspiciously convenient murder, under the circumstances, but even if the solicitor spoke up, nothing could have been *proved.*"

"By screaming, Lord Hull spoiled everything," I said, "as he had been spoiling things all his life. The house was roused. Jory must have been in a total panic, frozen to the spot the way a deer is by a bright light. It was Stephen Hull who saved the day . . . or Jory's alibi, at least, the one which had him sitting on the bench under the stairs when his father was murdered. Stephen rushed down the hall from the music room, smashed the door open, and must have hissed at Jory to get over to the desk with him, at once, so it would look as if they had broken in togeth—"

I broke off, thunderstruck. At last I understood the glances which had been flashing between Holmes and Lestrade. I understood what they must have seen from the moment I showed them the trick hiding place: *it could not have been done alone.* The killing, yes, but the rest . . .

"Stephen said he and Jory met at the study door," I said slowly. "That he, Stephen, burst it in and they entered together, discovered the body together. He lied. He might have done it to protect his brother, but to lie so well when one doesn't know what has happened seems . . . seems . . ."

"*Impossible,*" Holmes said, "is the word for which you are searching, Watson."

"Then Jory and Stephen went in on it together," I said. "They planned it together . . . and in the eyes of the law, both are guilty of their father's murder! My God!"

"Not both of them, my dear Watson," Holmes

said in a tone of curious gentleness. "*All* of them."

I could only gape.

He nodded. "You have shown remarkable insight this morning, Watson; you have, in fact, burned with a deductive heat I'll wager you'll never generate again. My cap is off to you, dear fellow, as it is to any man who is able to transcend his normal nature, no matter how briefly. But in one way you have remained the same dear chap you've always been: while you understand how good people can be, you have no understanding of how black they *may* be."

I looked at him silently, almost humbly.

"Not that there was much blackness here, if half of what we've heard of Lord Hull was true," Holmes said. He rose and began to pace irritably about the study. "Who testifies that Jory was with Stephen when the door was smashed in? Jory, naturally. Stephen, naturally. But there are two other faces in this family portrait. One belongs to William, the third brother. Do you concur, Lestrade?"

"Yes," Lestrade said. "If this is the straight of the matter, William also had to be in on it. He said he was halfway down the stairs when he saw the two of them go in together, Jory a little ahead."

"How interesting!" Holmes said, eyes gleaming. "*Stephen* breaks in the door — as the younger and stronger of course he must — and so one would expect simple forward momentum would have carried him into the room first. Yet William, halfway down the stairs, saw *Jory* enter first. Why was that, Watson?"

I could only shake my head numbly.

"Ask yourself whose testimony, *and whose tes-*

timony alone, we can trust here. The answer is the only witness who is not part of the family: Lord Hull's man, Oliver Stanley. He approached the gallery railing in time to see Stephen enter the room, and that is just as it should have been, since Stephen was alone when he broke it in. It was *William,* with a better angle from his place on the stairs, who said he saw Jory precede Stephen into the study. William said so because he had seen Stanley and knew what he *must* say. It boils down to this, Watson: we know Jory was inside this room. Since both of his brothers testify he was *outside,* there was, at the very least, collusion. But as you say, the smooth way they all pulled together suggests something far more serious."

"Conspiracy," I said.

"Yes. Do you recall my asking you, Watson, if you believed all four of them simply walked wordlessly out of that parlor in four different directions after they heard the study door locked?"

"Yes. Now I do."

"The *four* of them." He looked briefly at Lestrade, who nodded, and then back at me. "We know Jory had to have been up and off and about his business the moment the old man left the parlor in order to reach the study ahead of him, yet all four of the surviving family — including Lady Hull — say they were in the parlor when Lord Hull locked his study door. The murder of Lord Hull was very much a family affair, Watson."

I was too staggered to say anything. I looked at Lestrade and saw an expression on his face I had never seen there before nor ever did again;

a kind of tired sickened gravity.

"What may they expect?" Holmes said, almost genially.

"Jory will certainly swing," Lestrade said. "Stephen will go to jail for life. William Hull may get life, but will more likely get twenty years in Wormwood Scrubs, a kind of living death."

Holmes bent and stroked the canvas stretched between the legs of the coffee-table. It made that odd hoarse purring noise.

"Lady Hull," Lestrade went on, "may expect to spend the next five years of her life in Beechwood Manor, more commonly known to the inmates as Poxy Palace . . . although, having met the lady, I rather suspect she will find another way out. Her husband's laudanum would be my guess."

"All because Jory Hull missed a clean strike," Holmes remarked, and sighed. "If the old man had had the common decency to die silently, all would have been well. Jory would, as Watson says, have left by the window, taking his canvas with him, of course . . . not to mention his trumpery shadows. Instead, he raised the house. All the servants were in, exclaiming over the dead master. The family was in confusion. How shabby their luck was, Lestrade! How close was the constable when Stanley summoned him?"

"Closer than you would believe," Lestrade said. "Hurrying up the drive to the door, as a matter of fact. He was passing on his regular rounds, and heard a scream from the house. Their luck *was* shabby."

"Holmes," I said, feeling much more comfortable in my old role, "how did you know a constable was so nearby?"

"Simplicity itself, Watson. If not, the family would have shooed the servants out long enough to hide the canvas and 'shadows.' "

"Also to unlatch at least one window, I should think," Lestrade added in a voice uncustomarily quiet.

"They *could* have taken the canvas and the shadows," I said suddenly.

Holmes turned toward me. "Yes."

Lestrade raised his eyebrows.

"It came down to a choice," I said to him. "There was time enough to burn the new will or get rid of the hugger-mugger . . . this would have been just Stephen and Jory, of course, in the moments after Stephen burst in the door. They — or, if you've got the temperature of the characters right, and I suppose you do, *Stephen* — decided to burn the will and hope for the best. I suppose there was just enough time to chuck it into the stove."

Lestrade turned, looked at it, then looked back. "Only a man as black as Hull would have found strength enough to scream at the end," he said.

"Only a man as black as Hull would have required a son to kill him," Holmes rejoined.

He and Lestrade looked at each other, and again something passed between them, some perfectly silent communication from which I myself was excluded.

"Have you ever done it?" Holmes asked, as if picking up on an old conversation.

Lestrade shook his head. "Once came damned

close," he said. "There was a girl involved, not her fault, not really. I came close. Yet . . . that was only one."

"And here there are four," Holmes returned, understanding him perfectly. "Four people ill-used by a villain who should have died within six months anyway."

At last I understood what they were discussing.

Holmes turned his gray eyes on me. "What say you, Lestrade? Watson has solved this one, although he did not see all the ramifications. Shall we let Watson decide?"

"All right," Lestrade said gruffly. "Just be quick. I want to get out of this damned room."

Instead of answering, I bent down, picked up the felt shadows, rolled them into a ball, and put them in my coat pocket. I felt quite odd doing it: much as I had felt when in the grip of the fever which almost took my life in India.

"Capital fellow, Watson!" Holmes cried. "You've solved your first case, become an accessory to murder, and it's not even tea-time! And here's a souvenir for myself — an original Jory Hull. I doubt it's signed, but one must be grateful for whatever the gods send us on rainy days." He used his pen-knife to loosen the artist's glue holding the canvas to the legs of the coffee-table. He made quick work of it; less than a minute later he was slipping a narrow canvas tube into the inner pocket of his voluminous greatcoat.

"This is a dirty piece of work," Lestrade said, but he crossed to one of the windows and, after a moment's hesitation, released the locks which held it and opened it half an inch or so.

"Say it's dirty work undone," Holmes said in a tone of almost hectic gaiety. "Shall we go, gentlemen?"

We crossed to the door. Lestrade opened it. One of the constables asked him if there was any progress.

On another occasion Lestrade might have shown the man the rough side of his tongue. This time he said shortly, "Looks like attempted robbery gone to something worse. I saw it at once, of course; Holmes a moment later."

"Too bad!" the other constable ventured.

"Yes," Lestrade said, "but at least the old man's scream sent the thief packing before he could steal anything. Carry on."

We left. The parlor door was open, but I kept my head down as we passed it. Holmes looked, of course; there was no way he could not have done. It was just the way he was made. As for me, I never saw any of the family. I never wanted to.

Holmes was sneezing again. His friend was twining around his legs and miaowing blissfully. "Let me out of here," he said, and bolted.

An hour later we were back at 221B Baker Street, in much the same positions we had occupied when Lestrade came driving up: Holmes in the window-seat, myself on the sofa.

"Well, Watson," Holmes said presently, "how do you think you'll sleep tonight?"

"Like a top," I said. "And you?"

"Likewise, I'm sure," he said. "I'm glad to be away from those damned cats, I can tell you that."

891

"How will Lestrade sleep, d'you think?"

Holmes looked at me and smiled. "Poorly tonight. Poorly for a week, perhaps. But then he'll be all right. Among his other talents, Lestrade has a great one for creative forgetting."

That made me laugh.

"Look, Watson!" Holmes said. "Here's a sight!" I got up and went to the window, somehow sure I would see Lestrade riding up in the wagon once more. Instead I saw the sun breaking through the clouds, bathing London in a glorious late-afternoon light.

"It came out after all," Holmes said. "Marvellous, Watson! Makes one happy to be alive!" He picked up his violin and began to play, the sun strong on his face.

I looked at his barometer and saw it was falling. That made me laugh so hard I had to sit down. When Holmes asked — in tones of mild irritation — what the matter was, I could only shake my head. I am not, in truth, sure he would have understood, anyway. It was not the way his mind worked.

Umney's Last Case

The rains are over. The hills are still green and in the valley across the Hollywood hills you can see snow on the high mountains. The fur stores are advertising their annual sales. The call houses that specialize in sixteen-year-old virgins are doing a land-office business. And in Beverly Hills the jacaranda trees are beginning to bloom.

— Raymond Chandler,
The Little Sister

I. The News from Peoria.

It was one of those spring mornings so L.A.-perfect you keep expecting to see that little trademark symbol — ® — stamped on it somewhere. The exhaust of the vehicles passing on Sunset smelled faintly of oleander, the oleander was lightly perfumed with exhaust, and the sky overhead was as clear as a hardshell Baptist's conscience. Peoria Smith, the blind paperboy, was standing in his accustomed place on the corner of Sunset and Laurel, and if that didn't mean God was in His heaven and all was jake with the world, I didn't know what did.

Yet since I'd swung my feet out of bed that

893

morning at the unaccustomed hour of 7:30 A.M., things had felt a little off-kilter, somehow; a tad woozy around the edges. It was only as I was shaving — or at least showing those pesky bristles the razor in an effort to scare them into submission — that I realized part of the reason why. Although I'd been up reading until at least two, I hadn't heard the Demmicks roll in, squiffed to the earlobes and trading those snappy one-liners that apparently form the basis of their marriage.

Nor had I heard Buster, and that was maybe even odder. Buster, the Demmicks' Welsh Corgi, has a high-pitched bark that goes through your head like slivers of glass, and he uses it as much as he can. Also, he's the jealous type. He lets loose with one of his shrill barking squalls every time George and Gloria clinch, and when they aren't zinging each other like a couple of vaudeville comedians, George and Gloria usually *are* clinching. I've gone to sleep on more than one occasion listening to them giggle while that mutt prances around their feet going *yarkyarkyark* and wondering how difficult it would be to strangle a muscular, medium-sized dog with a length of piano-wire. Last night, however, the Demmicks' apartment had been as quiet as the grave. It was passing strange, but a long way from earth-shattering; the Demmicks weren't exactly your perfect life-on-a-timetable couple at the best of times.

Peoria Smith was all right, though — chipper as a chipmunk, just as always, and he'd recognized me by my walk even though it was at least an hour before my usual time. He was wearing a baggy CalTech sweatshirt that came down to his thighs and a pair of corduroy knickers that showed off his scabby knees. His hated white cane leaned casually against the side of the card-table he did business on.

"Say, Mr. Umney! Howza kid?"

Peoria's dark glasses glinted in the morning sunlight, and as he turned toward the sound of my step with my copy of the *L.A. Times* held up in front of him, I had a momentary unsettling thought: it was as if someone had drilled two big black holes into his face. I shivered the thought off my back, thinking that maybe the time had come to cut out the before-bedtime shot of rye. Either that or double the dose.

Hitler was on the front of the *Times*, as he so often was these days. This time it was something about Austria. I thought, and not for the first time, how at home that pale face and limp forelock would have looked on a post-office bulletin board.

"The kid is just about okay, Peoria," I said. "In fact, the kid is as fine as fresh paint on an outhouse wall."

I dropped a dime into the Corona box resting atop Peoria's stack of newspapers. The *Times* is a three-center, and overpriced at that, but I've been dropping that same chip into Peoria's change-box since time out of mind. He's a good kid, and making good grades in school — I took it on myself to check that last year, after he'd helped me out on the Weld case. If Peoria hadn't shown up on Harris Brunner's houseboat when he did, I'd still be trying to swim with my feet cemented into a kerosene drum, somewhere off Malibu. To say I owe him a lot is an understatement.

In the course of that particular investigation (Peoria Smith, not Harris Brunner and Mavis Weld), I even found out the kid's real name, although wild horses wouldn't have dragged it out of me. Peoria's father took a permanent coffee-break out a ninth-floor office window on Black Friday, his mother's the only white frail working in that goofy Chinese laundry down on La Punta, and the kid's blind. With all that, does the world need to know they hung Francis on him when he was too young to fight back? The defense rests.

If anything really juicy happened the night before, you almost always find it on the front page of the *Times,* left side, just below the fold. I turned the newspaper over and saw that a bandleader of the Cuban persuasion had suffered a heart attack while dancing with his female vocalist at The Carousel in Burbank. He died an hour later at L.A. General. I had some sympathy for the maestro's widow, but none for the man himself. My opinion is that people who go dancing in Burbank deserve what they get.

I opened to the sports section to see how Brooklyn had done in their doubleheader with the Cards the day before. "How about you, Peoria? Everyone holding their own in your castle? Moats and battlements all in good repair?"

"I'll say, Mr. Umney! Oh, boy!"

Something in his voice caught my attention, and I lowered the paper to take a closer look at him. When I did, I saw what a gilt-edged shamus like me should have seen right away: the kid was all but busting with happiness.

"You look like somebody just gave you six tickets to the first game of the World Series," I said. "What's the buzz, Peoria?"

"My mom hit the lottery down in Tijuana!" he said. "Forty thousand bucks! We're rich, brother! *Rich!*"

I gave him a grin he couldn't see and ruffled his hair. It popped his cowlick up, but what the hell. "Whoa, hold the phone. How old are you, Peoria?"

"Twelve in May. *You* know that, Mr. Umney, you gave me a polo-shirt. But I don't see what that has to do with —"

"Twelve's old enough to know that sometimes people get what they *want* to happen mixed up with what actually *does* happen. That's all I meant."

"If you're talkin about daydreams, you're right — I *do* know all about em," Peoria said, running his hands over the back of his head in an effort to make his cowlick lie down again, "but this ain't no daydream, Mr. Umney. It's real! My Uncle Fred went down and picked up the cash yest'y afternoon. He brought it back in the saddlebag of his Vinnie! I smelled it! Hell, I *rolled* in it! It was spread all over my mom's bed! Richest feeling I ever had, let me tell you — forty-froggin-thousand smackers!"

"Twelve may be old enough to know the difference between daydreams and what's real, but it's not old enough for that kind of talk," I said. It sounded good — I'm sure the Legion of Decency would have approved two thousand per cent — but my mouth was running on automatic pilot, and I barely heard what was coming out of it. I was too busy trying to get my brain wrapped around what he'd just told me. Of one thing I was absolutely positive: he'd made a mistake. He *must* have made a mistake, because if it was true, then Peoria wouldn't be standing here anymore when I came by on my way to my office in the Fulwider Building. And that just couldn't be.

I found my mind returning to the Demmicks, who for the first time in recorded history hadn't played any of their big-band records at full volume before retiring, and to Buster, who for the first time in recorded history hadn't greeted the sound of George's latchkey turning in the lock with a fusillade of barks. The thought that something was off-kilter returned, and it was stronger this time.

Meanwhile, Peoria was looking at me with an expression I'd never expected to see on his honest, open face: sulky irritation mixed with exasperated humor. It was the way a kid looks at a windbag uncle who's told all his stories, even the boring ones, three or four times.

"Ain't you picking up on this newsflash, Mr. Umney? We're *rich!* My mom ain't going to have to press shirts for that damned old Lee Ho anymore, and I ain't going to have to sell papers on the corner anymore, shiverin when it rains in the winter and havin to suck up to those nutty old bags who work down at Bilder's. I can quit actin like I died and went to heaven every time some blowhard leaves me a nickel tip."

I started a little at that, but what the hell — I wasn't a nickel man. I left Peoria seven cents, day in and day out. Unless I was too broke to afford it, of course, but in my business an occasional stony stretch comes with the territory.

"Maybe we ought to go up to Blondie's and have a cup of java," I said. "Talk this thing over."

"Can't. It's closed."

"*Blondie's?* The hell you say!"

But Peoria couldn't be bothered with such mundane stuff as the coffee shop up the street. "You ain't heard the best, Mr. Umney! My Uncle Fred knows a doctor up in Frisco — a specialist — who thinks he can do something about my eyes." He turned his face up to mine. Below the cheaters and his too-thin nose, his lips were trembling. "He says it might not be the optic nerves after all, and if it's not, there's an operation . . . I don't understand all the technical stuff, but I could see again, Mr. Umney!" He reached out for me blindly . . . well, of course he did. How else *could* he reach out? "*I could see again!*"

He clutched at me, and I gripped his hands and squeezed them briefly before pushing them gently away. There was ink on his fingers, and I'd been feeling so good when I got up that I'd put on my new chalk worsted. Hot for summer, of course, but the whole city is air-conditioned these days, and besides, I was feeling naturally cool.

I didn't feel so cool now. Peoria was looking up at me, his thin and somehow perfect newsboy's face troubled. A little breeze — scented with oleander and exhaust — ruffled his cowlick, and I realized that I could see it because he wasn't wearing his tweed cap. He looked somehow naked without it, and why not? *Every* newsboy should wear a tweed cap, just like every shoeshine boy should wear a beanie cocked way back on his head.

"What's the matter, Mr. Umney? I thought you'd be happy. Jeepers, I didn't *have* to come out here to this lousy corner today, you know, but I did — I even got here early, because I kinda had an idea *you'd* get here early. I thought you'd be happy, my mom hittin the lottery and me gettin a chance at an operation, but you ain't." Now his voice trembled with resentment. "You ain't!"

"Yes I am," I said, and I *wanted* to be happy — part of me did, anyway — but the bitch of it was that he was mostly right. Because it meant things would change, you see, and things weren't *supposed* to change. Peoria Smith was supposed to be right here, year in and year out, with that perfect cap of his tilted back on hot days and pulled down low on rainy ones, so that the raindrops dripped off the bill. He was always supposed to be smiling, was never supposed to say "hell" or "frogging," and most of all, he was supposed to be *blind.*

"You *ain't!*" he said, and then, shockingly, he pushed his card-table over. It fell into the street, papers flapping everywhere. His white cane rolled into the gutter. Peoria heard it go and bent down to get it. I could see tears coming out from beneath his dark glasses and go rolling down his pale, thin cheeks. He started groping for the cane, but it had fallen near me and he was going the wrong way. I felt a sudden strong urge to haul off and kick him in his blind newsboy's ass.

Instead, I bent over, got his stick, and tapped him lightly on the hip with it.

Peoria turned, quick as a snake, and snatched it. Out of the corner of my eye I could see pictures of Hitler and the recently deceased Cuban band-leader flapping all over Sunset Boulevard — a bus bound for Van Ness snored through a little drift of them, leaving a bitter tang of diesel fumes behind. I hated the way those newspapers looked, fluttering here and there. They looked messy. Worse, they looked *wrong*. Utterly and completely *wrong*. I fought another urge, as strong as the first one, to grab Peoria and shake him. To tell him he was going to spend the morning picking up those newspapers, and I wasn't going to let him go home until he'd gotten every last one.

It occurred to me that less than ten minutes ago, I'd been thinking that this was the perfect L.A. morning — so perfect it deserved a trademark symbol. And it *had* been, dammit. So where had things gone wrong? And how had it happened so fast?

No answers came, only an irrational but powerful voice from inside, telling me that the kid's mother *couldn't* have won the lottery, that the kid *couldn't* stop selling newspapers, and that, most of all, the kid couldn't see. Peoria Smith was supposed to be blind for the rest of his life.

Well, it's got to be something experimental, I thought. *Even if the doctor up in Frisco isn't a quack, and he probably is, the operation's bound to fail.*

And, bizarre as it sounds, the thought calmed me down.

"Listen," I said, "we got off on the wrong foot this morning, that's all. Let me make it up to you. We'll go down to Blondie's and I'll buy you breakfast. What do you say, Peoria? You can dig into a plate of bacon and eggs and tell me all ab—"

901

"Fuck you!" he shouted, shocking me all the way down to my shoes. "Fuck you and the horse you rode in on, you cheap gumshoe! You think blind people can't tell when people like you are lying through their teeth? Fuck you! And keep your hands off me from now on! I think you're a faggot!"

That did it — no one calls me a faggot and gets away with it, not even a blind newsboy. I forgot all about how Peoria had saved my life during that Mavis Weld business; I reached for his cane, meaning to take it away from him and whack him across the keister with it a few times. Teach him some manners.

Before I could get it, though, he hauled off and slammed the cane's tip into my lower belly — and I *do* mean lower. I doubled up in agony, but even while I was trying to keep from howling with pain, I was counting my blessings; two inches lower still and I could have quit peeping for a living and gotten a job singing soprano in the Palace of the Doges.

I made a quick, reflexive grab for him anyway, and he brought the cane down on the back of my neck. Hard. It didn't break, but I heard it crack. I figured I could finish the job when I caught him and ran it into his right ear. I'd show him who was a faggot.

He backed away from me as if he'd caught my brainwave, and threw the cane into the street.

"Peoria," I managed. Maybe it still wasn't too late to catch sanity by the shirttail. "Peoria, what the hell's wrong with —"

"*And don't call me that!*" he screamed. "*My*

*name's Francis! Frank! You're the one who started
calling me Peoria! You started it and now everyone
calls me that and I hate it!"*

My watering eyes doubled him as he turned and
fled across the street, heedless of traffic (of which
there was currently none, luckily for him), hands
held out in front of him. I thought he would trip
over the far curb — was looking forward to it,
in fact — but I guess blind people must keep a
pretty good set of topographical survey maps in
their heads. He jumped onto the sidewalk as nimbly as a goat, then turned his dark glasses back
in my direction. There was an expression of crazed
triumph on his tear-streaked face, and the dark
lenses looked more like holes than ever. Big ones,
as if someone had hit him with two large-caliber
shotgun rounds.

"*Blondie's is gone, I toldja!*" he screamed. "*My
mom says he upped and ran away with that redhead
floozy he hired last month! You should be so lucky,
you ugly prick!*"

He turned and went running up Sunset in that
strange way of his, with his splayed fingers held
out in front of him. People stood in little clusters
on both sides of the street, looking at him, looking at the papers fluttering in the street, looking
at me.

Mostly looking at me, it seemed.

This time Peoria — well, okay, Francis — made
it as far as Derringer's Bar before turning to deliver
one final salvo.

"*Fuck you, Mr. Umney!*" he screamed, and ran
on.

II. Vernon's Cough.

I managed to pull myself erect and make my way across the street. Peoria, aka Francis Smith, was long gone, but I wanted to put those blowing newspapers behind me, too. Looking at them was giving me a headache that was somehow worse than the ache in my groin.

On the far side of the street I stared into Felt's Stationery as if the new Parker ball-point pen in the window was the most fascinating thing I'd ever seen in my life (or maybe it was those sexy imitation-leather appointment books). After five minutes or so — time enough to commit every item in the dusty show-window to memory — I felt capable of resuming my interrupted voyage up Sunset without listing too noticeably to port.

Questions circled in my mind the way mosquitoes circle your head at the drive-in in San Pedro when you forget to bring along an insect stick or two. I was able to ignore most of them, but a couple got through. First, what the hell had gotten into Peoria? Second, what the hell had gotten into me? I kept slapping at these uncomfortable queries until I got to Blondie's City Eats, Open 24 Hrs, Bagels Our Specialty, on the corner of Sunset and Travernia, and when I got that far, they were driven out in a single wallop. Blondie's had been on that corner for as long as I could remember — the sharpies and the hustlers and the hipsters and the hypes going in and going out, not to mention the debs, the dykes, and the dopes. A famous silent-movie star was once arrested for murder as he was coming out of Blondie's, and I myself had concluded a nasty piece of business there not so long ago, shooting a coked-up fashion-plate named Dunninger who had killed three hopheads in the aftermath of a Hollywood dope party. It was also the place where I'd said goodbye to the silver-haired, violet-eyed Ardis McGill. I'd spent the rest of that lost night walking in a rare Los Angeles fog which might have only been behind my eyes . . . and trickling down my cheeks, by the time the sun came up.

Blondie's closed? Blondie's gone? Impossible, you would have said — more likely that the Statue of Liberty should have disappeared from her barren lick of rock in New York Harbor.

Impossible but true. The window which had once held a mouth-watering selection of pies and cakes was soaped over, but the job had been done indifferently, and I could see a nearly empty room through the stripes. The lino looked filthy and barren. The grease-darkened blades of the overhead fans hung down like the propellers of crashed airplanes. There were a few tables left, and six or eight of the familiar red-upholstered chairs piled on them with the legs sticking up, but that was all . . . except for a couple of empty sugar-shakers tumbled in one corner.

I stood there trying to get it into my head, and it was like trying to get a big sofa up a narrow flight of stairs. All that life and excitement, all that late-night hustle and surprise — how could it be ended? It didn't seem like a mistake; it seemed like a blasphemy. For me Blondie's had summed up all the glittering contradictions that

905

surround L.A.'s essentially dark and loveless heart; I had sometimes thought Blondie's *was* L.A. as I had known it over the last fifteen or twenty years, only drawn small. Where else could you see a mobster eating breakfast at 9:00 P.M. with a priest, or a diamond-decked glamorpuss sitting on a counter-stool next to a grease-monkey celebrating the end of his shift with a hot cup of java? I suddenly found myself thinking of the Cuban bandleader and his heart attack again, this time with considerably more sympathy.

All that fabulous starry City of Lost Angels *life* — do you get it, chum? Are you picking up this newsflash?

The sign hung in the door read CLOSED FOR RENOVATIONS, REOPENING SOON, but I didn't believe it. Empty sugar-shakers lying in the corner do not, in my experience, indicate renovations in progress. Peoria had been right: Blondie's was history. I turned away and went on up the street, but now I walked slowly and had to consciously order my head to stay up. As I approached the Fulwider Building, where I've kept an office for more years than I like to think about, an odd certainty gripped me. The handles of the big double doors would be wrapped up in a thick tow-chain and held with a padlock. The glass would be soaped over in indifferent stripes. And there would be a sign reading CLOSED FOR RENOVATIONS, REOPENING SOON.

By the time I reached the building, this nutty idea had taken over my mind with the force of a compulsion, and not even the sight of Bill Tuggle, the rummy CPA from the third floor, going inside could quite dispel it. But seeing is believing, they say, and when I got to 2221, I saw no chain, no sign, and no soap on the glass. It was just the Fulwider, the same as ever. I went into the lobby, smelled the familiar odor — it reminds me of the pink cakes they put in the urinals of public men's rooms these days — and glanced around at the same ratty palm trees overhanging the same faded red tile floor.

Bill was standing next to Vernon Klein, world's oldest elevator operator, in Car 2. In his frayed red suit and ancient pillbox hat, Vernon looks like a cross between the Philip Morris bellboy and a rhesus monkey which has fallen into an industrial steam-cleaning machine. He looked up at me with his mournful basset-hound eyes, which were watering from the Camel pasted in the middle of his mouth. His peepers should have gotten used to the smoke years ago; I couldn't remember ever having seen him without a Camel parked in that same position.

Bill moved over a little, but not far enough. There wasn't room enough in the car for him to move far enough. I'm not sure there would have been room in Rhode Island for him to move far enough. Delaware, maybe. He smelled like bologna which has spent a year or so marinating in cheap bourbon. And just when I thought it couldn't get any worse, he belched.

"Sorry, Clyde."

"Well, you certainly ought to be," I said, waving the air in front of my face as Vern slid the gate across the front of the car and prepared to fly us to the moon . . . or at least to the seventh floor.

"What drainpipe did you spend the night in, Bill?"

Yet there was something comforting about that smell — I'd be lying if I said there wasn't. Because it was a *familiar* smell. It was just Bill Tuggle, odoriferous, hung over, and standing with his knees slightly bent, as if someone had filled the crotch of his underpants with chicken salad and he'd just realized it. Not pleasant, nothing about that morning's elevator ride was pleasant, but it was at least *known*.

Bill gave me a sick smile as the elevator began to rattle upward but said nothing.

I swung my head in Vernon's direction, mostly to get away from the smell of overbaked accountant, but whatever small talk I'd been meaning to make died in my throat. The two pictures which had hung over Vern's stool since the beginning of time — one of Jesus walking on the Sea of Galilee while his boatbound disciples gawped at him and the other of Vern's wife in a buckskin-fringed Sweetheart of the Rodeo outfit and a turn-of-the-century hairdo — were both gone. What had replaced them shouldn't have been shocking, especially in light of Vernon's age, but it hit me like a barge-load of bricks just the same.

It was a card, that's all — a simple card showing the silhouette of a man fishing on a lake at sunset. It was the sentiment printed below the canoe that floored me: HAPPY RETIREMENT!

You could have doubled the way I felt when Peoria told me he might see again and still have come up short. Memories flickered through my mind with the speed of cards being shuffled by a riverboat gambler. There was the time Vern

908

broke into the office next to mine to call an ambulance when that nutty dame, Agnes Sternwood, first tore my phone out of the wall and then swallowed what she swore was drain-cleaner. The "drain-cleaner" turned out to be nothing but crystals of raw sugar, and the office Vern broke into turned out to be a high-class horse parlor. So far as I know, the guy who leased the place and slapped MacKenzie Imports on the door is still receiving his annual Sears Roebuck catalogue in San Quentin. Then there was the guy Vern cold-conked with his stool just before he could ventilate my guts; that was the Mavis Weld business again, of course. Not to mention the time he brought his daughter to me — what a babe *she* was! — when she got involved with that dirty-picture racket.

Vern retiring?

It wasn't possible. It just wasn't.

"Vernon," I asked, "what kind of joke is this?"

"No joke, Mr. Umney," he said, and as he brought the elevator car to a stop on Three, he began to hack a deep cough I'd never heard in all the years I'd known him. It was like listening to marble bowling balls rolling down a stone alley. He took the Camel out of his mouth, and I was horrified to see the end of it was pink, and not with lipstick. He looked at it for a moment, grimaced, then replaced it and yanked back the accordion grille. "*Thuh-ree*, Mr. Tuggle."

"Thanks, Vern," Bill said.

"Remember the party on Friday," Vernon said. His words were muffled; he'd taken a handkerchief spotted with brown stains out of his back pocket and was wiping his lips with it. "I sure would admire for you to come." He glanced at me with his rheumy eyes, and what was in them scared the bejabbers out of me. Something was waiting for Vernon Klein just around the next bend in the road, and that look said Vernon knew all about it. "You too, Mr. Umney — we been through a lot together, and I'd be tickled to raise a glass with you."

"Wait a minute!" I shouted, grabbing Bill as he tried to step out of the elevator. "You wait just a God damned minute, both of you! *What* party? What's going on here?"

"Retirement," Bill said. "It usually happens at some point after your hair turns white, in case you've been too busy to notice. Vernon's party is going to be in the basement on Friday afternoon. Everybody in the building's going to be there, and I'm going to make my world-famous Dynamite Punch. What's the matter with you, Clyde? You've known for a month that Vern was finishing up on May thirtieth."

That made me angry all over again, the way I'd been when Peoria called me a faggot. I grabbed Bill by the padded shoulders of his double-breasted suit and gave him a shake. "The hell you say!"

He gave me a small, pained smile. "The hell I don't, Clyde. But if you don't want to come, fine. Stay away. You've been acting *poco loco* for the last six months, anyhow."

I shook him again. "What do you mean, *poco loco?*"

"Crazy as a loon, nutty as a fruitcake, two wheels off the road, out to lunch, playing without a full

910

deck — any of those ring a bell? And before you answer, just let me inform you that if you shake me one more time, even a *little* shake, my guts are going to explode straight out through my chest, and not even dry-cleaning will get *that* mess off your suit."

He pulled away before I could do it again even if I'd wanted to and started down the hall with the seat of his pants hanging somewhere down around the level of his knees, as per usual. He glanced back just once, while Vernon was sliding the brass gate across. "You need to take some time off, Clyde. Starting last week."

"What's gotten into you?" I shouted at him. "What's gotten into *all* of you?" But by then the inner door was closed and we were headed up again — this time to Seven. My little slice of heaven. Vern dropped his cigarette butt into the bucket of sand that squats in the corner, and immediately stuck a fresh one in his kisser. He popped a wooden match alight with his thumbnail, set the fag on fire, and immediately started coughing again. Now I could see fine drops of blood misting out from between his cracked lips. It was a gruesome sight. His eyes had dropped; they stared vacantly into the far corner, seeing nothing, hoping for nothing. Bill Tuggle's B.O. hung between us like the Ghost of Binges Past.

"Okay, Vern," I said. "What is it and where are you going?"

Vernon had never been one to wear out the English language, and that at least hadn't changed. "It's Big C," he said. "On Saturday I catch the Desert Blossom to Arizona. I'm going to live with

911

my sister. I don't expect to wear out my welcome, though. She might have to change the bed twice." He brought the elevator to a stop and rattled the gate back. "*Seven,* Mr. Umney. Your little slice of heaven." He smiled at that just as he always did, but this time it looked like the kind of smile you see on the candy skulls down in Tijuana, on the Day of the Dead.

Now that the elevator door was open, I smelled something up here in my little slice of heaven that was so out of place it took a moment for me to recognize it: fresh paint. Once it was noted, I filed it. I had other fish to fry.

"This isn't right," I said. "You know it isn't, Vern."

He turned his frightening vacant eyes on me. Death in them, a black shape flapping and beckoning just beyond the faded blue. "What isn't right, Mr. Umney?"

"You're supposed to be *here,* damn it! Right *here!* Sitting on your stool with Jesus and your wife over your head. Not *this!*" I reached up, grabbed the card with the picture of the man fishing on the lake, tore it in two, put the pieces together, tore it in four, and then gave them the toss. They fluttered to the faded red rug on the floor of the elevator car like confetti.

"S'posed to be right here," he repeated, those terrible eyes of his never leaving mine. Beyond us, two men in paint-splattered coveralls had turned to look in our direction.

"That's right."

"For how long, Mr. Umney? Since you know everything else, you can probably tell me that, can'tcha? How long am I supposed to keep drivin this damned car?"

"Well . . . forever," I said, and the word hung between us, another ghost in the cigarette-smokey elevator car. Given a choice of ghosts, I guess I would have picked Bill Tuggle's B.O. . . . but I wasn't given a choice. Instead, I said it again. "Forever, Vern."

He dragged on his Camel, coughed out smoke and a fine spray of blood, and went on looking at me. "It ain't my place to give the tenants advice, Mr. Umney, but I guess I'll give you some, anyway — it being my last week and all. You might consider seeing a doctor. The kind that shows you ink-pitchers and you say what they look like."

"You can't retire, Vern." My heart was beating harder than ever, but I managed to keep my voice level. "You just can't."

"No?" He took his cigarette out of his mouth — fresh blood was already soaking into the tip — and then looked back at me. His smile was ghastly. "The way it looks to me, I ain't exactly got a choice, Mr. Umney."

III. Of Painters and Pesos.

The smell of fresh paint seared my nose, overpowering both the smell of Vernon's smoke and Bill Tuggle's armpits. The men in the coveralls were currently taking up space not far from my office door. They had put down a dropcloth, and the tools of their trade were spread out all along it — tins and brushes and turp. There were two step-ladders as well, flanking the painters like scrawny bookends. What I wanted to do was to run down the hall, kicking the whole works every whichway as I went. What right had they to paint these old dark walls that glaring, sacrilegious white?

Instead, I walked up to the one who looked as if it might take a two-digit number to express his IQ and politely asked what he and his fellow mug thought they were doing. He glanced around at me. "Hellzit look like? I'm givin Miss America a finger-frig and Chick there's puttin rouge on Betty Grable's nippy-nips."

I'd had enough. Enough of them, enough of everything. I reached out, grabbed the quiz-kid under the armpit, and used my fingertips to engage a particularly nasty nerve that hides up there. He screamed and dropped his brush. White paint splattered his shoes. His partner gave me a timid doe-eyed look and took a step backward.

"If you try taking off before I'm done with you," I snarled, "you're going to find the handle of your paint-brush so far up your ass you'll need a boat-hook to find the bristles. You want to try me and see if I'm lying?"

He stopped moving and just stood there on the edge of the dropcloth, eyes darting from side to side, looking for help. There was none to be had. I half-expected Candy to open my door and look out to see what the fracas was, but the door stayed firmly closed. I turned my attention back to the quiz-kid I was holding onto.

"The question was simple enough, bud — what the hell are you doing here? Can you answer it, or do I give you another blast?"

I twiddled my fingers in his armpit just to refresh his memory and he screamed again. *"Paintin the hall! Jeezis, can't you see?"*

I could see, all right, and even if I'd been blind, I could *smell*. I hated what both of those senses were telling me. The hallway wasn't *supposed* to be painted, especially not this glaring, light-reflecting white. It was supposed to be dim and shadowy; it was supposed to smell like dust and old memories. Whatever had started with the Demmicks' unaccustomed silence was getting worse all the time. I was mad as hell, as this unfortunate fellow was discovering. I was also scared, but that was a feeling you get good at hiding when carrying a heater in a clamshell holster is part of the way you make your living.

"Who sent you two dubs down here?"

"Our *boss*," he said, looking at me as if I were crazy. "We work for Challis Custom Painters, on Van Nuys. The boss is Hap Corrigan. If you want to know who hired the cump'ny, you'll have to ask h—"

"It was the owner," the other painter said quietly. "The owner of this building. A guy named Samuel Landry."

I searched my memory, trying to put the name of Samuel Landry together with what I knew of the Fulwider Building and couldn't do it. In fact, I couldn't put the name of Samuel Landry together with anything . . . yet for all that it seemed almost to chime in my head, like a church-bell you can

915

hear from miles away on a foggy morning.

"You're lying," I said, but with no real force. I said it simply because it was something to say.

"Call the boss," the other painter said. Appearances could be deceiving; he was apparently the brighter of the two, after all. He reached inside his grimy, paint-smeared coverall and brought out a little card.

I waved it away, suddenly tired. "Who in the name of Christ would want to paint this place, anyway?"

It wasn't them I was asking, but the painter who'd offered me the business card answered just the same. "Well, it brightens the place up," he said cautiously. "You gotta admit that."

"Son," I asked, taking a step toward him, "did your mother ever have any kids that lived, or did she just produce the occasional afterbirth like you?"

"Hey, whatever, whatever," he said, taking a step backward. I followed his worried gaze down to my own balled-up fists and forced them open again. He didn't look very relieved, and I actually didn't blame him very much. "You don't like it — you're coming through loud and clear on that score. But I gotta do what the boss tells me, don't I? I mean, hell, that's the American way."

He glanced at his partner, then back to me. It was a quick glance, really no more than a flick, but in my line of work I'd seen it more than once, and it's the kind of look you file away. *Don't bother this guy,* it said. *Don't bump him, don't rattle him. He's nitro.*

916

"I mean, I've got a wife and a little kid to take care of," he went on. "There's a Depression going on out there, you know."

Confusion came over me then, drowning my anger the way a downpour drowns a brushfire. *Was there a Depression going on out there? Was there?*

"I know," I said, not knowing anything. "Let's just forget it, what do you say?"

"Sure," the painters agreed, so eager they sounded like half of a barbershop quartet. The one I'd mistakenly tabbed as half-bright had his left hand buried deep in his right armpit, trying to get that nerve to go back to sleep. I could have told him he had an hour's work ahead of him, maybe more, but I didn't want to talk to them anymore. I didn't want to talk to anyone or see anyone — not even the delectable Candy Kane, whose humid glances and smooth, subtropical curves have been known to send seasoned street-brawlers reeling to their knees. The only thing I wanted to do was to get across the outer office and into my inner sanctum. There was a bottle of Robb's Rye in the bottom lefthand drawer, and right now I needed a shot in the worst way.

I walked down toward the frosted-glass door marked CLYDE UMNEY PRIVATE INVESTIGATOR, restraining a renewed urge to see if I could drop-kick a can of Dutch Boy Oyster White through the window at the end of the hall and out onto the fire-escape. I was actually reaching for my doorknob when a thought struck me and I turned back to the painters . . . but slowly, so they wouldn't believe I was being gripped by some new seizure. Also, I had an idea that if I turned too

917

fast, I'd see them grinning at each other and twirling their fingers around their ears — the looney-gesture we all learned in the schoolyard.

They weren't twirling their fingers, but they hadn't taken their eyes off me, either. The half-smart one seemed to be gauging the distance to the door marked STAIRWELL. Suddenly I wanted to tell them that I wasn't such a bad guy when you got to know me; that there were, in fact, a few clients and at least one ex-wife who thought me something of a hero. But that wasn't a thing you could say about yourself, especially not to a couple of bozos like these.

"Take it easy," I said. "I'm not going to jump you. I just wanted to ask another question."

They relaxed a little. A very little, actually.

"Ask it," Painter Number Two said.

"Either of you ever played the numbers down in Tijuana?"

"*La lotería?*" Number One asked.

"Your knowledge of Spanish stuns me. Yeah. *La lotería.*"

Number One shook his head. "Mex numbers and Mex call houses are strictly for suckers."

Why do you think I asked you? I thought but didn't say.

"Besides," he went on, "you win ten or twenty thousand pesos, big deal. What's that in real money? Fifty bucks? Eighty?"

My mom hit the lottery down in Tijuana, Peoria had said, and I had known something about it wasn't right even then. *Forty thousand bucks . . . My Uncle Fred went down and picked up the cash yest'y afternoon. He brought it back in the*

918

saddlebag of his Vinnie!

"Yeah," I said, "something like that, I guess. And they always pay off that way, don't they? In pesos?"

He gave me that look again, as if I was crazy, then remembered I really was and readjusted his face. "Well, yeah. It *is* the Mexican lottery, you know. They couldn't very well pay off in dollars."

"How true," I said, and in my mind I saw Peoria's thin, eager face, heard him saying, *It was spread all over my mom's bed! Forty-froggin-thousand smackers!*

Except how could a blind kid be sure of the exact amount . . . or even that it really was money he was rolling around in? The answer was simple: he couldn't. But even a blind newsboy would know that *la lotería* paid off in pesos rather than in dollars, and even a blind newsboy had to know you couldn't carry forty thousand dollars' worth of Mexican lettuce in the saddlebag of a Vincent motorcycle. His uncle would have needed a City of Los Angeles dump truck to transport that much dough.

Confusion, confusion — nothing but dark clouds of confusion.

"Thanks," I said, and headed for my office.

I'm sure that was a relief for all three of us.

IV. Umney's Last Client.

"Candy, honey, I don't want to see anybody or take any ca—"

I broke off. The outer office was empty. Candy's desk in the corner was unnaturally bare, and after a moment I saw why: the IN/OUT tray had been dumped into the trash basket and her pictures of Errol Flynn and William Powell were both gone. So was her Philco. The little blue stenographer's stool, from which Candy had been wont to flash her gorgeous gams, was unoccupied.

My eyes returned to the IN/OUT tray sticking out of the trash can like the prow of a sinking ship, and for a moment my heart leaped. Perhaps someone had been in here, tossed the place, kidnapped Candy. Perhaps it was a case, in other words. At that moment I would have welcomed a case, even if it meant some mug was tying Candy up at this very moment . . . and adjusting the rope over the firm swell of her breasts with particular care. Any way out of the cobwebs that seemed to be falling around me sounded just peachy to me.

The trouble with the idea was simple: the room hadn't been tossed. The IN/OUT was in the trash, true enough, but that didn't indicate a struggle; in fact, it was more as if . . .

There was just one thing left on the desk, placed squarely in the center of the blotter. A white envelope. Just looking at it gave me a bad feeling. My feet carried me across the room just the same, however, and I picked it up. Seeing my name written across the front of the envelope in Candy's wide loops and swirls was no surprise; it was just another unpleasant part of this long, unpleasant morning.

I ripped it open and a single slip of note-paper fell out into my hand.

Dear Clyde,

I have had all of the groping and sneering I'm going to take from you, and I am tired of your ridiculous and childish jokes about my name. Life is too short to be pawed by a middle-aged divorce detective with bad breath. You did have your good points Clyde but they are getting drownded out by the bad ones, especially since you started drinking all the time.

Do yourself a favor and grow up.

Yours truely,
Arlene Cain

P.S.: *I'm going back to my mother's in Idaho. Do not try to get in touch with me.*

I held the note a moment or two longer, looking at it unbelievingly, then dropped it. One phrase from it recurred as I watched it seesaw lazily down toward the already occupied trash basket: *I am tired of your ridiculous and childish jokes about my name.* But had I ever known her name was anything *other* than Candy Kane? I searched my mind as the note continued its lazy — and seemingly endless — swoops back and forth, and the answer was an honest and resounding no. Her name had *always* been Candy Kane, we'd joked about it many a time, and if we'd had a few rounds of office slap-and-tickle, what of that? She'd always enjoyed it. We both had.

921

Did she enjoy it? a voice spoke up from somewhere deep inside me. *Did she* really, *or is that just another little fairytale you've been telling yourself all these years?*

I tried to shut that voice out, and after a moment or two I succeeded, but the one that replaced it was even worse. That voice belonged to none other than Peoria Smith. *I can quit actin like I died and went to heaven every time some blowhard leaves me a nickel tip,* he said. *Ain't you picking up on this newsflash, Mr. Umney?*

"Shut up, kid," I said to the empty room. "Gabriel Heatter you ain't." I turned away from Candy's desk, and as I did, faces passed in front of my mind's eye like the faces of some lunatic marching band from hell: George and Gloria Demmick, Peoria Smith, Bill Tuggle, Vernon Klein, a million-dollar blonde who went under the two-bit name of Arlene Cain . . . even the two painters were there.

Confusion, confusion, nothing but confusion.

Head down, I trudged into my office, closed the door behind me, and sat at the desk. Dimly, through the closed window, I could hear the traffic out on Sunset. I had an idea that, for the right person, it was still a spring morning so L.A.-perfect you expected to see that little trademark symbol stamped on it somewhere, but for me all the light had gone from the day . . . inside as well as out. I thought about the bottle of hooch in the bottom drawer, but all of a sudden even bending down to get it seemed like too much work. It seemed, in fact, a job akin to climbing Mount Everest in tennis shoes.

The smell of fresh paint had penetrated all the way into my inner sanctum. It was a smell I ordinarily liked, but not then. At that moment it was the smell of everything that had gone wrong since the Demmicks hadn't come into their Hollywood bungalow bouncing wisecracks off each other like rubber balls and playing their records at top volume and throwing their Corgi into conniptions with their endless billing and cooing. It occurred to me with perfect clarity and simplicity — the way I'd always imagined great truths must occur to the people they occur to — that if some doctor could cut out the cancer that was killing the Fulwider Building's elevator operator, it would be white. *Oyster* white. And it would smell just like fresh Dutch Boy paint.

This thought was so tiring that I had to put my head down with the heels of my palms pressed against my temples, holding it in place . . . or maybe just keeping what was inside from exploding out and making a mess on the walls. And when the door opened softly and footsteps entered the room, I didn't look up. It seemed like more of an effort than I was able to make at that particular moment.

Besides, I had the strange idea that I already *knew* who it was. I couldn't put a name to my knowledge, but the step was somehow familiar. So was the cologne, although I knew I wouldn't be able to name it even if someone had put a gun to my head, and for a very simple reason: I'd never smelled it before in my life. How could I recognize a scent I'd never smelled before, you ask? I can't answer that one, bud, but I did.

Nor was that the worst of it. The worst of it was this: I was scared nearly out of my mind. I've faced blazing guns in the hands of angry men, which is bad, and daggers in the hands of angry women, which is a thousand times worse; I was once tied to the wheel of a Packard automobile that had been parked on the tracks of a busy freight line; I have even been tossed out a third-story window. It's been an eventful life, all right, but nothing in it had ever scared me the way the smell of that cologne and that soft footstep scared me.

My head seemed to weigh at least six hundred pounds.

"Clyde," a voice said. A voice I'd never heard before, a voice I nevertheless knew as well as my own. Just that one word and the weight of my head went up to an even ton.

"Get outta here, whoever you are," I said without looking up. "Joint's closed." And something made me add, "For renovations."

"Bad day, Clyde?"

Was there sympathy in that voice? I thought maybe there was, and somehow that made things worse. Whoever this mug was, I didn't want his sympathy. Something told me that his sympathy would be more dangerous than his hate.

"Not so bad," I said, supporting my heavy, aching head with the palms of my hands and looking down at my desk-blotter for all I was worth. Written in the upper lefthand corner was Mavis Weld's number. I sent my eyes tracing over it again and again — BEverley 6-4214. Keeping my eyes on the blotter seemed like a good idea. I didn't know who my visitor was, but I knew I didn't want to see him. Right then it was the only thing I *did* know.

"I think maybe you're being a little . . . disingenuous, shall we say?" the voice asked, and it was sympathy, all right; the sound of it made my stomach curl up into something that felt like a quivering fist soaked with acid. There was a creak as he dropped into the client's chair.

"I don't exactly know what that word means, but by all means, let's say it," I agreed. "And now that we have, why don't you rise up righteous, Moggins, and shift on out of here. I'm thinking of taking a sick day. I can do that without much argument, you see, because I'm the boss. Neat, the way things work out sometimes, isn't it?"

"I suppose so. Look at me, Clyde."

My heart stuttered but my head stayed down and my eyes kept tracing over BEverley 6-4214. Part of me wondered if hell was hot enough for Mavis Weld. When I spoke, my voice came out steady. I was surprised but grateful. "In fact, I might take a whole year of sick days. In Carmel, maybe. Sit out on the deck with the *American Mercury* in my lap and watch the big ones come in from Hawaii."

"Look at me."

I didn't want to, but my head came up just the same. He was sitting in the client's chair where Mavis had once sat, and Ardis McGill, and Big Tom Hatfield. Even Vernon Klein had sat there once, when he got those pictures of his daughter wearing nothing but an opium grin and her birthday suit. Sitting there with the same patch of California sun slanting across his features — features

925

I most certainly *had* seen before. The last time had been less than an hour ago, in my bathroom mirror. I'd been scraping a Gillette Blue Blade over them.

The expression of sympathy in his eyes — in *my* eyes — was the most hideous thing I'd ever seen, and when he held out his hand — held out *my* hand — I felt a sudden urge to wheel around in my swivel chair, get to my feet, and go running straight out my seventh-floor office window. I think I might even have done it, if I hadn't been so confused, so totally lost. I've read the word *unmanned* plenty of times — it's a favorite of the pulpsmiths and sob-sisters — but this was the first time I'd ever actually felt that way.

Suddenly the office darkened. The day had been perfectly clear, I would have sworn to that, but a cloud had crossed the sun just the same. The man on the other side of the desk was at least ten years older than I was, maybe fifteen, his hair almost completely white while mine was still almost all black, but that didn't change the simple fact — no matter what he was calling himself or how old he looked, he was me. Had I thought his voice sounded familiar? Sure. The way your own voice sounds familiar — although not quite the way it sounds inside your own head — when you hear it on a recording.

He picked my limp hand up off the desk, shook it with the briskness of a real-estate agent on the make, then dropped it again. It hit the desk-blotter with a plop, landing on Mavis Weld's telephone number. When I raised my fingers, I saw that Mavis's number was gone. In fact, *all* the numbers

I'd scratched on the blotter over the years were gone. It was as clear as . . . well, as clear as a hardshell Baptist's conscience.

"Jesus," I croaked. "Jesus Christ."

"Not at all," the older version of me sitting in the client's chair on the other side of the desk said. "Landry. Samuel D. Landry. At your service."

V. An Interview with God.

Even as rattled as I was, it only took me two or three seconds to place the name, probably because I'd heard it such a short time ago. According to Painter Number Two, Samuel Landry was the reason why the long dark hall leading to my office was soon going to be oyster white. Landry was the owner of the Fulwider Building.

A crazy idea suddenly occurred to me, but its patent craziness did nothing to dim the sudden blaze of hope which accompanied it. They — whoever *they* are — say that everyone on the face of the earth has a double. Maybe Landry was mine. Maybe we were identical twins, unrelated doubles who had somehow been born to different parents and ten or fifteen years out of step in time with each other. The idea did nothing to explain the rest of the day's high weirdness, but it was something to hang onto, damn it.

"What can I do for you, Mr. Landry?" I asked. I was trying like hell, but my voice was no longer quite steady. "If it's about the lease, you'll have to give me a day or two to get squared around. It seems my secretary just discovered she had pressing business back home in Armpit, Idaho."

Landry paid absolutely no attention to this feeble effort on my part to shift the focus of the conversation. "Yes," he said in a musing tone of voice, "I imagine it's been the granddaddy of bad days . . . and it's my fault. I'm sorry, Clyde — really. Meeting you in person has been . . . well, not what I expected. Not at all. For one thing, I like you quite a bit better than I expected to. But there's no going back now." And he fetched a deep sigh. I didn't like the sound of it very much.

"What do you mean by that?" My voice was trembling worse than ever now, and the blaze of hope was dying. Lack of oxygen inside the cave-in site which had once been my brain seemed to be the cause.

He didn't answer right away. He leaned over instead, and grasped the handle of the slim leather case leaning against the front leg of the client's chair. The initials stamped on it were S.D.L., and I deduced that my weird visitor had brought it in with him. I didn't win the Shamus of the Year Award in 1934 and '35 for nothing, you know.

I had never seen a case quite like it in my life — it was too small and too slim to be a briefcase, and it was fastened not with buckles and straps but with a zipper. I'd never seen a zipper quite like this one, either, now that I thought about it. The teeth were extremely tiny, and they hardly looked like metal at all.

But the oddities only *began* with Landry's luggage. Even setting aside his uncanny older-brother

928

resemblance to me, Landry looked like no businessman I'd ever seen in my life, and certainly not one prosperous enough to own the Fulwider Building. It's not the Ritz, granted, but it *is* in downtown L.A., and my client (if that was what he was) looked like an Okie on a good day, one which had included a bath and a shave.

He was wearing blue jeans pants, for one thing, and a pair of sneakers on his feet . . . except they didn't look like any sneakers I'd ever seen before. They were great big clumpy things. What they *really* looked like were the shoes Boris Karloff wears as part of his Frankenstein get-up, and if they were made of canvas, I'd eat my favorite Fedora. The word written up the sides in red script looked like the name of a dish on a Chinese carry-out menu: REEBOK.

I looked down at the blotter which had once been covered with a tangle of telephone numbers, and suddenly realized that I could no longer remember Mavis Weld's, although I must have called it a billion times only this past winter. That feeling of dread intensified.

"Mister," I said, "I wish you'd state your business and get out of here. Come to think of it, why don't you skip the talking and just go right to the getting-out part?"

He smiled . . . tiredly, I thought. That was the other thing. The face above the plain open-collared white shirt looked terribly tired. Terribly sad, as well. It said the man who owned it had been through things I couldn't even dream of. I felt some sympathy for my visitor, but what I mostly felt was fear. And anger. Because it was *my* face, too, and the bastard had apparently gone a long way toward wearing it out.

"Sorry, Clyde," he said. "No can do."

He put his hand on that tiny, cunning zipper, and all at once Landry opening that case was the last thing in the world I wanted. To stop him I said, "Do you always go visiting your tenants dressed like a guy who makes his living following the cabbage crop? What are you, one of those eccentric millionaires?"

"I'm eccentric, all right," he said. "And it won't do you any good to draw this business out, Clyde."

"What gave you that ide—"

Then he said the thing I'd been dreading, and put out the last tiny flicker of hope at the same time. "I know *all* your ideas, Clyde. After all, I'm *you.*"

I licked my lips and forced myself to speak; anything to keep him from yanking that zipper. Anything at all. My voice came out husky, but at least it *did* come out.

"Yeah, I noticed the resemblance. I'm not familiar with the cologne, though. I'm an Old Spice man, myself."

His thumb and finger remained pinched on the zipper, but he didn't pull it. At least not yet.

"But you like this," he said with perfect assurance, "and you'd use it if you could get it down at the Rexall on the corner, wouldn't you? Unfortunately, you can't. It's Aramis, and it won't be invented for another forty years or so." He glanced down at his weird, ugly basketball shoes. "Like my sneakers."

"The devil you say."

"Well, yes, I suppose the devil might come into it somewhere," Landry said, and he didn't smile.

"Where are you from?"

"I thought you knew." Landry pulled the zipper, revealing a rectangular gadget made of some smooth plastic. It was the same color the seventh-floor hall was going to be by the time the sun went down. I'd never seen anything like it. There was no brand name on it, just something that must have been a serial number: T-1000. Landry lifted it out of its carrying case, thumbed the catches on the sides, and lifted the hinged top to reveal something that looked like the telescreen in a Buck Rogers movie. "I come from the future," Landry said. "Just like in a pulp magazine story."

"You come from Sunnyland Sanitarium, more like it," I croaked.

"But not *exactly* like a pulp science-fiction story," he went on, ignoring what I'd said. "No, not exactly." He pushed a button on the side of the plastic case. There was a faint whirring sound from inside the gadget, followed by a brief, whistling beep. The thing sitting on his lap looked like some strange stenographer's machine . . . and I had an idea that that wasn't far from the truth.

He looked up at me and said, "What was your father's name, Clyde?"

I looked at him for a moment, resisting an urge to lick my lips again. The room was still dark, the sun still behind some cloud that hadn't even been in sight when I came in off the street. Landry's face seemed to float in the gloom like an old, shrivelled balloon.

"What's that got to do with the price of cu-

cumbers in Monrovia?" I asked.

"You don't know, do you?"

"Of course I do," I said, and I did. I just couldn't come up with it, that was all — it was stuck there on the tip of my tongue, like Mavis Weld's phone number, which had been BAyshore something-or-other.

"How about your mother's?"

"Quit playing games with me!"

"Here's an easy one — what high school did you go to? Every red-blooded American man remembers what school he went to, right? Or the first girl he ever went all the way with. Or the town he grew up in. Was yours San Luis Obispo?"

I opened my mouth, but this time nothing came out.

"Carmel?"

That sounded right . . . and then felt all wrong. My head was whirling.

"Or maybe it was Dusty Bottom, New Mexico."

"Cut the crap!" I shouted.

"Do you know? *Do* you?"

"Yes! It was —"

He bent over. Rattled the keys of his strange steno machine.

"San Diego! Born and raised!"

He put the machine on my desk and turned it around so I could read the words floating in the window above the keyboard.

"San Diego! Born and raised!"

My eyes dropped from the window to the word stamped into the plastic frame surrounding it.

"What's a Toshiba?" I asked. "Something that comes on the side when you order a Reebok dinner?"

"It's a Japanese electronics company."

I laughed dryly. "Who're you kidding, mister? The Japs can't even make wind-up toys without getting the springs in upside down."

"Not now," he agreed, "and speaking of now, Clyde, when *is* now? What year is it?"

"1938," I said, then raised a half-numb hand to my face and rubbed my lips. "Wait a minute — 1939."

"It might even be 1940. Am I right?"

I said nothing, but I felt my face heating up.

"Don't feel bad, Clyde; you don't know because *I* don't know. I always left it vague. The time-frame I was trying for was actually more of a *feel* . . . call it Chandler American Time, if you like. It worked like gangbusters for most of my readers, and it made things simpler from a copy-editing standpoint as well, because you can never exactly pinpoint the passage of time. Haven't you ever noticed how often you say things like 'for more years than I can remember' or 'longer ago than I like to think about' or 'since Hector was a pup'?"

"Nope — can't say that I have." But now that he mentioned it, I *did* notice. And that made me think of the *L.A. Times*. I read it every day, but exactly which days were they? You couldn't tell from the paper itself, because there was never a date on the masthead, only that slogan which reads "America's Fairest Newspaper in America's Fairest City."

"You say those things because time doesn't really pass in this world. It is . . ." He paused, then smiled. It was a terrible thing to look at, that smile, full of yearning and strange greed. "It is one of its many charms," he finished.

I was scared, but I've always been able to bite the bullet when I felt it really needed biting, and this was one of those times. "Tell me what the hell's going on here."

"All right . . . but you're already beginning to know, Clyde. Aren't you?"

"Maybe. I don't know my dad's name or my mom's name or the name of the first girl I ever went to bed with because *you* don't know them. Is that it?"

He nodded, smiling the way a teacher would smile at a pupil who's made a leap of logic and come up with the right answer against all odds. But his eyes were still full of that terrible sympathy.

"And when you wrote San Diego on your gadget there and it came into my head at the same time . . ."

He nodded, encouraging me.

"It isn't just the Fulwider Building you own, is it?" I swallowed, trying to get rid of a large blockage in my throat that had no intention of going anywhere. "You own everything."

But Landry was shaking his head. "Not *everything*. Just Los Angeles and a few surrounding areas. This version of Los Angeles, that is, complete with the occasional continuity glitch or made-up addition."

"Bull," I said, but I whispered the word.

"See the picture on the wall to the left of the door, Clyde?"

I glanced at it, but hardly had to; it was Washington crossing the Delaware, and it had been there since . . . well, since Hector was a pup.

Landry had taken his plastic Buck Rogers steno machine back onto his lap, and was bending over it.

"Don't do that!" I shouted, and tried to reach for him. I couldn't do it. My arms had no strength, it seemed, and I could summon no resolve. I felt lethargic, drained, as if I had lost about three pints of blood and was losing more all the time.

He rattled the keys again. Turned the machine toward me so I could read the words in the window. They read: *On the wall to the left of the door leading out to Candy-Land, Our Revered Leader hangs . . . but always slightly askew. That's my way of keeping him in perspective.*

I looked back at the picture. George Washington was gone, replaced by a photo of Franklin Roosevelt. F.D.R. had a grin on his face and his cigarette holder jutting upward at that angle his supporters think of as jaunty and his detractors as arrogant. The picture was hanging slightly askew.

"I don't need the laptop to do it," he said. He sounded a little embarrassed, as if I'd accused him of something. "I can do it just by concentrating — as you saw when the numbers disappeared from your blotter — but the laptop helps. Because I'm used to writing things down, I suppose. And then editing them. In a way, editing and rewriting are the most fascinating parts of the job, because that's where the final changes — usually small but often crucial — take place and the picture really comes into focus."

935

I looked back at Landry, and when I spoke, my voice was dead. "You made me up, didn't you?"

He nodded, looking strangely ashamed, as if what he had done was something dirty.

"When?" I uttered a strange, croaky little laugh. "Or is that the right question?"

"I don't know if it is or isn't," he said, "and I imagine any writer would tell you about the same. It didn't happen all at once — that much I'm sure of. It's been an ongoing process. You first showed up in *Scarlet Town,* but I wrote that back in 1977 and you've changed a lot since then."

1977, I thought. A Buck Rogers year for sure. I didn't want to believe this was happening, wanted to believe it was all a dream. Oddly enough, it was the smell of his cologne that kept me from being able to do that — that familiar smell I'd never smelled in my life. How could I have? It was Aramis, a brand as unfamiliar to me as Toshiba.

But he was going on.

"You've grown a lot more complex and interesting. You were pretty one-dimensional to start with." He cleared his throat and smiled down at his hands for a moment.

"What a pisser for me."

He winced a little at the anger in my voice, but made himself look up again, just the same. "Your last book was *How Like a Fallen Angel.* I started that one in 1990, but it took until 1993 to finish. I've had some problems in the interim. My life has been . . . interesting." He gave the word an ugly, bitter twist. "Writers don't do their best work during interesting times, Clyde. Take my word for it."

I glanced at the baggy way his hobo clothes hung on him and decided he might have a point there. "Maybe that's why you screwed up in such a big way on this one," I said. "That stuff about the lottery and the forty thousand dollars was pure guff — they pay off in pesos south of the border."

"I knew that," he said mildly. "I'm not saying I don't goof up from time to time — I may be a kind of God in this world, or *to* this world, but in my own I'm perfectly human — but when I *do* goof up, you and your fellow characters never know it, Clyde, because my mistakes and continuity lapses are part of your truth. No, Peoria was lying. I knew it, and I wanted *you* to know it."

"Why?"

He shrugged, again looking uneasy and a little ashamed. "To prepare you for my coming a little, I suppose. That's what all of it was for, starting with the Demmicks. I didn't want to scare you any more than I had to."

Any private eye worth his salt has a pretty good idea when the person in the client's chair is lying and when he's telling the truth; knowing when the client is telling the truth but purposely leaving gaps is a rarer talent, and I doubt if even the geniuses among us can tap it all the time. Maybe I was only tapping it now because my brainwaves and Landry's were marching in lock-step, but I *was* tapping it. There was stuff he wasn't telling me. The question was whether or not I should call him on it.

What stopped me was a sudden, horrible intuition that came waltzing out of nowhere, like a ghost oozing out of the wall of a haunted house. It had to do with the Demmicks. The reason they'd been so quiet last night was because dead people don't engage in marital spats — it's one of those rules, like the one that says crap rolls downhill, that you can pretty much count on through thick and thin. From almost the first moment I'd met him, I'd sensed there was a violent temper under George's urbane top layer, and that there might be a sharp-clawed bitch lurking in the shadows behind Gloria Demmick's pretty face and daffy demeanor. They were just a little too Cole Porter to be true, if you see what I mean. And now I was somehow sure that George had finally snapped and killed his wife . . . probably their yappy Welsh Corgi, as well. Gloria might be sitting propped up in the bathroom corner between the shower and the toilet right now, her face black, her eyes bulging like old dull marbles, her tongue protruding between her blue lips. The dog was lying with its head in her lap and a wire coathanger twisted around its neck, its shrill bark stilled forever. And George? Dead on the bed with Gloria's bottle of Veronals — now empty — standing beside him on the night-table. No more parties, no more jitterbugging at Al Arif, no more frothy upper-class murder cases in Palm Desert or Beverly Glen. They were cooling off now, drawing flies, growing pale under their fashionable poolside tans.

George and Gloria Demmick, who had died inside this man's machine. Who had died inside this man's *head*.

"You did one lousy job of not scaring me," I said, and immediately wondered if it would have been possible for him to do a good one. Ask yourself this: how do you get a person ready to meet God? I'll bet even Moses got a little hot under the robe when he saw that bush start to glow, and I'm nothing but a shamus who works for forty a day plus expenses.

"*How Like a Fallen Angel* was the Mavis Weld story. The name, Mavis Weld, is from a novel called *The Little Sister*. By Raymond Chandler." He looked at me with a kind of troubled uncertainty that had some small whiff of guilt in it. "It's an *hommage*." He said the first syllable so it rhymed with Rome.

"Bully for you," I said, "but the guy's name rings no bells."

"Of course not. In your world — which is my version of L.A., of course — Chandler never existed. Nevertheless, I've used all sorts of names from his books in mine. The Fulwider Building is where Chandler's detective, Philip Marlowe, had *his* office. Vernon Klein . . . Peoria Smith . . . and Clyde Umney, of course. That was the name of the lawyer in *Playback*."

"And you call those things *hommages?*"

"That's right."

"If you say so, but it sounds like a fancy word for plain old copying to me." But it made me feel funny, knowing that my name had been made up by a man I'd never heard of in a world I'd never dreamed of.

Landry had the good grace to flush, but his eyes didn't drop.

"All right; perhaps I *did* do a little pilfering. Certainly I adopted Chandler's style for my own, but I'm hardly the first; Ross Macdonald did the same thing in the fifties and sixties, Robert Parker did it in the seventies and eighties, and the critics decked them with laurel leaves for it. Besides, Chandler learned from Hammett and Hemingway, not to mention pulp-writers like —"

I held up my hand. "Let's skip the lit class and get down to the bottom line. This is crazy, but —" My eyes drifted to the picture of Roosevelt, from there they went to the eerily blank blotter, and from there they went back to the haggard face on the other side of the desk. "— but let's say I believe it. What are you doing here? What did you come for?"

Except I already knew. I detect for a living, but the answer to that one came from my heart, not my head.

"I came for *you*."

"For me."

"Sorry, yes. I'm afraid you'll have to start thinking of your life in a new way, Clyde. As . . . well . . . a pair of shoes, let's say. You're stepping out and I'm stepping in. And once I've got the laces tied, I'm going to walk away."

Of course. Of course he was. And I suddenly knew what I had to do . . . the only thing I *could* do.

Get rid of him.

I let a big smile spread across my face. A tell-me-more smile. At the same time I coiled my legs under me, getting them ready to launch me across the desk at him. Only one of us could leave this office, that much was clear. I intended to be the one.

"Oh, *really?*" I said. "How fascinating. And what happens to me, Sammy? What happens to the shoeless private eye? What happens to Clyde —"

Umney, the last word was supposed to be my last name, the last word this interloping, invading thief would ever hear in his life. The minute it was out of my mouth I intended to leap. The trouble was, that telepathy business seemed to work both ways. I saw an expression of alarm dawn in his eyes, and then they slipped shut and his mouth tightened with concentration. He didn't bother with the Buck Rogers machine; I suppose he knew there was no time for it.

" 'His revelations hit me like some kind of debilitating drug,' " he said, speaking in the low but carrying tone of one who recites rather than simply speaking. " 'All the strength went out of my muscles, my legs felt like a couple of strands of *al dente* spaghetti, and all I could do was flop back in my chair and look at him.' "

I flopped back in my chair, my legs uncoiling beneath me, unable to do anything but look at him.

"Not very good," he said apologetically, "but rapid composition has never been a strong point of mine."

"You bastard," I rasped weakly. "You son of a bitch."

"Yes," he agreed. "I suppose I am."

"Why are you doing this? Why are you stealing my life?"

His eyes flickered with anger at that. "*Your* life? You know better than that, Clyde, even if you don't want to admit it. It isn't your life at all.

941

I made you up, starting on one rainy day in January of 1977 and continuing right up to the present time. I gave you your life, and it's mine to take away."

"Very noble," I sneered, "but if God came down here right now and started yanking *your* life apart like bad stitches in a scarf, you might find it a little easier to appreciate my point of view."

"All right," he said, "I suppose you've got a point. But why argue it? Arguing with one's self is like playing solitaire chess — a fair game results in a stalemate every time. Let's just say I'm doing it because I can."

I felt a little calmer, all of a sudden. I had been down this street before. When they got the drop on you, you had to get them talking and keep them talking. It had worked with Mavis Weld and it would work here. They said stuff like *Well, I suppose it won't hurt you to know now* or *What harm can it do?*

Mavis's version had been downright elegant: *I want you to know, Umney — I want you to take the truth to hell with you. You can pass it on to the devil over cake and coffee.* It really didn't matter what they said, but if they were talking, they weren't shooting.

Always keep em talking, that was the thing. Keep em talking and just hope the cavalry would show up from somewhere.

"The question is, why do you *want* to?" I asked. "It's hardly the usual thing, is it? I mean, aren't you writer types usually content to cash the checks when they come, and go about your business?"

"You're trying to keep me talking, Clyde. Aren't you?"

That hit me like a sucker-punch to the gut, but playing it down to the last card was the only choice I had. I grinned and shrugged. "Maybe. Maybe not. Either way, I really do want to know." And there was no lie in that.

He looked unsure for a moment longer, bent over and touched the keys inside that strange plastic case (I felt cramps in my legs and gut and chest as he stroked them), then straightened up again.

"I suppose it won't hurt you to know now," he said finally. "After all, what harm can it do?"

"Not a bit."

"You're a clever boy, Clyde," he said, "and you're perfectly right — writers very rarely plunge all the way into the worlds they've created, and when they do I think they end up doing it strictly in their heads, while their bodies vegetate in some mental asylum. Most of us are content simply to be tourists in the country of our imaginations. Certainly that was the case with me. I'm not a fast writer — composition has always been torture for me, I think I told you that — but I managed five Clyde Umney books in ten years, each more successful than the last. In 1983 I left my job as regional manager for a big insurance company and started to write full-time. I had a wife I loved, a little boy that kicked the sun out of bed every morning and put it to bed every night — that's how it seemed to me, anyway — and I didn't think life could get any better."

He shifted in the overstuffed client's chair, moved his hand, and I saw the cigarette burn Ardis

McGill had put in the overstuffed arm was also gone. He voiced a bitterly cold laugh.

"And I was right," he said. "It couldn't get any better, but it *could* get a whole hell of a lot worse. And did. About three months after I started *How Like a Fallen Angel,* Danny — our little boy — fell out of a swing in the park and bashed his head. Cold-conked himself, in your parlance."

A brief smile, every bit as cold and bitter as the laugh had been, crossed his face. It came and went at the speed of grief.

"He bled a lot — you've seen enough head-wounds in your time to know how they are — and it scared the crap out of Linda, but the doctors were good and it *did* turn out to be only a concussion; they got him stabilized and gave him a pint of blood to make up for what he'd lost. Maybe they didn't have to — and that haunts me — but they did. The real problem wasn't with his head, you see; it was with that pint of blood. It was infected with AIDS."

"Come again?"

"It's something you can thank your God you don't know about," Landry said. "It doesn't exist in your time, Clyde. It won't show up until the mid-seventies. Like Aramis cologne."

"What does it do?"

"Eats away at your immune system until the whole thing collapses like the wonderful one-hoss shay. Then every bug circling around out there, from cancer to chicken pox, rushes in and has a party."

"Good Christ!"

His smile came and went like a cramp. "If you

944

say so. AIDS is primarily a sexually transmitted disease, but every now and then it pops up in the blood supply. I suppose you could say my kid won big in a very unlucky version of *la lotería*."

"I'm sorry," I said, and although I was scared to death of this thin man with the tired face, I meant it. Losing a kid to something like that . . . what could be worse? Probably something, yeah — there's always something — but you'd have to sit down and think about it, wouldn't you?

"Thanks," he said. "Thanks, Clyde. It went fast for him, at least. He fell out of the swing in May. The first purple blotches — Kaposi's sarcoma — showed up in time for his birthday in September. He died on March 18, 1991. And maybe he didn't suffer as much as some of them do, but he suffered. Oh yes, he suffered."

I didn't have the slightest idea what Kaposi's sarcoma was, either, and decided I didn't want to ask. I knew more than I wanted to already.

"You can maybe understand why it slowed me down a little on your book," he said. "Can't you, Clyde?"

I nodded.

"I pushed on, though. Mostly because I think make-believe is a great healer. Maybe I *have* to believe that. I tried to get on with my life, too, but things kept going wrong with it — it was as if *How Like a Fallen Angel* was some kind of weird bad-luck charm that had turned me into Job. My wife went into a deep depression following Danny's death, and I was so concerned with her that I hardly noticed the red patches that had started breaking out on my legs and stomach and

945

chest. And the itching. I knew it wasn't AIDS, and at first that was all I was concerned with. But as time went on and things got worse . . . have you ever had shingles, Clyde?"

Then he laughed and clapped the heel of his hand to his forehead in a what-a-dunce-I-am gesture before I could shake my head.

"Of course you haven't — you've never had more than a hangover. Shingles, my shamus friend, is a funny name for a terrible, chronic ailment. There's some pretty good medicine available to help alleviate the symptoms in my version of Los Angeles, but it wasn't helping me much; by the end of 1991 I was in agony. Part of it was general depression over what had happened to Danny, of course, but most of it was the agony and the itching. That would make an interesting book title about a tortured writer, don't you think? *The Agony and the Itching, or, Thomas Hardy Faces Puberty.*" He voiced a harsh, distracted little laugh.

"Whatever you say, Sam."

"I say it was a season in hell. Of course it's easy to make light of it now, but by Thanksgiving of that year it was no joke — I was getting three hours of sleep a night, tops, and I had days when it felt like my skin was trying to crawl right off my body and run away like The Gingerbread Man. And I suppose that's why I didn't see how bad it was getting with Linda."

I didn't know, *couldn't* know . . . but I did. "She killed herself."

He nodded. "In March of 1992, on the anniversary of Daniel's death. Over two years ago now."

A single tear tracked down his wrinkled, prematurely aged cheek, and I had an idea that he had gotten old in one hell of a hurry. It was sort of awful, realizing I had been made by such a bush-league version of God, but it also explained a lot. My shortcomings, mainly.

"That's enough," he said in a voice which was blurred with anger as well as tears. "Get to the point, you'd say. In my time we say cut to the chase, but it comes to the same. I finished the book. On the day I discovered Linda dead in bed — the way the police are going to find Gloria Demmick later today, Clyde — I had finished one hundred and ninety pages of manuscript. I was up to the part where you fish Mavis's brother out of Lake Tahoe. I came home from the funeral three days later, fired up the word-processor, and got started right in on page one-ninety-one. Does that shock you?"

"No," I said. I thought about asking him what a word-processor might be, then decided I didn't have to. The thing in his lap was a word-processor, of course. Had to be.

"You're in a decided minority," Landry said. "It shocked what few friends I had left, shocked them plenty. Linda's relatives thought I had all the emotion of a warthog. I didn't have the energy to explain that I was trying to save myself. Frog them, as Peoria would say. I grabbed my book the way a drowning man would grab a life-ring. I grabbed *you*, Clyde. My case of the shingles was still bad, and that slowed me down — to some extent it kept me *out*, or I might have gotten here sooner — but it didn't stop me. I started getting a little better — physically, at least — right around the time I finished the book. But when I *had* finished, I fell into what I suppose must have been my own state of depression. I went through the edited script in a kind of daze. I felt such a feeling of regret . . . of *loss* . . ." He looked directly at me and said, "Does any of this make any sense to you?"

"It makes sense," I said. And it did. In a crazy sort of way.

"There were lots of pills left in the house," he said. "Linda and I were like the Demmicks in a lot of ways, Clyde — we really did believe in living better chemically, and a couple of times I came very close to taking a couple of double handfuls. The way the thought always came to me wasn't in terms of suicide, but in terms of wanting to catch up to Linda and Danny. To catch up while there was still time."

I nodded. It was what I'd thought about Ardis McGill when, three days after we'd said toodle-oo to each other in Blondie's, I'd found her in that stuffy attic room with a small blue hole in the center of her forehead. Except it had been Sam Landry who had really killed her, and who had accomplished the deed with a kind of flexible bullet to the brain. Of course it had been. In my world Sam Landry, this tired-looking man in the hobo's pants, was responsible for *everything*. The idea should have seemed crazy, and it did . . . but it was getting saner all the time.

I found I had just energy enough to swivel my chair and look out my window. What I saw some-how did not surprise me in the least: Sunset Boulevard and all that surrounded it had frozen solid. Cars, buses, pedestrians, all stopped dead in their tracks. It was a Kodak snapshot world out there, and why not? Its creator could not be bothered with animating much of it, at least for the time being; he was still caught in the whirlpool of his own pain and grief. Hell, I was lucky to still be breathing myself.

"So what happened?" I asked. "How did you get here, Sam? Can I call you that? Do you mind?"

"No, I don't mind. I can't give you a very good answer, though, because I don't exactly know. All I know for sure is that every time I thought of the pills, I thought of you. What I thought specifically was, 'Clyde Umney would never do this, and he'd sneer at anyone who did. He'd call it the coward's way out.' "

I considered that, found it fair enough, and nodded. For someone staring some horrible ailment in the face — Vernon's cancer, or the misbegotten nightmare that had killed this man's son — I might make an exception, but take the pipe just because you were depressed? That was for pansies.

"Then I thought, 'But that's Clyde Umney, and Clyde is make-believe . . . just a figment of your imagination.' That idea wouldn't live, though. It's the dumbbells of the world — politicians and lawyers, for the most part — who sneer at imagination, and think a thing isn't real unless they can smoke it or stroke it or feel it or fuck it. They think that way because they have no imagination themselves, and they have no idea of its power. I knew better. Hell, I ought to — my imagination has been buying my food and paying the mortgage for the last ten years or so.

"At the same time, I knew I couldn't go on living in what I used to think of as 'the real world,' by which I suppose we all mean 'the only world.' That's when I started to realize there was only one place left where I could go and feel welcome, and only one person I could be when I got there. The place was here — Los Angeles, in 1930-something. And the person was you."

I heard that faint whirring sound coming from inside his gadget again, but I didn't turn around.

Partly because I was afraid to.

And partly because I no longer knew if I could.

VI. Umney's Last Case.

On the street seven stories below, a man was frozen with his head half-turned to look at the woman on the corner, who was climbing up the step of the eight-fifty bus headed downtown. She had exposed a momentary length of beautiful leg, and this was what the man was looking at. A little farther down the street a boy was holding out his battered old baseball glove to catch the ball frozen in mid-air just above his head. And, floating six feet above the street like a ghost called up by a third-rate swami at a carnival séance, was one of the newspapers from Peoria Smith's overturned table. Incredibly, I could see the two photographs on it from up here: Hitler above the fold, the recently deceased Cuban bandleader below it.

Landry's voice seemed to come from a long way off.

"At first I thought that meant I'd be spending the rest of my life in some nut-ward, thinking I was you, but that was all right, because it would only be my *physical* self locked up in the funny-farm, do you see? And then, gradually, I began to realize that it could be a lot more than that . . . that maybe there might be a way I could actually . . . well . . . slip all the way in. And do you know what the key was?"

"Yes," I said, not looking around. That whir came again as something in his gadget revolved, and suddenly the newspaper frozen in mid-air flapped off down the frozen Boulevard. A moment or two later an old DeSoto rolled jerkily through the intersection of Sunset and Fernando. It struck the boy wearing the baseball glove, and both he and the DeSoto sedan disappeared. Not the ball, though. It fell into the street, rolled halfway to the gutter, then froze solid again.

"You do?" He sounded surprised.

"Yeah. Peoria was the key."

"That's right." He laughed, then cleared his throat — nervous sounds, both of them. "I keep forgetting that you're me."

It was a luxury I didn't have.

"I was fooling around with a new book, and not getting anywhere. I'd tried Chapter One six different ways to Sunday before realizing a really interesting thing: Peoria Smith didn't like you."

That made me swing around in a hurry. "The hell you say!"

"I didn't think you'd believe it, but it's the truth,

951

and I'd somehow known it all along. I don't want to convene the lit class again, Clyde, but I'll tell you one thing about my trade — writing stories in the first person is a funny, tricky business. It's as if everything the writer knows comes from his main character, like a series of letters or dispatches from some far-off battle zone. It's very rare for the writer to have a secret, but in this case I did. It was as if your little part of Sunset Boulevard were the Garden of Eden —"

"I never heard it called *that* before," I remarked.

"— and there was a snake in it, one I saw and you didn't. A snake named Peoria Smith."

Outside, the frozen world that he'd called my Garden of Eden continued to darken, although the sky was cloudless. The Red Door, a nightclub reputedly owned by Lucky Luciano, disappeared. For a moment there was just a hole where it had been, and then a new building filled it — a restaurant called Petit Déjeuner with a window full of ferns. I glanced up the street and saw that other changes were going on — new buildings were replacing old ones with silent, spooky speed. They meant I was running out of time; I knew this. Unfortunately, I knew something else, as well — there was probably not going to be any nick in this bundle of time. When God walks into your office and tells you He's decided he likes your life better than His own, what the hell are your options?

"I junked all the various drafts of the novel I'd started two months after my wife's death," Landry said. "It was easy — poor crippled things that they were. And then I started a new one. I called

952

it . . . can you guess, Clyde?"

"Sure," I said, and swung around. It took all my strength, but what I suppose this geek would call my "motivation" was good. Sunset Strip isn't exactly the Champs Elysées or Hyde Park, but it's my world. I didn't want to watch him tear it apart and rebuild it the way *he* wanted it. "I suppose you called it *Umney's Last Case.*"

He looked faintly surprised. "You suppose right."

I waved my hand. It was an effort, but I managed. "I didn't win the Shamus of the Year Award in 1934 and '35 for nothing, you know."

He smiled at that. "Yes. I always *did* like that line."

Suddenly I hated him — hated him like poison. If I could have summoned the strength to lunge across the desk and choke the life out of him, I would have done it. He saw it, too. The smile faded.

"Forget it, Clyde — you wouldn't have a chance."

"Why don't you get out of here?" I grated at him. "Just get out and let a working stiff alone?"

"Because I can't. I couldn't even if I wanted to . . . and I don't." He looked at me with an odd mixture of anger and pleading. "Try to look at it from my point of view, Clyde —"

"Do I have any choice? Have I ever?"

He ignored that. "Here's a world where I'll never get any older, a year where all the clocks are stopped at just about eighteen months before World War II, where the newspapers always cost three cents, where I can eat all the eggs and red meat I want and never have to worry about my cholesterol level."

"I don't have the slightest idea what you're talking about."

He leaned forward earnestly. "No, you don't! And that's exactly the point, Clyde! This is a world where I can *really* do the job I dreamed about doing when I was a little boy — I can be a private eye. I can go racketing around in a fast car at two in the morning, shoot it out with hoodlums — knowing they may die but I won't — and wake up eight hours later next to a beautiful *chanteuse* with the birds twittering in the trees and the sun shining in my bedroom window. That clear, beautiful California sun."

"My bedroom window faces west," I said.

"Not anymore," he replied calmly, and I felt my hands curl into strengthless fists on the arms of my chair. "Do you see how wonderful it is? How perfect? In this world, people don't go half-mad with itching caused by a stupid, undignified disease called shingles. In this world, people don't go gray, let alone bald."

He looked at me levelly, and in his gaze I saw no hope for me. No hope at all.

"In this world, beloved sons never die of AIDS and beloved wives never take overdoses of sleeping pills. Besides, you were *always* the outsider here, not me, no matter how it might have felt to you. This is *my* world, born in my imagination and maintained by my effort and ambition. I loaned it to you for awhile, that's all . . . and now I'm taking it back."

"Finish telling me how you got in, will you do

that much? I really want to hear."

"It was easy. I tore it apart, starting with the Demmicks, who were never much more than a lousy imitation of Nick and Nora Charles, and rebuilt it in my own image. I took away all the beloved supporting characters, and now I'm removing all the old landmarks. I'm pulling the rug out from under you a strand at a time, in other words, and I'm not proud of it, but I *am* proud of the sustained effort of will it's taken to pull it off."

"What's happened to you back in your own world?" I was still keeping him talking, but now it was nothing but habit, like an old milk-horse finding his way back to the barn on a snowy morning.

He shrugged. "Dead, maybe. Or maybe I really have left a physical self — a husk — sitting catatonic in some mental institution. I don't think either of those things is really the case, though — all of this feels too real. No, I think I made it all the way, Clyde. I think that back home they're looking for a missing writer . . . with no idea that he's disappeared into the storage banks of his own word-processor. And the truth is I really don't care."

"And me? What happens to me?"

"Clyde," he said, "I don't care about that, either."

He bent over his gadget again.

"Don't!" I said sharply.

He looked up.

"I . . ." I heard the quiver in my voice, tried to control it, and found I couldn't. "Mister, I'm afraid. Please leave me alone. I know it's not really my world out there anymore — hell, in here, either — but it's the only world I'll ever come close to knowing. Let me have what's left of it. Please."

"Too late, Clyde." Again I heard that merciless regret in his voice. "Close your eyes. I'll make it as fast as I can."

I tried to jump him — I tried as hard as I could. I didn't move so much as an iota. And as far as closing my eyes went, I discovered I didn't need to. All the light had gone out of the day, and the office was as dark as midnight in a coalsack.

I sensed rather than saw him lean over the desk toward me. I tried to draw back and discovered I couldn't even do that. Something dry and rustly touched my hand and I screamed.

"Take it easy, Clyde." His voice, coming out of the darkness. Coming not just from in front of me but from everywhere. *Of course,* I thought. *After all, I'm a figment of his imagination.* "It's only a check."

"A . . . check?"

"Yes. For five thousand dollars. You've sold me the business. The painters will scratch your name off the door and paint mine on before they leave tonight." He sounded dreamy. "Samuel D. Landry, Private Detective. It's got a great ring, doesn't it?"

I tried to beg and found I couldn't. Now even my voice had failed me.

"Get ready," he said. "I don't know exactly what's coming, Clyde, but it's coming now. I don't think it'll hurt." *But I don't really care if it does* — that was the part he didn't say.

That faint whirring sound came out of the blackness. I felt my chair melt away beneath me, and suddenly I was falling. Landry's voice fell with me, reciting along with the clicks and taps of his fabulous futuristic steno machine, reciting the last two sentences of a novel called *Umney's Last Case*.

" 'So I left town, and as to where I finished up . . . well, mister, I think that's my business. Don't you?' "

There was a brilliant green light below me. I was falling toward it. Soon it would consume me, and the only feeling I had was one of relief.

" 'THE END,' " Landry's voice boomed, and then I fell into the green light, it was shining through me, *in* me, and Clyde Umney was no more.

So long, shamus.

VII. The Other Side of the Light.

All that was six months ago.

I came to on the floor of a gloomy room with a humming in my ears, pushed myself to my knees, shook my head to clear it, and looked up into the bright green glare I'd fallen through, like Alice through the looking glass. I saw a Buck Rogers machine that was the big brother of the one Landry had brought into my office. Green letters shone on it and I pushed myself to my feet so I could read them, absently running my fingernails up and down over my lower arms as I did so:

*So I left town, and as to where I finished up
. . . well, mister, I think that's my business. Don't
you?*

And below that, capitalized and centered, two
more words:

THE END.

I read it again, now running my fingers over
my stomach. I was doing it because there was
something wrong with my skin, something that
wasn't exactly painful but *was* certainly bother-
some. As soon as it rose to the fore in my mind,
I realized that weird sensation was going on everywhere — the nape of my neck, the backs of
my thighs, in my crotch.

Shingles, I thought suddenly. *I've got Landry's
shingles. What I'm feeling is itching, and the reason
I didn't recognize it right away is because —*

"Because I've never *had* an itch before," I said,
and then the rest of it clicked into place. The click
was so sudden and so hard that I actually swayed
on my feet. I walked slowly across to a mirror
on the wall, trying not to scratch my weirdly crawling skin, knowing I was going to see an aged version of my face, a face cut with lines like old dry
washes and topped with a shock of lackluster white
hair.

Now I knew what happened when writers somehow took over the lives of the characters they had
created. It wasn't exactly theft after all.

More of a swap.

I stood staring into Landry's face — *my* face,
only aged fifteen hard years — and felt my skin

tingling and buzzing. Hadn't he said his shingles had been getting better? If this was better, how had he endured worse without going completely insane?

I was in Landry's house, of course — my house, now — and in the bathroom off the study, I found the medication he took for his shingles. I took my first dose less than an hour after I came to on the floor below his desk and the humming machine on it, and it was as if I had swallowed his life instead of medicine.

As if I'd swallowed his whole life.

These days the shingles are a thing of the past, I'm happy to report. Maybe it just ran its course, but I like to think that the old Clyde Umney spirit had something to do with it — Clyde was never sick a day in his life, you know, and although I seem to always have the sniffles in this run-down Sam Landry body, I'll be damned if I'll give in to them . . . and since when did it hurt to turn on a little of that positive thinking? I think the correct answer to that one is "since never."

There have been some pretty bad days, though, the first one coming less than twenty-four hours after I showed up in the unbelievable year of 1994. I was looking through Landry's fridge for something to eat (I'd pigged out on his Black Horse Ale the night before and felt it couldn't hurt my hangover to eat something) when a sudden pain knifed into my guts. I thought I was dying. It got worse, and I *knew* I was dying. I fell to the kitchen floor, trying not to scream. A moment or two later, something happened, and the pain eased.

Most of my life I've been using the phrase "I

don't give a shit." All that has changed, starting that morning. I cleaned myself up, then climbed the stairs, knowing what I'd find in the bedroom: wet sheets in Landry's bed.

My first week in Landry's world was spent mostly in toilet-training myself. In my world, of course, nobody ever went to the bathroom. Or to the dentist, for that matter, and my first trip to the one listed in Landry's Rolodex is something I don't even want to think about, let alone discuss.

But there's been an occasional rose in this nest of brambles. For one thing, there's been no need to go job-hunting in Landry's confusing, jet-propelled world; his books apparently continue to sell very well, and I have no problem cashing the checks that come in the mail. My signature and his are, of course, identical. As for any moral compunctions I might have about doing that, don't make me laugh. Those checks are for stories about *me*. Landry only wrote them; I lived them. Hell, I deserved fifty thou and a rabies shot just for getting within scratching distance of Mavis Weld's claws.

I expected to have problems with Landry's so-called friends, but I suppose a heavy-duty shamus like me should have known better — would a guy with any real friends want to disappear into a world he'd created on the soundstage of his own imagination? Not likely. Landry's friends were his son and his wife, and they were dead. There are acquaintances and neighbors, but they seem to accept me as him. The woman across the street throws me puzzled glances from time to time, and her little girl cries when I come near even though I used to baby-sit for them every now and then (the woman *says* I did, anyway, and why would she lie?), but that's no big deal.

I have even spoken to Landry's agent, a guy from New York named Verrill. He wants to know when I'm going to start a new book.

Soon, I tell him. Soon.

Mostly I stay in. I have no urge to explore the world Landry pushed me into when he pushed me out of my own; I see more than I want to on my once-weekly trip to the bank and the grocery store, and I threw a bookend through his awful television machine less than two hours after I figured out how to use it. It doesn't surprise me that Landry wanted to leave this groaning world with its freight of disease and senseless violence — a world where naked women dance in nightclub windows, and sex with them can kill you.

No, I spend my time inside, mostly. I have re-read each of his novels, and each one is like leafing through the pages of a well-loved scrapbook. And I've taught myself to use his word-processing machine, of course. It's not like the television machine; the screen is similar, but on the word-processor, you can make whatever pictures *you* want to see, because they all come from inside your own head.

I like that.

I've been getting ready, you see — trying sentences and discarding them the way you try pieces in a jigsaw puzzle. And this morning I wrote a few that seem right . . . or *almost* right. Want to hear? Okay, here goes:

*When I looked toward the door, I saw a very chas-
tened, very downcast Peoria Smith standing there.
"I guess I treated you pretty bad the last time I saw
you, Mr. Umney," he said. "I came to say I'm sorry."
It had been over six months, but he looked the same
as ever. And I do mean the same.*

"You're still wearing your cheaters," I said.

*"Yeah. We tried the operation, but it didn't work."
He sighed, then grinned and shrugged. In that moment he looked like the Peoria I'd always known.
"What the hey, Mr. Umney — bein blind ain't so
bad."*

It isn't perfect; sure, I know that. I started out
as a detective, not a writer. But I believe you can
do just about anything, if you want to bad enough,
and when you get right down to where the cheese
binds, this is a kind of keyhole-peeping, too. The
size and shape of the word-processor keyhole are
a little different, but it's still looking into other
people's lives and then reporting back to the client
on what you saw.

I'm teaching myself for one very simple reason:
I don't want to be here. You can call it L.A. in
1994 if you want to; I call it hell. It's awful frozen
dinners you cook in a box called a "microwave,"
it's sneakers that look like Frankenstein shoes, it's
music that comes out of the radio sounding like
crows being steamed alive in a pressure-cooker,
it's —

Well, it's *everything.*

I want my life back, I want things the way they
were, and I think I know how to make that happen.

You're one sad, thieving bastard, Sam — may
I still call you that? — and I feel sorry for you

. . . but sorry only stretches so far, because the operant word here is *thieving*. My original opinion on the subject hasn't changed at all, you see — I still don't believe that the ability to create conveys the right to steal.

What are you doing right this minute, you thief? Eating dinner at that Petit Déjeuner restaurant you made up? Sleeping beside some gorgeous honey with perfect no-sag breasts and murder up the sleeve of her negligee? Driving down to Malibu with carefree abandon? Or just kicking back in the old office chair, enjoying your painless, odorless, shitless life? What are you doing?

I've been teaching myself to write, that's what *I've* been doing, and now that I've found my way in, I think I'll get better in a hurry. Already I can almost see you.

Tomorrow morning, Clyde and Peoria are going to go down to Blondie's, which has re-opened for business. This time Peoria's going to take Clyde up on that breakfast offer. That will be step two.

Yes, I can almost see you, Sam, and pretty soon I will. But I don't think you'll see me. Not until I step out from behind my office door and wrap my hands around your throat.

This time nobody goes home.

Head Down

AUTHOR'S NOTE: I am breaking in here, Constant Reader, to make you aware that this is *not* a story but an essay — almost a diary. It originally appeared in *The New Yorker* in the spring of 1990.

S.K.

Head down! Keep your head *down!*"

It is far from the most difficult feat in sports, but anyone who has ever tried to do it will tell you that it's tough enough: using a round bat to hit a round ball squarely on the button. Tough enough so that the handful of men who do it well become rich, famous, and idolized: the Jose Cansecos, the Mike Greenwells, the Kevin Mitchells. For thousands of boys (and not a few girls), their faces, not the face of Axl Rose or Bobby Brown, are the ones that matter; their posters hold the positions of honor on bedroom walls and locker doors. Today Ron St. Pierre is teaching some of these boys — boys who will represent Bangor West Side in District 3 Little League tournament play — how to put the round bat on the round ball. Right now he's working with a kid named Fred Moore while my son, Owen, stands nearby, watching closely. He's due in St. Pierre's hot seat next.

964

Owen is broad-shouldered and heavily built, like his old man; Fred looks almost painfully slim in his bright green jersey. And he is not making good contact.

"Head down, Fred!" St. Pierre shouts. He is half-way between the mound and home plate at one of the two Little League fields behind the Coke plant in Bangor; Fred is almost all the way to the backstop. The day is a hot one, but if the heat bothers either Fred or St. Pierre it does not show. They are intent on what they are doing.

"Keep it *down!*" St. Pierre shouts again, and unloads a fat pitch.

Fred chips under it. There is that chinky aluminum-on-cowhide sound — the sound of someone hitting a tin cup with a spoon. The ball hits the backstop, rebounds, almost bonks him on the helmet. Both of them laugh, and then St. Pierre gets another ball from the red plastic bucket beside him.

"Get ready, Freddy!" he yells. "Head down!"

Maine's District 3 is so large that it is split in two. The Penobscot County teams make up half the division; the teams from Aroostook and Washington counties make up the other half. All-Star kids are selected by merit and drawn from all existing district Little League teams. The dozen teams in District 3 play in simultaneous tournaments. Near the end of July, the two teams left will play off, best two out of three, to decide the district champ. That team represents District 3 in State Championship play, and it has been a long time — eighteen years — since a Bangor team

965

made it into the state tourney.

This year, the State Championship games will be played in Old Town, where they make the canoes. Four of the five teams that play there will go back home. The fifth will go on to represent Maine in the Eastern Regional Tournament, this year to be held in Bristol, Connecticut. Beyond *that,* of course, is Williamsport, Pennsylvania, where the Little League World Series happens. The Bangor West players rarely seem to think of such dizzy heights; they will be happy just to beat Millinocket, their first-round opponent in the Penobscot County race. Coaches, however, are allowed to dream — are, in fact, almost *obligated* to dream.

This time Fred, who is the team joker, *does* get his head down. He hits a weak grounder on the wrong side of the first-base line, foul by about six feet.

"Look," St. Pierre says, taking another ball. He holds it up. It is scuffed, dirty, and grass-stained. It is nevertheless a baseball, and Fred eyes it respectfully. "I'm going to show you a trick. Where's the ball?"

"In your hand," Fred says.

Saint, as Dave Mansfield, the team's head coach, calls him, drops it into his glove. "Now?"

"In your glove."

Saint turns sideways; his pitching hand creeps into his glove. "Now?"

"In your hand. I think."

"You're right. So watch my hand. Watch my hand, Fred Moore, and wait for the ball to come out in it. You're looking for the ball. Nothing else.

966

Just the ball. I should just be a blur to you. Why would you want to see me, anyway? Do you care if I'm smiling? No. You're waiting to see how I'll come — sidearm or three-quarters or over the top. Are you waiting?"

Fred nods.

"Are you watching?"

Fred nods again.

"O.K.," St. Pierre says, and goes into his short-arm batting-practice motion again.

This time Fred drives the ball with real authority: a hard sinking liner to right field.

"All *right!*" Saint cries. "That's *all right,* Fred Moore!" He wipes sweat off his forehead. "Next batter!"

Dave Mansfield, a heavy, bearded man who comes to the park wearing aviator sunglasses and an open-neck College World Series shirt (it's a good-luck charm), brings a paper sack to the Bangor West-Millinocket game. It contains sixteen pennants, in various colors. BANGOR, each one says, the word flanked by a lobster on one side and a pine tree on the other. As each Bangor West player is announced on loudspeakers that have been wired to the chain-link backstop, he takes a pennant from the bag Dave holds out, runs across the infield, and hands it to his opposite number.

Dave is a loud, restless man who happens to love baseball and the kids who play it at this level. He believes there are two purposes to All-Star Little League: to have fun and to win. Both are important, he says, but the most important thing is to keep them in the right order. The pennants are not a sly gambit to unnerve the opposition but just for fun. Dave knows that the boys on both teams will remember this game, and he wants each of the Millinocket kids to have a souvenir. It's as simple as that.

The Millinocket players seem surprised by the gesture, and they don't know exactly what to do with the pennants as someone's tape player begins to warble out the Anita Bryant version of "The Star-Spangled Banner." The Millinocket catcher, almost buried beneath his gear, solves the problem in unique fashion: he holds his Bangor pennant over his heart.

With the amenities taken care of, Bangor West administers a brisk and thorough trouncing; the final score is Bangor West 18, Millinocket 7. The loss does not devalue the souvenirs, however; when Millinocket departs on the team bus, the visitors' dugout is empty save for a few Dixie cups and Popsicle sticks. The pennants — every single one of them — are gone.

"Cut *two!*" Neil Waterman, Bangor West's field coach, shouts. "Cut *two,* cut *two!*"

It's the day after the Millinocket game. Everyone on the team is still showing up for practice, but it's early yet. Attrition will set in. That is a given: parents are not always willing to give up summer plans so their kids can play Little League after the regular, May–June season is over, and sometimes the kids themselves tire of the constant grind of practice. Some would rather be riding their bikes, trying to hang ten on their skateboards, or just hanging around the community pool and checking out the girls.

"Cut *two!*" Waterman yells. He is a small, compact man in khaki shorts and a Joe Coach crewcut. In real life he is a teacher and a college basketball coach, but this summer he is trying to teach these boys that baseball has more in common with chess than many would ever have believed. Know your play, he tells them over and over again. Know who it is you're backing up. Most important of all, know who your cut man is in every situation, and be able to hit him. He works patiently at showing them the truth that hides at the center of the game: that it is played more in the mind than with the body.

Ryan Iarrobino, Bangor West's center fielder, fires a bullet to Casey Kinney at second base. Casey tags an invisible runner, pivots, and throws another bullet to home, where J. J. Fiddler takes the throw and tosses the ball back to Waterman.

"Double-play ball!" Waterman shouts, and hits one to Matt Kinney (not related to Casey). Matt is playing shortstop at practice today. The ball takes a funny hop and appears to be on its way to left center. Matt knocks it down, picks it up, and feeds to Casey at second; Casey pivots and throws to Mike Arnold, who is on first. Mike feeds it home to J.J.

"All right!" Waterman shouts. "Good job, Matt Kinney! *Good job!* One-two-one! You're covering, Mike Pelkey!" The two names. Always the two names, to avoid confusion. The team is lousy with Matts, Mikes, and guys named Kinney.

The throws are executed flawlessly. Mike Pelkey, Bangor West's number two pitcher, is right where he's supposed to be, covering first. It's a move he doesn't always remember to make, but this time he does. He grins and trots back to the mound as Neil Waterman gets ready to hit the next combination.

"This is the best Little League All-Star team I've seen in years," Dave Mansfield says some days after Bangor West's trouncing of Millinocket. He dumps a load of sunflower seeds into his mouth and begins to chew them. He spits hulls casually as he talks. "I don't think they can be beaten — at least not in this division."

He pauses and watches as Mike Arnold breaks toward the plate from first, grabs a practice bunt, and whirls toward the bag. He cocks his arm back — then holds the ball. Mike Pelkey is still on the mound; this time he has forgotten that it is his job to cover, and the bag is undefended. He flashes Dave a quick guilty glance. Then he breaks into a sunny grin and gets ready to do it again. Next time he'll do it right, but will he remember to do it right during a game?

"Of course, we can beat ourselves," Dave says. "That's how it usually happens." And, raising his voice, he bellows, *Where were you, Mike Pelkey? You're s'posed to be covering first!*"

Mike nods and trots over — better late than never.

"Brewer," Dave says, and shakes his head. "Brewer at their field. That'll be tough. Brewer's *always* tough."

Bangor West does not trounce Brewer, but they

win their first "road game" without any real strain. Matt Kinney, the team's number one pitcher, is in good form. He is far from overpowering, but his fastball has a sneaky, snaky little hop, and he also has a modest but effective breaking pitch. Ron St. Pierre is fond of saying that every Little League pitcher in America thinks he's got a killer curveball. "What they think is a curve is usually this big lollipop change," he says. "A batter with a little self-discipline can kill the poor thing."

Matt Kinney's curveball actually curves, however, and tonight he goes the distance and strikes out eight. Probably more important, he walks only four. Walks are the bane of a Little League coach's existence. "They kill you," Neil Waterman says. "The walks kill you every time. Absolutely no exceptions. Sixty per cent of batters walked score in Little League games." Not in this game: two of the batters Kinney walks are forced at second; the other two are stranded. Only one Brewer batter gets a hit: Denise Hewes, the center fielder, singles with one out in the fifth, but she is forced at second.

After the game is safely in the bag, Matt Kinney, a solemn and almost eerily self-possessed boy, flashes Dave a rare smile, revealing a set of neat braces. "She could *hit!*" he says, almost reverently.

"Wait until you see Hampden," Dave says dryly. "They *all* hit."

When the Hampden squad shows up at Bangor West's field, behind the Coke plant, on July 17th, they quickly prove Dave right. Mike Pelkey has pretty good stuff and better control than he had against Millinocket, but he isn't much of a mystery to the Hampden boys. Mike Tardif, a compact kid with an amazingly fast bat, rips Pelkey's third pitch over the left-field fence, two hundred feet away, for a home run in the first inning. Hampden adds two more runs in the second, and leads Bangor West 3–0.

In the third, however, Bangor West breaks loose. Hampden's pitching is good, Hampden's hitting is awesome, but Hampden's fielding, particularly infielding, leaves something to be desired. Bangor West puts three hits together with five errors and two walks to score seven runs. This is how Little League is most often played, and seven runs should be enough, but they aren't; the opposition chips stubbornly away, getting two in its half of the third and two more in the fifth. When Hampden comes up in the bottom of the sixth, it is trailing by only three, 10–7.

Kyle King, a twelve-year-old who started for Hampden this evening and then went to catcher in the fifth, leads off the bottom of the sixth with a double. Then Mike Pelkey strikes out Mike Tardif. Mike Wentworth, the new Hampden pitcher, singles to deep short. King and Wentworth advance on a passed ball, but are forced to hold when Jeff Carson grounds back to the pitcher. This brings up Josh Jamieson, one of five Hampden home-run threats, with two on and two out. He represents the tying run. Mike, although clearly tired, finds a little extra and strikes him out on a one-two pitch. The game is over.

The kids line up and give each other the custom-ordained high fives, but it's clear that Mike isn't the only kid who is simply exhausted after the match; with their slumped shoulders and lowered heads, they all look like losers. Bangor West is now 3–0 in divisional play, but the win is a fluke, the kind of game that makes Little League such a nerve-racking experience for spectators, coaches, and the players themselves. Usually sure-handed in the field, Bangor West has tonight committed something like nine errors.

"I didn't sleep all night," Dave mutters at practice the next day. "Damn, we were outplayed. We should have lost that game."

Two nights later, he has something else to feel gloomy about. He and Ron St. Pierre make the six-mile trip to Hampden to watch Kyle King and his mates play Brewer. This is no scouting expedition; Bangor has played both clubs, and both men have copious notes. What they are really hoping to see, Dave admits, is Brewer getting lucky and putting Hampden out of the way. It doesn't happen; what they see isn't a baseball game but gunnery practice.

Josh Jamieson, who struck out in the clutch against Mike Pelkey, clouts a home run over everything and into the Hampden practice field. Nor is Jamieson alone. Carson hits one, Wentworth hits one, and Tardif hits a pair. The final score is Hampden 21, Brewer 9.

On the ride back to Bangor, Dave Mansfield chews a lot of sunflower seeds and says little. He rouses himself only once, as he wheels his old green Chevy into the rutted dirt parking lot beside the Coke plant. "We got lucky Tuesday night, and they know it," he says. "When we go down there

Thursday, they'll be waiting for us."

The diamonds on which the teams of District 3 play out their six-inning dramas all have the same dimensions, give or take a foot here or an outfield gate there. The coaches all carry the rule book in their back pockets, and they put it to frequent use. Dave likes to say that it never hurts to make sure. The infield is sixty feet on each side, a square standing on the point that is home plate. The backstop, according to the rule book, must be at least twenty feet from home plate, giving both the catcher and a runner at third a fair chance on a passed ball. The fences are supposed to be 200 feet from the plate. At Bangor West's field, it's actually about 210 to dead center. And at Hampden, home of power hitters like Tardif and Jamieson, it's morelike 180.

The most inflexible measurement is also the most important: the distance between the pitcher's rubber and the center of the plate. Forty-six feet — no more, no less. When it comes to this one, nobody ever says, "Aw, close enough for government work — let it go." Most Little League teams live and die by what happens in the forty-six feet between those two points.

The fields of District 3 vary considerably in other ways, and a quick look is usually enough to tell you something about the feel any given community has for the game. The Bangor West field is in bad shape — a poor relation that the town regularly ignores in its recreation budget. The undersurface is a sterile clay that turns to soup when the weather is wet and to concrete when the weather is dry, as it has been this summer. Watering has kept most of the outfield reasonably green, but the infield is hopeless. Scruffy grass grows up the lines, but the area between the pitcher's rubber and home plate is almost completely bald. The backstop is rusty; passed balls and wild pitches frequently squirt through a wide gap between the ground and the chain link. Two large, hilly dunes run through short-right and center fields. These dunes have actually become a home-team advantage. Bangor West players learn to play the caroms off them, just as Red Sox left fielders learn to play caroms off the Green Monster. Visiting fielders, on the other hand, often find themselves chasing their mistakes all the way to the fence.

Brewer's field, tucked behind the local IGA grocery and a Marden's Discount Store, has to compete for space with what may be the oldest, rustiest playground equipment in New England; little brothers and sisters watch the game upside down from the swings, their heads down and their feet in the sky.

Bob Beal Field in Machias, with its pebble-pocked-skin infield, is probably the worst of the fields Bangor West will visit this year; Hampden, with its manicured outfield and neat composition infield, is probably the best. With its picnic area beyond the center-field fence and a rest-room-equipped snack bar, Hampden's diamond, behind the local VFW hall, looks like a rich kids' field. But looks can be deceiving. This team is a combination of kids from Newburgh and Hampden, and Newburgh is still small-farm and dairy country. Many of these kids ride to the games in old cars with primer paint around the headlights and mufflers held in place by chicken wire; they wear sunburns they got doing chores, not while they were hanging out at the country-club swimming pool. Town kids and country kids. Once they're in uniform, it doesn't much matter which is which.

Dave is right: the Hampden-Newburgh fans are waiting. Bangor West last won the District 3 Little League title in 1971; Hampden has never won a title, and many local fans continue to hope that this will be the year, despite the earlier loss to Bangor West. For the first time, the Bangor team really feels it is on the road; it is faced with a large hometown rooting section.

Matt Kinney gets the start. Hampden counters with Kyle King, and the game quickly shapes up as that rarest and richest of Little League commodities, a genuine pitchers' duel. At the end of the third inning, the score is Hampden 0, Bangor West 0.

In the bottom of the fourth, Bangor scores two unearned runs when Hampden's infield comes unglued once more. Owen King, Bangor West's first baseman, comes to bat with two on and one out. The two Kings, Kyle on the Hampden team and Owen on the Bangor West team, are not related. You don't need to be told; a single glance is enough. Kyle King is about five foot three. At six foot two, Owen King towers over him. Size differences are so extreme in Little League that it's easy to feel disoriented, the victim of hallucination.

Bangor's King raps a ground ball to short. It's a tailor-made double play, but the Hampden shortstop does not field it cleanly, and King, shucking his two hundred or so pounds down to first at top speed, beats the throw. Mike Pelkey and Mike Arnold scamper home.

Then, in the top of the fifth, Matt Kinney, who has been cruising, hits Chris Witcomb, number eight in Hampden's order. Brett Johnson, the number nine hitter, scorches one at Casey Kinney, Bangor West's second baseman. Again, it's a tailor-made double-play ball, but Casey gives up on it. His hands, which have been automatically dipping down, freeze about four inches off the ground, and Casey turns his face away to protect it from a possible bad hop. This is the most common of all Little League fielding errors, and the most easily understood; it is an act of naked self-preservation. The stricken look that Casey throws toward Dave and Neil as the ball squirts through into center field completes this part of the ballet.

"It's O.K., Casey! Next time!" Dave bawls in his gravelly, self-assured Yankee voice.

"New batter!" Neil shouts, ignoring Casey's look completely. "New batter! Know your play! We're still ahead! Get an out! Just concentrate on getting an out!"

Casey begins to relax, begins to get back into the game, and then, beyond the outfield fences, the Hampden Horns begin to blow. Some of them belong to late-model cars — Toyotas and Hondas and snappy little Dodge Colts with U.S. OUT OF CENTRAL AMERICA and SPLIT WOOD NOT ATOMS stickers on the bumpers. But most of the

Hampden Horns reside within older cars and pick-up trucks. Many of the pick-ups have rusty doors, FM converters wired up beneath the dashboards, and Leer camper caps built over the truck beds. Who is inside these vehicles, blowing the horns? No one seems to know — not for sure. They are not parents or relatives of the Hampden players; the parents and relatives (plus a generous complement of ice-cream-smeared little brothers and sisters) are filling the bleachers and lining the fence on the third-base side of the diamond, where the Hampden dugout is. They may be local guys just off work — guys who have stopped to watch some of the game before having a few brewskis at the VFW hall next door — or they may be the ghosts of Hampden Little Leaguers Past, hungry for that long-denied State Championship flag. It seems at least possible; there is something both eerie and inevitable about the Hampden Horns. They toot in harmony — high horns, low horns, a few fog-horns powered by dying batteries. Several Bangor West players look uneasily back toward the sound.

Behind the backstop, a local TV crew is preparing to videotape a story for the sports final on the eleven o'clock news. This causes a stir among some of the spectators, but only a few of the players on the Hampden bench seem to notice it. Matt Kinney certainly doesn't. He is totally intent on the next Hampden batter, Matt Knaide, who taps one turf shoe with his aluminum Worth bat and then steps into the batter's box.

The Hampden Horns fall silent. Matt Kinney goes into his windup. Casey Kinney drops back into position just east of second, glove down. His face says it has no plans to turn away if the ball is hit to him again. The Hampden runners stand expectantly on first and second. (There is no leading away from the bag in Little League.) The spectators along the opposing arms of the diamond watch anxiously. Their conversations die out. Baseball at its best (and this is a very good game indeed, one you would pay money to see) is a game of restful pauses punctuated by short, sharp inhalations. The fans can now sense one of those inhalations coming. Matt Kinney winds and fires.

Knaide lines the first pitch over second for a base hit, and now the score is 2–1. Kyle King, Hampden's pitcher, steps to the plate and sends a low, screeching line drive straight back to the mound. It hits Matt Kinney on the right shin. He makes an instinctive effort to field the ball, which has already squiggled off toward the hole between third and short, before he realizes he is really hurt and folds up. Now the bases are loaded, but for the moment no one cares; the instant the umpire raises his hands, signalling time out, all the Bangor West players converge on Matt Kinney. Beyond center field, the Hampden Horns are blowing triumphantly.

Kinney is white-faced, clearly in pain. An ice pack is brought from the first-aid kit kept in the snack bar, and after a few minutes he is able to rise and limp off the field with his arms around Dave and Neil. The spectators applaud loudly and sympathetically.

Owen King, the erstwhile first baseman, becomes Bangor West's new pitcher, and the first batter he must face is Mike Tardif. The Hampden

Horns send up a brief, anticipatory blat as Tardif steps in. King's third pitch goes wild to the backstop. Brett Johnson heads home; King breaks toward the plate from the mound, as he has been taught to do. In the Bangor West dugout, Neil Waterman, his arm still around Matt Kinney's shoulders, chants, *"Cover-cover-COVER!"*

Joe Wilcox, Bangor West's starting catcher, is a foot shorter than King, but very quick. At the beginning of this All-Star season, he did not want to catch, and he still doesn't like it, but he has learned to live with it and to get tough in a position where very few small players survive for long; even in Little League, most catchers resemble human Toby jugs. Earlier in this game he made an amazing one-handed stab of a foul ball. Now he lunges toward the backstop, flinging his mask aside with his bare hand at the same instant he catches the rebounding wild pitch. He turns toward the plate and tosses to King as the Hampden Horns chorus a wild — and premature, as it turns out — bray of triumph.

Johnson has slowed down. On his face is an expression strikingly similar to that worn by Casey Kinney when Casey allowed Johnson's hard-hit grounder to shoot through the hole. It is a look of extreme anxiety and trepidation, the face of a boy who suddenly wishes he were someplace else. *Anyplace* else. The new pitcher is blocking the plate.

Johnson starts a halfhearted slide. King takes the toss from Wilcox, pivots with surprising, winsome grace, and tags the hapless Johnson out easily. He walks back toward the mound, wiping sweat from his forehead, and prepares to face Tardif once more. Behind him, the Hampden Horns have fallen silent again.

Tardif loops one toward third. Kevin Rochefort, Bangor's third baseman, takes a single step backward in response. It's an easy play, but there is an awful look of dismay on his face, and it is only then, as Rochefort starts to freeze up on what is an easy pop fly, that one can see how badly the whole team has been shaken by Matt's injury. The ball goes into Rochefort's glove, and then pops out when Rochefort — dubbed Roach Clip first by Freddy Moore and then by the whole squad — fails to squeeze it. Knaide, who advanced to third while King and Wilcox were dealing with Johnson, has already broken for the plate. Rochefort could have doubled Knaide up easily if he had caught the ball, but here, as in the majors, baseball is a game of ifs and inches. Rochefort doesn't catch the ball. He throws wild to first instead. Mike Arnold has taken over there, and he is one of the best fielders on the team, but no one issued him stilts. Tardif, meanwhile, steams into second. The pitchers' duel has become a typical Little League game, and now the Hampden Horns are a cacophony of joy. The home team has their thumping shoes on, and the final score is Hampden 9, Bangor West 2. Still, there are two good things to go home on: Matt Kinney is not seriously hurt, and when Casey Kinney got another tough chance in the late innings he refused to choke, and made the play.

After the final out is recorded, the Bangor West players trudge into their dugout and sit on the

981

bench. This is their first loss, and most of them are not coping with it very gracefully. Some toss their gloves disgustedly between their dirty sneakers. Some are crying, others look close to tears, and no one is talking. Even Freddy, Bangor's quipmaster general, has nothing to say on this muggy Thursday evening in Hampden. Beyond the center-field fence, a few of the Hampden Horns are still tooting happily away.

Neil Waterman is the first person to speak. He tells the boys to get their heads up and look at him. Three of them already are: Owen King, Ryan Iarrobino, and Matt Kinney. Now about half the squad manages to do as he's asked. Several others, however — including Josh Stevens, who made the final out — continue to seem vastly interested in their footgear.

"Get your *heads* up," Waterman says again. He speaks louder this time, but not unkindly, and now they all manage to look at him. "You played a pretty good game," he says softly. "You got a little rattled, and they ended up on top. It happens. It doesn't mean they're better, though — that's something we're going to find out on Saturday. Tonight all you lost was a baseball game. The sun will still come up tomorrow." They begin to stir around on the bench a little; this old homily has apparently not lost its power to comfort. "You gave what you had tonight, and that's all we want. I'm proud of you, and you can be proud of yourselves. Nothing happened that you have to hang your heads about."

He stands aside for Dave Mansfield, who surveys his team. When Dave speaks, his usually loud voice is even quieter than Waterman's. "We knew when we came down here that they had to beat us, didn't we?" he asks. He speaks reflectively, almost as if he were talking to himself. "If they didn't, they'd be out. They'll be coming to our field on Saturday. That's when *we* have to beat *them*. Do you want to?"

They are all looking up now.

"I want you to remember what Neil told you," Dave says in that reflective voice, so unlike his practice-field bellow. "You are a team. That means you love each other. You love each other — win or lose — because you are a team."

The first time anyone suggested to these boys that they must come to love each other while they were on the field, they laughed uneasily at the idea. Now they don't laugh. After enduring the Hampden Horns together, they seem to understand, at least a little.

Dave surveys them again, then nods. "O.K. Pick up the gear."

They pick up bats, helmets, catching equipment, and stuff everything into canvas duffel bags. By the time they've got it over to Dave's old green pick-up truck, some of them are laughing again.

Dave laughs with them, but he doesn't do any laughing on the ride home. Tonight the ride seems long. "I don't know if we can beat them on Saturday," he says on the way back. He is speaking in that same reflective tone of voice. "I want to, and *they* want to, but I just don't know. Hampden's got mo on their side, now."

Mo, of course, is momentum — that mythic force which shapes not only single games but whole seasons. Baseball players are quirky and superstitious at every level of play, and for some reason the Bangor West players have adopted a small plastic sandal — a castoff of some young fan's baby doll — as their mascot. They have named this absurd talisman Mo. They stick it in the chain-link fence of the dugout at every game, and batters often touch it furtively before stepping into the on-deck circle. Nick Trzaskos, who ordinarily plays left field for Bangor West, has been entrusted with Mo between games. Tonight, for the first time, he forgot to bring the talisman.

"Nick better remember Mo on Saturday," Dave says grimly. "But even if he remembers . . ." He shakes his head. "I just don't know."

There is no admission charge to Little League games; the charter expressly forbids it. Instead, a player takes around a hat during the fourth inning, soliciting donations for equipment and field maintenance. On Saturday, when Bangor West and Hampden square off in the year's final Penobscot County Little League game, at Bangor, one can judge the growth of local interest in the team's fortunes by a simple act of comparison. The collection taken up at the Bangor-Millinocket contest was $15.45; when the hat finally comes back in the fifth inning of the Saturday-afternoon game against Hampden, it's overflowing with change and crumpled dollar bills. The total take is $94.25. The bleachers are full; the fences are lined; the parking lot is full. Little League has one thing in common with almost all American sports and business endeavors: nothing succeeds like success.

Things start off well for Bangor — they lead 7–3 at the end of three — and then everything falls apart. In the fourth inning, Hampden scores six runs, most of them honest. Bangor West doesn't fold, as it did after Matt Kinney was hit in the game at Hampden — the players do not drop their heads, to use Neil Waterman's phrase. But when they come to bat in the bottom of the sixth inning they are down by a score of 14–12. Elimination looks very close and very real. Mo is in its accustomed place, but Bangor West is still three outs away from the end of its season.

One kid who did not need to be told to get his head up following Bangor West's 9–2 loss was Ryan Iarrobino. He went two for three in that game, played well, and trotted off the field *knowing* he had played well. He is a tall kid, quiet, with broad shoulders and a shock of dark-brown hair. He is one of two natural athletes on the Bangor West team. Matt Kinney is the other. Although the two boys are physical opposites — Kinney slim and still fairly short, Iarrobino tall and well muscled — they share a quality that is uncommon in boys their age: they trust their bodies. Most of the others on the Bangor West squad, no matter how talented, seem to regard feet, arms, and hands as spies and potential traitors.

Iarrobino is one of those boys who seem somehow more *there* when they are dressed for some sort of competition. He is one of the few kids on either team who can don batting helmets and not look like nerds wearing their mothers' stewpots. When Matt Kinney stands on the mound and throws a baseball, he seems perfect in his place and time. And when Ryan Iarrobino steps into the right-hand batter's box and points the head of his bat out toward the pitcher for an instant before raising it to the cocked position, at his right shoulder, he also seems to be exactly where he belongs. He looks dug in even before he settles himself for the first pitch: you could draw a perfectly straight line from the ball of his shoulder to the ball of his hip and on down to the ball of his ankle. Matt Kinney was built to throw baseballs; Ryan Iarrobino was built to hit them.

Last call for Bangor West. Jeff Carson, whose fourth-inning home run is really the difference in this game, and who earlier replaced Mike Wentworth on the mound for Hampden, is now replaced by Mike Tardif. He faces Owen King first. King goes three and two (swinging wildly for the fences at one pitch in the dirt), then lays off a pitch just inside to work a walk. Roger Fisher follows him to the plate, pinch-hitting for the ever-gregarious Fred Moore. Roger is a small boy with Indian-dark eyes and hair. He looks like an easy out, but looks can be deceptive; Roger has good power. Today, however, he is overmatched. He strikes out.

In the field, the Hampden players shift around and look at each other. They are close, and they know it. The parking lot is too far away here for the Hampden Horns to be a factor; their fans settle for simply screaming encouragement. Two women wearing purple Hampden caps are standing behind the dugout, hugging each other joyfully. Several other fans look like track runners waiting for the starter's gun; it is clear they mean to rush onto the field the moment their boys succeed in putting Bangor West away for good.

Joe Wilcox, who didn't want to be a catcher and ended up doing the job anyway, rams a one-out single up the middle and into left-center field. King stops at second. Up steps Arthur Dorr, the Bangor right fielder, who wears the world's oldest pair of high-top sneakers and has not had a hit all day. This time he rifles one, but right at the Hampden shortstop, who barely has to move. The shortstop whips the ball to second, hoping to catch King off the bag, but he's out of luck. Nevertheless, there are two out.

The Hampden fans scream further encouragement. The women behind the dugout are jumping up and down. Now there are a few Hampden Horns tootling away someplace, but they are a little early, and all one has to do to know it is to look at Mike Tardif's face as he wipes off his forehead and pounds the baseball into his glove.

Ryan Iarrobino steps into the right-hand batter's box. He has a fast, almost naturally perfect swing; even Ron St. Pierre will not fault him on it much.

Ryan swings through Tardif's first pitch, his hardest of the day — it makes a rifle-shot sound as it hits Kyle King's glove. Tardif then wastes one outside. King returns the ball; Tardif meditates briefly and then throws a low fastball. Ryan looks at it, and the umpire calls strike two. It has caught the outside corner — maybe. The ump says it did, anyway, and that's the end of it.

Now the fans on both sides have fallen quiet, and so have the coaches. They're all out of it. It's only Tardif and Iarrobino now, balanced on the last strike of the last out of the last game one of these teams will play. Forty-six feet between these two faces. Only, Iarrobino is not watching Tardif's *face*. He is watching Tardif's *glove*, and somewhere I can hear Ron St. Pierre telling Fred, *You're waiting to see how I'll come — sidearm, three-quarters, or over the top.*

Iarrobino is waiting to see how Tardif will come. As Tardif moves to the set position, you can faintly hear the *pock-pock, pock-pock* of tennis balls on a nearby court, but here there is only silence and the crisp black shadows of the players, lying on the dirt like silhouettes cut from black construction paper, and Iarrobino is waiting to see how Tardif will come.

He comes over the top. And suddenly Iarrobino is in motion, both knees and the left shoulder dipping slightly, the aluminum bat a blur in the sunlight. That aluminum-on-cowhide sound — *chink*, like someone hitting a tin cup with a spoon — is different this time. A *lot* different. Not *chink* but *crunch* as Ryan connects, and then the ball is in the sky, tracking out to left field — a long shot that is clearly gone, high, wide, and handsome into the summer afternoon. The ball will later be recovered from beneath a car about 275 feet away from home plate.

The expression on twelve-year-old Mike Tardif's face is stunned, thunderstruck disbelief. He takes one quick look into his glove, as if hoping to find the ball still there and discover that Iarrobino's dramatic two-strike, two-out shot was only a hideous momentary dream. The two women behind the backstop look at each other in total amazement. At first, no one makes a sound. In that moment before everyone begins to scream and the Bangor West players rush out of their dugout to await Ryan at home plate and mob him when he arrives, only two people are entirely sure that it did really happen. One is Ryan himself. As he rounds first, he raises both hands to his shoulders in a brief but emphatic gesture of triumph. And, as Owen King crosses the plate with the first of the three runs that will end Hampden's All-Star season, Mike Tardif realizes. Standing on the pitcher's rubber for the last time as a Little Leaguer, he bursts into tears.

"You gotta remember, they're only twelve," each of the three coaches says at one time or another, and each time one of them says it, the listener feels that he — Mansfield, Waterman, or St. Pierre — is really reminding himself.

"When you are on the field, we'll love you and you will love each other," Waterman tells the boys again and again, and in the wake of Bangor's eleventh-hour, 15–14 win over Hampden, when they all did love each other, the boys no longer laugh at this. He continues, "From now on, I'm going to be hard on you — very hard. When you're playing, you'll get nothing but unconditional love from me. But when we're practicing on our home field some of you are going to find out how loud I can yell. If you're goofing off, you're going to sit down. If I tell you to do something and you don't do it, you're going to sit down. Recess is over, guys — everybody out of the pool. This is where the hard work starts."

A few nights later, Waterman hits a shot to right during fielding practice. It almost amputates Arthur Dorr's nose on the way by. Arthur has been busy making sure his fly is zipped. Or inspecting the laces of his Keds. Or some damn thing.

"*Arthur!*" Neil Waterman bellows, and Arthur flinches more at the sound of that voice than he did at the close passage of the baseball. "*Get in here!* On the bench! *Now!*"

"But —" Arthur begins.

"In here!" Neil yells back. "You're on the pine!"

Arthur trots sullenly in, head down, and J. J. Fiddler takes his place. A few nights later, Nick Trzaskos loses his chance to hit away when he fails to bunt two pitches in five tries or so. He sits on the bench by himself, cheeks flaming.

Machias, the Aroostook County/Washington County winner, is next on the docket — a two-out-of-three series, and the winner will be District 3 champion. The first game is to be played at the Bangor field, behind the Coke plant, the second at Bob Beal Field in Machias. The last game, if needed, will be played on neutral ground between the two towns.

As Neil Waterman has promised, the coaching staff is all encouragement once the national anthem has been played and the first game starts.

"That's all right, no damage!" Dave Mansfield cries as Arthur Dorr misjudges a long shot to right and the ball lands behind him. "Get an out, now! Belly play! Let's just get an out!" No one seems to know exactly what "belly play" is, but since it seems to involve winning ball games, the boys are all for it.

No third game against Machias is necessary. Bangor West gets a strong pitching performance from Matt Kinney in the first one and wins 17–5. Winning the second game is a little tougher only because the weather does not cooperate: a drenching summer downpour washes out the first try, and it is necessary for Bangor West to make the 168-mile round trip to Machias twice in order to clinch the division. They finally get the game in, on the twenty-ninth of July. Mike Pelkey's family has spirited Bangor West's number two pitcher off to Disney World in Orlando, making Mike the third player to fade from the team, but Owen King steps quietly in and pitches a five-hitter, striking out eight before tiring and giving way to Mike Arnold in the sixth inning. Bangor West wins, 12–2, and becomes District 3 Little League champ.

At moments like these, the pros retire to their air-conditioned locker rooms and pour champagne over each other's heads. The Bangor West team goes out to Helen's, the best (maybe the only) restaurant in Machias, to celebrate with hot dogs, hamburgers, gallons of Pepsi-Cola, and mountains of French fries. Looking at them as they laugh at each other, razz each other, and blow napkin pellets through their straws at each other, it is impossible not to be aware of how soon they will discover gaudier modes of celebration.

For now, however, this is perfectly O.K. — great, in fact. They are not overwhelmed by what they have done, but they seem tremendously pleased, tremendously content, and entirely *here*. If they have been touched with magic this summer, they do not know it, and no one has as yet been unkind enough to tell them that it may be so. For now they are allowed the deep-fried simplicities of Helen's, and those simplicities are quite enough. They have won their division; the State Championship Tournament, where bigger and better teams from the more heavily populated regions downstate will probably blow them out, is still a week away.

Ryan Iarrobino has changed back into his tank top. Arthur Dorr has a rakish smear of ketchup on one cheek. And Owen King, who struck terror into the hearts of the Machias batters by coming at them with a powerful sidearm fastball on 0-2 counts, is burbling happily into his glass of Pepsi. Nick Trzaskos, who can look unhappier than any boy on earth when things don't break his way, looks supremely happy tonight. And why not? Tonight they're twelve and they're winners.

Not that they don't remind you themselves from time to time. Halfway back from Machias after the first trip, the rainout, J. J. Fiddler begins to wriggle around uneasily in the back seat of the car he is riding in. "I gotta go," he says. He clutches at himself and adds ominously, "Man, I gotta go bad. I mean big time."

"J.J.'s gonna do it!" Joe Wilcox cries gleefully. "Watch this! J.J.'s gonna flood the car!"

"Shut up, Joey," J.J. says, and then begins to wriggle around again.

He has waited until the worst possible moment

992

to make his announcement. The eighty-four-mile trip between Machias and Bangor is, for the most part, an exercise in emptiness. There isn't even a decent stand of trees into which J.J. can disappear for a few moments along this stretch of road — only mile after mile of open hayfields, with Route 1A cutting a winding course through them.

Just as J.J.'s bladder is going to DEFCON-1, a providential gas station appears. The assistant coach swings in and tops up his tank while J.J. splits for the men's room. "Boy!" he says, brushing his hair out of his eyes as he jogs back to the car. "That was close!"

"Got some on your pants, J.J.," Joe Wilcox says casually, and everyone goes into spasms of wild laughter as J.J. checks.

On the trip back to Machias the next day, Matt Kinney reveals one of the chief attractions *People* magazine holds for boys of Little League age. "I'm sure there's one in here someplace," he says, leafing slowly through an issue he has found on the back seat. "There almost always is."

"What? What are you looking for?" third baseman Kevin Rochefort asks, peering over Matt's shoulder as Matt leafs past the week's celebs, barely giving them a look.

"The breast-examination ad," Matt explains. "You can't see everything, but you can see quite a lot. Here it is!" He holds the magazine up triumphantly.

Four other heads, each wearing a red Bangor West baseball cap, immediately cluster around the magazine. For a few minutes, at least, baseball is the furthest thing from these boys' minds.

The 1989 Maine State Little League Championship Tournament begins on August 3, just over four weeks after All-Star play began for the teams involved. The state is divided into five districts, and all five send teams to Old Town, where this year's tourney is to be held. The participants are Yarmouth, Belfast, Lewiston, York, and Bangor West. All the teams but Belfast are bigger than the Bangor West All-Stars, and Belfast is supposed to have a secret weapon. Their number one pitcher is this year's tourney wunderkind.

The naming of the tourney wunderkind is a yearly ceremony, a small tumor that seems to defy all attempts to remove it. This boy, who is anointed Kid Baseball whether he wants the honor or not, finds himself in a heretofore unsuspected spotlight, the object of discussion, speculation, and, inevitably, wagering. He also finds himself in the unenviable position of having to live up to all sorts of pretournament hype. A Little League tournament is a pressure situation for any kid; when you get to Tourney Town and discover you have somehow become an instant legend as well, it's usually too much.

This year's object of myth and discussion is Belfast's southpaw Stanley Sturgis. In his two outings for Belfast he has chalked up thirty strikeouts — fourteen in his first game, sixteen in his second. Thirty K's in two games is an impressive statistic in any league, but to fully understand Sturgis's accomplishment one has to remember that Little League games consist of only six innings. That means that 83 per cent of the outs Belfast recorded with Sturgis on the hill came on strikeouts.

Then there is York. All the teams that come to the Knights of Columbus field in Old Town to compete in the tourney have excellent records, but York, which is undefeated, is the clear favorite to win a ticket to the Eastern Regionals. None of their players are giants, but several of them are over five-ten, and their best pitcher, Phil Tarbox, has a fastball that may top seventy miles an hour on some pitches — extravagant by Little League standards. Like Yarmouth and Belfast, the York players come dressed in special All-Star uniforms and matching turf shoes, which make them look like pros.

Only Bangor West and Lewiston come wearing mufti — which is to say, shirts of many colors bearing the names of their regular-season team sponsors. Owen King wears Elks orange, Ryan Iarrobino and Nick Trzaskos wear Bangor Hydro red, Roger Fisher and Fred Moore wear Lions green, and so on. The Lewiston team is dressed in similar fashion, but they have at least been provided with matching shoes and stirrups. Compared with Lewiston, the Bangor team, dressed in a variety of baggy gray sweatpants and nondescript street sneakers, looks eccentric. Next to the other teams, however, they look like out-and-out ragamuffins. No one, with the possible exception of the Bangor West coaches and the players themselves, takes them very seriously. In its first article on the tourney the local newspaper gives more coverage to Sturgis, of Belfast, than it does to the entire Bangor West team.

Dave, Neil, and Saint, the odd but surprisingly

effective brain trust that has brought the team this far, watch Belfast take infield and batting practice without saying much. The Belfast kids are resplendent in their new purple-and-white uniforms — uniforms that have not worn so much as a speck of infield dirt until today. At last, Dave says, "Well, we finally got here again. We did that much. Nobody can take that away from us."

Bangor West comes from the district in which the tournament is being held this year, and the team will not have to play until two of the five teams have been eliminated. This is called a first-round bye, and right now it's the biggest, perhaps the only, advantage this team has. In their own district, they looked like champions (except for that one awful game against Hampden), but Dave, Neil, and Saint have been around long enough to know that they are now looking at an entirely different level of baseball. Their silence as they stand by the fence watching Belfast work out acknowledges this eloquently.

In contrast, York has already ordered District 4 pins. Trading pins is a tradition at the regional tournaments, and the fact that York has already laid in a supply tells an interesting tale. The pins say York means to play with the best of the East Coast, in Bristol. The pins say they don't think Yarmouth can stop them; or Belfast, with its wunderkind southpaw; or Lewiston, which clawed its way to the Division 2 championship through the losers' bracket, after dropping their first game 15–12; or, least of all, fourteen badly dressed pipsqueaks from the west side of Bangor.

"At least we'll get a chance to play," Dave says,

"and we'll try to make them remember we were here."

But first Belfast and Lewiston have *their* chance to play, and after the Boston Pops has steamed through a recorded version of the national anthem, and a local writer of some repute has tossed out the obligatory first pitch (it sails all the way to the backstop), they have at it.

Area sports reporters have spilled a lot of ink on the subject of Stanley Sturgis, but reporters are not allowed on the field once the game starts (a situation caused by a mistake in the rules as they were originally laid out, some of them seem to feel). Once the umpire has commanded the teams to play ball, Sturgis finds himself on his own. The writers, the pundits, and the entire Belfast hot-stove league are now all on the other side of the fence.

Baseball is a team sport, but there is only one player with a ball at the center of each diamond and only one player with a bat at the diamond's lowest point. The man with the bat keeps changing, but the pitcher remains — unless he can no longer cut it, that is. Today is Stan Sturgis's day to discover the hard truth of tourney play: sooner or later, every wunderkind meets his match.

Sturgis struck out thirty men in his last pair of games, but that was District 2. The team Belfast is playing today, a tough bunch of scrappers out of Lewiston's Elliot Avenue League, is a different plate of beans altogether. They are not as big as the boys from York and don't field as smoothly as the boys from Yarmouth, but they are pesky and persistent. The first batter, Carlton Gagnon, personifies the gnawing, clawing spirit of the team. He singles up the middle, steals second, is sacrificed to third, then bolts home on a steal play sent in from the bench. In the third inning, with the score 1–0, Gagnon reaches base again, this time on a fielder's choice. Randy Gervais, who follows this pest in the lineup, strikes out, but before he does, Gagnon has gone to second on a passed ball and stolen third. He scores on a two-out base hit by Bill Paradis, the third baseman.

Belfast comes up with a run in the fourth, briefly making a game of it, but then Lewiston puts them, and Stanley Sturgis, away for good, scoring two in the fifth and four more in the sixth. The final tally is 9–1. Sturgis strikes out eleven, but he also gives up seven hits, while Carlton Gagnon, Lewiston's pitcher, strikes out eight and allows only three hits. When Sturgis leaves the field at the end of the game, he looks both depressed and relieved. For him the hype and hoopla are over. He can quit being a newspaper sidebar and go back to being a kid again. His face suggests that he sees certain advantages in that.

Later, in a battle of the giants, tourney favorite York knocks off Yarmouth. Then everybody goes home (or, in the case of the visiting players, back to their motels or to the homes of their host families). Tomorrow, Friday, it will be Bangor West's turn to play while York waits to meet the winner in the closer.

Friday comes in hot, foggy, and cloudy. Rain threatens from first light, and an hour or so before Bangor West and Lewiston are scheduled to square off the rain comes — a deluge of rain. When this sort of weather struck in Machias, the game was quickly cancelled. Not here. This is a different field — one with a grass infield instead of dirt — but that isn't the only factor. The major one is TV. This year, for the first time, two stations have pooled their resources and will telecast the tournament final statewide on Saturday afternoon. If the semifinal between Bangor and Lewiston is postponed, it means trouble with the schedule, and even in Maine, even in this most amateur of amateur sports, the one thing you don't jiggle is the media's schedule.

So the Bangor West and Lewiston teams are not dismissed when they come to the field. Instead, they sit in cars or cluster in little groups beneath the candy-striped canvas of the central concession booth. Then they wait for a break in the weather. And wait. And wait. Restlessness sets in, of course. Many of these kids will play in bigger games before their athletic careers end, but this is the biggest to date for all of them; they are pumped to the max.

Someone eventually has a brainstorm. After a few quick phone calls, two Old Town schoolbuses, gleaming bright yellow in the drenching rain, pull up to the nearby Elks Club, and the players are whisked off on a tour of the Old Town Canoe Company factory and the local James River paper mill. (The James River Corporation is the prime buyer of ad time on the upcoming championship telecast.) None of the players look particularly happy as they climb aboard the buses; they don't look much happier when they arrive back. Each player is carrying a small canoe paddle, about the right size for a well-built elf. Freebies from the canoe factory. None of the boys seem to know just what they should do with the paddles, but when I check later they're all gone, just like the Bangor pennants after that first game against Millinocket. Free souvenirs — good deal.

And there will be a game after all, it seems. At some point — perhaps while the Little Leaguers were watching the fellows at the James River mill turn trees into toilet paper — the rain stopped. The field has drained well, the pitcher's mound and the batters' boxes have been dusted with Quick-Dry, and now, at just past three in the afternoon, a watery sun takes its first peek through the clouds.

The Bangor West team has come back from the field trip flat and listless. No one has thrown a ball or swung a bat or run a single base so far today, but everybody already seems tired. The players walk toward the practice field without looking at each other; gloves dangle at the ends of arms. They walk like losers, and they talk like losers.

Instead of lecturing them, Dave lines them up and begins playing his version of pepper with them. Soon the Bangor players are razzing each other, catcalling, trying for circus catches, groaning and bitching when Dave calls an error and sends someone to the end of the line. Then, just before Dave is ready to call the workout off and take them over to Neil and Saint for batting practice, Roger Fisher steps out of the line and bends over with his glove against his belly. Dave goes to him at once, his smile becoming an expression of concern. He wants to know if Roger is all right.

"Yes," Roger says. "I just wanted to get this." He bends down a little farther, dark eyes intent, plucks something out of the grass, and hands it to Dave. It is a four-leaf clover.

In Little League tournament games, the home team is always decided by a coin toss. Dave has been extremely lucky at winning these, but today he loses, and Bangor West is designated the visiting team. Sometimes even bad luck turns out to be good, though, and this is one of those days. Nick Trzaskos is the reason.

The skills of all the players have improved during their six-week season, but in some cases attitudes have improved as well. Nick started deep on the bench, despite his proven skills as a defensive player and his potential as a hitter; his fear of failure made him unready to play. Little by little, he has begun to trust himself, and now Dave is ready to try starting him. "Nick finally figured out that the other guys weren't going to give him a hard time if he dropped a ball or struck out," St. Pierre says. "For a kid like Nick, that's a big change."

Today, Nick cranks the third pitch of the game to deep center field. It is a hard, rising line drive, over the fence and gone before the center fielder has a chance to turn and look, let alone cruise back and grab it. As Nick Trzaskos rounds second and slows down, breaking into the home-run trot all these boys know so well from TV, the fans behind the backstop are treated to a rare sight:

Nick is grinning. As he crosses home plate and his surprised, happy teammates mob him, he actually begins to laugh. As he enters the dugout, Neil claps him on the back, and Dave Mansfield gives him a brief, hard hug.

Nick has also finished what Dave started with his game of pepper: the team is fully awake now, and ready to do some business. Matt Kinney gives up a lead-off single to Carl Gagnon, the pest who began the process of dismantling Stanley Sturgis. Gagnon goes to second on Ryan Stretton's sacrifice, advances to third on a wild pitch, and scores on another wild pitch. It is an almost uncanny repetition of his first at bat against Belfast. Kinney's control is not great this afternoon, but Gagnon's is the only run the team from Lewiston can manage in the early going. This is unfortunate for them, because Bangor comes up hitting in the top of the second.

Owen King leads off with a deep single; Arthur Dorr follows with another; Mike Arnold reaches when Lewiston's catcher, Jason Auger, picks up Arnold's bunt and throws wild to first base. King scores on the error, putting Bangor West back on top, 2–1. Joe Wilcox, Bangor's catcher, scratches out an infield hit to load the bases. Nick Trzaskos strikes out his second time up, and that brings Ryan Iarrobino to the plate. He struck out his first time up, but not now. He turns Matt Noyes's first pitch into a grand-slam home run, and after an inning and a half the score is Bangor West 6, Lewiston 1.

Up to the sixth, it is an authentic four-leaf-clover day for Bangor West. When Lewiston comes to bat for what the Bangor fans hope will be the last time, they are down by a score of 9–1. The pest, Carlton Gagnon, leads off and reaches on an error. The next batter, Ryan Stretton, also reaches on an error. The Bangor fans, who have been cheering wildly, begin to look a little uneasy. It's hard to choke when you're eight runs ahead, but not impossible. These northern New Englanders are Red Sox fans. They have seen it happen many times.

Bill Paradis makes the jitters worse by singling sharply up the middle. Both Gagnon and Stretton come home. The score is now 9–3, runner on first, nobody out. The Bangor fans shuffle and look at each other uneasily. *It can't really get away from us this late in the game, can it?* their looks ask. The answer is, Of course, you bet it can. In Little League, anything can and often does happen.

But not this time. Lewiston scores one more time, and that's it. Noyes, who fanned three times against Sturgis, fans for the third time today, and there is finally one out. Auger, Lewiston's catcher, hits the first pitch hard to the shortstop, Roger Fisher. Roger booted Carl Gagnon's ball earlier in the inning to open the door, but he picks this one up easily and shovels it to Mike Arnold, who feeds it on to Owen King at first. Auger is slow, and King's reach is long. The result is a game-ending 6–4–3 double play. You don't often see around-the-horn d.p.'s in the scaled-down world of Little League, where the base paths are only sixty feet long, but Roger found a four-leaf clover today. If you have to chalk it up to anything, it might as well be that. Whatever you chalk it up

1003

to, the boys from Bangor have won another one, 9–4.

Tomorrow, there are the giants from York.

It is August 5, 1989, and in the state of Maine only twenty-nine boys are still playing Little League ball — fourteen on the Bangor West squad and fifteen on York's team. The day is an almost exact replica of the day before: hot, foggy, and threatening. The game is scheduled to begin promptly at 12:30, but the skies open once again, and by 11 it looks as though the game will be — must be — cancelled. The rain comes pouring down in buckets.

Dave, Neil, and Saint are taking no chances, however. None of them liked the flat mood the kids were in when they returned from their impromptu tour of the day before, and they have no intention of allowing a repeat. No one wants to end up counting on a game of pepper or a four-leaf clover today. If there *is* a game — and TV is a powerful motivator, no matter how murky the weather — it will be for all the marbles. The winners go on to Bristol; the losers go home.

So a makeshift cavalcade of vans and station wagons driven by coaches and parents is assembled at the field behind the Coke plant, and the team is ferried the ten miles up to the University of Maine field house, a barnlike indoor facility where Neil and Saint rally them through their paces until the boys are soaked with sweat. Dave has arranged for the York team to use the field house, too, and as the Bangor team exits into the overcast the York team, dressed in their natty blue uniforms, troops in.

The rain is down to isolated dribbles by three o'clock, and the ground crew works frantically to return the field to playable shape. Five makeshift TV platforms have been constructed on steel frames around the field. In a nearby parking lot is a huge truck with MAINE BROADCASTING SYSTEM LIVE REMOTE painted on the side. Thick bundles of cable, held together with cinches of electrician's tape, lead from the cameras and the temporary announcer's booth back to this truck. One door stands open, and many TV monitors glimmer within.

York hasn't arrived from the field house yet. The Bangor West squad begins throwing outside the left-field fence, mostly to have something to do and keep the jitters at bay; they certainly don't need to warm up after the humid hour they just spent at the University. The camerapersons stand on their towers and watch the ground crew try to get rid of the water.

The outfield is in fair shape, and the skin parts of the infield have been raked and coated with Quick-Dry. The real problem is the area between home plate and the pitcher's mound. This section of the diamond was freshly resodded before the tournament began, and there has been no time for the roots to take hold and provide some natural drainage. The result is a swampy mess in front of home plate — a mess that slops off toward the third-base line.

Someone has an idea — an inspiration, as it turns out — that involves actually removing a large section of the wounded infield. While this is being done, a truck arrives from Old Town High School and two industrial-size Rinsenvacs are off-loaded.

Five minutes later, the ground crew is literally vacuuming the subsurface of the infield. It works. By 3:25, the groundkeepers are replacing chunks of sod like pieces in a large green jigsaw puzzle. By 3:35, a local music teacher, accompanying herself on an acoustic guitar, is winging her way through a gorgeous rendition of "The Star-Spangled Banner." And at 3:37 Bangor West's Roger Fisher, Dave's dark-horse pick to start in place of the absent Mike Pelkey, is warming up. Did Roger's find of the day before have anything to do with Dave's decision to start him instead of King or Arnold? Dave only puts his finger on the side of his nose and smiles wisely.

At 3:40, the umpire steps in. "Send it down, catcher," he says briskly. Joey does. Mike Arnold makes the sweep tag on the invisible runner, then sends the baseball on its quick journey around the infield. A TV audience that stretches from New Hampshire to the Maritime Provinces of Canada watches as Roger fusses nervously with the sleeves of his green jersey and the gray warm-up shirt he wears beneath it. Owen King tosses him the ball from first base. Fisher takes it and holds it against his hip.

"Let's play ball," the umpire invites — an invitation that umpires have been extending to Little League players for fifty years now — and Dan Bouchard, York's catcher and leadoff hitter, steps into the box. Roger goes to the set position and prepares to throw the first pitch of the 1989 State Championship game.

Five days earlier:

Dave and I take the Bangor West pitching staff up to Old Town. Dave wants them all to know how the mound feels when they come up here to play for real. With Mike Pelkey gone, the staff consists of Matt Kinney (his triumph over Lewiston still four days in the future), Owen King, Roger Fisher, and Mike Arnold. We get off to a late start, and as the four boys take turns throwing, Dave and I sit in the visitors' dugout, watching the boys as the light slowly leaves the summer sky.

On the mound, Matt Kinney is throwing one hard curve after another to J. J. Fiddler. In the home dugout, across the diamond, the three other pitchers, their workouts finished, are sitting on the bench with a few teammates who have come along for the ride. Although the talk comes to me only in snatches, I can tell it's mostly about school — a subject that comes up with greater and greater frequency during the last month of summer vacation. They talk about teachers past and teachers future, passing on the anecdotes that form an important part of their preadolescent mythology: the teacher who blew her cool during the last month of the school year because her oldest son was in a car accident; the crazy grammar-school coach (they make him sound like a lethal combination of Jason, Freddy, and Leatherface); the science teacher who supposedly once threw a kid against his locker so hard the kid was knocked out; the home-room teacher who will give you lunch money if you forget, or if you just say you forgot. It is junior high apocrypha, powerful stuff, and they tell it with great relish as twilight closes in.

Between the two dugouts, the baseball is a white streak as Matt throws it again and again. His rhythm is a kind of hypnosis: Set, wind, and fire. Set, wind, and fire. Set, wind, and fire. J.J.'s mitt cracks with each reception.

"What are they going to take with them?" I ask Dave. "When this is all over, what are they going to take with them? What difference does it make for them, do you think?"

The look on Dave's face is surprised and considering. Then he turns back to look at Matt and smiles. "They're going to take each other," he says.

It is not the answer I have been expecting — far from it. There was an article about Little League in the paper today — one of those think pieces that usually run in the ad-littered wasteland between the obituaries and the horoscopes. This one summarized the findings of a sociologist who spent a season monitoring Little Leaguers, and then followed their progress for a short time thereafter. He wanted to find out if the game did what Little League boosters claim it does — that is, pass on such old-fashioned American values as fair play, hard work, and the virtue of team effort. The fellow who did the study reported that it did, sort of. But he also reported that Little League did little to change the *individual* lives of the players. School troublemakers were still school troublemakers when classes started again in September; good scholars were still good scholars; the class clown (read Fred Moore) who took June and July off to play some serious Little League ball was still the class clown after Labor Day. The sociologist found exceptions; exceptional play some-times bred exceptional changes. But in the main this fellow found that the boys were about the same coming out as they were going in.

I suppose my confusion at Dave's answer grows out of my knowledge of him — he is an almost fanatic booster of Little League. I'm sure he must have read the article, and I have been expecting him to refute the sociologist's conclusions, using the question as a springboard. Instead, he has de-livered one of the hoariest chestnuts of the sports world.

On the mound, Matt continues to throw to J.J., harder than ever now. He has found that mystic place pitchers call "the groove," and even though this is only an informal practice session to famil-iarize the boys with the field, he is reluctant to quit.

I ask Dave if he can explain a little more fully, but I do so in a gingerly way, half expecting that I am on the verge of hitting a hitherto unsuspected jackpot of clichés: night owls never fly in the day-time; winners never quit and quitters never win; use it, don't lose it. Maybe even, God save us, a little Hummm, baby.

"Look at them," Dave says, still smiling. Some-thing in that smile suggests he may be reading my mind. "Take a good look."

I do. There are perhaps half a dozen of them on the bench, still laughing and telling junior high school war stories. One of them breaks out of the discussion long enough to ask Matt Kin-ney to throw the curve, and Matt does — one with a particularly nasty break. The boys on the bench all laugh and cheer.

"Look at those two guys," Dave says, pointing. "One of them comes from a good home. The other one, not so good." He tosses some sunflower seeds into his mouth and then indicates another boy. "Or that one. He was born in one of the worst sections of Boston. Do you think he'd know a kid like Matt Kinney or Kevin Rochefort, if it wasn't for Little League? They won't be in the same classes at junior high, wouldn't talk to each other in the halls, wouldn't have the slightest idea the other one was alive."

Matt throws another curve, this one so nasty J.J. can't handle it. It rolls all the way to the backstop, and as J.J. gets up and trots after it the boys on the bench cheer again.

"But this changes all that," Dave says. "These boys have played together and won their district together. Some come from families that are well-to-do, and there's a couple from families as poor as used dishwater, but when they put on the uniform and cross the chalk they leave all that on the other side. Your school grades can't help you between the chalk, or what your parents do, or what they don't do. Between the chalk, what happens is the kids' business. They tend it, too, as well as they can. All the rest —" Dave makes a shooing gesture with one hand. "All left behind. And they know it, too. Just look at them if you don't believe me, because the proof is right there."

I look across the field and see my own kid and one of the boys Dave has mentioned sitting side by side, heads together, talking something over seriously. They look at each other in amazement, then break out laughing.

"They played together," Dave repeats. "They practiced together, day after day, and that's probably even more important than the games. Now they're going into the State Tournament. They've even got a chance to win it. I don't think they will, but that doesn't matter. They're going to be there, and that's enough. Even if Lewiston knocks them out in the first round, that's enough. Because it's something they did together between those chalk lines. They're going to remember that. They're going to remember how that felt."

"Between the chalk," I say, and all at once I get it — the penny drops. Dave Mansfield *believes* this old chestnut. Not only that, he can *afford* to believe it. Such clichés may be hollow in the big leagues, where some player or other tests positive for drugs every week or two and the free agent is God, but this is not the big leagues. This is where Anita Bryant sings the national anthem over battered PA speakers that have been wired to the chain-link behind the dugouts. This is where, instead of paying admission to watch the game, you put something in the hat when it comes around. If you want to, of course. None of these kids are going to spend the off-season playing fantasy baseball in Florida with overweight businessmen, or signing expensive baseball cards at memorabilia shows, or touring the chicken circuit at two thousand bucks a night. When it's all free, Dave's smile suggests, they have to give the clichés back and let you own them again, fair and square. You are once more allowed to believe in Red Barber, John Tunis, and the Kid from Tomkinsville. Dave

Mansfield believes what he is saying about how the boys are equal between the chalk, and he has a right to believe, because he and Neil and Saint have patiently led these kids to a point where *they* believe it. They do believe it; I can see it on their faces as they sit in the dugout on the far side of the diamond. It could be why Dave Mansfield and all the other Dave Mansfields across the country keep on doing this, year after year. It's a free pass. Not back into childhood — it doesn't work that way — but back into the dream.

Dave falls silent for a moment, thinking, bouncing a few sunflower seeds up and down in the palm of his hand.

"It's not about winning or losing," he says finally. "That comes later. It's about how they'll pass each other in the corridor this year, or even down the road in high school, and look at each other, and remember. In a way, they're going to be on the team that won the district in 1989 for a long time." Dave glances across into the shadowy first-base dugout, where Fred Moore is now laughing about something with Mike Arnold. Owen King glances from one to the other, grinning. "It's about knowing who your teammates are. The people you had to depend on, whether you wanted to or not."

He watches the boys as they laugh and joke four days before their tournament is scheduled to begin, then raises his voice and tells Matt to throw four or five more and knock off.

Not all coaches who win the coin toss — as Dave Mansfield does on August 5, for the sixth time in nine postseason games — elect to be the home team. Some of them (the coach from Brewer, for instance) believe the so-called home-team advantage is a complete fiction, especially in a tournament game, where neither team is actually playing on its home field. The argument for being the visitors in a jackpot game runs like this: At the start of such a game, the kids on both teams are nervous. The way to take advantage of those nerves, the reasoning goes, is to bat first and let the defending team commit enough walks, balks, and errors to put you in the driver's seat. If you bat first and score four runs, these theorists conclude, you own the game before it's barely begun. QED. It's a theory Dave Mansfield has never subscribed to. "I want my lasties," he says, and for him that's the end of it.

Except today is a little different. It is not only a tournament game, it is a *championship* tournament game — a *televised* championship game, in fact. And as Roger Fisher winds and fires his first pitch past everything for ball one, Dave Mansfield's face is that of a man who is fervently hoping he hasn't made a mistake. Roger knows that he is a spot starter — that Mike Pelkey would be out here in his place if Pelkey weren't currently shaking hands with Goofy down in Disney World — but he manages his first-inning jitters as well as one could expect, maybe a little better. He backs off the mound following each return from the catcher, Joe Wilcox, studies the batter, fiddles with his shirtsleeves, and takes all the time he needs. Most important of all, he understands how necessary it is to keep the ball in the lowest quarter of the strike zone. The York lineup is packed with power from top to bottom. If Roger makes a mistake and gets one up in the batter's eyes — especially a batter like Tarbox, who hits as powerfully as he throws — it's going to get lost in a hurry.

He loses the first York batter nevertheless. Bouchard trots down to first, accompanied by the hysterical cheers of the York rooting section. The next batter is Philbrick, the shortstop. He bangs the first pitch back to Fisher. In one of those plays that sometimes decide ball games, Roger elects to go to second and try to force the lead runner. In most Little League games, this turns out to be a bad idea. Either the pitcher throws wild into center field, allowing the lead runner to get to third, or he discovers that his shortstop has not moved over to cover second and the bag is undefended. Today, however, it works. St. Pierre has drilled these boys well on their defensive positions. Matt Kinney, today's shortstop, is right where he's supposed to be. So is Roger's throw. Philbrick reaches first on a fielder's choice, but Bouchard is out. This time, it is the Bangor West fans who roar out their approval.

The play settles most of Bangor West's jitters and gives Roger Fisher some badly needed confidence. Phil Tarbox, York's most consistent hitter as well as their ace pitcher, strikes out on a pitch low and out of the strike zone. "Get him next time, Phil!" a York player calls from the bench. "You're just not used to pitching this slow!"

But speed is not the problem the York batters are having with Roger; it's location. Ron St. Pierre has preached the gospel of the low pitch all season long, and Roger Fisher — Fish, the boys call him — has been a quiet but extremely attentive student during Saint's ball-yard seminars. Dave's decisions to pitch Roger and bat last look pretty good as Bangor comes in to bat in the bottom of the first. I see several of the boys touch Mo, the little plastic sandal, as they enter the dugout.

Confidence — of the team, of the fans, of the coaches — is a quality that can be measured in different ways, but whatever yardstick you choose, York comes out on the long side. The hometown cheering section has hung a sign on the lower posts of the scoreboard. YORK IS BRISTOL BOUND, this exuberant Fan-O-Gram reads. And there is the matter of those District 4 pins, all made up and ready for trading. But the clearest indicator of the deep confidence York's coach has in his players is revealed in his starting pitcher. All the other clubs, including Bangor West, pitched their number one starter in their first game, bearing an old playoff axiom in mind: if you don't get a date, you can't dance at the prom. If you can't win your prelim, you don't have to worry about the final. Only the coach from York ran counter to this wisdom, and pitched his number two starter, Ryan Fernald, in the first game, against Yarmouth. He got away with it — by a whisker — as his team outlasted Yarmouth, 9–8. That was a close shave, but today should be the payoff. He has saved Phil Tarbox for the final, and while Tarbox may not be technically as good as Stanley Sturgis, he's got something going for him that Sturgis did not. Phil Tarbox is *scary*.

Nolan Ryan, probably the greatest fastball pitcher ever to play the game of baseball, likes to tell a story about a Babe Ruth League tournament game he pitched in. He hit the opposing team's leadoff batter in the arm, breaking it. He hit the second batter in the head, splitting the boy's helmet in two and knocking him out for a few moments. While this second boy was being attended to, the number three batter, ashen-faced and trembling, went up to his coach and begged the man not to make him hit. "And I didn't blame him," Ryan adds.

Tarbox is no Nolan Ryan, but he throws hard and he is aware that intimidation is the pitcher's secret weapon. Sturgis also threw hard, but he kept the ball low and outside. Sturgis was polite. Tarbox likes to work high and tight. Bangor West has got to where they are today by swinging the bat. If Tarbox can intimidate them, he will take the bats out of their hands, and if he does that Bangor is finished.

Nick Trzaskos doesn't come anywhere near a leadoff home run today. Tarbox strikes him out with an intimate fastball that has Nick ducking out of the box. Nick looks around unbelievingly at the home-plate umpire and opens his mouth to protest. "Don't say a word, Nick!" Dave blares from the dugout. "Just hustle back in there!" Nick does, but his face has resumed its former narrow look. Once inside the dugout, he slings his batting helmet disgustedly under the bench.

Tarbox will try to work everyone but Ryan Iarrobino high and tight today. Word on Iarrobino has got around, and not even Phil Tarbox, confident as he appears to be, will challenge him. He works Ryan low and outside, finally walking him. He also walks Matt Kinney, who follows Ryan, but now he is high and tight again. Matt has superb reflexes, and he needs them to avoid being hit, and hit hard. By the time he is awarded first base, Iarrobino is already at second, courtesy of a wild pitch that came within inches of Matt's face. Then Tarbox settles down a little, striking out Kevin Rochefort and Roger Fisher to end the first inning.

Roger Fisher continues to work slowly and methodically, fiddling with his sleeves between pitches, glancing around at his infield, occasionally even checking the sky, possibly for UFOs. With two on and one out, Estes, who reached on a walk, breaks for third on a pitch that bounces out of Joe Wilcox's glove and lands at his feet. Joe recovers quickly and guns the ball down to Kevin Rochefort at third. The ball is waiting for Estes when he arrives, and he trots back to the dugout. Two out; Fernald has gone to second on the play.

Wyatt, York's number eight hitter, dribbles one up the right side of the infield. The ball's progress is slowed further by the soggy condition of the ground. Fisher goes for the ball. So does King, the first baseman. Roger grabs it, then slips on the wet grass and *crawls* for the bag, ball in hand. Wyatt beats him easily. Fernald comes all the way home on the play to score the first run of the game.

If Roger is going to crack, one would expect it to happen right here. He checks his infield, and examines the ball. He appears ready to pitch, and then steps off the rubber. His sleeves, it seems, are not quite to his liking after all. He takes his time fixing them while Matt Francke, the York batter, grows old and mouldy in the batter's box. By the time Fisher finally gets around to throwing, he all but owns Francke, who hits an easy hopper to Kevin Rochefort at third. Rochefort throws on to Matt Kinney, forcing Wyatt. Still, York has drawn first blood and leads, 1–0, at the end of an inning and a half.

Bangor West doesn't put any runs on the board in the second inning, either, but they score against Phil Tarbox just the same. The rangy York pitcher trotted off the mound with his head up at the end of the first inning. Going in after pitching the second, he trudges with his head down, and some of his teammates glance at him uneasily.

Owen King, who bats first in Bangor's half of the second, isn't intimidated by Tarbox, but he is a big boy, much slower than Matt Kinney. After running the count full, Tarbox tries to jam him inside. The fastball runs up and in — too much of both. King is hit hard in the armpit. He falls to the ground, clutching the hurt place, too stunned to cry at first, but obviously in pain. Eventually, the tears do come — not a lot of them, but real tears, for all that. At six foot two and over two hundred pounds, he's as big as a man, but he's still only twelve and not used to being hit by seventy-mile-an-hour inside fastballs. Tarbox immediately rushes off the mound toward him, his face a mask of concern and contrition. The umpire, already bending over the downed player, waves him off impatiently. The on-duty paramedic who hurries out doesn't even give Tarbox a second look. The fans do, however. The fans are giving him all kinds of second looks.

"Take him out before he hits someone else!" one yells.

"Pull him before someone *really* gets hurt!" another adds, as if being hit in the ribcage by a fastball weren't really getting hurt.

"Warn im, ump!" a third voice chimes in. "That was a deliberate brushback! Warn im what happens if he does it again!"

Tarbox glances toward the fans, and for a moment this boy, who has formerly radiated a kind of serene confidence, looks very young and very uncertain. He looks, in fact, the way Stanley Sturgis did as the Belfast-Lewiston game neared its conclusion. As he goes back to the mound, he slams the ball into his glove in frustration.

King, meanwhile, has been helped to his feet. After making it clear to Neil Waterman, the paramedic, and the umpire that he wants to stay in the game and is capable of doing so, he trots down to first base. Both sets of fans give him a solid round of applause.

Phil Tarbox, who of course had no intention of hitting the leadoff batter in a one-run game, immediately shows how shaken he is by grooving one right down the middle to Arthur Dorr. Arthur, the second-smallest boy in Bangor West's starting lineup, accepts this unexpected but welcome gift by driving it deep to right center.

King is off at the crack of the bat. He rounds third, knowing he can't score but hoping to draw the throw that will assure Arthur of second base, and, as he does, the wet conditions become a factor.

The third-base side of the diamond is still damp. When King tries to put on the brakes, his feet go out from under him and he lands on his ass. The relay has come in to Tarbox, and Tarbox will not risk a throw; he charges King, who is making feeble efforts to regain his feet. At the end, Bangor's biggest player just raises his arms in an eloquent, touching gesture: *I surrender.* Thanks to the slippery conditions, Tarbox now has a runner on second with one out instead of runners on second and third with none out. It is a big difference, and Tarbox displays his renewed confidence by striking out Mike Arnold.

Then, on his third pitch to Joe Wilcox, the next batter, he hits him smack in the elbow. This time, the cries of outrage from the Bangor West fans are louder, and tinged with threat. Several of them direct their ire at the home-plate umpire, demanding that Tarbox be taken out. The ump, who understands this situation completely, does not bother even to warn Tarbox. The stricken look on the boy's face as Wilcox jogs shakily down to first undoubtedly tells him it isn't necessary. But York's manager has to come out and settle the pitcher down, to point out the obvious: *You have two outs and first base was open anyway. There's no problem.*

But for Tarbox there *is* a problem. He has hit two boys this inning, hit both of them hard enough to make them cry. If that weren't a problem, he would need a mental examination.

York puts together three singles to score two runs in the top of the third, opening up a 3–0 lead. If these runs, both solidly earned, had come

1020

in the top of the first, Bangor would have been in serious trouble, but when the players come in for their raps they look eager and excited. There is no feeling among them that the game is lost, no whiff of failure.

Ryan Iarrobino is Bangor's first batter in the bottom of the third, and Tarbox works him carefully — too carefully. He has begun to aim the ball, and the result is fairly predictable. With the count at 1-2, he plinks Iarrobino on the shoulder. Iarrobino turns and pounds his bat once on the ground — whether in pain, frustration, or anger is impossible to tell. Most probably it is all three. Reading the mood of the crowd is much easier. The Bangor fans are on their feet, yelling angrily at Tarbox and at the ump. On the York side, the fans are silent and bewildered; it is not the game they were expecting. As Ryan trots down to first, he glances over at Tarbox. It is brief, that glance, but it seems clear enough: *That's the third time, you. Make it the last time.*

Tarbox confers briefly with his coach, then faces Matt Kinney. His confidence is in shambles, and his first pitch to Matt, a wild one, suggests that he wants to continue pitching this game about as much as a cat wants a bubble bath. Iarrobino beats York catcher Dan Bouchard's throw to second easily. Tarbox walks Kinney. The next batter is Kevin Rochefort. After two failed bunt attempts, Roach settles back and allows Phil Tarbox the chance to dig his hole a little deeper. He does, walking Kevin after having him 1-1. Tarbox has now thrown more than sixty pitches in less than three innings.

Roger Fisher also goes 3-2 with Tarbox, who is now relying almost exclusively on soft breaking stuff; he seems to have decided that if he does hit another batter he will not hit him hard. There is no place to put Fish; the bases are jammed. Tarbox knows it and takes a calculated risk, grooving another one, believing Fish will lay off in the hope of a walk. Roger snaps hungrily at it instead, bouncing one between first and second for a base hit. Iarrobino trots home with Bangor's first run.

Owen King, the player who was at bat when Phil Tarbox started to self-destruct, is the next batter. The York coach, suspecting his ace will work even less successfully to King this time, has seen enough. Matt Francke comes in to relieve, and Tarbox becomes York's catcher. As he squats behind the plate to warm Francke up, he looks both resigned and relieved. Francke doesn't hit anyone, but he is unable to stop the bleeding. At the end of three innings, Bangor West has only two hits, but they lead York, 5–3.

It is now the fifth inning. The air is full of gray moisture, and the YORK IS BRISTOL BOUND banner tacked to the scoreboard uprights has begun to sag. The fans look a little saggy themselves, and increasingly uneasy. *Is* York Bristol bound? *Well, we're supposed to be,* their faces say, *but it's the fifth inning now, and we're still two runs behind. My God, how did it get so late so early?*

Roger Fisher continues to cruise, and in the bottom of the fifth Bangor West puts what appear to be the final nails in York's coffin. Mike Arnold leads off with a single. Joe Wilcox sacrifices pinch-runner Fred Moore to second, and Iarrobino doubles off Francke, scoring Moore. This brings Matt Kinney to the plate. After a passed ball advances Ryan to third, Kinney hits an easy grounder to short, but it squirts off the infielder's glove and Iarrobino trots home.

Bangor West takes the field jubilantly, owning a 7–3 lead and only needing three more outs.

When Roger Fisher takes the mound to face York in the top of the sixth, he has thrown ninety-seven pitches, and he's a tired boy. He shows it at once by walking pinch-hitter Tim Pollack on a full count. Dave and Neil have seen enough. Fisher goes to second base, and Mike Arnold, who has been warming up between innings, takes over on the mound. He is ordinarily a good reliever, but it's not his day. Tension, maybe, or maybe it's just that the damp dirt of the mound has caused a change in his normal motion. He gets Francke to fly out, but then Bouchard walks, Philbrick doubles, and Pollack, the runner charged to Fish, scores, and Bouchard is held up at third; by itself, Pollack's run means nothing. The important thing is that York now has runners on second and third, and the potential tying run is coming to the plate. The potential tying run is someone with a very personal interest in getting a hit, because he is the main reason York is only two outs away from extinction. The potential tying run is Phil Tarbox.

Mike works the count to 1-1, and then throws a fastball right down the middle of the plate. In the Bangor West dugout, Dave Mansfield winces and raises one hand toward his forehead in a warding-off gesture even as Tarbox begins his swing. There is the hard sound of Tarbox accomplishing that most difficult of baseball feats: using the round bat to hit the round ball squarely on the button.

Ryan Iarrobino takes off the instant Tarbox connects, but he runs out of room much too early. The ball clears the fence by twenty feet, bangs off a TV camera, and bounces back onto the field. Ryan looks at it disconsolately as the York fans go mad, and the entire York team boils out of the dugout to greet Tarbox, who has hit a three-run homer and redeemed himself in spectacular fashion. He does not step on home plate but *jumps* on it. His face wears an expression of near-beatific satisfaction. He is mobbed by his ecstatic teammates; on his way back to the dugout, his feet are barely allowed to touch the ground.

The Bangor fans sit in silence, utterly stunned by this awful reversal. Yesterday, against Lewiston, Bangor flirted with disaster; today they have swooned in its arms. Mo has changed sides again, and the fans are clearly afraid that this time it has changed for good. Mike Arnold confers with Dave and Neil. They are telling him to go on back and pitch hard, that the game is only tied, not lost, but Mike is clearly a dejected, unhappy boy.

The next batter, Hutchins, hits an easy two-hopper to Matt Kinney, but Arnold is not the only one who is shaken; the usually dependable Kinney boots the ball, and Hutchins is on. Andy Estes pops out to Rochefort at third, but Hutchins advances to second on a passed ball. King grabs Matt Hoyt's pop-up for the third out, and Bangor West is out of trouble.

The team has a chance to put it away in the bottom of the sixth, except that doesn't quite happen, either. They go one-two-three against Matt Francke, and all at once Bangor West is in its first extra-innings game of postseason play, tied 7–7 with York.

During the game against Lewiston, the muddy weather eventually unravelled. Not today. As Bangor West takes the field in the top of the seventh, the skies grow steadily darker. It's now approaching six o'clock, and even under these conditions the field should still be clear and fairly bright, but fog has begun to creep in. Watching a videotape of the game would make someone who wasn't there believe something was wrong with the TV cameras; everything looks listless, dull, underexposed. Shirtsleeve fans in the center-field bleachers are becoming disembodied heads and hands; in the outfield, Trzaskos, Iarrobino, and Arthur Dorr are discernible chiefly by their shirts.

Just before Mike throws the first pitch of the seventh, Neil elbows Dave and points out to right field. Dave immediately calls time and trots out to see what's the matter with Arthur Dorr, who is standing bent over, with his head almost between his knees.

Arthur looks up at Dave with some surprise as he approaches. "I'm O.K.," he says in answer to the unspoken question.

"Then what in hell are you doing?" Dave asks.

"Looking for four-leaf clovers," Arthur responds.

Dave is too flabbergasted, or too amused, to lecture the boy. He simply tells Arthur it might be more appropriate to look for them after the game is over.

Arthur glances around at the creeping fog before looking back at Dave. "I think by then it's gonna be too dark," he says.

With Arthur set to rights, the game can continue, and Mike Arnold does a creditable job — possibly because he's facing the substitute-riddled bottom of York's order. York does not score, and Bangor comes up in the bottom of the seventh with another chance to win it.

They come close to doing just that. With the bases loaded and two out, Roger Fisher hits one hard up the first-base line. Matt Hoyt is right there to pounce on it, however, and the teams change sides again.

Philbrick flies out to Nick Trzaskos to open the eighth, and then Phil Tarbox steps in. Tarbox is not finished working Bangor West over yet. He has regained his confidence; his face is utterly serene as he takes Mike's first pitch for a called strike. He swings at the next one, a pretty decent changeup that bounces off Joe Wilcox's shin guard. He steps out of the box, squats with the bat between his knees, and concentrates. This is a Zen technique the York coach has taught these boys — Francke has done it several times on the mound while in tight spots — and it works for Tarbox this time, along with a little help from Mike Arnold.

Arnold's final pitch to Tarbox is a hanging curve up in the batter's eyes, exactly where Dave and Neil hoped no pitch would be today, and Tarbox creams it. It goes deep to left center, high over the fence. There is no camera stanchion to stop this one; it ends up in the woods, and the York fans are on their feet again, chanting "Phil-Phil-Phil" as Tarbox circles third, comes down the line, and jumps high in the air. He doesn't just jump on home plate; he *spikes* it.

Nor, it seems at first, will that be all. Hutchins bangs a single up the middle and gets second on an error. Estes follows this by hitting one to third, and Rochefort throws badly to second. Luckily, Roger Fisher is backed up by Arthur Dorr, saving a second run, but now York has guys at first and second with only one out.

Dave calls Owen King in to pitch, and Mike Arnold moves over to first. Following a wild pitch that moves the runners up to second and third, Matt Hoyt bangs one on the ground to Kevin Rochefort. In the game that Bangor West lost to Hampden, Casey Kinney was able to come back and make the play after committing an error. Rochefort does it today, and in spades. He comes up with the ball, then holds it for a moment, making sure Hutchins isn't going to break for the plate. *Then* he throws across the diamond to Mike, getting the slow-running Matt Hoyt by two steps. Considering the wringer these boys have been through, it is an incredibly canny piece of baseball. Bangor West has recovered itself, and King works Ryan Fernald — who hit a three-run homer against Yarmouth — perfectly, nipping at the corners, using his weirdly effective sidearm delivery to supplement the over-the-top fastball. Fernald pops weakly to first and the inning is over. At the end of seven and a half, York leads Bangor, 8–7. Six of York's RBIs belong to Philip Tarbox.

Matt Francke, York's pitcher, is as tired as

Fisher was when Dave finally elected to replace him with Mike Arnold. The difference is that Dave *had* a Mike Arnold and, behind Mike, an Owen King. The York coach has no one; he used Ryan Fernald against Yarmouth, making him ineligible to pitch today, and now it's Francke forever.

He starts off the eighth well enough, striking out King. Arthur Dorr comes up next, one for four on the day (a double off Tarbox). Francke, obviously struggling now but just as obviously determined to finish this game, goes full with Arthur, then serves one up that's way outside. Arthur trots down to first.

Mike Arnold comes up next. It wasn't his day on the mound, but he does well this time at the plate, laying down a perfect bunt. The intent is not to sacrifice; Mike is bunting for the base hit, and almost gets it. But the ball will not quite die in that soggy patch between home and the pitcher's mound. Francke snatches it, glances toward second, and then elects to go to first. Now there are two men out with a runner at second. Bangor West is an out away from the end.

Joe Wilcox, the catcher, is up next. With the count 2-1, he hits a chalk hugger up the first-base line. Matt Hoyt grabs it, but just an instant too late; he takes the ball less than half a foot into foul territory, and the first-base umpire is right there to call it. Hoyt, who has been ready to charge the mound and embrace Matt Francke, instead returns the ball.

Now the count on Joey is 2-2. Francke steps off the rubber, stares straight up into the sky, and concentrates. Then he steps back on and delivers one high and out of the strike zone. Joey goes for it anyway, not even looking, swinging in self-defense. The bat makes contact with the ball — pure luck — and it bounces foul. Francke does the concentration bit again, then throws — just outside. Ball three.

Now comes what may be the pitch of the game. It *appears* to be a high strike, a game-ending strike, but the umpire calls ball four. Joe Wilcox trots down to first base with a faint expression of disbelief on his face. It is only later, watching the slow-motion replay on the TV tape of the game, that one can see how right, and how good, the umpire's call was. Joe Wilcox, so anxious that he is pinwheeling the bat in his hands like a golf club right up to the moment of the pitch, rises on his tiptoes as the ball approaches, and this is the reason it appears to be letter-high to him as it crosses the plate. The umpire, who never moves, discounts all of Joe's nervous tics and makes a major league call. The rules say you cannot shrink the strike zone by crouching; by the same token, you cannot expand it by stretching. If Joe hadn't gone up on his toes, Francke's pitch would have been throat-high instead of letter-high. So, instead of becoming the third out and ending the game, Joe becomes another base runner.

One of the TV cameras was trained on York's Matt Francke as he made the pitch, and it caught a remarkable image. A video replay shows Francke light up as the ball breaks downward just a moment too late to earn the strike. His pitching hand comes up in a victorious fisted salute. At this moment, he begins to move to his right, toward the York dugout, and the umpire blocks him out. When he returns to view a second later, his expression has become one of unhappiness and incredulity. He does not argue with the call — these kids are taught not to do that in their regular seasons, and to never, never, *never* do it in a championship situation — but as he prepares to work the next batter Francke appears to be crying.

Bangor West is still alive, and as Nick Trzaskos approaches the plate they come to their feet and begin to yell. Nick is obviously hoping for a free ride, and he gets one. Francke walks him on five pitches. It is the eleventh walk given up by York pitching today. Nick trots down to first, loading the bases, and Ryan Iarrobino steps in. Again and again, it has been Ryan Iarrobino in these situations, and now it is Ryan once more. The Bangor West fans are on their feet, screaming. The Bangor players crowd the dugout, fingers hooked through the mesh, watching anxiously.

"I can't believe it," one of the TV commentators says. "I can't believe the script of this game."

His partner chips in, "Well, I'll tell you what. Either way, this is how both teams would want the game to end."

As he speaks, the camera offers its own ghastly counterpoint to the comment by focusing on the stricken face of Matt Francke. The image strongly suggests that this is the *last* thing the York lefty wanted. Why would he? Iarrobino has doubled twice, walked twice, and been hit by a pitch. York hasn't retired him a single time. Francke throws high and outside, then low. These are his 135th and 136th pitches. The boy is exhausted. Chuck

1030

Bittner, the York manager, calls him over for a brief conference. Iarrobino waits for the conference to end, then steps in again.

Matt Francke concentrates, head back and eyes closed; he looks like a baby bird waiting to be fed. Then he winds up and throws the last pitch of the Maine Little League season.

Iarrobino has not been watching the concentration bit. His head is down; he is only watching to see how Francke will come, and his eyes never leave the ball. It is a fastball, low and tailing toward the outside corner of the plate. Ryan Iarrobino dips a little. The head of the bat whips around. He catches all of this one, really cranks it, and as the ball flies out of the park to deep right-center field, his arms shoot up over his head and he begins to tap-dance deliriously down the first-base line.

On the mound, Matt Francke, who was twice within inches of winning his game, lowers his head, not wanting to look. And as Ryan rounds second and starts back toward home, he seems to finally understand what he has done, and at that point he begins to weep.

The fans are in hysterics; the sports commentators are in hysterics; even Dave and Neil seem close to hysterics as they block the plate, making room for Ryan to touch it. Rounding third, he passes the umpire there, who is still twirling one magisterial finger in the gray air, signalling home run.

Behind the plate, Phil Tarbox takes off his mask and walks away from the celebration. He stamps his foot once, his face clenched with deep frustration. He walks off-camera and out of Little

1031

League for good. He will play Babe Ruth ball next year, and probably he will play it well, but there will be no more games like this for Tarbox, or for any of these boys. This one is, as they say, in the books.

Ryan Iarrobino, laughing, crying, holding his helmet on his head with one hand and pointing straight up to the gray sky with the other, leaps high, comes down on home plate, and then leaps again, straight into the arms of his teammates, who bear him away in triumph. The game is over; Bangor West has won, 11–8. They are Maine's 1989 Little League Champions.

I look toward the fence on the first-base side and see a remarkable sight: a forest of waving hands. The parents of the players have crowded against the chain-link and are reaching across the top to touch their sons. Many of the parents are also in tears. The boys all wear identical expressions of happy disbelief, and all these hands — hundreds of them, it seems — wave toward them, wanting to touch, wanting to congratulate, wanting to hug, wanting to *feel*.

The boys ignore them. Later, there will be touches and hugs. First, however, there is business to take care of. They line up and slap hands with the boys from York, crossing at home plate in the ritual manner. Most of the boys on both teams are crying now, some so hard they can barely walk.

Then, in the instant before the Bangor boys go to the fence, where all those hands are still waving, they surround their coaches and pummel them and each other in joyful triumph. They have held on to win their tournament — Ryan and Matt, Owen and Arthur, Mike and Roger Fisher, finder of four-leaf clovers. At this moment they are cheering each other, and everything else will just have to wait. Then they break for the fence, going toward their crying, cheering, laughing parents, and the world begins to turn in its ordinary course once again.

"How long are we gonna keep on playing, Coach?" J. J. Fiddler asked Neil Waterman after Bangor clinched the division against Machias.

"J.J.," Neil replied, "we're gonna play until someone makes us stop."

The team that finally made Bangor West stop was Westfield, Massachusetts. Bangor West played them in the second round of the Eastern Regional Little League Championship, at Bristol, Connecticut, on August 15th, 1989. Matt Kinney pitched for Bangor West and threw the game of his life, striking out nine, walking five (one intentional), and giving up only three hits. Bangor West, however, got only one hit off Westfield pitcher Tim Laurita, and that one belonged, predictably enough, to Ryan Iarrobino. The final score was 2–1, Westfield. Credit Bangor's one RBI in the game to King, on a bases-loaded walk. Credit the game-winning RBI to Laurita, also on a bases-loaded walk. It was a hell of a game, a purist's game, but it couldn't match the one against York.

In the pro world, it was a bad year for baseball. A future Hall of Famer was banned from the sport for life; a retired pitcher shot his wife and then took his own life; the commissioner suffered a fatal heart attack; the first World Series game to be played at Candlestick Park in over twenty years was postponed when an earthquake shook north-ern California. But the majors are only a small part of what baseball is about. In other places and in other leagues — Little League, for instance, where there are no free agents, no salaries, and no gate admissions — it was a pretty fine year. The Eastern Regional Tournament winner was Trumbull, Connecticut. On August 26, 1989, Trumbull beat Taiwan to win the Little League World Series. It was the first time an American team had won the Williamsport World Series since 1983, and the first time in fourteen years that the winner had come from the region in which Bangor West plays.

In September, the Maine division of the United States Baseball Federation voted Dave Mansfield amateur coach of the year.

Brooklyn August

(FOR JIM BISHOP)

In Ebbets Field the crabgrass grows
(where Alston managed)
row on row
      as the day's axle turns into twilight
      I still see them, with the green smell
      of just-mown infield grass heavy
      in the darkening end of the day:
      picked out by the right-field floods, just
      turned on and already assaulted by
      battalions of circling moths
      and bugs on the night shift;
      below, old men and offduty taxi drivers
      are drinking big cups of Schlitz in the
        75¢ seats,
      this Flatbush as real as velvet Harlem streets
      where jive packs the jukes in the June of '56.
In Ebbets Field the infield's slow
and seats are empty, row on row
      Hodges is hulked over first, glove stretched
      to touch the throw from Robinson at third,
      the batters' boxes float in the ghost-glow
      of this sky-filled Friday evening
      (Musial homered early, Flatbush is down by 2).

Newcombe trudged to an early shower through
a shower of popcorn and newspaper headlines.
Carl Erskine is in now and chucking hard but
Johnny Podres and Clem Labine are heating
in case he blows up late;
he can, you know, they all can
In Ebbets Field they come and go
and play their innings, blow by blow
    time's called in the dimness of the 5th
    someone chucked a beer at Sandy Amoros
       in right
    he spears the empty cup without a word
    and hands it to a groundkeeper chewing
       Mail Pouch
    while the faceless fans cry down juicy Brooklyn
       vowels,
    a plague on both their houses.
    Pee Wee Reese leans on his knees west of
       second
    Campanella gives the sign
    with my eyes closed I see it all
    smell steamed franks and 8 pm dirt
    can see those heavenly shades of evening
    they swim with angels above the stadium dish
    as Erskine winds and wheels and throws
       low-inside:

Notes

Not long after I published *Skeleton Crew,* my previous book of short stories, I spoke to a reader who told me how much she had liked it. She had been able to ration the stories out, she said — one a night for about three weeks. "I skipped the notes at the end, though," she said, keeping a close eye on me as she said it (I think she believed I might leap upon her in my anger at this terrible affront). "I'm one of those people who don't want to know how the magician does his tricks."

I simply nodded and told her that was her perfect right, not wanting to get into a long, involved discussion on the subject when I had errands to run, but I have no errands this morning, and I want to make two things perfectly clear, as our old pal from San Clemente used to say. First, I don't care if you read the notes that follow or not. It's your book, and you can wear it on your head in a horserace for all of me. Second, I am *not* a magician and these are *not* tricks.

That's not to say there isn't magic involved in writing; I happen to believe that there is, and that it twines around fiction with particular luxuriance. The paradox is this: magicians don't have anything to do with magic, as most of them will readily admit. Their undeniable wonders — doves from handkerchiefs, coins from empty pitchers, silk scarves from empty hands — are achieved through exhaustive practice and well-tested misdirections and sleights of hand. Their talk of "ancient secrets of the Orient" and "the forgotten lore of Atlantis" is so much patter. I suspect that, by and large, stage-magicians would deeply identify with the old joke about the out-of-towner who asks the New York beatnik how to get to Carnegie Hall. "Practice, man, practice," the beatnik replies.

All that goes for writers, too. After twenty years of writing popular fiction and being dismissed by the more intellectual critics as a hack (the intellectual's definition of a hack seems to be "an artist whose work is appreciated by too many people"), I will gladly testify that craft is terribly important, that the often tiresome process of draft, redraft, and then draft again is necessary to produce good work, and that hard work is the only acceptable practice for those of us who have some talent but little or no genius.

Still, there *is* magic in this job, and it comes most frequently at that instant when a story pops into a writer's head, usually as a fragment but sometimes as a complete thing (and having that happen is a little like being hit by a tactical nuke). The writer can later relate where he was when that happened, and what the elements were that combined to give him his idea, but the *idea itself* is a new thing, a sum greater than its parts, something that is created from nothing. It is, to paraphrase Marianne Moore, a real toad in an imaginary garden. So you need not fear to read the notes that follow on the grounds that I will spoil the magic by telling you how the tricks work.

There are no tricks to real magic; when it comes to real magic, there is only history.

It *is* possible to spoil a story which hasn't been read yet, however, and so if you're one of those people (one of those *awful* people) who feel a compulsion to read the last thing in a book first, like a willful child who is determined to eat his or her chocolate pudding before touching the meatloaf, I'm going to invite you to get the hell out of here, lest you suffer what may be the worst of all curses: disenchantment. For the rest of you, here is a whirlwind tour of how some of the stories in *Nightmares and Dreamscapes* happened to happen.

"Dolan's Cadillac" — I'd guess the train of thought which led to this story is pretty obvious. I was idling my way through one of those seemingly endless road-repair sites where you breathe a lot of dust, tar, and exhaust and sit looking at the ass end of the same station wagon and the same I BRAKE FOR ANIMALS bumper sticker for what feels like about nine years . . . only the car in front of me that day was a big green Cadillac Sedan DeVille. As we inched our way past an excavation where huge cylinders of pipe were being laid, I remember thinking, *Even a car as big as that Cadillac would fit in there.* A moment later I had the idea of "Dolan's Cadillac" firmly in place, fully developed, and none of the narrative elements ever changed so much as an iota.

That is not to say the story was an easy birth; it most definitely was not. I have never been so daunted — so nearly overwhelmed, in fact — by technical details. Now I'll give you what the

Reader's Digest likes to call A Personal Glimpse: although I like to think of myself as a literary version of James Brown (the self-styled "Hardest-Working Man in Show Business"), I am an extremely lazy sod when it comes to research and technical details. I have been twigged again and again by readers and critics (most accurately and humiliatingly by Avram Davidson, who writes for the *Chicago Tribune* and *Fantasy and Science Fiction* magazine) for my lapses in these areas. When writing "Dolan's Cadillac," I came to realize that this time I could not simply fudge my way through, because the story's entire underpinning depended on various scientific details, mathematical formulae, and the postulates of physics.

If I had discovered this unpalatable truth sooner — before I had roughly 15,000 words already invested in the story of Dolan, Elizabeth, and Elizabeth's Poe-esque husband, that is — I undoubtedly would have consigned "Dolan's Cadillac" to The Department of Unfinished Stories. But I *didn't* discover it sooner, I *didn't* want to stop, and so I did the only thing I could think of: I called my big brother and asked for help.

Dave King is what we New Englanders call "a piece of work," a child prodigy with a tested IQ of over 150 (you will find reflections of Dave in Bow-Wow Fornoy's genius brother in "The End of the Whole Mess") who went through school as if on a rocket-sled, finishing college at eighteen and going right to work as a high-school math teacher at Brunswick High. Many of his remedial algebra students were older than he was. Dave was the youngest man ever to be elected Town

Selectman in the state of Maine, and was a Town Manager at the age of twenty-five or so. He is a genuine polymath, a man who knows something about just about everything.

I explained my problems to my brother over the telephone. A week later I received a manila envelope from him and opened it with a sinking heart. I was sure he'd sent me the information I needed, but I was equally sure it would do me no good; my brother's handwriting is absolutely awful.

To my delight, I found a videocassette. When I plugged it in, I saw Dave sitting at a table piled high with dirt. Using several toy Matchbox cars, he explained everything I needed to know, including that wonderfully ominous stuff about the arc of descent. Dave also told me that my protagonist would have to use highway equipment in order to bury Dolan's Cadillac (in the original story he did it by hand), and explained exactly how to jump-start the big machines your local Highway Department is apt to leave around at various road-repair sites. This information was extremely good . . . a little *too* good, in fact. I changed just enough so that if anyone tries it according to the recipe in the story, nothing will happen.

One last point about this story: when it was finished, I hated it. Absolutely *loathed* it. It was never published in a magazine; it simply went into one of the cardboard boxes of Bad Old Stuff I keep in the hallway behind my office. A few years later, Herb Yellin, who publishes gorgeous limited editions in his function as head of Lord John Press, wrote and asked if he could do a limited edition of one of my short stories, preferably an unpublished one. Because I love his books, which are small, beautifully made, and often extremely eccentric, I went out into what I think of as the Hallway of Doom and hunted through my boxes to see if there was anything salvageable.

I came across "Dolan's Cadillac," and once again time had done its work — it read a lot better than I remembered, and when I sent it to Herb, he agreed enthusiastically. I made further revisions and it was published in a small Lord John Press edition of about five hundred copies. I have revised it again for its appearance here, and have changed my opinion of it enough to have put it in the lead-off position. If nothing else, it's a kind of archetypal horror story, with its mad narrator and its account of a premature burial in the desert. But this particular story really isn't mine anymore; it belongs to Dave King and Herb Yellin. Thanks, guys.

"Suffer the Little Children" — This story is from the same period as most of the stories in *Night Shift*, and was originally published in *Cavalier*, as were most of the stories in that 1978 collection. It was left out because my editor, Bill Thompson, felt the book was getting "unwieldy" — this is the way editors sometimes tell writers that they have to cut a little before the price of the book soars out of sight. I voted to cut a story called "Gray Matter" from *Night Shift*. Bill voted to cut "Suffer the Little Children." I deferred to his judgement, and read the story over carefully before deciding to include it here. I like it quite a lot

— it feels a little bit like the Bradbury of the late forties and early fifties to me, the fiendish Bradbury who revelled in killer babies, renegade undertakers, and tales only a Crypt-Keeper could love. Put another way, "Suffer the Little Children" is a ghastly sick-joke with no redeeming social merit whatever. I like that in a story.

"The Night Flier" — Sometimes a supporting character in a novel catches a writer's attention and refuses to go away, insisting he has more to say and do. Richard Dees, the protagonist of "The Night Flier," is such a character. He originally appeared in *The Dead Zone* (1979), where he offers Johnny Smith, the doomed hero of that novel, a job as a psychic on his awful paper, the supermarket tabloid *Inside View*. Johnny throws him off the porch of his dad's house, and that was supposed to be the end of him. Yet here he is again.

Like most of my stories, "The Night Flier" started off as nothing but a lark — a vampire with a private pilot's license, how amusingly *modrun* — but it grew as Dees grew. I rarely *understand* my characters, any more than I understand the lives and hearts of the real people I meet every day, but I find that it's sometimes possible to *plot* them, as a cartographer plots his or her maps. As I worked on "The Night Flier," I began to glimpse a man of profound alienation, a man who seemed to somehow sum up some of the most terrible and confusing things about our supposedly open society in the last quarter of the century. Dees is the essential unbeliever, and his confrontation with the Night Flier at the end of the story recalls that

George Seferis line I used in *'Salem's Lot* — the one about the column of truth having a hole in it. In these latter days of the twentieth century, that seems to be all too true, and "The Night Flier" is mostly about one man's discovery of that hole.

"Popsy" — Is this little boy's grandfather the same creature that demands Richard Dees open his camera and expose his film at the conclusion of "The Night Flier"? You know, I rather think he is.

"It Grows on You" — A version of this story was originally published in a University of Maine literary magazine called *Marshroots* back in the early seventies, but the version in this book is almost entirely different. As I read through the original story, I began to realize that these old men were actually the survivors of the debacle described in *Needful Things*. That novel is a black comedy about greed and obsession; this is a more serious story about secrets and sickness. It seems a fitting epilogue to the novel . . . and it was great to glimpse some of my old Castle Rock friends one last time.

"Dedication" — For years, since I first met and was appalled by a now-dead famous writer, whom I will not name here, I have been troubled by the question of why some enormously talented people turn out to be such utter shits in person — woman-pawing sexists, racists, sneering elitists, or cruel practical jokers. I'm not saying that *most* talented or famous people are this way, but I have met enough who are — including that one undeniably great writer — to wonder why. This story was written as an effort to answer that question to my own satisfaction. The effort failed, but I was at least able to articulate my own unease, and in this case, that seemed enough.

It's not a very politically correct story, and I think a lot of readers — the ones who want to be scared by the same comfy old bogies and fun-house demons — are going to be outraged by it. I hope so; I've been doing this job for quite awhile now, but I like to think I'm not quite ready for the old rocking chair yet. The stories in *Nightmares and Dreamscapes* are, for the most part, the sort that critics categorize (and then all too often dismiss, alas) as horror stories, and the horror story is supposed to be a kind of evil-tempered junkyard dog that will bite you if you get too close. This one bites, I think. Am I going to apologize for that? Do you think I should? Isn't that — the risk of being bitten — one of the reasons you picked this book up in the first place? I think so. And if you get thinking of me as your kindly old Uncle Stevie, a sort of end-of-the-century Rod Serling, I will try even harder to bite you. To put it another way, I want you to be a little bit afraid every time you step into my parlor. I want you unsure about how far I'll go, or what I may do next.

Now that I've said all that, just let me add that if I really thought "Dedication" needed to be defended, I never would have offered it for publication in the first place. A story that can't serve as its own defense lawyer doesn't *deserve* to be published. It's Martha Rosewall, the humble maid, who wins this battle, not Peter Jefferies, the big-shot writer, and that should tell the reader all he or she needs to know about where my sympathies lie.

Oh, one other thing. It seems to me now that this story, originally published in 1985, was a trial cut for a novel called *Dolores Claiborne* (1992).

"The Moving Finger" — My favorite sort of short story has always been the kind where things happen just because they happen. In novels and movies (save for movies starring fellows like Sylvester Stallone and Arnold Schwarzenegger), you are supposed to explain *why* things happen. Let me tell you something, friends and neighbors: I *hate* explaining why things happen, and my efforts in that direction (such as the doctored LSD and resultant DNA changes which create Charlie McGee's pyrokinetic talents in *Firestarter*) aren't very good. But real life very rarely has what movie producers are this year calling "a motivation through-line" — have you noticed that? I don't know about you, but nobody ever issued me an instruction manual; I'm just muddling along as best I can, knowing I'm never going to get out of it alive but trying not to fuck up too badly in the meantime.

In short stories, the author is sometimes still allowed to say, "This happened. Don't ask me why." The story of poor Howard Mitla is that sort of tale, and it seems to me that his efforts to deal with the finger that pokes out of his bathroom drain during a quiz-show form a perfectly valid metaphor for how we cope with the nasty surprises life holds in store for all of us: the tumors, the accidents, the occasional nightmarish coincidence. It is the unique province of the fantasy story to be able to answer the question "Why do bad things happen to good people?" by replying, "Feh — don't ask." In a tale of fantasy, this gloomy answer actually seems to satisfy us. In the end, it may be the genre's chief moral asset: at its best, it can open a window (or a confessional screen) on the existential aspects of our mortal lives. It ain't perpetual motion . . . but it ain't bad, either.

"You Know They Got a Hell of a Band" — There are at least two stories in this book about what the lead female character here thinks of as "the peculiar little town." This is one; "Rainy Season" is the other. There will be readers who may think I've visited "the peculiar little town" once or twice too often, and some may note similarities between these two pieces and an earlier story of mine, "Children of the Corn." There *are* similarities, but does that mean "Band" and "Season" are lapses into self-imitation? It's a delicate question, and one each reader must answer for him- or herself, but my answer is no (of *course* it is, what else am I gonna say?).

There's a big difference, it seems to me, between working in traditional forms and self-imitation. Take the blues, for instance. There are really only two classic guitar chord-progressions for the blues, and those two progressions are essentially the same. Now, answer me this — just because John Lee Hooker plays almost everything he ever wrote in the key of E or the key of A, does that mean he's running on auto-pilot, doing the same thing over and over again? Plenty of John Lee Hooker fans (not to mention fans of Bo Diddley, Muddy Waters, Furry Lewis, and all the other greats) would say it doesn't. It's not the key you *play* it in, these blues *aficionados* would say; it's the soul you *sing* it with.

Same thing here. There are certain horror-tale archetypes which stand out with the authority of mesas in the desert. The haunted-house story; the return-from-the-grave story; the peculiar-little-town story. It's not really about what it's about, if you can dig that; this is, by and large, the literature of the nerve-endings and the muscle-receptors, and as such, it's really about what you *feel*. What I felt here — the impetus for the story — was how authentically creepy it is that so many rockers have died young, or under nasty circumstances; it's an actuarial expert's nightmare. Many younger fans view the high mortality rate as romantic, but when you've boogied your way from The Platters to Ice T, as I have, you start to see a darker side, a crawling kingsnake side. That's what I've tried to express here, although I don't think the story really starts to move and groove and creep and crawl until the last six or eight pages.

"Home Delivery" — This is probably the only story in the book which was written to order. John Skipp and Craig Spector (*The Light at the End, The Bridge,* plus several other good horror splatterpunk-ish novels) came up with the idea of an anthology of stories exploring what things would be like if George Romero's zombies from his *Dead* trilogy (*Night of, Dawn of, Day of*) took over the world. The concept fired off in my imagination like a Roman candle, and this story, set off the coast of Maine, was the result.

"My Pretty Pony" — In the early eighties, Richard Bachman was struggling to write a novel called (naturally enough, I suppose) *My Pretty Pony*. The novel was about an independent hit-man named Clive Banning who is hired to put together a string of like-minded psychopaths and kill a number of powerful crime figures at a wedding. Banning and his string succeed, turning the wedding into a bloodbath, and are then double-crossed by their employers, who begin picking them off, one by one. The novel was to chronicle Banning's efforts to escape the cataclysm he had induced.

The book was a bad piece of work, born in an unhappy time of my life when a lot of things which had been working pretty well for me up until then suddenly fell over with a resounding crash. Richard Bachman died during this period, leaving two fragments behind: an almost complete novel called *Machine's Way* under *his* pseudonym, George Stark, and six chapters of *My Pretty Pony*. As Richard's literary executor, I worked *Machine's Way* up into a novel called *The Dark Half* and published it under my own name (I did acknowledge Bachman, however). *My Pretty Pony* I junked . . . except for a brief flashback in which Banning, while waiting to begin his assault on the wedding party, remembers how his grandfather instructed him on the plastic nature of time. Finding that flashback — marvellously complete, almost a short story as it stood — was like finding a rose growing

1049

in a junkheap. I plucked it, and I did so with great gratitude. It turned out to be one of the few good things I wrote during an extremely bad year.

"My Pretty Pony" was originally published in an overpriced (and overdesigned, in my humble opinion) edition produced by the Whitney Museum. It was later issued in a slightly more accessible (but still overpriced and overdesigned, in my humble opinion) edition by Alfred A. Knopf. And here, I am pleased to see it, polished and slightly clarified, as it probably should have been in the first place — just another short story, a little better than some, not so good as others.

"Sorry, Right Number" — Remember how I started off, about a billion pages ago, talking about *Ripley's Believe It or Not*? Well, "Sorry, Right Number" almost belongs in it. The idea occurred to me as a "teleplaylet" one night on my way home from buying a pair of shoes. It came as a "visual," I suppose, because the telecast of a film plays such a central part. I wrote it, pretty much as it is presented here, in two sittings. My West Coast agent — the one who does film deals — had it by the end of the week. Early the following week, Steven Spielberg read it for *Amazing Stories,* a TV series which he then had in production (but which had not yet begun to air).

Spielberg rejected it — they were looking for *Amazing Stories* that were a little more upbeat, he said — and so I took it to my long-time collaborator and good friend, Richard Rubinstein, who then had a series called *Tales from the Darkside* running in syndication. I won't say Richard blows his nose on happy endings — he likes a happily-ever-after as well as anyone, I think — but he's never shied away from a downer; he was the guy who got *Pet Sematary* made, after all (*Pet Sematary* and *Thelma and Louise* are, I think, the only major Hollywood films to end with the death of a major character or characters since the late 1970s).

Richard bought "Sorry" the day he read it, and had it in production a week or two later. A month after that, it was telecast . . . as a season premiere, if my recollection serves. It is still one of the fastest turns from in-the-head to on-the-screen that I've ever heard of. This version, by the way, is my first draft, which is a little longer and a little more textured than the final shooting script, which for budgetary reasons specified just two sets. It is included here as an example of another kind of story-telling . . . different, but as valid as any other.

"The Ten O'Clock People" — During the summer of 1992 I was walking around downtown Boston, looking for an address that kept eluding me. I eventually found the place I was looking for, but before I did, I found this story. My address-hunt took place around ten in the morning, and as I walked I began to notice groups of people clustered in front of every expensive highrise building, groups that made no sociological sense. There were carpenters hobnobbing with business-men, janitors shooting the breeze with elegantly coiffed women in power clothes, messengers passing the time of day with executive secretaries.

After I'd puzzled over these groups — *granfalloons* Kurt Vonnegut never imagined — for half an hour or so, the penny dropped: for a certain class of American city dweller, addiction has turned the coffee-break into the cigarette-break. The expensive buildings are now all no-smoking zones as the American people go calmly about one of the most amazing turnabouts of the twentieth century; we are purging ourselves of our bad old habit, we are doing it with hardly any fanfare, and the result has been some very odd pockets of sociological behavior. Those who refuse to give up their bad old habit — the Ten O'Clock People of the title — constitute one of these. The story is intended as no more than a simple amusement, but I hope it says something interesting about a wave of change which has, temporarily, at least, re-created some aspects of the separate-but-equal facilities of the forties and fifties.

"The House on Maple Street" — Remember Richard Rubinstein, my producer friend? He was the guy who sent me my first copy of Chris Van Allsburg's *The Mysteries of Harris Burdick*. Richard attached a note in his spiky handwriting: "You'll like this" was all it said, and all it really *needed* to say. I *did* like it.

The book purports to be a series of drawings, titles, and captions by the eponymous Mr. Burdick — the stories themselves are not in evidence. Each combination of picture, title, and caption serves as a kind of Rorschach inkblot, perhaps offering more of an index to the reader/viewer's mind than to Mr. Van Allsburg's intentions. One of my favorites shows a man with a chair in his hand — he is obviously prepared to use it as a bludgeon if he needs to — looking at a strange and somehow *organic* bulge under the living-room carpet. "Two weeks passed and it happened again," the caption reads.

Given my feelings about motivation, my attraction to this sort of thing should be clear. *What* happened again after two weeks? I don't think it matters. In our worst nightmares, there are only pronouns for the things which chase us back to wakefulness, sweating and shuddering with horror and relief.

My wife, Tabitha, was also taken with *The Mysteries of Harris Burdick,* and it was she who suggested that each member of our family write a short story based on one of the pictures. She wrote one; so did our youngest son, Owen (then twelve). Tabby chose the first picture in the book; Owen chose one in the middle; I chose the last one. I have included my effort here, with the kind permission of Chris Van Allsburg. There's no more to add, except that I've read a slightly bowdlerized version of the tale to fourth- and fifth-graders several times over the last three or four years, and they seem to like it a great deal. I have an idea that what they really get off on is the idea of sending the Wicked Stepfather off into the Great Beyond. *I* certainly got off on it. The story has never been published before, mostly because of its tangled antecedents, and I am delighted to offer it here. I only wish I could offer my wife's and son's stories as well.

"The Fifth Quarter" — Bachman again. Or maybe George Stark.

"Umney's Last Case" — A *pastiche* — obviously — and paired with "The Doctor's Case" for that reason, but this one is a little more ambitious. I have loved Raymond Chandler and Ross Macdonald passionately since I discovered them in college (although I find it both instructive and a little scary to note that, while Chandler continues to be read and discussed, Macdonald's highly praised Lew Archer novels are now little-known artifacts outside the small circle of *livre noir* fans), and I think again it was the *language* of these novels which so fired my imagination; it opened a whole new way of seeing, one that appealed fiercely to the heart and mind of the lonely young man I was at that time.

It was also a style which was lethally easy to copy, as half a hundred novelists have discovered in the last twenty or thirty years. For a long time I steered clear of that Chandlerian voice, because I had nothing to use it for . . . nothing to say in the tones of Philip Marlowe that was *mine*.

Then one day I did. "Write what you know," the Wise Old Dudes tell us poor cometary remnants of Sterne and Dickens and Defoe and Melville, and for me, that means teaching, writing, and playing the guitar . . . though not necessarily in that order. As far as my own career-within-a-career of writing about writing goes, I'm reminded of a line I heard Chet Atkins toss off on *Austin City Limits* one night. He looked up at the audience after a minute or two of fruitless guitar-tuning and said, "It took me about twenty-five years to find out I wasn't very good at this part of it, and by then I was too rich to quit."

Same thing happened to me. I seem destined to keep going back to that peculiar little town — whether you call it Rock and Roll Heaven, Oregon; Gatlin, Nebraska; or Willow, Maine — and I also seem destined to keep going back to what I do. The question which haunts and nags and won't ever completely let go is this one: Who am I when I write? Who are *you*, for that matter? Exactly what is happening here, and why, and does it matter?

So, with these questions in mind, I pulled on my Sam Spade fedora, lit up a Lucky (metaphorically speaking, these days) and started to write. "Umney's Last Case" was the result, and of all the stories in this volume, it's the one I like the best. This is its first publication.

"Head Down" — My first writing for pay was sports writing (for awhile I was the entire sports department of the weekly *Lisbon Enterprise*), but that didn't make this any easier. My proximity to the Bangor West All-Star team when it mounted its unlikely charge on the State Championship was either pure luck or pure fate, depending on where you stand in regard to the possible existence of a higher power. I tend toward the higher power thesis, but in either case, I was only there because my son was on the team. Nevertheless, I quickly realized — more quickly than Dave Mansfield, Ron St. Pierre, or Neil Waterman, I think — that something pretty extraordinary was either happening or trying to happen. I didn't want to write about it, particularly, but something kept telling me I was *supposed* to write about it.

My method of working when I feel out of my depth is brutally simple: I lower my own head and run as fast as I can, as long as I can. That was what I did here, gathering documentation like a mad packrat and simply trying to keep up with the team. For a month or so it was like living inside one of those corny sports novels with which many of us guys have whiled away our duller afternoon study-halls: *Go Up for Glory, Power Forward,* and occasional bright standouts like John R. Tunis's *The Kid from Tomkinsville.*

Hard or not, "Head Down" was the opportunity of a lifetime, and before I was done, Chip McGrath of *The New Yorker* had coaxed the best nonfiction writing of my life out of me. I thank him for that, but I owe the most thanks to Owen and his teammates, who first made the story happen and then gave me permission to publish my version of it.

"Brooklyn August" — It pairs with "Head Down," of course, but there's a better reason for putting it here, at what is almost the end of this long book: it has escaped the wearisome cage of its creator's questionable reputation and lived its own placid life quite apart from him. It has been reprinted several times in various anthologies of baseball *curiosa,* and appears to have been selected upon each occasion by editors who seem not to have the slightest idea of who I'm supposed to be or what it is I'm supposed to do. And I really like that.

Okay; stick it on the shelf and take care of yourself until we meet again. Read a few good books, and if one of your brothers or sisters falls down and you see it happen, pick him or her up. After all, next time *you* might be the one who needs a hand . . . or a little help getting that pesky finger out of the drain, for that matter.

Bangor, Maine
September 16, 1992

The Beggar and the Diamond

AUTHOR'S NOTE: This little story — a Hindu parable in its original form — was first told to me by Mr. Surendra Patel, of Scarsdale, New York. I have adapted it freely and apologize to those who know it in its true form, where Lord Shiva and his wife, Parvati, are the major characters.

One day the archangel Uriel came to God with a downcast face. "What troubles you?" God asked.

"I have seen something very sad," Uriel replied, and then pointed between his feet. "Down there."

"On earth?" God asked with a smile. "Oh! No shortage of sadness there! Well, let us see."

They bent over together. Far below they saw a ragged figure trudging slowly along a country road on the outskirts of Chandrapur. He was very thin, this figure, and his legs and arms were covered with sores. Dogs frequently chased after him, barking, but the figure never turned to strike at them with his staff even when they nipped at his heels; he simply trudged onward, favoring his right leg as he walked. At one point a number of handsome, well-fed children with wicked smiling faces boiled out of a large house and threw stones at the ragged man when he held his empty begging bowl out to them.

"Go away, you nasty thing!" one of them cried. "Go away into the fields and die!"

At this, the archangel Uriel burst into tears.

"Now, now," God said, clapping him on the shoulder. "I thought you were made of sterner stuff."

"Yes, no doubt," Uriel said, drying his eyes. "It's just that the fellow down there seems to sum up everything which has ever gone wrong for all the sons and daughters of the earth."

"Of course he does," God replied. "That is Ramu, and that is his job. When he dies, another will hold it. It is an honorable job."

"Perhaps," Uriel said, covering his eyes with a shudder, "but I cannot bear to watch him do it. His sorrow fills my heart with darkness."

"Darkness is not allowed here," said God, "and therefore I must take steps to change what has brought it to you. Look here, my good archangel."

Uriel looked and saw that God was holding a diamond as big as a peacock's egg.

"A diamond of this size and quality will feed Ramu for the rest of his life, and keep his descendants unto the seventh generation," God remarked. "It is, in fact, the finest on the earth. Now . . . let us see . . ." He leaned forward on His hands and knees, held the diamond out between two gauzy clouds, and let it drop. He and Uriel marked its fall closely, watching as it struck the center of the road upon which Ramu walked.

The diamond was so large and so heavy that Ramu would no doubt have heard it strike the earth had he been a younger man, but his hearing had failed quite severely in the last few years, along with his lungs and his back and his kidneys. Only his eyesight remained as keen as it had been when he was one-and-twenty.

As he struggled up a rise in the road, unaware of the huge diamond which lay gleaming and flashing on the far side in the hazy sunshine, Ramu sighed deeply . . . then stopped, bent over his staff, as his sigh turned into a fit of coughing. He held onto his staff with both hands, trying to weather the fit, and just as it was easing, the staff — old and dry and almost as worn-out as Ramu himself — snapped with a dry crack, pitching Ramu into the dust.

He lay there, looking up at the sky and wondering why God was so cruel. "I have outlived all those I loved the most," he thought, "but not those I hate. I have grown so old and ugly that the dogs bark at me and the children throw stones at me. I have had nothing but scraps to eat these last three months, and no decent meal with family and friends for ten years or more. I am a wanderer on the face of the earth with no home to call my own; tonight I will sleep under a tree or a hedge with no roof to keep the rain off. I am covered with sores, my back aches, and when I pass water I see blood where no blood should be. My heart is as empty as my begging bowl."

Ramu slowly got to his feet, unaware that less than sixty feet and a dry bulge of land hid his still-keen glance from the world's largest diamond, and looked up at the hazy blue sky. "God, I am unlucky," he said. "I do not hate You, but I fear

You are not my friend, nor any man's friend."

Having said this, he felt a little better and resumed his trudge, pausing only to pick up the longer piece of his broken staff. As he walked, he began to reproach himself for his self-pity and for his ungrateful prayer.

"For I do have a few things to be grateful for," he reasoned. "The day is extraordinarily beautiful, for one thing, and although I have failed in many respects, my vision remains keen. Think how terrible it would be if I were blind!"

To prove this to himself, Ramu closed his eyes tightly and shuffled along with his broken staff stretched out in front of him, as a blind man uses his cane. The darkness was terrible, stifling, and disorienting. He soon had no idea if he was moving on as he had been, or if he was wandering off to one side of the road or the other, and might soon go tumbling into the ditch. The thought of what could happen to his old, brittle bones in such a fall frightened him, but he kept his eyes firmly shut and continued to forge ahead.

"This is just the thing to cure you of your ingratitude, old fellow!" he told himself. "You will spend the rest of the day remembering that you may be a beggar, but at least you are not a *blind* beggar, and you will be happy!"

Ramu did not walk into the ditch on either side, but he *did* begin to drift off to the right of the road as he topped the rise and started down the far side, and this was how he walked past the huge diamond which lay glowing in the dust; his left foot missed it by less than two inches.

Thirty yards or so farther on, Ramu opened his

eyes. Bright summer sunshine flooded them, and seemed to flood his mind, as well. He looked with gladness at the dusty blue sky, the dusty yellow fields, the beaten-silver track of the road upon which he walked. He marked the passage of a bird from one tree to the next with laughter, and although he never turned once to see the huge diamond which lay close behind him, his sores and his aching back were forgotten.

"Thank God for sight!" he cried. "Thank God for that, at least! Perhaps I shall see something of value on the road — an old bottle worth money in the bazaar, or even a coin — but even if I do not, I shall look my fill. Thank God for sight! Thank God for God!"

And, well satisfied, he set off again, leaving the diamond behind. God then reached down and scooped it up, replacing it beneath the mountain in Africa from which He had taken it. Almost as an afterthought (if God can be said to have afterthoughts), He plucked up an ironwood branch from the veldt and dropped it onto the Chandrapur Road, as He had dropped the diamond.

"The difference is," God told Uriel, "our friend Ramu will find the branch, and it will serve him as a staff for the rest of his days."

Uriel looked at God (as nearly as anyone — even an archangel — can look at that burning face, at least) uncertainly. "Have You given me a lesson, Lord?"

"I don't know," God responded blandly. "Have I?"